AIR BRI

&

THE STRANGE LAND

Also by Hammond Innes

FICTION

Wreckers Must Breathe
The Trojan Horse
Attack Alarm
Dead and Alive
The Lonely Skier
Maddon's Rock
The Killer Mine
The Blue Ice
The White South
The Angry Mountain
Campbell's Kingdom
The Wreck of the Mary Deare
The Doomed Oasis
The Land God Gave to Cain
Atlantic Fury
The Strode Venturer
Levkas Man
Golden Soak
North Star
The Big Footprints
The Last Voyage
Solomons Seal
The Black Tide
High Stand
Medusa
Isvik
Target Antarctica
Delta Connection

TRAVEL

Harvest of Journeys
Sea and Islands

HISTORY

The Conquistadors

Hammond Innes was born in Sussex in 1913 and died in 1998. He wrote thirty international bestsellers, all reissued by Pan. He also wrote a superb history of the Conquistadors, two books of his world travels and sailing, and an evocative illustrated book on East Anglia. It was in the early fifties, with books like *The Lonely Skier*, *Campbell's Kingdom*, *The White South* and *The Wreck of the Mary Deare*, all of them filmed, that he achieved international fame.

HAMMOND INNES

AIR BRIDGE & THE STRANGE LAND

PAN BOOKS

Air Bridge first published 1951 by William Collins
First published 1997 by Pan Books
The Strange Land first published 1954 by William Collin
First published in paperback by Fontana,
an imprint of William Collins, 1964 with a new author's note
First published 1997 by Pan Books

This omnibus edition published 2004 by Pan Books
an imprint of Pan Macmillan Ltd
Pan Macmillan, 20 New Wharf Road, London N1 9RR
Basingstoke and Oxford
Associated companies throughout the world
www.panmacmillan.com

ISBN 0 330 43260 5

1 3 5 7 9 8 6 4 2

A CIP catalogue record for this book is available from the British Library.

Printed and bound in Great Britain by
Mackays of Chatham plc, Chatham, Kent

AIR BRIDGE

For
Daphne and Bill

NOTE

In the sections of this book dealing with the Berlin Airlift I am indebted to the Royal Air Force, who flew me into blockaded Berlin and who gave me every facility for studying the lift both on the ground and in the air. I should like to take this opportunity of expressing my appreciation of the Air Ministry's willingness to assist me and of the friendly co-operation I received from lift personnel at Wunstorf and Gatow at a time when they were very overworked.

It is inevitable, in a story of this nature, that the types of aircraft and the titles of air-force personnel should be those that operated at the time and at the bases concerned. I wish to make it clear, therefore, that the story is not founded on anything that actually occurred and, in particular, that the characters in the story who hold official positions are entirely fictional.

CHAPTER ONE

It was dark and I was very tired. My head ached and my mind was confused. The road ran uphill between steep banks and there were trees with gaunt branches spread against the pale glimmer of the Milky Way. At last I reached the level and the high banks gave place to hedges. Through a gap I caught a glimpse of an orange moon lying on its back on the far side of a ploughed field. Nothing stirred. All life seemed frost-bound in the cold of night. I stood for a moment, exhausted, my knees trembling weakly and the sweat drying like cold steel against my skin. A little wind ran chill fingers through the bare spikes of the quick-thorn and I went on then, driven by the shivers that ran through my body. It was the reaction after the crash. I had to find somewhere to lie up – a barn, anything, so long as it was warm. And then I had to get out of the country. I was meeting the wind now, even as I walked, it chilled the sweat on my body. My steps no longer rang firm. The sound of them became a shuffle that was lost every now and then in the lashing of the trees in a small copse.

The country around was quite flat now – a familiar flatness. The sharp edges of a large rectangular building stood for a moment black against the moon. It was there for an instant, gaunt and recognisable, and then it was lost behind the high earth mounds of a dispersal point. I stopped, my body suddenly rigid. The dispersal point and that distant glimpse of a hangar confirmed what I had already sensed almost automatically. The flatness that stretched before me was an aerodrome.

If I could get a plane! Damn it – I'd done it before. And it had been far more difficult then. I could remember the fir trees and the feel of the sand, almost silver in the moonlight, and the dark shadows of men against the hangar lights. The picture was so vivid in my mind that the same surge of excitement took told of me now, tensing my nerves, giving me strength. I turned quickly and slid into the woods.

It was less cold in the woods or else the sudden urgency of hope gave me warmth as well as energy. It was darker, too. I might have lost my sense of direction, but always there was Jupiter, like a candle flickering amongst the branches, to show me the way the road had run. The trees clutched at me, whipping across my face, and in a moment I felt the warm trickle of blood from the cut on my forehead. The thick, salt warmth of it reached my tongue as I licked at the corner of my mouth. But it didn't hurt. In fact, I barely noticed it. I was intent upon one thing, and one thing only – a plane.

I came out of the wood on the very edge of the perimeter track, a fifty yard wide ribbon of tarmac, rutted and hillocked by the frosts and marked with the dead stalks of summer's weeds. Left and right it seemed to stretch to the horizon, and across the track was the airfield, a bleak, open hilltop, black under the moon, for the grass was gone and it was all plough. The curve of that hilltop was smooth and even like the curvature of the earth's surface, a section of a globe hung against the stars. The only relief to that impression of void was away to the left where the black edge of a hangar seemed to be shouldering the moon up the sky.

I stood there for a moment, conscious again of the wind cutting through my clothing as the sense of emptiness drained the excitement out of me. The story of the ploughed-up grassland, the dead weed stalks and the frost-broken tarmac was evident in the dead atmosphere of the place. The airfield was deserted. It was one of the great bomber stations that had died with the end of the war. It was easy to see it as it had been, full of activity with the roar of planes coming in from a raid – big, graceful shapes, in silhouette against the flarepath, settling clumsily on to the runway. This sort of place had been my life for six and a half years. Now the planes only existed as ghosts in my mind. All about me was empty desolation, a slow disintegration moving inevitably back to the land from which it had sprung up.

With a feeling of hopelessness I started along the

perimeter track towards the hangars. They would be just derelict shells, but at least they would give me shelter for the night. I felt suddenly sick and very tired – a little scared, too. The desolation of that airfield ate into me, bringing with it an awareness of my own loneliness.

The perimeter track seemed unending, growing wider and more desolate at every stumbling step as the wind thrust into my stomach till it chilled and stiffened my spine. Dizziness overtook me. It was the crash, of course, and the awful crack I'd got on the head. And then a flicker of hope came to steady me. The hangars now loomed black against the moon, big rectangular skeletons slowly crumbling away. But at the far end of the concrete apron there was one that looked whole and solid. The line of windows along its side was intact and reflected a glimmer of starlight.

I quickened my pace. It was just possible that some private owner, a local farmer or landowner, kept his plane up here on this deserted aerodrome. That was the hope that sent me hurrying across the apron to the deep shadows of the hangars. And as I slid from one hangar to the next I prayed to God there would be petrol in the tanks.

I was a fool perhaps to build my hopes on such slender foundations as the fact that one hangar was intact. But when you're desperate you clutch at anything. Before I'd even reached the hangar I was already mentally in the cockpit of some tiny aircraft winging my way through the night towards France. I knew exactly how the coast would look as it slid beneath me and how the Channel would be gently corrugated at right angles to my line of flight as the waves reflected the slanting rays of the moon. I could see myself checking in at the little hotel in Montmartre where I'd stayed several times before and then after a rest, going to Badouin's office. Badouin would fix it all for me. Everything would be all right as soon as I'd seen Badouin.

I reached the hangar and stood for a moment in the shadow of its bulk. I was panting. But I no longer felt sick or dizzy. I was trembling slightly, but that was just nerves. I had plenty of energy. Nothing could stop me now. I slid round the corner of the building and along the face of the huge sliding doors.

My luck was in, for the little wicket door in the centre yielded to the touch of my hand, revealing a dark void full of vague shadows. I stepped inside and closed the door. It was still and very cold with that queer musty smell of damp on concrete. Some glimmer of moonlight seemed to penetrate into the rear of the hangar, for the shadows resolved themselves into the nose and wings of a large four-engined plane. It was facing me head-on and it seemed enormous in the gloom of the hangar.

The incredible luck of it! I ducked under the port wing and moved along the fuselage, running my hand along the cold metal of it, searching for the door.

'So. His work is not to be remembered.'

I stopped with a jerk. It was a girl's voice that had spoken.

A man answered her: 'I'm sorry. War is a dirty business.'

'But the war is finished.'

'Yes, but you lost it, remember.'

'And because Germany loses a war, my father must suffer? My father has suffered enough, I think.'

'Your father is dead.' The brutal words were said in a hard, matter-of-fact voice.

A silence followed. Peering over the tailplane I could see the outline of two figures against the steady glow of a pressure lamp. The man was short, thick-set and powerful-looking and as he moved towards the girl he unmasked the lamp so that its dim light showed me the litter of a workbench running the width of the hangar and the dark shadow of a belt-driven machine lathe.

I turned quickly. The lamplight was glowing on the metal of the plane and as I slid along the fuselage towards the door I saw that it was a Tudor and its inboard engine was missing.

If I had gained the door unnoticed I should not now be setting down what must surely be the most extraordinary story of the Berlin Airlift. But my foot caught against some scrap metal and with the sudden clang of sheet tin I froze.

'Who's that?' It was the man's voice and it had the drive of a man accustomed to absolute authority. 'So you've got friends here, have you?' The beam of a torch swept the plane and then spotlighted me with its dazzling light. 'Who are you? What do you want?'

I just stood there, blinking in the glare, incapable of movement, panic lifting my heart into my mouth.

The torch moved suddenly. There was a click by the wall and the sound of an engine starting up outside. Then lights glowed and brightened.

The man was facing me across the tail of the plane now and he had a gun in his hand. He wasn't tall, but he was immensely broad across the shoulders. He was thick through like a bull and he held his head slightly forward as though about to charge. I hardly noticed the girl.

'Well, who are you?' the man repeated and began to move in on me. He came slowly and inevitably like a man sure of his ability to handle a situation.

I broke and ran. I wasn't going to be caught like this, trapped in a hangar, accused of attempting to steal an aircraft as well as a car. If once I could get to the shelter of the woods I'd still have a chance. I ducked under the wings with the sound of his feet pounding on the concrete behind me. As I wrenched open the door of the hangar he shouted at me in German: '*Halt! Halt, Du Verrückter!*' That damned language with its memory of endless, unbearable days of prison and the nagging fear of the escape gave me a last burst of energy.

I shot through the door and in a moment I was out on the perimeter track racing for the dark line of the woods. I crossed the concrete of the runway-end, my breath a wild hammering in my throat. My mind had become confused so that I seemed to be running again from the tunnel mouth to the dark anonymity of the fir woods. At any moment I expected to hear the deep bay of the dogs and my skin crawled between my shoulder blades just as it had done that night in Germany so long ago, cringing in anticipation of the shattering impact of a bullet. The concrete was broken and matted with weeds. Then I was on plough with the clay clinging to my shoes and the sound of my flight deadened in the sticky earth.

I stumbled and clawed my way to the woods. I heard my pursuer crash into the undergrowth close behind me. Branches whipped across my face. I barely noticed them. I found a path and then lost it again in a tangle of briar that tore at my clothes. I fought my way through it to find that he'd skirted the brambles and was level with me. I started to double back, but the undergrowth was too thick. I turned and faced him then.

I didn't stop to think. I went straight for him. God knows what I intended to do. I think I meant to kill him. He had shouted at me in German and my mind had slipped back to that earlier time when I had been nearly hunted down. His fist struck my arm with numbing force and I closed with him, my fingers searching for his windpipe. I felt the knobbly point of his Adam's apple against the ball of my thumb, heard him choke as I squeezed. Then his knee came up and I screamed in agony. My hands lost their grip and as I doubled up I saw him draw his fist back. I knew what was coming and I was powerless to stop it. His fist seemed huge in a shaft of moonlight and then it shattered into a thousand fragments as it broke against my jaw.

What followed is very confused in my mind. I have a vague memory of being half-led, half-carried over ground that seemed to rise and fall in waves. Then I was lying on a camp bed in an office full of bright lights. I was being interrogated, first in German, then in English. There was only one person there – the man who had hit me. I didn't see any sign of the girl. He sat in a chair, leaning over me so that his big, solid head seemed hung in space, always on the verge of falling on me and crushing me. I tried to move, but my hands and feet were bound. The light was above me and to the left. It was very bright and hurt my eyes. My jaw ached and my head throbbed and the interrogation went on and on through periods of black-out. I remember coming round once with a cry of pain as the searing burn of disinfectant entered the wound on my forehead. After that I slept.

When I woke it was daylight. I lay staring at the ceiling and wondering why it was plain, untreated concrete. The walls were bare brick. In the opposite corner the mortar had crumbled away and there was a long, jagged crack stuffed with newspaper. Slowly the events of the night before came back to me – the airfield, the hangar, the struggle in the woods.

I sat up with a jerk that sent a stab of pain shooting through my head. My jaw was painful and slightly swollen, the cut on my forehead was covered with lint secured by adhesive tape. There was a patch of dried blood on the grey Army blanket that had been pulled over me. I swung my legs out of bed and then sat there for quite a while staring at the unfamiliar room and fingering my jaw.

It was quite a small room and had obviously been used as an office. There was a cheap desk with a portable typewriter in its case, an old swivel chair, a steel filing cabinet and an untidy litter of books and papers. The books, I saw at a glance, were all technical manuals – engineering, mechanics, aviation. They were thick with dust. The floor was of bare boards and a rusty stove stood against one wall, the chimney running out through a roughly-patched hole in the ceiling. The windows were barred and looked out on to a pile of rubble and a vista of broken brick foundations, half-covered with dead sorrel stalks. There was an air of disintegration about the place. My gaze focused and held on the bars of the windows. They were solid iron bars set in cement. I turned quickly to the door with a feeling of being trapped. It was locked. I tried to find my shoes, but they had been removed. Panic seized hold of me then and I stood quite still in the middle of the room in my stockinged feet and fought it down.

I got control of myself at last, but I was overcome with a feeling of sickness and lay down on the bed. After a time the sickness passed and my brain became active again. I was in a hell of a spot! Oh, I was being quite honest with myself then. I knew I'd tried to kill a man. I could remember the feel of his windpipe against my thumb. The question was, did he know that I'd meant to kill him?

I looked slowly round the room. The iron bars, the locked door, the removal of my shoes – he knew all right.

My hand groped automatically for my cigarette-case. My jacket hung over the back of a chair and as I felt for the case, my fingers touched the inside breast pocket. It was empty. My wallet was gone.

I found the case and lit a cigarette. And then I leaned back. That wallet had contained something more important than money – it had contained my pilot's certificate and my false identity. Hell! He'd only to read the papers . . . I dragged at my cigarette, trying to think through the throbbing ache of my head. I had to get out of here. But how? How? My eyes roved desperately over the room. Then I glanced at my watch. It was eight-fifteen. Probably the papers had arrived already. In any case he would have phoned the police.

A door slammed somewhere beyond the brickwork of the walls. I sat up, listening for the sound of footsteps. All I could hear was the beating of my heart and the buzzing of a fly trapped in a web at the corner of the window. Nobody came. Time passed slowly. Occasionally I heard the sound of movement somewhere in the depths of the building. At eight thirty-five a car drew up at the back. There was the slam of a door and the sound of voices. Five minutes later the car drove off.

I couldn't stand it any more. The feeling of impotence was getting on my nerves. In a sudden mood of anger I got up and beat on the panels of the door.

Footsteps approached, a heavy, solid tread, boots ringing metallic on concrete. Then a voice asked, 'Are you awake?'

'Of course I'm awake,' I replied angrily. 'Do you mind opening the door?'

There was a moment's pause and then the voice said, 'That depends. I'm a bit cautious after last night. You damn nearly throttled me.'

I didn't say anything and a moment later the key turned in the lock and he opened the door. It was the same man all right – short and broad and very solid. He had thick dark hair slightly grizzled at the temples and a wide jaw that seemed to compress his lips into a thin, determined line. He was dressed in oil-stiff overalls and the silk scarf round his neck didn't entirely hide the livid marks left by my fingers.

'I'm sorry – about last night,' I murmured.

He didn't come in, but stood there in the gap of the doorway, his legs slightly straddled, staring at me. He had hard, slate-grey eyes. 'Forget it.' His voice was more friendly than his eyes. 'Have you had a look at yourself in the mirror? Afraid I made a bit of a mess of your jaw.'

There was an awkward silence. Somehow I couldn't bring myself to ask when the police would arrive. 'I'd like to get cleaned up,' I said.

He nodded. 'Down the passage.' He stood aside to let me pass. But though he didn't seem angry, I noticed he took good care to keep well out of my reach.

Outside I found myself in a brick passageway filled with sunlight. An open doorway showed the woods crowding right up to the side of the building and through the lacework of the trees I caught a glimpse of the flat, bare expanse of the airfield. It all looked very quiet and peaceful. Through that door lay freedom and as though he read my thoughts, he said, 'I shouldn't try wandering about outside, Fraser. The police are searching this area.'

'The police?' I swung round, staring at him, trying to understand the sense behind his words.

'They've found the car. You'd crashed it about half-way down Baydon Hill.' He glanced up at my fore-head. 'I did the best I could with the cut. You've probably scarred yourself for life, but I don't think any dirt has got into it.'

I didn't understand his attitude. 'When are the police coming for me?' I asked.

'We'll discuss that later,' he said. 'Better get cleaned up first. The lavatory is at the end there.'

Feeling dull and rather dazed I went on down the passage. I could hear him following behind me. Then his footsteps stopped. 'I've left my shaving kit out for you. If there's anything you want, shout.' And then he added, 'I'm just knocking up some breakfast. How many eggs would you like – two?'

'If you can spare them,' I mumbled. I was too astonished at the calmness of his attitude to say any-thing else.

'Oh, I'm all right for eggs. A girl brings them from the farm each day with the milk.' A door opened on the sound of sizzling fat and then closed. I turned to find myself alone in the passage. Freedom beckoned through the sunlit doorway at the end. But it was hopeless. He wouldn't have left me alone like that if he hadn't known it was hopeless. I turned quickly and padded down the corridor in my stockinged feet.

The lavatory was small with an open window looking out on to a tangle of briar. It was a reminder of service quarters with its cracked basin, broken utility seat and initials and other pencil scratchings still visible on the crumbling plaster. A shaving kit had been left out for me and a towel. Hung on a nail on the window frame was a cracked mirror. I stared at myself in the pock-marked surface. I wasn't a particularly pleasant sight. Apart from the black stubble that I'd met every day for at least fifteen years, the side of my jaw was puffed and swollen, producing a queer variation of colour from red to dark purple and culminating in an ugly split of dried blood. My eyes were sunk back in dark sockets of exhaustion, the whites bloodshot and wild-looking, and to cap it all was a broad strip of adhesive tape running right across the right side of my forehead.

'You bloody fool,' I said aloud. It was like talking to a stranger, except that the lips of the face in the glass moved in echo of my words. I almost laughed at the thought that I'd wanted to try and escape into the outside world looking like that.

I looked better after I'd shaved – but not much better. I'd had to leave the stubble round the swollen side of my jaw and it gave me a queer, lop-sided appearance. The cold water had freshened me up a bit, but the dark shadows round my eyes remained and there was still the adhesive tape across my forehead.

'Breakfast's ready.'

I turned to find him standing in the doorway. He nodded for me to go ahead and at the same time stepped slightly back. 'You're taking no chances,' I said. The bitterness in my voice was for myself, not for him.

'Last door on the right,' he said as though I hadn't spoken.

Inside was a trestle table, the sort we'd had in forward bases. Two plates heaped with bacon and eggs and fried bread steamed slowly and there was a pot of tea. 'By the way, my name's Saeton. Bill Saeton.'

'I gather – you know my name.' My voice trembled slightly. He was standing just inside the door, solid and immovable like a rock, his eyes fixed on my face. The personality of the man seemed to grow in silence, dominating me and filling the room.

'Yes, I think I know all about you,' he said slowly. 'Sit down.'

His voice was remote, impersonal. I didn't want to sit down. I wanted my shoes and my wallet. I wanted to get out of there. But I sat down all the same. There was something compelling about the way he stood there, staring at me. 'Can I have my wallet, please?'

'Later,' was all he said. He sat down opposite me, his back to the window, and poured the tea. I drank thirstily and then lit a cigarette.

'I thought you said you could manage two eggs.'

'I'm not hungry,' I answered, drawing the smoke

deep down into my lungs. It soothed me, easing the tension of my nerves. 'When are they coming for me?' I asked. I had control of my voice now.

He frowned. 'Who?' he asked, his mouth crammed full.

'The police,' I said impatiently. 'You've phoned them, haven't you?'

'Not yet.' He pointed his fork at my plate. 'For God's sake relax and get some breakfast inside you.'

I stared at him. 'You mean they don't know I'm here?' I didn't believe him. Nobody would calmly sit down to eat his breakfast with a man who'd tried to throttle him the night before unless he knew the authorities were on their way. Then I remembered the car and the way he'd advised me not to wander about outside. 'The police were here about half an hour ago, weren't they?' I asked him.

For an answer he reached over to a side table and tossed me the morning paper. I glanced down at it. The story was there in bold headlines that ran half-across the front page: PALESTINE FLIGHT FOILED – Police Prevent Another Plane Leaving Country Illegally – Mystery of 'Mr Callahan'. It was all there in the opening paragraph of leaded type – the whole wretched story.

I pushed the paper away and said, 'Why didn't you hand me over?' I spoke without looking up. I had a peculiar sense of being trapped.

'We'll talk about that later,' he said again.

He spoke as though he were talking to a child and suddenly anger came to bolster my courage. What was he doing living alone up here on this deserted aerodrome tinkering about with a Tudor in the dead of night? Why hadn't he rung the police? He was playing some sort of cat-and-mouse game with me and I wanted to get it over. If it had to come, let it come now, right away. 'I want you to call the police,' I said.

'Don't be a fool! Get some breakfast inside you. You'll feel better then.'

But I'd got to my feet. 'I want to give myself up.' My voice trembled. It was part anger, part fear. There was something wrong with this place. I didn't like it. I didn't like the uncertainty of it. I wanted to get it over.

'Sit down!' He, too, had risen and his hand was on my shoulder, pressing me down. 'Nervous reaction, that's all.'

'There's nothing wrong with my nerves.' I shook his hand off and then I was looking into his eyes and somehow I found myself back in my seat, staring at my plate.

'That's better.'

'What are you keeping me here for?' I murmured. 'What are you doing up here?'

'We'll talk about it after breakfast.'

'I want to talk about it now.'

'After breakfast,' he repeated.

I started to insist, but he had picked up the paper and ignored me. A feeling of impotence swept over me. Almost automatically I picked up the knife and fork. And as soon as I'd started to eat I realised I was hungry – damnably hungry. I hadn't had anything since midday yesterday. A silence stretched over the table. I thought of the trial and the prison sentence that must inevitably follow. I might get a year, possibly more after resisting arrest, hitting a police officer and stealing a car. The memory of those eighteen months in Stalag Luft 1 came flooding back into my mind. Surely to God I'd had enough of prison life! Anything rather than be shut up again. I looked across at Saeton. The sunlight was very bright and though I screwed up my eyes, I couldn't see his expression. His head was bent over the newspaper. The quiet impassive way he sat there, right opposite me, gave me a momentary sense of confidence in him and as I ate a little flicker of hope slowly grew inside me.

'When you've finished we'll go up to the hangar.' He lit a cigarette and turned to the inside of the paper. He didn't look up as he spoke.

I hurried through the rest of the meal, and as soon as I'd finished he got up. 'Put your jacket on,' he said. 'I'll get your shoes.'

The air struck quite warm for November as we went out into the sunlight but there was a dank autumnal smell of rotting vegetation. A berberis gleamed red against the gold of the trees and there were some rose bushes half-covered with the dead stalks of bindweed. It had been a little garden, but now the wild had moved in.

We crossed the garden and entered a path leading through the woods. It was cold and damp amongst the trees though the trunks of the silver birch saplings were dappled with sunlight. The wood thinned and we came out on the edge of the airfield. The sky was crystal clear, bright blue with patches of cumulus. The sun shone white on the exposed chalk of a dispersal point. Far away, beyond the vast curve of the airfield, a line of hills showed the rounded brown of downland grass. The place was derelict with disuse – the concrete of the runways cracked and sprouting weeds, the buildings that dotted the woods half-demolished into rubble, the field itself all ploughed up for crops. Only the hangar, fifty yards away to our left, seemed solid and real.

'What's the name of this airfield?' I asked Saeton.

'Membury.'

'What are you doing living up here on your own?'

He didn't answer and we continued in silence. We turned the corner of the hangar and walked to the centre of the main doors. Saeton took out a bunch of keys and unlocked the wicket door that I'd pushed open the previous night. Inside, the musty smell of concrete and the damp chill was familiar. Both the inboard engines of the plane were missing. It had a sort of toothless grin. Saeton pressed his hand against the door till the lock clicked and then led the way to the back of the hangar where the workbench stretched along the wall. 'Sit down,' he said, indicating a stool. He drew up another with his foot and sat down facing me. 'Now then—' He took my wallet from his pocket and spread the contents on the oil-black wood of the bench. 'Your name is Neil Leyden Fraser and you're a pilot. Correct?'

I nodded.

He picked up my passport. 'Born at Stirling in 1915, height five-eleven, eyes brown, hair brown.

Picture quite flattering compared with what you look like at the moment.' He flicked through the pages. 'Back and forth from the Continent quite a bit.' He looked up at me quickly. 'Have you taken many planes out of the country?'

I hesitated. But there was no point in denying the thing.

'Three,' I said.

'I see.' His eyes didn't move from my face. 'And why exactly did you engage in this somewhat risky business?'

'Look,' I said, 'if you want to get me under cross-examination hand me over to the police. Why haven't you done so already? Do you mind answering me that?'

'No. I'm quite prepared to tell you why – in a moment. But until I have the answer to the question I've just asked I can't finally make up my mind whether to hand you over or not.' He leaned forward then and tapped my knee. 'Better tell me the whole thing. I'm the one person, outside of the organisers of your little racket, who knows that you're the pilot calling himself "Callahan". Am I right?'

There was nothing I could say. I just nodded.

'All right then. Either I can give you up or I can stay quiet. That places me in the position of judge. Now, why did you get mixed up in this business?'

I shrugged my shoulders. 'Why the hell does anyone get mixed up in something illegal? I didn't know it was illegal. It wasn't at first anyway. I was just engaged to pilot a director of a British firm of exporters. His business took him all over Western Europe and the Mediterranean. He was a Jew. Then they asked me to ferry a plane out. They said it was being exported to a country where the British weren't very popular and suggested that for the trip I used a name that was more international. I agreed and on arrival in Paris I was given papers showing my name as "Callahan".'

'It was a French plane?'

'Yes. I took it to Haifa.'

'But why did you get mixed up with these people in the first place?'

'Why the hell do you imagine?' I demanded angrily. 'You know what it was like after the war. There were hundreds of pilots looking around for jobs. I finished as a Wing Co. I went and saw my old employers, a shipbuilding yard on the Clyde. They offered me a £2 rise – £6 10s. a week. I threw their offer back in their faces and walked out. I was just about on my uppers when this flying job was offered to me. I jumped at it. So would you. So would any pilot who hadn't been in the air for nearly a year.'

He nodded his head slowly. 'I thought it'd be something like that. Are you married?'

'No.'

'Engaged?'

'No.'

'Any close relatives who might start making inquiries if Neil Fraser disappeared for a while?'

'I don't think so,' I answered. 'My mother's dead.

My father remarried and I'm a bit out of touch with him. Why?'

'What about friends?'

'They just expect me when they see me. What exactly are you driving at?'

He turned to the bench and stared for a while at the contents of my wallet as though trying to make up his mind. At length he picked up one of the dog-eared and faded photographs I kept in the case. 'This is what interested me,' he said slowly. 'In fact, it's the reason I didn't ring the police last night and denied that I'd seen anything of you when they came this morning. Picture of you with W.A.A.F. girlfriend. On the back it's got – *September, 1940: Self and June outside our old home after taking a post-blitz cure.*' He held it out to me and for the first time since I'd met him there was a twinkle in his eyes. 'You look pretty tipsy, the pair of you.'

'Yes,' I said. 'We were tight. The whole place collapsed with us in it. We were lucky to get out alive.'

'So I guessed. It was the ruins that interested me. Your old home was a maintenance hangar, wasn't it?'

'Yes. Kenley Aerodrome. A low-flying daylight raid – it pretty well blew the place to bits. Why?'

'I figured that if you could describe a maintenance hangar as your home in 1940 you probably knew something about aero-engines and engineering?'

I didn't say anything and after staring at me for a moment he said impatiently, 'Well, do you know anything about aero-engines or don't you?'

'Yes,' I said.

'Practical – or just theory? Given specifications and tools can you build an engine?'

'What are you getting at?' I asked. 'What do you [illegible]'

'Just answer my questions. Can you operate a lathe, do milling, grinding and boring, screw cutting and drilling?'

'Yes.' And then I added, 'I don't know very much about jets. But I'm pretty sound on all types of piston engines.'

'I see. And you're a pilot?'

'Yes.'

'When did you become a pilot?'

'In 1945, after I escaped from Germany.'

'Why?'

'I don't know. I wanted a change. In 1944 I was posted to bombers as flight engineer. I started learning to fly. Then we were shot down. I escaped early in 1945 and remembered enough about flying to pinch a Jerry plane and crash-land at an airfield back home. Shortly after that I got my wings.'

He nodded vaguely as though he hadn't been listening. He had turned slightly on his stool and was staring sombrely at the gleaming fuselage of the Tudor. His eyes caught a shaft of sunlight from the high windows and seemed to gleam with some inner fire. Then he turned back to me. 'You're in a spot, aren't you?' It wasn't said unpleasantly – more a statement of fact. 'But I'll make you a proposition. See that engine over there?' I turned. It stood against the wall and was chocked up on wooden blocks. 'That's finished – complete. It's hand-built, mostly right here in this hangar. Well, that's one of them. But there's got to be another before I can get this crate into the air.' He nodded towards the Tudor. 'It's due to fly on the Berlin Airlift on 25th January – fuel freighting. We've got the tanks installed. Everything's ready. All we need is a second engine. We've started on it already. But I'm pressed for time. That first one took us six months. And now Carter, who's been working on it with me, is getting impatient. I'm a pilot, not an engineer. If he walks out on me, which is what he threatens to do, I'll have to pack up – unless I've got somebody else to carry on.' He looked at me, eyes narrowed slightly. 'Well, what about it? Can you build another engine like that, if necessary on your own?'

'I don't know,' I said. 'I haven't examined it and I don't know what equipment you've got.' My eyes roved quickly along the bench, noting the lathes, the racks of taps, boxes of dies, the turning tools, the jigs and the welding equipment. 'I should think I could,' I added.

'Good.' He got up as though it were settled and went over to the completed engine. He stood there staring at it, and then he turned away from it with a quick, impatient movement of his shoulders as though throwing off something that was constantly at the back of his mind. 'You won't get any pay. Free board and lodging, beer, cigarettes, anything that is absolutely necessary. You'll work up here until the thing's complete. After that . . . well, we'll see. If things work out the way they should, then you won't lack a permanent job if you want it.'

'You seem to be taking my acceptance rather for granted,' I said.

'Of course I am,' he said, swinging round on me. 'You've no alternative.'

'Look – just what's your racket?' I demanded. 'I'm in enough trouble without getting deeper—'

'There's no racket,' he cut in angrily. 'I run a company called Saeton Aircraft Ltd, and I rent these premises from the Air Ministry. It's all perfectly legal.'

'Then why pick on a lonely spot like this? And last night – you were scared of something. And you shouted at me in German. Why in German? And who was the girl?'

He came towards me then, his head thrust forward, his thick neck hard with the tautness of the muscles. 'Take my advice, Fraser – accept my offer and don't ask questions.' His jaw was so tight that the words came through his teeth.

I had got to my feet now. 'Are you sure you haven't pinched this plane?' I asked. Damn it! He wasn't going to get me in a worse mess.

For a moment I thought he was going to strike me. But instead he turned away with a little laugh. 'No. No, I didn't pinch it.' He rounded on me and added violently, 'Nor this engine, nor these tools, all this equipment. There's three years of my life in this hangar – three years of sweating my guts out, improvising, struggling, trying to make fools see that if only . . .' He stopped suddenly. Then in a voice into which he had forced mildness he said, 'You've nothing to worry about, Fraser. It's all perfectly legal. And once this plane is in the air and—' He was interrupted by someone banging on the hangar door. He hesitated and then glanced at me. 'That could be the police. Which is it to be – complete the second engine for me or do I hand you over? You'll be quite safe up here in a day or so,' he added.

The banging on the door seemed to merge with the hammering of my heart. The possibility of arrest, which had gradually receded, now became real and instant. But I had already succumbed to a flicker of hope that had grown up inside me. 'I'll stay,' I said.

He nodded as though there had never been any doubt of it. 'Better nip into the fuselage. You can hide in the toilet at the rear. They won't think of looking for you there.'

I did as he suggested and climbed into the fuselage. In the dark belly of the plane I could just make out the shape of three large elliptical tanks up for'ard. I heard the click of the door being opened and the sound of voices. The door slammed to and for a moment I thought they'd left the hangar. But then their footsteps were echoing on the concrete as they came down towards the bench. There was the drone of a man's voice, low and urgent. Then Saeton cut him short: 'All right. Throw in your hand if you want to. But we'll talk about it back at the quarters, not here.' His voice was hard and angry.

'For God's sake, Bill, be reasonable. I'm not throwing in my hand. But we can't go on. You know that as well as I do.' They had stopped close beside the fuselage. The man was breathing heavily as though he were out of breath. He had a slight cockney accent and his voice was almost pleading. 'Can't you understand – I'm broke. I haven't a bean.'

'Well, nor have I,' Saeton said harshly. 'But I don't whine about it. In three months from now—'

'It's been two years already,' the other put in mildly.

'Do you think I don't know how long it's been?' Saeton's voice softened. 'Listen, Tubby, in three months we'll be on top of the world. Think of it, man – only three months. Surely to God you can pull in your belt and stick it as long as that after all we've been through together?'

The other grunted. 'But you're not married, are you chum?'

'So your wife's been getting at you. That's it, is it? I ought to have known it. Well, if you think your wife's going to stop me from getting that plane into the air . . .' Saeton had been lashing himself into a fury, but he stopped suddenly. 'Let's go back to the quarters. We can't talk here.'

'No,' the other said obstinately. 'I'll say what I've got to say here.'

'We're going back to quarters,' Saeton said gently. 'We'll talk about it over a cup of tea.'

'No,' the other repeated, still in the same obstinate tone. 'We'll talk it over here and now if you don't mind. I'm not going to have you rowing Diana for something that isn't her—'

'Diana!' Saeton's voice was suddenly harsh. 'You haven't brought her back—'

'She's down at the quarters now,' the other said stolidly.

'At the quarters! You bloody fool! This is no place for a woman. They can't keep their mouths shut and—'

'Diana won't talk. Besides, she's nowhere else to go.'

'I thought she was sharing a flat with a friend in London.'

'Damn it, man,' the other shouted, 'can't you understand what I'm trying to tell you? We're broke. I'm overdrawn by twenty quid and the bank has warned me I've got to settle my overdraft within three months.'

'What about your wife? Didn't she have a job?'

'She got fed up and chucked it.'

'And you're supposed to throw up all you've worked for just because she's bored. That's typical of a woman. If you can take it, why can't she? Doesn't she understand—'

'It's no good kicking at Diana,' the other cut in. 'She's not to blame. She's stuck it pretty well if you ask me. Now it's come to this – either I find a job that'll bring us in some money so that we can live together like normal human beings, or else—'

'I see.'

'You don't see at all,' the other snapped, his voice rising on a note of anger. 'All you can think of is the engines. You're so crazy about them you don't behave like a human being at all. Well, I'm not made that way. I'm married and I want a home. I'm not busting up my marriage because of your engines.'

'I'm not asking you to go to bed with them, am I?'

Saeton snarled. 'Well, all right. If you're so in love with your matrimonial pleasures that you can't see the future that's within your grasp—'

'I think you'd better withdraw that remark.' The man's voice was low and obstinate.

'Oh God!' Saeton exploded. 'All right, I withdraw it. But for Christ's sake, Tubby, stop to think what you're doing.'

It seemed to me it was about time I showed myself. I slammed the toilet door and stomped across the steel-sheeted floor of the plane. From the open door of the fuselage I could see them standing, staring up at me. Saeton's companion was dressed in an old pair of grey flannels and leather-patched sports jacket – a round, friendly little man with a shock of unruly hair. His fresh, ruddy complexion contrasted oddly with Saeton's hard, leathery features. By comparison he looked quite boyish though he was about my age. Little creases of fat crinkled the corners of his eyes giving them a permanent twinkle as though he were perpetually on the verge of laughter. 'Who's this?' he asked Saeton.

'Neil Fraser. He's an engineer, and he's come up here to work with us on that last engine.'

'My successor, eh?' the other said quickly. 'You knew I'd be leaving.'

'Don't be a fool. Of course, I didn't. But I knew time was getting short. With an extra hand—'

'How much are you paying him?'

'Oh, for God's sake!' Saeton exclaimed angrily. 'His keep. That's all.' He turned to me. 'Fraser. This is

Tubby Carter. He built the engine I've just shown you. Did you fix that toilet door?'

'Yes,' I said. 'It's all right now.' I got down and shook Carter's hand.

'Fraser is an old friend of mine,' Saeton explained.

Carter's small, button-brown eyes fixed themselves on my face in a puzzled frown. 'You look as though you've been in a rough house.' His eyes stared at me, unwinking, as I searched desperately for some reasonable explanation.

It was Saeton who supplied the answer. 'He got mixed up in some trouble at a night-club.'

But Carter's eyes remained fixed on my face. 'Neil Fraser.' He seemed to be turning the name over in his mind and my heart sank. Suppose the police had discovered who Callahan was. After all, I'd only seen one of the daily papers. 'Are you a pilot by any chance?'

I nodded.

'Neil Fraser.' His face suddenly lit up and he snapped his fingers. '101 Bomber Squadron. You were the type who made a tunnel escape from prison camp and then pinched a Messerschmitt and flew it back to England. We met once – remember? At Mildenhall.' He turned to Saeton. 'How's that for a photographic memory, eh? I never forget a face.' He laughed happily.

Saeton glanced at me with sudden interest. Then he turned to Carter. 'You stay here with Fraser and talk over your boyhood memories. I'm going to have a word with Diana.'

'No, you don't, Bill.' Carter had caught his arm as

he turned away. 'This is between you and me. You leave Diana out of this.'

Saeton stopped. 'It's all right, Tubby,' he said and his voice was almost gentle. 'I won't upset your wife, I promise you. But before she forces you into some dead-end job she must be given the facts. The situation has altered since you left on Saturday. With Fraser here we can still get on to the airlift on schedule.'

'It took us six months to build that one.' Carter nodded to the completed engine.

'That included tests,' Saeton answered. 'And we came up against snags. Those have been ironed out now. Damn it, surely she'll have the sense to give you two months longer. As for money, leave that to me. I'll wring some more out of Dick if I have to squeeze it out of him with my bare hands. It's a pity he's such a —' He stopped abruptly, his lips compressed as though biting on the words. 'You stay here. I'll talk to Diana. She's no fool. No woman is when it comes to looking to the future. We've got all the metal and castings. All we've got to do is build the damned thing.' His eyes swung towards the plane. 'Then we'll have 'em all licked.' He stood staring at it as though by mere effort of will he could get it into the air. Then almost reluctantly his gaze came back to Carter. 'You can have that front room that used to be the office. It'll work out. You'll see. She can do the cooking for us. That'll keep her busy, and it'll give us more working time.'

'I tell you, her mind's made up,' Carter said wearily.

Saeton laughed. It was a slightly cynical laugh. 'No woman's mind is ever made up,' he said. 'They're constructed for the purpose of having their minds made up for them. How else do you imagine the human race survives?'

Carter stood quite still watching Saeton as he left the hangar. Then he turned and went straight over to the end of the workbench by the telephone and took down a pair of overalls. As he got into them he glanced at me curiously. 'So you're an engineer?' He zipped up the front of the overalls. Then he went over to a small petrol engine and started it up. 'We're working on the pistons at the moment.' He pulled a big folder towards me across the bench and opened it out. There were sheaves of fine pencil drawings. 'Here we are. Those are the specifications. You can work a lathe?' I nodded. He took me down the bench. The lathe was an ex-R.A.F. type, the sort we'd had in the maintenance hangar at Kenley. The belt drive was running free. With a quick movement of his hand he engaged it and at the same time picked up a half-turned block of bright metal. 'Okay, then, go ahead. Piston specifications: five-inch diameter, seven-inch depth, three-ring channels, two to be drilled for oil disposal, and there's a three-quarter inch hole for the gudgeon-pin sleeve. And for the love of Mike don't waste metal. This outfit's running on a shoe-string, as you've probably gathered.'

It was some time since I'd worked at a lathe. But it's a thing that once you've learnt you never forget. He stood over me for a time and it made me nervous. But as the shavings of metal ran off the lathe my confidence returned. My mind ceased to worry about the events of the last twenty-four hours. It became concentrated entirely in the fascination of turning a piece of mechanism out of a lump of metal. I ceased to be conscious of his presence. Hands and brain combined to recapture my old skill, and pride of craftsmanship took hold of me as the shape of the piston slowly emerged from the metal.

When I looked up again Carter was leaning over the specifications, his eyes staring at a bolt he was screwing in and out of a nut. His mind was outside the shop, worrying about his own personal problems. He looked up and caught my eye. Then he threw the bolt down and came towards me.

I bent to my work again and for a time he stood watching me in silence. At length he said, 'How long have you known Saeton?'

I didn't know what to say so I didn't answer him. 'Saeton was a Coastal Command pilot.' The metal whirled under my hands, thin silver slivers streaming from it. 'I don't believe you've ever met him before in your life.'

I stopped the lathe. 'Do you want me to balls this up?' I said.

He was fidgeting with the metal shavings. 'I was just wondering—' He stopped then and changed his line of approach. 'What do you think of him, eh?' He was looking directly at me now. 'He's mad, of course. But it's the madness that builds empires.' I could see he worshipped the man. There was a boy's admiration in his voice. 'He thinks he'll lick every charter company in the country once he gets into the air.'

'They're most of them on the verge of bankruptcy anyway,' I said.

He nodded. 'I've been with him for two years now. Working in partnership, you know. We had one plane flying – single-engined job. But that crashed.' His fingers strayed back to the metal shavings. 'He's a crazy devil. Incredible energy. The hell of it is his enthusiasm is infectious. When you're with him you believe what he wants you to believe. Did you hear what we were talking about when you were fixing that door?'

'Part of it,' I said guardedly.

He nodded absently. 'My wife's got a will of her own. She's American. Do you think he'll persuade her to agree to give me three months more?' He picked up a block of metal destined to be the next piston. 'He's right, of course. With the three of us working at it we ought to be able to complete the second engine in two months.' He sighed. 'Having come this far I'd like to see it through to the end. This place has become almost a part of me.' He turned slowly and stared at the tail-plane of the aircraft. 'I'd like to see her flying.'

I couldn't help him so I started the lathe again and he moved off along the bench and began work on an induction coil.

Half an hour later Saeton returned. He came and stood over me as I measured the diameter of the piston-head with a screw micrometer. Carter moved along the bench. 'Well?' he asked, his voice hesitant.

'Oh, she agrees,' Saeton said. His manner was offhand, but when I glanced at him I saw that he was pale as though he'd driven himself hard to get her agreement. 'She'll bring lunch up to us here.'

Carter stared at him almost unbelievingly. Then suddenly his eyes crinkled and his face fell into its natural mould of smiling good humour. 'Well, I'm damned!' he said and went whistling down the bench back to his induction coil.

'I see you know how to handle a lathe,' Saeton said to me. And then with sudden violence, 'By God! I believe we'll do it in a couple of months.'

And then the phone rang.

He started and the light died out of his face as though he were expecting this call. He went slowly down the bench and lifted the receiver. His face gradually darkened as he bent over the instrument and then he shouted, 'You're selling out on me? Don't be a fool, Dick . . . Of course, I understand . . . But wait a minute. Listen, damn you! I've got another man up here. Two months, that's all I'm asking . . . Well, six weeks then . . . No, of course I can't guarantee anything. But you've got to hang on a bit longer. In a couple of months we'll have it in the air . . . Surely you can hang on a couple of months? . . . All right, if that's the way you feel. But come down and see me first . . . Yes. A thing like this needs talking over . . . Tomorrow, then. All right.'

He replaced the receiver slowly. 'Was that Dick?' Carter asked.

Saeton nodded. 'Yes. He's had an offer for the aircraft and all the equipment here. He's threatening to sell us up.' He picked up a stool and sent it spinning across the hangar. 'God damn him, why can't he understand we're on the verge of success at last?'

Carter said nothing. I returned to my lathe. Saeton hesitated and then seized hold of the folder of specifications. For a moment he held it in his hands as though about to tear it across. His face was dark with passion. Then he flung it down and went over to the engine standing on its blocks against the wall. He pressed a switch and the thing roared into life, a shattering, earsplitting din that drowned all sound of my lathe. And he stood watching it, caressing it with his eyes as though all his world was concentrated in the live, dinning roar of it.

CHAPTER TWO

As I worked at the lathe and the day wore on, it slowly dawned on me what an incredible stroke of luck I had had. It was as though I had been given another chance. And this was legal. I might not have taken Saeton's word for it, but the presence of Tubby Carter proved there was nothing wrong with the set-up. He was so unquestionably honest. With him working beside me the whole thing became ordinary, matter-of-fact.

Saeton was different. It wasn't that I didn't trust the man. But he was a human dynamo, full of nervous, violent energy. The mercurial emotionalism of the Celt seemed mixed with a Saxon stolidity and singleness of purpose and I felt he was capable of anything. He was a born leader with that vital spark that can kindle enthusiasm in others, the type that can whip the dull heart of the mob into thundering passion. His strength was that he didn't need the support of others. It was all there inside him. He showed that when he switched off the thundering din of that one engine and turned with a grim concentration to the job of winding the armature of a starter motor. The structure of his life was crumbling about him. His partner was selling him up. But he didn't discuss it. He threw himself into the work that littered the bench with the silent preoccupation of a man who can see the finished article in his mind's eye.

Something of his drive and purpose seemed to enter into the two of us as we worked beside him. And the fascination of seeing a part of a complicated machine take shape under my hands so engrossed me that I lost all sense of time. I didn't notice Carter's wife bring in our lunch. Saeton pushed a mug of tea and some sandwiches along the bench to me and I ate whilst I worked. He and Carter did the same.

The only interruption was just after we'd switched on the light plant, shortly after four. There was a banging on the door. Saeton shouted to know who it was and a voice answered, 'The police.' I looked up at him from the lathe, my heart suddenly in my mouth. I had so completely lost myself in the work that the reminder that the authorities were searching for me came as a shock.

Saeton tossed me a flash-mask. 'Put that on,' he ordered crisply. 'The oxy-acetylene equipment is at the end of the bench there.' I saw Carter looking at me curiously. Then I had the mask on and was hurrying across to the oxygen cylinders.

By the time Saeton came back with a police inspector and a sergeant I had the flame going and was cutting across a piece of scrap metal. 'Just routine,' the

Inspector said as he asked for our identity cards. He glanced at them idly, talking to Saeton all the time. 'Thought we'd take a look round Membury before we packed it in. But he'll be out of the district by now. Probably out of the country in some private plane. Still, we'll just take a look round – in case. Quite a handy place, an old aerodrome, for a man to lie up.' He handed back our cards. 'No fear of his pinching your plane, anyway, sir. Can't fly a plane with two of its engines missing, can you?'

'No,' Saeton answered and he didn't join in the Inspector's good-humoured laughter.

They left then and I put the flash-mask aside and got back to my lathe with a feeling that the last hurdle had been overcome. I was safe now. So long as I remained at Membury I was safe.

But as we worked on in the evening I was conscious of Carter watching me periodically from the other end of the bench. We knocked off at about eight. I was pretty tired by then and I might have felt depressed, but Saeton clapped his hand on my shoulder. 'You're a better acquisition than I'd dared to hope,' he said, and that word of praise lifted me above physical tiredness. 'It's a pity though,' he added.

'What's a pity?' Carter asked.

'That Dick Randall doesn't know anything about engineering,' he answered. 'If he could understand just how much we've achieved in one single day with the three of us working without interruption for meal-getting, then he'd realise how close we are to success.'

It was cold outside the hangar and the biting north

wind made the cut on my forehead ache as though the bone had been smashed. Back at the quarters there was a smell of roasting chicken. We cleaned ourselves up and then gathered in the front room. The trestle table had been covered. It was only an old curtain, but it gave it a more friendly air. The table was laid for four. Saeton crossed to a cupboard and brought out glasses and a bottle of whisky. 'I thought you were broke,' Carter said.

Saeton laughed. 'Only bankrupts can afford to be spendthrifts.' But though he laughed, there was no laughter in his eyes. 'No point in hoarding when Randall may sell us out tomorrow.'

The click of high-heeled shoes sounded on the concrete of the passage outside and Saeton sprang to open the door.

Diana Carter was such a contrast to her husband that she produced in me a sense almost of shock. She was a product of the war, a hard, experienced-looking woman with a wide, over-thick mouth and hennaed hair. There was nothing homely about her. She swept in, a flash of red dirndl skirt and tawny hair with eyes that matched the green of her jersey and a motion of the body that was quite uninhibited. Her glance went straight to Saeton and then fell to the bottle. 'What are we celebrating, Bill?' Her voice was deep and throaty with just the trace of an American accent.

'The fact that we're broke,' Saeton answered, handing her a glass. 'Randall's selling us up tomorrow. Then you and Tubby can go and raise a family in peace.'

She made a face at him and raised her glass. 'You'll talk him out of it,' she said. 'But I'll need some curtains, tablecloths, bed-linen and china. I'm not going to live in a pig-sty. And we're short of beds.' Her gaze had fastened on me. It was a curiously personal stare and her green eyes were a little too narrow, a little too close.

Saeton introduced us. Her eyes strayed to the adhesive tape across my forehead. But all she said was, 'Where is he going to sleep?'

'I'll fix him up,' Saeton answered.

She nodded, her gaze concentrated on him. 'Two months, you said, didn't you, Bill?' There was a sort of breathlessness about her that contrasted pleasantly with the essentially masculine atmosphere of the hangar. And the gleam of excitement in her eyes made me think she found it more interesting keeping house for three men on this lonely airfield than sharing a flat in London with a girlfriend. 'Who's the girl that comes with the milk and eggs in the morning?' she asked.

'Oh, she works at the farm,' Saeton answered carelessly. 'Her name is Else.'

'She behaved more like a camp-follower than a land-girl.' She was looking at her husband as she said this, but then she switched her gaze back to Saeton. 'Yours?'

'Really, Diana!' Saeton picked up the bottle and refilled her glass. 'Have you managed to make the room opposite habitable?'

'After nearly a day's work – yes. Was she cook here before I came?'

'She came in and did things for us in the evening sometimes,' Saeton admitted. 'By arrangement with the farm.'

'I thought she looked at me like a cat that sees the cream whipped away from under her nose.' It wasn't said banteringly. Her tone was hard and her eyes searched her husband's face. 'I guess I dug in my heels just in time.' There was a bitter clutching in her voice. She was the sort of woman who would always be wanting the thing that had just been put out of her reach. Slowly she turned and faced Saeton again. 'Is she foreign? She has a queer way of talking.'

Saeton nodded. 'Yes, she's German. A D.P. Her name is Else Langen.' He seemed reluctant to talk about her. 'Suppose we have some food now, Diana?'

She nodded and finished her drink. As she turned to go, she paused. 'So long as I'm here tell her to confine her activities to outside help.'

Saeton laughed. 'I'll tell her.' And he went on chuckling quietly to himself after Diana had left the room, as though at some private joke.

To my surprise Diana proved to be a good cook. The meal was excellent, but before it was over the warmth of the oil stove and the whisky had made me drowsy. I'd had a long day and not much sleep the night before and as they were planning to start work again at seven, I decided to go straight to bed. Saeton fixed me up with a camp bed in one of the back rooms. But for a long time I lay awake, hearing the murmur of their voices. It wasn't so much the cold that seeped up through the canvas of the bed that kept me awake as the fact that so much had happened since I had arrived at Membury. My mind was chock-full of half-digested impressions, all of them slightly fantastic, like a dream.

But the thing that stood out in my mind was that this was the beginning of a new life for me. I was safe up here at Membury. Whatever the future of Saeton's outfit, it served my purpose. I'd stay here for a time and then, when the hunt had died down, I'd leave and get a job. I wouldn't bother about flying. I'd go back to engineering. My day's work had taught me that I was still an engineer, and there was no shortage of jobs for engineers.

The only thing that worried me as I drifted off to sleep was that Saeton's company would pack up before it was safe for me to venture again into the outside world. All that seemed to stand between it and failure was the personality of the man. And yet, somehow, that seemed sufficient.

We breakfasted next morning at six-thirty. Diana got the meal for us, an old blue dressing-gown over her nightdress, her face freshly made-up. We ate in silence by the light of an oil lamp, the threat of foreclosure hanging bleakly over the table, like the reluctant daylight. Diana's eyes kept straying to Saeton's face as though searching for something there that she needed. He didn't once look up. He ate with the fierce concentration of a man to whom the act of feeding is a necessary interruption to the day's work. Tubby Carter, on the other hand, ate with a leisurely enjoyment.

As I went down the passage after breakfast to get my overalls, I passed an open door and paused at the sight of a bed made up on the floor in the far corner. Hanging on the wall was the jacket Saeton had worn the previous night. The man had given me his own camp bed. I don't know whether this had any direct bearing on my actions later, but I know that at the time it made me feel part of a team and that from that moment I wanted Saeton to win out and get his plane on to the airlift.

There was no hesitation when we reached the hangar, no discussion. We went straight on with the jobs we had left the night before. But as we worked I was conscious of a mounting tension. Several times Saeton paused and glanced impatiently at his watch. A nerve twitched at the skin of his temple. But he worked steadily, unhurriedly, as though the day stretched ahead with absolute security.

Diana brought coffee shortly after eleven. She tossed the morning paper to me with a little secret smile and then turned to Saeton. 'Well, he's here.'

'Randall?'

'Yes.'

'Then why the devil didn't you bring him up here with you?'

'I told him to wait. He's talking to that girl from the farm. I thought you'd like to know he's got someone with him.'

'Someone with him?' He jerked round towards her. 'A man?'

'Yes.'

'What sort of a man?'

'Short, slightly bald, with glasses and—'

'I don't want to know what he looks like. What's his business?'

'I haven't asked him.' She seemed to enjoy baiting him with the mystery.

'Well, what's he look as though he does?' he asked angrily.

'He's dressed in a dark suit and a Homburg. I guess he might be something in the City – a lawyer maybe.'

'A lawyer! My God! Don't say he's brought his solicitor with him. Go and tell them to wait. I'll be down right away. And get rid of that girl.' He was scrambling out of his overalls, cursing softly to himself, as her heels click-clacked across to the door of the hangar. When he had his jacket on, he picked up a mug of coffee and drank it slowly as though steadying himself, controlling the violence that seemed on the verge of erupting from him. At length he turned to Carter. 'We've got to convince him, Tubby,' he said in a tight, controlled voice.

The other nodded. 'But don't lose your temper, Bill, like you did last time. It only makes him stutter. If he was an engineer—'

'Well, he's not an engineer,' Saeton snapped. 'He's just a jerk that's been left fifty thousand by an adoring aunt.' He thrust his hands into his pockets. 'All right. I won't lose my temper – provided he shows some sense.' He turned then and walked quickly out of the hangar as though he were going to something unpleasant and wanted to get it over.

Carter watched him go and then shrugged his shoulders. 'Trouble is, every time he meets Randall he acts as though he's a steam hammer driving sense into a block of pig iron.'

'What's Randall like?' I asked. I wasn't really interested. This was none of my business. I had picked up the paper and was searching through it for a follow-up to the 'Callahan' story of the previous day.

'Oh, he's not a bad fellow really. Got more money than sense, that's all.'

I had found what I wanted now, a paragraph on an inside page stating that the police believed 'Callahan' had left the country. I folded the paper and laid it on the bench. There was nothing for me to worry about. I looked across at Carter. 'Why does Randall want to sell up?' I asked.

Carter shrugged. 'Bored, I suppose. He's not really interested in aircraft. Horse racing is what he lives for. Besides, three years is a long time.'

I glanced at the plane and then back again to Carter. There was something here I didn't understand. It had been at the back of my mind and now that I didn't have to worry about myself any more it came to the fore. 'It doesn't take three years to get a plane into the air,' I said.

Carter looked up at me guardedly. 'Hasn't Saeton told you anything about these engines? I thought you were an old friend of his?'

I didn't pursue the matter, but turned back to the lathe.

It must have been about half an hour later that Saeton came in, his face dark with anger. With him was a tall, erect-looking man with a brushed-up ginger moustache and rather prominent eyes. He wore tweed trousers and a cloth cap and the open neck of his sheepskin jacket was filled with a brilliant blue and gold silk scarf. Behind them trotted a soft, plump little man with a brief-case.

Saeton went straight over to Carter. 'You can pack up work on that induction coil, Tubby. We're through.' His voice was hard and vicious.

Carter sat back on his stool, still holding the coil in his hands as though he didn't want to let it go, and stared at Randall unbelievingly. 'Doesn't he understand we only need two more months?' he asked Saeton. 'With Fraser here—'

'I've told him all that,' Saeton cut in. 'But we're not dealing with Randall. We're dealing with Mr Reinbaum here.' He nodded to the plump little man whose white fingers were fidgeting with the lock of his brief-case. 'He holds the mortgages.'

'I don't understand,' Carter said slowly. 'Those mortgages were given to Dick as security for money he advanced to the company. How does this fellow Reinbaum come into it?'

Randall cleared his throat awkwardly. 'I borrowed money on the mortgages,' he said.

'Well, surely if you repay the money—'

'We've been over all this,' Saeton cut in impatiently. 'Randall has lost heavily – betting.' The word came out with an explosive violence. 'Reinbaum has received an offer for the plane and all our tools and equipment and Randall has agreed to close.'

'It is out of the question that we should receive a

better offer,' Reinbaum said. He had a soft, slightly foreign voice.

'The offer,' Saeton said harshly, 'is twenty-five thousand for the whole box of tricks. That's just two thousand more than the mortgages.'

'But that means winding up the company,' Carter said. 'Randall can't do that unless one of us agrees. Together we out-vote him. Under the articles of the company—'

'Please, Mr Carter,' Reinbaum interrupted. 'It is not a question of voluntary liquidation.'

'You mean your going to force us into liquidation?' Carter asked and there as an obstinate note in his voice that made me suddenly respect him.

'The damnable part of it is,' Saeton said angrily, 'that when Randall advanced us that last five thousand his solicitor insisted that since it was for material for building the engines, the engines themselves must be included in the mortgage.' He swung round on Randall. 'By God!' he said. 'If it wasn't that I'd swing for it, I'd—' He turned quickly and started to pace up and down, his hands clenched as he fought down the fury that mottled his features. He stopped as he came face to face with the completed engine. Then he reached up to the wall and pressed the starter switch. The engine turned, coughed twice and roared into life. The hangar shook to the thundering din of it. He turned to Randall. 'Come here, Dick,' he shouted. 'Look at it! Feel the power of it! That engine is ready for installation.' He waved his thick hand at the bench. 'The second is already taking shape. In a month it will be finished. In six weeks we'll be on test. And on the 25th January, we'll be on the airlift. In two months you'll be director of a company owning the most talked-of plane in the world. Think of it! Saeton Aircraft freighter slashes fuel costs! My God, man, haven't you any ambition? We'll make a fortune, and all I'm asking you for is two months. You've carried the company for nearly three years. Another two months isn't much to ask.'

So that was it! Saeton had something new in engine design, something that would reduce fuel consumption. His wasn't the first company that had come to grief trying to pursue this particular mirage, and yet the vibrance in his voice, the sheer gripping enthusiasm of the man carried conviction. I stared at Randall. Surely he would give Saeton those two months? I wanted to see those engines finished now. I wanted to see them in the air, to see them tested. If Saeton succeeded. . . .

But Randall was shaking his head. 'I'm s-sorry, Bill.' He was stuttering now in his embarrassment. 'I'm p-pretty well cleaned out, you know.'

'You mean you've lost so heavily you can't buy those mortgages back?' Saeton was staring at him hard.

Randall nodded.

'But what about your horses, your car, that house down at Hatfield?'

The other stared at him. 'But dash it,' he exclaimed. 'I can't sell the house. It's been in the family for generations. And I won't sell my horses.' His face was flushed and there was an obstinate look in his eyes. 'I'm sorry, Bill,' he said again. 'But you've had all the money you're going to get out of me. My solicitor warned me against—'

'Oh, damn your solicitor!' Saeton shouted. 'Can't you understand that in two months' time—' He didn't finish. He had seen the obstinate look in Randall's eyes and he turned away in disgust. His hand reached out and switched off the engine. The din gradually died away. Saeton's hand tightened on the boss where the propellor would be fitted as he turned slowly and faced Reinbaum. 'So it comes to this – we're dealing direct with you, Mr Reinbaum. Is that correct?' His voice was quiet and controlled.

Reinbaum beamed and bowed slightly.

'What are your terms for allowing us to continue with the fitting out of the plane?'

Reinbaum shook his head. 'I'm sorry, Mr Saeton. I do not speculate.'

'I've given you some idea of what we're doing here,' Saeton said. 'Surely we can come to some arrangement?'

'The offer I have for your plane and the equipment here is conditional on acceptance within forty-eight hours.' Reinbaum spread his hands in a little apologetic gesture. 'Unless you can pay what is due on the mortgages I must foreclose.'

'You know damn well we can't pay. In two months—'

'I want the money now, Mr Saeton.' The softness was leaving Reinbaum's voice.

'But if you wait two months . . .' Saeton's voice was desperate. 'Two months isn't long. In two months' time I'll have all the backing . . .'

'I repeat, if you cannot pay what is due, then—' Reinbaum shrugged his shoulders.

Saeton turned away and in the light from the high windows I caught a glint of tears in his eyes. He went slowly over to the bench and stood there, fiddling with the armature he'd spent so many laborious hours winding, his back towards us.

'Well, I think that is settled then,' Reinbaum said, glancing up at Randall, whose face was stiff and wooden. 'We had better go now, Major.'

In a flash I saw my refuge up here on this aerodrome disappearing. But it wasn't only that. I believed in Saeton. I wanted to see these engines in the air. The money I had made ferrying planes and on currency deals wasn't honest money. I didn't care what happened to it. Probably it would be better if I threw it away and I might as well throw it away on this. 'Just a moment,' I said as Reinbaum and Randall were turning away. 'Is it one of the mortgages that has fallen due?'

Randall shook his head. 'No. It's the interest on them.'

'The interest on them?' I exclaimed. 'How much?'

'Eleven hundred and fifty,' Randall murmured.

I turned to Saeton 'Can't you raise that?' I said. 'You could sell something.'

He shook his head. 'There's nothing here that isn't essential,' he said dully. 'If we sold any part of the equipment we couldn't go on. Besides, it's all mortgaged. Everything in this hangar is mortgaged.'

'But surely you've got some money of your own?' I persisted.

'Blast you!' he shouted, swinging round on me. 'You don't have to hammer the truth of this home to me. I don't possess any money at all. For the past month we've lived on credit. My bank account is overdrawn to the tune of more than a hundred pounds. Carter is in the same boat. And don't for God's sake start asking me if I haven't any friends. I haven't any friends to the tune of eleven hundred quid.' He turned to Randall and Reinbaum. 'Now get the hell out of here, the pair of you. Take what action you like.'

They turned to go.

'Just a minute,' I called to them. 'The amount is eleven hundred and fifty?'

It was Reinbaum who answered. 'The exact amount is eleven hundred and fifty-two pounds four shillings and sevenpence.'

'Then perhaps you would make me out a receipt,' I said. I had got my wallet out and was extracting my cheque book.

He stood there staring at me as though a pit had suddenly opened at his feet. 'A receipt, please, Mr Reinbaum,' I repeated.

He came slowly towards me. 'How do I know that your cheque will be honoured? I do not give a receipt—'

'You have the law to protect you in a case like that,' I said. 'Can I see the documents proving that you are the legal possessor of these mortgages?' I was enjoying myself, enjoying the sudden surprised silence that descended on the hangar. Nobody spoke, and Reinbaum stared at me with baffled eyes. For some reason he didn't want to be paid. I thought of how I had got that money and I was suddenly glad I'd ferried those planes. Somehow this made the racket worth while.

Saeton was the first to come to life. 'Just a minute, Fraser. Apart from the fact that I can't allow you to do this, it won't help you know. We owe money. Also we've got to be carried for two months.'

'I realise that,' I said. 'What's the absolute minimum that will carry you to the flying stage?'

He hesitated. 'About another thousand.' His voice suddenly took on new life. 'You see, we've got the metal and the castings. We've got everything. All we need is to cover some of the bills that'll come in and our living—' His sudden excitement faded and his words stopped. 'To carry us and pay the interest on these mortgages you've got to have nearly two thousand five hundred.'

I sat down and wrote out Reinbaum's cheque. 'Who shall I make it out to?' I asked him.

'Weiner, Reinbaum and Company,' he answered sullenly.

As I entered the amount on the cheque counterfoil Saeton touched my shoulder. 'Have you really got two thousand five hundred in your account?' he asked almost unbelievingly.

'Not in my account,' I answered. 'But with my life policy I'm good for that much.'

He didn't say anything, but his hand gripped my shoulder for a moment.

I checked the documents Reinbaum reluctantly produced from his brief-case. Then I gave him the cheque and got his receipt. All this time Saeton had been standing over us and as the little man straightened up, he said, 'It was the engines you wanted, wasn't it, Reinbaum?' There was a dangerous quietness about his voice.

'I do not want anything,' Reinbaum answered him. 'Only the moneys.' But I don't think he expected Saeton to believe him, for he added quickly, 'My clients are interested in the charter business.'

'And who exactly are your clients?' Saeton asked in the same quiet voice.

'I am sorry. I cannot tell you that.'

Saeton took him gently by the collar. 'It was the engines they wanted, wasn't it? Somebody tipped them off that you held the mortgages.' He turned to Randall. 'Had you borrowed on these mortgages when you were down here last, in October?' he asked.

'I'm not sure,' Randall answered unwillingly. 'Possibly.'

'Did you mention it to anyone – Else, for instance?'

Randall flushed. 'I may have done. I can't remember. I—'

'You tell a stray D.P. and you don't tell me.' Saeton's face was white with anger. 'And you're a director of my company. My God!' He picked little Reinbaum up by his collar with his two hands and shook him. 'Who are these clients of yours?' he shouted, and I thought he'd break the little man apart.

Reinbaum's spectacles fell to the ground. His plump white hand moved agitatedly with a flash of gold. 'Please,' he cried. 'I will have the police—'

'Oh, no you won't.' Saeton laughed through his clenched teeth. 'You've no friends here. They'll swear I never laid a finger on you. Now, then. Who are your clients?' He shook the man till he screamed and then he flung him away like a discarded sack. Reinbaum stumbled, caught his foot against a stool and went sprawling on to the dusty concrete. 'Well?' Saeton demanded, standing over him.

The man was fumbling blindly for his glasses. Saeton kicked them over to him and then picked up the brief-case, searching through it, strewing the papers he'd discarded over the floor. He found what he wanted in the end, holding it up, his eyes darkening with anger as he read it. 'My God!' he exclaimed. 'So that's it.' He stuffed the letter into the pocket of his jacket and stared down at Reinbaum. 'How did they discover I'd got the prototype?' he demanded. 'How did they know that?' He turned away as Reinbaum shook his head obstinately. 'All right. It doesn't matter.' He tossed the brief-case and the rest of the papers on to the man's prostrate body. 'Now, get out!'

Reinbaum seized hold of the case, bundled the documents into it and fled.

'Well, that's that,' Saeton said. He was standing there in the centre of the hangar like a bull that has disposed of one matador and is glaring round in search of the next. His gaze fixed on Randall. 'Do you realise what you've done? You bloody nearly—' His mouth clamped shut and he came steadily down the hangar. 'You're not fit to be a director of a company.' He stopped and Randall muttered inarticulate apologies. 'Sit down,' Saeton said, his voice shaking with anger. 'Now write me out a letter of resignation.'

'Suppose I refuse to resign?' Randall's face was pale and though his head was turned towards Saeton his eyes slid away from him.

'Refuse to resign!' There were white patches under Saeton's eyes. 'Whilst we've been slaving our guts out up here to build something worth while, what have you been doing? Gambling. Gambling with the future of my company. Well, Carter and I aren't working twenty-four hours a day to make a fortune for a man who has never done a thing to help us, who—'

'That's not true,' Randall answered. 'Who brought the thing out of Germany in the first place? You'd never have got it back here unless I'd smuggled it out in one of my vehicles. Who's paid for all the development work? Every time you've asked for money—'

'It's all covered by those mortgages,' Saeton cut in, his voice suddenly quiet. 'You've never risked a penny, whilst Carter and I have sunk everything we had without security. The company owes you nothing, except a fee for smuggling the prototype out, and I'll see you're paid for that. As for the mortgages, it's not my fault you've borrowed on them and gambled away the proceeds.' He paused for breath. 'You've only yourself to blame, Dick,' he added, almost gently. He pulled a pen out of his pocket and pushed it into Randall's hand. 'I suggest "pressure of other business".

Randall hesitated. But Saeton was standing over him and there was something compelling in the quietness of the man, the whiteness of his face. Randall glanced up once and then the pen was scratching at the paper Carter had thrust in front of him.

As soon as Randall had signed it, Saeton took it from him, glanced at it quickly and then slipped it into his pocket. 'And now for God's sake get Reinbaum off the airfield before I murder the little bastard.'

Randall stood up, hesitating as he faced us. I thought for a moment he was going to say something, but the hostile silence was too much for him. He turned away and we watched him go, heard the door click shut, and then we were alone in the hangar. Saeton pulled out his handkerchief and mopped his face. 'Christ!' he said. 'I didn't expect to come out of that with the company still intact.' His gaze came round to me. 'About the luckiest thing I ever did was to tell you you could stay on up here.' He rubbed his hands and his voice was suddenly cheerful as he said, 'Well, that leaves us short of the necessary three directors, Tubby. I suggest, therefore, as an acknowledgment of our gratitude to him for saving the company in its hour of need, we invite Mr Fraser to join the board.' Relief had brought a hint of laughter to his voice. 'Will you second that, Tubby?'

Carter glanced quickly across at me. I was conscious of a fractional hesitation, and then he said, 'Yes. I second that.'

Saeton came over and clapped me on the shoulder. 'You're now a director of Saeton Aircraft Ltd, entitled to a yearly salary of £2,500.' He gave a quick laugh. 'It's never been paid yet.' And then he added, 'But some day – soon now—' He stopped. His voice had become serious. 'Fraser, I can't thank you enough. God knows why you did it, but' – he gripped my hand – 'I can't tell you—' His voice broke off as though the words he sought were inadequate and he just stood there, wringing my hand. 'Why did you do it, eh? Why?' He was suddenly laughing. 'I can't forget little Reinbaum's face when you asked him for that receipt.' He laughed till the tears ran down his face. Then, with a quick change to brusqueness: 'Well, why did you do it?'

'I don't quite know,' I answered awkwardly. 'I wanted to, that's all.' I turned away, embarrassed by the sudden emotionalism in his voice.

There was a moment's silence, and then he said abruptly, 'Well, let's get back to work.' The sense of purpose was back in his eyes now and it gave me an odd feeling of closeness to him as I went over to my lathe and picked up the half-completed piston.

But somehow I couldn't concentrate. Randall's words came between me and my work. I'd been caught out in a racket once and I didn't want any more of it. If they were smuggling foreign patents. . . .

I switched off the lathe and went over to Saeton. He was seated on a stool, working on the armature again with the fierce concentration of a man who holds the future in his hands. He looked up at me as I stood over him. 'Well, what is it?' he asked impatiently.

'I want all the cards on the table,' I said. 'I don't like working in the dark – not any more.'

He stared at me, his jaw clamped shut, an angry frown creasing his forehead. I watched the thick hand resting on the bench slowly clench into a fist. His eyes had hardened and narrowed with the clenching of his hand. I was looking at the man who had hit me two nights ago in the woods on the edge of the airfield.

'Well?'

I hesitated. But I had to know where I stood. The hours I had spent working at that lathe had given me a new sense of confidence in myself. 'Come on, man, let's have it,' he snapped. 'What's on your mind?'

'This aero engine of yours' – I nodded to the gleaming bulk standing against the wall on its wooden chocks – 'you didn't design it, did you?'

'So that's it. You think I've filched somebody else's design, do you?'

'I didn't say that,' I answered, feeling suddenly uncertain under the cold anger of his gaze. 'I simply want to know whether you designed it.'

'Of course I didn't design it,' he snapped. 'You're not a fool. You know damn well I don't know enough about engineering to design an aero engine.' He had risen slowly to his feet and was standing in what seemed to be a characteristic attitude, legs slightly straddled, head thrust forward. 'I suppose, now you've bought your way into the thing, you think you're entitled to throw your weight about.' The violence died out of him and in a milder tone he added, 'If you must know, it's a bit of wartime loot. One day I'll tell you the whole story. But not now.'

'Who owns the patent?' I asked.

'I do,' he snapped. 'The prototype was never completed. For a man in your position, you've a devilish sensitive conscience.' He sat down abruptly. 'For God's sake let's get on. We've wasted enough time already.'

I had barely got back to my lathe when there was a knock at the door of the hangar. 'See who it is, Fraser,' Saeton said. 'If it's Randall I won't talk to him.'

But it wasn't Randall. It was Diana, and with her was a girl in a faded brown smock. I knew her at once. She was the girl who had been talking with Saeton in the hangar that first night I had come to Membury. She had recognised me, too, for she caught her breath and stared at me as though I were something unexpected, and her broad forehead contracted in a frown that gave her pleasant, quiet features a brooding look.

'She wants to see Bill,' Diana said.

I pulled open the door and they came in, the girl hesitating over the sill as though she feared a trap. Then she was walking down the hangar, her head erect, her shoulders squared.

Saeton looked up, saw her and jumped to his feet. 'What the devil are you doing here?' His thick eyebrows were dragged down, his body tense.

The girl didn't flinch. Her eyes roved quickly along the bench. They were wide, intelligent eyes, and they seemed to miss nothing. Finally they came to rest on the completed engine and their expression seemed to change, to soften.

'Did you bring her here, Diana?' Saeton's voice was harsh.

'Yes. She wanted to see you.'

'I don't care who she wanted to see,' he stormed. 'Get her out of here.' He got control of himself and turned to me. 'Take her outside and find out what she wants. I won't have people walking in and out of this place as though it were a railway station.' But almost immediately he changed his mind. 'All right. I'll talk to her.' He strode down the hangar. The girl hesitated, her eyes lingering a moment on the litter of the work bench, then she turned and followed him.

'That's a queer girl,' Diana said to her husband. 'When Randall was here she hung around the quarters like a cat on hot bricks. After a time she went out on to the airfield, and the next I saw of her she came flying through the woods, her face white and her eyes wet with tears. Had she been in a concentration camp or something?'

'Her father died in one,' Carter answered. 'That's all I know.'

Saeton came back then, his face angry, the muscles at the side of his jaw swollen with the clenching of his teeth.

'What did she want?' Diana asked.

He didn't appear to hear her question. He strode straight past her and seated himself at the bench again. 'Will you bring lunch for the three of us up here at one-thirty,' he said.

Diana hesitated. But his manner didn't encourage questions. 'All right,' she said and left the hangar. I turned back to my lathe, but all the time I was trying to remember the scrap of conversation I'd overheard that night in the hangar.

Twice I glanced at Saeton, but each time his expression stopped me from putting the question that was on the tip of my tongue. At length I said, 'Who is that girl?'

His head jerked up. 'That was Else,' he said.

'What was her father's work?'

His fist crashed down on the bench. 'You ask too many damned questions,' he shouted.

I felt the shock of his violence as though it was a physical blow and went quickly over to the lathe. But a moment later he was at my side. 'I'm sorry, Neil,' he said quietly. 'Don't worry if I lose my temper now and then.' His hand reached out and gripped my arm and he waved his free hand to the litter of parts on the bench. 'I feel sometimes as though these were my organs and I was being slowly manufactured and pieced together. If anything happened to prevent the completion of the whole thing—' He didn't finish and the grip on my arm slowly relaxed. 'I'm a bit tired, that's all. It'll be like this until we're in the air.'

CHAPTER THREE

Time stood still for me on Membury aerodrome in the weeks that followed. November slid into December and I scarcely noticed it. We rose at six and started work at seven. There was coffee around eleven and we had our lunch and our tea at the work bench. Breakfast and dinner were the only meals we had back at the quarters, dinner anywhere between seven-thirty and nine according to how the work ran. Tempers were short and the working hours long, and though Diana Carter talked about Prince Charles and the fighting in Palestine and the opening of Tegel airport, it meant nothing to me, for I didn't read the papers. My life was the cold, grey cavern of the hangar; I lived and dreamed engineering and the world outside Membury ceased to exist.

And yet through it all ran a thread of pure excitement. Saeton never gave me a briefing on the engines. He left me to find out for myself and as the Satan Mark II, which was what he called it, took shape under our hands, my sense of excitement mounted.

The difference lay mainly in the system of ignition and the method of fuel injection. High-pressure injectors delivered filtered fuel to the combustion chambers. Injector timing replaced ignition timing and there was a complicated system for metering the fuel, the flow having to be adjusted constantly in relation to altitude. It was essentially a compression ignition motor and though it was a long way removed from the diesel design, it was soon clear to me that the man who had made the original design must have been a diesel expert.

It took us just over five weeks to build that second engine and all the time it was a race – our skill against my bank balance, with the airlift date looming ever nearer.

It was a queer life, the four of us alone up on that derelict airfield, held there by Saeton's tenacity and the gradual emergence of that second engine. I got to know Tubby Carter and his wife well, and they were as different as two people could be. Maybe that was why they had got married. I don't know. They were an oddly assorted pair.

Tubby was a stolid, unimaginative man, round of face and round of figure with rolls of fat across his stomach and sides that gave him the appearance of a man-sized cupid when stripped. His nature was happy and friendly. He was one of the nicest men I have ever met, and one of the most uninteresting. Outside of flying and engineering, he knew nothing of the world, accepting it and ignoring it so long as it let him get on with his job. What had caused this unenterprising son of a Lancashire poultry farmer to take to flying I never discovered. He had started in a blacksmith's shop and when that closed down he had got a job in a foundry producing farm equipment. He was one of those men who shift along on the tide of life and the tide had drifted him into a motor factory and so into the engineering side of the aircraft industry. That he had started to fly because he wanted to would have been quite out of character. I imagine it just happened that way and his stolidity would have made him an ideal flight engineer in any bomber crew.

When I think of Tubby, it is of a happy child, whistling gently between his teeth. He was like a fat, cheerful mongrel, something of a cross between airedale and pug. His eyes were brown and affectionate and if he'd had a tail it would have wagged every time anybody spoke to him. But when I think of him as a man, then it is only his hands I remember. His hands were long and slender, and quite hairless like the rest of him – very different from Saeton's hands. Give those hands a piece of metal and ask them to produce something out of it and he grew to man's stature in an instant, all his being concentrated in his fingers, his face wreathed in a smile that crinkled his eyes, and his short, fat lips pursed as he whistled endlessly at the work. He was a born engineer, and though he was a child in other respects, he had a streak of obstinacy that took the place of initiative. Once he had been persuaded on a course of action, nothing would deflect him. It was this tenacity that made one respect as well as like him.

His wife was so different it was almost unbelievable. Her father had been a railroad construction engineer. He had been killed when she was seventeen, crushed by a breakdown crane toppling on its side. In those seventeen years she had travelled most of America and had acquired a restless taste for movement and the atmosphere of the construction camps. Her mother, who had been half-Italian, had died in childbirth and Diana had been brought up in a masculine world. She had many of a man's qualities – a decisiveness, the need of a goal to aim for and a desire for strong leadership. She was also a woman, with a good deal of the hot passion of the Italian.

After her father's death she became a nurse. And when Pearl Harbor came she was one of the first to volunteer for overseas service. She had come to England as a W.A.A.C. in 1943 and had been stationed at a B17 station near Exeter. That was where she had met Tubby. They had met again in France and had been married at Rouen in 1945. Later she had worked for a short time in the Malcolm Club Organisation, whilst Tubby was flying with Transport Command.

I have said that she was a hard, experienced-looking woman. Certainly that was my first impression. But then I had expected somebody altogether younger and softer. She was several years older than Tubby and her life had not been an easy one. Her brother had been working for the Opel people in Germany, and with no family and no friends, she had been very much on her own in the big hospital in New York. She would never talk about this period. She had endless stories to tell of the railroad camps and of her service life in Britain, France and Germany. But I never heard her talk of her life in that New York hospital.

Tubby she treated rather as a child. I learned later that she had had an operation that had made it impossible for her to have any children of her own. Whether this had anything to do with it, I don't know. But I do know this, that right from the start she was fascinated by Saeton. She breathed in the atmosphere of drive and urgency that he created as though it were life itself. I had a feeling that in him she found all the excitement and her girlhood again, as though he recreated for her the life she had led with her father on the railroads of America.

But though I got to know these two well, Saeton himself remained a mystery. What his background was I never discovered. It was as though he had sprung like a phoenix from the flames of war complete with his looted engine and the burning dream of a freighter fleet tramping the airways of the world. He'd talk and he'd conjure visions, but he never talked about himself. He had been a test pilot before the war. He knew South America, particularly Brazil, and he'd flown for an oil company in Venezuela. He'd done some gold prospecting in South Africa. But as to who his family were, what they did and where he'd been born and brought up, I still have no idea. Nor have I any knowledge of how he came to be a pilot.

He was the sort of person that you accept as a

finished article. His personality was sufficient in itself. I felt no urge to rummage around the backstairs of his life. He seemed to have no existence outside of the engines. He even slept with them after that scene with Randall as though he were afraid an attempt might be made to steal them. When he had warned me that his temper would be short until we were in the air, it was no understatement. His moods were violent and when nervous or excited he used his tongue like a battering ram. I remember the day after I had promised to finance the company he came up to me as I was working at the lathe. 'I think you agreed to cover us over the building period.' His voice was angry, almost belligerent. 'I want some money.'

I began to apologise for not having settled the financial details with him before, but he cut me short: 'I don't want your apologies. I want a cheque.' The rudeness of his tone jolted me. But it was typical of the man, and if I expected deference on account of my financial standing in the company he made it clear I wasn't going to get it.

He wanted the money right away to meet some bills and I had to go back to the quarters for my cheque book. That was how I first came into real contact with Else, the fifth character in this extraordinary story. She was standing at the entrance to the quarters, calling for Diana.

'She's just taken coffee up to the hangar,' I said.

The girl turned at the sound of my voice. She wore the same brown overall that she'd worn the previous day when Diana had brought her to the hangar and in her hands she held four very still but sharp-eyed fowls. 'I have bring these,' she said, making a slight movement of her hands that caused the one cockerel to beat his wings angrily.

'I didn't know we were having a feast tonight,' I said.

'No, no. Mrs Carter starts to keep chicken for you, I think.' The girl's voice, with its marked foreign accent, was like a breath of the old life, a reminder of brief meetings in bars and hotel bedrooms that is all in the way of memories that most pilots take out of the cities where they touch down.

'She'll be back in a minute,' I said. 'If you and the chickens can wait.' I started to move through the door and then stopped and we stood there for a moment smiling at each other, not saying anything.

'You are partners with Mr Saeton now?' she said at last.

'Yes.'

She nodded and her gaze strayed to the trees that screened us from the hangar. Her face was rather square, the cheekbones high, the skin pale and dappled with freckles. Her nose tipped up slightly at the end as though she'd pressed it too often against windows as a kid. She wore no make-up and her eyebrows were thick and fair, like the untidy mop of her hair that blew in the wind. She turned to me slowly and her lips parted as though she were about to say something, but she just stood there looking up at me with a frown as though by staring at me she could resolve some riddle that puzzled her. Her eyebrows were dragged down at the corners and her eyes shifted from the adhesive tape on my forehead to meet mine with a direct, level gaze. They were the colour of mist in a mountain valley – a soft grey.

'What were you doing up at the hangar the other night?' I had asked the question without thinking.

Her lips moved slightly at the corners. She had a very mobile mouth. 'Perhaps I ask you why you run away, eh?'

For an instant I thought she had connected me with the police inquiries in the neighbourhood. But then she asked, 'Are you an engineer?' and I knew it was all right.

'Yes,' I said.

'And you work on the engines with Mr Saeton?'

I nodded.

'Then perhaps we meet again, yes?' She smiled and thrust the birds into my hands. 'Will you please give these to Mrs Carter.' She half-turned to go and then hesitated. 'When you do not know what to do with yourself, perhaps you come and talk with me. It is very lonely up here sometimes.' She turned then and walked across the clearing and as I watched her disappear amongst the trees I felt excitement singing through my blood.

The story of Else Langen was a jig-saw puzzle that I had to piece together, bit by bit. I asked Saeton about her that night, but all he'd say was that she was a German D.P. 'Yes, but what's her story?' I persisted. 'Tubby says her father died in a concentration camp.'

He nodded.

'Well?' I asked.

His eyes narrowed. 'Why are you so interested in her?' he demanded. 'Have you been talking to the girl?'

'I had a few words with her this morning,' I admitted.

'Well, keep clear of her.'

'Why?'

'Because I tell you to,' he growled. 'I don't trust her.'

'But you had her cooking here for you.'

'That was—' He stopped and his jaw stiffened. 'Have some sense,' he added. 'The girl's German and this engine we're working on was first designed in Germany.'

'Is that why you're sleeping up at the hangar now?' I asked. 'Are you suggesting that the girl—'

'I'm not suggesting anything,' he snapped. 'I'm just telling you to keep clear of her. Or is it too much to expect you to keep your hands off a woman for five weeks?'

The sneer in his voice brought me to my feet. 'If you think—'

'Oh, for God's sake, Neil. Sit down. All I'm asking you to do is not to get talking to anyone outside of the four of us here. For your sake as well as mine,' he added pointedly.

I might have taken his advice if the monotony of our life hadn't got on my nerves. Perhaps monotony is the wrong word. It was tension really. The work itself was exciting enough. But we never relaxed. The four of us were cooped up together, never leaving the aerodrome, always in the same atmosphere of pressure, always in each other's company. Within a fortnight the strain was beginning to tell. Tubby ceased to whistle at the bench and his round, cheerful face became morose, almost sulky. Diana did her best, but her chatter was hard and brittle against the solid background of long hours in the hangar. Saeton became impossible – tense and moody, flying into a rage at the slightest provocation or at nothing at all.

The atmosphere got on my nerves. I had to find some relaxation, and automatically it seemed I began thinking of Else more and more often. *It is very lonely up here sometimes*. I could see the lift of her eyebrows, the smile in her eyes and the slight spread of the corners of her mouth. *When you do not know what to do with yourself* . . . The invitation couldn't have been plainer. I brooded over it at my work, and particularly I brooded over Diana's suggestion that the girl had been a camp-follower. Saeton hadn't denied it. In the end I asked Tubby about it. 'I wasn't interested in her, if that's what you mean,' he answered 'I don't go for foreign women.'

'What about Saeton?' I asked.

'Bill?' He shrugged his shoulders. 'I wouldn't know.' And then he added almost viciously. 'They all fall for him. He's got something that appeals to women.'

'And she fell for him?'

'She was always around before Diana came.' He glanced up at me from the fuel pump he was assembling and his eyes crinkled. 'The monastic life getting you down? Well, you shouldn't have much trouble with Else. Randall used to take her out in his car when he visited us up here.'

It was a warm, soft night despite a clear sky and after dinner I said I'd take a stroll. Saeton looked across at me quickly, but he said nothing and a moment later I was striding through the still dampness of the woods, my heart suddenly light with the sense of relief at escaping at last from the atmosphere of the aerodrome. A track ran from the quarters down to the road and a little farther on I found the gates of the Manor. A light shone through the trees and the gentle putter of an electric light plant sounded across the silence of the lawns. An owl flapped like a giant moth to the shelter of the trees.

I went round to the side of the house, and through an uncurtained window saw Else standing over a table rubbing salt into a large ham. Her sleeves were rolled up and her face was flushed. She was a big, well-built girl with a full bosom and wide shoulders. She looked soft and pleasant, working there in that big kitchen and I found myself tingling with the desire to touch her, to feel the warm roundness of her body under my hands. I stood there for quite a while, watching her, liking the capable movements of her hands and the glowing concentration of her features. At length I moved to the door and knocked.

She smiled when she saw who it was. 'So! You have become bored, eh?'

'I thought you might like to come for a walk,' I said. 'It's a warm night.'

'A walk?' She looked up at me quickly. 'Yes. Why not? Come into the kitchen whilst I go and dress myself in some clothes.'

It was a big kitchen, warm and friendly, with bacon hanging from hooks in the ceiling and bunches of dried herbs and a smell of chicken. 'You like cream?' She produced a bowl full of thick cream, a loaf of bread and some home-made jam. 'Help yourself please. I will be one minute, that is all.'

I hadn't tasted cream in years and I was still eating when she returned. 'You like to take some back with you? Mrs Ellwood will not mind. She is a very 'ospitable woman.'

'No. No thanks.' I should have to explain to Saeton where it had come from.

She looked at me with a slight frown, but she made no comment. 'Come. I take you to the pond. It is very funny there at night. The frogs croak and there are many wild things.'

We went round behind the outbuildings, through the farmyard and out into a grass field. 'There are mushrooms here in the autumn. What is your name?'

'Neil Fraser.'

'Do you like working at the airfield?'

'Yes.' I spoke without thinking, conscious only of her nearness and of the fact that she hadn't hesitated to come out with me.

'It is going well, I hope?'

'Yes. Very well.'

'When will you have finished the engines?'

I took her hand. Her fingers were warm and soft in mine. She raised no objection.

'Well?'

'I'm sorry,' I said. 'What was it you asked?'

'When will you finish? When do you fly?'

'I don't know,' I said. 'In about a month.'

'So soon?' She fell silent. We were in the woods again now on a path that ran downhill. The night air rustled gently among the tall, spear-like shafts of the osiers. I tightened my grip on her hand, but she didn't seem to notice, for she asked if I were a flier and then began to talk about her brother who had been in the *Luftwaffe*.

'Where is he now?' I asked.

She was silent for a moment, and then she said, 'He is dead. He was shot down over England.' She glanced up at me, her face serious. 'Do you think we shall ever be at peace – Germany and England?'

'We're at peace now,' I answered.

'Oh, now! Now you are the victors. You occupy us with your troops. But it is not peace. There is no treaty. Germany is not permitted to join any international organisation. We cannot trade. Everything is taken from us.'

I didn't say anything. I wasn't interested in a political argument. I didn't want to be reminded that she was German. I just wanted her companionship, her warmth, the feel of her close to me. The screen of osiers parted and we were looking down a steep bank to a dew pond. It was fringed with reeds and the still surface in the centre was like a plate of burnished pewter reflecting the stars. 'It is beautiful here, yes?' The cry of a night bird jarred the stillness and a frog croaked. The stillness and the wintry beauty of it brought the blood hammering to my throat. I reached out and caught her by the shoulder twisting her round so that her neck lay in the curve of my arm. Then I bent and kissed her.

For a moment she was limp in my arms, her lips soft and open against mine. Then her body became rigid and her mouth tightened. She fought me off with a sudden and intense fury. For a moment we struggled, but she was strong and my passion subsided with the obstinacy of her resistance and I let her go. 'You – you—' She stood there speechless, panting with the effort she had made. 'Because I am German and you are English you think I should lie on my back for you? *Verfluchter Kerl! Ich hasse Sie!*' She turned, tears of anger on her face, and fled up the path. In an instant the screen of osiers had swallowed her and I was alone by the pond with the protesting croak of the frogs.

Saeton was just leaving when I got back to the quarters. 'What have you been up to?' he said, looking up at me from under his shaggy eyebrows. 'That cut of yours has opened up again.'

I put my hand to my forehead and my fingers came away sticky with blood. Else must have scratched the scab as she fought me off. 'It's nothing,' I said. 'A branch of a tree caught me, that's all.'

He grunted and went out into the night towards the hangar. As I passed the door of the Carters' home I heard Diana say, 'All right. But any time I like the

Malcolm Club will . . .' I was back in the tense atmosphere of our own little world and I'd destroyed my one chance of escape. I went to bed feeling depressed and angry with myself, for Else had been right – I had treated her as though she were a piece of occupied territory to be bought for a bar of chocolate.

The next day we had visitors. Diana rang through on the field telephone. 'There's an R.A.F. officer here and a Mr Garside of the Ministry of Civil Aviation. They want to speak to Bill.' I had answered the phone and I passed on the message to Saeton. He jumped to his feet as though I'd cracked a stock whip. 'Tell her they're not to come up here. I'll see them over at the quarters.' He searched quickly along the bench, picking up odd parts that lay amongst the junk at the back. 'Tubby. Take these out the back somewhere and hide them. Go over the whole bench and see that there's nothing left of the old engine here. I'll hold them at the quarters for five or ten minutes.'

'They may only have come to check over the plane prior to airworthiness tests,' Tubby said.

'Maybe. But I'm taking no chances. You'd better keep in the background, Neil.'

He hurried out of the hangar and Tubby searched frantically along the bench, picking up parts and stuffing them into a canvas tool bag. I stood watching him, wondering whether my identity had been discovered.

Tubby had barely returned from hiding the bag when Saeton brought the two men into the hangar. 'These are my two engineers,' he said. 'Carter and

Fraser. Tubby, this is Wing-Commander Felton, R.A.F. Intelligence, and Garside, Civil Aviation. Well, now, what exactly do you want to look at?' Saeton was forcing himself to be genial, but I could see by the way his head was hunched into his shoulders that he was angry.

'Well, if you did take it, I don't imagine you'd be fool enough to leave the prototype lying about,' the R.A.F. officer said. 'We'd like to have a look at the design you're working on.'

'I'm sorry,' Saeton said. 'That's the one thing I can't allow you to do. You can have a look at the finished engine, but the design remains secret until we're in the air.'

'You're not being very helpful,' the Intelligence Officer said.

'Why should I be?' Saeton demanded angrily. 'A German company complains that an English concern is working on a pet project of their own and immediately they have the support of our own people and you come rushing up here to investigate.'

'As far as I'm concerned the Germans can stew in their own juice,' Felton replied. 'But they've persuaded Control Commission the matter needs investigating. My instructions come from B.A.F.O. H.Q. Garside here is acting at the direct request of Control Commission.'

'Have the Rauch Motoren sent over the plans of their prototype?' Saeton asked.

'No.'

'Then how can you check from my plans whether I've lifted their design?'

The Intelligence Officer glanced at his companion. 'According to my information,' Garside said, 'they claim that the plans were looted with the prototype.'

'The plans can be withdrawn.'

'The designer is dead. The fools arrested him in the middle of his work for alleged complicity in the July 20 bomb plot.'

'Then they've only themselves to blame,' Saeton said.

'How did you know that it was the Rauch Motoren who had lodged the complaint?' the R.A.F. officer asked.

'I've admitted already that it was seeing their prototype that gave me the idea,' Saeton answered. His voice was quiet. He was keeping a tight hold of himself. 'The same company has already made an effort to get control of my outfit through a gentleman called Reinbaum who now holds the mortgages on the plane and equipment here.' He turned and faced the two of them. 'What exactly are the authorities trying to do? Do they want a German company to produce a new type of aero engine in preference to a British concern? Carter and I have worked for nearly three years on this. If we'd pinched their prototype and it was so far advanced that they were ready to go into production with it, surely we'd have been in the air now, instead of mortgaged to the hilt and still working to produce a second engine?'

The two men glanced at each other. 'So long as it

can't be proved that you looted the thing . . .' The R.A.F. officer shrugged his shoulders. 'The trouble with Control Commission is that they think in terms of supporting the Jerries. You don't have to worry as far as I'm concerned, Saeton. Three years ago I was bombing the beggars and if you'd looted the complete article . . .' He turned to his companion. 'What's your view, Garside?'

The other looked helplessly round the hangar. 'Even if it was looted,' he said slowly, 'it would be very difficult to prove it now.' He turned to Saeton. 'In any case, you've done three years' work on your engines. My advice is, get it patented as soon as possible. Doubtless the Patents Office will compare your design with the German company's, if they can produce one and if they put in a claim.'

'I notified Headquarters at the time I saw the Rauch Motoren prototype,' Saeton said.

The R.A.F. officer nodded. 'Yes, I've looked over your report. Had the devil's own job digging it out of its pigeon hole in the Air Ministry. You acted perfectly correctly as far as the authorities were concerned. You don't have to worry about that. But as Garside says – get your patents. Every day you delay, German pressure is becoming more effective.' He held out his hand to Saeton. 'Well, good luck!'

'You'd better come and have some coffee before you drive back,' Saeton suggested and he shepherded them out of the hangar.

'Well, what's all that about, Tubby?' I asked as the door of the hangar closed behind them.

'Just that our problems won't be over even when we get into the air,' he answered and went back to the bench.

Saeton was looking pleased with himself when he came back. 'What I didn't tell them,' he said with a grin, 'is that the designs are already with the Patents Office. If the German company want to put in a claim they'll have to get busy.'

'Do you think Randall had anything to do with that visit?' Tubby asked.

'Randall? Of course not. If they got hold of Randall, then there would be trouble.'

At dinner that night he announced that he was going to London. 'I want to have a word with Dick,' he said. 'Also it's time I saw the patents people.'

Diana paused, with her fork half-way to her mouth. 'How long will you be gone, Bill?' Her voice was tense.

'A couple of days.'

'Two days!'

It's strange how you can live with people and not notice what's happening right under your nose because it happens so gradually. Tubby glanced at his wife, his face pale, his body very still. The atmosphere had suddenly become electric. In the way she had spoken she had betrayed herself. She was in love with Saeton. And Tubby knew it. Saeton knew it, too, for he didn't look at her and answered too casually: 'I shall be away one night. That's all.'

It was queer. Nothing of any importance had been said, and yet it was as though Diana had shouted her infatuation from the middle of the runway. She had stripped herself naked with that too interested, too tense query and her repetition of the time as though it were eternity. Silence hung over the table like a storm that has revealed itself in one lightning stab but has still to break.

Tubby's hand had clenched into a fist and I waited for the moment when he'd fling the trestle table over and round on Saeton. I'd seen men break like that during the war, sane, solid men pushed over the edge by nerves strung too taut through danger, monotony and the confined space of a small mess.

But he had that essential stolidity, that Saxon aversion for the theatrical. The scrape of his chair as he thrust it back shattered the silence. 'I'm going out for a breath of air.' His voice trembled slightly. That was the only indication of the angry turmoil inside him – that and his eyes, which showed bright and angry in the creases of fat. His cheeks quivered slightly as he turned from the table. He shut the door quite softly behind him and his footsteps rang on the frozen earth outside and then died away into the woods.

The three of us sat there for a moment in a stunned silence. Then Saeton said, 'You'd better go and talk to him, Diana. I don't want him walking out on me. Without him, we'd be lost.'

'Can't you think of anything but your engines?' The violence of her emotion showed in her voice and in her eyes.

He looked at her then. There was something in his face I couldn't fathom – a sort of bitterness, a mixture of desire and frustration. 'No,' he said. The one word seemed drawn out of the depths of his being.

Diana leaned quickly forward. Her face was white, her eyes very wide and she was breathing as though she were making a last desperate effort in a race. 'Bill. I can't go on like this. Don't you understand—'

'I didn't ask you to come here,' his voice rasped. 'I didn't want you here.'

'Do you think I don't know that?' She seemed to have forgotten my presence entirely. Both of them had. Their eyes were at grips with each other, face to face with something inside them that had to come out. 'But I'm here. And I can't go on like this. You dominate everything. You've dominated me. I don't care how long you're away. But I can't—' She stopped then and looked at me as though aware of my presence for the first time.

I started to get to my feet, but Saeton leaned quickly forward and gripped my arm. 'You stay here, Neil,' he said. I think he was scared to be left alone with her. Still gripping my arm as though clutching hold of something solid and reasonable, he turned and looked at her. 'Go and find Tubby,' he said. His voice was suddenly cold and unemotional. 'He needs you. I don't.'

She stared at him, her lips trembling. She wanted to fight him, to beat at his resistance till it was down. But I think the essential truth of his words struck home, for suddenly there were tears in her eyes, tears of anger, and she turned and fled from the room. We heard the door of her room slam and it muffled the sound of her sobs.

Saeton's fingers slowly released their grip of my wrist. 'Damn all women to hell!' he muttered savagely.

'Do you want her?' I had put the question without thinking.

'Of course I do,' he answered, his voice tight as a violin string and trembling with his passion. 'And she knows it.' He gave a growl of anger and got to his feet. 'But it isn't her I want. Any woman would do. She knows that, too – now.' He was pacing up and down and I saw him feel automatically in his pocket for a cigarette. 'I've been lost to the world up here too long. God! Here I am with the future almost within my grasp, with everything I've dreamed of coming to the verge of reality, and it can all be thrown in jeopardy because a woman senses my primitive need.'

'You could send her away?' I suggested.

'If she goes, Tubby goes, too. Tubby loves her more than he loves himself or his future.' He turned and looked at me. 'And Diana loves him, too. This is merely—' He hesitated. And then almost bitterly, 'You know, Neil, I don't think I'm capable of love. It isn't a word I understand. Else knew that. I thought she'd see me through this period of monasticism. But when it came to the point, she wanted something I wasn't prepared to give her.' He laughed harshly. 'Diana is different. But she's got Tubby. She's driven by nothing more than an urge for excitement. There's that in women, too. The constant craving for novelty, conquest. Why the hell can't she be satisfied with what she's got already?' His hand gripped my shoulder. 'Go and find Tubby, will you, Neil. Tell him . . . Oh, tell him what you like. But for Christ's sake smooth him down. I can't get this engine to the flying stage. Nor can you. He's been in it from the beginning. The prototype didn't work, you know. For months I studied engineering, made inquiries, picked other people's brains. I produced a modified version, flew it in an old Hurricane and crashed it. Then I found Tubby and with his genius for improvisation we built one that worked. Go and talk to him. He's got to stay here, for another month at any rate. If he doesn't, you've lost your money.'

I found Tubby in the hangar and I think it was then that I first really admired him. He was quietly working away, truing up a bearing assembly that had been giving trouble. He stopped me before I could say anything. 'Bill sent you to talk to me, didn't he?'

I nodded.

He put the bearing down. 'Tell him that I understand.' And then, more to himself than to me: 'It's not his fault. It's something Diana wants that he's got. It was there inside her before she ever came here – a restlessness, an urge for a change. I thought by bringing her up here—' He moved his hand in a helpless gesture. 'It'll work itself out. She ought to have had a child, but—' He sighed. 'Tell Bill it's all right. I won't blame him so long as he gives me no cause. It'll work itself out,' he repeated. And then added quietly: 'In time.'

Saeton left next morning on the old motor bike

which was their sole form of transport. And it was only after he'd gone that I realised how much the whole tempo of the place depended on him. Without the driving enthusiasm of his personality it all seemed flat. Tubby worked with the concentration of a man trying hard to lose himself in what he was making. But it was a negative drive. For myself I found the time hang slowly on the hands of my watch and I determined to go down to the farm that evening and make it up with Else. Somehow I hadn't been able to get her out of my mind. I think it was her presence in the hangar with Saeton that first night that I'd arrived at Membury that intrigued me. The obvious explanation I had proved to be wrong. Now, suddenly, I was filled with an urgent desire to get at the truth. Also I was lonely. I suppose any girl would have done – then. But she was the only one available and as soon as Tubby and I knocked off I went down to the Manor.

The kitchen curtains were drawn and when I knocked at the door it wasn't Else who opened it. A small, grey-haired woman stood framed against the light, a swish of silk at her feet and the scent of jasmine clinging on the air. 'I was looking for Else Langen,' I explained awkwardly.

She smiled. 'Else is upstairs dressing. Are you from the aerodrome? Then you must be Mr Fraser. Won't you come in? I am Mrs Ellwood.' She closed the door behind me. 'You must find it very cold up at the airfield now. I really think Mr Saeton should get some proper heating put in. I've told him, any time he or his friends want a little home comfort to come over and see us.

But he's always so busy.' We were in the kitchen now and she went over to the Aga cooker and stirred vigorously at the contents of a saucepan, holding her dressing-gown close around the silk of her dress. 'Have you had dinner, Mr Fraser?'

'No. We have it later—'

'Then why not stay and have some food with us? It's only stew, but—' She hesitated. 'I'm cook tonight. You see, we're going to the Red Cross dance at Marlborough. It's for Else, really. Poor child, she's hardly been anywhere since she came to us. Of course, she's what they call a D.P. and she's here as a domestic servant – why do they call them D.P.s? – it's so depressing. But whether she's a servant or not, I don't think it right to keep a young thing shut away here without any life. You people at the aerodrome are no help. We never see anything of you. And it is lonely up here. What do you think of Else? Don't you think she's pretty, Mr Fraser?'

'I think she's very pretty,' I murmured.

She cocked an eye at me. She was like a little grey-haired sparrow and I had a feeling that she missed nothing. 'Are you doing anything tonight, Mr Fraser?'

'No, I was just going to—'

'Then will you do something for me? Will you come to this dance with us? It would be a great kindness. You see, I had arranged for my son, who works with the railways at Swindon, to come over, but this afternoon he rang up to say he had to go to London. I wouldn't mind if it were an English girl. But you know what country places are. And after all' – she lowered her voice – 'she is German. It would be a kindness.'

'But I've no clothes,' I murmured.

'Oh!' She waved the spoon at me like a little fairy godmother changing me into evening clothes on the spot. 'That's all right, I'm certain. You're just about my son's size. Come along and we'll see.'

And of course the clothes fitted. It was that sort of a night. By the time I had changed the three of them were assembled in the big lounge hall. Colonel Ellwood was pouring drinks from a decanter that sparkled in the firelight. He was a tall, very erect man with grey hair and a long, serious face. His wife fluttered about with a rustle of silk. And Else sat in a big winged chair staring into the fire. She was dressed in very deep blue and her face and shoulders were like marble. She looked lonely and a little frightened. She didn't look up as I came in. She seemed remote, shut away in a world of her own. Only when Mrs Ellwood called to her did she turn her head. 'I think you know Mr Fraser.' She saw me then and her eyes widened. For an awful moment I thought she was going to run from the room, but then she said, 'Good evening,' in a cold, distant voice and turned back to the fire.

She hardly said a word all through dinner and when we were together in the back of the car she drew away from me and sat huddled in her corner, her face a white blur in the reflected light of the headlights. Not until we were dancing together in the warmth of the ballroom did she break that frigid silence and then I think it was only her sense of loneliness in that alien gathering that made her say, 'Why did you come?'

'I was lonely,' I said.

'Lonely?' She looked up at me then. 'You have your – friends.'

'I happen to work there – that's all,' I said.

'But they are your friends.'

'Three weeks ago I had never met any of them.'

She stared at me. 'But you are a partner. You put up money.' She hesitated. 'Why do you come here if you do not know them?'

'It's a long story,' I answered and holding her close in the swing of the music I suddenly found myself wanting to tell her. But instead I said, 'Else. I want to apologise for the other night. I thought—' I didn't know how to put it, so I said, 'That first night I came to Membury – why were you in the hangar with Saeton?'

Her grey eyes lifted to my face and then to the cut on my forehead. 'That also is a long story,' she said slowly. And then in a more friendly tone: 'You are a strange person.'

'Why did Saeton think I was a friend of yours that night?' I asked. 'Why did he call to me in German?'

She didn't answer for a moment and I thought she was going to ignore the question. But at length she said, 'Perhaps I tell you some day.' We danced in silence for a time. I have said that she was a big girl, but she was incredibly light on her feet. She was like thistledown in my arms and yet I could feel the warm strength of her under my hand. The warmth and the music were going to my head, banishing loneliness and the tension of the past weeks. 'Why did you come to the farm tonight?' she asked suddenly.

'To see you,' I answered.

'To apologise?' She was smiling for the first time. 'You did not have to.'

'I told you – I was lonely.'

'Lonely!' Her face seemed to harden. 'You do not know what that word means. Please, I would like a drink.' The music had stopped and I took her over to the bar. 'Well, here is to the success of those engines!' Her tone was light, but as she drank her eyes were watching me and they did not smile. 'Why do you not drink? You are not so crazy about those engines as Mr Saeton, eh?' She used the word crazy in its real sense.

'No,' I said.

She nodded. 'Of course not. For him they are a part of his nature now – a great millstone round his neck.' She hesitated and then said, 'Everyone makes for himself on this earth some particular hell of his own. With Saeton it is these engines, *ja*?' She looked up into my face again. 'When are they finished – when do you fly them?'

I hesitated, but there was no reason why she shouldn't know. Living so close at the Manor she would see us in the air. 'With luck we'll be in the air by Christmas. Airworthiness tests are fixed for the first week in January.'

'So!' A sudden mood of excitement showed in her eyes. 'Then you go on to the air bridge. I hope your friend Saeton is happy then.' Her voice trembled slightly. She was suddenly tense and the excitement in her eyes had changed to bitterness.

'Why are you so interested in Saeton?' I asked her.

'Interested – in Saeton?' She seemed surprised, almost shocked.

'Are you in love with him?' I asked.

Her face hardened and she bit at her lower lip. 'What has he been saying?'

'Nothing,' I answered.

'Then why do you ask me if I am in love with him? How can I be in love with a man I hate, a man who has—' She stopped short, staring at me angrily. 'Oh!' she exclaimed. 'You are so stupid. You do not understand nothing – nothing.' Her fingers were white against the stem of the glass as she sought for words.

'Why do you say you hate him?' I asked.

'Why? Because I offer him the only thing I have left to offer – because I crawl to him like a dog—' Her face was suddenly white with anger. 'He only laugh. He laugh in my face, I tell you, as though I am a common – *Nutte*.' She spat the word out as though she were hating herself as well as Saeton. 'And then that Carter woman comes. He is a devil,' she whispered and then turned quickly away from me and stared miserably at the crowded bar. 'You talk of loneliness! That is what it is to be lonely. Here, with all these people. To be away from one's own people, a stranger in a—'

'You think I don't understand,' I said gently. 'I was eighteen months in a prison camp in Germany.'

'That is not the same thing. There you are still with your own peoples.'

'Not after I escaped. For three weeks I was alone in Germany, on the run.'

She stared up at me and gave a little sigh. 'Then perhaps you do understand. But you are not alone here.'

I hesitated, and then I said, 'More alone than I have ever been.'

'More alone than—' She stopped and gazed at me unbelievingly. 'But why is that?'

I took her arm and guided her to a seat. I had to tell her now. I had to tell someone and she was a German, alone in England – my story was safe with her. I told her the whole thing, sitting there in an alcove near a roaring fire with the sound of dance music in my ears. When I had finished she put her hand on mine. 'Why did you tell me?'

I shrugged my shoulders. I didn't know myself. 'Let's dance,' I said.

We didn't talk much after that. We just seemed to lose ourselves in the music. And then Mrs Ellwood came and said we must go as her husband had to start work early the next morning. In the car going back Else didn't talk, but she no longer shrank into her corner of the seat. Her shoulder leant against mine and when I closed my hand over hers she didn't withdraw. 'Why are you so silent?' I asked.

'I am thinking of Germany and what fun we could have had there – in the old days. Do you know Wiesbaden?'

'Only from the air,' I answered and then wished I had not said that as I saw her lips tighten.

'Yes, of course – from the air.' She took her hand away and seemed to withdraw into herself. She didn't speak again until the car was climbing the hill to Membury, and then she said very quietly, 'Do not come to see me again, Neil.'

'Of course I shall,' I said.

'No.' She said it almost violently, her eyes staring at me out of the darkness. Her hand gripped mine. 'Please try to understand. We are like two people who have caught sight of each other for a moment through a crack in the wall that separates us. Whatever the S.S. do to my father, I am still a German. I must hold fast to that, because it is all I have left now. I am German, you are English, and also you are working—' She stopped and her grip on my hand tightened. 'I like you too much. Do not to come again, please. It is better so.'

I didn't know what to say. And then the car stopped. We were at the track leading up to the quarters. 'You can return the clothes in the morning,' Mrs Ellwood said. I got out and thanked them for the evening. As I was about to shut the car door, Else leaned forward. 'In England do you not kiss your partners goodnight?' Her face was a pale circle in the darkness, her eyes wide. I bent to kiss her cheek, but found her lips instead. 'Goodbye,' she whispered.

The Ellwoods were chuckling happily as they drove off. I stood watching until the red tail-light had turned into the Manor drive and then I went up the track to the quarters, wondering about Else.

It was to be nearly three weeks before I saw Else again, for Saeton returned the following evening with the news that the Air Ministry now wanted the plane on the airlift by 10th January, and airworthiness tests had been fixed for 1st January.

In the days that followed I plumbed the depths of physical exhaustion. I had neither the time nor the energy for anything else. And it went on, day after day, one week dragging into the next with no let-up, no pause. Saeton didn't drive. He led. He did as long as we did at the bench, then he went back to the hangar, typing letters far into the night, ordering things, staving off creditors, running the whole of the business side of the company. My admiration for the man was boundless, but somehow I had no sympathy for him. I could admire him, but I couldn't like him. He was inhuman, as impersonal as the mechanism we pieced together. He drove us with the sure touch of a coachman who knew just how to get the last ounce out of his horses, but didn't care a damn what happened to them in the end so long as he made the next stage on time.

But it was exciting. And it was that sense of excitement that carried me through to Christmas. The airfield hardened to iron as the cold gripped it. The runways gleamed white with frost in the sunshine on fine days. But mostly it was grey and cold with the ploughed-up earth black and ringing hard and metallic like solidified lava. There was no heating in the hangar. It had the chill dank smell of a tomb. Only the work kept us warm as we lathered ourselves daily into a sweat of exhaustion.

Saeton was working for engine completion on 20th

December, installation by 23rd December and first test on Christmas Day. It was a tight schedule, but he wanted a clear week for tests. But though we worked far on into the night, we were behind schedule all the time and it was not until Christmas Eve that we completed that second engine.

The final adjustments were made at eight-thirty in the evening. We were dead beat and we stood in front of the gleaming mass of metal in a sort of daze. None of us said a word. We just stood back and looked at it. I produced a packet of cigarettes and tossed one to Saeton. He lit it and drew the smoke into his lungs as though smoke alone could ease the tension of his nerves. 'All right, fill her up with oil, Tubby, and switch on the juice. I'll get Diana. She'd like to be in on this.' He went over to the phone and rang the quarters. I helped fill up with oil. We checked that there was petrol in the wall tank, tightened the unit of the petrol feed and switched on.

There was a tense silence as we waited for Diana. Five weeks' work stood before us and a touch of the starter button would tell us whether we'd made a job of it. It wasn't like an engine coming out of a works. There everything moves with an inevitable progression from the foundry and the lathes and the electrical shop to the assembly and the final running in. This was different. Everything had been made by hand. One tiny slip in any of the precision work . . . I thought of how tired we were. It seemed incredible that everything would work smoothly.

A knock on the door of the hangar sounded

incredibly loud in the silence. Tubby went to the door and let his wife in. 'Well, there it is, Diana,' Saeton said, pointing to the thing. His voice trembled slightly. 'Thought you'd like to see what your cooking has given birth to.' Our laughter was uneasy, forced. 'Okay, Tubby. Let her go.' He turned away with a quick nervous twist of his shoulders and walked down to the far end of the bench. He wasn't going to touch that starter switch himself. He wasn't even going to watch. He stood with his back towards us, puffing at his cigarette, his hands playing aimlessly with the pieces of metal lying on the bench.

Tubby watched him, hesitating.

'Go on – start it.' Saeton's voice was a rasp.

Tubby glanced at me, swallowed nervously and crossed to the starter motor which was already connected up. He pressed the switch. It groaned, overloaded with the stiffness of the metal. The groaning sound went on and on. He switched off and went over to the engine, his practised eye running over it, checking. Then he went back to the starter motor. The groaning sound was faster now, moving to a hum. There was a sharp explosion. The engine rocked. The hum of the starter took over again and then suddenly the stillness of the hangar was shattered by a roar as the motor picked up. The whole building seemed to shake. Tubby switched off, hurried to the engine and adjusted the controls. When he started it again, the roar settled to a steady, glorious hum of power, smooth and even like the dynamos of a power station.

Saeton ground out his cigarette and came back

along the bench. His face was shining with sweat. 'She's okay,' he shouted above the din. It was part statement, part question. Tubby looked up from the controls and his fat, friendly face was creased in a happy grin and he nodded. 'Carburation wants a bit of adjustment and the timing on that—'

'To hell with the adjustments,' Saeton shouted. 'We'll do those tomorrow. All I care about at the moment is that she goes. Now switch the damned thing off and let's go and have a drink. My God, we've earned it.'

The roar died away as Tubby cut off the juice. The hangar was suddenly still again. But there was no tension in the stillness now. We were all grinning and slapping each other on the back. Tubby caught hold of his wife and hugged her. She had caught our mood of relief. Her eyes were shining and she just didn't seem able to contain her excitement. 'Anybody else like a kiss?' I was nearest to her and she reached up and touched her lips to mine. Then she turned and caught hold of Saeton. She pressed her lips to his, her hands tightening on his overalls. He caught hold of her shoulders and pushed her away almost roughly. 'Come on. Let's get a drink.' His voice was hoarse.

Saeton had kept a bottle of whisky for this moment. 'Here's to the airlift!' he said.

'To the airlift!' we echoed.

We drank it neat, talking excitedly of how we'd manage the installation, what the first test flight would show, how the plane would behave on two engines. Saeton planned to use the outboard engines for take-off only. With the extra power developed by the Satan Mark II all flying would be done on the two engines. We bridged in our excitement all the immediate problems and talked instead of how we should develop the company, what planes we should buy, what routes we should operate, whose works we should take over for mass production. In a flash the bottle was empty. Saeton wrung the last drop out of it and smashed it on the concrete floor. 'That's the best bottle of Scotch I've ever had and I won't have it lying on any damned rubbish heap,' he shouted. His eyes were dilated with the drink and his own excitement.

Our glasses suddenly empty, we stood around looking at them in silence. It seemed a pity to end the evening like this. Saeton apparently felt the same. 'Look, Tubby,' he said. 'Suppose you nip on the old bike and run down into Ramsbury. Bring back a couple of bottles. Doesn't matter what it costs.' He glanced at me. 'Okay, Neil? It's your money.' And as I nodded, he clapped my arm. 'You won't regret having backed us. If you live to be as old as Methuselah you'll never make a better investment than this. More Scotch, Tubby!' He waved his arm expansively. 'Get on your charger, boy, and ride like hell. This bloody dump is out of Scotch. Come on. We'll hold your stirrups for you and we'll be out to cheer you as you ride back, bottles clanking in your saddle-bags.'

We were all laughing and shouting as we trooped out to the store-room where the bike was housed. Tubby roared off, his face beaming, his hand whacking at the rear of the bike as he flogged through the gears.

His tail-light disappeared through the trees and we fell suddenly silent. Saeton passed his hand across his eyes. 'Let's go in,' he said moodily and I saw that the nerves at the corners of his eyes were twitching. He was near to breaking point. We all were. A good drink would do us good and I suddenly thought of Else. 'What about making it a party?' I said. 'I'll go down and see the Ellwoods.' I knew they wouldn't come, but I thought Else might. Saeton tried to stop me, but I was already hurrying down the track and I ignored him.

A light was on over the front door of the farm. It looked friendly and welcoming.

Mrs Ellwood answered my ring. 'It's you, Mr Fraser.' She sounded surprised. 'We thought you must have left.'

'We've been very busy,' I murmured.

'Come in, won't you?'

'No, thank you. I just came down to say we're having a party. I wondered if you and Colonel Ellwood could come up for a drink. And Else,' I added.

Her eyes twinkled. 'It's Else you're wanting, isn't it? What a pity! We've been expecting you all this time and now you come tonight. Else has had to go to London. Something about her passage. She's going back to Germany, you know.'

'To Germany?'

'Yes. Oh, dear, it's all very sudden. And what we shall do without her I don't know. She's been such a help.'

'When is she going?' I asked.

'In a few days' time, I imagine. It was all very

unexpected. Just after that dance. She got a letter to say her brother was very ill. And now there is some trouble about her papers. Do come and see her before she goes.'

'Yes,' I murmured. 'Yes, I'll come down one evening.' I backed away trying to remember if Else had said she had a second brother. 'Goodnight, Mrs Ellwood. Sorry you won't join us.' I heard the door close as I started back down the drive. Hell! The evening suddenly seemed flat. A feeling of violent anger swept through me. Damn the girl. Why for God's sake, couldn't she be home this evening of all evenings?

I took a short cut through the woods. I was just in sight of the quarters when I heard the snap of a twig behind me. I glanced over my shoulder and saw the figure of a man emerging out of the darkness. 'Who's that?' he asked. The voice was Tubby's.

'Neil,' I said. 'Did you get the Scotch?'

For an answer I heard the clank of bottle against bottle. 'Bloody bike ran out of petrol just up the road.' His voice was thick. He'd either had several at the pub or he'd opened one of the bottles. 'What are you doing, looking for fairies?'

'I've just been down to the farm,' I said.

'Else, eh?' He laughed and slipped his arm through mine.

We went on in silence. A lighted widow showed through the trees like a homing beacon. We came out of the woods and there was the interior of the dining-room. Saeton and Diana were there, standing very close together, a bottle on the table and drinks in their hands. 'I wonder where they got that?' Tubby murmured. 'Come on. We'll give them a surprise.'

We had almost reached the window when Diana moved. She put down her drink and moved closer to Saeton. Her hand touched his. She was talking. I could hear the murmur of her voice through the glass of the window. Tubby had stopped. Saeton took his hand away and turned towards the door. She caught hold of him, swinging him round, her head thrown back, laughing at him. The tinkle of her laughter came out to us in the cold of the night air.

Tubby moved forward. He was like a man in a dream, compelled to go to the window as though drawn there by some magnetic influence. Saeton was standing quite still, looking down at Diana, his hard, leathery face unsoftened, a muscle twitching at the corner of his mouth. Standing there in the darkness facing that lighted window it was like watching a puppet show. 'All right. If you want it that way.' Saeton's voice was harsh. It came to us muffled, but clear. He knocked back his drink, set down the glass and seized hold of her by the arms. She lay back in his grip, her hair hanging loose, her face turned up to him in complete abandon.

Saeton hesitated. There was a bitter set about his mouth. Then he drew her to him. Her arms closed around his neck. Her passion was to me something frightening. I was so conscious all the time of Tubby standing there beside me. It was like watching a scene from a play, feeling it through the senses of a character who had yet to come on. Saeton was fumbling at her dress, his face flushed with drink and quite violent. Then suddenly he stiffened. His hands came away from her. 'That's enough, Diana,' he said. 'Get me another drink.'

'No, Bill. It's me you want, not drink. You know you do. Why don't you—'

But he took hold of her hands and tore them from his neck. 'I said get me another drink.'

'Oh God! Don't you understand, darling?' Her hand touched his face, stroking it, smoothing out the deep-etched lines on either side of the mouth. 'You want me. You know you do.'

Tubby didn't move. And I stood there, transfixed by his immobility.

Saeton's hands slowly reached out for Diana, closed on her and then gripped hold of her and hurled her from him. She hit the edge of the table and clutched at it. He took two steps forward, standing over her, his head thrust slightly forward. 'You little fool!' he said. 'Can't you understand you mean nothing to me. Nothing, do you hear? You're trying to come between me and something that is bigger than both of us. Well, I'm not going to have everything wrecked.'

'Go on,' she cried. 'I know I don't rate as high as that bloody engine of yours. But you can't go to bed with an engine. And you can with me. Why don't you forget it for the moment? You know you want me. You know your whole body's crying out for—'

'Shut up!'

But she couldn't shut up. She was laughing at him, goading him. 'You never were cut out for a monk. You lie awake at nights thinking about me. Don't you? And I lie awake thinking about you. Oh, Bill, why don't you—'

'Shut up!' His voice shook with violence and the veins were standing out on his forehead, hard and knotted.

Her voice dropped to a low murmur of invitation. I could no longer hear the words. But the sense was there in her face, in the way she looked at him. His hands came slowly out, searching for her. Then suddenly he straightened up. His hand opened out and he slapped her across the face – twice, once on each cheek. 'I said – shut up! Now get out of here.'

She had staggered back, her hand to her mouth, her face white. She looked as though she were going to cry. Saeton reached out for the bottle. 'If you'd had any sense you'd have given me that drink.' His voice was no longer hard. 'Next time, pick somebody your own size.' He tucked the bottle under his arm and turned to go. But he hesitated at the door, looking back at her. I think he was going to say something conciliatory. But when he saw the blazing fury in her eyes, his face suddenly hardened again. 'If you start any trouble between me and Tubby,' he said slowly, 'I'll break your neck. Do you understand?' He wrenched open the door and disappeared.

A moment later the outer door of the quarters opened and we were spotlighted in the sudden shaft of light. Saeton stopped. 'How long have you two been—' He slammed the door. 'I hope you enjoyed your rubbernecking. I'm going over to the hangar.' His footsteps rang on the iron-hard earth as his figure merged into the darkness of the woods.

Neither of us moved for a moment. Utter stillness surrounded us, broken only by the muffled sound of Diana's sobs where she lay across the table, her head buried in her hands amongst the litter of glasses. I felt the chill glass of the bottles as Tubby thrust them into my hands. 'Take these over to the hangar,' he said in a strangled voice.

I watched him as he opened the door of the quarters and went inside, walking slowly, almost unwillingly. I didn't move for a moment. I seemed rooted to the spot. Then the door of the dining-room opened and I saw him enter. I'd no desire to stand in as audience on another painful scene. I turned quickly and hurried through the woods after Saeton.

When I entered the hangar, Saeton was sitting on the work bench staring at the new engine and drinking out of the bottle. 'Come in, Neil.' He waved the bottle at me. 'Have a drink.' His voice was slurred, almost unrecognisable. God knows how much he'd drunk in the short time it had taken me to get to the hangar.

I took the bottle from him. It was brandy and more than half-empty. The liquid ran like fire down my throat and I gasped.

'You saw the whole thing, I suppose?' he asked.

I nodded.

He laughed, a wild, unnatural sound. 'What will Tubby do?'

'I don't know,' I said.

He got off the bench and began pacing up and

down. 'Why did he ever let her come here? It was no place for her. She likes plenty going on – lots of people, excitement, plenty of noise and movement. Why don't men learn to understand their wives? Let's forget about it.' He waved his arm angrily. 'What have you got there – Scotch?' He came over and picked up one of the bottles from the bench where I'd placed it. 'Thank God we've got some liquor, anyway.' He glanced at the bottle of brandy which I still held. 'Queer, a woman hiding away a bottle like that.' He unscrewed the top of a whisky bottle.

'Haven't you had enough?' I suggested.

He gave me a glassy stare. 'It's Christmas Eve, isn't it? And the engine is finished. I could drink a bloody vat.' He raised the bottle to his lips and drank, rocking slightly back on to his heels and then forward on to his toes. 'Funny, isn't it?' he muttered hoarsely, wiping his lips with the back of his hand. 'You start out with the idea of celebrating and before you know where you are you're trying to drown your sorrows. Neil, old man.' His free hand reached out and fastened around my shoulders. 'Tell me something. Be honest with me now. I want an honest reply. Do you like me?'

I hesitated. If I'd been as drunk as he was it wouldn't have mattered. But I was comparatively sober and he knew it.

His arm slipped away from my shoulders and he staggered away from me towards the engine. He stood in front of it and addressed it. 'You bastard!' he said. Then he lurched round towards me. 'I haven't a friend in the world,' he said and there was a frightful bitterness in his voice which caught on a sob of self-pity. 'Not a friend in the whole wide world,' he repeated. 'Diana was right. An engine is something you create, not a living being. God damn it! I don't care. Do you hear me? – I don't care. I don't give a damn for the whole human race. If they don't like me, why should I care? I don't need anything from them. I'm building something of my own. And that's all I care about, do you hear? I don't give a damn—' He turned suddenly at the sound of the hangar door opening.

It was Tubby. He came slowly down the hangar. 'Give me a drink,' he said.

Saeton handed him the bottle. Tubby raised it to his lips and gulped, Saeton watching him, his body tense. 'Well?' he asked. And then as Tubby didn't answer he added, 'For God's sake say something, can't you? What happened?'

Tubby raised his eyes and looked at Saeton. But I don't think he saw him. His hand strayed to the leather belt that supported his trousers. 'I thrashed her,' he said in the same flat tone. 'She's packing now.'

'Packing?' Saeton's voice was suddenly hard and crisp. In that moment he seemed to shake off all the effects of the drink.

'I've telephoned for a taxi.'

Saeton strode over to him and caught hold of him by his jacket. 'You can't walk out on me now, Tubby. In a few days we'll be making our first test flight. After all this time.'

'Can't you forget about your engine for just one night?' Tubby's voice was tired. There was a sort of hopelessness about it. 'I want some money, Saeton. That's what I came up to see you about.'

Saeton laughed suddenly. 'There isn't any money. You know that. Not until we're on the airlift.' The sudden sense of domination was back in his voice and I knew that he had seen how he could keep Carter with us.

'How much do you want, Tubby?' I asked, feeling for my wallet.

Saeton rounded on me, his face heavy with anger. 'If you think the two of us can get the plane into the air, you're crazy,' he said. 'For one thing the margin of time is too small. For another there may be alterations to make. Neither you nor I—' He turned away with a quick, angry shrug.

'How much do you want?' I asked again.

'A fiver.' He came across to me and I gave him the notes. 'I hate to do this, Neil, but . . .' His voice tailed away.

'Forget it,' I said. 'Are you sure that will be enough?'

He nodded. 'It's only to get Diana to London. She'll stay with her friends. She's got a job waiting for her. It's just to see her through for a few days. She's going back to the Malcolm Club. She worked for them during the war and they've been wanting her back ever since the airlift got under way.' He stuffed the money into his pocket. 'She'll pay you back.'

He turned to leave the hangar, but Saeton stopped him. 'They employ girls at the Malcolm Club, not engineers. What are you going to do?'

Tubby looked at him. 'I'm staying here,' he said. 'I promised I'd see you into the air and I'll keep my promise. After that—'

But Saeton wasn't listening. He came across the hangar like a man who had been reprieved. His eyes were alight with excitement, his whole face transfigured. 'Then it's okay. You're not walking out on me.' He caught hold of Tubby's hand and wrung it. 'Then everything's all right.'

'Yes,' Tubby answered, withdrawing his hand. 'Everything's all right, Bill.' But as he turned away I saw there were tears in his eyes.

Saeton stood for a moment, watching him go. Then he turned to me. 'Come on, Neil. Let's have a drink.' He seized hold of the opened bottle of Scotch. 'Here's to the test flight!'

There was only room for one thing in the man's mind. With a sick feeling I turned away. 'I'm going to bed,' I said.

CHAPTER FOUR

It wasn't until the following day that I realised how much Diana had been doing for us. It wasn't only that she'd cooked our food, made our beds, kept the place clean and neat and done all the little odd jobs that are so boring and yet are an essential part of the act of living. She'd done more than that. By her brightness, her cheerfulness – her mere presence – she had cushioned the tense exhaustion of our effort. She had provided a background for us in which we could momentarily relax and gather strength for another day's sustained effort. The place seemed flat without her.

I cooked the breakfast that morning. Tubby hadn't got back until the early hours. He looked all in when I called him. His round, friendly face was hollow and drained of all its natural cheerfulness. And Saeton looked like death when he came across from the hangar. His face was grey and the corners of his eyes twitched nervously. He was suffering from a hangover.

But I think it was more than that. He was hating himself that morning. There was something inside of him that drove him on. It wasn't exactly ambition. It was something more urgent, more essentially a part of his nature – a frustrated creative urge that goaded him, and I think he'd been fighting it through the long, drunken hours of the night. He wasn't a normal human being. He was a cold, single-purposed machine. And I think that part of him was at war with his Celtic blood.

It was the grimmest Christmas I have ever had. We spent the day in bench tests on the new engine and in getting the first engine in position in the nacelle. The hangar was equipped with overhead gear for this purpose. It had been a maintenance hangar in the days when the Americans had had the aerodrome. Without that gear I don't know how we should have done it. But no doubt Saeton had thought of that when he decided to rent the hangar. I was looking after the commissariat and though it was all canned food that I served it took time. I was thankful that we were so near the end of our work.

It wasn't only the fact that Diana had gone. There was Tubby. No set-back ever discouraged him and his cheery grin had seen me through many bad moments. But now his end of the bench was silent. He didn't whistle any more and there was no friendly grin to cheer me. He worked with stolid, urgent drive as though the work itself, as well as Saeton, stood between him and his wife. It was only then that I realised how much I had leaned on his good-natured optimism. He had never asked me any questions. To this day I don't know how much he knew about me. He had just accepted me and in his acceptance and in his solid ordinariness he had created an atmosphere that had made the aerodrome reality and the past somehow remote.

That was all gone now. A sense of impermanence crept into the hangar as though we were on the fringe of the outside world and I began to worry about the future, wondering whether, when we flew out of Membury, the police would get on my trail again. I suddenly found myself in dread of the outside world.

That first day after Diana's departure was hell. A tenseness brooded over us in the din of the hangar where the new engine was being run in on the bench. But on the following day Saeton had recovered from his hangover. He came down at six-thirty and got our breakfast. He didn't talk much but a quiet, steadying confidence radiated from him. I never admired him more than I did then. The following day would see the work of installation completed. He was face-to-face with the first test flight. Three years of work were concentrated on the results of that one day. The previous flying tests had resulted in the plane crashing and the man's nerves must have been stretched to the uttermost. But he never showed it. He set out to instil confidence in us and renew our interest and enthusiasm. A forced cheerfulness would have been fatal. He didn't make that mistake. He did it by the force of his personality, by implanting in us his own feelings. The mood sprang from deep within him and was natural and real. I felt as though he had stretched out his hand to lift me up to his own pitch of excitement. And Tubby felt it, too. It didn't start him whistling again at his work and there was no good-natured grin, but as we heaved on the pulley chains to jockey the second engine into position for lowering into its nacelle I suddenly realised that his heart was in it again.

We didn't knock off that night till past ten. By then the two engines were in position. All we had to do the next day was connect them up, fix the airscrews and prepare the plane for the first test. 'Think she'll make it, Tubby?' Saeton asked.

'She'd better.' Tubby spoke through his teeth and there was a gleam in his eyes as he stared up at the plane as though already he saw her winging into Gatow on those two engines we had sweated blood to produce.

I knew then that everything was all right. In one day Saeton had quietly and unobtrusively overlaid Tubby's bitterness with enthusiasm for the plane and an overwhelming interest in the outcome of the flight.

December 28 – a Tuesday – was the last day of preparation. As the light faded out of the sky we slid back the doors of the hangar and started up the two motors. The work bench whitened under a film of cement dust kicked up by the backlash of the two props. Nobody cared. Tubby and I stood in the dust and grinned at each other as Saeton revved the motors and the whole fuselage quivered against the grip of the brakes. As the noise died down and the props slowly jerked to a standstill, Tubby gripped my arm. 'By God!' he said. 'They work. It's good to see something you've made running as smoothly as that. I've never built an engine from scratch before,' he added.

We were building castles in the air that night as we sat over the remaining bottle of Scotch. The airlift was only our springboard. Between us we swept past the work-out into the airways of the world. Saeton's imagination knew no common bounds. He drew a picture for us of planes tramping the globe, able to cut steamer rates as well as steamer schedules, of a huge assembly line turning out freighters, of a gigantic organisation running freight to the ultimate ends of the earth. 'The future of the passenger plane lies in jets,' he said. 'But freight will go to any company that can offer the lowest rates.' He was standing over us and he leaned down, his eyes shining, and gripped the two of us by the shoulder. 'It's queer. Here we are, just three ordinary types – broke to the wide and living on credit – and tomorrow, in the air over this derelict airfield, we shall fly the first plane of the biggest freight organisation the world has ever seen. We're going to be the most talked-of people in the world in a few months' time. It's been tough going up here.' He grinned. 'But not half as tough as it's going to be. You'll look back on this period as a holiday when we start to get organised.'

And then, with one of those abrupt changes of mood, he sat down. 'Well, now, let's get tomorrow sorted out. To begin with I'd rather not taxi out of the hangar. You never know, something may go wrong and she may swing. Neil. You know the Ellwoods. Suppose you go down and arrange for them to send one of their tractors up here. I'd like it here by eight.' He turned to Tubby. 'Ground tests will take most of the morning I expect. But I'd like to be in the air by midday. How are we fixed for petrol? Are all the tanks full?'

Tubby shook his head. 'No. Only the main tanks. They're about two-thirds full.'

'That'll do.'

'What about checking over the controls?' Tubby asked. 'I'd like to run over the plane itself.'

'We did it after she was flown in,' Saeton said.

'Yes, I know, but I feel—'

'We haven't time, Tubby. She came in all right and we went over her before we finally closed the purchase. If she was all right then, she's all right now. Neil, go and fix that tractor, will you? The sooner we get to bed the better. I want everyone to be fresh tomorrow.' He jerked back his chair and got to his feet. 'A lot depends on it.' He pushed his hand through his thick hair and grinned. 'Not that I shall get much sleep. I'm too darned excited. I haven't felt so excited since I did my first solo. If we pull this off—' He laughed nervously as though he were asking too much of the gods. 'Good-night.' He turned quickly and went out.

I glanced at Tubby. He was tying endless knots in a piece of string and humming a little tune. He was nervous, too. So was I. It wasn't only the test flight. For me there was the future. Membury had been a refuge, and now the outside world was crowding in on us. I pushed back my chair. 'I'll go and arrange about the tractor,' I said, but I was thinking of Else. I needed to feel that there was somebody, just one person in the world that cared what happened to me.

The Manor seemed in darkness, but I could hear the sound of the light plant and when I rang Else opened the door to me. 'I was afraid you might have gone already,' I said.

'I leave on Monday,' she said. 'You wish to come in?' She held the door open for me and I went through into the lounge where a great log blazed in the open hearth. 'Colonel and Mrs Ellwood have gone out for this evening.' She turned quickly towards me. 'Why have you come?'

'I wanted to arrange with Colonel Ellwood for a tractor tomorrow.'

'To bring the airplane out of the hangar?'

I nodded. 'We're flying tests tomorrow.'

'*Das ist gut*. It will be good to see those engines in the air.' Her tone was excited. 'But—' She hesitated and the excitement died out of her, leaving her face blank and miserable. 'But he will not be here to see.' She turned back to the fire and almost automatically took a cigarette from the box on a side table and lit it. She didn't speak for a long time, just standing there, drawing the smoke into her lungs and staring into the fire. Something told me not to say anything. Silence hung between us in the flickering firelight, but there was nothing awkward about it. It was a live, warm silence. And when at length she spoke, the intimacy wasn't broken. 'It has been such a long time.' The words were whispered to the fire. She was not in the room. She was somewhere far away in the reaches of her memory. She turned slowly and saw me again. 'Sit down, please,' she said and offered me a cigarette. 'You remember I ask you not to come here again?'

I nodded.

'I say that a wall separates us.' She pushed back her hair with a quick, nervous gesture. 'I was afraid I will talk to you because I am too much alone. Now you are here and—' She shrugged her shoulders and stared into the fire again. 'Have you ever wished for something so much that nothing else matter?' She didn't seem to expect a reply and after a moment she went on. 'I grew up in Berlin, in a flat in the Fassenenstrasse. My mother was a cold, rather nervous person with a passion for music and pretty clothes. My brother Walther was her life. She lived through him. It was as though she had no other existence. My father and his work did not mean anything to her. She knew nothing about engineering.' She shifted her gaze from the fire and stared at me with a bitter smile. 'I think I was never intended to be born. It just happened. My father never spoke about it, but that I think is what happen, for I was born eight years after my brother when my mother was almost forty.' Her smile ceased suddenly. 'I think perhaps it was a painful birth. I grew up in a world that was cold and unfriendly. I seldom saw my father. He was always working at some factory outside Berlin. When I left school I took a secretarial course and became a typist in the Klockner-Humboldt-Deutz A.G. There I fell in love with my boss.' She gave a bitter laugh. 'It was not difficult for him. I had not had much love. He took me away to Austria for the ski-ing and for a few months we shared a little apartment – just a bedroom really. Then he got bored and I cried myself into a nervous breakdown. That was when I first really met my father. My mother did not wish to be bothered with me, so she sent me to stay with him in Wiesbaden. This was in 1937.'

Her gaze had gone back to the fire. 'My father was wonderful,' she went on, speaking slowly. 'He had never had anyone to help him before. I looked after the flat and did all his typing. We made excursions down the Rhine and took long walks in the Black Forest. His hair was white even then, but he was still like a boy. And for my part, I became engrossed in his work. It fascinated me. I was not interested in men. I could not even bear for a man to touch me any more. I lived and breathed engineering, enjoying the exactness of it. It was something that had substance, that I could believe in. I think my father was very impressed. It was the first time he discovered that women also have brains. He sent me to the University at Frankfurt where I took my engineering *staatsexamen*. After that I return to Wiesbaden to work as my father's assistant in the engine works there. That was in 1941. We were at war then and my father is engaged on something new, something revolutionary. We work on it together for three years. For us nothing else matters. Oh, I know that my father does not like the régime, that he is in touch with old friends who believe that Germany is doomed under Hitler. But apart from the air raids, it is quiet at Wiesbaden and we work at the designing board and at the bench, always on the same thing.'

She threw her cigarette into the fire. Her face was very pale, her eyes almost luminous in the firelight as she turned to me. 'They came when we were working in the engine shop – two officers of Himmler's S.S. They arrested him there in the middle of our work. They said he was something to do with the attempt on Hitler's life. It was a lie. He had nothing to do with the conspiracy. But he had been in contact with some of the people who were involved, so they took him away. They would not even wait for me to get him some clothes. That was on the 27th July, 1944. They took him to Dachau and I never saw him again.' Her lips trembled and she turned away, stretching her hand down for another cigarette.

'What did you do?' I asked.

'Nothing. There was nothing I could do. I try to see him, of course. But it is hopeless. I can do nothing. Suddenly we have no friends. Even the company for whom he has worked for so long can do nothing. The *Herr Direktor* is very sympathetic, but he has instructions not to employ me any more. So, I go back to Berlin, and a few days later we hear my father is dead. It means little to my mother, everything to me. My world has ceased. Within a month Walther also is dead, shot down over England. They give him the Iron Cross and my mother has a breakdown and I have to nurse her. Her world also is gone. Her son, the pretty clothes, the music and the chatter all have disappeared and the Russians take Berlin. I do not think she wished to live any longer after Walther's death. She never leave her bed until she died in October of last year.'

'And you looked after her all that time?' I asked, since she seemed to expect some comment.

She nodded. 'I have never been so miserable. And then, when she is dead, I begin to think again about my father and his work. I go to Wiesbaden. But the designs, the experimental work is all disappeared. There is nothing left. However, the Rauch Motoren is still in business and they are willing for me to try to—' Her voice died away as though she could not find the right words.

'To try and recover the engines?' I suggested.

'*Ja.*'

'And that is why you are here at Membury?' It was so obvious now she had told me about her father, and I couldn't help but admire her pluck and tenacity.

She nodded.

'Why have you told me all this?' I asked.

She shrugged her shoulders and kicked at the big oak log, sending a shower of sparks up the chimney. 'I do not know.' Then she suddenly flung up her head and looked straight at me almost defiantly. 'Because I am alone. Because I have always been alone since they took him away. Because you are English and do not matter to me.' She was like an animal that is cornered and has turned at bay. 'You had better go now. I have told you, we are on two sides of a wall.'

I got slowly to my feet and went towards her. 'You're very bitter, aren't you?' I said.

'Bitter?' Her eyes stared at me angrily. 'Of course I am bitter. I live for one thing now. I live for the day when my father's work will be recognised, when he will be known as one of the greatest of Germany's engineers.' The fire suddenly died out of her and she turned away from me. 'What else have I to live for?' Her voice sounded desperately unhappy.

I reached out and put my hand on her shoulder, but she shook me off. 'Leave me alone. Do not touch me.' Her voice was sharp, almost hysterical. And then in a moment her mood changed and she turned towards me. 'I am sorry. You cannot help. I should not have talked like this. Will you go now, please?'

I hesitated. 'All right,' I said. Then I held out my hand. 'Goodbye, Else.'

'Goodbye?' Her fingers touched mine. They were very cold despite the warmth of the fire. 'Yes. I suppose it is goodbye.'

'Will you give my message to Colonel Ellwood? We would like his heaviest tractor at the airfield at eight o'clock.'

'I will tell him.' She lifted her eyes to mine. 'And you fly the test tomorrow?' Her fingers tightened on my hand. '*Alles Gute!*' Her eyes were suddenly alive, almost excited. 'I will watch. It will be good to see those engines in the air – even if no one knows it is his work.' The last few words were little more than a whisper.

She came with me to the door then and as she stood there framed in the soft light of the lounge, she said, 'Neil!' She had a funny way of saying it, almost achieving the impossible and pronouncing the vowels individually. 'If you come to Berlin sometimes I live at

Number fifty-two, Fassenenstrasse. That is near the Kurfurstendamm. Ask for – Fräulein Meyer.'

'Moyor?'

'*Ja*. Else Meyer. That is my real name. To come here I have to have the papers of some other girl. You see – I am a Nazi. I belong to the *Hitler-Jugend* before – before they kill my father.' Her lips twitched painfully. 'Good-bye,' she said quickly. Her fingers touched mine and then the door closed and I was alone in the dark cold of the night. I didn't move for a moment and as I stood there I thought I heard the sound of sobbing, but it may only have been the wind.

It was a long time beforc I got to sleep that night. It was such a pitiful story, and yet I couldn't blame Saeton. I was English – she was German. The wall between us was high indeed.

Next morning the memory of her story was swamped in the urgent haste of preparations for tests. It was a cold, grey day and it was raining. A low curtain of cloud swept across the airfield. But nobody seemed to mind. Our thoughts were on the plane. Apparently Else had delivered my message, for promptly at eight o'clock a big caterpillar tractor came trundling across the tarmac apron leaving a trail of clay and chalk clods on the wet, shining surface of the asphalt. We slid the hangar doors back and hitched the tractor to the plane's undercarriage.

It gave me a sense of pride to see that gleaming Tudor nose slowly out of the hangar. It no longer had the toothless grin that had greeted me every morning for the past five weeks. It was a complete aircraft, a purposeful, solid-looking machine, fully engined and ready to go. The tractor dragged it to the main runway and then left us.

'Well, let's get moving,' Saeton said and swung himself up into the fuselage. I followed him. Tubby wheeled out the batteries and connected up. First one engine and then another roared into life. Saeton's hand reached up to the four throttle levers set high up in the centre of the windshield. The engine revs died down as he trimmed the motors. Tubby came in through the cockpit door and closed it. 'What about parachutes?' he asked.

Saeton grinned. 'They're back in the fuselage, you old Jonah. And they're okay. I packed them myself last night.'

The engines roared, the fuselage shivering violently as the plane bucked against the wheel brakes. I was in the second pilot's seat, checking the dials with Saeton. Tubby was between us. Fuel, oil pressure and temperature gauges, coolant temperature, rev meters – everything was registering correctly. 'Okay,' Saeton said. 'Ground tests.' He released the brakes and we began to move forward down the shining surface of the runway. Left rudder, right rudder – the tail swung in response. Landing flaps okay. Tail controls okay. Brakes okay. For an hour we roared up and down the runways, circling the perimeter track, watching fuel consumption, oil indicators, the behaviour of the plane with four motors running and then with the two new inboard engines only. Tubby stood in the well between the two pilots' seats, listening, watching the dials and scribbling notes on a pad.

At length Saeton brought the plane back to the apron opposite the hangar and cut the engines. 'Well?' he asked, looking down at Tubby. His voice seemed very loud in the sudden silence.

For answer Tubby raised his thumb and grinned. 'Just one or two things. I'd like to check over the injection timing on that starboard motor and I want to have a look at the fuel filters. We got a slight drop in revs and she sounded a bit rough.'

Saeton nodded and we climbed out. As we did so I saw a movement in the trees that screened the quarters. It was Else. Saeton had seen her, too. 'What's that girl doing up here?' he muttered angrily. Then he turned quickly to me. 'Did you tell her we were flying tests this morning?'

'Yes,' I said.

'I thought I warned you to keep away from her.' He glared at me as though I were responsible for her presence there on the edge of the airfield. Then he switched his gaze to the fringe of trees. Else had disappeared. 'It's about time the authorities took some action about her.'

'How do you mean?' I asked.

'She's here on false papers. Her name isn't really Langen.'

'I know that – now,' I said. And then suddenly I understood what he was driving at. 'Do you mean to say you've reported her to the authorities?'

'Of course. Do you think I want her snooping

around the place, sending reports to the Rauch Motoren. They'd no right to let her into the country.'

'Haven't you done that girl enough harm?' I said angrily.

'Harm?' He glanced at me quickly. 'How much do you know of her story?' he asked.

'I know that it was her father who designed these engines,' I said. 'She worked on them with him.' I caught hold of his arm. 'Why don't you come to terms with her?' I said. 'All she really wants is recognition for her father.'

He flung my hand off. 'So she's got round you, as she got round Randall – as she nearly got round me. She's just a little tart trading her body for the glorification of the fatherland.'

I felt a sudden urge to hit him. 'Don't you understand anybody?' I exclaimed through clenched teeth. 'She loved her father. Can't you understand that all she wants is recognition for his work?'

'Recognition!' He gave a sneering laugh. 'It's Germany she loves. They killed her father, but still it is Germany she thinks of. She offered to be my mistress if I'd allow the Rauch Motoren to manufacture the engines. My engines! The engines Tubby and I have worked on all these years! She traded on my weakness, on the fact that I was alone up here, and if Diana hadn't come—' He half-shrugged his shoulders as though shaking off something he didn't like. 'Her father has got about as much to do with these engines as you have.'

'Nevertheless,' I said, 'it was his prototype you stole—'

'Stole! Damn it, man, a country that has gone through what we have on account of the blasted Germans has a right to take what it wants. If Professor Meyer had completed the development of those engines—' He stopped and stared at me angrily. 'You bloody fool, Neil. Why waste your sympathy on the girl or her father? She was a good little Nazi till the S.S. took Meyer to Dachau. And Meyer was a Nazi too.' His lips spread in a thin, bitter smile. 'Perhaps you're not aware that Professor Meyer was one of the men who developed the diesel engine for use in bombers. London is in his debt to the tune of many hundreds of tons of bombs. My mother was killed in the blitz of 1940.' He turned away, his shoulders hunched, his hands thrust deep into his pockets, and walked across the tarmac to the hangar. I followed slowly, thinking of the tangled pattern of motive that surrounded these engines.

For over an hour Tubby worked on the engine. Then he checked over the others. It was just on one o'clock when he climbed down and pulled the gantry away. 'Okay,' he said. 'There's nothing more I can do.'

'All right,' Saeton said. 'Let's have a bit of food.' His voice was over-loud as though by speaking like that he could convince us of his confidence. I glanced at the plane. The rain clouds had broken up and she was caught in a gleam of watery sunlight. It was one thing doing ground tests, quite another to commit ourselves to the take-off. But she looked just like any other

Tudor. It was difficult to realise, seeing her standing there on the tarmac, that this wasn't to be a routine flight.

Saeton had brought a loaf and some cheese and butter up from the quarters. We ate it in the hangar, none of us talking, all of us, I think, very conscious of the emptiness of the place and of the aircraft standing out there on the apron waiting for us. As soon as we'd finished we got into our flying kit and went out to the plane. Saeton insisted we wear our parachutes.

Once more we sat in the cockpit – Saeton and I in the pilots' seats, Tubby in the well between us – the engines ticking over. Saeton's hand reached out for the throttle levers. The engines revved and we moved away across the apron, along the perimeter track and swung on to the runway end, the concrete stretching ahead of us, a broad white path shining wet in the sunlight. 'Okay?' Saeton looked at us. His jaw had broadened with the clenching of the muscles. His features looked hard and unsmiling. Only his eyes mirrored the excitement that held him in its grip.

'Okay,' Tubby said. I nodded. Again Saeton's hand reached up for the throttle levers, pressing them slowly down with his palm. The four motors roared in unison. The fuselage shuddered violently as the thrust of the props fought the brakes.

Then he released the brakes and we started forward.

I won't pretend I wasn't nervous – even a little scared. But it was overlaid by the sense of excitement. At the same time it was difficult to realise fully the danger. Viewed from the cockpit all the engines looked ordinary standard models. There was nothing to bring home to us the fact that those inboard engines were the work of our own hands – only the memory, now distant, of the countless hours we'd worked at them in the hangar. In a sense it was nothing more than I'd done hundreds of times before – a routine take-off.

I tried to concentrate on the dials, but as we gathered speed my eyes strayed to the concrete streaming beneath us, faster and faster, and thence to the ploughed verge of the runway and to the woods beyond. I caught a glimpse of the quarters through a gap in the trees. It suddenly seemed like home. Would we ever again sit at the trestle table drinking Scotch in celebration of success? Would we again lounge in those hard, uncomfortable chairs talking of a huge freighter fleet and our plans for a constant stream of aircraft tramping the globe? And as these questions appeared in my mind, my stomach suddenly became an empty void as panic hit me. Suppose those pistons I'd worked on when I first arrived were not quite true? Suppose . . . A whole stream of ugly possibilities flooded through my mind. And what about the engine that had been completed before I arrived? My hands tightened automatically on the control column as I felt the tail lift.

I glanced at Saeton. His face was tense, his eyes fixed unblinkingly ahead, one hand on the throttles, the other on the control column. I saw his left foot kick at the rudder to counter a sudden swing of the tail. The end of the runway was in sight now. It ran slightly downhill and a bunch of oaks was rushing to meet us.

No chance now of pulling up. We were committed to the take-off. The new starboard engine was still running a little rough. The tail swung. Left rudder again. I held my breath. God! He was leaving it late. I should have been watching the rev counters and the airspeed indicator. But instead my eyes were fixed on the trees ahead. They seemed to fill all my vision.

Then the control column eased back under my tense, clutched hands. The wheels bumped wildly on a torn-up piece of concrete. The starboard motor still sounded rough, the tail swung and the engine notes changed to a quieter drone. We were riding air, smooth, steady, the seat lifting me upwards as the trees slid away below us. Through the side window I saw Membury dropping away to a black circle of plough criss-crossed by the white pattern of runways and circled by the darker line of the perimeter track, the hangars small rectangles that looked like toys. We were airborne and climbing steeply, the full thrust of the motors taking us up in a steady, circling climb.

I glanced at Saeton. His body had relaxed into the shape of his seat. That was the only sign he gave of relief. 'Check undercarriage up,' he shouted to me as he levelled out. I glanced out of the side window. The starboard wheel was up inside the wing casing and I nodded. His eyes remained hard and alert, scanning the instrument panel. Tubby was jotting down notes as he read the dials. Oil Pressure 83–Oil Temp. 68–Coolant Temp. 90–Revs 2,300, with the exception of the inboard starboard engine, which read 2,270–Vacuum Pressure 4½ ins. – Height 1,500. We cruised around for a bit, checking everything, then we began to climb. Oil Pressure 88–Oil Temp. 77–Coolant Temp. 99–Revs 2,850 plus 9–Vacuum Pressure 4½. I glanced at my watch. Rate of climb 1,050 feet a minute.

At 6,000 Saeton levelled out. 'Okay to cut out the other motors?' He glanced down at Tubby, who nodded, his face unsmiling, his eyes almost lost in their creases of fat as he screwed them up against the sun which drove straight in through the windshield. At the same moment I saw the outboard engine slow. The individual blades of the prop became visible as it began to feather. The noise in the cockpit had lessened, so had the vibration. We were flying on our own motors only. Airspeed 175. Height 6,300. Still climbing. Swindon lay below us as we turned east, banking sharply.

The two motors hummed quietly. Saeton pulled back the control column. The nose of the plane lifted. We were climbing on the two engines only. Six thousand five hundred. Seven thousand. Eight thousand. Rate of climb 400 feet per minute. Half a dozen banking turns, then a long dive to 4,000 and up again. The motors hummed happily. The starboard engine was a shade rough perhaps, and engine revs were a little below those of the port motor. But there was plenty of power there.

Saeton levelled out. 'I could do with a cigarette.' He was grinning happily now, all tension smoothed out of his face. 'From now on we can forget all the hours we've slaved at those engines. They're there. They exist. We've done what we set out to do.'

Tubby was smiling, too, his face wreathed in a happy grin. He hummed a little tune.

We swung south over White Horse Hill. The racing gallops at Lambourne showed like age-old tracks along the downs. Climb, turn, dive – for two hours we flew the circuit of the Marlborough downs. Then at last Saeton said, 'Okay. Let's go back and get some tea. Tomorrow we'll do take-off and landing tests. Then we'll try her under full load and check petrol consumption.'

'I want that starboard motor back on bench tests first,' Tubby shouted.

Saeton nodded vaguely. For him it was all settled. He'd proved the motors. It only remained to get them to the highest pitch of efficiency. 'Okay,' he answered. 'We've plenty of time. I'll fix airworthiness tests for the latter part of next week.' He eased the control column forward and we slid down towards the rounded brown humps of the downs. Ramsbury airfield slid away beneath us, the Kennet showing like a twisting ribbon of steel in the cold light of the sinking sun. Membury opened out on the hill ahead of us. The two outboard motors started into life.

'Ready to land?'

We nodded.

Saeton looked down through the side window. 'There's a bottle of whisky down there.' He grinned as we peered down at the felted roof of our quarters. 'Pity Diana isn't here to see this.' He said it without thinking. I glanced at Tubby. His face gave no sign that he'd heard. 'Better get your undercarriage down,' Tubby said.

Saeton laughed. 'If you think I'm going to prang the thing now, you're wrong.' His hand reached down and found the undercarriage release switch automatically. He pulled it up and glanced out of his side window. Then he turned quickly, peered down at the lever and jerked at it. In the tenseness of his face I read sudden panic. I turned to my own side window and craning forward, peered back at the line of the wing. 'The starboard wheel is down,' I reported.

Saeton was flicking at the switch. 'It's the port wheel,' he said, staring out of his window. 'The bloody thing's jammed.' I don't think he was frightened for himself. The panic that showed in his face was for all our achievement that could be set at nought by a crash landing.

'I told you we ought to check over the plane,' Tubby shouted back, peering forward over the lever.

'That's a hell of a lot of use now,' Saeton's voice rasped through his clenched teeth. 'Neil. Take over. Climb to 7,000 whilst we try and sort this bastard out. Tubby, see if she'll come down on the hand gear.'

I felt the control column go slack under my hands as he eased himself out of his seat. I took hold of it, at the same time reaching out for the throttle levers. The engines responded to my touch and Membury dropped away from us as I pulled the control column back and climbed under full power, banking steadily. Saeton and Tubby were trying to wind the port wheel down, but the handle seemed to be alternately jamming and running free.

At 7,000 feet I levelled out. They had the

floorboards up and Tubby was head down in the gap. A steady blast of bitterly cold air roared into the cockpit. For an hour I stooged round and round over Membury. And at the end of that hour Tubby straightened up, his face blue with cold and stood there blowing on his fingers. 'Well?' Saeton demanded.

Tubby shook his head. 'Nothing we can do,' he said. 'The connecting rod is snapped. A fault probably. Anyway, it's snapped and there's no way of lowering the port side undercarriage.'

Saeton didn't speak for a moment. His face was grey and haggard. 'The best we can hope for then is to make a decent pancake landing.' His voice was a flat monotone as though all the weariness of the last few weeks had crowded in on him at this moment. 'You're absolutely sure there's nothing we can do?' he asked Tubby.

The other shook his head. 'Nothing. The connecting rod has snapped and—'

'All right. You said that once. I'm not that dense.' He had pulled a packet of cigarettes out of his pocket. He handed it to me. I took one and he lit it for me. It was a measure of his acceptance of the facts of the situation. He would never have smoked in the cockpit unless he had abandoned all hope.

'The light's fading,' I said. 'And we haven't much gas left.'

He nodded, drawing in a lungful of smoke.

'Better make for Upavon,' Tubby shouted. It was an R.A.F. Station and I knew what was in his mind. There would be crash squads there and ambulances.

'No. We'll go back to Membury,' Saeton answered. 'You two get aft. Have the door of the fuselage open. I'll take you over the airfield at 3,000 feet. Wind's easterly, about Force 2. Jump just before I cross the edge of the field.' He climbed back into his seat. 'All right, Neil. I'll take over now.' I felt the pressure of his hands as he gripped the other control column and I let go of mine. Tubby started to protest, but Saeton rounded on him. 'For God's sake do as you're told. Jump at the edge of the field. No point in more than one of us getting hurt. And as you so tactfully point out, it's my fault. Of course we should have checked the plane.' Out of the tail of my eye I saw the starboard wheel folding into the wing again.

'I'm sorry, Bill,' Tubby said. 'I didn't mean—'

'Don't argue. Get aft. You, too, Fraser.' His voice was almost vicious in his wretchedness. And then with that quick change of mood: 'Good luck, both of you.'

I had hesitated, half-out of my seat. His face was set in a grim mask as he stared straight ahead of him, thrusting the control column forward, dipping the nose to a long glide towards the airfield. Tubby jerked his head for me to follow him and disappeared through the door that communicated with the fuselage. 'Good luck!' I murmured.

Saeton's eyes flicked towards me and he gave a bitter laugh. 'I've had all the good luck I need,' he snarled. I knew what he meant. Whether he came out of the plane alive or dead, he was finished. For a moment I still hesitated. I had a crazy idea that he might intend to crash the plane straight into the ground.

'What the hell are you waiting for?'

'I think I'd better stay,' I said. If I stayed he'd be forced to make an attempt to land.

He must have sensed what was at the back of my mind, for he suddenly laughed. 'You don't know very much about me, do you, Neil?' The snarl had gone out of his voice. But his eyes remained hard and bitter. 'Go on. Get back aft with Tubby, and don't be a fool. I don't like heroics.' And then suddenly shouting at me: 'Get aft, man. Do you hear? Or have I got to come down there myself and throw you out?' His eyes narrowed. 'Ever jumped before?'

'Once,' I answered, my mind mirroring the memory of that night landing in the woods of Westphalia, hanging in the straps with my parachute caught in a tree and my arm broken.

'Scared, eh?' The sneer was intentional. I knew that. He was goading me to jump. And yet I reacted. I reacted as he wanted me to because I was scared. I'd always been scared of having to bale out after that one experience. 'Of course I'm not scared,' I snapped and turned and moved awkwardly to the fuselage, the weight of my parachute bouncing against my buttocks.

Tubby already had the door of the fuselage open. The rush of air made it bitterly cold. The plane was turning now over the hangars, losing height rapidly. He didn't say anything. You haven't room for anything else in your mind when you are faced with a jump. We caught a glimpse of the quarters, looking very neat and snug in its little patch of trees. I could even make out the hen-run at the back with the white dots of two or three fowl. Then we were banking for the run-in. The trees slid away under us. I saw the snaking line of the road coming up from Ramsbury. Then, over Tubby's shoulder, I made out the edge of the airfield. He glanced at me with a quick, nervous grin, gripped my arm tightly and then, still looking at me, fell outwards into space.

I watched his body turn over and over. Saw his hand pull at the release of his parachute. The canopy of nylon blossomed like a flower and his body steadied, swinging rhythmically.

We were right over the airfield now. My limbs felt cold and stiff. The sweat stood out on my forehead. I heard Saeton scream at me to jump, saw him clambering out of the pilot's seat. He was going to leave the controls, come aft and throw me out. I closed my eyes quickly, gripped the cold metal of the release lever and fell forward into the howl of the slipstream. My legs swung over the back of my neck. Opening my eyes I saw the sky, the sun, the horizon coming up the wrong way as though I were in a loop, the airfield rolling under me. Then I jerked at the release; jerked at it again and again in desperate fear that it wouldn't work.

Suddenly my shoulders were wrenched from their sockets, the inside of my legs cut by the hard pull of the straps. My legs fell into place. Sky and earth sorted themselves out. I was dangling in space, no wind, no sound – only the fading roar of the plane as it climbed, a black dot over the far side of the airfield. Above me the white cloud of the parachute swung gently, beautifully, the air-hole showing a dark patch of sky. Twisting my head I saw Tubby touch the ground, roll over and over in a perfect drill landing. Then he was scrambling to his feet, pulling in his parachute, legs braced against the drag of it, emptying the air till it lay in an inert white fold at his feet.

Travelling with the light wind the air was quite still. It was as though I were suspended there over the airfield for all eternity. There seemed to be no movement. Time and space stood still as I dangled like a daylight firework. The drone of the plane had died away. It had vanished as though it had never been. The stillness was all-pervading, pleasant, yet rather frightening.

Though the movement was imperceptible my position gradually altered in relation to the ground. I was gliding steadily along the line of the east-west runway. I tried to work out my angle of drop in relation to the trees bordering the airfield near the quarters. But it was quite impossible to gauge the rate of fall. All I know is that one moment I was dangling up there, apparently motionless, and the next the concrete end of the runway was rushing up to meet me.

I hit the concrete with my legs too firmly braced for the shock. I hit it as though I'd jumped from a building into the street. The jar of the touchdown ran up my spine and hammered at my head and then all was confusion as my parachute harness jerked me forward. I had the sense to throw up my arms and duck my head into the protection of my shoulder as I hit the concrete.

I remember being pitched forward and over and then there was a stunning blow on the front of my head and I lost consciousness.

I couldn't have been out for long because I came round to find myself being slowly dragged along the concrete by my shoulders. I dug my hands and feet in, anchoring myself for a moment. Blood ran down my face and dripped into a crack in the concrete. Somebody shouted to me and I caught hold of the strings of the parachute, struggling to fold it as I'd been taught to do. But I hadn't the strength. I dropped back, half-unconscious, a feeling of terrible lassitude running along my muscles.

The pull of my shoulders slackened. Somebody stooped over me and fingers worked at the harness buckles. 'Neil! Are you all right? Please.'

I looked up then. It was Else. 'What – are you doing here?' I asked. I had some difficulty in getting my breath.

'I came to see the test. What has happened? Why have you jumped?'

'The undercarriage,' I said.

'The undercarriage? Then it is not the engines? The engines are all right?'

'Yes, the engines are all right. It's the undercarriage. Won't come down.' I looked up at her and saw that she was staring up into the sky, her eyes alight with some emotion that I couldn't understand. 'Why are you so excited?' I asked her.

'Because—' She looked down at me quickly, her mouth clamped shut. 'Come. I help you up now.' She placed her hands under my arms. The world spun as I found my feet and leaned heavily against her, waiting for the aerodrome to stop spinning. Blood trickled into my mouth and I put my hand to my forehead. It was the old cut that had reopened and I thought: *This is where I came in*. 'What about Tubby? Is he all right?'

'Yes. He is coming here now.'

I shook the blood out of my eyes. A small dot was running down the runway. He shouted something. I didn't understand at first. Then I remembered Saeton and the aircraft. Ambulance! Of course. The quarters were not five hundred yards away. 'Quick, Else. I must get to the phone.' A muscle in one of my legs seemed to have been wrenched. It was hell running. But I made it in the end and seized hold of the telephone. My voice when I spoke to the operator was a breathless sob. She put me through to the Swindon hospital and then to the fire brigade. Tubby came in as I finished phoning. 'Ambulance and fire brigade coming,' I said.

'Good! You'd better lie down, Neil. Your head looks bad.'

'I'm all right,' I said. 'What about the plane?' The need for action had given me strength.

'Saeton's stooging round over the field at about 5,000 feet using up his remaining gas.' He turned to Else. 'You'd better get some water on to heat. He may be a bit of a mess when we get him in.' She nodded quickly and hurried out to the kitchen. 'What's that girl doing here?' he asked me. But he didn't seem to expect an answer, for he went straight out to the airfield. I followed him.

Looking up into the sun brought a blinding pain to my eyes, but by screwing them up I could see the glint of the plane as it banked. The air was very still in the shelter of the woods and the sound of the engines seemed quite loud. Time passed slowly. We stood there in silence, waiting for the inevitable moment when the plane would cease its interminable circling and dive away over the horizon for the final approach. My legs began to feel weak and I sat down on the ground. 'Why don't you go and lie down?' Tubby asked. His voice sounded irritable.

'I'll stay here,' I said. I wasn't thinking of Saeton then. I was thinking of the plane. There it was, flying perfectly. Only that damned undercarriage stood between us and success. It seemed a hard twist of fate.

'I have arrange plenty of hot water.' It was Else. She had a steaming bowl with her and she plumped down beside me. 'Now we can fix that cut, eh?' I winced as the hot water touched the open cut across my forehead. The water smelt strongly of disinfectant. Then she bandaged my head and it felt better. 'That is finished. Now you look like you are a wounded man.'

'So I am,' I said. Her face hung over me, framed by the darkening blue of the sky. She looked young and soft and rather maternal. My head was in her lap. I could feel the softness of her limbs against the back of my skull. We should have been lying like that in a hay field in May. The distant drone of the aircraft was like the sound of bees. I caught the gleam of its wings just beyond her hair.

'Where the devil's the ambulance?' Tubby demanded. 'He's coming in now.'

I glanced at my watch. It was twenty minutes since I'd phoned. 'They'll be here in about ten minutes,' I told him.

He grunted a curse. 'They'll be here too late then.'

I could see the plane gliding over Ramsbury, a black dot against the sunset. I thought of the engine we had laboured to complete all these weeks, of Saeton alone up there at the controls. The pain of my head was nothing then. My eyes were trained on the sky over Ramsbury and every fibre of my being was concentrated on the plane, which was banking sharply as it disappeared behind the trees, turning for the final approach.

It seemed an age before it appeared again. Then suddenly it was there over the end of the runway, hanging like a great, clumsy bird over the trees, dropping towards the concrete, its landing flaps down, the props turning slowly. I scrambled to my feet and began to run. Tubby was running, too. Saeton levelled out for the touchdown and as the gap between plane and concrete lessened, the aircraft seemed to gather speed till it was rushing towards us.

Then the belly hit the concrete. Pieces of metal were flung wide. There was a horrible scraping. But when the sound reached me the plane had bounced several feet above the runway. It came down then with a splintering crash, swivelling round, the fuselage breaking up as the tail disintegrated, grinding the concrete to puffs of powder, the metal sheeting stripping from her belly like tinplate. She slewed broadside, tipping crazily, righted herself, straightened up and broke in half. The appalling grinding sound went on for a second after she had stopped. Then there was a sudden, frightening silence. The plane lay there, a crumpled wreck, unnaturally still. Nothing moved. The sunset was just as red, the trees just as black, nothing had changed as though the aerodrome had taken no interest in the accident. Somebody had pranged a plane. It had happened here countless times during the war. Life went on.

Tubby was running towards the machine. For a second I stood rooted to the spot, my stomach quivering in expectation of the sudden blossoming of the wreck into a blazing fury of fire. But it just lay there, inert and lifeless, and I, too, started to run.

We got Saeton out. There was a lot of blood, but it was from his nose. He was unconscious when we laid him on the concrete, his hand badly cut and a livid bruise across his forehead. But his pulse beat was quite strong. Tubby loosened his collar and almost immediately his eyes opened, staring up at us blankly. Then suddenly there was life behind them and he sat up with a jerk that brought a groan from his lips. 'How's the plane? Is she—' His voice stopped as his eyes took in the wreck. 'Oh, God!' he murmured. He began to swear then – a string of obscene oaths that ignored Else's presence and were directed solely at the plane.

'The engines are all right,' Tubby said consolingly.

'What's the good of engines without a plane?' Saeton snarled. 'I got the tail too low.' He began swearing again.

'You better lie back,' Tubby said. 'There's nothing you can do about the plane. Just relax now. The ambulance will be here in a minute.'

'Ambulance?' He glared at us. 'What damn' fool phoned for an ambulance?' He got out his handkerchief and wiped some of the blood from his face. 'Get down to the main road and stop them,' he ordered Tubby hoarsely. 'Tell them it's all right. Tell them there wasn't any crash after all – anything, so long as you get them away from here without them coming on to the airfield.'

'But even if you're all right, there's Neil here needing treatment,' Tubby said.

'Then take him with you and pack him off to hospital. But I don't want them on the field. I don't want them to know we've crashed.'

'But why?' Tubby asked.

'Why?' Saeton passed his hand across his eyes and spat blood on to the concrete. 'I don't know why. I just don't want anyone to know about this. Now for God's sake stop arguing and get down to the road.'

Tubby hesitated. 'That nose of yours looks as though it's broken,' he said. 'And there may be something else—'

'There's nothing else broken,' Saeton snarled. 'If there is I'll get to a doctor under my own steam. Now get going.'

Tubby glanced at me. 'I'm all right,' I said. He nodded and started at a steady trot across the field towards the quarters. Saeton struggled to his feet and stood there, swaying weakly, staring at the wreckage, bitter, black despair in his eyes. Then, as he turned away, he caught sight of Else and his thick hands clenched with sudden violence of purpose. 'I thought you were going back to Germany,' he said hoarsely.

'I go on Monday.' Her eyes were wide and she looked frightened.

'Wanted to be in at the death, eh? You timed it nicely.'

'I do not understand.'

'You do not understand, eh?' he mimicked her crudely. 'I suppose you don't understand what happened up there?' He was moving towards her, staggering slightly, the sweat standing out in great drops on his forehead and running down into his eyes. 'Well, the connecting rod was snapped. We couldn't lower the undercarriage. That surprises you, eh? You didn't know the connecting rod was broken.'

The expression on his face held me rooted to the spot. It was a bloody mask of hatred. Else stood quite still, her eyes wide, her mouth slightly open. And then suddenly she was talking, talking fast, the words tumbling out of her as though in themselves they could form a barrier between herself and what was moving so inevitably upon her. 'I do not touch your plane. I have nothing to do with what has happened. Please. You must believe me. Why should I do this thing? These are my father's engines – my father's and mine. I wish them to fly. I wish to see them in the air. It is all I have left of him. It is the work we do together. He was happy then, and I was happy also. I want them to fly. I want them—'

'Your father's engines!' The contempt in his voice stopped her like a slap in the face. 'They're my engines. Mine. Your father's engine wouldn't work. It crashed. I broke my leg trying to fly the bloody thing. It was no good. We had to start again. All over again. A new design.'

She flung up her head then, facing him like a tigress defending her young. 'It is not a new design. It is different, but it is the same principle. Those engines belong to him. They are—'

He laughed. It was a wild, violent sound. 'You've smashed what I've lived for for three years. You're happy now, aren't you? You think now that Germany will get control of them again. But she won't.' He was very close to her now. 'You tried to kill us. Well, now I'm going to—'

'That's a lie!' she cried. 'I have nothing to do with it. Nobody has touched the airplane.'

'Then why are you here – on the spot, gloating—'

'Oh, will you never understand?' she cried furiously. 'I come to see them up there in the air. They are my father's work. Do you think it is no excitement for me to see them fly? Please, I have nothing to do with the crash.' His hands had reached out to her and gripped her shoulders. She was suddenly pleading. 'I have done nothing – nothing. You must believe what I say.'

But he didn't seem to hear her. 'You tried to kill us,' he whispered hoarsely. 'You tried to smash everything I have worked for. First you try to bribe me with your body. Then you try to get control of my company.

When you don't succeed you try to destroy what I've worked for. If you can't get what you want you must destroy it. That is the German in you. Everything you touch, you destroy. And always you work for Germany.'

'Not for Germany,' she cried. 'Only for my father. Everything I do, I do for my father. Why could you not give him the credit for what he do?'

'You're a part of the Germany I've hated since I was a kid,' he went on, his voice thick as though clotted with blood, his hands gripping her violently, fumbling blindly for her throat. 'My father in one war, my mother in another. All you can do is smash and break things. And now I'm going to break you – break you in little pieces.'

Her eyes stared wildly as his blunt fingers dug into her neck. Then she began to struggle, and in that instant I came to life and moved forward. But I needn't have bothered. His hands clawed at her clothes and his body slowly sagged against her, his knees giving under him and pitching him forward on to his face.

Saeton had fainted.

Else stared down at him, fear and horror stamped on her face. I think she thought he was dead. 'I didn't do anything to the airplane.' The words were a strangled sob. 'Neil!' She glanced wildly at me. 'Nobody touched the airplane. You must believe that.'

Saeton moved suddenly, his fingers digging into the earth, scrabbling at it as he tried to rise, and when he had pushed himself up on to his knees, she broke and ran.

Tubby came back and we got Saeton to the quarters and put him to bed. His ribs were badly bruised, but nothing seemed to be broken. It was more shock than anything else. Still half-dazed he ordered us to get one of Ellwood's tractors and have the wreckage dragged into the hangar. He wanted it done that night. He seemed to have an unreasoned, instinctive urge to get the evidence of failure under cover as quickly as possible. It was as though he felt none of his own injuries, only the hurts of the aircraft and wanted to let it crawl away into the dark like a dog to lick its wounds.

By ten o'clock that night it was done and all trace of the crash landing was concealed behind the closed doors of the hangar. The plane was a hell of a mess. The tractor took it in in two pieces, the tail having ripped off completely as soon as we began to drag the wreck along the concrete. Saeton himself came out to the runway to make sure there was no trace of the accident left.

Whether the plan had formed in his mind then, I can't be certain. Personally, I don't think so. It was a matter of instinct rather than planning. If nobody knew we had crashed there might still be a chance. At any rate, if the idea was in his mind, it didn't show that evening as we sat over a drink and tried to sort out the future.

Tubby was through. That was clear from the start. 'I'm going back to flying,' he said. His tone was obstinate and quite final. 'You know Francis Harcourt? He's got two Tudors on the tanking lift, and he's back in England now negotiating the purchase of two more.

Just before Christmas he wrote asking me to join him as a flight engineer.'

'And you've accepted?' Saeton asked.

For answer Tubby produced an envelope from his pocket. It was already stamped and sealed.

'We've still a month before we're due on the airlift – if we hold the Air Ministry to their first date,' Saeton said quietly.

'A month!' Tubby grunted. 'Six months wouldn't see that kite ready to fly – six months and a lot of money.' He leaned forward and caught Saeton by the arm. 'Listen, Bill. I've worked with you for nothing for just on two years. I haven't got a bean out of it. If you think I can go on any longer, you're crazy. Anyway, where the hell would you get the money from? You've cleaned me out. You've just about cleaned Neil out. We owe money all over the place. The company is broke – finished.' His voice softened as he saw the bitter set of Saeton's mouth below the bandages. 'I'm sorry, chum. I know what this means to you. But you've got to face the facts. We can't go on.'

'Can't we? Well, I say we can. I don't know how – yet. But I'll find a way. You'll see me on the airlift next month. I'll do it somehow.' His voice was trembling, but it had no conviction, only violence. His fist beat at the table. 'If you think I'm going to let a little bitch of a German destroy everything I've worked for, you're wrong. I don't care what it costs me, I'll get those engines into the air.'

'How do you know she was responsible for what happened?' I asked.

'Of course she was,' he snarled. 'Either her or one of the Rauch Motoren agents.'

'You can't be certain,' I said.

'Can't be certain! Damn it, man, how else could it have happened? She tracked me down to this airfield. How she did it I don't know. But suddenly she arrived at the Manor and because we were short-handed I got her to come up and cook and clean for us in the evenings. I thought she was just a D.P. It never occurred to me she was Professor Meyer's daughter.'

'When did you discover who she really was?' I asked.

'That night you arrived and found us together in the hangar.' He suddenly clicked his fingers. 'She must have done it then. It's the only time she's ever been alone in the hangar.'

'Are you seriously suggesting the girl filed through the undercarriage connecting rod?' Tubby asked.

'She an engineer, isn't she? And she had about half an hour up there on her own. She couldn't be sure the plan to buy up the outfit through Randall's mortgages would succeed. Anyway, what's it matter?' he added, his tone suddenly rising. 'Finding out whether it was German thoroughness or a natural break won't put the crate back into the air. We'll sort it out tomorrow.' He spoke through clenched teeth and his hands trembled as he thrust back his chair. I think he was in the grip of a bitter, raging anger, on the verge of tears. The man was dead beat anyway and his nerves must have been just about stretched to the edge of screaming hysteria.

He had risen to his feet and he stood, staring at Tubby. 'Are you going to post that letter?'

'Yes,' Tubby answered.

'All right.' The veins on Saeton's forehead seemed to swell. 'But remember this: join Harcourt's outfit and you're through with this company. Understand?'

'I understand,' Tubby said in a level tone.

'You bloody fool!' Saeton said, and went out, slamming the door.

I was pretty tired and my head ached. I followed him out and was asleep almost before my head touched the pillow.

I awoke in a mood of despair. My job was gone and I was broke. The future was bleak. I longed to be back at the bench, driven beyond physical endurance to complete something that I believed in.

It was a chill, grey morning, frost riming the windows and the wind moaning round the building. Tubby produced tea and bacon and eggs in a mood of contrition for deserting us. Breakfast did nothing to lift us out of our gloom. We ate in silence and went out to the hangar. I suppose in the five weeks I had been there I had gradually come to identify my future with the plane. Seeing it lying there in the drab light, its metal all broken and twisted, the tail completely severed and lying like a piece of discarded junk gave me a sense of sudden loneliness. This was the end of our work together. We were no longer a team, but three individuals going our own separate ways. It was this, I think, that made me feel so wretched. I'd felt safe here and complete. I'd been doing something I'd come to believe in and there had been a goal to work for. Now there was nothing.

We cleared the torn metal away from the fuselage, working to reach the undercarriage and find out what had gone wrong. It was a useless investigation. Whatever we discovered, it wouldn't help us. We worked slowly, almost unwillingly, and in silence. Shortly before eleven the phone rang. It was Harcourt asking for Tubby. Saeton and I stood listening. 'Yes . . . Yes, I'll be there. Diana is already in Germany . . . Well, maybe she'll fix it to get to the Gatow canteen . . . Fine. I'll meet you there.' Tubby's eyes gleamed excitedly and he was whistling happily to himself as he replaced the receiver.

'Well, when do you leave?' Saeton barked in the hard, impersonal tone he used when he wished to hide his own feelings.

'He wants me down at Northolt at ten o'clock tomorrow,' Tubby answered.

'Then you'd better get moving,' Saeton said abruptly.

'It's all right. I'll get a train this evening. I don't want to leave without knowing what the trouble was.'

'Hell, man! What difference does it make?'

'I'd like to know all the same,' Tubby answered woodenly.

Saeton turned away with a shrug of his shoulders. 'Well, let's get on with the post-mortem.'

It was useless for him to pretend that he didn't care what had caused the break. He did care. He was looking for something to fight. He was that sort. But when we got to the connecting rod it showed a clean break and unmistakable signs of faulty casting.

'So it wasn't Else after all,' I said.

'No.' He threw the broken rod on to the concrete and turned away. 'Better see if you can fix Fraser up with a job on the airlift,' he said to Tubby over his shoulder, and he slammed out of the hangar.

Tubby left that afternoon and with his departure a tense, brooding gloom settled on the quarters. Saeton was impossible. It wasn't only that he wouldn't talk. He prowled up and down, constantly, irritably on the move, lost in his own morose thoughts. He was racking his brains for a means of getting on the airlift with the engines by 25th January. Once he turned to me, his eyes wild, his face looking grey and slightly crazy with his nose covered with adhesive plaster. 'I'm desperate,' he said. 'I'd do anything to get hold of a plane. Anything, do you hear?'

At that moment I was prepared to believe he'd commit murder if he were sure of getting another aircraft as a result of it. The man was desperate. It showed in his eyes, in the way he talked. He hadn't given up hope. I think that was what made the atmosphere so frightening. He wasn't quite sane. A sane man would see that the thing was impossible. But he wouldn't he was still thinking in terms of getting those engines into the air. It was incredible – incredible and frightening. No man should be driven by such violent singleness of purpose. 'You're crazy,' I said.

'Crazy?' He laughed and his laugh was pitched a shade too high. Then he suddenly smiled in an odd, secretive way. 'Yes, perhaps you're right. Perhaps I am crazy. All pioneers are crazy. But believe me, I'll get into the air if I have to steal a plane.' He stopped then and stared at me fixedly in an odd sort of way. Then he smiled again. 'Yes,' he said slowly, reflectively. 'I'll get on to the airlift somehow.' He went out then and I heard his feet dragging slowly down the frostbound path until the sound lost itself in the noise of the wind blowing through the trees.

I went down to the Manor to see Else. I wanted to tell her that we knew she had had nothing to do with the failure of the undercarriage, that it was in fact an accident. But she had already gone. She had taken the afternoon train to London because she had to be at Harwich early the following morning to catch the boat. I returned to the quarters feeling that my last link with the past few weeks had gone.

The next two days were hell. I just drifted, clinging desperately to Membury, to the hangar and the quarters. I just couldn't nerve myself to face the outside world. I was afraid of it; afraid of the fact that I had no job and only a few pounds left in my account. The memory of Else haunted me. God knows why. I wasn't in love with her. I told myself that a hundred times. But it made no difference. I needed a woman, someone to attach myself to. I was as rudderless as the wreck lying in the hangar.

To give me something to do Saeton had told me to get to work with the oxy-acetylene cutter and clean up the mess. It was like operating on the broken body of a friend. We lifted our two engines out of her and she looked like a toothless old hag waiting for the inevitable end. I could have wept for what might have been. A thousand times I remembered those supreme moments up in the air over Membury when we had climbed, superbly, majestically, on the power of the engines we'd made. I had felt then as though all the world lay within my grasp. And now I was cleaning up the wreck, cutting out the sections that had been torn to strips of tin by the concrete of the runway.

Saeton didn't even pretend that we were working to repair the plane. And yet he wasn't morose any more. There was a sort of jauntiness in the way he walked and every now and then I'd catch him watching me with a soft, secretive smile. His manner wasn't natural and I found myself wishing that he'd begin cursing again, wishing he'd make up my mind for me by throwing me off the place.

Well, I had my wish in the end. He made up my mind for me. But it wasn't at all the way I had expected it. It was the third evening after Tubby's departure. We were back in the quarters and the phone rang. Saeton leapt up eagerly and went into the office, the room that Tubby and Diana had had as a bedroom. I heard the murmur of his voice and then the sound of the bell as he replaced the receiver. There was a pause before his footsteps came slowly across the passage and the door of the mess room opened.

He didn't close it immediately, but stood there, framed in the doorway, staring at me, his head sunk into his shoulders, his chin thrust slightly out, a queer glint of excitement in his eyes. 'That was Tubby,' he said slowly. 'He's found you a job.'

'A job?' I felt a tingle of apprehension run along my nerves. 'What sort of a job?'

'Flying for the Harcourt Charter Company.' He came in and shut the door. His movements were oddly slow and deliberate. He reminded me of a big cat. He sat himself down on the trestle table. His thick, powerful body seemed to tower above me. 'You're to pilot one of Harcourt's new Tudors. I got on to Tubby two days ago about it and he's fixed it.'

I began to stammer my thanks. My voice sounded odd and far away from me, as though it were somebody else speaking. I was in a panic. I didn't want to leave Membury. I didn't want to lose that illusion of security the place had given me.

'You're to meet Harcourt at Northolt for lunch tomorrow,' Saeton went on. 'One o'clock in the canteen. Tubby will be there to introduce you. It's an incredible piece of luck.' The excitement had spread from his eyes to his voice now. 'The pilot he had engaged has gone down with pneumonia.' He stopped and stared at me, his face faintly flushed as though he had been drinking, his eyes sparkling like a kid that sees the thing he's dreamed of come true at last. 'How much do these engines we've built mean to you, Neil?' he asked suddenly.

I didn't know quite what to say. But apparently he didn't expect an answer, for he added quickly, 'Listen. Those engines are okay. You've seen that for yourself. You've got to take my word for it about the saving in fuel consumption. It's about 50 per cent. Tubby and I proved that in the bench tests on the first engine. Now, suppose we got into the air as planned on January 10—'

'But we can't,' I cried. 'You know very well—'

'The engines are all right, aren't they? All we need is a new plane.' He was leaning down over me now, his eyes fixed on mine as though trying to mesmerise me. 'We've still got a chance, Neil. Harcourt's planes are Tudors. In a few days' time you'll be at Wunstorf and flying into Berlin. Suppose something went wrong with the engines over the Russian Zone?' He paused, watching for my reaction. But I didn't say anything. I suddenly felt ice-cold inside. 'All you've got to do is to order your crew to bale out,' he went on, speaking slowly as though talking to a child. 'It's as easy as that. A little play-acting, a little organised panic and you'll be alone in the cockpit of a Tudor. All you've got to do then is to make straight for Membury.'

I stared at him foolishly. 'You *are* crazy,' I heard myself say. 'You'd never get away with it. There'd be an inquiry. The plane would be recognised when they saw it again. Harcourt's not a fool. Besides—'

He stopped me with a wave of his hand. 'You're wrong. To begin with an inquiry would show nothing. The crew would say the plane had made a forced landing in the Russian Zone. The Russians would deny it. Nobody would believe them. As for the plane being recognised, why should it? Nobody knows we've crashed our machine here. At least they don't know how badly. All that happens is that a plane disappears on the Berlin Airlift and on January 10 another flies in to take its place. Harcourt's all right – he gets his insurance. The country's all right, for the number of Tudors remains the same. God, man – it sticks out a mile. You'll make a fortune. We'll both of us make a fortune.'

'You'd never get away with it,' I repeated obstinately.

'Of course I'll get away with it. Why should they ever suspect anything? And if they did, what then? Look. Part numbers and engine numbers can be altered to those of our wrecked Tudor. Our own two engines will be in her. As for our own plane, we'll cut it up into small bits. You've already started on that work. In a few days we could have the whole plane in fragments. A load of those fragments can be strewn over Russian territory. The rest we'll dump in that pond over on the far side of the airfield. God! It's too easy. All I need is for you to fly Harcourt's plane back here.'

'Well, I won't do it,' I said angrily.

'Do you want the Germans to be the first to produce these engines?' His hand came out and gripped my shoulder. 'Just think before you refuse. Damn it, haven't you a spark of adventure in you? A slight risk and this country can have the biggest fleet of freighters in the world – a global monopoly.' His eyes were blazing and I suddenly felt scared. The man was a fanatic.

'I won't do it,' I repeated stubbornly.

'When you've flown the plane in here all we have to do is drop you just inside the British Zone,' he went on.

'You report back to Wunstorf with the story that you made a forced landing in the Russian Zone and got back under your own steam across the frontier. It's child's play.'

'I won't do it.'

He gave an ugly laugh. 'Scared, eh?'

I hesitated, trying to sort out in my mind whether it was because I was scared or whether my refusal was on moral grounds. I couldn't sort it out. All I knew was that I didn't want to be mixed up in anything like this. I wanted to forget that sense of being hunted. I didn't want ever again to have anything on my conscience, to have to run and hide – I didn't want to be afraid of the world any more.

He suddenly let go my arm. 'All right,' he said, and I didn't like the softness in his voice and the way he smiled down at me. 'All right, if that's the way you feel.' He paused, watching me with an odd expression in his eyes. 'Do you remember the other evening I said I'd do anything to get hold of a plane?'

I nodded.

'Well, I meant that. I meant every word of it. I said I was desperate. I am desperate. If one man's life stood between me and getting into the air, I'd kill that man. I'd brush him out of my way without a thought. Bigger things than a single life are involved. It's not just my own future I'm thinking of. Don't think that. I happen to believe in my country. And I believe that these engines are the greatest contribution I can make to my country. There's nothing I won't do to see these engines are operated by a British concern. Nothing. Nothing.'

His voice had risen and there was a wild look in his eyes. 'Forget about yourself. Forget about me. Won't you do this for your country?'

'No,' I said.

'God, man! You fought for your country in war. You risked your life. Have some imagination. Can't you fight for her in peacetime? I'm not asking you to risk your life. All I'm asking you to do is to fly that plane back here. What's the trouble? You're not damaging Harcourt. Or is it the risk you're afraid of? I tell you, there isn't any risk. Do it the way I've planned it and you're as safe as houses. You've nothing to be afraid of.'

'I'm not afraid,' I answered hotly.

'What's the trouble then?'

'I just don't like it and I won't do it.'

He sighed and eased himself off the edge of the table. 'All right. If that's the way you want it—' He stood for a moment, looking down at me. The room was suddenly very silent. I felt my nerves tightening so that I wanted to shout at him, to do anything to relieve the tension. At length he said, 'If you don't do what I want you to I'll turn you over to the police.' He spoke quite flatly and my inside seemed to curl up into a tight ball. 'You were in a prison camp, weren't you? You know what it's like then. Three years in prison is quite a slice out of a man's life. Do you think you could stand it? You'd go mad, wouldn't you? You were on the edge of hysteria when you came here. You're all right now, but in prison—'

'You bastard!' I screamed at him, suddenly finding

my voice. I called him a lot of other names. I had got to my feet and I was trembling all over, the sweat breaking out in prickling patches across my scalp and trickling down my forehead. I was cold with fear and anger. And he just stood there, watching me, his shoulders hunched a little forward as though expecting me to charge him, a quiet, confident smile on his lips.

'Well?' he said as I paused for breath. 'Which is it to be?'

'You're crazy,' I cried. 'And you're trying to drive me crazy, too. I won't do it. Suppose one of the crew were killed? Suppose they did discover what had happened? And if I did it – then I'd have something on you. You wouldn't stand for that. Somehow you'd get rid of me. You're not doing this for your country. You're doing it for yourself. Your love of power is driving you – driving you over the edge of reason. You can't get away with a thing like—'

'Which is it to be?' he cut in, his lips tightening and his voice suddenly cold and metallic. 'Do you take this job with Harcourt or do I telephone the police? I'll give you half an hour to make up your mind.' He hesitated and then said slowly, 'Just remember what it's like to be locked away in a cell, seeing the sun through iron bars, with no hope – and no future when you get out. I'm offering you a flying job – and a future. Now sit down and make up your mind.' He turned abruptly then and went out.

With the closing of the door the room seemed suddenly empty and silent. The key grated in the lock. It was like the turning of the key in the solitary confinement cells – only there the door had been of metal and had clanged. Stalag Luft I, with its lines of huts, the barbed wire, the endless march of the guards, the searchlights at night, the deadly monotony, was there in my mind, as vivid as though I had only just escaped. Surely to God I'd had enough of life behind bars. Surely to God. . . .

CHAPTER FIVE

I won't attempt to defend my decision. Saeton had asked me to steal a plane and I agreed to do it. I must take full responsibility, therefore, for all that happened afterwards as a result of that decision.

We went down to Ramsbury and in the smoky warmth of the pub that faces the old oak, he went over the plan in detail. I know it sounds incredible – to steal a plane off such a highly organised operation as the Berlin Airlift and then, after replacing two of the engines, to fly it back to Germany and operate it from the same airfield from which it had been stolen. But he had it all worked out. And when he had gone over all the details, it didn't seem incredible any more.

The devil of it was the man's enthusiasm was infectious. I can see him now, talking softly in the hubbub of the bar, his eyes glittering with excitement, smoking cigarette after cigarette, his voice vibrant as he reached out into my mind to give me the sense of adventure that he felt himself. The essence of his personality was that he could make others believe what he believed. In any project, he gave himself to it so completely that it was impossible not to follow him. He was a born leader. From being an unwilling participant, I became a willing one. Out of apparent failure he conjured the hope of success, and he gave me something positive to work for. I think it was the daring of the plan that attracted me more than anything else. And, of course, I was up to the hilt in the thing financially. I may have thought it was money better thrown away considering how I'd got it, but no one likes to be broke when he is shown a way to make a fortune. The only thing he didn't allow for was the human factor.

As we left the pub he said, 'You'll be seeing Tubby tomorrow. Don't tell him anything about this. You understand? He's not to know. His family were Methodists.' He grinned at me as though that explained everything that constituted Tubby Carter's make-up.

Early the following morning Saeton drove me to Hungerford Station. Riding behind him on the old motor bike through the white of the frozen Kennet valley I felt a wild sense of exhilaration. For over five weeks I hadn't been more than a few miles from Membury aerodrome. Now I was going back into the world. Twenty-four hours ago I should have been scared at the prospect, afraid that I might be picked up by the police. Now I didn't think about it. I was bound for Germany, riding a mood of adventure that left no room in my mind for the routine activities of the law.

Tubby met me at Northolt. 'Glad to see you, Neil,' he said, beaming all over his face, his hand gripping my arm. 'Bit of luck Morgan going sick. Not that I wish the poor chap any harm, but it just happened right for you. Harcourt leaves for Wunstorf with one of the Tudors this evening. You're flying a test with him this afternoon in our plane.'

I glanced at him quickly. 'Our plane?'

He nodded, grinning. 'That's right. You're skipper. I'm engineer. A youngster called Harry Westrop is radio operator and the navigator is a fellow named Field. Come on up to the canteen and meet them. They're all here.'

I could have wished that Tubby wasn't to be a member of the crew. I immediately wanted to tell him the whole thing. Maybe it would have been better if I had. But I remembered what Saeton had said, and seeing Tubby's honest, friendly features, I knew Saeton was right. It was out of the question. Duty, not adventure, was his business in life. But it was going to make it that bit more difficult when I ordered the crew to bale out.

I began to feel nervous then. It was a long time since I'd flown operationally, a long time since I'd skippered an air crew. We went into the bar, and Tubby introduced me to the rest of the crew. Westrop was tall and rather shy with fair, crinkly hair. He was little more than a kid. Field was much older, a small, sour-looking man with sharp eyes and a sharper nose. 'What are you having, skipper?' Field asked. The word 'skipper' brought back memories of almost-forgotten nights of bombing. I ordered a Scotch.

'Field is just out of the R.A.F.,' Tubby said. 'He's been flying the airlift since the early days at Wunstorf.'

'Why did you pack up your commission?' I asked him.

He shrugged his shoulders. 'I got bored. Besides, there's more money in civil flying.' He looked at me narrowly out of his small, unsmiling eyes. 'I hear you were in 101 Squadron. Do you remember—' That started the reminiscences. And then suddenly he said: 'You got a gong for that escape of yours, didn't you?'

I nodded.

He looked at the ceiling and pursed his thin lips. I could see the man's mind thinking back. 'I remember now. Longest tunnel escape of the war and then three weeks on the run before—' He hesitated and then snapped his fingers. 'Of course. You were the bloke that flew a Jerry plane out, weren't you?'

'Yes,' I said. I was feeling suddenly tight inside. Any moment he'd ask me what I'd been doing since then.

'By Jove! That's wizard!' Westrop's voice was boyish and eager. 'What happened? How did you get the plane?'

'I'd rather not talk about it,' I said awkwardly.

'Oh, but dash it. I mean—'

'I tell you, I don't want to talk about it.' Damn it! Suppose his parachute didn't open? I didn't want any hero-worship. I must keep apart from the crew until after the first night flight.

'I only thought—'

'Shut up!' My voice sounded harsh and violent.

'Here's your drink,' Tubby said quietly, pushing the

glass towards me. Then he turned to Westrop. 'Better go and check over your radar equipment, Harry.'

'But I've just checked it.'

'Then check it again,' Tubby said in the same quiet voice. Westrop hesitated, glancing from Tubby to me. Then he turned away with a crestfallen look. 'He's only a kid,' Tubby said and picked up his drink. 'Well, here's to the airlift!' *Here's to the airlift!* I wondered whether he remembered the four of us drinking that toast in the mess room at Membury. It all seemed a long time ago. I turned to Field. 'What planes were you navigating on the lift?' I asked him.

'Yorks,' he replied. 'Wunstorf to Gatow with food for the bloody Jerry.' He knocked back his drink. 'Queer, isn't it? Just over three years ago I was navigating bombers to Berlin loaded with five hundred pounders. Now, for the last four months I've been delivering flour to them – flour that's paid for by Britain and America. Do you think they'd have done that for us?' He gave a bitter laugh. 'Well, here's to the Ruskies, God rot 'em! But for them we could have been a lot tougher.'

'You don't like the Germans?' I asked, glad of the change in conversation.

He gave me a thin-lipped smile. 'You should know about them. You've been inside one of their camps. They give me the creeps. They're a grim, humourless lot of bastards. As for Democracy, they think it's the biggest joke since Hitler wiped out Lidice. Ever read Milton's *Paradise Lost*? Well, that's Germany. Don't let's talk about it. Do you know Wunstorf?'

'I bombed it once in the early days,' I said.

'It's changed a bit since then. So has Gatow. We've enlarged them a bit. I think you'll be quite impressed. And the run in to Gatow is like nothing you've ever done before. You just go in like a bus service, and you keep rolling after touchdown because you know damn well there's either another kite coming down or taking off right on your tail. But they'll give you a full briefing at Wunstorf. It's reduced to a system so that it's almost automatic. Trouble is it's bloody boring – two flights a day, eight hours of duty, whatever the weather. I tried for B.O.A.C., but they didn't want any navigators. So here I am, back on the airlift, blast it!' His gaze swung to the entrance. 'Ah, here's the governor,' he said.

Harcourt was one of those men born for organisation, not leadership. He was very short with a small, neat moustache and sandy hair. He had tight, rather orderly features and a clipped manner of speech that finished sentences abruptly like an adding machine. His method of approach was impersonal – a few short questions, punctuated by sharp little nods, and then silence while shrewd grey eyes stared at me unblinkingly. Lunch was an awkward affair carried chiefly by Tubby. Harcourt had an aura of quiet efficiency about him, but it wasn't friendly efficiency. He was the sort of man who knows precisely what he wants and uses his fellow creatures much as a carpenter uses his tools. It made it a lot easier from my point of view.

Nevertheless, I found the test flight something of an ordeal. It was the machine that was supposed to be on test. He'd only just taken delivery. But I knew as we walked out to the plane that it was really I who was being tested. He sat in the second pilot's seat and I was conscious all through the take-off of his cold gaze fixed on my face and not on the instrument panel.

Once in the air, however, my confidence returned. She handled very easily and the fact that she was so like the one we'd flown only a few days before made it easier. Apparently I satisfied him, for as we walked across the airfield to the B.E.A. offices, he said, 'Get all the details cleared up, Fraser, and leave tomorrow lunchtime. That'll give you a daylight flight. I'll see you in Wunstorf.'

We left Northolt the following day in cold, brittle sunshine that turned to cloud as we crossed the North Sea. Field was right about Wunstorf. It had changed a lot since I'd been briefed for that raid nearly eight years ago. I came out of the cloud at about a thousand feet and there it was straight ahead of me through the windshield, an enormous flat field with a broad runway like an autobahn running across it and a huge tarmac apron littered with Yorks. There were excavations marking new work in progress and a railway line had been pushed out right to the edge of the field. Beyond it stretched the Westphalian plain, grim and desolate, with a line of fir-clad hills marching back along the horizon.

I came in to land through a thick downpour. The runway was a cold, shining ribbon of grey, half-obscured by a haze of driven rain. I went in steeply, pulled back the stick and touched down like silk. I was glad about that landing. Somehow it seemed an omen.

I kicked the rudder and swung on to the perimeter track, the rain beating up from the concrete and sweeping across the field so that the litter of planes became no more than a vague shadow in the murk.

'Dear old Wunstorf!' Field's voice crackled over the intercom. 'What a dump! It was raining when I left. Probably been raining ever since.'

A truck came out to meet us. We dumped our kit in it and it drove us to the airport buildings. They were a drab olive green; bleak utilitarian blocks of concrete. The Operations Room was on the ground floor. I reported to the squadron leader in charge. 'If you care to go up to the mess they'll fix you up.' Then he saw Field. 'Good God! You back already, Bob?'

'A fortnight's leave, that's all I got out of getting demobilised,' Field answered.

'And a rise in pay I'll bet.' The squadron leader turned to me. 'He'll get things sorted out for you. Report here in the morning and we'll let you know what your timings are.'

The station commander came in as he finished speaking, a big blond Alsatian at his heels. 'Any news of that Skymaster yet?' he asked.

'Not yet, sir,' replied the squadron leader. 'Celle have just been on again. They're getting worried. It's twenty minutes overdue. There's been a hell of a storm over the Russian Zone.'

'What about the other bases?'

'Lübeck, Fuhlsbuttel, Fassberg – they've all made negative reports, sir. It looks as though it's force-landed somewhere. Berlin are in touch with the Russians, but so far Safety Centre hasn't reported anything.'

'Next wave goes out at seventeen hundred, doesn't it? If the plane hasn't been located by then have all pilots briefed to keep a lookout for it, will you?' He turned to go and then stopped as he saw us. 'Back in civvies, eh, Field? I must say it doesn't make you look any smarter.' He smiled and then his eyes met mine. 'You must be Fraser.' He held out his hand to me. 'Glad to have you with us. Harcourt's up at the mess now. He's expecting you.' He turned to the squadron leader. 'Give the mess a ring and tell Wing-Commander Harcourt that his other Tudor has arrived.'

'Very good, sir.'

'We'll have a drink sometime, Fraser.' The station commander nodded and hurried out with his dog.

'I'll get you a car,' the squadron leader said. He went out and his shout of '*Fahrer!*' echoed in the stone corridor.

The mess was a huge building; block on block of grey concrete, large enough to house a division. When I gave my name to the German at the desk he ran his finger down a long list. 'Block C, sir – rooms 231 and 235. Just place your baggage there, please. I will arrange for it. And come this way, gentlemen. Wing-Commander Harcourt is wishing to speak with you.' So Harcourt retained his Air Force title out here! We followed the clerk into the lounge. It had a dreary waiting-room atmosphere. Harcourt came straight over. 'Good trip?' he asked.

'Pretty fair,' I said.

'What's visibility now?'

'Ceiling's about a thousand,' I told him. 'We ran into it over the Dutch coast.'

He nodded. 'Well, now we've got six planes here.' There was a touch of pride in the way he said it and this was reflected in the momentary gleam in his pale eyes. He'd every reason to be proud. There was only one other company doing this sort of work. How he'd managed to finance it, I don't know. He'd only started on the airlift three months ago. He'd had one plane then. Now he had six. It was something of an achievement and I remember thinking: *This man is doing what Saeton is so desperately wanting to do*. I tried to compare their personalities. But there was no point of similarity between the two men. Harcourt was quiet, efficient, withdrawn inside himself. Saeton was ruthless, genial – an extrovert and a gambler.

'Fraser!'

Harcourt's voice jerked me out of my thought. 'Yes?'

'I asked you whether you're okay to start on the wave scheduled for 10.00 hours tomorrow?'

I nodded.

'Good. We've only two relief crews at the moment so you'll be worked pretty hard. But I expect you can stand it for a day or two.' His eyes crinkled at the corners. 'Overtime rates are provided for in your contracts.' He glanced at his watch. 'Time I was moving. There's a wave due to leave at seventeen hundred. Field knows his way around.'

He left us then and we went in search of our rooms.

It was a queer place, the Wunstorf Mess. You couldn't really call it a mess – aircrews' quarters would be a more apt description. It reminded me of an enormous jail. Long concrete corridors echoed to ribald laughter and the splash of water from communal washrooms. The rooms were like cells, small dormitories with two or three beds. One room we went into by mistake was in darkness with the blackout blinds drawn. The occupants were asleep and they cursed us as we switched on the light. Through the open doors of other rooms we saw men playing cards, reading, talking, going to bed, getting up. All the life of Wunstorf was here in these electrically-lit, echoing corridors. In the washrooms men in uniform were washing next to men in pyjamas quietly shaving as though it were early morning. These billets brought home to me more than anything the fact that the airlift was a military operation, a round-the-clock service running on into infinity.

We found our rooms. There were two beds in each. Carter and I took one room; Westrop and Field the other. Field wandered in and gave us a drink from a flask. 'It's going to be pretty tough operating six planes with only two relief crews,' he said. 'It means damn nearly twelve hours' duty a day.'

'Suits me,' I replied.

Carter straightened up from the case he was unpacking. 'Glad to be back in the flying business, eh?' He smiled.

I nodded.

'It won't last long,' Field said.

'What won't?' I asked.

'Your enthusiasm. This isn't like it was in wartime.' He dived across the corridor to his room and returned with a folder. 'Take a look at this.' He held a sheet out to me. It was divided into squares – each square a month and each month black with little ticks. 'Every one of these ticks represents a trip to Berlin and back, around two hours' flying. It goes on and on, the same routine. Wet or fine, thick mist or blowing half a gale, they send you up regular as clockwork. No let-up at all. Gets you down in the end.' He shrugged his shoulders and tucked the folder under his arm. 'Oh, well, got to earn a living, I suppose. But it's a bloody grind, believe you me.'

After tea I walked down to the airfield. I wanted to be alone. The rain had stopped, but the wind still lashed at the pine trees. The loading apron was almost empty, a huge, desolate stretch of tarmac shining wet and black in the grey light. Only planes undergoing repairs and maintenance were left, their wings quivering soundlessly under the stress of the weather. It was as though all the rest had been spirited away. The runways were deserted. The place looked almost as empty as Membury.

I turned back through the pines and struck away to the left, to the railway sidings that had been built out to the very edge of the landing field. A long line of fuel wagons was being shunted in, fuel that we should carry to Berlin. The place was bleak and desolate. The country beyond rolled away into the distance, an endless vista of agriculture, without hedges or trees. Something of the character of the people seemed inherent in that landscape – inevitable, ruthless and without surprise. I turned, and across the railway sidings I caught a glimpse of the wings of a four-engined freighter – symbol of the British occupation of Germany. It seemed suddenly insignificant against the immensity of that rolling plain.

We were briefed by the officer in charge of Operations at nine o'clock the following morning. By ten we were out on the perimeter track waiting in a long queue of planes, waiting our turn with engines switched off to save petrol. Harcourt had been very insistent about that. 'It's all right for the R.A.F.,' he had said. 'The taxpayer foots their petrol bill. We're under charter at so much per flight. Fly on two engines whenever possible. Cut your engines out when waiting for take-off.' It made me realise how much Saeton had to gain by the extra thrust of those two engines and their lower fuel consumption.

The thought of Saeton reminded me of the thing I'd promised to do. I wished it could have been this first flight. I wanted to get it over. But it had to be a night flight. I glanced at Tubby. He was sitting in the second pilot's seat, the earphones of his flying helmet making his face seem broader, his eyes fixed on the instrument panel. If only I could have had a different engineer. It wasn't going to be easy to convince him.

The last plane ahead of us swung into position, engines revving. As it roared off up the runway the voice of Control crackled in my earphones. '*Okay, Two-five-two. You're clear to line up now. Take off right away.*' Perhaps it was as well to fly in daylight first, I thought, as I taxied to the runway end and swung the machine into position.

We took off dead on time at 10.18. For almost three-quarters of an hour we flew north-east making for the entry to the northern approach corridor for Berlin. '*Corridor beacon coming up now*,' Field told me over the inter-com. '*Turn on to 100 degrees. Time 11.01. We're minus thirty seconds*.' That meant we were thirty seconds behind schedule. The whole thing was worked on split-second timing. Landing margin was only ninety seconds either side of touch-down timing. If you didn't make it inside the margin you just had to overshoot and return to base. The schedule was fixed by timings over radar beacons at the start and finish of the air corridor that spanned the Russian Zone. Fixed heights ensured that there were no accidents in the air. We were flying Angels three-five – height 3,500 feet. Twenty miles from Frohnau beacon Westrop reported to Gatow Airway.

As we approached Berlin I began to have a sense of excitement. I hadn't been over Berlin since 1945. I'd been on night raids then. I wondered what it would look like in daylight. Tubby seemed to feel it, too. He kept on looking down through his side window and moving restlessly in his seat. I pushed my helmet back and shouted to him. 'Have you seen Berlin from the air since the war?'

He nodded abstractedly. 'I was on transport work.'

'Then what are you so excited about?' I asked.

He hesitated. Then he smiled – it was an eager, boyish smile. 'Diana's at Gatow. She's working in the

Malcolm Club there. She doesn't know I'm on the airlift.' He grinned. 'I'm going to surprise her.'

Westrop's voice sounded in my earphones, reporting to Gatow Airway that we were over Frohnau beacon. We switched to contact with Traffic Control, Gatow. '*Okay, Two-five-two. Report again at Lancaster House.*' So Diana was at Gatow. It suddenly made the place seem friendly, almost ordinary. It would be nice to see Diana again. And then I was looking out of my side window at a bomb-pocked countryside that merged into miles of roofless, shattered buildings. There were great flat gaps in the city, but mostly the streets were still visible, bordered by the empty shells of buildings. From the air it seemed as though hardly a house had a roof. We were passing over the area that the Russians had fought through. Nothing seemed to have been done about it. It might have happened yesterday instead of four years ago.

Over the centre of the city Field gave me my new course and Westrop reported to Gatow Tower, who answered, '*Okay, Two-five-two. Report at two miles. You're Number Three in the pattern.*'

There was less damage here. I caught a glimpse of the Olympic stadium and then the pine trees of the Grunewald district were coming up to meet me as I descended steeply. Havel Lake opened out, the flat sheet of water across which the last survivors from the Führer Bunker had tried to escape, and Westrop reported again. '*Clear to land, Two-five-two,*' came the voice of Gatow Control. 'Keep rolling after touchdown. There's a York close behind you.'

I lowered undercarriage and landing flaps. We skimmed the trees and then we were over a cleared strip of woods dotted with the posts of the night landing beacons with the whole circle of Gatow Airport opening up and the pierced steel runway rising to meet us. I levelled out at the edge of the field. The wheels bumped once, then we were on the ground, the machine jolting over the runway sections. I kept rolling to the runway end, braked and swung left to the off-loading platform.

Gatow was a disappointment after Wunstorf. It seemed much smaller and much less active. There were only five aircraft on the apron. Yet this field handled more traffic than either Tempelhof in the American Sector or Tegel in the French. As I taxied across the apron I saw the York behind me land and two Army lorries manned by a German labour team, still in their field grey, nosed out to meet it. I went on, past the line of Nissen huts that bordered the apron, towards the hangars. Two Tudor tankers were already at Piccadilly Circus, the circular standing for fuel off-loading. I swung into position by a vacant pipe. By the time we had switched off and got out of our seats the fuselage door was open and a British soldier was connecting a pipeline to our fuel tanks.

'Where's the Malcolm Club?' Tubby asked Field. His voice trembled slightly.

'It's one of those Nissen huts over there,' Field answered, pointing to the off-loading apron. He turned to me. 'Know what the Army call this?' He waved his hands towards the circular standing. 'Remember they called the cross-Channel pipeline PLUTO? Well, this one's called PLUME – Pipeline-under-mother-earth. Not bad, eh? It runs the fuel down to Havel where it's shipped into Berlin by barge. Saves fuel on transport.'

We were crossing the edge of the apron now, walking along the line of Nissen huts. The first two were full of Germans. 'Jerry labour organisation,' Field explained.

'What about the tower?' I asked. Above the third Nissen hut was a high scaffolding with a lookout. It was like a workman's hut on stilts.

'That's the control tower for the off-loading platform. All this is run by the Army – it's what they call a FASO. Forward Airfield Supply Organisation. Here's the Malcolm Club.' A blue board with R.A.F. roundel faced us. 'Better hurry if you want some coffee.'

Tubby hesitated. 'She may not be on duty,' he murmured.

'We'll soon see,' I said and took his arm.

Inside the hut the air was warm and smelt of fresh-made cakes. A fire glowed red in an Army-type stove. The place was full of smoke and the sound of voices. There were about four aircrews there, in a huddle by the counter. I saw Diana immediately. She was in the middle of the group, her hand on the arm of an American Control officer, laughing happily, her face turned up to his.

I felt Tubby check and was reminded suddenly of that night at Membury when he and I had stood outside the window of our mess. Then Diana turned and saw us. Her eyes lit up and she rushed over, seizing hold of Tubby, hugging him. Then she turned to me and kissed me, too. 'Harry! Harry!' She was calling excitedly across the room. 'Here's Tubby just flown in.' She swung back to her husband. 'Darling – remember I told you my brother Harry was in Berlin. Well, here he is.'

I saw the stiffness leave Tubby's face. He was suddenly grinning happily, shaking the big American's hand up and down, saying, 'My God! Harry. I should have recognised you from your photograph. Instead, I thought you were some boyfriend of Diana's.' He didn't even bother to hide his relief, and Diana never seemed to notice that anything had been wrong. She was taken too much by surprise. 'Why didn't you tell me you were flying in?' she cried. 'You devil, you. Come on. Let's get you some coffee. They only give you a few minutes here.'

I stood and watched her hustling him to the bun counter, wondering whether he had told her what had happened at Membury, wondering what she'd say if she knew I was going to ditch him in the Russian Zone.

'You must be Fraser.' Her brother was at my elbow. 'I've heard a lot about you from Di. My name's Harry Culyer, by the way.' He had Diana's eyes, but that was all they had in common. He had none of her restlessness. He was the sort of man you trust on sight; big, slow-spoken, friendly. 'Yes, I've heard a lot about you and a crazy devil called Saeton. Is that really his name?' He gave a fat chuckle. 'Seems apt from what Di told me.'

I wondered how much she had told him. 'Are you connected with the airlift?' I asked him.

He shook his head. 'No, I'm attached to the Control Office of the U.S. Military Government. I used to work for the Opel outfit before the war so they figured I'd have to stay on in some sort of uniform and keep an eye on vehicle production in the Zone. Right now I guess you could do with some coffee, eh?'

The coffee was thick and sweet. With it was a potted meat sandwich and a highly-coloured cake full of synthetic cream. 'Cigarettes?' I said, offering him a packet.

'Well, thanks. That's one of the troubles here in Berlin. Cigarettes are damned hard to come by. And it's worse for your boys. They're down to about fifteen a day. Well, what do you think of Gatow?' He laughed when I told him I was disappointed. 'You expected to find it littered with aircraft, eh? Well, that's organisation. Tempelhof is the same. They've got it so that these German labour teams turn the planes round in about fifteen minutes.'

'What brings you out to Gatow?' I asked him. 'Just paying Diana a visit?'

'Sort of. But I got a good excuse,' he added with a grin. 'I had to interview a German girl who has just got a job out here as a checker in your German Labour Organisation. Some trouble about her papers and we urgently need her down at Frankfurt. That's why I came up to Berlin.'

'You're not stationed here then?' I asked.

'No. I'm normally in the Zone. It's nice and quiet

down there – by comparison. I just been talking to your SIB major over there. The stories that man can tell!'

'What's he doing up at Gatow?' I asked.

'Oh, there's been some trouble with the Russians. This is your first trip, isn't it? Well, you see those trees on the other side of the airfield?' He nodded through the windows. 'That's the frontier over there.'

'The Russian Sector?'

'No. The Russian Zone. Last night Red Army guards opened up on a German car just after it had been allowed through the frontier barrier into the British Sector. Then their troops crossed the frontier and pushed the car back into their Zone under the nose of the R.A.F. Regiment. Your boys are pretty sore about it.'

'You mean the car was shot up in British territory?' I asked.

He laughed. 'Seems that sort of thing is happening every day in this crazy town. If they want somebody, they just drive into the Western Sectors and kidnap them.' The corners of his eyes crinkled. 'From what I hear our boys do the same in the Eastern Sector.'

An R.A.F. orderly called to me from the door. 'Two-five-two ready, sir.'

'Well, I guess that's your call. Glad to have met you, Fraser.'

'Neil!' Diana caught hold of my arm. 'Tubby has just told me – about the crash.' She glanced quickly at Tubby who was saying goodbye to her brother. 'What's Bill doing now?' she asked in a quick whisper. I didn't know what to say so I kept my mouth shut. 'Oh, don't be silly. I've got over that. But I know how it must have hit him. Where is he now?'

'He's still at Membury,' I said. And then added, 'He's sticking the plane together with sealing wax.'

'You don't mean to say he's still going on with it?'

'Look – I've got to go now,' I said. 'Goodbye, Diana.'

She was staring at me with a puzzled frown. 'Goodbye,' she said automatically.

Outside it was still raining. We climbed into the plane and taxied out to the runway. '*You're clear to line up now, Two-five-two. Two-six-O a-concrete – angels three-five.*' We flew out along the single exit corridor and were back in Wunstorf in good time for lunch. A letter was waiting for me at the mess. The address was typed and the envelope was postmarked 'Baydon'. *Dear Neil. Just to let you know I have almost completed the break-up. I have a flare path now. All you have to do is buzz once and I'll light you in. Good luck. Bill Saeton.* As I folded the letter Tubby came into the room. 'Message from Harcourt. We're not on the 1530 wave. He's switched us to 2200. Says the other boys need a night's sleep.'

So it had come. I had a sudden sick feeling.

He peered at me anxiously. 'You feeling all right, Neil?'

'Yes. Why?'

'You look pretty pale. Not nervous, are you? Damn it, you've no reason to be. You had enough experience of night-flying during the war.' His gaze fell to the letter in my hand but he didn't say anything and I tore it into small pieces and stuffed them into my pocket.

'Better turn in then if we're going to fly all night,' I said.

But I knew I shouldn't sleep. Hell! Why did I have to agree to this damn-fool scheme? I was scared now. Not scared of the danger. I don't think it was that. But what had seemed straightforward and simple over a drink in the pub at Ramsbury seemed much more difficult now that I was actually a part of the airlift. It seemed utterly crazy to try and fly a plane out of this organised bus service of supply delivery. And I had to convince a crew that included Tubby Carter that they had got to bale out over the Russian Zone. The menace of the Zone had already gripped me. I lay and sweated on my bed, listening to the 1530 wave taking off, knowing that mine was the next wave, scared that I should bungle it.

At tea I could eat nothing, but drank several cups, smoking cigarette after cigarette, conscious all the time of Tubby watching me with a puzzled, worried expression. Afterwards I walked down to the field in the gathering dusk and watched the planes pile in, a constant stream of aircraft glimmering like giant moths along the line of the landing lights. I saw my own plane, Two-five-two, come in, watched it swing into position on the loading apron and the crew pile out, and I hung on, waiting for the maintenance crew to finish servicing it. At last it stood deserted, a black shape against the wet tarmac that glistened with the reflection of the lights. I climbed on board.

Saeton and I had discussed this problem of simulating engine failure at great length. The easiest method would have been simply to cut off the juice. But the fuel cocks were on the starboard side, controlled from the flight engineer's seat. We had finally agreed that the only convincing method was to tamper with the ignition. I went forward to the cockpit and got to work on the wiring behind the instrument panel. I had tools with me and six lengths of insulated wire terminating in small metal clips. What I did was to fix two wires to the back of three of the ignition switches. These wires I led along the back of the instrument panel and brought out at the extreme left on my own side. All I had to do when I wished to simulate engine failure was to clip each pair of wires together and so short out the ignition switches. That would close the ignition circuit and stop the plugs sparking.

It took me the better part of an hour to fix the wires. I was just finishing when a lorry drove up. There was the clatter of metal and the drag of a pipe as they connected the fuel lorry to the tanks in the port-hand wing. The lorry's engine droned as it began refuelling.

I waited, conscious already of a fugitive, guilty feeling. Footsteps moved round the plane. Rather than be caught crouched nervously in the cockpit of my own machine, I went aft down the fuselage, climbing round the three big elliptical tanks and dropping on to the asphalt. I started to walk away from the plane, but the beam of a torch picked me out and a voice said, 'Who's that?'

'Squadron-Leader Fraser,' I answered, reverting

automatically to my service title. 'I've just been checking over something.'

'Very good, sir. Goodnight.'

'Goodnight,' I answered and went hurriedly across to the terminal building and along the road to the mess. I went up to my room and lay on my bed, trying to read. But I couldn't concentrate. My hands were trembling. Time dragged by as I lay there chain-smoking. Shortly after seven-thirty the door opened and Westrop poked his head into the room. 'You coming down to dinner, sir?'

'May as well,' I said.

As we went down the echoing corridors and along the cinder paths to the mess, Westrop chattered away incessantly. I wasn't listening until something he said caught my attention. 'What's that about a crash?' I asked.

'Remember when we arrived here yesterday – the station commander was talking about a Skymaster that was missing?' he said. 'Well, they made a forced landing in Russian territory. I got it from a flight lieutenant who's just come off duty at Ops. One of our crews sighted the wreck this afternoon. The Russians have apparently denied all knowledge of it. What do you think happens to crews who get landed in the Russian Zone?'

'I don't know,' I said shortly.

'The flight lieutenant said they were probably being held for interrogation. He didn't seem worried about them. But they might be injured. Do you think the Russians would give them medical treatment, sir? I mean' – he hesitated – 'well, I wouldn't like to have a Russian surgeon operate on me, would you?'

'No.'

'What do you think they hope to gain by this sort of thing? Everybody seems convinced they're not prepared to go to war yet. They've stopped buzzing our planes. That seems to prove it. They got scared when they crashed that York. I was talking to an R.E. major this afternoon. He said the trouble was their lines of communication. Their roads are bad and their railways from Russia to Eastern Germany are only single track. But I think it's more than that, don't you, sir? I mean, they can't possibly be as good as us technically. They could never have organised a thing as complicated as the airlift, for instance. And then their planes – they're still operating machines based on the B 29s they got hold of during the war.' He went on and on about the Russians until at length I couldn't stand it any more. 'Oh, for God's sake,' I said. 'I'm sick and tired of the Russians.'

'Sorry, sir, but—' He paused uncertainly. 'It's just – well, this is my first operational night flight.'

It was only then that I realised he'd been talking because he was nervous. I thought: *My God! The poor kid's scared stiff of the Russians and in a few hours' time I'm going to order him to jump*. It made me feel sick inside. Why wasn't my crew composed entirely of Fields? I didn't care about Field. I'd have ordered him to jump over wartime Berlin and not cared a damn. But Tubby and this child. . . .

I forced myself to eat and listened to Westrop's

chatter all through the meal. He had a live, inquiring mind. He already knew that we had to cover seventy miles of the Russian Zone in flying down the Berlin approach corridor. He knew, too, all about Russian interrogation methods – the round-the-clock interrogation under lights, the solitary confinement, the building up of fear in the mind of the victim. 'They're no better than the Nazis, are they?' he said. 'Only they don't seem to go as far as physical torture – not against service personnel.' He paused and then said, 'I wish we wore uniform. I'm certain, if anything like that happened, we'd be better off if we were in R.A.F. uniform.'

'You'll be all right,' I answered without thinking.

'Oh, I know we shan't have to make a forced landing,' he said quickly, mistaking what had been in my mind. 'Our servicing is much better than the Yanks' and—'

'I wouldn't be too sure of that,' I cut in. 'Have a cigarette and for God's sake stop talking about forced landings.'

'I'm sorry, sir. It was only—' He took the cigarette. 'You must think me an awful funk. But it's odd – I always like to know exactly what I'm facing. It makes it easier, somehow.'

Damn the kid! I'd always felt just like that myself. 'I'll see you at the plane at 21.46,' I said and got quickly to my feet. As I went out of the dining-hall I glanced at my watch. Still an hour to go! I left the mess and walked down to the airfield. The night was cold and frosty, the sky studded with stars. The apron was full of the huddled shapes of aircraft, looking clumsy and unbeautiful on the ground. Trucks were coming and going as the FASO teams worked to load them for the next wave. I leaned on the boundary fence and watched them. I could see my own plane. It was the left-hand one of a line of Tudors. Fuel loading and maintenance crews had completed their work. The planes stood deserted and silent. The minutes dragged slowly by as I stood, chilled to the marrow, trying to brace myself for what I had to do.

The odd thing is I never thought of refusing to carry out my part of the plan. I could have raised technical difficulties and put it off until gradually Saeton lost heart. Many times since I have asked myself why I didn't do this, and I still don't really know the answer. I like to think that Saeton's threat of exposing my identity to the police had nothing to do with it. Certainly the audacity of the thing had appealed to me. Also I believed in Saeton and his engines and the airlift had only served to increase their importance in my eyes. Moreover, my own future was involved. I suppose the truth is that my attitude was a combination of all these things. At any rate, as I stood there on the edge of Wunstorf airfield waiting for zero hour, it never occurred to me not to do it.

At last my watch told me it was nine-fifteen. I went slowly back to the mess. Tubby came in as I was getting into my flying kit. 'Well, thank God the weather's cleared,' he said cheerfully. 'I wouldn't want to be talked down by GCA the first time we went in by night.' GCA is Ground Control Approach, a means of blind landing where the plane lands on instructions from an officer operating radar gear at the edge of the runway.

By nine-fifty we were climbing into the plane. Our take-off time was 22.36 and as I lifted the heavy plane into the starlit night my hands and stomach felt as cold as ice. Tubby was checking the trim of the engines, his hand on the throttle levers. I groped down and found one of my three pairs of wires and touched the ends of them together. The inboard port motor checked. It worked all right. I glanced quickly at Tubby. He had taken his hand from the throttles and was listening, his head on one side. Then he turned to me. 'Did you hear that engine falter?' he shouted.

I nodded. 'Sounded like dirt in the fuel,' I called back.

He stayed in the same position for a moment, listening. Then his hand went back to the throttles. I glanced at the airspeed indicator and then at my watch. Three-quarters of an hour to Restorf beacon at the entrance of the air corridor.

The time dragged. The only sound was the steady drone of the engines. Twice I half-cut the same motor out. On the second occasion I did it when Tubby had gone aft to speak to Field. I held the wires together until the motor had cut out completely. Tubby suddenly appeared at my elbow as I allowed it to pick up again. 'I don't like the sound of that engine,' he shouted.

'Nor do I,' I said.

He stood quite still, listening. 'Sounded like ignition. I'll get it checked at Gatow.'

I glanced at my watch. It was eleven-sixteen. Any minute now. Then Field's voice crackled in my ears. 'We're over the corridor beacon now. Right on to 100 degrees. We're minus ten seconds.' I felt ice cold, but calm, as I banked. My stomach didn't flutter any more. I leaned a little forward, feeling for the metal clips. One by one I fastened them together in their pairs. And one by one the engines died, all except the inboard starboard motor. The plane was suddenly very quiet. I heard Tubby's muttered curse quite distinctly. 'Check ignition!' I shouted to him. 'Check fuel!' I made my voice sound scared. The airspeed indicator was dropping, the luminous pointer swinging back through 150, falling back towards the 100 mark. The altimeter needle was dropping, too, as the nose tilted earthwards. 'We're going down at about 800 a minute,' I shouted.

'Ignition okay,' he reported, his hand on the switches. 'Fuel okay.' His eyes were frantically scanning the instrument panel. 'It's an electrical fault – ignition, I think. The bastards must have overlooked some loose wiring.'

'Anything we can do?' I asked. 'We're down to three thousand already.'

'Doubt it. Not much time.'

'If you think there's anything we can do, say so. Otherwise I'm going to order the crew to bale out.' I had kept my inter-com mouthpiece close to my lips so that Field and Westrop could hear what we were saying.

Tubby straightened up. 'Okay. We'd better bale out.' His face looked stiff and strained in the light of the instrument panel.

'Get your parachutes on,' I ordered over the intercom. 'Field. You go aft and get the fuselage door open. We may have to ditch her.' Out of the tail of my eye I saw the two of them struggling with their parachutes. Field shouted something to Westrop and a moment later the bags containing the other two parachutes were slid on to the floor of the cockpit. 'Get back to the fuselage door,' I told Westrop. 'I'll send Carter aft when I want you to jump.' I glanced at the altimeter dial. 'Height two-six,' I called to Tubby.

He straightened up. 'Nothing I can do,' he said. 'It's in the wiring somewhere.'

'Okay,' I said. 'Get aft and tell the others to jump. Give me a shout when you're jumping.'

He stood there, hesitating for a moment. 'Okay.' His hand gripped my arm. 'See you in the Russian Zone.' But he still didn't move and his hand remained gripping my arm. 'Would you like me to take her while you jump?' he asked.

I realised suddenly that he was remembering the last time I'd jumped, over Membury. He thought my nerve might have gone. I swallowed quickly. Why did he have to be so bloody decent about it? 'Of course not,' I said sharply. 'Get aft and look after yourself and the others.'

His eyes remained fixed on mine – brown, intelligent eyes that seemed to read my mind. 'Good luck!' He turned and dived quickly through towards the fuselage. Leaning out of my seat, I looked back and watched him climbing round the fuel tanks. I could just see the others at the open door of the fuselage. Tubby joined them. Westrop went first, then Field. Tubby shouted to me. 'Jump!' I called to him. The plane skidded slightly and I turned back to the controls, steadying her.

When I looked back down the length of the fuselage there was no one there. I was alone in the plane. I settled myself in my seat. Height one thousand six hundred. Airspeed ninety-five. I'd take her down to a thousand feet. That should put her below the horizon of the three who had jumped. Through the windshield I saw a small point of light moving across the sky – the tail-light of one of the airlift planes holding steadily to its course. I wondered if those behind could see me. In case, I banked away and at the same time broke one of the wire contacts. The outboard port engine started immediately as I unfeathered the prop.

As I banked out of the traffic stream a voice called to me – 'You bloody fool, Neil. You haven't even got your parachute on.' I felt sudden panic grip me as I turned to find Tubby coming back into the cockpit.

'Why the hell haven't you jumped?'

'Plenty of time now,' he said calmly. 'Perhaps the other engines will pick up. I was worried about you, that's why I came back.'

'I can look after myself,' I snapped. 'Get back to that door and jump.'

I think he saw the panic in my eyes and misunderstood it. His gaze dropped to my parachute still in its canvas bag. 'I'll take over whilst you get into your parachute. With two engines we might still make Gatow.'

He was already sliding into the second pilot's seat now and I felt his hands take over on the controls. 'Now get your 'chute on, Neil,' he said quietly.

We sat there, staring at each other. I didn't know what the hell to do. I glanced at the altimeter. The needle was steady at the thousand mark. His eyes followed the direction of my gaze and then he looked at me again and his forehead was wrinkled in a puzzled frown. 'You weren't going to jump, were you?' he said slowly.

I sat there, staring at him. And then I knew he'd got to come back to Membury with me. 'No,' I said. And with sudden violence, 'Why the hell couldn't you have jumped when I told you?'

'I knew you didn't like jumping,' he said. 'What were you going to do – try and crash land?'

I hesitated. I'd have one more shot at getting him to jump. I edged my left hand down the side of my seat until I found the wires that connected to the ignition switch of that outboard port motor. I clipped them together and the motor died. 'It's gone again,' I shouted to him. I switched over to the automatic pilot. 'Come on,' I said. 'We're getting out.' I slid out of my seat and gripped him by the arm. 'Quick!' I said, half-pulling him towards the exit door.

I think I'd have done it that time, but he glanced

back, and then suddenly he wrenched himself free of my grip. I saw him reach over the pilot's seat, saw him tearing at the wires, and as he unfeathered the props the motors picked up in a thrumming roar. He slid into his own seat, took over from the automatic pilot and as I stood there, dazed with the shock of discovery, I saw the altimeter needle begin to climb through the luminous figures of its dial.

Then I was clambering into my seat, struggling to get control of the plane from him. He shouted something to me. I don't remember what it was. I kicked at the rudder bar and swung the heavy plane into a wide banking turn. 'We're going back to Membury,' I yelled at him.

'Membury!' He stared at me. 'So that's it! It was you who fixed those wires. You made those boys jump—' The words seemed to choke him. 'You must be crazy. What's the idea?'

I heard myself laughing wildly. I was excited and my nerves were tense. 'Better ask Saeton,' I said, still laughing.

'Saeton!' He caught hold of my arm. 'You crazy fools! You can't get away with this.'

'Of course we can,' I cried. 'We have. Nobody will ever know.' I was so elated I didn't notice him settling more firmly into his seat. I was thinking I'd succeeded. I'd done the impossible – I'd taken an aircraft off the Berlin airlift. I wanted to sing, shout, do something to express the thrill it gave me.

Then the controls moved under my hands. He was dragging the plane round, heading it for Berlin. For a moment I fought the controls, struggling to get the ship round. The compass wavered uncertainly. But he held on grimly. He had great strength. At length I let go and watched the compass swing back on to the lubber lines of our original course.

All the elation I had felt died out of me. 'For God's sake, Tubby,' I said. 'Try to understand what this means. Nobody's going to lose over this. Harcourt will get the insurance. As for the airlift, in a few weeks the plane will be back on the job. Only then it will have our engines in it. We'll have succeeded. Doesn't success mean anything to you?' Automatically I was using Saeton's arguments over again.

But all he said was, 'You've dropped those boys into Russian territory.'

'Well, what of it?' I demanded hotly. 'They'll be all right. So will Harcourt. And so will we.'

He looked at me then, his face a white mask, the little lines at the corners of his eyes no longer crinkled by laughter. He looked solid, unemotional – like a block of granite. 'I should have known the sort of person you were when you turned up at Membury like that. Saeton's a fanatic. I can forgive him. But you're just a dirty little crook who has—'

He shouldn't have said that. It made me mad – part fear, part anger. Damn his bloody high and mighty principles! Was he prepared to die for them? I reached down for the wires. My fingers were trembling and numb with the cold blast of the air that came in through the open doorway aft, but I managed to fasten the clips. The engines died away. The cabin was suddenly silent, a ghostly place of soft-lit dials and our reflections in the windshield. We seemed suddenly cut off from the rest of the world. A white pin-point of light slid over us like a star – our one contact with reality, a plane bound for Berlin.

'Don't be a fool, Fraser!' Tubby's voice was unnaturally loud in the stillness.

I laughed. It wasn't a pleasant sound. My nerves were keyed to the pitch of desperation. 'Either we fly to Membury,' I said, 'or we crash.' My teeth were clenched. It might have been a stranger's voice. 'You can jump if you want to,' I added, nodding towards the rear of the cockpit where the wind whistled.

'Unfasten those wires!' he shouted. And when I made no move he said, 'Get them unfastened and start the motors or I'll hurt you.'

He was fumbling in the pocket beside his seat and his hand came out holding a heavy spanner. He let go the controls then. The plane dipped and slid away to port. Automatically I grasped the control column and righted her. At the same time he rose in his seat, the spanner lifted in his hand.

I flung myself sideways, lunging out at him. The spanner caught me across the shoulder and my left arm went numb. But I had hold of his flying suit now and was pulling him towards me. He had no room to use the spanner again. And at the same moment the plane dropped sickeningly. We were flung into the aisle and fetched up against the fuel tanks in the fuselage.

For a moment we stood there, locked together, and then he fought to get clear of me, to get back to start the motors again. I was determined he shouldn't. I'd take him down into the ground rather than fly on to Gatow to be accused of having attempted to take a plane off the airlift. I clutched hold of him, pinning his arms, bracing myself against the tanks. The plane lurched and we were flung between the tanks into the main body of the fuselage where the wind roared in through the open doorway. That lurch flung us against the door to the toilet, breaking us clear of each other. He raised the spanner to strike at me again and I hit him with my fist. The spanner descended, striking my shoulder again. I lashed out again. My fist caught his jaw and his head jerked back against the metal of the fuselage. At the same moment the plane seemed to fall away. We were both flung sideways. Tubby hit the side of the open doorway. I saw his head jerk back as his forehead caught a protruding section of the metal frame. Blood gleamed red in a long gash and his jaw fell slack. Slowly his legs gave under him.

As he fell I started forward. He was falling into the black rectangle of the doorway. I clutched at him, but the plane swung, jerking me back against the toilet door. And in that instant Tubby slid to the floor, his legs slowly disappearing into the black void of the slip-stream. For an instant his thick torso lay along the floor, held there by the wind and the tilt of the plane. I could do nothing. I was pinned by the tilt of the plane, forced to stand there and watch as his body began to slide outwards, slowly, like a sack, the outstretched hands making no attempt to hold him. For a second he was there, sliding slowly out across the floor, and then the slip-stream whisked him away and I was alone in the body of the plane with only the gaping doorway and a thin trickle of blood on the steel flooring to show what had happened.

I shook myself, dazed with the horror of it. Then I closed the door and went for'ard. Almost automatically my brain registered the altimeter dial. Height 700. I slipped into the pilot's seat and with trembling fingers forced the wires apart. The engines roared. I gripped the control column and my feet found the rudder bar. I banked and climbed steeply. The lights of a town showed below me and the snaking course of a river. I felt sick at the thought of what had happened to Tubby. Height two-four. Course eight-five degrees. I must find out what had happened to Tubby.

I made a tight, diving turn and levelled out at five hundred feet. I had to find out what had happened to him. If he'd regained consciousness and had been able to pull his parachute release . . . Surely the cold air would have revived him. *God! Don't let him die*. I was sobbing my prayer aloud. I went back along the course of the river, over the lights of the town. A road ran out of it, straight like a piece of tape and white in the moonlight. Then I shut down the engines and put down the flaps. This was the spot where Tubby had fallen. I searched desperately through the windshield. But all I saw was a deserted airfield bordered by pine woods and a huddle of buildings that were no more than empty shells. No sign of a parachute, no comforting mushroom patch of white.

I went back and forth over the area a dozen times.

The aerodrome and the woods and the bomb-shattered buildings stood out clear in the moonlight, but never a sign of the white silk of a parachute.

Tubby was dead and I had killed him.

Dazed and frightened I banked away from the white graveyard scene of the shattered buildings. I took the plane up to 10,000 feet and fled westward across the moon-filled night. Away to the right I could see the lines of planes coming in along the corridor, red and green navigation lights stretching back towards Lübeck. But in a moment they were gone and I was alone, riding the sky, with only the reflection of my face in the windshield for company – nothing of earth but the flat expanse of the Westphalian plain, white like a salt-pan below me.

CHAPTER SIX

There was no problem of navigation to distract my mind on the homeward run. The earth lay like a white map below me. I found the North Sea at Flushing, crossed the southern extremity of it, flying automatically, and just as automatically picked up the Thames estuary, following the curves of the river till it met the Kennet. And all the time I was remembering every detail of what had happened. It seemed such a waste that he should die like that. And all because he'd called me a crook. My face, ghostly in the windshield, seemed to reflect the bitterness of my thoughts.

I had three hours in which to sort the thing out and face it. But I didn't face it. I know that now. I began that flight hating myself. I ended it by hating Saeton. It was he who had forced me into it. It was he, not I, who was responsible for Tubby's death. By the time I was over the Kennet I had almost convinced myself of that.

I dropped to a thousand feet in a mood of cold fury, picked up Ramsbury and swung north-east. The trees of Baydon Hill were a dark line and there, suddenly, were the hangars of Membury and, as I swept low over the field, I caught a glimpse of the quarters nestled snugly in their clearing in the woods. All just as I had left it. Nothing changed. Only a man dead and the moon bathing everything in a white unreal light.

I had no need of any flares. I skidded in a tight, vicious turn, dropped flaps and undercarriage, and slammed the machine down on to the runway not caring whether I smashed it up in the violence of my anger.

Saeton was at the hangar and came running out to meet me as I cut the engines. He was waiting for me as I stepped out on to the concrete, his face alive with excitement. 'Well done, Neil! Magnificent!' He seized my hand and wrung it.

I flung him off. I couldn't say anything. The words choked in my throat. He was gazing at the plane, caressing it with his eyes, like a father who has been presented with another son to replace one that has died. My hands clenched with the desire to hit out, to smash the eagerness of his face.

Then he turned and met my gaze. 'What's the trouble?' His hand reached out and caught my arm in a hard, unyielding grip. His voice was urgent, his mood tuned to mine.

I faced him then, my guts screwed up in a tight little knot in my belly and my teeth clenched.'Tubby's dead,' I said.

'Dead?' His fingers dug into the muscles of my arm

and he stared at me hard. Then his grip relaxed. 'What happened?' he asked, in a flat tone.

I told him what had happened – how Tubby's body had slumped unconscious through the fuselage door, how I'd searched the area and found no sign of a parachute. When I had finished he turned and stared at the plane. Then he shook himself. 'All right. Let's get the plane into the hangar.'

'The plane!' I heard myself laugh. 'I tell you, Tubby's dead.'

'All right,' he said angrily. 'So he's dead. There's nothing you or I can do about it.'

'Diana was at Gatow,' I told him. 'She's working at the Malcolm Club there. I saw her yesterday.' I was remembering the sudden radiance of her face as she turned and found Tubby standing beside me.

'What's Diana got to do with it?' he asked angrily. 'She'll get over it. Now give me a hand with the hangar doors. We've got to get this plane under cover right away.'

Anger burst like a torrent inside me. 'My God! You callous bastard! You don't care who's killed so long as you get your bloody engines into the air. Nothing else matters to you. Can't you understand what's happened? He was unconscious when he fell through the door. And now he's lying out there beside a disused airfield in the Russian Zone. He's dead, and you killed him,' I screamed. 'And all you can think about is the plane. You haven't the decency even to say you're sorry. He was straight and honest and decent, and you wipe the memory off your mind as though he were no more than—'

He hit me then, across the face with the flat of his hand. 'Shut your mouth!' His voice trembled, but it was without anger or violence. 'It doesn't occur to you, I suppose, that I was fond of Tubby? He was the nearest I ever had to a friend in my life.' He said that slowly as though he were explaining something to himself. Then he turned away, his shoulders hunched, his hands thrust into his trouser pockets as though he didn't trust them in the open. 'Now come and help me get the hangar doors opened.'

I followed him dully, tears stinging the back of my eyeballs, blurring the white naked brilliance of the scene. He opened the wicket door, undid the bolts of the main doors and between us we slid them back. Moonlight flooded into the hangar, showing it strangely empty. The crashed Tudor was gone. All that remained of it was a jumbled heap of broken metal piled along each side of the hangar walls. And at the far end the bench with its lathes and machine tools stood deserted and silent. The whole place reeked of Tubby. I could see him beside me at that bench, whistling his flat, unending tunes, a grin crinkling his cheerful, sweaty face.

The engines of the plane roared. The vague outline of Saeton's head showed behind the glass of the windshield as he turned it and taxied into the hangar. Between us we got the doors closed again. 'We'll go back to the quarters now,' he said. 'You need a drink.' His hand gripped my shoulder. 'I'm sorry, Neil. I should have let you blow off steam. You've had a hell of a night.'

'I can't get the memory of Tubby out of my mind,' I said, more to myself than to him.

We walked through the woods in silence and went into the mess room. Nothing had changed – the same trestle table, the four chairs and the cupboard in the corner. But there were just the two of us now. I stood there, feeling cold and numb. 'Sit down,' he said, 'and I'll get you a drink.' He returned in a few minutes with two tumblers of whisky and a bundle of maps. 'Knock that back,' he said gently. 'You'll feel better then.'

As I drank he shuffled through the maps, picked out one and spread it flat on the table. 'Now then, where exactly did it happen?'

'I'd rather not talk about it,' I said dully.

He nodded. 'I understand how you feel. But I must get it pin-pointed whilst it's still vivid in your mind. Now. Here's Restorf at the entrance to the corridor. How soon did you cut out the engines?'

'About three minutes after Field had reported that we'd passed the entrance beacon,' I answered.

'Field was your navigator?'

'Yes.'

'Speed?'

'About one-sixty knots.' I put down my tumbler. 'What are you going to do?'

'I don't know yet.'

'Tubby's dead,' I said bitterly. 'He was unconscious when he went through the door. I searched the whole area. There wasn't any sign of a parachute. There's nothing we can do.' I looked at him, the beginnings of a decision forming in my mind. 'I must give myself up.'

'What good do you think that will do?' he demanded harshly.

I shook my head. 'None.' My voice was bitter. 'But I can't go on like this. Do you know what he called me? He called me a dirty little crook. That's what started it all.' I stared down at my drink. 'He was right, too. That's what hurt. First the 'Callahan' business. Now, this. Saeton, I can't go on with it. It'd drive me crazy. All the time I'd be thinking—'

'Stop thinking about yourself,' he snapped. The vein on the side of his forehead was beginning to throb.

'We killed him,' I said dully. 'Between us, we killed him.'

'We did nothing of the sort,' he replied angrily. 'It was an accident.'

'He tried to stop me taking the plane. In the eyes of the law it would be—'

'Damn the law! So you told him what you were doing?'

'I had to. He came back after the others had jumped.' I wiped my hand across my eyes. 'I've made up my mind,' I said. 'I can't go on—'

'Oh, for God's sake!' he cried. And then he leaned towards me, his eyes fixed on mine. 'You think I'm callous about Tubby's death, don't you?' His gaze dropped slowly to the map and he shrugged his shoulders. 'Maybe it's happened too often before – men going out and not coming back. I had nearly a year in command of a bomber station out in France. I lost fifty-five in that year – just boys I knew who passed through my life and were gone. Maybe I got hardened to it.' His eyes lifted and fastened on me again. 'But Tubby wasn't just a boy I knew. Damn it, we worked together for two years, side-by-side on the same project with the same end in view. When you told me he was dead, I could have killed you. You've bungled it, and through your bungling you've killed the one man I was really fond of. And now you have the bloody nerve to say you won't go through with the rest of the plan. Get this into your head, Neil. If you don't go through with it, you make Tubby's death utterly pointless. If it was necessary for him to die that a British company should get a world lead in air-freight transport, well and good. But if you're now going to—'

'I must tell the police the whole thing,' I repeated obstinately.

'Why? Telling the police won't help. You say Tubby is dead. All right then. He's dead. But for the love of God let's see to it that his death was to some purpose.' He slewed the map round towards me. 'Now then. You dropped Field and the other fellow about there – correct? What happened then?'

'I banked away out of the traffic stream,' I answered, my voice trembling. 'Then Tubby came back to the cockpit. He knew I was scared of jumps. He came back to make sure I got out. We were at about a thousand feet—'

'And then?'

'Christ!' I said. 'Don't you see? It was because he was so bloody decent. That was why he died. Because he was so bloody decent. He was afraid I wouldn't jump. He was going to take the controls . . .' I was almost sobbing.

Saeton pushed the tumbler into my hand. 'Drink up,' he said. The drink produced a little oasis of warmth in the cold pit of my stomach. 'You're at a thousand feet. What happened then?'

I swallowed another mouthful. 'I was on two motors then. I cut one. I nearly convinced him. He was just going aft again when he saw the clips. He took control then and turned the machine back into the corridor.'

'I see. And you tried to persuade him to make for Membury. That's when you told him our plan?'

'That's right. But he wouldn't. His Methodist upbringing. You told me about that. You warned me . . .' My mind was confused now. I felt damnably tired.

He shook my shoulder. 'Then you had a fight. That's what you told me.'

'Yes. He called me a dirty little crook. That made me mad. I cut the engine out then. I told him either we crashed or he let me take over. That's when he came at me with a spanner. The rest you know.' My eyelids felt heavy. I couldn't keep them open. 'What are you going to do?' I mumbled.

'How long between his returning to the cockpit and the fight?'

'Five minutes – ten minutes. I don't know.'

'What height were you when Tubby went out through the fuselage door?'

'I don't know. Yes. Wait a minute. About seven hundred. I climbed to over two thousand and then went down to five hundred again to search for him.'

'You mentioned a disused airfield.'

'Yes.' My head nodded forward uncontrollably and I felt him shaking me. 'There was a small town. There was a river, too, and a road ran north, quite straight, past the edge of the airfield.' I stared at him dully. He was peering at the map, marking off distances with a rule. 'Can you find it?' I asked.

He nodded. 'Yes. Hollmind. No doubt of it.'

'What are you going to do?' I asked again.

'Nothing much we can do,' he said. 'But an old friend of mine is at Lübeck, flying Daks. I'll cable him and have him search the area as he flies over in daylight.'

I nodded vaguely. I couldn't keep my eyes open.

'You're dead beat, Neil. Better get some sleep.' His voice sounded miles away. I felt his hands under my arm. 'Come on, old chap.'

I think Saeton must have put something in my drink, for I don't remember anything more until I woke to sunlight streaming into the familiar, comfortless little room. It had never done that before and when I glanced at my watch I found it was past two. I was still in my clothes and I had slept for nearly twelve hours. I fumbled for a cigarette, lit it and lay back.

The events of the night before came back to me then, like some nightmare half forgotten in waking. Tubby's death was no longer vivid in my memory. The whole thing had an unreal quality, until I went across to the hangar and saw the plane with Saeton already at work on the inboard engines.

'Feeling better?' he asked. 'I left some food out for you. Did you find it?'

'No.' I walked round to the front of the machine and saw that he had already got the starboard engine out. The single-purposed drive of the man was incredible.

'I'm having difficulty with the securing nuts of this engine,' he said. 'Can you come up and give me a hand?'

I didn't move. I stood there, staring at the shining sweep of the wings – hating the plane, hating Saeton, and hating myself worst of all. Slowly my eyes travelled from the plane to the litter of the hangar. God, how the man must have worked whilst I'd been at Wunstorf! He'd cut the old machine to pieces with an oxy-acetylene cutter; wings, tail, fuselage were a jumble of unrecognisable fragments piled along the walls. Only the engines were left intact.

He climbed down from the wheeled gantry. 'Snap out of it, Neil!' His voice was hard, almost violent. 'Put your overalls on and get to work on that engine.' His face, close to, looked grey and haggard, his eyes shadowed with sleeplessness. He looked old. 'I'm going to get some sleep.' He cleared a space for himself on the bench and lay down. He kept his eyes open until I'd climbed the gantry and started work. After that he didn't stir until I switched the light plant on.

He brought some food over then and we worked on together until we had the port engine lowered on to the concrete floor. It was then eight forty-five. 'Nearly news time,' I said and lit a cigarette, my hands trembling.

We got the news on the plane's radio. There was nothing in the summary. With the earphones clamped to my ears the announcer's voice seemed to be there in my head, telling me of political wrangles, strikes, a depression over Iceland, anything but what I wanted to hear. Right at the end, however, he paused. There was a rustle of paper and then his voice was back in my ears and I gripped the edge of the seat.

News has just come in that the Tudor aircraft, missing on the airlift since last night, has crashed in the Russian Zone of Germany. Two members of the crew, who baled out, crossed the frontier into the British Zone this morning. They are R. E. Field, navigator, and H. L. Westrop, radio operator. According to their report, the plane's engines failed shortly after it had turned into the northern approach corridor to Berlin and the captain ordered the crew to bale out. Still missing are N. L. Fraser, pilot, and R. C. Carter, flight engineer. The pilot of one of the planes following the missing Tudor has reported seeing a single parachute open at about a thousand feet. It was clearly visible in brilliant moonlight. As Field and Westrop came down together, it is thought that this parachute may belong to one of the other two members of the crew. So far the Russians have denied that any plane crashed in their territory or that they hold any of our aircrews. The plane was a Tudor tanker belonging to the Harcourt Charter Company. Squadron Leader Neil Fraser escaped from Germany during the war by flying out a Messerschmitt after—

I switched it off and removed my headphones. *A single parachute!* 'Do you think he's alive?' The sudden relief of hope made my voice unsteady. Saeton made no answer. He was staring down the fuselage at nothing in particular. 'A single parachute! That must be Tubby. The others went out together. They came down together. The news said so.'

'We'll see what the papers say tomorrow.' Saeton got to his feet.

I caught hold of his arm as he passed me. 'What's the matter? Aren't you glad?'

He looked down at me, his eyes grey like slate. 'Of course, I'm glad.' There was no enthusiasm in his voice.

His reaction left me with a sense of depression. The report was third or fourth hand. The pilot might have been seeing two parachutes as one. It might mean nothing – or everything. I got out on to the floor of the hangar and stood, staring at the plane. If only Saeton hadn't taken the inboard engines out. If the machine had been left as I had brought it in, we could have gone over, landed on that disused airfield and searched the area. It was a crazy idea, but it stuck in my mind.

And as though Saeton had also thought of that, he pressed straight on with the installation of the first of our own engines. We finished it at three in the morning. But even then I couldn't sleep. My mind kept on seeing that single parachute, a white mushroom of silk in the moonlight, picturing Tubby forced to consciousness by the rush of cold air, tugging at the release. Pray God the papers carried more detail.

I was up at eight. The quarters were silent. There was no sign of Saeton. I thought he must be over at the hangar until I found a note on the mess table to say he'd gone into Baydon for the papers. By the time I'd cooked the bacon he was back. I saw at once he had some news. There was a gleam of excitement in his eyes and his face looked younger as though all the sleeplessness had been wiped away. 'What is it?' I asked breathlessly. 'Have they found him?'

'No.'

'What then?'

'Take a look at that.' He handed me a teleprint.

Your plane urgently required Wunstorf to replace Tudor tanker missing stop Ministry Civil Aviation agree rush C of A stop Report Wunstorf soonest possible notifying your E.T.A. Signed Aylmer B.E.A.

I handed it back to him. 'I suppose you didn't bother to see what the papers say about the crew of the plane?'

'Can't you get your mind off what's happened?' he demanded irritably.

'No,' I said. 'I can't. Have you got the papers?'

'Here you are.' He handed me a whole bundle of newspapers. 'They tell us nothing that we didn't know last night.'

I glanced quickly through them as he went past me to get his breakfast. All the reports were the same. It was obviously a hand-out. The only difference was that in two cases the position at which the pilot had seen that single parachute was given. The position was two miles north of Hollmind.

When I entered the mess room again Saeton was already there, the teleprint beside his plate. He was making notes whilst he ate. I thrust the paper in front of him. 'Have you seen that?' I asked.

He nodded, looking up at me, his mouth full.

'It means Tubby is alive,' I cried. 'He must have come to and pulled the release.'

'I hope you're right,' was all he said.

'What else could it mean?' I demanded.

'You remember I said I'd cable a friend of mine at Lübeck? I phoned it through that morning. This morning I got his reply. I'll read it to you.' He pulled a second teleprint out of his pocket and read it out to me. '*Regret no trace of Carter or Fraser stop All aircraft ordered from dawn third to keep sharp lookout Hollmind area stop Routes staggered to cover limits of Corridor stop Visibility perfect stop Two parachutes reported near frontier belonging Westrop Field stop No wreckage, parachute or signal reported target area stop Sorry signed Manning*.' He pushed it into my hand. 'Read it yourself.'

'It doesn't prove anything,' I said. 'He may have been hurt.'

'If he were he would have made some signal – smoke or something.' He turned back to his breakfast.

'He may not have been able to. He may have been unconscious.'

'Then his parachute would have been seen.'

'Not necessarily. Hollmind airfield is surrounded

by a belt of pine woods. His parachute could easily have been invisible from the air if he'd come down in the woods.'

'If he'd landed in the woods his parachute would have been caught in the trees. It would be clearly visible.'

'Then maybe he was seen coming down and picked up by a Russian patrol or some Germans.' I felt suddenly desperate. Tubby had to be alive. My mind clung desperately to the slender hope of this report of a parachute near Hollmind.

Saeton looked up at me again then. 'What time did Tubby drop?'

'I don't know. It must have been just near eleven-thirty.'

'On the evening of the second?'

I nodded.

'Within a few hours all pilots had been ordered to keep a sharp lookout. That means that from dawn onwards there was a constant stream of aircrews overhead searching the area. Do you seriously suggest that in the intervening seven hours of darkness Tubby would have been picked up?'

'There was a moon,' I said desperately.

'All right – five hours of moonlight. If Tubby pulled his parachute release, then he would still have been there on the ground at dawn. If he were hurt, then he wouldn't have been able to do anything about his parachute and it would have been clearly visible from above. And if he wasn't injured, then he'd have been able to signal.' He hesitated. 'On the other hand, if he never regained consciousness—'

'My God!' I said. 'I believe you want him dead.'

He didn't say anything, ignoring me as I stood over him with my hands clenched. 'I've got to know what happened,' I cried. I caught hold of his shoulder. 'Can't you understand? I can't go through life thinking myself a murderer. I've got to go out there and find him.'

'Find him?' He looked at me as though I were crazy.

'Yes, find him,' I cried. 'I believe he's alive. I've got to believe that. If I didn't believe that—' I moved my hand uncertainly. Couldn't the man see how I felt about it? 'If he's dead, then I killed him. That's murder, isn't it? I'm a murderer then. He's got to be alive.' I added desperately, 'He's got to be.'

'Better get on with your breakfast.' The gentleness was back in his voice. Damn him! I didn't want kindness, I wanted something to fight. I wanted action. 'When will the plane be ready?' I demanded thickly.

'Sometime tomorrow,' he answered. 'Why?'

'That's too late,' I said. 'It's got to be tonight.'

'Impossible,' he answered. 'We'll barely have got the second motor installed by this evening. Then there's the tests, refuelling, loading the remains of the old Tudor, fixing the—'

'The remains of the old Tudor?' I stared at him. 'You mean you're going through with the plan? You'll leave Tubby out there another whole day just because—'

'Tubby's dead,' he said, getting to his feet. 'The

sooner you realise that, the better. He's dead and there's nothing you can do about it.'

'That's what you want to believe, isn't it?' I sneered. 'You want him dead because if he isn't dead, he'd give the whole game away.'

'I told you how I feel about Tubby.' His face was white and his tone dangerously quiet. 'Now shut up and get on with your breakfast.'

'If Tubby's dead,' I said, 'I'll do exactly what he would have done if he'd been alive. I'll go straight to the authorities—'

'Just what is it you want me to do, Fraser?'

'Fly over there,' I said. 'It's no good a bunch of bored aircrews peering down at those woods from a height of three thousand or more. I want to fly over the area at nought feet. And if that doesn't produce any result, then I want to land at Hollmind airfield and search those woods on foot.'

He stood looking at me for a moment. 'All right,' he said.

'When?' I asked.

'When?' He hesitated. 'It's Tuesday today. We'll have the second engine installed this evening. To-morrow I'll fly down for the C of A. Could be Friday night.'

'Friday night!' I stared at him aghast. 'But good God!' I exclaimed. 'You're not going to leave Tubby out there whilst you get a certificate of airworthiness? You can't do that. We must go tonight, as soon as we've—'

'We'll go as soon as I've got the C of A.' His tone was final.

'But—'

'Don't be a fool, Neil.' He leaned towards me across the table. 'I'm not leaving without a C of A. When I leave it's going to be for good. I'll be flying direct to Wunstorf. We'll call at Hollmind on the way. You must remember, I don't share your optimism. And now get some breakfast inside you. We've got a lot to do.'

'But I must get there tonight,' I insisted. 'You don't understand. I feel—'

'I know very well how you feel,' he said sharply. 'Anybody would feel the same if he'd caused the death of a good man like Tubby. But I'm not leaving without a C of A and that's final.'

'But the C of A might take a week,' I said. 'Often it takes longer – two weeks.'

'We'll have to chance that. Aylmer of B.E.A. has said the Civil Aviation inspectors will rush it through. All right. I'm banking on it taking two days. If it takes longer, that's just too bad. Now get some breakfast inside you. The sooner we get to work, the sooner you'll be at Hollmind.'

There was nothing I could do. I got up slowly and fetched my bacon.

'Another thing,' he said as I sat down again. 'I'm not landing at Hollmind except in moonlight. If it's a pitch black night, you'll have to jump.'

I felt my stomach go cold at the thought of another jump. 'Why not go over in daylight?'

'Because it's Russian territory.'

'You mean because those engines are more important—'

'For God's sake stop it, Neil.' His voice was suddenly violent. 'I've made a bargain with you. To land there at night will be dangerous enough. But I'm willing to do it – for the sake of your peace of mind.'

'But not for Tubby?'

He didn't answer. I knew what he was thinking. He was thinking that if I'd described the scene accurately Tubby couldn't be alive. But at least he had agreed to look for him now and I held on to that.

The urge to find him drove me to work as I'd never worked the whole time I'd been at Membury. I worked with a concentrated frenzy that narrowed my world down to bolts and petrol unions and the complicated details of electrical wiring. Yet I was conscious at the same time of Saeton's divergent interest. The clack of his typewriter as he cleared up the company's business, the phone calls instructing the men he'd picked as a crew to report to R.A.F. Transport Command for priority flights to Bückeburg for Wunstorf – all reminded me that, whatever had happened, his driving purpose was still to get his engines on to the Berlin airlift. And I hated him for his callousness.

It was past midnight when the second engine was in and everything connected up. Saeton left at dawn the next morning. The pipes were all frozen and we got water by breaking the ice on the rainwater butt. Membury was a frozen white world and the sun was hazed in mist so that it was a dull red ball as it came up over the downs. The mist swallowed the Tudor almost immediately. I turned back to the quarters, feeling shut in and wretched.

The next two days were the longest I ever remember. To keep me occupied Saeton had asked me to proceed with the cutting up of the old aircraft into smaller fragments. It occupied my hands. Nothing more. It was an automatic type of work that left my mind free to think. I couldn't leave the airfield. I couldn't go anywhere or see anybody. Saeton had been very insistent on that. If I showed my face anywhere and was recognised then he wouldn't go near Hollmind. It meant I couldn't even visit the Ellwoods. I was utterly alone and by Friday morning I was peering out of the hangar every few minutes searching the sky, listening for the drone of the returning Tudor.

It was Saturday afternoon that Saeton got in. He had got his C of A. His crew were on their way to Wunstorf. 'If it's clear we'll go over tonight,' he said. And we got straight on with the work of preparing for our final departure. We tanked up and he insisted on filling the fuselage of the plane with pieces of the old Tudor. He was still intent on going through with his plan. He kept on talking about the airworthiness tests. 'The inspectors were pretty puzzled by the engines,' he said. 'But I managed to avoid any check on petrol consumption. They know they're a new design. But they don't know their value – not yet.' The bastard could think of nothing else.

Dusk was falling as we finished loading. The interior of the hangar was still littered with debris, but

Saeton made no attempt to dispose of it. We went back to the quarters. Night had fallen and I had seen the last of Membury. When the moon rose I should be in Germany. I lay in my blankets, barely conscious of the gripping cold, my thoughts clinging almost desperately to my memory of the place.

Saeton called me at ten-thirty. He had made tea and cooked some bacon. As soon as he had finished his meal he went out to the hangar. I lingered over a cigarette, unwilling to leave the warmth of the oil stove, thinking of what lay ahead of me. At length Saeton returned. He was wearing his heavy, fleece-lined flying jacket. 'Ready?'

'Yes, I'm ready,' I said and got slowly to my feet.

Outside it was freezing hard, the night crystal clear and filled with stars. Saeton carried the oil stove with him. At the edge of the woods he paused for a moment, staring at the dark bulk of the hangar with the ghostly shape of the plane waiting for us on the apron. 'A pity,' he said gruffly. 'I've got fond of this place.' When we reached the plane he ordered me to get the engines warmed up and went on to the hangar. He was gone about five minutes. When he climbed into the cockpit he was breathing heavily as though he had been running. His clothes smelt faintly of petrol. 'Okay. Let's get going.' He slid into the pilot's seat and his hand reached for the throttle levers. But instead of taxi-ing out to the runway, he slewed the plane round so that we faced the hangar. The wicket door was still open and a dull light glowed inside. We sat there, the screws turning, the air frame juddering. 'What are we waiting for?' I asked.

'Just burning my boats behind me,' he said.

The rectangular opening of the hangar door flared red and I knew then what he had wanted the oil stove for. There was a muffled explosion and flames shot out of the gap. The whole interior of the hangar was ablaze, a roaring inferno which almost drowned the sound of our engines.

'Well, that's that,' Saeton said. He was grinning like a child who has set fire to something for fun, but his eyes as he looked at me reflected a more desperate mood. Another explosion shook the hangar and flames licked out of the shattered windows at the side. Saeton reached up to the throttle levers, the engines roared and we swung away to the runway end.

A moment later we turned our backs on the hangar and took off into the frosted night. At about a thousand feet Saeton banked slightly for one last glimpse of the field. It was a great dark circle splashed with an orange flare at the far end. As I peered forward across Saeton's body the hangar seemed to disintegrate into a flaming skeleton of steel. At that distance it looked no bigger than a Guy Fawkes bonfire.

We turned east then, setting course for Germany. I stared at Saeton, seeing the hard inflexible set of the jaw in the light of the instrument panel. There was nothing behind him now. The past to him was forgotten, actively erased by fire. There would be nothing at Membury but molten scraps of metal and the congealed lumps of the engines. As though he knew what I was thinking he said, 'Whilst you were sleeping this evening I went over this machine erasing old numbers and stamping in our own.' There was a tight-lipped smile on his face as he said this. He was warning me that there would be no proof, that I would not be believed if I tried to accuse him of flying Harcourt's plane.

The moon rose as we crossed the Dutch coast, a flattened orange in the east. The Scheldt glimmered below us and then the snaking line of water gave place to frosted earth. 'We're in Germany now,' Saeton shouted, and there was a note of triumph in his voice. In Germany! This was the future for him – the bright, brilliant future to replace the dead past. But for me . . . I felt cold and alone. There was nothing here for me but the memory of Tubby's unconscious body slumping through the floor of this very machine – and farther back, tucked away in the dark corners of my mind, the feel of branches tearing at my arm, the sight of the barbed wire and the sense of being hunted.

My brain seemed numb. I couldn't think and I flew across the British Zone of Germany in a kind of mental vacuum. Then the lights of the airlift planes were below us and we were in the corridor, flying at five thousand feet. Saeton put the nose of the machine down, swinging east to clear the traffic stream and then south-west at less than a thousand with all the ground laid bare in brilliant moonlight, a white world of unending, hedgeless fields and black, impenetrable woods.

We found Hollmind, turned north and in an instant

we were over the airfield. Saeton pressed the mouthpiece of his helmet to his lips. 'Get aft and open the fuselage door.' His voice crackled in my ears. 'You can start shovelling the bits out just as soon as you like. I'll stooge around to the north of the airfield.' I hesitated and he looked across at me. 'You want me to land down there, don't you?' he said. 'Well, this machine's heavily overloaded. And that runway hasn't been used for four years. It's probably badly broken up by frost and I'm not landing till the weight's out of the fuselage. Now get aft and kick the load out of her.'

There was no point in arguing with him. I turned and went through the door to the fuselage. The dark bulk of the fuel tanks loomed in front of me. I climbed round them and then I was squeezing my way through the litter of the old Tudor that was piled to the roof. Jagged pieces of metal caught at my flying suit. The fuselage was like an old junk shop and it rattled tinnily. I found the fuselage door, flung it back and a rush of cold air filled the plane. We were flying at about two thousand now, the countryside, sliding below us, clearly mapped in the white moonlight. The wings dipped and quivered as Saeton began to bank the plane. Above me the lights of a plane showed driving south-east towards Berlin with its load of freight; below, the snaking line of a river gleamed for an instant, a road running straight to the north, the black welt of a wood, and then the white weave of ploughed earth.

The engines throttled back and I felt the plane check as Saeton applied the air brakes. I caught hold of the nearest piece of metal, dragged it to the wind-filled gap and pushed it out. It went sailing into the void, a gleam of tin twisting and falling through the slip-stream. Soon a whole string of metal was falling away behind us like pieces of silver paper. It was like the phosphorescent gleam of the log line of a ship marking the curve of our flight as we banked.

By the time I'd pitched the last fragment out and the floor of the fuselage was clear, I was sweating hard. I leaned for a moment against the side of the fuselage, panting with the effort. The sweat on me went cold and clammy and I began to shiver. I pulled the door to and went for'ard. 'It's all out now,' I told Saeton.

He nodded. 'Good! I'm going down now. I'll take the perimeter of Hollmind airfield as my mark and fly in widening circles from that. Okay?' He thrust the nose down and the airfield rose to meet us through the windshield. The concrete runways gleamed white, a huge cross. Then we were skimming the field, the starboard wing-tip down as we banked in a right turn. He was taking it clockwise so that I had a clear, easy view of the ground through my side window. 'Keep your eyes skinned,' he shouted. 'I'll look after the navigation.'

Round and round we circled, the airfield sliding away till it was lost behind the trees. There was nothing but woods visible through my window, an unending stream of moon-white Christmas trees sliding away below me. My eyes grew dizzy with staring at them, watching their spiky tops and the dark shadows rushing by. The leading edge of the wing seemed to be cutting through them, we were so low. Here and there they thinned out, vanishing into patches of plough or the gleam of water. The pattern repeated itself like flaws in a wheel as we droned steadily on that widening circle.

At last the woods had all receded and there was nothing below us but plough. Saeton straightened the plane out then and climbed away to the north. 'Well?' he shouted.

But I'd seen nothing – not the glimmer of a light, no fire, no sign of the torn remains of parachute silk – nothing but the fir trees and the open plough. I felt numb and dead inside. Somewhere amongst those woods Tubby had fallen – somewhere deep in the dark shadows his body lay crumpled and broken. I put the mouthpiece of my helmet to my lips. 'I'll have to search those woods on foot,' I said.

'All right,' Saeton's voice crackled back. 'I'll take you down now. Hold tight. It's going to be a bumpy touchdown.'

We banked again and the airfield reappeared, showing as a flat clearing in the woods straight ahead of us. Flaps and undercarriage came down as we dropped steeply over the firs. The concrete came to meet us, cracked and covered with the dead stalks of weeds. Then our wheels touched down and the machine was jolting crazily over the uneven surface. We came to rest within a stone's throw of the woods, the nose of the machine facing west. Saeton followed me out on to the concrete. No light showed in all the huge, flat expanse of the field. Nobody came to challenge us. The place was as derelict and lonely as Membury. Saeton thrust a paper package into my hand. 'Bread and cheese,' he said. 'And here's a flask. You may need it.'

'Aren't you coming with me?' I asked.

He shook his head. 'I'm due at Wunstorf at 04.00. Besides, what's the use? We've stooged the area for nearly an hour. We've seen nothing. To search it thoroughly on foot would take days. It doesn't look much from the air, but from the ground—' He shook his head again. 'Take a look at the size of this airfield. Just to walk straight across it would take you half an hour.'

I stood there, staring at the dark line of the woods, the panic of loneliness creeping up on me. 'I won't be long,' I said. 'Surely you can wait an hour for me – two hours perhaps?' The plane was suddenly important to me, my link with people I knew, with people who spoke my own language. Without it, I'd be alone in Germany again – in the Russian Zone.

His hand touched my arm. 'You don't seem to understand, Neil,' he said gently. 'You're not part of my crew – not yet. You're the pilot of a plane that crashed just north of here. I couldn't take you on to Wunstorf even if you wanted to come. When you've finished your search, make for Berlin. It's about thirty-five miles to the south-east. You ought to be able to slip across into the British Sector there.'

I stared at him. 'You mean you're leaving me here?' I swallowed quickly, fighting off the sudden panic of fear.

'The arrangement was that I should fly you back to Germany and drop you there. As far as I'm concerned that plan still holds. All that's different is that I've landed you and so saved you a jump.'

Anger burst through my fear, anger at the thought of him not caring a damn about Tubby, thinking only of his plans to fly his engines on the airlift. 'You're not leaving me here, Saeton,' I cried. 'But I must know whether he's alive or dead.'

'We know that already,' he said quietly.

'He's not dead,' I cried. 'He's only dead in your mind – because you want him dead. He's not dead, really. He can't be.'

'Have it your own way.' He shrugged his shoulders and turned away towards the plane.

I caught him by the shoulder and jerked him round. 'All right, he's dead,' I shouted. 'If that's the way you want it. He's dead, and you've killed him. The one friend you ever had! Well, you've killed your one friend – killed him, just as you'd kill anyone who stood between you and what you want.'

He looked me over, measuring my mood, and then his eyes were cold and hard. 'I don't think you've quite grasped the situation,' he said slowly. 'I didn't kill Tubby. You killed him.'

'Me?' I laughed. 'I suppose it wasn't your idea that I should pinch Harcourt's Tudor? I suppose that's your own machine standing there? You blackmailed me into doing what you wanted. My God! I'll see the world knows the truth. I don't care about myself any more. What happened to Tubby has brought me to my senses.

You're mad – that's what you are. Mad. You've lost your reason, all sense of proportion. You don't care what you do so long as your dreams come true. You'll sacrifice everything, anyone. Well, I'll see you don't get away with it. I'll tell them the truth when I get back. If you'd got a gun you'd shoot me now, wouldn't you? Or are you only willing to murder by proxy? Well, you haven't got a gun and I'll get back to Berlin somehow. I'll tell them the truth then. I'll—'

I paused for breath and he said, 'Telling the truth won't help Tubby now – and it won't help you either. Try to get the thing clear in your mind, Fraser. Tubby's dead. And since you killed him it's up to you to see that his death is to some purpose.'

'I didn't kill him,' I shouted. 'You killed him.'

He laughed. 'Do you think anybody will believe you?'

'They will when they know the facts. When the police have searched Membury, when they have examined that plane and they've interrogated—'

'You've nothing to support your story,' he said quietly. 'The remains of Harcourt's plane are strewn over the countryside just north of here. Field and Westrop will say that you ordered them to bale out, that the engines had packed up. You yourself will be reporting back from the area of the crash. As for Membury, there's nothing left of the hangar now except a blackened ruin.'

I felt suddenly exhausted. 'So you knew what I'd do. You knew what I was going to do back there at

Membury. You fooled me into pushing out that load of scrap. By God—'

'Don't start using your fists,' he cut in sharply. 'I may be older than you, but I'm heavier – and tougher.' His feet were straddled and his head was thrust forward, his hands down at his sides ready for me.

I put my hands slowly to my head. 'Oh, God!' I felt so weak, so impotent.

'Get some sense into your head before I see you again,' he said. 'You can still be in this thing with me – as my partner. It all depends on your attitude when you reach Berlin.'

For answer I turned away and walked slowly towards the woods.

Once I glanced back. Saeton was still standing there, watching me. Then, as I entered the darkness of the trees, I heard the engines roar. Through needle-covered branches I watched the machine turn and taxi to the runway end. And then it went roaring across the airfield, climbing, a single white light, like a faded comet, dwindling into the moonlit night, merging into the stars. Then there was silence and the still shadows of the woods closed round me. I was alone – in the Russian Zone of Germany.

CHAPTER SEVEN

For a long time after the plane had disappeared I stood there on the fringe of the woods gazing at the empty expanse of the airfield. A small wind whispered in the upper branches of the fir trees and every few minutes there was the distant drone of a plane – airlift pilots flying down the corridor to Berlin. Those were the only sounds. The cold seeped through my flying suit, stiffening my limbs, and at length I turned and walked into the woods. A few steps and I had lost the airfield. The trees closed round me and I was in a world apart. It was very still there in the woods, even the sound of my footsteps was muffled by the carpet of pine needles. I could still hear the planes, but I couldn't see them. The branches of the trees cut me off from the sky and only a ghostly radiance told me that the moon still filled the world with its white light.

I found a path and followed it to the earth mound of an old dispersal point. The frost-cracked concrete was a white blaze in the moonlight, cutting through the dark ranks of the trees to the open plain of the airfield. I stopped there to consider what I should do. My mind went back to the scene in the plane. We had been flying almost due south when Tubby's body slid through the open doorway. I had gone straight back to the cockpit and then I had looked through my side window and seen Hollmind airfield below me. That meant that Tubby had gone out north and slightly west of the field.

I followed the line of the concrete till I came out on to the edge of the airfield and turned left, walking in the shadow of the woods till I reached the north-west extremity of the field. Buildings began there, shapeless heaps of broken rubble. I skirted these and entered the woods again, following a path that ran in the direction I wanted to go.

It was four o'clock when I began my search. I remember thinking that Saeton would be at Wunstorf. The plane would be parked on the loading apron in the row of Tudors where it had stood before. Only the crew would be different – and the numbers and the engines. He'd be reporting to Ops and checking in at the mess, finding a bed in the echoing concrete corridors of that labyrinth that housed the human force of the airlift. He'd be one of them now, getting up when the world was asleep, going to bed when others were shaving. In a few hours perhaps it would be his plane I'd hear droning over on its way to Berlin. He'd be up there, with success ahead of him, whilst I was down in these grim, dark woods, searching for the body of the man who'd given two years to help him build those engines. Damn it, it wasn't even his plane. It was my plane. Nothing was really his. Even the design of the engines he'd pinched from Else's father.

Blind anger drove everything else out of my head for a moment. Then I steadied myself, forcing my mind to concentrate on the thing I'd set myself to do. I decided to walk east and west, backwards and forwards on a two mile front working gradually northwards. The impossibility of complete coverage was apparent from the start. I had a small pocket compass, that was all. The trees, fortunately, were well spaced out, but they were all alike. There was nothing to guide me. It was obvious that at some points I should be covering the same ground twice, maybe three times, whilst at other times I should be leaving large gaps uncovered. But it was the only course open to me and with a feeling of hopelessness I turned west on my first beat. It was past five when I came to the western fringe of the woods and looked across the dreary flatness of the Mecklenburg plain with the moon dipping over it towards the horizon. And in that time I had stopped a hundred times to investigate a deeper shadow, a dead branch that looked like an arm or a patch of white where a beam of direct moonlight shone on the bark of a pine trunk.

Dawn found me at the end of the eastward beat. The daylight penetrated slowly into the woods, a slight lightening of the deeper shadows, a paling of the moon's whiteness. I didn't really see it until I was in a clearing that showed me the bomb-battered ruins of the hangars that lay along the north fringe of Hollmind airfield. It was a grey dawn, still, but pitilessly cold, with great cloud banks rolling in from the north and the feel of snow in the air.

I ate two sandwiches and took a nip from the flask Saeton had given me. There was rum in that flask and I could feel the warmth of it trickling into my stomach. But as I turned westward again on my third beat I was already tired. There was no breath of wind. The woods seemed frozen into silence. The only sound was the drone of aircraft. That sound had been with me all the time. It was monotonous, unending. But God, how glad I was of it! That sound was my one link with the world, with reality. And as the daylight increased, I began to look for the planes in the gaps in the trees. At last I saw one. It was flying across my line of march at about three thousand feet, the thick belly unmistakable – a York. That meant that it had come from Wunstorf. The men in that plane would have breakfasted before dawn with the electric lights on and the mess warm with the smell of hot radiators and food. They had hot food in their bellies and hot coffee.

I stood there in the clearing, watching the plane till it was out of sight, the smell of coffee stronger than the smell of the pines, remembering a shop I'd known as a kid that had a big grinder always working in the window, spilling its fragrance into the street. As the plane disappeared over the tops of the trees another came into sight, exactly the same, flying the same route, flying the same height. I watched another and another. All Yorks. All exactly the same. It was as though they were on an endless belt going behind the trees, like those little white clay airgun targets you find at fairs.

The smell of coffee lingered with me as I went on into the sombre gloom of the woods.

Shortly after midday it began to snow, the flakes drifting gently down out of the leaden sky, dark, widely-spaced specks until they landed and were transformed to little splashes of virgin white. It was less cold after the snow began to fall. But by then I was feeling sleepy, exhausted and hungry. There were two sandwiches left and half a flask of rum. I saved them for the night and stumbled on.

On my eighth beat I found a crumpled piece of metal. It was lodged in the branches of a tree – a piece of the tailplane of the Tudor Saeton had pranged at Membury. It didn't seem possible that it was less than twelve hours since I'd slung that fragment out of the open door of the fuselage with these woods flashing by below me.

An hour later I nearly walked into a Russian patrol. I was almost on top of them before I heard the low murmur of their voices. They were in a group, short men with round, sallow faces, black boots and brown tunics buttoned to the neck. The soldiers leaned on their rifles while two officers bent over a piece of metal that gleamed dully.

I wondered what they'd make of these scraps of metal scattered through the woods as I slipped past them and continued eastward. The snow thickened and the sky darkened. Patches of white showed in the gaps between the trees and these I had to avoid for fear of leaving footprints. In the gathering darkness and my growing weakness every shadow became a Russian soldier. My progress became wretchedly slow. Finally it was too dark to go on and I dug a hole for myself close under the low-sweeping branches of a large fir and lay down in it, covering myself with pine needles.

I finished the two sandwiches and drank the rest of the rum. But within an hour the warmth of the rum had completely evaporated; the cold of the night moved in on me, gripping my limbs like a steel sheet. Sleep was impossible. I lay and shivered, my mind a blank, my body in a coma of misery. The cold covered everything. The snow became hard and powdery, the trees cracked.

By midnight I was so frozen that I got to my feet and stamped and swung my arms. My breath hung like smoke in front of my face. The snow clouds had passed. Stars shone frosty-clear above my head and the moon had risen showing me a beautiful, fairy-white world of Christmas trees.

I started moving westward, walking blindly, not really caring where I went so long as I got some warmth into my limbs. And that was how I found Tubby's flying helmet. I just stumbled on it lying on a patch of snow. I suppose what had happened was that it had been caught on one of the branches of a tree and when the snow weighed the branch down it had slipped to the ground.

I don't remember feeling any excitement. I think I was too numbed with cold to have any feelings at all. And I had no sense of surprise either. I had been so determined to find him that it hadn't occurred to me that I should fail. I have always believed that if you go out for a thing hard enough, you get it in the end, and I didn't bother to consider the virtual impossibility of the task I had set myself. But though I had found his helmet I could find no trace of Tubby himself. There was just the helmet. Nothing else.

After a thorough search of the area I returned to the spot where the helmet had lain. The trees were very thick and in the darkness of the shadows it was impossible to see whether there was anything lodged in the branches. In the end I climbed to the top of the tree that overhung the spot. With my head thrust above the snow-laden branches I looked over a plain of white spikes that glistened in the moonlight. By shaking the tree I got rid of most of the snow. The needle foliage looked very green, but there was no sign of anything that would prove that this was the spot where Tubby had fallen.

I was half-way down the tree, back in the world of half-light and shadows, when my hand slid from the gritty surface of the bark to something softer. My fingers closed on it, feeling the smoothness of light material. I didn't need to look at it to know that this was nylon. I pulled at it and my hand came away with a torn strip of parachute silk about the length of a scarf.

I was excited then. That strip of nylon silk showed that Tubby had pulled his parachute release before he hit the ground and I went tumbling down the tree, oblivious of the snow that fell on my neck and trickled in icy streams down my back, oblivious of everything but that single fact – Tubby wasn't dead. He might have hurt himself, but he'd regained consciousness, he'd pulled the release and his parachute had opened. And I realised then how the fear of finding him, a mangled, blood-stained heap of broken bones and torn flesh, had haunted me. In a frenzy I searched the area again, trampling the snow in my haste to find out what had happened to him after he'd crashed through the trees.

But the snow hid all trace.

At length, utterly exhausted, I sat down on a dry patch of ground with my back against the bole of a tree and lit one of my last cigarettes. I had searched the area in a circle extending about fifty yards from the spot where I had come upon the helmet. I had found no trace of him. Clearly one of two things had happened – either he had been all right and had left the area on foot or else he had been injured and some woodman had found him and got him away. Or perhaps it had been the Russians who'd found him. Maybe the patrol I'd seen in the afternoon had come upon him and carted him off to Hollmind. The possibility that he might be dead was nagging at me again. I had to be sure that he was alive.

I got to my feet again. I would have to widen my search, radiate out until I found some trace. I began walking again, circling out from the spot where the helmet had lain. The snow helped me here, for all I had to do was walk outside the footprints I'd made on my previous circuit. The moon was high overhead now and it was much lighter under the trees. At four o'clock in the morning, after walking for over two hours in a widening circle, I stumbled upon a broad track running through the woods. One side of the track was sheltered by the trees and was clear of snow and there I found the marks of a farm cart. I traced it back to a spot where it had stood for some time. The tracks did not continue. They finished there and I knew then that Tubby was either dead or injured. Cold and wretched, I turned westward and followed the track till it left the shelter of the woods and ran out into the bitter flatness of ploughed land that was all white under the moon.

The wheel tracks were lost under the snow now, but the track was still visible – two deep ruts swinging south-west towards a Christmas card huddle of steep-roofed farm buildings. As I approached I saw the yellow glow of a light. It came from the half-open door of a barn. Inside the barn a man was filling sacks with potatoes from a deep, square hole in the floor. Wooden boards heavy with earth were stacked against the heaped-up straw and earth had been piled near the door.

The man must have sensed my presence, for he suddenly paused in his work and looked straight at me where I stood in the gaping doorway. He was short and wiry with a broad forehead and his eyes looked startled and afraid. '*Wer sind Sie? Was wollen Sie?*'

'I am an English flier,' I replied in German. 'I am looking for a friend of mine who may be injured.'

He put down his fork and came towards me, his dark, frightened eyes peering first at my face, then at my clothes. 'Come in then and close the door please. The wind blow it open I think.' He fixed the latch with trembling fingers. 'I was afraid it was the Russians.' He laughed nervously. 'They want everything – all my crops. For the East, you know.' His speech was jerky. 'To feed our pigs we must keep something.' He held the lantern close to me, still examining me uncertainly. Apparently he was finally satisfied, for he lowered the lantern and said, 'You look tired. You walk far, yes.'

'What has happened to my friend?' I asked 'He was brought here, wasn't he? Is he – is he dead?' I waited, dreading his answer.

He shook his head slowly. '*Nein*. He is not dead. But he injure himself very much when he land in the trees. Now you lie down in the straw there. I must finish my work before it is light. Then I get you something to eat, eh?'

But I wasn't listening. 'Thank God!' I breathed it aloud. Tubby was alive. He was alive and I'd found him. I hadn't killed him after all. I felt suddenly light-headed. I wanted to laugh. But once I started to laugh I felt I should never stop. I held my breath, fighting to control myself. Then I stumbled into the straw, sinking into it, relaxing, knowing I had done everything I could and that God had been with me. I had found Tubby and he wasn't dead. 'When did you find him?' I asked.

'Four days ago,' the man answered. He had returned to his work.

'And you have not handed him over to the Russians?'

He paused with a forkful of potatoes. 'No, we do

not hand him to the Russians. You have to thank my wife for that. Our daughter is in Berlin. She live in the French Sector with her husband who work on the railways there. But for the air bridge, she would be like us – she would be under the Russians.'

I mumbled my thanks. My head kept nodding. It was very warm and comfortable there in the straw. 'Is he badly hurt?'

'*Ja*. He is not so good. Several ribs are broken and his arm and he has concussion. But he is conscious. You can speak with him.'

'He should have a doctor.' My voice sounded very far away. I couldn't keep my eyes open.

'You do not have to worry. Our doctor is coming here to see him every day. He is a good doctor and he do not love the Russians because they take him to the East for a year to work with our prisoners. Once he meet my son. My son, Hans, is a prisoner of the Russians since 1945. Before that he is in North Africa and Italy and then on the Eastern front. I do not see him now for almost six years. But soon I hope he will come home. We have had two letters . . .'

His voice droned pleasantly and my eyelids closed. I dreamt I was back in Stalag Luft I, but the guards all wore tight-necked brown tunics and black knee-length boots, and there was always snow and no hope of release or escape – only the hope of death. They kept on interrogating me, trying to get me to admit that I'd killed Tubby – there were intensely bright lights and they kept on shaking me . . . I woke to find the farmer bending over me, shaking my shoulder. 'Wake up, Herr

Fraser.' He pronounced the 's' sharply and not as a 'z'. 'It is seven o'clock. We will have some food now and then you can talk with your friend.'

'You know my name?' I murmured sleepily. And then I felt in my breast pocket. My papers were still there. He must have put them back after examining them. I clambered stiffly to my feet. I was cold and very tired.

'I think perhaps we put your flying clothes under the straw, eh? I do not wish my men to know I have a British flier here. By talking, one of them might be given my farm. That is something they learn from the Nazis.' He said the word 'Nazis' unemotionally as one might talk of an avalanche or some other act of God.

When I had hidden my flying suit he took me across the farmyard to the house. It was a cold, bleak dawn, heavy with leaden cloud that promised more snow. Overhead I heard the drone of the planes flying in to Berlin, but I couldn't see them, for the ceiling was not much more than a thousand.

My memory of the Kleffmanns' house is vague; a memory of warmth and the smell of bacon, of a big kitchen with a great, clumsy, glowing stove and a bright-eyed, friendly little woman with wisps of greying hair and the slow, sure movements of one who lives close to the earth and whose routine never changes. I also remember the little bedroom high up under the roof where Tubby lay, his fat cheeks strangely hollow, his face flushed with fever and his eyes unnaturally bright. The ugly, patterned wallpaper with butterflies flying up vertical strips was littered with photographs of Hans Kleffmann who would some day come back from Russia and meet his mother and father again for the first time in six years. There were photographs of him as a baby, as a boy at the school in Hollmind, in the uniform of the Nazi Youth Organisation and finally in the uniform of the Wehrmacht – against the background of the Hradcany Palace in Prague, in a Polish village, with the Eiffel Tower behind him, in the desert leaning on a tank, in Rome with St. Peter's Dome over his left shoulder. And there were a few less formal snaps – Hans in bathing shorts on the Italian Riviera, Hans with a dark-haired girl in Naples, Hans ski-ing in the Dolomites. Hans filled that room with the nostalgia of a boy's life leading inevitably, irrevocably to the Russian prison camp. They showed me a letter. It was four lines long – *I am well and the Russians treat me very kindly. The food is good and I am happy. Love, Hans.*

Tubby, lying in that small, neatly austere bed, was an intruder.

He was asleep when I went in. The Kleffmanns left me sitting by his bed whilst they got on with the business of the farm. Tubby's breath came jerkily and painfully but he slept on and I had a long time in which to become familiar with Hans. It's almost as though I had met him, I got to know him so well from those faded photographs – arrogant and fanatical in victory, hard-faced and bitter in defeat. There in that room I was face to face with the Germany of the future, the Germany that was being hammered out on the vulcan forge of British, American and Soviet policy. I found my eyes turning back repeatedly to the grim, relentless face in the photograph taken at Lwow in the autumn of 1944 and comparing it with the smiling carefree kid in knickerbockers taken outside the Hollmind school.

Then Tubby opened his eyes and stared at me. At first I thought he wasn't going to recognise me. We stared at each other for a moment and then he smiled. He smiled at me with his eyes, his lips a tight line constricted by pain. 'Neil! How did you get here?'

I told him, and when I'd finished he said, 'You came back. That was kind of you.' He had difficulty in speaking and his voice was very weak.

'Are they looking after you all right?' I asked awkwardly.

He nodded slowly. 'The old woman is very kind. She treats me as though I were her son. And the doctor does his best.'

'You ought to be in hospital,' I said.

He nodded again. 'But it's better than being in the hands of the Russians.'

'Thank God you're alive anyway,' I said. 'I thought—' I hesitated and then said, 'I was afraid I'd killed you. You were unconscious when you went out through the door. I didn't mean it, Tubby. Please believe that.'

'Forget it,' he said. 'I understand. It was good of you to come back.' He winced as he took a breath. 'Did you take the plane back to Saeton?'

'Yes,' I said. 'It's got our engines in now and Saeton's at Wunstorf. They ordered him over immediately to replace Harcourt's Tudor.'

His mouth opened to the beginning of a laugh and then he jerked rigid at the pain it caused him.

'You ought to be in hospital,' I said again. 'Listen,' I added. 'Do you think you could stand another journey in that cart, up to Hollmind airfield?'

I saw him clench his teeth at the memory.

'Could you stand it if you knew at the end there would be a hospital and everything in the way of treatment you need?'

The sweat shone on his forehead. 'Yes,' he breathed, so quietly that I could hardly hear him. 'Yes, I'd face it again if I knew that. Maybe the doc here would fix me up with a shot of morphia. But they've so little in the way of drugs. They've been very kind, but they're Germans, and they haven't the facilities for . . .' His voice trailed away.

I was afraid he was going to fade into unconsciousness and I said quickly, 'I'm going now, Tubby. Tonight I'll start out for Berlin. I'll make it just as quickly as I can. Then, within a few hours, I'll be back with a plane and we'll evacuate you from Hollmind. Okay?'

He nodded.

'Goodbye then for the moment. I'll get through somehow and then we'll get you to a hospital. Hold on to that. You'll be all right.'

The corners of his lips twitched in a tight smile. 'Good luck!' he whispered. And then as I rose from the bed, his hand came out from beneath the sheets and closed on mine. 'Neil!' I had to bend down to hear him. 'I want you to know – I won't say anything. I'll leave things as I find them. The plane crashed. Engine failure – ignition.' His voice died away and his eyes closed.

Bending close to him I could hear the sob of his breathing. I reached under his pillow for his handkerchief to wipe the sweat from his forehead. The handkerchief was dark with blood. I knew then that his lung was punctured. I wiped his forehead with my own handkerchief and then went quietly out of Hans's little bedroom and down the dark stairs to the kitchen.

They gave me a bed and I slept until it was dark. Then, after a huge meal by the warmth of the kitchen stove, I said goodbye to the Kleffmanns. 'In a night or two,' I told them, 'I will be back with a plane and we'll get him away.'

'*Gut! Gut!*' The farmer nodded. 'It is better so. He is very bad, I think. Also it is dangerous for us having him here in the farm.'

Frau Kleffmann came towards me. She had a bulky package in her hand. 'Here is food for your journey, Herr Fraser – some chicken and some bread and butter and apples.' She hesitated. 'If anything happens, do not worry about your friend. He is safe here. We will look after him. There has been war between us, but my Hans is in Russia. I will care for your friend as I would have others care for Hans if he is sick. *Auf wiedersehen!*' Her gnarled hand touched my arm and her eyes filled with tears. She turned quickly to the stove.

The farmer accompanied me to the door. 'I try to arrange for you to ride in a lorry who go once a week to Berlin with potatoes. But' – he spread his hands hopelessly – 'the driver is sick. He do not go tonight. If you go three miles beyond Hollmind there is a café there for motor drivers. I think you will perhaps get a ride there.' He gave me instructions how to by-pass Hollmind and then shook my hands. '*Viel Glück*, Herr Fraser. Come soon, please, for your friend. I fear he is very sick.'

More snow had fallen during the day, but now the clouds had been swept away by a bitter east wind and the night was cold and clear. The moon had not yet risen, but the stars were so brilliant that I had no difficulty in seeing my way as soon as my eyes became accustomed to the darkness. High above me the airlift planes droned at regular three-minute intervals – I could see their navigation lights every now and then, green and red dots moving steadily through the litter of stars and the drift of the Milky Way. The white pinpoint of their tail-lights pointed the way to Berlin for me. I had only to follow them through the night sky and I should arrive at Gatow. For them Gatow was twenty minutes flying time. But for me. . . .

I turned south on the hard straight road that led to the town of Hollmind, wondering how long the journey would take me. The snow was deep and crisp under my feet. Kleffmann had given me an old field-grey Wehrmacht greatcoat and a Wehrmacht forage cap; Hans's cast-off clothing. For the first time since I'd landed in Germany I felt warm and well-fed.

Nothing stirred on the road. The snow seemed to have driven all transport off it. My footsteps were muffled and I walked in a deep silence. The only sound was the drone of the planes overhead and the hum of the wind in the telegraph wires. I reached the fork where the road branched off that I was to take in order to by-pass Hollmind. There was a signboard there – Berlin 54 km.

Fifty-four kilometres isn't far; not much more than thirty miles. A day's march. But though I had had a good rest, I was still tired and very stiff. I was wearing shoes and my feet were blister-sore. And there was the cold. For a time the warmth of exercise kept it out, but, as I tired, the sweat broke out on my body and chilled into a clammy, ice-cold film, and then the wind cut through my clothing and into my flesh, seeming to blow straight on to my spine. God, it was cold! For miles, it seemed, I walked along by-roads through unmarked snow and there was no traffic. I must have missed the turning back on to the Berlin road, for it was almost midnight when I finally found it again and I saw no transport café – only dark woods and the illimitable miles of white agricultural land, flat and windswept.

Several times I tried to thumb a lift. But each time the heavy, long-nosed German trucks ignored me, thundering by in a shower of snow that spattered icily on my face. However the fourth truck I waved to stopped and a voice called out, '*Wohin, Freund?*'

'Berlin,' I shouted.

There was a pause and then a Red Army soldier clambered down from the cabin. He was sleepy and he'd left his rifle in the truck. That was the only thing that saved me. He asked me in vile German for my papers. Fortunately the edge of the road was wooded. I dived into the dark shelter of the pines, ignoring the branches that lashed at my face, running until I was exhausted.

Dawn found me trudging through powdery snow along a narrow side road flanked with trees, following blindly the drone of the airlift planes. It was a blood-red dawn, wild and violent and full of cold. The sun was a misty red disc above the pines. I staggered into the shelter of the woods, ate Frau Kleffmann's chicken and bread, wrapped myself in pine needles and slept.

All that day I slept, if you can call it sleep. It was more like a bone-chilled coma. I suppose I was suffering from mental as well as physical exhaustion. At all events I found the present and the past inextricably mixed in my mind, so that the urge to reach Berlin became confused with the urge to get out of Germany and I was back in those cold, wretched, starved weeks of escape.

Night came at last, cold and black. There were no stars. I stumbled to the road and headed south-east, the drone of the planes my only guide. I passed through a small town, not bothering to note its name, joined a broader road where the snow had been churned up by traffic, and the first truck that came along stopped beside me. In the headlights I saw that the country bordering the road was flat. If there had been woods I should almost certainly have dived into them. But it was bare, open plain. '*Wo wollen Sie hin, mein Lieber?*' the driver called.

'Berlin,' I heard myself answer in a cracked, trembling voice. Any moment I expected the brown, tunic-clad figure of a Red Army man to jump out and face me. But all that happened was that the driver called, '*Kommen Sie rauf, Kamerad. Ich fahre auch nach Berlin.*'

It was almost too good to be true. I hauled myself up into the cabin. The driver was alone. There was no mate with him. The gears ground and the old vehicle lurched forward, wheels spinning in the snow. The cabin was hot and stuffy and smelt comfortingly of exhaust fumes. '*Was wollen Sie in Berlin?*' the driver asked.

'Work,' I answered him gruffly in German.

'Out of Russia into the Western Sectors, eh?' He grinned at me. He was a small, hard-bitten little man with ferrety eyes. 'Well, I don't blame you. If I thought there was a trucking job for me in the Western Sectors I'd be across the border in no time. But I have a wife and family up in Lübeck. Every night I come down this same road. Sometimes I wish I was up there flying the air bridge. I was in the *Luftwaffe*, you know. Radio operator. Had a little radio business before the war. But now, of course, it is finished. There are so few radio sets. It is better to drive a truck. But those bastards up there get to Berlin a lot quicker than I do. My wife always tells me . . .'

He went on and on about himself and the drone of his voice merged with the engine and the eternal distant hum of aircraft throbbing through the clouds. My head nodded, sleepy with the sudden, unaccustomed warmth of the cabin. His voice lost itself in the engine. I slept fitfully, conscious of the lights of a town, of a signboard caught in the headlights that said Berlin 27 km, of the unending dirty yellow of hard-packed snow slipping away beneath us.

And then finally he was shaking me. '*Aufwachen! Aufwachen! Berlin!*'

I opened my eyes blearily and surveyed unlit, slush-filled streets flanked by the empty, blasted shells of buildings which had not been touched since we'd smashed them to rubble five years ago. So this was Berlin! 'Where are you making for?' I asked him.

'Potsdam.' He peered at me out of the corners of his eyes. 'That's in the Russian Zone. Don't imagine you'll be wanting to go there.' He laughed mirthlessly, his breath whistling through broken front teeth.

'Where are we?' I asked.

'Oranienburg.' He was still looking at me out of the corners of his eyes. 'You are a Pole, no? You are not German. Not with that accent.'

I didn't say anything and he shrugged his shoulders. '*Na was, schadet es schon?*' He eased his foot on the accelerator pedal. 'Well, where do you wish to go, eh? In a few moments I turn right. I have to keep inside the Russian Zone. But if you follow this road it will lead you to Frohnau. Frohnau is in the French Sector.'

Frohnau! Frohnau beacon! Frohnau meant Berlin to every airlift pilot. But the warmth of the truck held me tight in my seat. Frohnau was many miles from Gatow. I should have to walk right across Berlin, more than twenty kilometres. 'Where do you go when you turn right?' I asked.

'Velten, Schönewald Airfield, Falkensee, Staaken

Airfield, past Gatow and then into Potsdam. Choose which you like. It's all the same to me.'

'You're going near Gatow?' I asked him.

His eyes narrowed. 'What do you want Gatow for, eh?' His voice was harsher. He braked violently and the lorry skidded as he swung right off the main Oranienburg-Berlin road. 'Why Gatow?' he repeated. And when I didn't say anything, he added slowly, 'Gatow is in the British Sector. It's owned by *die verdammten Tommies*. Night after night they come. *Die verfluchten Kerle!* I have send my family to my parents in Hamburg. Night after night the English come. They flatten Hamburg and the *Schweinehunde* kill both the kids – the boy was nine and the girl five. They were crushed when the building they shelter in collapses.' He stopped talking and stared at me. 'Why do you want Gatow, eh?'

'I have a job to go to in the British Sector,' I answered.

'What sort of a job?'

I thought desperately. Remembering the crowded Nissen huts at the edge of the off-loading apron at Gatow, I said, 'Labour corps. I have a friend who is a checker at Gatow, unloading the airlift planes.'

His lips tightened. 'You say airlift, when we always say air bridge. Why do you say airlift?' I shrugged my shoulders. 'Only *die verdammten* English and Americans call it airlift.' For a long time there was a tense silence in the cabin. We were entering Falkensee now. Staaken aerodrome lay ahead, and then Gatow. 'Please, your papers. I wish to see your papers.'

I hesitated. 'I have no papers,' I said. I felt empty and cold inside.

'So! No papers, eh?' He peered through the wind shield, searching the road ahead with his eyes. There were few lights. Falkensee was asleep. Then, far ahead in the gleam of the headlights, I saw two figures in the grey of the German police. The driver's foot checked on the accelerator and his eyes swung nervously to me. I knew what he was going to do then. I could see him working it out in his mind. There was only one thing for me to do. I felt with my hand for the handle of the door and pushed. It swung back violently and a stream of bitter air struck my face. I heard the door clang against the tin of the cabin, saw the rutted, slushy snow spraying up from the wheels, heard the driver shout as he leaned across to grip my arm – and I jumped.

I hit the snow with my feet and was flung down, striking the side of the lorry with my head. A sudden blackness enveloped me as the snow closed over my face. I could not have been out for more than a few seconds, for the lorry was still screeching to a halt, its horn blaring excitedly, as I lifted my head from the cold, gritty filth of the snow. I pressed myself upwards with my hands, feeling suddenly sick at the sight of my blood scarlet against the yellow, gravel-covered surface of the snow. Then I was on my feet and running for the shelter of a side-street, shouts echoing after me.

As I turned out of the main street, I looked over my shoulder and saw that the two German policemen were level with the stationary truck now and running towards me. Whistles shrilled. The side-street was narrow and flanked with the rubble ruins of shattered buildings. I scrambled over a pile of bricks and mortar and half staggered, half fell into a cleared space that had been the cellars of houses in the next street. An open doorway gaped black and I slid into the welcoming darkness and leaned panting against the wall almost oblivious in my fear of the nauseating smell of human excreta.

More whistles shrilled and voices shouted in the darkness outside. Boots climbed the mound of rubble up which I had scrambled. Mortar dust streamed down in a choking cloud in the open doorway. '*Hier, Kurt. Hierlang ist er gelaufen.*' The voice was heavy and menacing. The man was standing right above my hideout. There was a clatter of dislodged bricks higher up the crumbling rubble and a voice answered faintly, '*Nein. Komm hierlang. Hier kann er zur Friedrichstrasse durchkommen.*' The chase went thudding and slithering over my head and gradually faded into the distance.

All the time I had been standing there rigid. Now my muscles relaxed. I wiped the sweat from my forehead. My hand was gritty and I winced with the pain of the grit on raw flesh. It was the old cut in my forehead that had opened up. My hand came away, wet and sticky with my own blood. The moon was shining opaquely through low cloud and the faint, ghostly light of the doorless gap showed my hand all red and dripping. The blood was trickling down my face, getting into my eyes and into the corner of my mouth the way it had done that first time I'd come to Membury. Only there was grit in my mouth now, sharp and hard, setting my teeth on edge as I clenched them.

I wiped my hands on the inside of my clothes and then tied my handkerchief over the cut. For a long time I just stood there, trying to stop the trembling of my limbs. It was very cold. It seemed as though my body had no warmth and the wind cut like a knife through the gaping doorway – nervous reaction and the shock of my fall from the moving lorry! I wished to God I had some liquor with me, something to warm the frozen guts of my belly.

I moved at last and went out of the nauseous cell. I was facing a cleared strip where demolition gangs had been working. There was a railway and a line of loaded tip trucks. The snow was a thin layer of powder that had deepened into windy little drifts in the corners of still-standing masonry. Behind rose a hill of brick and rubble over which the gaunt finger of a building pointed a broken chimney at the pale, luminous clouds. There was no sound except the distant rumble of the airlift rolling into Gatow. The pursuit had moved on and lost me.

I stood for a moment, getting my bearings. This was Falkensee, a western suburb of Berlin. The sound of the planes landing and taking off from Gatow drew me as something familiar, friendly and homelike. I could almost smell the coffee and cakes in the Malcolm Club. But if I went direct to Gatow I should all the time be in the Russian Zone. To the east lay the British Sector and I knew it couldn't be far away. I faced into the wind and began to walk.

My left leg was very stiff and painful when I moved. I had grazed my knee-cap when I fell and had strained a muscle somewhere in the groin. But I didn't care about that. My one thought was to get out of the Russian Zone and into the British Sector. The sight of another human being sent me scuttling into the doorway or into the shadows of the broken buildings that flanked the streets. And yet, not more than two or three miles away in the same sort of streets I should be able to stop the first person I met and demand his help.

I twisted and turned through narrow, broken streets, always keeping the sound of Gatow over my right shoulder. At length I came out on to a broad highway that led almost due east. It was Falkenhagener Chaussee and it ran straight like a ruled line towards Spandau – and Spandau I knew was in the British Sector.

It was three o'clock in the morning and the Falkenhagener Chaussee seemed dead. Nothing stirred. The snow-powdered thoroughfare was deserted. The crumbling masses of the buildings were white mounds in the darkness marked occasionally by a still-standing wall, tottering skyward like some two-thousand-year-old tomb seen along the Appian Way. Somewhere in Berlin a train whistled like an owl in a forest of dead oaks. There were no lights, no people – no suggestion even that anything lived here. It was all devastation and slow, timeless ruin.

For an hour or more I limped along that arrow-straight road without seeing a living soul, with only the constant drone of Gatow to remind me I was still in a living world and to give me hope. Then at last, when I was tottering with weakness, I saw the distant gleam of lights shining on a road barrier. I was nearing the limits of the Russian Zone. That knowledge gave me fresh strength. I walked to within five hundred yards of the barrier and then turned down a side-street.

At a crossing a small truck slipped quietly eastward without lights. I followed it on to a quiet, rubble-packed track that ran close beside the railway. A goods train clanked noisily, a rattle of buffers that seemed to split the night it was so loud in the utter stillness.

For half an hour I walked eastward, searching the track ahead, trembling and scuttling into the shadows at every sign of movement. But always it was nothing but my eyes playing me tricks. And at the end of half an hour I knew I must have passed over into the British Sector. A blockade-running German lorry had shown me the way through the road checks.

I followed the railway right into Spandau and there a German railway worker going on duty at five in the morning directed me to a British Army M.T. Section. I must have looked a pretty sight, for all the time he was talking to me the German kept looking nervously about him and when he had given the directions I wanted he was almost running in his hurry to get away from me.

I found the place without difficulty. It was an R.A.O.C. Depot and a big board directed me into the sidings of what had once been a huge factory. I was trembling with fatigue and feeling sick with relief when I faced the German orderly who seemed to be the only person awake in the depot. At first he refused to do anything about me. His eyes were coldly contemptuous. I began to curse him in English, all the filthy words I could think of spewed off my tongue as I consigned the whole German race to perdition with tears of frustration hot on my eyeballs. Still he didn't move, and then I saw hanging on a peg a web belt complete with holster and revolver. I dived towards it, pulled the revolver out and thumbed forward the safety catch with trembling fingers. 'Now, get the duty officer,' I shouted. 'Quick! Or I shoot.'

The man hesitated and then hurried out, returning a few minutes later with a tall, lanky youth who had an officer's greatcoat wrapped over his pyjamas, a solitary pip gleaming on its shoulder. 'What's the trouble?' he asked sleepily, rubbing at his eyes.

'My name's Fraser,' I said. 'Squadron Leader Fraser. I've just got out of the Russian Zone. I've got to get to Gatow at once.'

He was staring at the weapon in my hand. 'Do you usually go about threatening people with revolvers?' He came across to me and took the revolver out of my hands. 'This is an Army revolver. Is it yours?'

'No,' I said. 'I got it there.' And I nodded to the belt hanging on the hook.

The lieutenant swung round on the orderly. 'What's that equipment doing there, Heinrich?'

They began a long discussion as to why an officer had left it in the orderly room. At length I shouted at him, 'For Christ's sake!'

He turned and stared at me blankly. 'Heinrich here

says you threatened him with this revolver,' he said accusingly.

'Look!' I couldn't keep my hands still, I was so angry. 'Can't you understand what I'm trying to tell you? I'm an R.A.F. officer. I'm a pilot on the airlift and my plane crashed at Hollmind. I've just got out of the Russian Zone. I must get to Gatow quickly. I want transport. Do you understand? Some transport. I've got to get to Gatow.' I was talking wildly. I knew that. I knew I must seem like a lunatic, but there was nothing I could do about it. My nerves were all to pieces.

'May I have a look at your papers, please?'

I fumbled for my wallet, dropping the papers on the floor in my nervous haste. The German orderly picked them up for me and handed them back with a click of the heels. His eyes were no longer contemptuous.

The lieutenant glanced through them. 'You say you crashed at Hollmind?'

I nodded.

'When?'

When? Was it the night before last or – no I mustn't say that. It was the original night he wanted, the night when Tubby had gone out through the door. My mind searched desperately for a date, but I'd lost all sense of time. 'Several days ago,' I mumbled. 'What's it matter when I crashed?'

'What's your base?'

'Wunstorf.'

'You were flying a York?'

'No. A Tudor tanker.'

'A Tudor. His face suddenly cleared and he gave me

a sheepish grin. 'I say, I'm awfully sorry, sir. Of course, I know who you are now. You're the chap who flew that Messerschmitt out of Germany during the war. I mean – well, there's been a lot about it in the papers. Nobody could find any trace of the plane and you and Carter were missing.' He looked at me, hesitating awkwardly. 'You look as though you've had a rough trip, sir. Are you all right? I mean, oughtn't I to run you down to a first-aid post?'

'I must get to Gatow, ' I said.

'Yes, of course. I'll drive you myself. I'll just put some things on. Won't be a jiffy.' He hesitated in the doorway. 'Would you like a cup of char? And you'd probably like to get cleaned up a bit. That's an awfully nasty cut you've got.'

He took me through to the washroom. The water was icy cold. However, I cleaned off some of the dirt and he produced a proper bandage from a first-aid kit. Then the German orderly appeared with a steaming tin mug of dark, sweet tea. Ten minutes later we were in an Army fifteen hundredweight roaring along the Wilhelmstrasse.

We turned left on to the Gatower Damm. I knew I was home then, for planes were thundering low overhead with their flaps down and the underbelly of the low cloud was illumined by the brilliant fire-glow of the sodium lights and high-intensity cross bars that marked the approach to Gatow.

We were stopped at the barrier to Gatow Airport and a corporal of the R.A.F. Police came out and peered at the car, a gleam of white-blancoed webbing against the blue of his battledress. Then he asked for our papers. 'Squadron Leader Fraser is just out of the Russian Zone,' my lieutenant explained quickly. 'He's the pilot of that Tudor that crashed.'

The corporal handed my papers back without looking at them. 'Glad you're safe, sir.' He drew himself up stiffly and saluted. The truck ground forward. 'Where do you want to go?' the lieutenant asked. 'Terminal building?'

All the time I'd been getting closer to Gatow I'd been wondering about what I should do when I got there. There was Diana. That was the first thing I had to do – tell Diana that Tubby was alive and safe. And I wanted to get hold of Saeton. Now that I was back in the organised life of Occupied Berlin I had a feeling that there might be difficulties raised about landing an R.A.F. plane in the Russian Zone. Officially it would be embarrassing. If the plane were captured by a Russian patrol the diplomatic repercussions would be endless and far-reaching. But if Saeton would land there unofficially . . . He had the nerve to do it. He wouldn't be hide-bound by regulations and diplomatic dangers. Saeton was the person I had to see. 'Will you take me straight to the Malcolm Club, please,' I said.

'Malcolm Club? That's down by FASO, isn't it?'

'That's right.'

'Sure you don't want to report in to Ops first?' he asked.

'No. The Malcolm Club, please.'

'Okay.'

The truck slipped down through the trees, past the

lighted entrance of the mess and then suddenly there were the yellow and purple runway and perimeter lights of Gatow with the concrete square box of the terminal building to the right, rising to the tall, lighted windows of the control tower. The truck turned left through the white-painted boundary fence, skirted a B.E.A. Skymaster and hummed across the tarmac which was streaked with a white, wind-driven powder of snow. The hangars were dark, rectangular shadows to our left and ahead the lights of Piccadilly Circus shone yellow, showing the PLUME standing empty of aircraft. Planes moved along the perimeter track, engines roaring, drowning the thinner sound of planes streaming in along the runway. Everything was normal, familiar. I might never have been outside the organised bus-service of the airlift.

We skirted Piccadilly Circus, tyres jolting rhythmically on the joints of the concrete, and then we were on the FASO apron where big arc lamps blazed and there was the bustle of planes and lorries and German off-loading teams. The control tower shack on its scaffold stilts stood high and dark above the line of Nissen huts.

'Shall I wait for you?' the lieutenant asked as he drew up at the roundel signboard of the Malcolm Club.

'No, thanks,' I said. 'I'll be all right now. And thank you very much for running me out.'

'Not at all.' He got down and opened the door for me, his hand steadying me as though he thought I were too weak to climb out on my own. 'Good-bye, sir. And good luck!' He gave me a parade ground salute.

I hesitated at the entrance of the club and stood watching him get back into his truck, turn and drive off. The red tail-light dwindled and was lost amongst the litter of lights. I stared at the planes coming in. They were Daks from Lübeck with coal. There was a line of them standing in the slush of the apron. I stared at them dully. A girl checker with the nearest German labour team looked up from her manifest and stared at me. She was big and fair-haired with high cheek bones. She reminded me of Else, except that she was covered in coal dust. I turned towards the entrance to the Malcolm Club, still hesitating, reluctant to go in. If Diana were there it would be all right. But if she weren't . . . I'd have to explain myself and the filthy state I was in and I should be surrounded by a barrage of questions as air crew after air crew came in and wanted to know the story of the crash.

A group of R.A.F. boys tumbled out of the hut, laughing and talking, bringing with them through the open doorway that familiar smell of coffee and cakes. There was no point in putting it off any longer – besides, the smell of the place had made me realise how hungry I was. I brushed quickly at my filthy clothing and pushed open the door.

It was hot inside, the stove roaring red and the place full of smoke and cheerful chatter. I crossed the long room, pushing my way towards the counter, conscious of the gradual fall of conversation as eyes fastened on my scarecrow figure. 'Is Mrs Carter here?' I asked the girl behind the counter. I had spoken quietly, but even so my voice sounded loud in the silence that had developed.

The girl looked nervously to the mute groups behind me. 'No,' she said. 'She doesn't come on until seven.'

I glanced at my watch. It was half-past six. 'I'll wait,' I said. 'Can I have some coffee and a plate of sandwiches, please?'

The girl hesitated. 'All right,' she said.

A hand touched my shoulder. I spun round and found myself facing a big blond man with a wide moustache. 'Who are you?' he asked. The silent circle of eyes echoed his question.

'My name's Fraser,' I answered.

'Fraser.' He turned the name over in his mouth as though searching for it in his memory. And then he suddenly boomed out, 'Fraser! You mean the pilot of that Tudor?'

'That's right,' I said.

'Fraser! Good Christ Almighty!' He seized hold of my hand. 'Don't know you from Adam, old man. But allow me to do the honours and welcome you back. You look about all in. Here, Joan – the coffee and sandwiches are on me. What happened? Come on, tell us all about it. We've got to go in a minute. What happened?' The circle of faces closed in like a pack of wolves, avid for news. Their eyes shone with excitement. Questions were hurled at me from all directions.

'There's nothing to tell,' I murmured awkwardly. 'The engines failed. The plane crashed near Hollmind.'

'And you've just got out of the Russian Zone?'

'Yes.' The girl thrust a cup of coffee and a plate of sandwiches into my hand. 'If you don't mind – I'd rather not talk about it.' The heat of the room was making my legs shake under me. 'I'm very tired. You must excuse me. I must sit down.'

Hands gripped my arms at the elbows and half-lifted me to one of the easy-chairs by the stove. 'You sit there and drink your coffee, old man. We'll have you fixed up in no time.'

'I must speak to Mrs Carter,' I insisted.

'All right. We'll get her for you.'

They left me then and I grasped the coffee cup in my hands, feeling the warmth of it spread up my arms, savouring the glorious, reviving smell of it. I could hear them talking about me in the background. Fresh air crews came in to replace others that went out to their planes. The word was passed on and they took up the story, talking about me in whispers.

Somebody came and squatted down on his haunches beside me. 'Glad to know you're back, Fraser,' he said. 'You must be the greatest escape merchant alive. All the boys back at Wunstorf will be glad as hell to know you're back. We thought you'd had it.'

'Wunstorf?' I stared at him. His face seemed vaguely familiar.

'That's right. Remember me? I'm the guy that was sitting right next to you at dinner that night you crashed. You were growling at Westrop for talking too much about the Russians. Seems he had second sight or something. I'll see that the station commander knows you're back.'

'Is the Wunstorf wave coming in now?' I asked.

'Yes. Just started to come in.'

'Is a man called Saeton flying a Tudor tanker on the lift yet?'

'Is he flying the lift!' The kid laughed. 'I'll say he is. Been flying for two days now and he's got the development section puzzled as hell. Flies on his two inboard engines all the time, except on take-off, and his fuel consumption is knocking holes the size of a hangar door in all the aero engine boys' ideas. He said you worked on the motors with him at one time. Boy, he's certainly got them guessing. Boffins from Farnborough are flying out tomorrow with the C.T.O. of the Ministry of Civil Aviation and a big pot from the Ministry of Supply. Saeton will be in shortly.'

'How soon?' I asked.

'About quarter of an hour. The Tudors aren't far behind us.'

An R.A.F. corporal pushed forward. He had a big web satchel with a red cross on it. 'I've got an ambulance outside, sir. Do you think you can walk to it or shall I get a stretcher in for you?'

'You can send your bloody ambulance away,' I said angrily. Why the devil couldn't they leave me alone? 'I'm not leaving here until I've seen Mrs Carter.'

The fellow hesitated. 'Very good, sir. I'll be back in a minute and then we'll get you patched up. Nasty cut you got there. Sure you're all right, sir?'

'Of course I'm all right,' I snapped. 'I've walked nearly twenty miles already tonight.'

'Very good, sir.' He went to the door and opened it, and at that moment Diana came in.

Her face, devoid of make-up, looked quite haggard. At sight of me she stopped as though she couldn't believe that I was really sitting there in an easy-chair beside the stove. 'So it *is* you.' She said it almost accusingly. Then she came slowly towards me. 'What happened? What have you done with Tubby? Why didn't you let him jump with the others?' Her voice trembled and there was a look of dull pain in her eyes.

'You needn't worry,' I said. 'He's safe.'

She stared at me. 'You're lying.' Her voice was suddenly hard. 'You know he's dead.'

'Tubby's all right,' I repeated. 'He's alive.'

'I don't understand.' Her voice had faded to a whisper. 'It can't be true. If you're alive, then it's Tubby whose body—' Her words died away in a choking sob.

'Tubby's alive,' I said again. I reached out and caught hold of her hand. Her fingers were cold and slack in mine. 'Diana. I want your help. He's alive, but he's injured and we've got to get him out. You've got to persuade Saeton to fly there and get him out.'

'What are you saying?' Her voice was flat and toneless.

I didn't understand her attitude. 'I thought you'd be glad,' I said. 'I came straight here to tell you.'

'Glad that you're alive?' She turned away. 'Of course I'm glad, only . . . I loved him,' she suddenly burst out. 'I loved him, I tell you.'

Somebody bent over me, an officer in R.A.F.

uniform with dark, boot-button eyes and a thin, aquiline nose. 'You're Fraser, aren't you?' he said. 'They just told me.'

'For God's sake!' I pushed him away. 'I'm trying to tell Mrs Carter something.'

'Yes, I heard. I think you'd better listen to me first. I'm the I.O. here. We know all about your plane. It crashed two miles north of Hollmind Airfield, dived straight into the ground.'

I stared at him. 'Who told you it crashed at Hollmind?' I demanded.

'The Russians.'

'The Russians?'

'Yes. After denying the whole thing for days, they came through with a report yesterday. They've found the wreckage in the woods north of Hollmind.' He leaned down and lowered his voice. 'They also found the remains of one body. We didn't know whether it was yours or Carter's.' His glance slid to Diana whose face was buried in her hands. 'Now you're safe, of course, we know whose it was.' He straightened up. 'Soon as you're ready, we'll go up to my office and I'll get a statement from you. I'll have to have a report ready for the station commander.'

I stared at him. Why should the Russians make such a report? It didn't make sense. I felt suddenly scared – scared that they wouldn't believe what I had to tell them.

CHAPTER EIGHT

The next quarter of an hour was a nightmare. I started by trying to convince the Intelligence Officer that the Russian report was nonsense. It was a mistake. He believed the information the Russians had given him. What's more, the lieutenant who had driven me to Gatow had reported to him after dropping me at the Malcolm Club. He knew that I'd held a German orderly up with a revolver. 'You don't know what you're saying – or what you're doing, Fraser,' he said. His voice was cold and practical. 'Better come up to my office and then I'll take you along to the sick bay.'

I thought of the little patrol of Red Army men in the woods near Hollmind. They knew damn well the plane hadn't dived into the ground. 'Can I see this report?' I asked him.

'It's up at my office now.'

'Does the report give any details?'

'Oh, yes. It's quite detailed. No question about it being your plane. They've even got the number –

Two-five-two.' He turned to the medical orderly who had returned. 'Take Mrs Carter back to her quarters.'

'Wait,' I said. If I couldn't convince him, at least I might be able to convince Diana. I pulled myself out of my seat and went over to her, catching hold of her shoulders and shaking her in my desperate urge to get her to concentrate on what I had to tell her. 'You've got to listen to me, Diana.' She lifted her head and stared at me through tear-dimmed eyes. 'I was with Tubby yesterday. He *is* alive.'

The desire to believe me was there in her face. Hope showed for an instant in her eyes, but then it died and she clenched her teeth. 'Take him away from me, please,' she said in a whisper.

The I.O. pulled my hand away from her shoulder. 'The Russians wouldn't say he was dead if he wasn't.' He pushed me gently back into the chair. 'Just take it easy. You're a bit upset – but it's no good raising Mrs Carter's hopes. Carter's dead. No question of that. Now all I want from you—'

'He's not dead,' I cut in angrily. 'He's badly injured, but he's alive. He's at a farm—'

'Stop it, Neil!' Diana screamed at me. 'For God's sake stop it! Why do you keep saying he's alive when you know he's dead? If it hadn't been for me,' she added in a lifeless tone, 'he'd never have taken the job. He'd still have been with Saeton. Bill wouldn't have crashed him. He'd have been all right with Bill. Oh, God!'

She was beside herself and I sat there staring at the misery which made her face look wild and wondering how the devil I could convince her that her husband was alive. I turned to the I.O. 'I want to see the station commander,' I said. 'I want a plane put at my disposal tonight. Do you think he'd do that?'

'What do you want a plane for?' His tone was the sort you use to placate an excited child and I saw him exchange a quick glance with the medical orderly.

'I want to fly to Hollmind Airfield,' I answered quickly. 'If I can land at Hollmind I can get Carter out.'

'Is that ambulance still here?' he asked the medical orderly.

'Yes, sir. Mr Fraser told me to send it away, but I thought I'd better—' He stared at me without finishing the sentence.

'Good! Come along, Fraser. You need a good, hot drink, warmth and a bed. We'll soon have you fixed up.' His hand was on my arm, gently but firmly raising me from my seat.

I flung him off. 'Can't you understand what I'm trying to tell you? Tubby Carter is alive. He didn't die in any crash.' It was on the tip of my tongue to say there hadn't been any crash, but I knew he wouldn't believe that, not unless I told him the whole story and I wasn't going to do that until I had seen Saeton. 'He's at a farm, being cared for by the local doctor. He's got a broken arm, several broken ribs and a pierced lung and he needs treatment.'

'Now, be reasonable, Fraser.' The I.O.'s hand was back on my arm. 'We all understand how you feel. But it's no good pretending he's alive just because you're worried that you jumped when he was still in the plane. We'll get all that sorted out later. Now come on up to the sick bay.'

So they were going to pin that on me! I felt the blood rush, hammering, to my head. Damn them! At least that wasn't the truth. I'd gone back for him, hadn't I? I felt a sense of utter frustration taking hold of me.

And then Diana's hand was on my arm. 'Why do you keep on talking about a farm?' she asked. The desire to believe me was back in her face.

I told her about the Kleffmanns then and about their son Hans. 'Tubby is lying in Hans's old room,' I said. I half-closed my eyes, forcing into my mind the picture of that room. 'The wallpaper has butterflies on it and it's littered with faded photographs of Hans. The bedstead is of iron and brass and the single dormer window looks out on to the roof of a barn.' I seized hold of her shoulder again. 'You've got to believe me, Diana. You've got to help me persuade Saeton to fly in to Hollmind tonight. Please – please, for God's sake believe what I'm trying to tell you.'

She stared at me and then she nodded slowly, half-dazed. 'I must believe you,' she said half to herself. Her eyes searched my face. 'You do know what you're saying, don't you? You aren't lying – just to protect yourself?'

'To protect myself?'

'Yes – so that we'd think you didn't leave him to—' She stopped and bit hold of her lip. 'No. I can't believe you'd do that. I guess you mean what you say.' She looked up quickly at the I.O. 'Leave us a minute. Do you mind? I'd like to talk to him.'

The I.O. hesitated and then turned away to the coffee counter.

'How did you know Bill was here?' She was leaning forward and the unexpectedness of her question nearly caught me off my guard. I was feeling wretchedly tired. The warmth of the stove was making me sleepy. I pushed my hand over my face. 'One of the air crews, a fellow from Wunstorf, told me,' I answered. I shook myself, trying to keep my mind clear. I mustn't tell her what really happened. If I did that Saeton wouldn't help me. 'Can you find out when he'll be in?' I asked her. 'I've got to speak to him. Once I get up there in the terminal building they'll start questioning me and then they'll push me off to hospital or something. Saeton must take me to Hollmind. Tubby's got to be flown out tonight.'

'Why are you so set on Bill going?' she asked.

'He was a friend of Tubby's,' I said. 'It was Tubby who got those engines made for him, wasn't it? Damn it, he owes Tubby that.'

'There's no other reason?' She hesitated, staring at me hard. 'You say you jumped, leaving Tubby in the plane?'

Again the quickness of her question almost caught me off my guard. 'I said nothing of the sort. Don't try and pin anything like that on to me,' I added angrily.

'Then why was he hurt and not you?'

'Because—' I dropped my head into my hand, pressing at the corners of my eyes with finger and thumb, trying to loosen the band of strain that was tightening across my forehead. 'I don't know,' I said wearily. 'For God's sake stop asking me questions. All I want you to do is to get Saeton for me.'

Diana caught hold of the lapels of my German greatcoat. 'You're lying!' Her voice hissed between her clamped teeth. 'You're lying, Neil. I know you are. You're hiding something. What is it? You must tell me what it is.' She was shaking me violently. 'What happened? What really happened?'

'Leave me alone, can't you?' I whispered. If only she'd leave me alone, let me think. 'Get Saeton,' I added. 'I want to talk to Saeton.'

'Something happened that night. Didn't it? Something happened. Neil – what was it? Please tell me what it was.' She was kneeling beside me now and her voice had risen hysterically. I could feel the sudden silence in the room, feel them staring at me – the regular air crew boys, men who knew nothing about my story, who would be judging me in the light of Diana clinging to my greatcoat and crying out, '*What happened? What happened that night?*'

'Wait till Saeton comes,' I said wearily.

'What's Bill got to do with it? Was he the cause of it?' she looked wildly round and then swung fiercely back on me. 'Will you talk if Bill is here? Will you tell me that really happened then?'

'Yes, if you'll get him to fly out to Hollmind tonight. He can land at the airfield and then we'll get Tubby out. Tubby will be all right then.'

'Hollmind is a disused aerodrome. I checked that

yesterday when I got the news. Are you sure he'll be able to land there?'

'He's done it once.'

'What do you mean?'

I pressed my head into my hand. 'Nothing,' I said. If I didn't get some sleep soon I'd be saying the first thing that came into my mind. 'I didn't mean anything,' I murmured. 'I don't know what I'm saying. I'm very tired, Diana. Get Saeton for me, will you; and stop asking me questions.'

She hesitated as though on the brink of another question. But all she said was, 'Bill isn't here yet.'

The I.O. was back at my side now. 'You want Saeton? He'll be here any minute now. The first Tudor has just come in. You worked with him on these engines of his, I understand?'

'Yes,' I didn't want to talk any more. The idea that the authorities wouldn't help me was firmly fixed in my mind. Saeton was the only man who could help me. I sat there, stupid with the warmth of the stove and the fatigue of my body, feeling the blood drying in a crust on my temple, watching the door. Air crews moved in and out and as they passed they stared at us silently as though we were some queer tableau entirely divorced from the solid, everyday routine of flying in and out of Berlin.

Then at last the door was pushed open and Saeton came striding in followed by his crew. He was almost past us before he saw me. He checked, rocking back on his heels as though for an instant he had been caught off balance. Then his features set themselves into a smile of welcome. 'Hallo, Neil!' He reached down and grasped my shoulder. 'Glad you're safe.' But I noticed that his eyes didn't light up with his face. They were hard as slate and withdrawn as though wrestling with the problem of my presence. He had a silk sweat rag knotted round his throat and his flying suit was unzipped, making him appear more solid than ever. 'Well, what happened? How did you get out?'

'I hitched a ride and walked the rest,' I said.

There was an awkward silence. He seemed to want to put a question, but his eyes slid to the others and he remained silent. I knew suddenly that he was nervous. I hadn't thought of him as a man who could ever be nervous, but as he lit a cigarette his hands were trembling. 'You've heard the news, have you? About the engines, I mean. They're proving even better than we expected – twenty per cent increase in power and a forty-five per cent reduction in fuel consumption. They're going to be—'

'Tubby is alive,' I said.

'Alive?' The echo of my statement was jerked out of him as though I'd hit him below the belt. Then he recovered himself. 'Are you sure? You're not—' He stopped, conscious of the silence of the others watching him. 'Where is he?'

'In a farmhouse near Hollmind Airfield.'

'I see.' He took a long pull at his cigarette. The news had jolted him and I could see he didn't know what to do about it. He glanced at Diana and then at the I.O. who drew him on one side. I saw the man's lips frame the words 'Russian report' and I could almost have laughed at the thought of an R.A.F. Intelligence Officer giving Saeton the details of what had happened to that plane when all the time it was sitting out there on the FASO apron unloading fuel.

At length Saeton said, 'All right. I'll see if I can get some sense out of him. Mind if I talk to him alone?'

The I.O. agreed and led Diana away. Saeton came and stood over me. He was smiling. 'For some reason the Russians have been very helpful,' he said. He was quite sure of himself again now. 'You've heard about this report, have you? They say they found the remains of one of the crew.' I made no comment. His head was in silhouette against the light. It hung over me as it had done that first night at Membury. And he was smiling. 'Well, how did you find him?' I told him about the search and when I had finished he said, 'So he's injured. Badly?'

'Broken arm and ribs and a pierced lung,' I said. 'We've got to get him out. He needs hospital treatment.'

'And if he doesn't get it?'

'I don't know,' I answered. 'There's a German doctor looking after him. But Tubby is pretty bad. I think he might die.'

'I see.' He ran his thumb along the blue line of his jaw. 'What are you going to do about it?'

'I can't do anything. That bloody little Intelligence Officer doesn't believe me. I want you to tell them you believe what I'm saying – persuade them to give us a plane.'

'Us?' He gave a quick laugh.

'Tubby won't talk,' I said quickly. 'He promised me.'

'I'm on the very edge of success,' he said and I realised that he had room for nothing else in that queer, urgent mind of his.

'Yes, I heard about that,' I said. 'Is it true officials are coming out from England?'

He nodded, his eyes lighting up. 'Everything's gone marvellously. First trip my flight engineer was staggered by the performance of the engines. Within twenty-four hours it was all over the mess at Wunstorf and R.A.F. engineers were flying the airlift with me, checking for themselves. Now the Ministry of Civil Aviation and the Ministry of Supply are sending their experts out, including a boffin from Farnborough. By this afternoon—'

'What about Tubby?' I said. 'You can't abandon him. You've got to get him out.'

'You should have thought about him before you told me you were going to the authorities as soon as you got back here.'

'I won't talk,' I said hastily. 'Nor will Tubby.'

'It's too late to say that now.' And then he added slowly, 'As far as I'm concerned Tubby is dead.'

He said it without any emotion and I stared up at him, seeing the hard line of his jaw, the cold slatiness of his eyes, unable to believe even then that he meant what he said.

'We've got to get him out,' I insisted.

He shrugged his shoulders. 'You know damn' well I can't accept your story. It would be fatal.'

I didn't believe him at first. 'You can't leave Tubby out there in the Russian Zone.'

'I'll do nothing to betray the belief of the authorities in this Russian report,' was his reply.

The full horror of what he was saying dawned on me slowly. 'You mean—' The words choked in my throat.

'I mean I'll do nothing,' he said.

All right. If he was as cold-blooded as that . . . 'Do you remember how you blackmailed me into stealing that plane?' I asked.

He nodded slowly, that cold smile back on his lips.

'Well, I'm going to blackmail you now,' I said. 'Either you fly me into Hollmind tonight to pick up Tubby or I tell the I.O. here everything – how I pinched the plane, how I nearly killed Tubby, how you altered the numbers and we strewed the wreckage of our old Tudor through the Hollmind woods and how you set fire to the hangar at Membury so that there would be no trace.'

'You think he'd believe you?' There was almost a sneer in his voice.

'Get him out, Saeton,' I whispered urgently. 'If you don't, I'll bust the whole game wide open. Understand?'

His eyes narrowed slightly. That was the only sign he gave that he took my threat seriously. 'Don't think I haven't taken care of the possibility of your reaching Berlin,' he said quietly. He glanced round at Diana and the I.O. and then in a louder voice: 'No wonder you get scared when it comes to jumping. You're about the most imaginative flier I ever met.' He turned and nodded to the I.O. 'I'm sorry,' he said. 'I can't get any sense out of him.' He drew the officer to one side. 'I'm afraid he's pretty bad. Concussion or something. He keeps on talking about pinching a plane and having a fight with Carter. I think he's all mixed up in his mind with that escape he did from Germany in 1944.' They began whispering together and I heard the I.O. mention the word 'psychiatrist'. Diana was staring at me dully, all hope gone from her eyes, her body slumped at the shoulders in an attitude of dejection. Saeton and the I.O. came back towards me and I heard Saeton saying, '. . . if we knew what happened when the plane crashed.'

'You know damn' well it didn't crash,' I jerked out. Sudden, overwhelming hatred of him swept me to my feet. 'I know what it is. You want Tubby dead. You know damn' well the credit for those engines is his. You want him dead.'

They stared at me like humans looking through bars at a caged animal. 'I'll get him away,' the I.O. whispered quickly to Saeton and Saeton nodded.

I turned to Diana then. She was the person I had to convince. She knew Saeton, knew the set-up – above all she was the only one of them that wanted to believe that Tubby was alive. 'Diana, you must listen to me,' I implored her. 'You've got to believe me. Tubby isn't dead. I saw him yesterday afternoon.' My head was swimming and I pressed my hands to my temples. 'No, it wasn't yesterday. It was the day before. He was badly injured, but he could talk. I promised I'd come back for him. If you love him, Diana, you've got to help me. You've got to make the people here believe—'

A hand grasped my shoulder and spun me round. 'Shut up!' Saeton's face was thrust close to mine. 'Shut up, do you hear? Tubby's dead. You're just saying this to cover yourself. Can't you realise how Diana feels? Until you turned up there was a good chance he was alive. Everybody thought the body the Russians found in the plane must be yours. You were the skipper. But you turn up. So it's Tubby who is dead, and now you try to raise false hopes in an effort to—'

I flung his hand off. 'You devil!' I said. 'You're the cause of all this. It's all your fault he's out there in the Russian Zone.' I turned to Diana. 'The plane didn't crash at all,' I cried. 'I flew it back to Membury. Saeton forced me to do it. Tubby tried to prevent me. There was a struggle and—' I could see they didn't believe me.

'Get him out of here,' I heard Saeton say. 'Get him out before he drives Mrs Carter crazy.' Hands closed on my arms and I was dragged across the room to the door. I screwed my head round and saw Saeton standing alone, his face grey and tired looking, and Diana was staring across at him, her lips trembling. Behind them the air crews stood in silence looking on. Then the door closed in my face and I was out in the grey dawn of Gatow Airfield with the roar of planes and the deliberate, operational movements of lorries and German labour teams.

I had a brief glimpse of the FASO apron, gleaming dully in its leaden mantle of slush. Close by a German labour team was hauling sacks of coal from the belly of a Dak and beyond it another Dak was swinging off the perimeter track and an R.A.F. corporal was signalling it into position. A lorry rolled past us to meet it. A sergeant of the R.A.F. Police had the ambulance doors open and I was bundled in. The Intelligence Officer climbed in beside me. The sergeant saluted stiffly and the doors closed, boxing us into a dark little world that shook with the roar of planes. A slight vibration of the stretcher bunk on which I had been sat told me the engine was running, and then we moved off, slithering on the wet surface as we swung round the fuel standing at Piccadilly Circus. 'Where are we going?' I asked the I.O.

'Sick bay,' he answered. 'I rang up Squadron Leader Gentry from the Malcolm Club. He's the M.O. He's expecting you.'

I was conscious of that sense of helplessness that comes to the individual when he is in process of being absorbed into the machine of an organised unit. Once I was in the M.O.'s clutches anything could happen – they'd regard any request as prejudicial to the patient's recovery. They might even drug me. 'I want to see the station commander,' I said.

The intelligence officer didn't answer. I repeated my request. 'Take my advice, Fraser,' he said coldly. 'See the M.O. first.'

I hesitated. Somehow his voice seemed to carry a note of warning. But I wasn't thinking about myself. I was thinking about Tubby. 'I've got to see the station commander,' I said.

'Well, you can't. I'm taking you to the M.O. Put your request to him if you want to.' In the half-light I could see his eyes watching me. 'I'm saying that for your own good.'

'For my own good?' His eyes had turned away as though breaking off the conversation. All I could see was the pale outline of his face under the peaked cap. 'I'm not worrying about myself,' I said. 'It's Carter I'm worried about.'

'I should have thought that was a waste of time now.'

The tone of his voice stung me. 'Civil airlift pilots come under R.A.F. for administration and discipline, don't they?' I asked. The line of his head nodded slowly. 'Very well, then. Take me to the station commander's office. That's a formal request.'

His eyes were back on my face again now. 'Have it your own way,' he said. 'But if you're fit enough to see the station commander, you're fit enough to see Squadron Leader Pierce, R.A.F. Police.' He turned and tapped on the partition separating us from the driver. A small hatch slid back. 'Terminal building first,' he ordered the driver.

'What did you mean about R.A.F. Police?' I asked.

'Pierce is very anxious to see you. Some question of an identity check.'

Identity check! 'What do you mean?' For a moment the thought of Tubby was thrust out of my mind. Identity check! Had Saeton talked about me? Was that what he meant when he had said he had taken care of the possibility of my reaching Berlin? Was this his attempt to discredit me? 'Whose instructions is he acting on?' I asked.

'I know nothing about it,' the I.O. answered in that same cold, deliberate voice.

Before I could question him further the ambulance had stopped and we were getting out. The terminal building was a lifeless hulk of concrete in the cloud-skimmed dawn. The tall windows of the control tower looked with dead eyes upon the runway where a single Tudor was lining up for take-off. There was no outward sign that this was the hub and heart of the world's busiest air traffic centre; beyond it the wings of a Dak widened against the dull cloud-scape over Berlin as it dropped towards the runway like a toy pulled by an unseen string. As we went through the swing doors the Tudor took off with a roar that split the dawn-cold stillness.

The I.O. took me up to the first floor. Little placards stood out from the doors of wood-partitioned offices; Flight Lieutenant Symes, Intelligence Officer – white on blue next to Public Relations. The I.O. pushed open the door. 'Wait here, will you, Fraser. I'll go down and see if the station commander has come in yet. He usually shows up about this time. Likes to have a look around before breakfast.' He turned to the medical orderly. 'You wait here with Mr Fraser, corporal.' He glanced at me quickly, but his eyes slid away from mine and I went into his office, wondering whether he thought I was going to try and escape. The corporal shut the door as I stood there listening to the I.O.'s footsteps fading down the wide corridor.

The office was a big one with two windows looking out across the standing and the hangars to the FASO apron still barely visible in the reluctant daylight of that bleak January morning. The arc lamps had been switched off, but runway and perimeter lights still burned, a complicated network of yellow and purple. The Dak was landing now and another Tudor was moving up the perimeter tracks towards the control tower. I could almost hear the pilot calling his number over the R/T, requesting permission from Traffic Control to taxi, and I wondered whether it was Saeton. Beyond the hangars lorries moved in a steady stream from the off-loading platform, moving slowly and positively towards Berlin with their loads of Ruhr coal.

'Fraser!'

I turned. The door behind me had opened and the I.O. was standing there, holding it open for a short, burly man in a wing commander's uniform. 'This is the station commander,' the I.O. said, closing the door and switching on the light.

'Sit down, Fraser.' The station commander nodded to a chair. 'Glad you got back all right. But I'm sorry about Carter.' His voice was quiet, impersonal. He placed his cap on the top of a steel filing cabinet and seated himself at the desk. In the naked lights I saw that the beaverboard walls of the office were covered with maps and charts, a kaleidoscope of colour – Russian tanks, Russian planes, survey maps of Berlin, Germany with the air corridors marked in white tape, a huge map of the British Zone dotted with flags bearing squadron numbers and a smaller map of

Eastern Germany covered with chinograph on which had been scribbled in different colours the numbers of Russian units. The whole room was a litter of secret and semi-secret information, most of it relating one way and another to the Russians. 'Understand you wanted to see me?' The slight rise of inflection in the station commander's voice at the end of the sentence was, I knew, my cue. But I hesitated, reluctant to commit myself to a line of approach. 'Well?'

I gripped hold of the wooden arms of the chair. The walls of the room were beginning to move again. It seemed very hot in there and the lights were blinding. 'I want a plane, sir. Tonight. Carter's alive and I've got to get him out. We can land at Hollmind. He's at a farm about three miles from the airfield.' The words came out in a rush, tumbling incoherently over each other, not a bit as I had intended. 'It would only take a couple of hours. The airfield's quite deserted and the runway is sound.'

'How do you know?'

I stared at him. It sounded like a trap, the way he barked the question at me. His face kept blurring so that I couldn't see his expression. 'How do I know?' I moved my fingers back and forth along the dirt-caked lines of my forehead. 'I just know,' I heard myself mumble. 'I just know. That's all.' I straightened my body up. 'Will you let me have a plane, sir – tonight?'

The door behind me opened and a squadron leader came over to the desk, a thin file in his hand. 'Here's the report you wanted, sir.' The man's eyes glanced curiously in my direction. 'I've rung for the M.O. and Pierce is in my office now. Shall I let him come up?'

The station commander glanced quickly across at me and then nodded. 'All right. Any further news about that threat of ack-ack practice in the exit corridor?'

'No more than we know already, sir. Air Safety Centre have lodged protests, but as far as we're concerned at the moment the Russians will be firing to 20,000 feet in the exit corridor. I don't think we're going to give way.'

'I should damn well hope not. They're just bluffing. They know what it means if they start shooting our boys down.' He gave a long sigh. 'All right, Freddie. But let me know as soon as you get any news.' The door closed and the station commander stared for a moment out through the windows to where another freighter was thundering down the runway. He watched it rise, watched it until it disappeared into the low cloud, a small speck carrying an air crew of four headed for base through the exit corridor. His eyes switched slowly to me. 'Where were we? Oh, yes. You claim Carter is alive.' He picked up the file his adjutant had brought in, opened it and handed me a slip of paper. 'Read that, Fraser. It's the Russian report on your aircraft.'

I took it and held it in my hands, the print blurring into solid, straight lines. I let my hand drop, not bothering to go through it. 'I know about this,' I said. 'It's completely phoney. It didn't dive into the ground. And they didn't find the charred remains of a body. They don't know anything about the plane – they're just guessing. The wreckage is strewn for miles around.

'How do you mean?' The station commander's voice was sharp and practical.

I pressed my fingers to my temples. How was I going to make them understand what had really happened? It was quite clear to me – ordinary and straightforward. But as soon as I tried to put it into words I knew it would sound fantastic.

'I think we'd better do it by questions, sir.' The I.O.'s voice seemed oddly remote, yet it rattled in my ears like the sharp, dry sound of a porcupine's quills. 'He's just about dead beat.'

'All right, Symes. Go ahead.'

I wanted to tell the station commander to let me tell it in my own way, but before I could say anything the I.O.'s sharp, insistent voice was saying, 'You claim Carter is alive, that he's lying injured at a farmhouse near Hollmind. Hollmind is thirty miles from the point where Westrop and Field jumped. That's almost ten minutes' flying time. What happened in those ten minutes? Didn't Carter jump with the others?'

'No.'

'He stayed in the plane with you?'

'Yes. He knew I didn't like jumping—' I was determined now that they should have every detail of the thing. If I told them everything, kept nothing back, they must believe me. 'We had to jump once before at Membury, when the undercarriage of Saeton's Tudor jammed; that's how he knew I was scared. He came back to see me out. Then I got the engines going and started to fly to Membury. He got angry then and—'

'You mean Gatow, don't you?'

'No, Membury.' I stared at him, trying to force him to understand that I meant Membury. 'I was taking the Tudor back to Membury. That's why I took the job with Harcourt. It was all planned. I was to steal a plane from the airlift and—' My voice trailed away as I saw the look of bewilderment on the station commander's face. If only they'd let me tell it my own way.

'I don't understand this sequence of events at all, Fraser.' His voice was kindly, but there was an underlying impatience. 'Go back to where you and Carter are alone in the plane. Westrop and Field had jumped. Who went out next?'

'Please—' I implored, 'let me tell it my own way. When I reached Membury—'

'Just answer my questions, will you, Fraser?' The voice was authoritative, commanding – it reminded me of Saeton's voice. 'Who jumped next?'

All my muscles seemed rigid with the violence of my need to tell it to them as a straight story. But I couldn't fight him. I hadn't the energy. It was so much easier just to answer the questions. 'Carter,' I said in a dull voice.

'But I thought you said he came back to see you out?'

'I pushed him out.'

'I see. You pushed him out.' I could tell by the tone in which he repeated the phrase that he didn't believe me. 'And then what happened?'

'I flew the plane back to Membury. It was moonlight all the way. I found the airfield quite easily and when I landed—'

'Please, Fraser . . . I want to get at what happened in that plane. Now try to help me. What happened after Carter went out? We know the plane dived into the ground. I want to know how—'

'It didn't dive into the ground,' I said. 'I told you what happened. I flew it back to Membury.'

He got up and came over to me. 'Now pull yourself together, please.' His hand pressed gently on my shoulder. 'We naturally want to know what happened. There's no question of the accuracy of the Russian report. They've even sent us a piece of the tailplane. The plane is yours all right. It has your flight number on it and it's unquestionably a Tudor. Now what caused it to crash?'

'It didn't crash,' I said wearily. 'I tell you, I flew it –

'Then if it didn't crash, how the devil are the Russians able to send us a sample of the wreckage that clearly shows it to be your plane?'

'I tell you, we put it there,' I replied desperately. 'We loaded it into the plane and flew it there. Saeton stooged around whilst I pushed the bits out. Then he landed me at Hollmind. That was when he flew out to Wunstorf to join the airlift. I searched all that night and all the next day for some trace of Carter. Then I found his helmet. It was just after the snow had started. It was lying on the snow and—'

'I just can't follow what you're saying,' the station

commander interrupted. 'Will you please stick to what happened in the plane.'

But before I could answer, the door of the room opened. 'Come in, Pierce. You, too, Gentry.' The station commander crossed over to the taller of the two men, drawing him aside and speaking to him in a low voice. I could see the two of them glancing covertly in my direction. Symes was beating an impatient tattoo on the edge of the desk with his long fingers, his dark eyes fixed curiously on my face.

I felt as though an invisible curtain was being lowered, separating me from contact with them, and I pulled myself to my feet. 'You don't understand,' I said angrily. 'I joined Harcourt's outfit in order to get hold of one of his planes. We'd crashed ours. It had to be replaced. We had to get hold of another plane in order to test the engines. Saeton was due on the airlift on the 25th. We had to have another plane. The only place we could get one was in Germany – off the airlift. It had to be a Tudor. That was why—' My voice trailed away as I saw them all staring at me as though I were crazy.

The man who was talking to the station commander said quietly, 'It's obvious he's had a nasty shock. He's suffering from some sort of mental disturbance – he's all mixed up with that escape he did. I'll get him down to the sick bay.'

The station commander stared at me and then nodded. 'All right. But I wish to God I could find out what happened to that plane of yours.'

'Nothing happened to it,' I cried angrily. 'There

was nothing wrong with it at all. I flew it back to Membury. All the Russians have found—'

'Yes, yes,' the station commander cut in impatiently. 'We've heard all about that. All right, Gentry. Take him down to the sick bay. Only for God's sake get some reasonable statement out of him as soon as possible.'

The M.O. nodded and started towards me. It was then that the other man stepped forward. 'Mind if I have a word with him first, sir?'

The station commander shrugged his shoulders. 'Just as you like, Pierce. I suppose you think in his present muddled state he's more likely to tell you the truth.' He gave a quick laugh. 'I hope you make better progress than we have.' He crossed to the door and paused with his hand on the handle. 'I'd like a word with you, Symes, after breakfast.'

The I.O. rose to his feet. 'Very good, sir.'

The door closed behind the station commander and as I slid wearily back into my seat the policeman came and leaned on the edge of the desk, his hard, slightly pitted features seeming to hang over me, a dark blur against the lights. 'My name's Pierce,' he said. 'R.A.F. Police. You're Fraser?'

I nodded hopelessly. All chance of a plane had vanished with the departure of the station commander and I felt drained and utterly exhausted. If only they'd let me tell my story the way I'd wanted to. But I knew that even then they wouldn't have believed me. Put into words it immediately became fantastic.

'Christian name's Neil Leyden?'

Again I nodded. It was stupid of him asking me my name when everybody in the room knew damn' well who I was.

'I've been instructed to ask you a few questions.' His voice was quiet, almost gentle; very different from his features. 'Do you remember the night of November 18th last year?'

I thought back. What an age it seemed. That was the night I'd arrived at Membury. 'Yes,' I said. 'I began working with Saeton that night.'

'At Membury?'

'Yes.'

'How did you get there – by car?'

'Yes, by car. There's no train service to Membury.'

'A car was found that night at the foot of Baydon Hill. That was your car, wasn't it?'

I stared at him, struggling to understand the drift of his questions. My hand reached up almost automatically to the crust of blood where my forehead was cut. 'I had a crash,' I said.

He nodded. 'You've another name, haven't you? Callahan.'

I started involuntarily. So that was it. This was what Saeton had meant. I stared up at him, meeting his steady gaze, knowing they'd got me and thinking that I might just as well have refused when Saeton had forced me to take that job with Harcourt. But it didn't matter now. So much had happened, nothing seemed to matter any more. It was as though in some queer way I was now paying the price for what I'd done to Tubby. 'Yes,' I said in a whisper. 'I'm Callahan.' And then in the silence that gripped the room I asked, 'What happens now?'

He shrugged his shoulders. 'It's nothing to do with me, old man. I'll send back a report to England. In due course I imagine you'll be flown back and they'll decide what they're going to do about you. There's no warrant for your arrest or anything like that at the moment.' He coughed awkwardly. 'Sorry to have to put the questions so soon after your escape from the Russian Zone. Now, I think you'd better go along with Squadron Leader Gentry here. It's time you had that cut cleaned up and you look as though you could do with a bit of rest. I shan't be worrying you again – not for some time anyway. So you can just relax.'

I thought how reasonable and logical his questions had been. If I could get him to do the questioning about what had happened to Tubby – they'd believe me then. I pulled myself to my feet again. He was already at the door. 'Just a minute,' I gasped, feeling the room reel. 'I've got to tell you something.' He had stopped in the doorway and was looking at me with a slight frown. 'You got this from Saeton, didn't you? It was Saeton who told the authorities who I was. You know why he did that? It was because he was afraid I'd talk. I didn't want to pinch the plane. But he made me do it. He said if I didn't he'd—' I closed my eyes trying to shut out the blurred movement of the room. The engines of a plane thundered on the perimeter track just outside the building. The windows rattled, the sound merging with the din in my ears. The sound was like the roar of a great fall; it went on and on. 'Don't you see?' I gasped. 'He blackmailed me—' My knees trembled and gave. Somebody called out something and I felt myself slipping. Hands caught hold of me as I fell, supporting me whilst my legs seemed to trickle away like used-up water from the base of my body. Everything was remote and indistinct as I slipped into unconsciousness.

I suppose they gave me something for I don't remember anything more till I woke up in bed with a nurse standing over me. 'Feeling better?' Her voice was gentle and soothing.

'Yes, thanks.' I closed my eyes, searching in my mind for what had happened, gradually piecing it together.

'Open your mouth, please. I want to take your temperature.' I obeyed her automatically and she pushed a thermometer under my tongue. 'You were a bit feverish when they brought you in and you've been talking a lot.'

'Delirious? What was I saying?'

'Keep your mouth closed now. All about your flight and a friend of yours in the Russian Zone. Squadron Leader Pierce was here for a time. They're flying you out tomorrow – that is if the M.O. says you're fit enough.'

'Flying me out tomorrow?' I thrust at the bed, forcing myself up into a sitting position. If they flew me out tomorrow nothing could ever be done about Tubby.

'Now don't get excited otherwise we shan't allow you to go.' Her hands touched my shoulders, pushing me gently back against the pillows.

My eyes went past her, searching the room. At least I was on my own. A single window rattled to the sound of planes behind black curtains. 'What's the time?' I mumbled the question, my tongue still closed over the thermometer.

'Don't talk, please. It's nearly seven and if you're good you can have some supper.' She reached down and took the thermometer out of my mouth, peering at it through her thick-lensed glasses. 'That's fine. We're back to normal now.' She shook it down with a neat, practised flick of the wrist. 'I'll get you some food. Are you hungry?'

I realised then what the faint feeling in the pit of my stomach was. I couldn't remember when I'd last had a meal. 'Very,' I said.

She smiled in her efficient, impersonal way. 'Just a minute, nurse,' I said as she was going out. 'I'm still at Gatow, aren't I?' She nodded. 'Will you get a message to someone for me? It's for Mrs Carter. She works in the Malcolm Club. I want her to come and see me – right away. It's urgent, tell her.'

'Mrs Carter. Is she the wife of your friend?' She nodded. 'I'll see she gets the message.'

She went out, closing the door, and I lay there staring at the light which hurt my eyes, listening to the planes coming in and taking off, and going over and over in my mind what I would say to Diana when she came. There must be no mistake this time. I had to convince her. She was my one hope. If they flew me out in the morning I'd be able to do nothing more for Tubby. And then I began to think about Saeton. I was angry then and I wished to God I had never met the man.

The nurse wasn't away long and when she returned she had a tray full of dishes. 'I brought you extra big helpings of everything,' she said. 'They told me you probably hadn't had a proper meal for some time.'

'What about Mrs Carter?' I asked. 'Is she coming?'

'I haven't been able to get your message to her yet.'

'You must,' I said desperately. 'Please, sister. It's urgent.'

'All right. Don't you fuss now. I'll see she gets your message. Now you eat that.'

I thanked her for the food and she left me. For a time I could think of nothing but the joy of eating again. I ate until I was full and then I lay back replete and the thought of Tubby was nagging at my mind again. Perhaps if I put it all down on paper . . . The thought excited me. That was the answer. If they read it as a straightforward report . . . I would address it to Squadron Leader Pierce. He had a logical, reasonable mind. They couldn't ignore it if it was sent to them in the form of a factual report. I lay there planning how I'd write it until the nurse returned.

'You must have been hungry,' she said as she saw the empty plates. 'You look better, too. The M.O. will be round later. I don't think you need be afraid he'll stop you from going out on the P 19 in the morning.'

'What about Mrs Carter? Did you get my message to her?' I asked.

'Yes. I went all the way down to the Malcolm Club myself. I'm sorry, Mr Fraser, but she won't see you.'

'Didn't you tell her it was urgent?' The sense of being boxed in with an invisible wall of disbelief was back with me again.

'Yes, I told her that. I even told her it might affect your recovery.'

'What did she say?'

'She said there was no point in her seeing you.'

I lay back and closed my eyes, feeling suddenly exhausted. What was the good of going on fighting? Then I remembered the report I was going to write. 'Can I have a pencil and some paper, please?'

She smiled. 'You want to write to your girl-friend?'

'Yes. Yes, that's it.' I nodded. 'Can I have them quickly, please. It's urgent. I must write now.'

She laughed. I remember it was a pleasant laugh. 'Everything is always urgent with you, isn't it?'

'I'd like a pen if possible,' I added. It would be better if it was written in ink. Somehow it seemed to make it more formal, more definite than if I scribbled it in pencil. 'Where are my clothes? There's a pen in my flying suit.'

'They're in the cupboard just outside. I'll get it for you. I haven't any note-paper, I'm afraid. Will typing paper do?'

'Yes, anything. Only hurry, please. I've got a lot to write and I want to get it finished before the M.O. comes round.'

But the M.O. didn't come round. Propped up in bed I set it all down right from the time of my arrival at Membury. I had no reason to hide anything now and my pen fairly flew over the paper. And when I was in the middle of it the door opened and Saeton walked in. He was dressed in his flying kit. 'Feeling better?' he asked as he crossed the room.

'I thought you were flying tests,' I said.

'So I am. But they can't spare tankers off the fuel run. The boffins are flying routine flights with me.'

It was odd how matter-of-fact our conversation was and Saeton kept it that way. He came over and sat down on my bed. 'Writing a report?'

'Yes.'

He nodded. 'I guessed you'd do that. It won't help you, you know, Neil – unless Tubby gets back to corroborate your statement.' He glanced at his watch. 'I've only got about five minutes so I'll say what I've got to say right away.' He hesitated as though marshalling his thoughts. 'You've put a lot of money and work into the company. I wouldn't want you to think I'm not grateful and I wouldn't want you to lose by it.' I think he meant that. 'You've seen Pierce?'

'Yes,' I said.

'And you've guessed that it was I who put them on to you?'

I nodded.

'Well, you didn't give me much alternative, did you? I was convinced Tubby was dead and you made it quite clear that if you didn't find him you'd give yourself up to the police. I couldn't risk that. I had to discredit you in advance.' He took a packet of cigarettes out of his pocket and tossed me one. His eyes were watching my face as he lit it for me. 'I'm very near to success now, Neil. I'm so near success that the authorities would be most unwilling to believe any report that you made. The Rauch Motoren have got the Americans behind them. If your report were accepted, it would mean a trial and the whole thing would become public. In those circumstances the Americans would bring pressure to bear on our people and the engines might have to be handed back to the Rauch Motoren. At best the design would become generally available for any company in any country. You see what I'm driving at?'

'You want me to keep my mouth shut?'

'Exactly. I want you to admit that the Russian report is correct.' I started to say something, but he held up his hand. 'I know it's tough on you. You'll go to jail for this Callahan business. But as an airlift pilot I don't imagine you'll get more than a year, perhaps less. After all, you've got a fine record. As for the fact that you came out of the crash alive, you could say it was Tubby, not you, who was scared of jumping.'

'Aren't you forgetting one thing?' I said.

'What's that?'

'That Tubby is alive.'

'I hadn't forgotten that.' He leaned closer to me, his eyes still on my face. 'I can cope with your evidence or Tubby's evidence, but not the two of you together.'

'What do you mean?'

'If you do as I want you to, it doesn't matter to me if Tubby does get out alive. A fantastic story told by a man who has been badly injured wouldn't carry much weight. Now as regards compensation for yourself. I'm prepared to offer you £10,000 and of course your position as a director of the firm would stand. And don't think I won't have the money to pay you. I'll have all the money I want in a few days' time.'

'And you'll leave Tubby to rot in that farmhouse?'

He shrugged his shoulders. 'I can't do anything about getting him out, if that's what you mean. If you admit the Russian report to be true, then I must accept it that he's dead.'

'And if I send in this report?' I asked.

He glanced at his watch and then got to his feet. 'Time I was going.' He paused, looking down at me. 'If you send in that report, nothing will come of it. That I can assure you. Without Tubby's corroborative evidence it will be disregarded. And I'll see to it that there is no corroborative evidence.'

I stared at him. His tone was so easy and natural it was difficult to believe that there was any sort of a threat behind his words. 'What do you mean by that?' I asked him.

'Think it out for yourself, Neil. But remember this. I haven't come all this way with those engines to be beaten now.'

'And either way Tubby doesn't get brought back for hospital treatment?'

He nodded. 'Either way Tubby remains where he is.'

'By God, you're a callous bastard,' I said. 'I thought he was the only man you were ever fond of?'

That touched him on the raw and his face darkened with sudden passion. 'Do you think I like the thought of him out there in the Russian Zone? But I can't help it. This thing is a lot bigger than the comfort of one man. I think I told you once that if one man stood between me and getting those engines into the air, I'd brush him aside. Well, that still holds good. As far as I'm concerned, Tubby is dead.' He glanced at his watch again. 'Well, think it over, Neil.' His tone was once more even and friendly. 'Either way you won't help Tubby, so you might just as well tear up that report.' He hesitated and then he said gently, 'We've come a long way together in a short time, Neil. I'd like to know that we were going on together. You've done all you could to help when the going was tough. Don't shut yourself out from the thing just as it's starting to go well. I'd like us to continue the partnership.' He nodded cheerily and opened the door. A moment later it had closed on his thick, burly figure and I was alone again.

I lay there for a moment going over in my mind that incredible conversation, appalled at Saeton's complete lack of any moral sense. This was the third time in our short acquaintance that he had forced a desperate choice on me. But this time it never entered my head to agree to his terms. I didn't even consider them. I was thinking only of Tubby. Somehow I had got to get him out.

I don't know quite when I reached the decision to get out of the sick bay. It just seemed to come as a logical answer to my problem. So long as I remained there, I should be taken out on the P 19 flight in the morning and then there would be no chance of doing anything for Tubby. On the other hand, if I were clear of Gatow, free of the whole organisation, then there might still be a chance.

As soon as I had reached that decision I set to work again on the report. By ten-fifteen it was done. After that I lay back, shielding my eyes from the light, waiting. Shortly before eleven the nurse came in. 'Lights not out yet?' She patted the pillows into place. 'You're looking tired now. My! What a lot you have written to your girl-friend.'

'It isn't to my girl-friend,' I said rather sharply. 'Where's the M.O.?'

'He's not coming to see you tonight. But don't worry. He'll be here first thing in the morning.'

The morning was no good. This must be read tonight by somebody in authority. 'Do you know Squadron Leader Pierce?' I asked.

'Of course.'

'Will you do something for me? Will you get this to him tonight?' I folded the numbered sheets across and handed them to her. 'Will you see that he gets it personally?'

'And I suppose it's urgent?' She smiled indulgently as she took the sheets from me. 'All right. I'll see he gets it if you promise to be a good boy and go to sleep.'

'I'll sleep if I know that will reach Pierce tonight. Will you promise that, sister? When he's read it, he'll understand the urgency.'

She nodded seriously, humouring me with an imitation of my own mood. 'Now, you go to sleep. Good-night.'

The room was suddenly in darkness as she

switched out the light. I had to suppress an urge to leap out of bed and go with her to the mess. But it wouldn't help. She'd only think I was mad and she'd call the M.O. and between them they'd drug me into a coma until I was on that damned plane and out of Berlin. The door closed with a decisive click and I lay there suddenly aware that I was alone again and all that stood between Tubby and complete disbelief of his need for help were a few flimsy sheets of paper in the hands of a nurse who thought I was slightly nuts.

I waited for about half an hour and then I slipped out of bed and groped my way to the door. A blast of cold air swept past me as I opened it. A blue-painted bulb showed me the top of some stairs and a corridor. The concrete flooring was bitterly cold against the soles of my feet.

I found the cupboard. My clothes were still there and I bundled them over my arm and slipped back into the room. It took me some time to dress in the dark, fumbling awkwardly with the laces of my cold, wet shoes, tugging at the zip of my flying suit. Finally I struggled into the heavy German greatcoat and jammed the forage cap over the bandages that circled my head.

Thinking back on it now I suppose I was still a little dazed with the exhaustion of the last few days, for I had no plan and as far as I can remember my mind made no effort to grapple with the problem of what I intended to do. I just knew I had to get out of the clutches of the Gatow authorities before they flew me out and, like an automaton who can only manage one idea at a time, I worked towards that end without a thought to the future.

As soon as I was dressed I felt my way to the door and opened it. The single blue-painted light bulb threw a weird light on to the empty corridor and the deserted stair-head. There was no sound except the intermittent murmur of the planes. I closed the door and went boldly down the stairs. There were two flights, each with its blue light, and then I was in the entrance hall. The light was bright here and a man's figure lounged by the open doorway where a car was drawn up. I hesitated. But there was no point in skulking in the shadows. I crossed the hall and went quickly out through the door to the accompaniment of a murmured '*Gute Nacht*' from the German driver who stood there.

I replied '*Gute Nacht*', my heart hammering against my ribs. But he made no move to stop me and in a moment the night had swallowed me with its blackness and its murmuring of the wind in the firs. I kept to the road, walking quickly, the sound of the planes on the airfield over my left shoulder, and in a few minutes I came out on to the road which ran from the entrance gates down past the mess to the terminal building. I recognised it at once in the lights of a Volkswagen saloon that went careering past me. I waited until its lights had completely disappeared and then I crossed the road and slipped into the sheltering anonymity of the fir woods.

I had no difficulty getting out of Gatow unobserved. I simply pressed on through the woods, keeping the sound of the airfield at my back. I had occasional glimpses of the lights of buildings and the swift rush of cars' headlights. The rest was utter blackness with the branches clutching at my bandaged head and roots tripping at my feet. I met no one and in a comparatively short time I was brought up by a wire boundary fence. After that I was in the open with the lights of a lorry showing me the Kladowerdamm and the way to Berlin.

There was some advantage in wearing Hans's discarded greatcoat and cap, for I was able to stop the first lorry that came along. The truck was a Bedford, one of a continuous line that moved through the night from the FASO apron to Berlin. I suppose the driver took me for one of the German labour teams slogging my way home. I climbed in and lay back on piled-up bags of flour that tickled my nostrils with their fine dust as we clattered over the pot-holed road.

We went into Berlin by way of the An Der Heer Strasse with its glimpse of Havel Lake where the Sunderlands had landed through the summer. There were lights along the An Der Heer Strasse, for the power, like that of Gatow itself, came from the Russian Zone. But darkness closed in with the trees of the Grunewald and the broad, straight line of the Kaiserdamm was like a dark cleft in the waste of ruins dimly seen from the swaying back of the lorry.

At length the truck slowed and the driver shouted to me, '*Wo wollen Sie hin?*'

'Anywhere in the centre of Berlin will do,' I answered in German.

'I drop you at the Gedachtniskirche.'

The Gedachtniskirche I knew – the Kaiser Wilhelm memorial church, one of the most conspicuous buildings in Berlin. It had been pointed out to me more than once during operational briefings. '*Danke schön*,' I said.

A few minutes later the lorry stopped again. Leaning out I saw a gigantic, ruined tower rearing above us into the darkness. A train hooted eerily and clattered by, wheels rattling hollow on the rails of a viaduct. I climbed over the tail-board and dropped to the ground. '*Danke schön*,' I called to the driver. '*Gute Nacht*.'

'*Gute Nacht*.' His voice was almost drowned in the roar of the engine as the heavily-laden lorry rolled on with its load of flour. I watched it disappear round the bend of the platz and then I was alone in the darkness with the monstrous hulk of the Gedachtniskirche above me, its colossal tower so battered by bombs that it looked as though it must topple into the street.

I turned and walked slowly up the Kurfurstendamm. This had been the Piccadilly of Berlin. Now it was a broken, ruined thoroughfare, the shops ground-floor affairs of wood and plaster board whose flimsy construction seemed constantly threatened by the rubble of the upper stories. There was no lighting in the Kurfurstendamm; all allied Berlin was under drastic power-cut now that fuel had to be flown in. But it was possible to see as though the thousands who huddled behind the broken façades of the buildings emanated a sort of radiance.

It was past midnight now, but despite the cold there were still prostitutes on the sidewalks, wandering up and down past the deserted street cafés. There were cars, too – black-marketeers' cars and taxis with American Negroes trading currency. Prowlers moved in the shadows, pimps and currency dealers, men who brushed by with a muttered, '*Fünf Ost für eine West.*' Bundles of rags lay huddled in doorways or dragged slowly along with a clop of wooden shoes as they searched the dustbins in the rich heart of Berlin.

I drifted up the Kurfurstendamm, only half conscious of the dim, shadowy life around me, my mind suddenly face-to-face with the problem of what I was going to do now. Until that moment my only thought had been to escape from the organised world that centred around the airlift at Gatow and so avoid being flown out on the P 19 passenger service in the morning. But now, in the heart of occupied Berlin, dressed half as a British civilian flier and half as a German labourer with no German money and no one I knew, I felt suddenly lost and slightly foolish.

But I wasn't cold any more and I had food inside me. My head was painful, but my mind was clear as I grappled with the problem. A dim figure slid past me with its muttered, '*Ich tausche Ost gegen West.*' I stopped him. 'Do you exchange English pounds?' I asked him in German.

'*Englische Pfunde?*'

'*Ja.*'

'You want Deutschmark or Bafs?'

'West Deutschmark,' I answered. 'What is the rate of exchange?'

'I give you thirty-two Deutschmark for one pound sterling.' Gold teeth glittered with a drool of saliva as the lights of a car slid past. The man had a wide-brimmed black hat and his face was swarthy with greasy sideboards. The long semitic nose was thrust inquisitively into my face. A Greek or perhaps a Pole – certainly not a German.

I changed ten pounds with this shadow of the Berlin underworld and with the Deutschmark forming a wad in the pocket of my flying suit I felt that the first hurdle was past. But what next? I stood on a corner by one of those circular poster hoardings that look like overgrown pillar boxes and wondered how I could get Tubby out of the Russian Zone. If I could get Tubby out, then there'd be no doubt about my story.

But in all Berlin I had no friend to help me.

CHAPTER NINE

To have no friends, no sense of security, in a city occupied by one's own people is not pleasant. There was no one I could turn to. I thought of Diana's brother – Harry Culyer. Maybe he was still in Berlin. But would he believe me when my own people didn't? And to contact any of the Allied headquarters and clubs would only be putting me back into the situation from which I had just been at such pains to escape.

I don't know what made me think of it. Maybe it was the prostitute who murmured in English, 'Hallo, darling,' from the shadowy gloom of the sidewalk. The soft warmth of her voice came like the nuzzling of a friendly bitch. And when I didn't turn away the dim shadow of her slunk to my side. 'You are American?' she asked. The power of the dollar was strong on the Kurfurstendamm.

'No. English,' I answered.

I saw her eyes, soft and hungry in the darkness, looking me over and noting my clothes. Probably she thought I was a deserter. Deserters would be bound to make for the Kurfurstendamm. But she asked no questions. All she said was, 'You come with me, honey? I have a room only two blocks away and it is comfortable.'

I didn't answer because her German accent had started a train of thought in my mind.

'Please come.' Her voice was suddenly desperate. 'I have been here all evening and I am hungry. You take me to a café. I know somewhere is cheap, very cheap.' Her hand reached out and slid along my arm. 'Please, honey. I sing for you, too, perhaps. I was in opera once. I only do this when my baby and I are hungry and nobody will pay to hear me sing. My name is Helga. You like me? I give you love and music – you forget everything. Come on, honey.' She dragged at my arm. 'Please, honey.'

'Where is the Fassenenstrasse?' I asked.

'It is just near here. You wish to go? I take you if you wish.' The voice was harder now, desperately urgent. 'Please. It is cold standing here. Please, honey.'

'All right,' I said. 'Take me there.'

'Okay.'

We moved off together up the wide cleft of the Kurfurstendamm, her hand clutching my arm. She was tall and her hip was level with mine, pressing against it. She hummed a little aria, something from Verdi. 'Where is this place you wish to go, honey?' she said, stopping at a corner. 'Here is the Fassenenstrasse. It runs right across the Kurfurstendamm. Which part do you wish?'

'I want Number 52,' I said. 'It's near the Savoy Hotel.'

'*Ach. So! Das Savoy.* It is this way.'

She took me down a tram-lined street and underneath the iron girders of a railway bridge, and then we passed the Hotel Savoy and were at Number 52. She stared at the blank face of the closed door. 'Why you bring me here?' she asked. 'This is not a club. We cannot eat here. Why you bring me, eh?'

'I have a friend here,' I said and tugged at the old-fashioned bell-pull. Then I pulled out my Deutschmark and gave her twenty. She stared at them. 'Go and get something to eat,' I said. 'And thank you for showing me the way.'

Her eyes looked up into my face unbelievingly. 'You do not want me?' She evidently saw that I didn't for she made no protest. Instead she reached up and kissed me. '*Danke schön.*' She turned away quickly and as the sound of her high heels faded away into the darkness I wondered whether perhaps she really was an opera singer with a baby and no job.

There was the rattle of a chain from the other side of the heavy door and then it opened, just a crack, and a woman's voice, old and hoarse and rather frightened, asked me what I wanted.

'I am a friend of Fräulein Langen,' I answered in German. 'I wish to see her please.'

'I do not know any Fräulein Langen.'

The door was closing and I put my foot against it.

'Fräulein Meyer, then.' And I added quickly, 'I have come all the way from England to see her.'

'*Aus England?*' There was a moment's pause. 'You are English?' The old woman spoke the words slowly as though she had learned the language at school.

'Yes,' I said. 'I am an English flier. Neil Fraser, tell her.'

The door opened to the full extent of the securing chain. Beady eyes stared at me through the crack. 'You do not look to be very English,' she said suspiciously. 'Where in England do you meet Fräulein Meyer?'

'At Membury,' I answered. 'I have had an accident. That's why I'm dressed like this.'

'Membury! So! It is very late, but come in. *Kommen Sie herein.*' The door opened. She closed it hastily behind me and in the darkness I heard the rattle of bolts and chain. 'We must be very careful. The Russians, you know. It is terrible. They come and take people away.' An electric torch gleamed faintly. 'Poor Fräulein Meyer. So pretty, so clever! And all this trouble over her papers.' I followed the old woman's shapeless figure up the stairs. The sound of our footsteps on the bare boards was very loud in the stillness of the house. 'I do not like to think what the Russians do to her if the English send her to the East Sector police. The Russians are brutes – *Schweinehunde*. They rape everyone.' A door opened as the torch finally gave out. A match spurted and rose in a steady flame as a candle was lit.

'*Was ist los, Anna?*' It was Else. Though I couldn't see her I recognised her voice.

'*Ein Mann aus England. Herr Fraser. Er sagt er kennt Sie von Membury her.*'

'Herr Fraser?' Else's tone was suspicious. The flame of the candle was lifted to my face. Through it I saw that she was peering at me with wide, frightened eyes, her dressing-gown clutched tightly round her. 'Neil! It is you?' She began to laugh then. I think it was relief at finding it really was me. 'You look so funny. Why are you in Berlin? And why do you dress yourself up in the uniform of the Wehrmacht?'

'It's a long story,' I said.

She smiled. 'Another long story? That is what you say before. Remember?'

'May I come in? I want to talk to you.'

'Yes, of course. I have only a bedroom now, but—' She glanced uncertainly at the old woman. 'So many peoples in Berlin have no homes,' she murmured. Then she glanced up at my face again and saw the bandages. 'You have hurt yourself again also.'

'I had an accident,' I said.

'Come in then,' she said and pushed open the door of her room. 'Anna. Have we any of that coffee left?'

'*Ja*, but for two cups only,' the old woman answered.

'It is so difficult now in Berlin. This blockade – it is worse than—' She shrugged her shoulders. 'Let us have the coffee, Anna. When it is finish, it is finish.'

'*Schön*.' The old woman tapped her torch on the banisters and it flickered into doubtful life. As she hobbled off down the stairs Else led me into her room and shut the door. It was a big room, furnished as part bedroom and part sitting room, with a couch under the window, a dressing-table covered with photographs and a big double bed in the corner. It had the fierce, penetrating cold of a room that has had no heat in it for a long time. 'Is your head all right?' she asked. 'Can I do anything for it?'

'No, it's all right,' I said. 'They fixed it for me at Gatow.'

'Gatow! When do you arrive at Gatow?'

'This morning.'

'So! It is you I see standing outside the Malcolm Club.'

I stared at her, remembering the girl checker with her face covered in coal dust. 'Are you working with the German Labour Organisation?' I asked.

'*Ja*.' She laughed. 'It is what you peoples call a very small world, eh?'

'But why?' I asked.

She shrugged her shoulders. 'I must work. Also I wish to be at Gatow to see if Mr Saeton get on to the airlift. It is most important that I find this thing out.'

'Well, he is. I've seen him today.'

She nodded. 'He make the first flight two days ago. And he has my father's engines. I know them by the sound. Tell me something, please. How does he manage to fly again so quickly? His own plane is crashed. It was finished. This cannot be the same airplane.'

'It isn't,' I said.

'But how does he get another? He have no money. You tell me so yourself. Did you get it for him?'

'Yes,' I said. She stared at me angrily and I added, 'Do you know what the word blackmail means?'

She nodded.

'Well, he blackmailed me into getting him another plane. I stole it off the airlift for him.'

'You stole it? I do not understand.'

I told her briefly what had happened then and when I had finished she stood there staring down at the flame of the candle. 'He is mad, that one,' she breathed. She turned to look at me and the corners of her mouth turned up momentarily in a smile. 'I think perhaps you are a little mad also.'

'Perhaps I was,' I said. 'You've no idea how glad I was to find that Tubby was alive.'

She nodded slowly.

'The trouble is Saeton won't do anything to get him out. He can't think of anything but the engines.'

She swung round on me. 'He is crazy. He is crazy, I tell you. It is as though – as though when he steal my father's work he start somethings and now he cannot stop.'

Her words were an echo of my own thoughts. My mind was on Tubby and I was wondering what Saeton would do when he discovered I had made a written report. He would brazen it out, say that I was suffering from delusions as a result of the crash, but all the time he would be thinking of Tubby out there in that farmhouse, the one man who by his mere existence threatened the whole future of what he was striving for. And as I thought about this, Saeton loomed in my mind as a sort of monster – a man who, as Else said, had started something that he could not stop. 'I must get Tubby out,' I said.

'Is that why you come to see me?'

I nodded, dimly aware that she wanted some other explanation of my visit. But I was too tired to pretend. Everything I had done since waking up in Gatow sick bay had been done because of Tubby. I was responsible for what had happened. I had to get him out. 'You've got to help me,' I said.

'Why should I?' Her voice was harder now. 'His wife work at the Malcolm Club. Let her help him.'

'But she thinks he's dead. I told you that.'

'If his wife think he is dead, why should not I?'

I stepped forward and caught her by the shoulders. 'You've got to help me, Else.'

'Why?' She was staring up at me, her eyes wide, almost calculating.

Why? I dropped my hands to my side and turned away. Why should this German girl I had met two or three times help me? 'I don't know why,' I said.

There was a knock at the door and the old woman came in with the coffee on a tray and a small oil lamp. '*Hier ist Ihr Kaffe, Fräulein Else*.'

'Do you keep some for yourself, Anna?' Else asked.

The old woman moved her head from side to side awkwardly. 'Just a little. Just for one cup.' Her beady eyes fastened on me. '*Soll ich aufbleiben um den Herrn hinauszulassen?*' Else spoke quickly to her in German and the old woman laughed. 'So!' She stared at me as though I were some strange animal. 'I do not meet one like that.' And still laughing to herself she sidled out and closed the door.

'What was all that about?' I asked.

Else looked across at me. 'She is worried for me, that is all. I tell her you are quite safe, but—' She turned away to hide her smile.

Her smile made me angry. 'Why didn't you tell her what happened when you took me to listen to the frogs?' I demanded.

'If I tell her that,' she said over her shoulder as she poured out the coffee, 'then she will want to see you go. And you must sleep. You look tired. I also am tired. I have to be up at six to catch the lorry to Gatow.'

I brushed my hand across my face. I was tired. 'Can you really put me up for the night?'

'Of course. If you do not mind the couch there. It is hard, but it is all right. I have to sleep there myself several times. Now, drink this please while it is hot.'

'But—' I stared at her. 'You mean sleep here – in this room?'

She looked up at me quickly. 'Have you some place in Berlin you can go then?'

'No,' I said. 'No, I've no place I can go now.'

'Very well then. It is settled. You sleep on the couch and I go back to my bed.' She went over to the bed and ripped off two of the blankets. 'There. We share the bedclothes. All right?' She put them on the couch. 'I am sorry I am not able to give you a room for yourself. Once we have the whole floor – seven rooms with bathroom, kitchen, everything. But part of the house is destroyed and there are many families homeless. So now, all I have is this one room.' She shrugged her shoulders. 'It is all right. But I do not like to share my kitchen with other peoples. Please, you will excuse me, but I am cold.' She slipped into the bed and reached for her coffee cup. 'Do you have a cigarette?'

I felt in my pocket. The nurse had given me a packet. 'Yes, here we are.' She took one and I lit it for her. Her eyes watched me over the flame and then she blew out a long streamer of smoke. 'Oh, it is so good to have a cigarette. I do not have one since I leave England.'

'Don't you get any at Gatow?' I asked.

'No. They do not give us any. I do not think there are very many for your own people.'

'Is the work hard?'

'No. Just checking the manifest of the cargo, so that nothing is missing. But it is a long time I am there and it is very cold on the airfield.'

I had sat down on the edge of the bed to drink my coffee. Perhaps it was the closeness – maybe it was just the strangeness of the circumstances, the two of us sharing that one room. At any rate that was the end of our small talk. There seemed nothing really to say and I sat there staring at her and absorbing the warmth of the coffee. Tired though I was I found the blood hammering in my veins. I suddenly found I wanted her. I wanted her more than I'd wanted anything in my life before. For the moment it seemed as though her competence and self-sufficiency were swept aside. She was just a rather pathetic, very attractive girl, sitting up in a double bed – and I wished to God she was sitting there waiting for me. But somehow I could do nothing about it. I didn't want to do anything to break the mood of that moment. If I had touched her I think she would have responded. But if that had happened then something would have gone that I desperately wanted. Instead of touching her, I said, 'Else, you've got to help me.'

She frowned and pulled her dressing-gown closer round her. 'To find your friend Carter?' she asked with a queer lift of the eyebrows that gave her a puzzled look.

I nodded. 'I've got to get him out of the Russian Zone.'

'It means so much to you?' The softness disappeared from her face. 'What happens if we do not get your friend out?'

'He may die,' I said.

'And if he die, what happens then?'

'There'll be no evidence to support my report of what happened.'

'And Saeton will go on flying my father's engines?'

'Yes. He'll get away with the whole thing.'

She nodded as though that were the answer she had expected. 'All right. I will do what I can.'

I started to thank her, but she cut me short. 'I do not do this thing for you, Neil. I do it because I wish to destroy Saeton.' Her hands were fastened tightly on the bedclothes, the cigarette burning unheeded in the saucer as she stared past me to the lamp. 'He has taken everything that is left of my father – the work we do together. I hate him. I hate him, I tell you.' She spat the words out through clenched teeth in the intensity of her feeling. 'He has no soul. He is a monster. That night you come to Membury, I offer him – I offer him myself. I know he want me. I do not love him. But I think I will barter my body for the recognition I want of my father's work. Do you know what he do? He laugh in my face.' She relaxed slowly and picked up her cigarette. 'Then you come into the hangar. After that I telephone to Reinbaum to go ahead and smash his company.' She gave a bitter little laugh. 'But you save it for him. Then he crash and I think that is the end of him. But you save him again.' She gave me a wry little smile. 'And now you wish me to help you. That is very funny.' She sat for a moment, quite still. Then with a quick movement of her fingers she stubbed out the cigarette. 'Okay, Neil. I do what I can. Now we must get some sleep. If I find somebody to take us into the Russian Zone it will be at night because it will be for the black market – perhaps tomorrow night.'

'You think you can find somebody?' I asked.

She nodded. '*Ja.* I think so. I have many friends among the drivers at Gatow. I will find someone who goes near Hollmind. There are many trucks going from the Western sectors into the Russian Zone. The Russians do not mind because they get things they want that way. I shall find someone.'

'I can't thank you enough,' I began, but she stopped me. 'You do not have to thank me. I do not do this for you. Goodnight.'

She snuggled down into the bedclothes. I had got to my feet and for a moment I stood there, hesitating, staring down at her. It seemed to me there were two Elses – the girl who excited me and was sweet and gentle, and the German who was revengeful and who would stop at nothing to do what she thought was right for her country and her father. 'Goodnight.' I turned heavily away and blew the lamp out.

In the heavy curtained darkness of the room I undressed to my underclothes and curled myself up on the couch under the blankets. It was bitterly cold in that room. It ate right into my bones. But then I thought of Tubby alone out there in that German farm-house, desperately hurt, and the cold didn't seem so bad. I prayed that Else would find some means of getting me there so that I could bring him back, so that I could prove that what I had said was true.

Neither the cold nor the constant racket of the airlift overhead kept me awake for long. I slept and in a moment it seemed the lamp was lit again and the old woman was in the room, talking to Else. I turned over and opened my eyes. Else was already up, brushing her hair. The old woman was standing by the door, a spluttering candle in her hand. 'I hope you are not too cold, Herr Fraser?' she said in German. It may have been my fancy but I thought her gnarled features had an expression of contempt as she said something very rapidly to Else.

'What did she say?' I asked as the bundle of old clothes disappeared through the door.

Else was giggling to herself. 'Nothing,' she said.

'She made some crack,' I said.

'You really wish to know?' She was smiling. 'She say you are not much like our boys, that if you are typical English then she do not understand how you win the war. Did you sleep well?'

'I slept all right,' I said curtly, wondering why the hell I hadn't shared Else's bed since that was apparently what had been expected of me.

'You were not cold?'

'It didn't stop me sleeping.'

'Now you are sulking. You do not want to pay any attention to Anna. She is old-fashioned, that is all. Now, please will you turn the other way. I have to wash.'

I turned over and faced the heavy curtains that covered the window. 'What time is it?' I asked.

'A quarter past five.'

'Good God!' I lay there feeling the cold numbing my body, thinking how tough Else must be. The room was icy and I could hear her splashing about with the water. 'Is that hot water?' I asked, thinking I would feel a lot better if I could have a shave.

'Of course not. We cannot heat water. Our fuel is for cooking only. If you stay here long you will get used to it.'

'Stay here long?' The problem of the future suddenly faced me. I was a fugitive in Berlin. I could not go back to my own people, not until Tubby was out of the Russian Zone. 'You must find some transport going to Hollmind tonight,' I said urgently. 'If I don't get him out soon he may—' Without thinking I had turned towards her and then the future and Tubby were driven out of my mind by the sight of Else leaning over the basin washing herself. She was naked to the waist, and her firm breasts looked big and warm in the soft lamplight.

She turned her head, conscious of my stillness, and for a moment her hands were still, holding the flannel, as she met my gaze. Water ran from her neck down her breasts and poured from her nipples into the basin. 'I thought I told you to turn the other way?' She laughed. It was an unselfconscious laugh. 'Do not stare at me as though you were hungry. Have you never seen a girl washing herself before?' She dipped the flannel into the water and began washing the soap from her face. It might have been the most natural thing in the world for her to have a man in her room watching her as she washed.

'Has this happened before?' I asked thickly.

'What?' Her words were half-obscured by the flannel.

'I didn't mean that,' I said quickly and turned to face the curtains again, the sight of her still a vivid picture on the retina of my brain.

She came and stood over me. I didn't hear her come across the room, for her feet were bare. I just sensed her standing there, looking down at me. Her fingers touched my hair.

'Sometimes I think you are very young, Neil. You do not know much about life. Or perhaps it is because we live among the ruins and when you do that you have not many conventions left. Life is very primitive in Berlin – like when we are in a yacht or up in the mountains.' She turned away with a little sigh. 'You would have liked it here in Germany before the war.'

She was dressed by the time the old woman brought breakfast up. 'It is not much,' Else said, as she handed me a plate of dark bread with a small piece of butter. 'But you will become accustomed to that if you stay here long.'

I hardly recognised her as the same person. She wore no make-up and she was padded out underneath a dirty raincoat so that she had no shape. Only her hair looked the same, golden silk in the soft glow of the lamp.

At ten to six she pulled on an old brown beret. 'Now I must go to catch the truck in the Kurfurstendamm. I think it is best if you do not go out. You have no papers and your shoes do not go with your Wehrmacht coat. Our police are very suspicious.' I held the door open for her, huddled against the cold in my borrowed greatcoat. 'Do not worry. I will find some way to get your friend out.'

I touched her hand. It was very cold. 'Thank you,' I said. 'You've been very kind and understanding.'

'I am not being kind,' she said almost sharply. 'I am doing this for myself. I would like to say differently, but—' She stared at me, her eyes very wide and troubled-looking. 'But it is the truth.' Her hand tightened on mine. 'One thing I wish you to know, however, I am glad it is something you want also. I am glad we both want this.' She said it quite fiercely as though she were angry with herself for what had gone before. Then she reached up and kissed me, pressing her lips to mine as though this alliance were something she had wanted badly. 'Do not worry. I fix something.'

'For tonight?' I asked.

'I hope so.'

She smiled and slipped out through the door. 'Do not go out – please.' Her footsteps sounded, quick and light on the stairs, disappearing into the dark vault of the house. I heard the front door open and close. Then there was silence and I shut the door and went back into the lamplit room that was so full of the girl who had just left me.

For some time I wandered round it, conscious of the alien heaviness of the furniture, of the photographs and particularly of her things that lay strewn about – clothes, books, sewing, an empty silver cigarette box, hair brushes, washing things, old papers, the tumbled bedclothes, her nightdress and the slippers she'd worn, all the litter of things that were Else when she herself was not there.

It was the photographs that I returned to. They were mostly of a big man with a short pointed beard and a high, domed forehead curving back to a mane of white hair. It was her father and the quiet, serious features with the slight droop at the corners of the mouth, the rather blunt nose and the lines of thought that furrowed the broad forehead reminded me of Else when she was puzzled by something. There was the suggestion of a twinkle in the lines at the corners of the eyes. But the face had none of Else's fierceness and passion. That she had got from her mother. Professor Meyer was a deeper, more thoughtful person than his daughter. This was particularly noticeable in the photographs of the two of them together. These were holiday snaps taken whilst climbing or on skis. But though the photographs showed her faults more clearly, I was glad of the opportunity to study her father. It explained so much of her that had puzzled me and I could understand more clearly her passionate loyalty to the work that she and this old man who was now dead had done together.

Very conscious of Else's presence in that room I returned to the couch and for a long time lay huddled under the blankets thinking about her and the peculiar relationship that was developing between the two of us. I tried to analyse my feelings, but I couldn't and in the end I went to sleep.

I didn't get up until past midday. The sky was overcast, the battered buildings opposite black in the bitter cold. Overhead the airlift planes droned steadily, but I could not see them. The old woman brought me some food – bread and some soup that was chiefly potatoes. She didn't attempt to talk to me. There was a barrier between us that was something more than a question of race. I found the answer in an old photograph album tucked away in a bookshelf, a picture of a little girl and an attractive, middle-aged nurse; underneath was written in an awkward, childish hand – *Ich und Anna*.

By five o'clock the light was fading and I could no longer decipher the unaccustomed German print of the book I was reading. I began to pace the room, wondering whether Else would have found transport to take me into the Russian Zone. My mood was a queer mixture of impatience and fear. It was bitterly cold.

Just after six I heard the sound of footsteps on the stairs. I checked in my pacing and listened. This wasn't the clumsy sound of wooden clogs on bare boards. It was a man's tread and he wore shoes. He didn't belong to the building.

The footsteps stopped on the landing outside and the old woman's clogs shuffled to the bedroom door. 'I do not know why she is not back already,' she said in German. 'But you can wait for her in her room.'

'Will she be long?' the man asked. His German was too lazy, too soft. In a panic I looked round for some place to conceal myself. But I was still standing in the middle of the room when the door opened.

'She always return at five. I do not know what has happened.' There was a knock at the door and the old woman opened it without waiting for permission. 'The gentleman here speaks your language. Perhaps you can talk to him while you are waiting for Fräulein Meyer.'

I had backed away towards the window. The old woman stood aside and Else's visitor came in. I saw his brown boots and the olive khaki of his trousers – an American. And then I looked at his face. 'Good God!' I exclaimed. It was Harry Culyer – Diana's brother. 'How did you know where I was?'

He stopped, staring at me. 'What makes you think I did, Fraser?'

'Didn't Diana send you?' I asked.

'Diana? No, of course not.'

'Why are you here then?'

'I might ask you the same question.' His gaze travelled quickly over the room, missing nothing and finally coming to rest on the Wehrmacht greatcoat I was wearing. 'So this is where you're hiding up. They told me at Gatow you'd disappeared from the sick bay.'

'You've been to the airport – today?'

He nodded. 'I've just come from there.'

'Did you see Diana?'

'Yes. Why?'

'She knows the truth now, doesn't she?' There was a puzzled frown on his face and I added quickly, 'She knows Tubby is alive now. She knows that, doesn't she?' My hands were sweating and I was almost trembling as I put the question.

'Alive? You know as well as I do he's dead.' He was leaning slightly forward, and his grey eyes were no longer friendly. 'So it's true what they told me about you.'

'What did they tell you?'

'Oh, just that you were a sick man. That's all.' He had thrown his hat on to the couch and he lowered his long body down beside it. 'When will the Meyer girl be back? I guess I must just have missed her at the airport.'

'I don't know,' I said. 'Did you see Pierce or the I.O.?'

'Yes, I saw them both.' He eyed me watchfully as though I was a strange dog that he was not quite sure of.

'I sent Pierce a report – a written report. Did he mention it?'

'No, he said nothing about a report.'

'Did he mention me at all?'

He lifted his eyes to my face. 'Suppose you stop

asking questions, Fraser?' His tone was abrupt, almost angry.

'But I must know,' I said. 'I must know what he said about me.'

'All right – if you want to know – he said you were – ill.' He was watching me closely as he said this, like a doctor examining a patient for reaction.

I slumped down on to the farther end of the couch. 'So he doesn't believe it even when he sees it in writing.' I felt suddenly very weary. It would be so much easier just to say no more, give myself up and go back to England to stand trial. 'I must get Tubby out,' I murmured. 'I must get him out.' I was speaking to bolster my determination, but of course he stared at me as though I was mad. 'You're waiting to see Else, are you?' I asked, and when he gave an abrupt nod, I added, 'Well, since you've nothing to do whilst you wait you may as well hear what happened that night in the corridor. I'd like to know whether you believe me.'

'Why don't you rest?' he suggested impatiently. 'You look just about all in.'

'Can I have a cigarette? I've finished all mine.'

He tossed me a packet. 'You can keep those.'

'Thanks.' I lit one. 'Just because you've been told I'm ill, it doesn't mean I can't remember what happened. The chief thing for you to know is this: Tubby is alive. And but for that bastard Saeton he'd be here in Berlin now. It's a pity your sister can't recognise the truth when she hears it.'

I had his interest then and I went straight on to tell him the whole thing.

I was just finishing when footsteps sounded on the stairs outside – Else's footsteps. She looked damnably tired as she pushed open the door. 'I've done it, Neil. We—' She stopped as she saw Culyer. 'I'm so sorry, Mr Culyer. Have you been waiting long?'

'It hasn't been long,' Culyer answered, rising to his feet. 'I've been talking to Fraser here – or rather, he's been talking to me.'

Else glanced quickly from one to the other of us. 'You know each other?'

'We met the other day – out at Gatow,' Culyer answered. 'I tried to catch you at the airport, Miss Meyer, but I guess you'd just gone.' He glanced awkwardly at me. 'Can we go somewhere and talk?' he asked her.

Else spread her hands in a quick gesture of despair. 'I am afraid this is the only room I have. You will not mind, Neil, if we talk about our own business for a moment, will you?'

She turned to Culyer. 'Have the British agreed? Shall I be permitted to go to Frankfurt?'

Culyer glanced hesitantly at me. Then he said, 'Yes, everything's fixed, Miss Meyer. As soon as your papers come through we'll fly you down to Frankfurt and then you can join Professor Hinkmann of the Rauch Motoren and get to work right away. Of course,' he added, 'you must realise Saeton is a jump or two ahead of us. His engines are flying right now.'

'Of course,' Else said. 'What about patents?'

'That is still undecided,' Culyer answered. 'We're pressing hard for refusal of patent on the grounds that it's largely your father's work. Mind you, Saeton's developed them to the flying stage, but I think our case may be strong enough for the whole thing to be left to sort itself out in open competition. Anyway, what I wanted to tell you was that the British have agreed for you to come to Frankfurt. I thought you'd want to know that right away.'

'Thank you – yes.' She hesitated and then asked, 'No questions about the papers I had in England?'

'No questions. They'll forget about that.'

Else turned and pulled off her beret. She stood for a moment staring at the large photograph of her father that stood above the huge oak tallboy. 'He would have been glad about this.' She suddenly swung round to Culyer again. 'It was Saeton who informed the British security officials about my papers, wasn't it?'

Culyer shrugged his shoulders. 'I don't think we need concern ourselves with that, Miss Meyer.'

'No, perhaps it is not important.' She turned to me. 'Saeton has requested the permission of the station commander to fly a plane to Hollmind.'

'To Hollmind?' I stared at her, hardly able to believe my ears. 'When?'

'Tonight.'

'Are you certain?' I asked urgently. 'How do you know?'

She smiled. 'I have friends at Gatow – a young officer of the R.A.S.C. tell me. Saeton is flying there to-night, just to make certain.'

For a second I was filled with relief. Saeton had realised he had been inhuman. He was going to get

Tubby out. And then Else's choice of words thrust themselves into my mind. *Just to make certain.* In an instant the monster I had built of Saeton was there again in my mind. 'Just to make certain,' I heard myself say aloud. 'My God! It can't be that. It can't be.'

'What's that you say?' Culyer asked uneasily.

But I was looking at Else, wondering whether she knew what was in my mind. 'It must be tonight,' I said.

'What must be tonight?' Culyer asked.

'Nothing,' Else said quickly. 'Please, Mr Culyer. I am very tired and I have some things to do.'

He looked uncertainly from one to the other of us and then picked up his hat. 'Okay, Miss Meyer. I'll be getting along then. As soon as the formalities are through I'll contact you.'

'Thank you.' She held the door open for him.

He hesitated on the threshold and his gaze swung back to me. He was obviously puzzled.

Else touched his arm. 'You will not say anything – about Mr Fraser. Please.'

He shrugged his shoulders. 'I guess it's none of my business anyway.'

But it was his business. He was Diana's brother. 'Will you be seeing your sister again?' I asked him.

He nodded. 'I'm going out to Gatow right now.'

'Will you give her a message? Will you tell her Tubby will be all right – that it's true what I said in that report, every word of it?'

He glanced across at Else. 'Do you know about this?'

Else nodded.

'And do you believe him? Do you believe Carter is still alive, the way he says he is?'

'Of course,' Else said.

Culyer shook his head slowly. 'I don't know what to think. But I'll give her your message, Fraser. Maybe if Saeton's flying out there—' He shrugged his shoulders. 'Goodnight, Miss Meyer. I hope we'll have this thing all tied up very shortly now. This project has great possibilities and my headquarters . . .'

He was still talking as Else lighted him to the stairs, but I wasn't listening. I was thinking of Tubby out there in that farmhouse. Saeton was flying to Hollmind. That was the thing that was still in my mind. I turned to the window. I had to get out there right away. I had to get there somehow. The door of the room closed and I swung round. Else was standing there, staring at me. 'Are you all right, Neil?' she asked.

'Yes, of course I'm all right,' I answered irritably. 'When you came in tonight – you started to say something?'

'Oh, yes. I have found a truck that is going into the Russian Zone. It is all fixed.'

'When for?' I asked. 'It must be tonight. I must get there tonight.'

She nodded. 'Yes. It is tonight.'

'Thank God!' I crossed the room and caught hold of her arms. 'How did you manage it?' I asked.

'Oh, I find out about it from one of the drivers at Gatow. We have to be at the corner of Fassenenstrasse and the Kantstrasse at ten-thirty.'

'Not before?' I thought of the short time it would take to fly. 'What time is Saeton leaving, do you know?'

She shook her head. 'That is something I cannot find out. But he will not dare to go till it is very late if he have to leave the plane on Hollmind airfield.'

That was true. 'How long will it take in this truck of yours?'

She shrugged her shoulders. 'We do not go the direct way. There are things to be delivered, you understand. Two or three hours perhaps.'

Two or three hours! I turned away. 'Couldn't the driver be persuaded to go there first?'

'I do not think so,' she replied. 'But I will talk to him. Perhaps if you have money—'

'You know I've no money,' I cut in. 'A few marks—'

'Then we will see.'

I stopped in my pacing and turned to her. 'We?' I asked. 'You don't mean you're coming into the Russian Zone?'

'But of course.'

I started to dissuade her. But she was quite determined. 'If I do not come the driver of the truck will not take you. It is a big risk for him. If we are stopped by the Red Army then there has to be some story that they can understand. It is better if you have a German girl with you.' She turned to the bed. 'Now please, I must rest. You also. I do not think you are too well.'

Not too well! That phrase kept recurring to me as I lay sleepless on the couch.

Else was asleep the instant she had climbed into her bed. But I had been resting all day. There was no sleep left in me and all the time I lay there, feeling the cold even through my clothes and listening to the sound of the airlift planes overhead, I kept on turning her words over in my mind. Was she herself uncertain of my story? Was that why she was coming – to see whether it was the truth or only the hallucinations of a sick man? I remembered how Culyer had reacted.

I must have fallen asleep in the end, for I woke in a sweat of fear that Tubby was dead and that the authorities at Gatow had been right in believing the Russian report.

And then I saw that Else was dressing and everything seemed suddenly normal and reasonable. We were going out of Berlin in a black market truck and in a few hours we should be coming back with Tubby. I was glad then that she was coming. If Tubby were dead, or if he didn't survive the journey back, then she would be witness to the fact that he had been at the farmhouse at Hollmind, that he had been alive.

We had some food and by ten-thirty we were at the corner of the Fassenenstrasse and the Kantstrasse. The truck was late and it was very cold. By eleven o'clock I was becoming desperate, convinced that something had gone wrong with her arrangements and that it would not come. Else, however, seemed quite resigned to waiting. 'It will come,' she kept saying. 'You see. It will come.'

Three-quarters of an hour late it ground to a stop beside us, one of those ugly, long-nosed German vehicles driven by a youth who was introduced to me as Kurt and whose jaw bore the purple markings of a bad burn. An older man was with him in the cab. We bundled into the back, climbing over packing cases piled to the roof to a cramped and awkward space that had been left for us. The gear cogs fought for a hold on each other, oil fumes seeped up from the floor, the packing cases jolted around us as we crawled out of Berlin.

We were nearly three hours in the back of that truck. We were cold and we both suffered from waves of nausea owing to the fumes. Periodically the truck stopped, packing cases were off-loaded and their place was taken by carcases of meat or sacks of flour. I cursed these delays, and at each stop it seemed more and more urgent that I should reach the farmhouse before Saeton.

At last all the packing cases had been off-loaded. We made one more stop, for poultry – there must have been hundreds of dead birds – and then at last through a rent in the canvas cover I saw that we had turned south. Shortly afterwards the truck stopped and I was told to get out and sit with the driver to direct him. We were then on the outskirts of Hollmind.

It was difficult to get my bearings after being cooped up in the body of the truck so long. However, I knew I had to get to the north of Hollmind and after taking several wrong turnings I at last found myself on a stretch of road that I remembered. By then the driver was getting impatient and he drove down it so fast that I nearly missed the track up to the farm and we had to back. The track was narrow and rutted and when he saw it the driver refused to take the truck up it. Else got down and did her best to persuade him, but he resolutely shook his head. 'If I go there,' he told her, 'I may get stuck. Also I do not know these people at the farm. The Red Army may be billeted there. Anything is possible. No. I wait for you here on the road. But hurry. I do not like to remain parked at the side of the road too long – it is very conspicuous.'

So Else and I went up the track alone, the ice crackling under our feet, the mud of the ruts black and hard like iron. 'How far?' she asked.

'About half a mile,' I said. My teeth were chattering and there was an icy feeling down my spine.

The lane branched and I hesitated, trying to remember which track I had come down that night that seemed so long ago.

'You have been here before, haven't you, Neil?' Else asked and there was a note of uncertainty in her voice.

'Of course,' I said and started up the left-hand fork. But it only led to a barn and we had to turn back and take the other fork. 'We must hurry,' Else whispered urgently. 'Kurt is a nervous boy. I do not wish for him to drive away and leave us.'

'Nor do I,' I said, thinking of the nightmare journey I had had into Berlin.

We were right this time and soon the shape of the farm buildings was looming up ahead of us against the stars. 'It's all right,' I said as the silhouette of the outbuildings resolved itself into familiar lines. 'This is the place.'

'So! The farm does exist. Your friend is alive.'

'Of course,' I said. 'I told you—'

'I am sorry, Neil.' Her hand touched my arm.

'You mean you weren't sure?'

'You were hurt and you look so ill. I do not know what to think. All I know is that it is urgent for you to come and that I must come with you.'

I could see the faint shape of her head. Her eyes looked very big in the darkness. I took hold of her hand. 'Come on,' I said. 'I hope to God—' I stopped then, for we had turned the corner of a barn and I saw there was a lamp on in the kitchen of the farmhouse. It was nearly two, yet the Kleffmanns hadn't gone to bed. The shadow of a man crossed the drawn curtains. I hurried across the yard and tapped on the window.

It was Kleffmann himself who answered my tap. He came to the back door and peered nervously out into the night. 'Herr Kleffmann!' I called softly. 'It's me – Fraser. Can we come in?'

'*Ja. Kommen Sie herein*. Hurry please.' As he stood back to let us through the door he turned his face towards the lamplight that came through from the kitchen. He looked startled, almost scared.

'Is he all right?' I asked.

'Your friend? Yes, he is all right. A little better, I think.'

I breathed a sigh of relief. 'We've got a truck waiting down on the road,' I said. 'This is Fräulein Meyer.'

He shook hands with Else. 'Come in. Come in, both of you.' He shut the door quickly and led us through into the kitchen. '*Mutter.* Here is Herr Fraser back again.'

Frau Kleffmann greeted me with a soft, eager smile, but her eyes strayed nervously to the stairs that led up from the kitchen. 'I do not understand,' she murmured uneasily in German. Then she turned to her husband and said, 'Why do they both come?'

I started to explain Else's presence and then I stopped. That wasn't what she had meant. Lying across the back of a chair was a heavy, fleece-lined flying jacket. Else had seen it, too. I turned to the Kleffmanns. They were standing quite still, staring towards the dark line of the stairs. From above us out of the silence of the house, came the sound of footsteps. They were coming down the stairs.

Else gripped my arm. 'What is it?' she whispered.

I couldn't answer her. My gaze was riveted to the stairs and all the muscles of my body seemed frozen in dread of the thing that was in my mind. The footsteps were heavy now on the bare boards of the landing. Then they were coming down the last flight. I saw the boots first and then the flying suit and followed the line of the zip to his face. 'Saeton!' The name came from my lips in a whisper. God! I'll never forget the sight of his face. It was grey like putty and his eyes burned in their sockets. He stopped at the sight of us and stood staring at me. Eyes and face were devoid of expression. He was like a man walking in his sleep.

'How's Tubby?' My voice was hoarse and grating.

'He's all right,' he answered, coming on down into the kitchen. 'Why did you have to come here?' His voice was flat and lifeless and it carried with it a terrible note of sadness.

'I came to get him out,' I said.

He shook his head slowly. 'It's no use now.'

'What do you mean?' I cried. 'You said he was all right. What have you done to him?'

'Nothing. Nothing that wasn't necessary.'

I started towards the stairs then, but he stopped me. 'Don't go up,' he said. And then slowly he added, 'He's dead.'

'Dead?' The shock of the word drove me to action. I thrust past him, but he caught me by the arm as I started up the stairs. 'It's no good, Neil. He's dead, I tell you.'

'But that is impossible!' Frau Kleffmann had retreated towards her chair by the fire. 'Only this morning the doctor is here and he say he will be well again. Now you say he is dead.'

Saeton pushed his hand across his eyes. 'It – it must have been a stroke – heart or something,' he muttered uncertainly.

'But only this evening he is laughing and joking with me,' Frau Kleffmann insisted. 'Is not that so, Frederick?' she asked her husband. 'Just before you come. I take him his food and he is laughing and saying I make him so fat he live up to his name.'

'Where is he?' Else whispered to me.

'Up at the top of the house. An attic. I'll go up and see what's happened.'

I started up the stairs again, but Saeton blocked my way.

'He's dead, I tell you. Dead. Going and looking at him won't help.'

I stared at him. The blackness of the eyes, the smallness of the pupils – the man seemed curled up inside himself and through the windows of those eyes I looked in on fear and the bitter, driven urge of something that had stepped out of the world's bounds. In sudden panic I flung him aside and leaped up the stairs. There was a small lamp on the landing and I picked it up as I turned to climb to the attic.

The door of Tubby's room was ajar and as I went in the lamplight picked out the photographs of Hans lining the walls. My eyes swung to the bed in the corner and then I stopped. From the tumbled bedclothes Tubby stared at me with fixed and bloodshot eyes. His face had a bluish tinge even in the softness of the lamplight. There was a froth of blood on his puffed lips and his tongue had swollen so that it had forced itself between his teeth. He had struggled a great deal before he had died, for in the wreck of the bed his body lay in a twisted and unnatural attitude.

Avoiding the fixed gaze of his eyes, I crossed the room and touched the hand that had reached clear of the bed and was hanging to the floor. The flesh was still warm.

Else came into the room then and stopped. 'So! It is true.' She looked across at me with a shudder. 'How does it happen?'

'Perhaps it was a stroke. Perhaps—' My voice

trailed away as I saw her eyes fasten on something that lay beside the bed.

'Look!' She shivered slightly, pointing to the pillow.

I bent and picked it up. It was damp and torn and bloody at the centre where Tubby had fought for air. The truth of how he had died was there in my hands.

'He did it,' she whispered. 'He killed him.'

I nodded slowly. I think I had known it all along. Tubby's wasn't the face of a man who had died a natural death. Poor devil! Alive he had threatened the future of Saeton's engines. Because of that Saeton had come all the way from Berlin to kill him, to smother him as he lay helpless on the bed. The force that had been driving Saeton all along had taken him to the final and irrevocable step. He had killed the man without whom the engines could never have been made, the one man whom he'd thought of as a friend. *If one man stood between me and success, I'd brush him aside.* I could remember how he had stood in the centre of the mess room at Membury and said that – and now he had done it. He had brushed Tubby aside. I dropped the pillow back on to the floor with a feeling of revulsion.

'I think he is mad.' Else's horrified whisper voiced my own thoughts. And at that moment I heard slow, heavy footsteps on the stairs. Saeton was coming back up to the attic. I wasn't prepared to face him yet. I reached for the door, closing it, my action unreasoned, automatic. I slid the bolt home and stood there, listening to the footsteps getting nearer.

'Come away from the door,' Else whispered urgently.

I stepped back and as I looked at her I saw she was scared.

The footsteps stopped outside the door and the handle turned. Then the thin deal boards bulged to the pressure of the man whose breathing I could hear. The room was very still as we waited. I think Else thought he would break the door down. I didn't know what I expected, all I knew was that I didn't want to talk to him. The silence in the room was heavy with suspense. Then his footsteps sounded on the stairs again as he went slowly down.

I opened the door and listened. There was the murmur of voices and then the side door closed with a bang. From the window I saw Saeton, looking big and squat in his flying jacket, cross the farmyard and go out through the gate by the barn. I felt relieved that he had left. It wasn't only that I didn't want to talk to him. I was scared of him. Perhaps Else's fear was infectious, but I think it would have come, anyway. The abnormal in its most violent form is a thing all sane men are afraid of. The initiative lies with the insane. It's that which is frightening.

I turned back to the door. 'I'll get Kleffmann,' I said. 'We must get his body down to the truck and take it back to Berlin.' Tubby's sightless eyes watched me in a fixed stare. I turned quickly and went down the stairs, conscious of Else's footsteps hurrying after me.

The kitchen looked just the same as when we had entered it. Frau Kleffmann sat huddled in her thick dressing-gown by the fire. Her husband paced nervously up and down. There was nothing in the warmth and friendliness of that room to indicate what had happened upstairs in the attic – only the tenseness. Frau Kleffmann looked up quickly as I entered. 'Is it true?' she asked. 'Is he dead?'

'Yes,' I said. 'He's dead.'

'It is unbelievable,' she murmured. 'And he was such a nice, friendly man.'

'Why did that other man – Herr Saeton – leave so quickly?' Kleffmann demanded.

I could see that he was suspicious, but there seemed no point in telling him what had happened. 'He was worried about his plane,' I said. 'Will you help me get Carter's body down? We are taking it back to Berlin.'

'*Ja*.' He nodded. '*Ja*, I think that is best.'

'Would you please find something for us to carry him on?' I asked Frau Kleffmann.

She nodded, rising slowly to her feet, a little dazed by what had happened.

'You stay here, Else,' I said and followed Kleffmann up the stairs to the attic again. We covered Tubby with a blanket and got his body down the steep, narrow stairs. Back in the kitchen Else and Frau Kleffmann had fixed a blanket over two broom handles. The improvised stretcher lay on the table and we put Tubby's body on it. Frau Kleffmann began weeping gently at the sight of his shrouded figure. I think she was remembering her son out there in a Soviet labour camp.

Else stood quite still, staring down at the shape huddled under the blanket.

'Will you help us to carry him down to the truck?' I asked Kleffmann.

'*Ja*. It is better that you take him away from here.' His voice trembled slightly and the sweat shone on his forehead. He had known as soon as he'd seen Tubby that the poor devil hadn't died naturally and he wanted to get the body out of his house, to be shot of the whole business. He hadn't said anything, but he knew who had done it and he was scared.

We picked the stretcher up, he at one end, I at the other. 'Come on, Else,' I said.

She didn't move and as I lifted the latch of the door she said, 'Wait!' Her voice was pitched high on a hysterical note. 'Do you think Saeton will let you go back to Berlin with – with that?' She came across the room, seizing hold of my arm and shaking it in the extremity of her fear. 'He cannot let either of us go back.'

I stood still, staring at her, the truth of what she was saying gradually sinking in.

'He is waiting for us – out there.' She jerked her arm towards the window.

I could see in her eyes that she was still remembering the sight of Tubby's face as he lay propped up in that bed. I lifted the stretcher back to the table and went towards the window. My hand was on the curtains to pull them back when Else seized my arm. 'Keep away from the window. Please, Neil.' I could feel the trembling of her body.

I turned irresolutely back into the room. Was he really waiting for us out there? The palms of my hands were damp with sweat. Saeton had never turned back from anything he had started. He wouldn't turn back now. Else and I were as fatal to him as a hangman's rope. A desperate feeling of weariness took hold of me so that my limbs felt heavy and my movements were slow. 'What do we do then?'

Nobody answered my question. They were all staring at me, waiting for me to make the first move. 'Have you got a gun here?' I asked Kleffmann.

He nodded slowly. '*Ja*. I have a shotgun.'

'That will do,' I said. 'Can I have it, please?'

He went out of the room and returned a moment later with the gun. It looked about the equivalent of an English 16 bore. He gave it to me together with a handful of cartridges. 'I'll go out by a window on the other side of the house,' I said. 'When I've gone, keep the doors bolted.' I turned to Else. 'I'll circle the house and then go down to the road and persuade Kurt to bring the truck up here.'

She nodded, her lips compressed into a tight line.

'If I find it's all clear, I'll whistle a bit of the Meistersingers. Don't open up until you hear that.' I turned to Kleffmann. 'Have you got another gun?'

He nodded. 'I have one I use for the rooks.'

'Good. Keep it by you.' I broke the gun I held in my hands and slipped a cartridge into each of the barrels. I felt like a man going out to finish off an animal that has run amok.

As I snapped the breech Else caught hold of my

hand. 'Be careful, Neil. Please. I – I do not know what I shall do if I lose you now.'

I stared at her, surprised at the intensity of feeling in her voice. 'I'll be all right,' I said. And then I turned to Kleffmann and asked him to show me to the other side of the house.

CHAPTER TEN

I dropped out near some bushes and slid into their shadow. Overhead the stars still shone, bright and cold, but to the west the sky was black with cloud. The wind seemed warmer now. I pulled my coat round me and slid along the wall of the house, ran past the gate to the farmyard and crouched in the shadow of the barn. I stood there, quite still, the barrel of the gun cold on the palm of my left hand, listening to the sounds of the night. One by one I identified them – the wind tapping the branch of a tree against the wooden side of the barn, a cow moving in its stall, the grunt of a pig, the tinkle of ice knocked from some guttering by the flutter of an owl. And over all these sounds the solid thumping of my heart.

I tried to tell myself that I was a fool to be standing out there, scared of every shadow that seemed to move, waiting with a gun in my hand. But every time I nearly convinced myself that I was being a fool, the memory of Tubby's face came to remind me that Saeton was now a killer. For a long time I stood quite still with my back against the wood of the barn, hoping that somewhere in the darkness round me I should hear a sound, see a movement that would prove he was really there. I longed to know, to end the suspense of waiting. But nothing stirred.

It was out of the question for me to stand there doing nothing till dawn. Kurt was waiting down on the road and he would not wait much longer. The thing to do was to go down there and get the truck up. If he left without us . . . The memory of that other journey into Berlin spurred me to action.

Moving warily I slid along the wall of the barn, past a piled-up heap of manure, through a litter of decaying farm machinery. A twig snapped under my feet. I stepped in a rut where the water was all frozen and the ice crunched under my weight. They were only little noises, but they sounded loud, and once away to the left, I thought I heard an answering movement. But when I stopped there was nothing but the sounds I had already identified.

I circled the farm without seeing any sign of Saeton. Then I started down the track to the road. I kept well clear of the ruts, moving slowly along the grass verge, brambles tearing at my trousers.

And then suddenly, out of the darkness ahead, the beam of a torch stabbed the night. As the dazzle of it touched my eyes I flung myself sideways. But I wasn't quick enough. There was a spurt of flame and the bullet thudded into my body, knocking me off my feet and sending me sprawling into the brambles that bordered the track. Boots crunched in the frozen ruts as the beam of the torch probed my shelter. I lifted the shotgun and fired at the torch. The kick of the gun wrenched me with pain, but the torch went out and above the sound of the shot I heard a cry. I fought my way through the thicket, the thorns tearing at my face and hands, all the right side of my body racked with pain. Behind the screen of brambles I crouched down and very gently ejected the spent shell and reloaded. My right hand had no strength in it. The fingers were stiff and clumsy and the cartridges sticky with blood. The click of the catch as I closed the breech seemed unnaturally loud in the stillness that had descended on the lane.

My eyes had been momentarily dazzled by the torch, but as they became accustomed to the darkness again I saw the line of the brambles bordering the track, and on either side of me and behind me the slope of the ground was visible against the stars. I was in a slight hollow. If he tried to circle me I should see him against the stars. The danger lay to my immediate front. The strange thing was that now I knew he was there and was at grips with him I was no longer afraid.

Away to my left on the main road the engine of a truck broke the silence, headlights cut a swathe through the night and began to move. Frightened by the shots Kurt was pulling out, leaving us to find our own way back to Berlin. I cursed under my breath as I listened to the sound of the engine dying away. Soon all that remained was a faint glow in the darkness to the south. Then that, too, was gone. The wind rustled in the brambles. A night bird cried its call. There was no other sound.

Then something moved in the bushes to my left. It moved again, nearer this time. I raised the gun to my shoulder. There was the sound of earth being dislodged and the rattle of dry bramble branches almost at my side. I fired at the sound. From behind me, echoing the sound of my own shot, the revolver smacked a bullet into the ground at my feet. I swung round, realising how he'd fooled me by throwing earth into the undergrowth. I saw his figure crouched against the stars and let off my second barrel at it. There was a grunt and a curse as something thudded to the ground. Desperately I broke my gun and fumbled in my pocket for the cartridges.

When the gun was loaded I started forward. I knew I had to finish it off now. If I didn't I should lose my nerve. I sensed that in the trembling of my hands. I had to finish it one way or the other. Crouched low I could see his body close to the ground as he waited for me. Whatever happened now I was close enough for the shotgun to be effective. I steeled myself to the jolt of a bullet hitting. I'd let him have both barrels. Wherever he got me I'd still have time to fire.

But I didn't have to. Even when I was so close I could have blown the top of his head off he did not move. He was crouched in an unnatural position, his head bent almost to the ground, his fingers dug deeply into the hard earth. Beside him his torch glimmered faintly in the starlight. The chromium was all wet and sticky as I picked it up and when I flicked it on I saw the metal was badly dented and filmed with blood. I turned him over on to his back and as I did so his service revolver slipped from between his fingers. His left arm was all bloody, the hand horribly pitted by the shot. There was a livid bruise above his left temple and the skin had split. But apart from this he didn't seem badly hurt and his breathing was quite natural. I think what had happened was that the main weight of my shot had struck the torch and flung it against the side of his head. There was no doubt that he'd been knocked clean out.

I picked up the revolver and slipped it into my pocket. I turned then and went back into the lane through a gap in the bramble hedge. It was fortunate that the torch hadn't been put out of action, because I was feeling dizzy and very faint as I staggered up the track and without its light I'm not at all sure I should have been able to find my way back to the farm.

I was pretty well all in by the time I reached the side door. I remember slumping against it, beating on it with my hands. But they had no strength and all I achieved was a faint scrabbling as I slid to the ground. Probably Else was listening for me. At any rate I never sang a bar of the Meistersingers, but when I came round I was in a chair by the kitchen fire and Else was cutting the blood-soaked clothes away from the wound in my shoulder. As she saw my eyes open her hand reached up and she pushed her fingers through my hair. 'You are always in the wars, Neil.' She smiled softly. 'I think you need someone to look after you.'

'Where's Kleffmann?' I asked her.

'*Hier.*' His big figure bent over me. 'What is it?'

I gave him the revolver and told him to go down the lane and get Saeton. 'If he's still there I don't think he'll give you much trouble,' I said.

'What happened?' Else asked.

As I told her Frau Kleffmann came in with a bowl of hot water. Else began to bathe the wound and the warmth of the water took some of the numbness out of it. 'I think the bullet is still there,' Else said after peering at the torn flesh with the aid of a torch.

'Well, patch me up the best you can,' I said. 'I've got to fly.'

'To fly?'

'Yes. The truck is gone. Kurt cleared off as soon as he heard our shots. Our only way out now is Saeton's plane.'

'But the airfield is more than a mile from here,' Else pointed out. 'I do not think you will be able to walk so far.'

'Perhaps not. We'll borrow a horse and cart from the Kleffmanns. I've no doubt they'll be only too glad to speed the parting guests.' I tried to smile at my little joke, but I didn't seem able to make the effort. I felt sick and tired. As soon as Else had finished dressing my wound I got her and Frau Kleffmann to harness one of the farm horses. They had got Tubby's body on to the cart and I was sitting in it by the time Kleffmann returned with Saeton. It was lucky that the farmer was a big man, for Saeton was still unconscious. He carried him slung over his shoulders in a fireman's lift and when he reached the cart he dumped the body into the muck of the farmyard like a sack of potatoes.

'Ready?' he asked me.

'Yes, I'm ready,' I said. I was anxious to be off. The plane was my only hope of getting back to Berlin. I knew the Kleffmanns wouldn't shelter us after what had happened, and every minute the plane stood out there in the airfield it ran the risk of being spotted by a Red Army patrol.

Else helped Kleffmann load Saeton's body on to the cart. Then he climbed up and clicked his tongue at the horse. Frau Kleffmann opened the gate for us. She spoke quickly and urgently to her husband. He nodded and the cart jolted over the frozen ruts into the lane. I called goodbye to her, but she did not answer. She just stood there, a frozen expression on her face, glad to see us go.

Kleffmann had returned the revolver to me and I kept my left hand on the butt as it lay in the pocket of my coat. My eyes were on Saeton's unconscious body as we jolted towards the woods. Rain clouds were spreading across the night sky and when we entered the woods it was as dark as pitch. Nobody spoke and the only sound was the creaking of the cart and an occasional snort from the horse. I kept my foot against Saeton's body. The cart jolted in the ruts and each jolt was like a knife stabbing at the blade of my shoulder. Else had seated herself so that I could lean against her and she seemed conscious of my pain, for when it was very bad she would slip her hand over my left arm.

We must have been about half-way through the

woods when Saeton stirred. He lay groaning for a moment and then he sat up. I could see his face, a pale oval in the darkness. My hand tightened automatically on the gun in my pocket. 'Don't move,' I told him. 'I've got a gun. If you move I'll shoot.'

There was a long silence. Then he said, 'That's you is it, Neil?'

'Yes,' I told him.

He was sitting up now and he gave a little cry of pain as he shifted his position. 'What happened?'

I didn't say anything. He could think it out for himself. The silence became heavy as the memory of Tubby's death came to all of us. 'Where's Tubby?' he asked at length. 'Did you – bury him?'

'No. His body is beside you in the cart.'

He said, 'My God! Why couldn't you leave him there?' And then silence descended on us again. I tried not to think of what Tubby looked like there under the blanket. The pain helped. It wrenched at my mind and made it difficult to think. I clung to the gun. If he made any move I'd use it. Maybe he sensed that, for he stayed quite still all the way through the woods.

At last we were out of the trees and dragging slowly across the flat expanse of the airfield. It was very dark. Isolated drops of rain began to fall. 'Where did you leave the plane?' I asked Saeton.

He didn't answer. Maybe he thought if he said nothing we might fail to find it. I peered anxiously into the darkness ahead. The cart jolted endlessly in the black void. Maybe the horse could see when we couldn't. At any rate the plane was suddenly there right in front of us, a shadowy, insubstantial shape. Kleffmann reined in the horse and turned to me. 'I think it is better if one of us goes and has a look round there.'

'I will go,' Else said. She eased herself gently away from me and dropped to the ground. In a moment the darkness had swallowed her. I waited, my nerves tense for the challenge of a Russian sentry. But no sound broke the stillness, only the soft whisper of the rain falling. Then Else was back. 'It is okay,' she whispered and we started forward again. Else was at the horse's head and she backed the cart against the door of the fuselage.

It was queer to think that that plane was the bridge between us and Berlin. Standing there, it was just an inert piece of metal. And yet with a pilot's direction it would set us down at Gatow. It seemed to me symbolic of the whole airlift, symbolic of the ingenuity of man to do the impossible, to jump in a few minutes from alien to friendly ground. But it required the direction of a pilot and my body cringed at the thought that it was I who had got to bridge that gap – in a night of black darkness, without a navigator and with a bullet wound in my shoulder. At least it was a Dakota. I don't think I could have handled a four-engined job.

Else helped Kleffmann to get Tubby's body into the fuselage. Saeton and I were alone in the cart. I saw him shift his position. 'Keep still!' I ordered him.

'What are you going to do?' he asked.

'Fly your plane back to Gatow.'

'What about me?'

'You're coming, too.'

There was a pause and then he said, 'You're wounded, aren't you?'

'Yes,' I said. 'But don't worry. I'll make it.'

'And if you don't?'

'If I don't you'll be able to take over and fly where you like.' It wasn't subtlety on my part that made me say that. But looking back on it I think that was why he didn't make a break for it there on Hollmind airfield. Maybe he was too weak. He had been out for a hell of a long time. But if he'd jumped from the cart right then he'd have had a chance.

Else and Kleffmann appeared at the fuselage door again. 'Get in!' I told Saeton. I had the gun in my hand now. 'And don't try anything,' I said. 'I'm quite willing to fire.'

He got up without a word. His movements were slow, but that was the only indication he gave that he had been hurt. I followed him, feeling sick and a little giddy as I moved my cramped limbs. Kleffmann dropped into the cart and picked up the reins, clicking his tongue to the horse. I called my thanks to him from the door of the fuselage, but he didn't answer. Where horse and cart had been there was nothing but the blackness of the airfield and only the faint creaking of the cart told me that a moment before it had stood there beside the plane.

'Herr Kleffmann is glad to go, I think,' Else said in a strained voice.

I couldn't blame him, but I wished I could have done something to compensate him for what had happened. He and his wife had been very good to Tubby. 'All right, got the door closed,' I said. I switched the lights on and for the first time I saw Saeton's face. It was streaked with mud and blood and the skin was quite white. His left arm hung limp at his side and blood trickled from his shot-pitted hand. 'Sit down,' I said.

He began to move towards the long line of seats that flanked the fuselage. Then he stopped and faced me again. 'Neil. Can't we come to an arrangement?'

'No,' I said. 'You know damn well we can't.'

'Because of Tubby?'

'Yes.'

He grunted and pushed his hand across his face, smearing the blood. 'It was necessary,' he said heavily. 'You made it necessary.'

'It was cold-blooded murder,' I said.

He shrugged his shoulders. 'You left me no alternative. It's a pity you can't see the wider issues. What's one man's life against what we planned?'

'The man was your friend,' I said.

'Do you think I enjoyed doing what I had to?' he said with a trace of anger. And then, almost to himself: 'He took time to die and he knew what I was going to do as I pulled the pillow from under his head. I hated doing it. And I hated you for making me do it.' My hand clenched round the butt of the revolver at his sudden violence. 'Now it's done,' he added, 'why not leave it at that? Why make his death pointless?'

It was the same argument that he'd used before when he had been trying to stop me making that report. The man could see things only from the standpoint of his own ambition. 'Sit down!' I said again and turned to Else. 'You'll have to watch him. Do you know how to use one of these?'

She took the gun from me and examined it. 'Is the safety catch on now or is it off?'

'It's off,' I told her.

She nodded. 'That is all I have to know. I understand how to use it.'

Saeton had sat down now. 'Sit over there,' I told her. 'And keep well away from him. If he moves from that seat, you're to shoot. You understand? Are you capable of firing just because a man moves?'

She glanced at Saeton. 'You do not have to worry. I know how to shoot.' Her hand had closed over the gun and she had the muzzle of it pointing towards Saeton. Her eyes were steady and her hand did not tremble. I knew she would fire if Saeton moved and I started forward towards the cockpit. But she put out her hand. 'Are you all right, Neil? Do you need some help?'

'I'll be all right,' I said.

She smiled and pressed my sound arm. 'Good luck!' she whispered.

But I wasn't so sure I would be all right. When I had struggled into the pilot's seat a wave of dizziness came over me and I had to fight it off. The engines started without difficulty and I left them running to warm up whilst I went back to the navigator's table and worked out my course. It would be easy enough getting back to Berlin once I had got the plane into the air. What worried me was the airlift. I could go in above the lift-stream, but when I was over Berlin I should have to come down to the line of flight of the other planes. Somehow I'd have to fit myself into the pattern and with the weather closing in I might have to do this in cloud. There would be a big risk of collision then.

For a moment I sat there, fighting a growing weakness and the frightened emptiness of my belly. I needn't go in to Berlin. I could make for one of the base airfields – Wunstorf, or Celle, which was nearer – or I could fly north to Lübeck, which was nearer still. But I had no navigator and I was very conscious of the fact that I was in no fit state to pilot a plane. Lübeck was the better part of 150 miles away, nearly an hour's flying, whereas I could be in Gatow in twenty minutes.

I reached up to the throttle levers and revved the engines. It would have to be Gatow. I switched on the twin spotlights, released the brakes and taxied out to the runway end. As I swung the plane into position for take-off I called to Else: 'All set? Have you fixed your safety belt?'

'Yes,' she called back. 'I am okay.'

'Fine,' I shouted and reached up to the throttle levers. Reaching up to control the engines stretched the muscles of my back and I bit my lip with the pain of my shoulder. My right hand was useless. To adjust the engines I had to let go of the control column. Again I was conscious of that feeling of emptiness in my stomach. I was a fool to try and fly in the state I was in. But there was no alternative. We had to get out of the Russian Zone.

The plane rocked and juddered as the engines revved. My eyes ran over the dials of the control panel. Everything was okay. I peered through the windshield. It was sheeting with rain now. The spotlights showed a few yards of weed-grown concrete streaming with water and then lost themselves in the steel curtain of the rain.

For a moment I hesitated, unwilling to commit myself to the take-off. Then, quickly, before reason could support my instinctive fear, I released the brakes and the plane began to move forward into the steel rods of the rain. The concrete came at me out of the murk and streamed beneath me, faster and faster. I braced my knees against the control column, steadying it as I adjusted the engines. Then the tail lifted and a moment later my hand was on the control column, pulling it back, pulling the plane up off the ground. Something slid away beneath us – it may have been a tree or the top of one of the ruined airfield buildings. After that I was alone in the lighted cockpit, riding smoothly through the inky blackness of the night, seeing nothing in the windshield but the water washing down it and the image of my own face, white in the glass.

I trimmed the engines and banked slowly on to my course, climbing all the time. At 7,000 feet I levelled out clear of the rain clouds in bright starlight and relaxed in my seat. I checked oil pressure and engine revs. Everything was okay. I felt drained of all energy. My eyelids closed for a second, and then I forced them open. It would be so easy to slip into unconsciousness. I fought off the faintness, holding myself against it as one does when one is tight and refusing to go under. I glanced at my watch. It was a quarter to five. By five o'clock I should be approaching Gatow. I was shivering with cold.

Once Else came through into the cockpit to see if I was all right. She looked tired and her eyes seemed very large in the pallor of her face. She held the gun firmly in her hand and her gaze was concentrated on the door to the fuselage as she spoke to me. 'Is Saeton all right?' I asked her.

'Yes.'

'Has he tried to move?'

'No. He do not try anything. I think he is dazed by what has happened. Also, he has lost much blood. He is very weak I think.' She put her hand on my arm. 'Can you land all right, do you think?'

'Yes,' I said. 'Better get back to your seat. And strap yourself in tight. I'll be going down in a few minutes.'

She nodded. 'Good luck, Neil!'

I didn't say anything and she went back into the fuselage. Below me I could just see the grey fluffy sea that marked the topside of the rain clouds. It was one thing piloting the plane up here in the clear, starlit night. But I had got to go down through that stuff. Somewhere, only a few minutes ahead of me, I had got to go down and contact a single square mile of ground through the impenetrable murk of the rain. The thought of it made me feel sick and I wished now that I had gone north to Lübeck. Maybe the weather would have been better at Lübeck. But I was committed now. It was no good turning back.

As I sat there in the cockpit, I was conscious of a growing sense of panic. To go on and on – that was all I wanted – to go on into infinity, into unconsciousness. Automatically I kept glancing at my watch. Just as automatically I pressed forward on the control column, as my watch came up to five, pushing the nose of the plane down. It was only years of operational training that enabled me to do that, for it was against all reason, against all the instinctive desire of mind and body. It meant action.

The clouds came up to meet me. From a flat sea of grey they became a tenuous, insubstantial drift of mist. Then the stars were blotted out and nothing was visible beyond the pulsating interior of the cockpit. I watched the altimeter dial – 6,000 – 5,500 – 5,000. Through my earphones I was picking up instructions from Gatow Airways to planes reporting over Frohnau: *Okay York 315. Channel A-able and call Controller.* And then another York was in my headphones reporting number and cargo at twenty miles. *York 270. Clear to Beacon.*

I pressed my A button for automatic radio tuning to Gatow Tower. *York 315. Clear to QSY. Channel D-dog and call Gatow director.*

Channel D-dog. That was Ground Control Approach! Things were bad down there. It meant ceiling zero and driving rain. It meant that I should have to do a controlled approach landing. I'd never done one before. I'd never been talked down in my life. We hadn't had those sort of aids when I had been flying on Ops. I cleared my throat and pressed my B button.

'Hallo, Gatow Airways!' I called. 'Hallo, Gatow Airways!'

Faint through the earphones came the answering voice from Gatow. '*Gatow Airways answering. Give your number and position please. Give your number and position please. Over.*'

'Hallo, Gatow. I have no number. This is Saeton's Dakota returning from Hollmind. Fraser piloting. I am now levelling out at Angels Five and will give you my position from Frohnau beacon. Can you direct me in please? Over.'

'*Gatow Airways answering. You cannot land at Gatow. I repeat, you cannot land at Gatow. Overshoot and proceed to Wunstorf. Proceed to Wunstorf. Acknowledge please. Over.*'

A wave of dizziness caught me and for a moment I thought I was going to black out. Then it had passed. 'Fraser answering. I must land at Gatow. I am injured. I must land at Gatow.' I started to tell them what had happened to Tubby and how Saeton was wounded, but they cut me short. '*Overshoot and proceed to Wunstorf. I repeat: Overshoot and proceed to Wunstorf.*'

'I cannot fly any farther,' I cried desperately. 'Am coming down. Repeat I am coming down.'

There was a pause. Then: '*Okay, Fraser. Give your position, please.*'

I looked quickly down at the instrument panel. The plane was fitted with a Sperry automatic pilot. 'I am going back now to get M/F bearings on Frohnau and Gatow. Off.'

I switched over to the automatic pilot and went

back to the navigator's desk. I got the M/F bearings and found that my position was almost directly over Spandau. I moved back to the cockpit and in sliding into the pilot's seat wrenched my arm so that I had to bite back the scream of pain that came to my throat. Half-collapsed over the control column I called Gatow again: 'Hallo, Gatow. Fraser calling. Am flying Angels Five directly above Spandau. Please direct me. Please direct me. Course now 085 degrees. Please direct me. Over.'

'Hallo, Fraser. Keep flying your present height and course. I will direct you in a few minutes. Give speed and acknowledge. Over.'

'Speed 135,' I answered. 'I await your directions. Over.'

I wiped the sweat from my forehead and disconnected the automatic pilot. Waves of nausea swept over me. My mind seemed a blank, unable to concentrate. Through the earphones came the sound of Gatow calling other planes. From the fuselage behind me I heard Saeton's voice call out, 'Fraser! Are you in trouble?'

'No,' I said. 'No, I'm all right.'

'If you want any help . . .'

But I didn't trust him. 'I'm all right,' I called back. 'Don't flap.' My throat felt dry. My tongue was like a piece of coarse flannel. I wanted to vomit.

'Hallo, Fraser. Gatow Airways calling Fraser. Can you hear me? Over.'

'Fraser answering. I hear you.' My voice sounded

weak and hoarse. *Oh God!* I breathed. *Let's get this over.*

'*GCA think they have located you. Channel D-dog and call Director.*'

'Roger, Gatow.' I pressed my D button, my hand trembling and damp with sweat. 'Hallo, Gatow Director. Fraser calling Gatow Director.'

A new voice, much clearer, sounded in my earphones. '*Turn 180 degrees, Fraser. Turn 180 degrees.*'

'Roger, Director.' I braced myself for the effort and shifted the control column, giving right rudder at the same time. The movement brought the sweat cold on my forehead again. I should never make it. I felt I just couldn't make it. The control column was heavy as lead. To work the rudder brought my shoulder in contact with the back of the seat. Pain seared through my neck and up into my head as I completed the turn and straightened out. God! This was going to be hell.

'*Thank you, Fraser,*' came the voice of the Director of Controlled Approach. '*I have now identified you. New course. Left on to 245 degrees and reduce height to 3,000. Acknowledge.*'

'Roger.' I turned the plane on to its new course, my senses strained to catch the director's voice. I felt sick with the strain. If only I had done one of these landings before! A sheet of water lashed against the windshield. The plane bucketed violently, wrenching at my shoulder as I moved to maintain course, the control column thrust forward, my eyes fixed on the altimeter dial and the luminous circle of the compass where the needle hovered at 245.

Else touched my arm. 'Are you all right, Neil? Can I do anything?'

'No,' I said. 'I'm all right. Just watch Saeton, that's all.'

She wiped the sweat from my forehead with her handkerchief. 'If you want me . . .'

'I'm all right,' I almost screamed at her. 'Strap yourself in. Go on. Fix your safety belt. We'll be going down in a minute.'

She hesitated. Her hand touched mine – a caress, a wish that she could help – and then she was gone and I was alone with the voice of GCA saying, '*Right on to 250 degrees now, Fraser. Right on to 250. Speed should be 120 now. You're doing fine. You'll be into the glide path soon. How are you feeling?*'

'I'm feeling all right,' I answered. I wasn't, but there was no point in telling him that my eyes found it difficult to focus on the instruments. The concentration was causing dizziness. *Hallo, York 270. Climb to 3,000 and return to base. Climb to 3,000 and return to base. Emergency landing ahead of you. Acknowledge. Over.* It was the voice of Gatow Director, clearing the way for me, and almost immediately 270 acknowledged. Then GCA was calling me again: '*Right on to 252 degrees now, Fraser.*' I shifted the rudder slightly and slid on to the new course. '*That's fine, Fraser. You're on the glide path now. Reduce speed to 100. Lower flaps and undercarriage. Two miles to touch-down. You're doing fine. Can you hear me? Over.*'

'Yes, I can hear you,' I answered.

A new voice came in: '*This is talk down. Don't acknowledge from now on. Check flaps and undercarriage. Reduce height by 500 feet per minute. Fine. Right two degrees. You're one and a half miles from touch-down now. You're fifty feet above the glide path. You're doing fine. Right on the glide path now. One mile to go. . . .*'

I could see nothing through the windshield – just my reflection, that was all. I stared at the instrument panel. The dials were blurred. I seemed conscious of nothing but the voice in my earphones. My whole body was tense, reacting to the GCA Director's instructions. The pain was blinding. My body seemed one screaming hell of pain. It shot along my nerves and jangled in my head like a burglar alarm. I could feel the nerves of my brain stretched taut. And I prayed – *God, don't let me black out now.*

'. . . *Half a mile to go now. You're coming in a little too steeply. You're below the glide path. Keep up, Fraser! Keep up!*' I jerked at the control column, cursing blindly to keep myself from screaming. '*That's fine. You're bang on now. Left one degree. You're coming in to touch-down now. Start to level out. You should be able to see the runway lights now. Level out! Level out! Look ahead and land visual.*'

I jerked at the control column, peering through the streaming windshield. A light showed – a row of lights. They were blurred and unreal. I felt the plane sag. I had pulled it up too hard. It sagged right down on to the lights, dropping on its belly, heavily, uncontrollably. The wheels hit and I screamed as the seat slashed up into my shoulder. For a second we were airborne and instinctively I applied left rudder and altered the position of the control column. We hit the deck again. But this time we stayed there. I sagged over the control column in a blinding sheet of pain and then I reached for the brakes and applied them. The plane swung – right rudder – but the wing dipped and suddenly we were pivoting to a stop and I blacked out.

I couldn't have been out long, for when I came round, Else was just coming through into the cockpit. 'Are you all right, Neil?'

I sat up slowly, feeling the stillness of the plane, the lack of motion. Thank God! We were on the ground. I wiped the cold sweat out of my eyes with the back of my hand. I was on the floor and outside the plane I heard voices and the sound of cars and then the roar of a plane landing close by. 'Yes,' I said weakly. 'I'm all right. What about you?'

'I had my safety belt fixed.' She had knelt down beside me and was loosening my collar. 'You were wonderful, Neil. Saeton said you were crazy to try it. He do not think you will do it. I do not think he want you to do it. And when you have done it he ask me . . .' She turned her head at a sound from the open door of the fuselage. 'They are coming now. You will soon be in hospital and then you will be able to rest.'

Figures appeared in the cockpit doorway. The faces were blurred and I pushed my hand across my eyes. 'What's all this about, Fraser?' It was the Wing Co. Flying. 'Because of you two planes have had to overshoot and return to base. You were told to proceed to Wunstorf . . .'

'Please,' Else interrupted him. 'He is hurt.'

'It's his own fault,' the wing commander snapped. 'If he'd done as he was told—'

'He is hurt with a bullet,' Else cut in. 'How can he go on to Wunstorf? Now please let the doctor see him. He is very bad I think.'

I caught hold of Else's arm with my left hand. 'Help me to my feet,' I said. She put her hands under my armpits and levered me up. I braced myself against the navigator's table, my eyes closed, fighting to maintain consciousness. The station commander appeared in the doorway. From very far away it seemed I heard him call for a medical orderly. Then he turned back to me. 'Before you go off in the ambulance, Fraser, perhaps you'll explain the extraordinary message you gave Airways.'

'What was that?' I asked uncertainly.

'Something about Carter having been murdered.'

I pushed the sweat out of my eyes again. God! I felt weak. 'He *was* murdered,' I said. 'Saeton killed him because he knew I would try to get him back from the Russian Zone. If I brought Carter back, then you would have to believe what I put in my report.' My vision had cleared slightly and behind the station commander I saw the figure of Squadron Leader Pierce. 'Do you believe me now?' I asked Pierce.

'Where's Saeton?' he asked. 'I thought you said you'd brought him back?'

'Why are you piloting the plane I let Saeton borrow?' the wing commander asked.

And then Pierce again: 'What have you done with Saeton?'

Questions, questions, questions – why the devil couldn't they leave me alone? 'You don't believe what I told you.' My voice was shrill. 'You don't believe me, do you? All right then.' I pushed them out of the way, staggering blindly as I stumbled into the body of the plane. 'Pierce,' I called, standing over the blanketed figure of Tubby still strapped along the seats. 'Take a look at that.'

Pierce pulled back the blanket. There was a gasp and a short heavy silence. 'So Carter was at your farmhouse at Hollmind.' He slowly put back the blanket. Then he turned to me and gripped my left arm. 'I'm sorry, Fraser. I've been rather dense. Now. Where's Saeton?'

I looked round. I couldn't see him and I glanced at Else. 'You were in charge of him. Where is he?' I asked.

She shrugged her shoulders. 'I do not know. After you land I come straight to the cockpit. I do not trouble myself with him any more.'

Pierce strode to the door. 'Sergeant! You were the first here. Did anybody leave the plane?'

'Yes, sir,' came the answer. 'A big, powerful-looking man.' There was a hurried exchange of words and then the sergeant added, 'He commandeered one of the jeeps. Said he had something urgent to report. He was injured, I think, sir. Leastways, there was a lot of blood on 'im.'

Pierce glanced at me. 'Did Saeton do that?' He nodded to the figure huddled under the blanket.

'Yes,' I said.

'Right. Sergeant! Take my jeep – find the man and arrest him. His name is Saeton.' Pierce turned and pushed his way up the fuselage. A moment later I heard him on the R/T to Emergency, ordering them to signal R.A.F Police to close all exit gates and patrol the standings where aircraft were parked.

Another plane thundered in down the runway. The station commander took my arm. 'I'm sorry, Fraser. It seems we've all made a mistake. Now we'll get you to the M.O.' He piloted me to the door. An ambulance was waiting. 'Ah, there you are, Gentry. Fraser's hurt. Better get him across to the sick bay right away.'

Else and the station commander helped me out of the fuselage. The rain drove in sheets across the runway lights. We were just moving across to the back of the ambulance when Pierce flung out of the plane shouting for a car. 'What is it, Pierce?' the station commander called.

'Saeton,' he shouted. 'Control have just come through on the R/T. Plane 481 – that's Saeton's Tudor – has just passed the tower, taxi-ing towards the runway. They've ordered him to stop, but he doesn't answer. They're calling an R.A.F. Regiment patrol car now.'

We halted and our eyes were turned eastwards towards the purple lights of the perimeter track. Faintly through the driving rain the lights of an aircraft showed, swinging on the last turn, moving forward to line up at the runway end. The driving squalls of rain periodically wiped it out, but a moment later we caught the roar of its engines and twin spotlights came hurtling through the murk towards us, went roaring past us and swept up and on into the night, a single white light that dwindled and was lost almost instantly. In the moment of its hissing, thundering passage past us I had recognised Saeton's Tudor – my Tudor – the cause of Tubby's death.

I felt suddenly sick at heart at the thought of Saeton getting away with it. There were the engines, too. They were Tubby's work as much as his. 'You must stop him,' I said to the station commander. 'Stop him!'

'Don't you worry,' was the reply. 'We'll get him. We'll send fighters up and force him down.'

I felt sorry then. I had asked for a man-hunt and it seemed I was going to get it. I shivered violently and the M.O. hustled me into the ambulance. All the way to the sick bay I was thinking about Saeton, alone up there in the cockpit of his plane. He was injured, like I had been. But there was no comforting goal for him, nothing for him to try for. He would eventually black out and then. . . .

'It is best he go like this,' Else said quietly.

I nodded. Perhaps it was best. But I couldn't help thinking about it. Where would he try to make for – Russia? One of the satellite countries? He could sell those engines to the Russians. He would be safe behind the Iron Curtain.

Again as though she had read my thoughts, Else said, 'You do not have to worry about Saeton. He is gone behind the Iron Curtain. Now I must work to reproduce the engines that we of the West have lost. And you must help, Neil. You are the only person now who know what those engines are like.'

I didn't say anything. I was only remembering that Saeton had fought in two wars for his country. He had murdered a man so that those engines would be produced in British factories. Surely he wouldn't barter them with the Russians for his life?

The M.O. wanted to put me straight to bed. But as soon as he had dressed my shoulder I insisted on being taken down to the Operations Room. He tried to make me remain in the sick bay, but somehow I couldn't face the thought of lying there, waiting for news. In the end he agreed to let me go, but before I left he gave me a dry overcoat and a blanket to wrap round me.

The Operations Room seemed crowded. There was the station commander and Pierce, the Wing Co. Flying and the I.O. Somebody tried to stop Else from coming in with me. I told him to go to hell, and then Harry Culyer was coming towards me. 'I just been down to the mortuary with Di,' he said. 'She asked me to tell you how much she appreciated . . .' His voice trailed off. 'She was pretty cut up, poor kid.'

'What's the news of Saeton?' I asked.

'They've got fighter squadrons up searching for him.'

The station commander turned at the sound of my voice. 'We'll get him,' he said. 'The weather's clearing to the west.'

'To the west?'

He nodded.

'He's flying westward?' I asked.

'Yes. One of our mobile radar outfits located him a few minutes back just south of Hanover.'

'Then he did not go to Russia?' Else exclaimed.

'Of course not,' I said.

'But why does he not go to the Soviet Zone? Is he so stupid he does not know he will be safe there? I do not understand.'

It was impossible for me to explain to the satisfaction of her logical German mind why Saeton had turned his back on the East, so I let it go. I found a chair and slumped into it. Reports were coming in all the time on an R/T loudspeaker, but I didn't listen. It was squadron-to-base stuff – the fighters reporting back. I didn't want to listen. It was horrible to think of Saeton up there being hounded by a pack of fighters. And he could so easily have turned eastwards.

The minutes dragged slowly by. Five-thirty . . . six . . . six-thirty. Dawn was breaking over the airfield. And then suddenly there was a whoop and somebody's voice was crackling over the radio: '*I've got him now. Flying at 10,000 feet, course slightly north of west. He is now over the Scheldt estuary. Making for England, home and beauty, I should say. What do I do now? Over.*'

'Tell that boy to start heading him off, back into Germany,' the station commander ordered. 'And get the rest of the squadron up with him.'

We followed it all in the R/T messages. In a moment the whole pack of them were buzzing round Saeton, beating him up, diving past his nose, flying just above him, trying to force him down and away from the coast. And I sat there and thought of Saeton alone there in the cockpit of the Tudor, his hand undressed and bleeding, and the fighters hurtling across the perspex so close that he could almost touch them. I could almost feel him wincing at each roar of a machine scraping at the paint of the aircraft. I remembered the pain I had suffered at each movement of the control column. God! It was horrible.

Intermittently the voice of a radio operator kept calling Saeton, ordering him to return to base, to return to Wunstorf. I sat rigid in my seat, expecting all the time to hear Saeton's voice come in. But he didn't answer. And as the minutes dragged by, the Operations Room, with its constant stream of instructions to planes coming in and the group of officers waiting, became unreal. In my mind I was there in the cockpit of the Tudor with Saeton. *He has turned north now. He has turned north. We are diving right across his nose, but we are making no impression. He won't turn back. The bastard won't alter course. What are your instructions please? We cannot fly any closer. Over.* The voice of the leader of the fighter squadron, excited, tensed up with the danger of the thing he was doing.

I didn't hear the reply. I was with Saeton, seeing him hunched over the control column, his face grey, the blood oozing between his fingers and sticky on the wheel. I could see him in my mind so clearly – solid and square, as immovable from his purpose as a bull who has seen the red of the matador's cloak. What was his purpose? What did he plan to do?

And as if in answer to my question the leader of the

squadron came back on the air. *He's putting his nose down now. We're over the North Sea.* And then more excited. *He's going into a power dive. He's trying to shake us off. He's going straight down now. My God! No, it's all right. F for Freddie swept right across his nose, but he's clear now. Thought they'd tangle that time. I'm right on his tail now. He's diving on full power. Air speed 320. I'm keeping right on his tail. He's going straight down. We're at 5,000 now. Four – three – two. My God! Isn't he ever going to pull out? I don't think he can pull out. He can't possibly pull out.*

There was a pause then. The fighter was pulling out of his dive. I knew the rest of it before the squadron leader came back on the air. *I've just pulled out and am banking. The Tudor drove straight into the sea. There's a great column of water. It's settling now. Can't see anything of the plane. There's just some slick on the surface of the sea. That's all. He went straight in. Never pulled out of that dive. Went slap in. Am returning to base now. Am returning the squadron to base.*

There was a heavy silence in the Operations Room, broken only by the squadron leader's voice calling his aircraft into formation. In that silence I had a strange feeling of loss. One shouldn't have any sympathy for a man like Saeton – his ambition had outrun the bounds of our social code, he had killed a man. And yet . . . There had been something approaching greatness in him. He was a man who had seen a vision.

I shifted stiffly in my chair and found that Else's hand was gripping mine. Culyer was the first to speak. 'Poor devil! He must have blacked out.'

But I knew he hadn't blacked out. Else knew it, too, for she said, 'He choose the best way.' There was a note of admiration in her voice.

'I'm sorry it had to end like that,' the station commander murmured. I think he was regretting his order to send fighters up.

I closed my eyes. I was feeling very tired.

'Fraser.'

I looked up. Culyer was standing over me.

'You worked on those engines with Saeton, didn't you?'

I nodded. I was too tired to speak.

'You know we were arranging for Miss Meyer here to get to work for us and the Rauch Motoren? Well, that's going to take time. Suppose we do a deal with the British? Suppose the two of you work on the project together?'

Still the engines! I wanted to say, 'Damn the bloody engines.' I wanted to tell him that they'd already cost the lives of two men. And then I looked up and saw Else watching me. There was excitement – a sort of longing – in her eyes. And then I knew what the future was.

'All right,' I said. 'We'll work on it together.'

Somehow that seemed to make sense – if we reproduced those engines for the West, then perhaps Saeton and Tubby would not have died for nothing. As soon as I had made the decision the tenseness inside me seemed to ease and I was relaxed for the first time in days. Else was smiling. She was happy. And despite the pain of my shoulder I think I was happy too.

THE STRANGE LAND

For
DOROTHY
This book in particular, because she acted as interpreter in addition to her usual role of reader and critic

AUTHOR'S NOTE TO THE NEW EDITION OF 1964

The Strange Land was first published in 1954. The setting is Tangier and Morocco and was the result of journeys my wife and I had made in North Africa two years previously. Morocco is now an independent kingdom, but at that time it was still a French Protectorate. The Protectorate dated from 1912, but in point of fact the final pacification of the remote south was not completed until the middle 30s. It was in this southern area – between the mountains of the High Atlas and the deserts of the Sahara – that we spent most of our time. In 1952 it was still known as the Zone of Insecurity and still a military area administered by Les Officiers des Affaires Indigènes through the Sheriffian Government of the Sultan. These officers supervised the building of roads, schools, hospitals, the collection of the Sultan's taxes, the tribunals of justice and arbitrated in the constant land disputes that had previously been settled by inter-tribal war. They were an élite corps, speaking both Berber and Arab and relying solely on the force of their personalities. They were the equivalent of our DCs except that they acted always *in loco parentis* to the Sheriffian Government and had no direct powers of enforcement.

The story of *The Strange Land* is, of course, fiction. But in the third section particularly I hope I have managed to convey not only the atmosphere of this primitive and exciting country on the edge of a vast desert, but also something of the work and achievements of a dedicated group of French officers who sacrificed their health and sometimes their lives for a people not their own.

Hammond Innes
Kersey, 1963

CONTENTS

PART ONE

INTERNATIONAL ZONE

1

PART TWO

THE MISSION

129

PART THREE

ZONE OF INSECURITY

167

PART ONE

INTERNATIONAL ZONE

CHAPTER ONE

The rain came in gusts out of a leaden sky. The flat-topped houses of the old Arab town climbed the hill like a cemetery of close-packed gravestones, windowless, lifeless, their whiteness accentuated by the dusk. There was still light enough for me to see the solitary palm tree above the old Sultan's Palace thrashing its fronds. It was straight like a flagstaff and black against the fading light of the western sky. Down in the harbour a siren blared, the sound of it cut off abruptly as the wind clutched at it. The wide, open space of the Zocco Grande – the big market – was deserted and runnelled by muddy streams of water. Naked lights already glimmered in the squalid huts, revealing the cracked mud of the walls and the still, wrapped bodies of the men who sat there drinking mint tea and smoking their tiny-bowled pipes of kif. An Arab passed me, carrying his slippers in his hand. His djellaba flapped in the wind and his bare feet were wide and splayed as they scuffed through the mud.

The Air France flight from Paris went over, a dull roar of engines in the murk of low-hung cloud. The plane was over two hours late, delayed by bad weather. Even so, it had left Paris only that morning. A day's flying and I could be in England. The rain would be soft and gentle there with the smell of things growing and the promise of spring. I hunched my shoulders into my raincoat and tried not to think of England. My home was Enfida now, close under the mountains of the High Atlas looking out across the flat, brown plain of Marrakech.

But Tangier is a restless, transient place. I had already been waiting three days; and all the time I had carefully avoided my old haunts, trying to tell myself that it was a sordid, unreal city, a sort of international Sodom and Gomorrah, and that the past was all done with. After all, it was here that I had made the big decision. It was here in Tangier that I had thought it all out and taken the plunge. It was crazy perhaps, but at least I was doing something real. And I had made some progress in the last five years; the French no longer regarded me with suspicion and the Berbers of the High Atlas accepted me without hostility. When Kavan arrived . . .

I half shrugged my shoulders. The sooner I got out of Tangier the better. It was an unsettling place and already the old fever, the desire for excitement, for taking a chance, had got hold of me. But Kavan would be in tonight, and tomorrow we should leave for Enfida where the white mountain peaks are seen through the grey mist of the olive trees and there are no planes roaring over to remind one of England.

The arch of the medina loomed ahead, the entrance to the Arab town and Es Siaghines, the street of the money changers. There were lights in some of the shops, but the street itself was deserted, the steep slope of the asphalt shining blackly. The money changers – operators of one of the world's few free bourses – were gone, and the narrow street was strangely silent. A bundle of rags, propped against a shuttered jeweller's shop, stirred and extended a brass bowl held in two filthy arm stumps.

The forgotten beggar and the deserted bourse seemed somehow symbolic of the bubble nature of Tangier, and I found myself suddenly loathing the place for what it was – crooked and greedy and shallow, a harlot city in a world at grips with the reality of a cold war.

The Zocco Chico was empty, the tables glistening forlornly in the light from the deserted cafés that surrounded it. The little market place was like an Italian piazza in the rain. I took the alley that leads past the grand mosque and went down the steps. The fronds of the palm trees lining the Avenue d'Espagne were waving wildly and the sea roared white along the sands; the noise of it mingled with the wind, so that the whole front was one continuous murmur of sound. Out in the harbour the lights of the anchored freighters shone on heaving, white-capped water. A plume of smoke rose from above the roof of the railway station and was whipped out across the mole in a long, white streamer. I pitied the poor devil I was waiting for and turned into José's Bar.

After all these years the place smelt the same – a combination of coffee, garlic, sour wine and bad sanitation. José was standing behind the bar counter. He looked fatter, greasier, more shifty, and his black hair as grizzled now. '*Muy buenas*, señor.' And then he stared. 'Señor Latham!' His face lit up with a smile, his brown teeth showing a grin that cracked the grey stubble. He wiped his hand on his apron and extended it to me across the counter. 'It is good to see you, señor. It is a long time – five, six years; I do not remember. Time goes so quick.'

'You've got a good memory, José,' I said.

'*Sí, sí*. A good memory is necessary in my business.' He turned and reached for a bottle. 'It is a Fundador, *sí*?'

'No, José. A coffee, that's all.'

'Ah, no, no, no.' He shook his head. 'I do not forget what you drink, and this is with me.' He poured two glasses. '*Salud*!'

'*Salud*!' I raised my glass. It was like old times. It seemed a long, long time ago.

'A terrible night, señor.'

'Terrible.' I glanced at my watch. It was nearly six. Youssef was late. But that meant nothing. Time meant nothing in an Arab world. 'How's business, José?' I asked. The place was almost empty.

He shrugged his shoulders. 'The season, she is finish now.' He meant the smuggling season. Not for nothing was José's called the 'Smuggler's Bar'. It used to be the haunt of half the riff-raff of the port, probably was still.

But the Mediterranean in December is no place for small boats. The business would be confined now to the bigger boats and the short runs across to Gib and Algeciras.

I turned and glanced round the café. It was a dreary little place. Yet there were times I could remember when it had seemed gay and bright and cheerful – but then that had been just after the war, late at night when the boys were in after a successful run and José sweating like a bull to keep the glasses filled. Now the piano in the corner was closed and the only music came from the radio, the tinkle of a guitar from some Spanish station. José's wife, Maria, hummed the tune tonelessly as she sat mending a shirt and watching the pots on the battered range. A child sat at her feet, cross-legged like an Arab and sucking a cork. The place had a tired, run-down air. Two sailors sat at a table engrossed in a game of cards and in the far corner, beyond the door, a girl sat alone, toying with a half-empty glass, whilst two tables away one of the currency boys, with long sideboards and a wide-brimmed hat, sat eyeing her speculatively. There was nobody else in the bar.

'Who's the girl?' I asked José. It was unusual for a girl to sit drinking alone in a place like José's.

He shrugged his shoulders. 'I never see her before, señor. I think she is new in Tangier.'

'She certainly must be,' I said. Didn't she know the sort of place José's was? 'You ought to have a notice up outside, José,' I said. ' "Abandon hope all girls who enter here." '

He frowned. 'I do not understand, señor.'

'Oh, yes you do.'

He glared at me angrily, and then he showed his decayed teeth like a bull terrier shifting a snarl to a smirk. '*Sí, sí* – always you are the joker, señor.'

I turned and glanced at the girl. She had a small, pinched, rather serious face with a finely shaped nose and an attractive mouth. Her skin was pale, accentuating her dark hair, and she had a high, rather bony forehead. She sat with her head a little on one side, staring out of the window, her mouth tightly puckered. There was something of the gamine about her that was appealing, and she wore no make-up, which again was something unusual.

She was apparently aware of my interest, for she glanced at me quickly out of the corners of her eyes. Then she was looking down at her fingers, which were twined round the stem of her glass as though to shatter it. Something about that quick, surreptitious glance had given her face an odd, almost furtive look. Perhaps it was the slant of her eyes. She was frowning now and her lips were no longer puckered, but compressed into a thin, hard line.

'She is not a Tangeroise,' José whispered across the bar.

'Of course not.'

'She is *inglésa* perhaps?'

But I shook my head. She didn't look English. I turned back to José. He still had that ugly smirk on his face. 'You are married per'aps now, señor?' he suggested.

'No.'

'You are still in the business then?'

'Smuggling?' I laughed. 'No,' I said. 'I'm a missionary now.'

'A missionary? You?' He let out a great guffaw that came to me hot with the smell of bad breath and garlic. 'You a missionary! *Sí, sí.* I understand. An *inglés* joke, eh?'

I didn't say anything. He'd never understand. How should he when I didn't understand myself? It was just that a man changed as he got older, that excitement palled – that kind of excitement anyway. It had happened to Paul. It had happened to any number of men.

'You are serious, señor?' His tone had changed.

'Yes, José – quite serious.'

He mumbled an apology and crossed himself, his fat face sagging. 'It is this place, señor, God is not here in Tangier.' And he crossed himself again.

And then the door swung open and Youssef came in.

'You're late, Youssef.'

He hung his head. 'Is wet, m'soor,' was all he said. His brown eyes stared up at me. The brown eyes and the big, hooked nose were all that was visible of him. The hood of his djellaba muffled his pock-marked features. He pushed the hood back with long, stained fingers till it showed the red of his tarbush. Little pools of water formed on the floor at his feet. 'Very wet, m'soor,' he said and shook his djellaba. 'Very bad night. Boat not come here. Stop other side, in Spain, I think.'

'Well, I don't,' I said. 'The weather's no worse than they'll have had in the Bay of Biscay. You have a drink, Youssef, and then get back to the douane.'

'Okay,' he said. 'But is no good, m'soor. Boat not in Spain, then is finish.'

There was a sudden tinkle of glass. It came from the corner where the girl was sitting. The stem of her glass had snapped. She sat, staring down at the dribble of wine that spilled across the oilcloth covering the table. Her long fingers still gripped the broken stem. Her face was very white. Again her eyes darted in my direction, apprehensive, furtive. Then she was picking up the pieces, her hand trembling slightly, and José was at her side, explaining volubly that glasses were difficult to get, that they were expensive. She fumbled in her bag and brought out a hundred-peseta note, which she handed to him, at the same time ordering another drink in English that was too grammatical, as though it were a language learned long ago and now unfamiliar. She had a soft, slightly husky voice, a whisper that was as pale and thin as her face.

'I take a *café* with you, m'soor,' Youssef said. 'After, I return to the douane. But is no good.'

'They'll come,' I said.

'*Insh'Allah*.' He shrugged his shoulders. He was a Christian, one of the few Arab Christians in Tangier, but he still used that inevitable, fatalistic phrase – *If Allah wills it*.

I was still watching the girl, wondering about her, and when José returned to the bar, I ordered two coffees and asked him what nationality he thought she was. He shrugged his shoulders. 'You are right,' he said. 'She speaks your language, señor, but she is not *inglésa*. She is not Spanish or French and she is not an *indigène*.

Perhaps she is Mexican.' He grinned. He had once had a Mexican girl to serve drinks, but his wife had thrown her out.

Youssef drank his coffee noisily, standing at the bar. He drank like a horse, sucking it up through his thick lips. Then he left. I went with him to the door and watched his flapping figure scurry down to the wharf like a rag blown on the wind. He was a clerk in the Customs office. He would know sooner than I could when the boat was sighted.

I stood there for a moment with the rain beating down on me, listening to the roar of the sea along the beach and thinking of the two men somewhere out there in the night, beating into the shelter of Tangier in a fifteen-ton ketch, fighting their way through the breaking seas towards the safety of the harbour. They had been sighted off Cape St Vincent the day I had arrived in Tangier and yesterday a freighter had reported them forty miles south-west of Cadiz. I prayed God that they would reach Tangier safely. It wasn't only a prayer for two men in peril on the sea. I needed Dr Kavan. I knew nothing about him, had never seen him, and I didn't understand why he had to come out to Tangier in an undermanned yacht, but I needed a doctor, a man who would give his life to the people I lived and worked among, who would give it for a pittance because it was what he wanted to do.

I went slowly back into the bar, conscious of the girl's eyes following me as I crossed the room. The place brought back old memories and I felt a momentary impatience, wishing Kavan would come so that I could get out of the town. José picked the bottle up. 'Don't you ever feel you want to go back to Spain?' I asked him.

'Spain?' He stared at me, the bottle poised in his hand. 'I fight in the Republican Army. What the hell for I go back to Spain, uhn?' The bottle tinkled against the rim of the glass as he poured. He pushed the drink across to me, not saying anything, his black eyes morose and withdrawn.

'I'm sorry,' I said. 'I didn't know.' I sipped the drink, looking across at him, seeing more now than the fat paunch held in by a leather belt and the matted, hairy chest and the grey, unshaven face, seeing for the first time the man behind the crumbling exterior, the man who had fought for an ideal.

I was still thinking about this, thinking how blind people are, seeing only the ugliness – until suddenly you catch a glimpse of the likeness of God in a man – and then the door was thrust open and the bar was suddenly full of noise. It was Big Harry and his crew. With them were the Galliani brothers and Kostos, the Greek. I had known them all in the old days. '*Muy buenas*, José,' Harry roared. 'Set 'em up. Drinks for everybody. The kid, too.' He bent down, swept José's little boy up and set him on the bar top. The child gurgled, putting his fat arms round the giant's neck, while the mother smiled coyly. 'Come on, José. Make it snappy. We're wet and tired and dam' thirsty. We just got in. An' we got somep'n to celebrate, ain't we, boys?' He grinned round at his crew and there was a murmur of assent.

He was a huge rock of a man dressed in a reefer

jacket with a peaked cap that looked several sizes too small for him crammed on to his cannon-ball of a head. He was an ex-Navy petty officer, one of the last of the big-time smugglers who had given Tangier the reputation it had had immediately after the war. Now it was all banking and export-import crookery and he was left to rule a roost that had become no more than a dung heap for Mediterranean small fry to root in. It was sad in a way.

He saw me and grinned and came staggering through the whole bunch of them like a tramp ploughing through a litter of bum boats. 'Well, Phip. Good God! Long time no see, eh? What you do for a living these days?' The big hand gripped my shoulder and the round, unshaven face was thrust close to mine. He still had a boyish look, even when liquored up – except for the eyes. 'Watcher drinking, cocker?'

'Same as you,' I said. 'Fundador.'

'*Ça va*. Make it eight, José. An' one fer yourself. We're celebrating.'

'Good run?' I asked him.

'Sure we had a good run. We always have good runs. Wet, that's all. Molto bloody wet.' He seized hold of the bottle on the counter and took a swig at it. 'Only we ain't the only ones to get wet tonight,' he said, grinning and wiping his mouth. 'There's a poor bastard out there . . . Christ! You never saw such a sight. We picked him up against the beam of Malabata. All plain sail an' going like a train. Couldn't see the boat fer spray. Jesus! There are some crazy bastards! Single-handed and full sail!'

I caught his elbow as he turned back to join his crew. 'What sort of boat was she?' I asked him.

'Ketch or yawl – couldn't be certain in the spotlight.'

'About fifteen tons?'

'Yeah, about that. Why? You know the boat?'

'If it's the boat I'm expecting, there should be two men on board her.'

'Well, this bloke was single-handed.'

'How do you know?'

'How do I know? Because there was only one bloke in the Goddamned boat, that's how.'

'In the cockpit?'

'Well, he wasn't standing in the bows, I can tell you. She was taking it green, right back as far as the coach-roofing.'

'The other fellow was probably below,' I said. 'In a storm that'd be the sensible—'

'What do you know about it?' He thrust his face close to mine. 'In a storm you shorten sail. This crazy bastard had full main and mizzen set, Number One jib and stays'l. If you don't believe me, ask one of the boys. They all saw it. He was a single-hander all right.'

Kostos thrust his long nose between us. He had a thin, acquisitive face and dark, restless eyes. 'How far is he, this boat?'

'About five miles.'

The Greek nodded. 'Good. That will be him. And you are right. He is alone – one man.'

'Well, that's fine.' Big Harry grinned. 'Kostos agrees with me. He's never seen the boat, but he agrees with me. That means I'm right, eh?'

Kostos smiled and tapped the side of his nose. 'Not a sparrow falls,' he said.

Big Harry roared with laugher and clapped him on the back. Then he turned and rolled back along the bar to join his crew. The Greek stared at me. He had grown sleeker and fatter with the years. When I had first come to Tangier he had been a pale, undernourished little runt of a man, inquisitive, restless, his grubby fingers prodding energetically into every pie. Now his hands were manicured, his clothes well cut and he had an air of flashy opulence. 'What do you want with Wade?' he asked me curiously.

'Wade?'

'Yes, Wade: the man who sails this boat into Tangier. What do you want with him?'

'Nothing.'

'Then why are you asking about the boat?'

'That's my business.'

He stared at me hard. The pupils of his eyes were the colour of sloes when the bloom has been rubbed off. An unpleasant silence stretched between us. I watched him trying to sum me up, trying to understand what I was doing back here in Tangier. 'You have been away from here a long time, Captain Lat'am,' he said, smiling. 'Things have changed. I have an organisation here now, several companies.' He paused significantly and then said, 'You like a drink?'

'No thank you,' I said.

He nodded and smiled. 'All right, Lat'am. But don't do nothing foolish.' He went back to his drink then and I wondered what his interest was in *Gay Juliet* and her skipper. I was wishing Dr Kavan had chosen a more conventional method of travelling out. I was wishing, too, that I hadn't decided to wait for the boat at this bar.

I seated myself at one of the tables. A newspaper lay there, the black print of the headlines ringed by the base of a wine glass. Idly, I picked it up. There had been trouble at Casablanca. There was always trouble at Casa, for it grew too fast and the people of the *bled* were herded in packing-case slums of indescribable squalor. And then I noticed the weather report. There was a gale warning, and heavy falls of snow were reported in the High Atlas. The pass of Tizi N Tichka, which linked Marrakech with Ouarzazate, was closed. I had never known the pass blocked so early in the year and I wondered if there had been snow at Enfida. I started thinking of the Mission then, wondering if it was all right and how Julie Corrigan was making out with the kids. George would be painting, of course. He never stopped painting. But Julie . . .

And then I was thinking of the girl again, alone there in the far corner of the bar. The rings of spilled wine had reminded me of how she had snapped the stem of her glass. I lowered the paper. She was still there, and she was staring out of the window, just as she had been when I had first noticed her. But there was nothing to see there; only the rain drops glistening on the glass and the lights of the ships out there in the blackness of the harbour. Her face and neck were reflected in the dark surface of the glass, disembodied and blurred, like the face and neck of a girl in an old painting.

And then I realised that it wasn't the world outside

nor the reflection of her own image that she saw there, but the bar and the men ranged along it under the naked lights, the whole room. I couldn't see her eyes, but somehow I knew that she was watching us all surreptitiously. And suddenly I knew, too, that she wasn't here by chance – she was here because she was waiting for somebody, or something. She had the tension and watchfulness and the resignation of a woman waiting. She was massaging nervously at the fingers of her left hand. I couldn't see whether she wore a wedding ring or not, but that was the finger she was massaging.

She turned her head then and our eyes met again. I heard Big Harry shouting to his crew, telling them to drink up and get the hell out of here and go on up to Maxie's with him, and all the time she seemed to be measuring me, trying to make up her mind about something.

Finally she got slowly to her feet. I watched her all the time she was coming across the café towards me. Her clothes were poor and did not fit very well, yet she moved easily and she had a good figure. She didn't smile as she reached my table. She just kept her eyes on mine and said, 'Do you mind please if I ask you something?'

'Go ahead,' I said, wondering what was coming.

She was nervous and her eyes looked scared. It gave her face a sort of beauty, that and the way her mouth puckered at the corners. 'You talk about a boat with the big sailor over there.' She nodded towards Big Harry. 'When will it come, please?'

'The boat?'

'Yes, the boat.'

A chair overturned with a crash as one of the crowd stumbled drunkenly. Harry was leading them out of the bar now.

'Are you waiting for *Gay Juliet*, too?'

She nodded her head solemnly. 'Yes, that is the name. When will it come, please?'

The street door was wide open now and the wind was blowing sand and dust along the floor. Surprisingly a glint of moonlight streaked the roadway outside. 'Soon,' I said. 'Big Harry saw her five miles out. That was probably an hour ago, maybe more.' The street door shut with a bang. 'Would you like to join me whilst you're waiting?' I suggested. And when she didn't answer I said, 'Why are you interested in the boat? Do you know one of them?'

She shook her head uncertainly, as though bewildered by the question.

'Who is it you're waiting for?' I asked. 'Is it Wade or Dr Kavan?'

Her eyes widened fractionally and her mouth opened as though she had caught her breath, but she still said nothing, and I asked her whether she would like a drink.

'It is kind of you. No.' She turned quickly and her heels click-clacked across the wooden floor to her table by the window.

I called to José for another coffee. It came in a cracked cup. A violent gust of wind shook the building. It went tearing and screaming round the walls, tugging at the tin roof. The door burst open and sand blew in along the floor in little, sifting runnels, bringing with it the wild sound of the sea along the beach. The girl shivered. I caught a glimpse of a big, bright moon sailing swiftly amongst torn fragments of cloud, and then José had shut the door again.

'A bad night, señor.' José crossed himself and I remembered that he'd been a fisherman in his youth.

Kostos hadn't left with Big Harry and his crowd. He was still standing at the bar, his long, thin nose dipping every now and then to the little glass of liqueur he held in his hand.

There was a conscious stillness about the half-empty bar. It was a silent watchful stillness, as though the whole place were waiting for something to happen. The girl glanced nervously at her watch and then stared resolutely out of the window. Moonlight filtered through on to her face, making it pale like a mask instead of living flesh and blood.

She was waiting for the boat, Kostos was waiting for it, too. All three of us were waiting for the boat, and I wondered what it was like out there in the wind and the waves. Tomorrow it would be hot again with that blazing North African sun heat that bleaches the houses of the kasbah whiter than bone. But right now it was gusting fifty or sixty knots and Big Harry had said the boat was being sailed single-handed. Suppose he were right? Suppose Kavan . . . I felt the need for prayer, but I couldn't, for I was thinking of my plans, not of the man. I didn't know the man. What I did know was that I'd never get another doctor for my Mission on my own terms the way I'd got Kavan. There was something odd about the man, of course. There had to be for him to come a thousand miles to a remote hill village for next to no money. But he had written – *I have the need to lose myself in work that is quite remote from everything that I have been striving for over many years. That part of my life is finished. Now I wish to make use of the art of healing I learned as a young man. It is better so and all I ask is that the work shall absorb me utterly . . .*

That section of his letter I knew by heart, for when you live a lonely life, cut off from the world among an alien people, and you plan to share that life with another man, a man you do not know, then you search urgently for any scrap that may give you some clue to the sort of person he is.

I was still wondering about him when the door opened and Youssef burst in. 'Come quick, m'soor,' he called, flapping urgently across to me, his hooked nose moist and blue with the wind. 'Quick. Is finish, the boat. Is to be a tragedy.' He caught hold of my arm. 'Quick. I show you.' The words spilled out of him in breathless puffs. The whole café was silent, listening.

I pulled him down into the chair beside me. 'Just tell me quietly what happened.'

He caught his breath. 'Is the wind – a terrible blow of wind. It take the roof from one of the warehouses and there is a little house down near the—'

'The boat,' I said, shaking him. 'Tell me about the boat.'

'*Oui*, m'soor. I tell you. Is finish – no good – *kaput*.'

'You mean it's sunk?'

'*Non, non*. Not sink. Is finish.'

'For heaven's sake, Youssef – what's happened?'

'Is the wind, m'soor. Is coming into Tangier, the boat, and I am watching it and there is terrible blow of wind and – pouff.' He blew out his lips and shrugged his shoulders. 'The big sail is finish and the boat is blown away.'

'Where? Where is it now?'

'Below the kasbah, m'soor. Per'aps he obtain the Baie des Juifs. I do not know.'

'What are they doing about it – the port authorities?'

'Nothing. They can do nothing. They have telephone to the police.' He shrugged his shoulders again. 'Is to be a tragedy.' He seemed to like the word. 'You come quick now. You see. I do not lie.'

I followed him out of the café then. The girl was standing, wide-eyed and shaken, by the door as I opened it. 'You'd better come, too,' I suggested.

Outside, the wind and the sea still roared along the beach, but the sky was clear now, a blue-black sky, studded with stars and dominated by the white orb of the moon which flung a glittering pathway across wind-white waters. Youssef clutched my arm and pointed. Beyond the roof of the Customs House, against the black blur of the sea, a patch of white showed, a rag hung momentarily above the waves and then lost in spray. It emerged again and, shielding my eyes from the wind, I saw vaguely the shape of a boat with heads'ls set and drawing. And then it was gone again, like a phantom boat, as the spray smothered it.

'Oh, God!' the girl whispered, and when I looked at her I saw her eyes were closed and her lips were moving silently.

I told Youssef to phone for a taxi and then I took her arm. 'Would you like a drink?' I had half turned her back towards the bar and, as Youssef opened the door, I saw Kostos momentarily outlined against the rectangle of light. He was staring along the line of the cliffs, watching the death struggles of the boat, and his hands were clasped together, the fingers pressed against the knuckles as though by mere physical effort of thrusting at his hands he could pull the boat through.

'Come on,' I said to the girl. 'A drink will do you good.'

But she remained quite still, resisting the pressure of my hand. 'No,' she whispered. 'I do not want a drink.'

She was trembling. I could feel her body shaking. 'Who do you know on the boat?' I asked her. She wasn't English. It had to be Kavan. 'Is it Dr Kavan?'

She nodded dumbly.

'You're a Czech then?' I said.

'My mother was Irish,' she answered as though that made some sort of difference.

I stared out across the docks to the moonlit fury of the sea. It was a wild, terrifying sight. The cliffs were black in shadow and the sea was white with driven spray and the backlash of the tide running around Cape Spartel. I was thinking about Kavan and how little I knew about him – just that he was a Czech and was thirty-eight years old and that he had been trained in his youth as a doctor. The Mission authorities in London had not been involved. This was a purely personal arrangement and the only information I had on him was what he had given me in those two letters – the first applying for the post in answer to my advertisement and the second informing me that he was sailing with a man called Wade in the fifteen-ton ketch *Gay Juliet*. I hadn't dared ask questions, for his had been the only application I had received. 'How did you know he was on the boat?' I asked the girl.

I thought for a moment that she hadn't heard my question and I glanced at her face. It was very pale in the moonlight and there were lines of strain at the corners of eyes and mouth. 'He told me,' she whispered. 'We still have means of communicating.' And her mouth was shut in a tight, hard line and I felt her body shake again, though she wasn't crying.

Youssef came back to us out of the bar. 'The taxi is coming, m'soor.'

The girl didn't move, didn't look at him. She was staring at the point where we'd last seen the boat. I wanted to ask her about Kavan, but it would have to wait. This wasn't the moment. She was racked with fear and there was a sort of desperate bitterness about her face. I looked round for Kostos, but he'd gone. And then a police jeep drove past and went through the dock gates and stopped at the Customs House.

The girl stopped trembling. She was suddenly incredibly still. And when I looked at her, she wasn't staring at the sea any more, but at the little group that had gathered about the jeep, gesticulating and pointing towards the cliffs where the boat had disappeared. Customs officers and police piled into the jeep and it turned and came racing past us again and disappeared down the Avenue d'Espagne, the red tail-light dwindling to a pinpoint. The girl found her voice then. 'What are the police going to do? Why have they been called?' Her voice was scared, a little breathless.

'The boat's in distress,' I reminded her.

'That is purely a job for the coastguards, not for the police.'

I shrugged my shoulders, not understanding her concern. 'There's a lot of smuggling goes on in Tangier,' I told her.

'Smuggling?' She repeated the word slowly as though she'd never heard it before. 'But if they—' She stopped suddenly as though biting back her words. And then she said, 'I suppose it does not matter. So long as they get him safe ashore. Nothing else matters.' But there was an odd reservation in her voice as though there were things worse than drowning.

The taxi arrived then and we got in and I ordered the driver to take us to the Pension de la Montagne. From the terrace there we should have a clear view right across Jews' Bay where the *oued* that the Europeans call Jews' River runs out into the sea. To go up to the kasbah meant walking and would take too long, and if we drove to the Marchan on this side of the bay, we should lose ourselves in a tangle of undergrowth and villas.

The girl sat very still as we drove up through the Place de France and out along the route de la Montagne. She didn't talk. She had her hands clasped tightly on her lap and her face, in the flash of the street lamps, was set and tense. We crossed the Pont des Juifs, and then the headlights were cutting up through a narrow road hemmed in by steep, walled banks, where the bougainvillea showed as splashes of bright purple on the walls of villas. At the bend halfway up la Montagne, we turned off on to a track, and in a moment we were in bright moonlight with a clear view of the sea below.

We left the taxi then and walked through the arched gateway of the *pension* and out on to the terrace. The wind caught us there, driving the breath back into our throats. The view was magnificent. On the dark slopes of the Marchan opposite, the lights of the villas shone like glow-worms, and beyond, the kasbah sprawled over its hill like a bone-white cemetery. Below us, the sea was deeply ridged and flecked with white. I shaded my eyes from the moon's glare and stared down along the line of the cliffs beyond to Marchan.

'Do you see it?' the girl asked.

'No.'

It was dark below the Marchan and all I could see was the white of the waves breaking. Then Youssef was pointing and I thought I saw the triangle of a sail. But it vanished as though it were a trick of the light. The girl saw it, too, and said, 'We must do something. Please can you do something?' There was a desperate urgency in her plea.

'There's nothing we can do,' I said. 'We can only wait until . . .' And then, suddenly, I saw the boat quite clearly. It had emerged from the shadow of the Marchan and was out in the moonlight. It was edging along the coast, close in and half-smothered by the break of the waves. The wind was driving it straight into the bay. 'They'll beach her in the bay,' I said. The yacht hadn't a hope of wearing the headland below us. 'Come on.' I caught her arm and we ran back to the taxi.

'Is there any hope for him?' she asked as the taxi turned and started back down the hill.

'I don't know,' I said. 'The sea looks pretty bad down there. But if the boat comes in close . . .' She was looking at me and there was a desperate pleading in her eyes, so that I felt her fear as though it were my own. 'Why does he mean so much to you?' I asked gently.

'He is my husband.' She said it so quietly, so softly, that I scarcely caught the words, only the meaning. And then in a sudden rush she added, 'We were engaged before the war. Christmas, 1938. And then in March the Germans came and, because he was a scientist, they forced him to go to Germany. We didn't see each other until after the war. Then he came back and we were married. We were married two years. Then the Russians came and he escaped to England. We only had those two years.' There was no bitterness in the way she said it, only a sort of hopeless resignation.

It seemed odd her talking about him whilst the man himself was fighting for his life down there in the bay and we were careering down the hill to be there when the boat struck. 'Why didn't you go to him in England?' I asked. 'If you could get to Tangier . . .' I felt the sentence unfinished, for she was staring at me, sudden fear and suspicion in her eyes.

'Who are you? Why are you here, waiting for him?' It was the same breathless rush of words, but difficult now, harder and more withdrawn.

'I'm Philip Latham,' I said. And then I began to

explain about the Mission and my need of a hospital and how we had so little money that I had despaired of ever getting a doctor out from England. And before I had finished, the taxi had swung off the road on to a track that ran down through a squalid, mud-walled village and finished on the banks of the *oued*.

The police jeep was parked there. And beside it was a big American car, its chromium glinting in the moonlight. She gave a little gasp and clutched my arm. She was staring at the jeep. 'Why can't they leave him alone?' she whispered. I stared at her, not understanding the cause of her outburst.

It was the car that puzzled me. The village was half a mile away and there was no villa near. 'Do you know whose car this is?' I asked Youssef.

But he shook his head. 'There are many American cars in Tangier, m'soor. Very expensive, very nice. Per'aps I have American car one day.' He grinned at me from beneath the hood of his djellaba. An American car was the dream of every Arab in Tangier.

We pushed past the jeep and hurried along the path that ran beside the *oued*. The pounding of the sea was hurled at us on the wind and soon a fine spray was drifting across our faces. Then we were out on a little bluff that was all coarse grass and sand, and there, straight ahead of us, was the yacht, its jib bellied out as it ran for the shore with the wind and sea behind it. A lone figure stood on the edge of the bluff, curiously insubstantial and ghostly in the driven spume and the moonlight. He turned as we came up. It was Kostos.

'What are you doing here?' I shouted to him.

His long face smiled at me. But he didn't say anything, only turned and stared out across the surging, foaming surf to where the boat was piling in, its bows lifting to a wave and then creaming forward on the break of it.

'Who is that man?' the girl asked me. 'He was there in the café. What does he want?'

'His name is Kostos,' I said. 'I think he's waiting for Wade.'

'Wade?'

'The owner of the boat.'

'Oh, I see.' She was staring down at the beach where a little group of officials stood at the water's edge, watching the boat. It was in the broken water now and I wondered how the poor devils who sailed her expected to get ashore through those thundering acres of surf.

A hand gripped my elbow and I turned to find Kostos at my side. 'Why do you come here, Lat'am?' he shouted at me. 'What is your interest in the boat?'

'What's yours?' I demanded.

He stared at me hard and then asked about the girl.

'She's come here to meet Kavan,' I told him.

'Who?'

'Dr Kavan,' I shouted.

'Kavan? But there is only Wade on the boat.'

'No. A Dr Kavan is with him.'

'I don't believe it.' He stared at me. 'Why should he bring Kavan? He would not be such a fool.' And then he caught hold of my arm. 'What do you know about this, Lat'am?'

But my attention switched to the boat then as she

lifted high on the curling crest of a breaker. I thought for a moment that she was going to broach-to; she swung almost broadside and then twisted back on to her pell-mell course of destruction, steadying in the surf and driving forward through the broken water, her bows half buried by the press of canvas for'ard. She was surging straight in towards us and I realised that the man at the helm had seen the channel cut by the *oued* and was driving her towards it. But the *oued* was only a trickle. The channel did not extend into the sands.

The tall mainmast quivered as she struck. She held there for a moment, her waterline showing like a red wound in the backwash, and then the next wave had piled in on top of her, jerking her forward, covering her with a seething cataract of foam like a half-submerged rock. And as the wave receded, a lone man fought his way for'ard to the bows. He wore a life jacket and for a moment he stood there, his head turned, watching the next wave climb and curl above the stern of the boat. I heard the girl give a cry that was as wild and forlorn as a sea bird's, and then the wave was breaking and the figure of the man plunged into the surf of it and was lost.

I ran down to the sands then. The little group by the water's edge had a rope, but they were arguing and gesticulating. They weren't going to risk their necks in that sea. I stripped off my clothes and seized the end of the rope and tied it round my waist. I could see the swimmer's head now. He was halfway between the yacht and the beach and he was being swept out again in the backwash of a wave. 'Hold that,' I shouted to one of the gendarmes, thrusting the end of the rope into his hand. And then I was wading out through the warmth of the water, letting the backwash carry me towards the dark head of the swimmer where he was being sucked into the break of the next wave.

I called to him as my legs were swept from under me, and then I was swimming. I met the on-coming breaker with my body flat, spearing through it, coming up with my ears singing with the rush of it, and then swimming hard with the rope tugging at my belly.

The yacht wasn't far now. It shifted in the break of a wave. The waves seemed huge in the moonlight. They piled in, one after the other, growing, white-capped mountains that rose up as though from some subterranean commotion, rose up to impossible heights and then toppled and fell with the crushing weight of tons of water. Their surf piled over me, flinging me shorewards, filling mouth, ears, eyes and nose full of the burning, sand-laden salt of the water.

I prayed to God that they would keep a firm hold on the rope, knowing no swimmer could get ashore through this unaided, and then I came up gasping for breath, searching desperately for the man I'd come in after. The tug of a backwash got me, tossed me into the maw of a breaker, which toyed with me and spewed me up out of its creaming back, and there he was, lying like a log not twenty yards to my left.

I put my head down and began to swim. Another wave piled over me and then I was seaward of him, treading water, waiting to hold him in the backwash. I caught him just as the next wave engulfed us. I got my fingers into his life jacket. and kicked with all my strength. And as we broke surface, I felt the rope tighten round my body, biting into my flesh as they held the two of us against the back-surge. And then they were dragging us in, my lungs fighting for breath against the constriction of the rope and the tug of the man's water-logged body.

After what seemed an age there came a wave that rolled us forward like logs before a wall of broken water, engulfed us and then subsided to leave my feet scrabbling desperately in a moving tide of sand.

After that there wasn't any danger any more, only the leaden weakness of my legs as I forced them to drag myself and my burden clear of the pull of the surf. Where the sea ended and the sands showed hard and white in the moonlight I staggered and fell forward on to my hands. I was completely drained of energy, utterly exhausted. They dragged us higher up the sands to safety and then fingers unknotted the rope from around my waist and began to rub my body to restore the circulation.

Slowly the blood pumped energy back into my limbs and I pulled myself into a sitting position. I saw the bay and the white surf in the moonlight and the lank hair lying across the man's bloodless face. He was short and thick-set and he had a round head set close into broad, powerful shoulders. One arm was bent across his chest. He looked like a little bearded Napoleon.

And then everything was blurred and I retched, emptying myself of the sea water that was in my lungs and stomach. I was sweating suddenly and very cold.

One of the Spanish Customs officers helped me to

my feet. And then Youssef was there. He had slipped out of his djellaba and he thrust it down over my head, whether to cover my nakedness or to keep me warm I don't know. The cloth was soft and it kept out the wind. I pulled it close round me, trying to control the shivering of my body. The girl was still standing up there on the bluff, her hands clasped together, her body leant forward as though she were on the point of rushing down on to the beach; but yet she did not move. She stayed up there as though her feet were somehow rooted to the spot.

The officials were all bending over the man I had pulled out of the sea. One of them had turned him over on his face and had begun to work on him, kneeling astride him and pressing rhythmically with the palms of his hands against the man's shoulders, thrusting down with all his weight. Kostos hovered uncertainly in the background. One of the police, a sergeant, caught hold of my hand and pumped it up and down and slapped me on the back as though by shaking my hand and congratulating me and telling me I was a brave man he could absolve himself from his failure to enter the water.

And all the time I stood there, feeling dazed, staring down at the face of the stranger that was pressed against the sand. It was a round, white face under the dark stubble of the beard, the lips slightly parted, blowing frothy bubbles. Then the eyes opened and they were bloodshot and wild in the moonlight. He began to retch with a ghastly concentration, and a pool of water appeared where his mouth touched the sand and trickled away under his body. He groaned, shook himself, and crawled slowly to his feet, swaying slightly and blinking his eyes. He stared at us for a moment, rubbed at the salt in his eyes with his knuckles, and then looked back at the yacht where it lay, canted over, the waves thundering across its decks.

'What about the other man?' I asked him.

He didn't seem to hear, so I caught him by the arm and repeated my question.

He looked at me then. There was blood trickling down from a cut on his head, a bright scarlet runnel of blood in the sand that covered his temple. His eyes were half closed and his mouth was a thin line as though compressed by pain. Then he looked past me at the police and the Customs officers and his eyes were wide open and I saw that he was fully conscious, his brain alive again.

The sergeant saw it, too. He stepped forward. 'Your name please, señor?' he asked in Spanish. The man didn't reply and the sergeant said, 'Are you Señor Kavan? Señor Jan Kavan, a resident of Great Britain?'

The man made some sort of sound, inarticulate as a grunt, as though somebody had punched him in the solar plexus. He was staring at the police, swaying slightly, his eyes immensely blue and wide open, dazed with shock. And then Kostos pushed his way through the little circle of officials. 'You are Mr Wade, yes?' He gripped the man's arm, shaking him. 'You do not bring anybody else with you, eh?'

The man shook his head dumbly.

'Good. I thought not. You are very fortunate man,

Mr Wade. One time I do not think you make it. But now, everything is all right, eh? I am Kostos.'

The man stared at him with the same concentration with which he had stared at the police. He was puzzled and uneasy. The sergeant cleared his throat and addressed Kostos. 'You know this man, Señor Kostos?'

'*Sí, sí.*' The Greek nodded emphatically. 'He is Mr Roland Wade – an Englishman. The yacht out there is called *Gay Juliet*. He has sailed it direct from England.'

'Is this correct, señor?' the sergeant asked.

The man I had pulled out of the sea stared wildly round the group, half-nodded and pushed his hand wearily through his hair. 'Please, I am cold. I must get some clothes. I'm very tired.'

The sergeant was sympathetic, but he was also correct. 'Have you anything by which to identify yourself, Señor Wade? Your passport? The certificate of registration of your boat? Entry into the International Zone of Tangier, you must understand, can only be permitted on production of the necessary passport.' It was really rather ridiculous, the pompous little sergeant demanding a passport from the poor devil there on the sands in the roar of the wind and the sea.

The man moved his hand in a vague, automatic gesture towards his breast pocket and let it fall limp at his side. His eyes closed and he swayed. I thought he was going to pass out. So did Kostos. We both caught hold of him at the same time. 'Can't you settle this in the morning, sergeant?' I said. 'The man is in no state to go through the immigration formalities now.'

The sergeant hesitated, frowning. He stared at the

stranger, whose body sagged heavily between the two of us. His eyes ceased to be impersonal, official, became sympathetic. '*Sí, sí.*' He nodded energetically. 'The formalities will be dealt with in the morning. For the moment, señor, I permit you to land.' He made an expansive, accommodating gesture, and looked round for confirmation from the Customs officers, who nodded agreement. They crowded round him then, bowing and offering him their congratulations at his miraculous escape from death.

'Help me get him out of here, Lat'm,' Kostos hissed.

'Mr Wade.' He shook the man's arm. 'I have a car waiting for you. Can you walk to my car?'

The officials had broken away from us and were going down the beach to recover their rope. The man seemed to pull himself together. 'I'm all right,' he mumbled. He had his eyes open again and was standing more firmly.

'What about the other man?' I asked him again.

'What other man?' His voice was slurred, almost inaudible against the sound of the surf.

'There were two of you on the boat.'

He shook his head slowly. 'No. Only myself. I am single-handed – all the way from England.' He spoke quickly, violently.

'You see,' Kostos said to me. 'It is as I tell you in the café. There is only Wade on the boat.' He tightened his hold on the man's arm. 'I have been expecting you.'

'Expecting me?' The man stared at him, his expression one of bewilderment. 'I don't understand.'

'I tell you. I am Kostos.'

'Leave it at that,' I said. 'He's about all in.'

'You keep out of this, Lat'am. Mr Wade.'

But the man had turned and was staring up the beach. And then he saw the girl and stopped. She was standing about ten yards away. She had her back to the moonlight and I couldn't see the expression on her face, but her hands were held slightly forward, her body too, as though she were entreating him to say he was her husband.

And for a moment I thought he knew her. His eyes had come suddenly alive and his mouth opened, but all he uttered was a sort of groan and then his eyes closed and his knees buckled slowly under him. The police sergeant ran forward, clicking his tongue. He bent over the man's body lying there in the sand and then he looked up at the girl. 'You know Señor Wade?' he asked.

She backed away slowly and shook her head. 'No. I do not know him.' Her body seemed suddenly slack as though all the strength had gone out of her with the realisation that the man was a stranger. She turned, slowly, reluctantly, her head bowed, and walked back alone across the bluff, back towards the taxi.

So Kostos was right. Kavan wasn't on the boat. I went and got my clothes and pulled them on. By the time I was dressed, the little party of officials, carrying the unconscious body of the man I had rescued, was climbing the bluff. Only Kostos still remained there on the wet, gleaming stretch of the sands. He was staring after the little cavalcade. I stared at them, too, wondering about Kavan. Had he changed his mind? Had he decided at the last minute not to sail in *Gay Juliet*? I felt tired and dispirited. And as I walked up the beach, I wasn't thinking about the girl. I was thinking of myself, of the people of Enfida and the mountain villages who needed a doctor, of the fact that the way to their confidence, to the success of my work, lay through medical aid.

Youssef was waiting for me at the foot of the bluff. I gave him his djellaba and we climbed through the wet sand. At the top of the bluff, I turned to look at the yacht again. A glint of metal caught my eye. Kostos was still there on the beach and he was ripping open the discarded life jacket with a knife. As I watched him, he flung the jacket down and started up the beach towards us.

I glanced at the yacht. The starboard shrouds had already parted and the mast was swaying wildly. It was only a matter of time before the whole thing broke up. It was cold there in the wind and spray and I turned and hurried after Youssef along the path beside the *oued*. We caught up with the others just as they reached the cars. They had halted beside the jeep, the half-conscious man held up between them. He was shivering violently and I suggested that he'd better come with me in the taxi. It would be warmer. The sergeant nodded. 'You will take him to the hospital, señor?'

Apparently the poor devil understood Spanish, for he caught hold of my arm in a quick, urgent movement. 'Not a hospital,' he said. 'There's nothing wrong with me; I just want some sleep, that's all.' He was scared of something. It was there in his eyes. They were imploring like the eyes of a stray dog. And I heard myself tell the sergeant that I would take him to my hotel. He asked me the name of it and I told him the Hotel Malabata. He glanced at the man and then nodded and climbed into his jeep.

I saw the look of relief in the man's eyes and then he had closed them and his body sagged as though he had suddenly relaxed his hold on consciousness. Youssef and I had to carry him to the taxi.

I had expected the girl to be sitting there, waiting for us. But she wasn't in the taxi and when I asked the driver whether he had seen her, he said 'No.' I turned and stared back along the path but there was no sign of her. I wondered whether to go and look for her, but I was cold and the man was just about all in. I decided the girl would have to look after herself and I got into the taxi. As we drove off I caught a glimpse of Kostos running towards us. He shouted something. I think it was the man's name. And then we were bumping our way back to the village and the road to Tangier, the police jeep following behind us.

CHAPTER TWO

It seemed a long drive back to Tangier. I felt tired and sick and dispirited, and the taste of the salt water I had swallowed was like a thick, furry film on my tongue. The man I had pulled out of the water lay slumped in his corner and I sat and stared at him, almost hating him. Why couldn't it be Kavan? If only one man was going to arrive in that boat, why couldn't it be . . . We were on a bend and his eyes suddenly flicked open and he grabbed at me. 'Look out! Hold on!' His voice was thick and blurred. He was back on the boat. Then he slumped back in the seat again and his head was lolling and he was mumbling to himself.

I should have realised the significance of his words immediately. But my brain was dulled with the cold and it only came to me slowly. That warning had been shouted to somebody. If in his mind he were back on the boat then he couldn't have been alone; there would have been no reason in shouting a warning if he were single-handed. In a sudden surge of anger I caught hold of him and shook him and shouted, 'What happened to Kavan? What have you done with him?' I was convinced now that Kavan had been on that boat.

But the man was dazed and only half conscious. He mumbled something I couldn't understand and then his head was lolling again to the movement of the car. The blood was caked on his temple and his face was grey with exhaustion. My mood changed from anger to pity and I leaned back and closed my eyes. I could find out about Kavan later. I was thinking what it must have been like at the helm of that yacht coming down through the Bay of Biscay and along the coasts of Spain and Portugal in winter. And then I began to think about Enfida again and how I had told the chiefs of all the villages about my plans and had persuaded them to send men down to help me build an extension to the house to act as a surgery and dispensary. They would shrug their shoulders and murmur *insh'Allah*. But it was a serious blow to my work. And it was no use pretending I should get another doctor. Kavan alone had replied to my advertisements. The salary I was able to offer was too small. I would have been able to stay on here in Tangier and run a few more cargoes. If I had done that . . .

It was stupid to think like that, but my mind was confused and angry. In my loneliness and isolation I had built too much upon Kavan, upon this idea of getting a doctor out to the mountain villages. I closed my eyes wearily, sinking back into a lassitude of exhaustion, too tired to face the thought of planning for the future again.

And then the taxi stopped and we were at the Hotel

Malabata. It was a small, cheap hotel occupying a part of one of those grey blocks of cracking concrete that cling to the escarpment above the Avenue d'Espagne. I pushed open the taxi door and stumbled out. The police jeep had parked behind us and they came and lifted the unconscious man out and carried him into the hotel. As I paid off the driver, an American car rolled quietly down the cobbled street, paused beside the taxi and then drove on. It was Kostos, and in the gleam of the street lighting I saw the hard, inquisitive stare of his eyes.

The hotel was full, but the patrone agreed to let the man share my room and they carried him up the stairs and laid him on the stiff, horsehair couch at the foot of the bed. The police and Customs officers left then with little bows, each of them shaking me by the hand and commending me for having saved the man's life. 'We will return in the morning, señor,' the sergeant said. 'For the formalities, you understand.' The Customs officers nodded. '*Buenas noches*, señor.'

'*Buenas noches*.'

They were gone and the door shut behind them and I stood there, shivering and staring down at the man on the couch. His eyes were closed and his body trembled uncontrollably with the cold. His skin had a wax-like transparency and the blue veins of his forehead showed through like the marks of an indelible pencil. I felt deathly tired. All I wanted to do was to get into my bed and sleep, and I wished I had ignored his plea and taken him straight to the French hospital. But he was here now and I was responsible for him. I sent Youssef for hot-water bottles and began to strip off his sodden clothing.

Below his oilskin jacket I found a waterproof bag hung by a line round his neck. It had the hard compactness of documents; the ship's papers presumably and the log. I tossed it onto the bed, making a mental note to have a look at it later. His sodden clothes I piled on the floor where they formed a little pool of water that trickled away across the bare tiles under the bed.

I was struggling to pull off his blue seaman's jersey when his eyes flicked open. They were incredibly blue. His hair was lank and his beard all grey with salt. Combined with the marble pallor of his face, it made him look like a corpse given back by the sea. He stared up at me. It was a fixed, glazed stare, without expression. His mouth opened, but no sound emerged from the cracked lips. He wiped his hand across his face, slowly, wearily, and then reached out automatically for something he imagined to be hanging above his head. 'Is it my watch already? I'm just coming.' His voice was dead and quite toneless.

Then, suddenly, there was consciousness in his eyes as they stared up at me and his forehead creased in a puzzled frown. He pushed himself up on his elbow with a quick-violent movement and stared wildly around the room. 'Who are you? What am I doing here?' His eyes had come back to my face and his voice was hard and urgent.

I started to explain and he nodded as though it were all coming back to him. 'Have the police gone?'

'Yes.'

'You were down on the beach, waiting for me, weren't you?'

'I was waiting for Kavan,' I said.

He nodded. 'Then you must be Philip Latham.'

'You know my name?' I stared at him. And then I caught hold of him, gripping his arm. 'How do you know my name's Philip Latham? Did Kavan tell you I'd be waiting here for him?' I shook him violently. 'What happened to him? He was on the boat, wasn't he? What happened to him?'

He stared at me. His eyes had a dazed look and he was frowning as though trying to concentrate his thoughts.

'What happened to Jan Kavan?' I repeated.

'Nothing.' His voice sounded dazed, and then in the same flat tone he added, 'I am Jan Kavan.'

'What?' I didn't understand for the moment. 'What was that you said?'

His eyes were suddenly wide open and he fought to raise himself. 'It's true, isn't it? You are Latham?'

'Yes. What did you mean just now?' I shouted at him. 'You said you were Kavan. What did you mean?'

'Yes. I am Kavan.' He said it wearily.

'But—' I stared at him stupidly. 'You're not Wade at all then,' I heard myself say.

'No. I told you. I'm Jan Kavan. I've come here to act as a doctor . . .'

'But you said you were Wade. Down there on the beach—'

'I never said I was Wade,' he said quickly.

'But you let Kostos think—' I stopped there. It was so unbelievable.

'I'm sorry,' he murmured. 'I wanted to tell you,

but—' He frowned. 'Who is that man Kostos? What did he want – do you know?'

'Nothing,' I said. 'He was meeting Wade, that's all.' It didn't matter about Kostos. It didn't matter about anything. Kavan was alive. He was here in my room. 'Did you check up on trachoma?' I asked. It was a stupid thing to ask of a man who was so utterly exhausted, but I couldn't help it. I couldn't think of anything but the fact that he was alive, that my dream of a doctor at the Mission was coming true. Eye diseases were the bane of the Berber people in their fly-ridden villages.

'Yes,' he said wearily. 'I checked up on everything – all the things I have forgotten.' He sighed and then said, 'When do we leave for your Mission?'

'As soon as you're fit enough to travel,' I said.

'Good.' He nodded and closed his eyes. I thought for a moment that he had lost consciousness again, but then his eyelids flicked back and he was looking up at me again. 'Is Kasbah Foum anywhere near your Mission?' he asked.

'Kasbah Foum?' It was an Arab name, meaning fort at the entrance. Probably it was somewhere down in the south, in the kasbah country beyond the High Atlas. 'No,' I replied. 'Why?'

'I have to go there. It's important. I have to go to Kasbah Foum.' He spoke in a whisper, his voice urgent. 'Wade told me that the Caid's son . . .' He stopped there and his eyes closed again.

That mention of Wade brought me back to the

problems of the moment. 'What happened to him?' I demanded. 'What happened to Wade?'

But he didn't answer. His eyes remained closed. It was then I began to get uneasy. The police would have to be informed that he was Kavan. And then there would be an investigation. It might take some days . . . 'Where's Wade?' I asked him again. And when he still didn't answer, I took hold of him and shook him. 'What happened to Wade?' I was certain he wasn't unconscious, and yet . . . 'You'll have to explain to the police,' I told him.

'The police?' His eyes flicked open again and he stared up at me. There was something near to panic in his face.

'They're coming here tomorrow.'

'Tomorrow.' He said it as though it were some distant thing like a mountain peak that had to be faced and overcome.

'It was Wade's boat,' I said. 'You couldn't have left England without him. He was the skipper. What happened? You must tell me what happened.'

'Wade's dead.' He said it in a flat, toneless voice. There was a sort of hopelessness in the way he said it.

So Wade was dead. Somehow I wasn't surprised or even shocked. Maybe I was too tired and my senses were dulled. All I knew was that if this was Kavan, then Wade had to be dead. And then I remembered how he'd said he was alone on the boat, that he'd come single-handed from England and an awful thought came into my mind. 'What happened?' I asked. 'For God's sake tell me what happened.'

He stared at me, his eyes clouded as though he were looking back through time to a scene that was indelibly imprinted on his mind. 'I don't know. I don't know how it happened. He just seemed to jump over the guardrail into the sea.'

There was a pause and then he lifted his head and stared up at me and it all came out of him in a rush. 'It was off Cape St Vincent. It had been blowing. The seas were terrible; great big seas, but not breaking then. It was night and I remember the St Vincent light was winking at us on the port quarter. There had been a bad storm, but the wind had dropped and it was a clear night. The sea was big and confused and there was a lot of movement. And we were tired. I was just coming on watch to relieve him. We were both of us in the cockpit. Then the jib sheet broke. The sail was flapping about and I had hold of the helm. It was difficult to hold the boat. She was yawing wildly and Wade jumped out of the cockpit to get the sail down. He was tired, that was the trouble. We were both of us tired. He jumped out of the cockpit straight into the sea. That was the way it seemed. He just jumped straight over the guardrail.'

He pushed his hand through his hair and glanced up at me. 'You believe me, don't you?' His voice was agitated. 'There was nothing I could do. The boat sunk away into a trough and then he was in the water. I saw him reach up to catch hold of the side and a wave came and he disappeared. I threw the lifebelt to him. I think he got hold of it. I don't know. It was dark. The moon had set. It took me a long time to go about single-handed and I didn't see him again, though I sailed round and round that area till dawn and for a long time after.'

He lay back, exhausted. 'That's all,' he said. 'That's how it happened. There was nothing I could do . . .' His voice trailed away. His eyes closed and he drifted into unconsciousness again, or maybe it was sleep. His face was relaxed, his breathing easier and more regular.

Youssef came back then with four wine bottles filled with hot water. I got some underclothes from my suitcase, wrapped them round the bottles and slipped them into the bed. Then we got Kavan stripped and I washed his body with hot water, rubbing hard with a towel to restore the circulation. His back and buttocks were covered with salt water sores, little nodules of suppuration that bled when I rubbed them. Patches of white, scabrous skin flaked away and his feet and hands were soft and wrinkled with long immersion.

'Is going to die?' Youssef asked.

'Of course not.' I spoke sharply, conscious of the Arab's fascination at the white European body lying naked and hurt and helpless. We got him on to the bed and I piled the blankets on top of him and then I sent Youssef for a doctor I had known, a Frenchman who had lived just across the Boulevard Pasteur.

Then at last I was free to slip out of my own damp clothes. I put on a dressing-gown and lit a cigarette. I would have liked a bath, but the hotel was inexpensive and Spanish and its occupants were expected to use the public baths or go without. I sat on the bed, thinking of the girl and their meeting on the beach. Of course, they had recognised each other. That was why he had collapsed. It was the shock of recognising her. He had said he was Wade and then she had turned away and disappeared. There was no longer any doubt in my mind. This man lying on my bed really was Jan Kavan. But why had he said he was Wade? That was the thing I couldn't understand. And he'd been scared of the police. Why?

I dragged myself to my feet and went over to the chair where my clothes lay. Both his letters were in my wallet – his original application and his note saying that he would be sailing with Wade on *Gay Juliet*.

Youssef returned as I was getting out my wallet. The French doctor had moved. Nobody seemed to know where he now lived. I looked at Kavan lying there on the farther side of the big double bed. His eyes were closed and he was breathing peacefully. It was sleep he needed more than a doctor. I let it go at that and paid Youssef off with two hundred peseta notes. Then I switched on the bedside lamp and checked through the letters.

It was the one in which he had applied for the post of doctor to the Mission that chiefly interested me. I knew it all, of course, but I was hoping that perhaps there was something I had missed, some little point that would now prove significant. I ran through it quickly . . .

I will be quite frank. I am 38 years old and I have not looked at a medical book since I obtained my degree. Nor have I at any time practised as a doctor. I studied at Prague, Berlin and Paris. My father was a specialist in diseases of the heart, and it was for him I passed my examinations. Already I was primarily interested in physics. All my life since then has been devoted to scientific research.

Normally I would not think of applying for a position as doctor, but I gather from your advertisement that you are in desperate need of one, that you can pay very little and that your Mission is in a remote area amongst backward people. I am a man of some brilliance. I do not think I should let you down or prove inadequate for the task. I am a Czech refugee and for personal reasons I wish to get out of England. I have the need to lose myself in work quite remote . . .

I folded the letter up and put it back in my wallet. He was a Czech refugee. He had been a scientist. He had personal reasons for wanting to leave England.

There was nothing there I had missed.

He had cabled acceptance of my offer. The final letter had merely announced that the French had given him a visa to work as a doctor in Morocco and that he would be sailing with Wade in the fifteen-ton ketch, *Gay Juliet*, leaving Falmouth on 24 November, and arriving Tangier by 14 December, all being well. He hadn't mentioned his wife, or even the fact that he was married. He hadn't explained his reasons for wanting such remote and out-of-the-way employment and he hadn't haggled over the ridiculously small salary which was all I had been able to offer him.

Then I remembered the oilskin bag. The answer to some, at any rate, of the things that were puzzling me might lie in the documents he'd salvaged. It's not a very nice thing to go prying into another man's papers, but in this case, I felt it was justified. I got up and began searching through the bedclothes. But I couldn't find it and I was afraid of waking him.

I didn't persist in the search. It was very cold in the room. North African hotels, with their bare, plaster walls and tiled floors are designed for the summer heat. Also I was tired. It could wait till morning. There was no point in trying to work it out for myself. When he was rested, he'd be able to explain the whole thing. I lay back again and switched off the light, pulling the blankets up round me. The moonlight cast the pattern of the window in a long, sloping rectangle on the opposite wall. I yawned and closed my eyes and was instantly asleep.

But it was only my body that was tired and probably this accounts for the fact that I awoke with such startling suddenness at the sound of movement in the room. The moonlight showed me a figure stooped over the couch at the foot of the bed. 'Who's that?' I called out.

The figure started up. It was one of the Arab hotel boys. I switched on the light. 'What are you doing in here?' I asked him in Spanish. 'I didn't send for you.'

'No, señor.' He looked scared and his rather too thick lips trembled slightly. He looked as though he had negro blood in him; so many of them did who came from the south. 'The patrone sent me to collect the clothes that are wet.' He held up some of Kavan's sodden garments. 'They are to be made dry.'

'Why didn't you knock and switch on the light?'

'I do not wish to disturb you, señor.' He said it quickly as though it were something he had expected to have to say, and then added, 'May I take them please?'

'All right,' I said. 'And you can take my jacket. That needs drying, too.' I got out of bed and emptied the pockets. Then I ran through Kavan's things. I thought he might have his wallet in one of the pockets of his windbreaker, but there was nothing but a jack-knife, an old briar, matches – the usual odds and ends of a man sailing a boat. 'Thank the patrone for me, will you?' The boy nodded and scurried out of the room. The door closed with a slam.

'Who was that? What is it?'

I turned quickly towards the bed and saw that Kavan was sitting bolt upright, a startled look on his face. 'It's all right,' I said. 'It was one of the hotel boys. He came for your wet things.'

Relief showed on his face and his head sank back against the pillows. 'I thought I was back on the boat,' he murmured. Though he was utterly exhausted, his mind still controlled his body, forcing it to react to unusual sounds, as though he were still at the yacht's helm. I thought of how it must have been at night out there in the Atlantic after Wade had gone overboard, and I crossed over to the window to draw the curtains and shut out the moonlight.

As I pulled the curtains, I glanced down into the street below. A movement caught my eyes. There was somebody standing down there in the shadow of a doorway on the opposite side of the street, standing quite still, staring up at the window. I could see the pale circle of a face, nothing more. And then the figure moved, walking quickly away, keeping to the shadows of the buildings. It was a European girl and where an alley entered the street, she crossed a patch of moonlight.

It was Kavan's wife.

She was in the shadows again now, walking quickly. I watched her until she turned at the end of the street, up towards the Boulevard Pasteur. I could have been mistaken, of course. But I knew I wasn't – the suède jacket and the crumpled skirt, the way she walked, the shape of the face with its high, bony forehead as she had stared up at me from the shadows. What had she wanted? She hadn't come into the hotel. She hadn't asked to see him. The natural thing . . .

'What is it? What are you staring at?'

I swung away from the window and saw that his eyes were watching me, and there was the same fearfulness in them that I had seen in his wife's eyes when she asked me who I was. 'I've just seen your wife,' I said. 'She was out there, looking up at the hotel.'

'My wife?'

'The girl who was on the beach.'

He stared at me. 'How do you know she is my wife?' For the first time I noticed the trace of a foreign accent.

'She told me,' I said.

He started to get out of bed then, but I stopped him. 'She's gone now.' And then I said, 'Why didn't you tell me you were Kavan down there on the beach? Surely you must have guessed who I was?'

'How should I? Besides—' He hesitated and

shrugged his shoulders. 'It is not the moment to say who I am.'

'Because of the police?' I asked. 'And then, when you saw your wife . . .' I hesitated, wondering how best to put it. 'She loves you,' I said. 'Surely you must know that? Somehow she got out of Czechoslovakia and came here to meet you, and when you saw her you turned your back on her. Surely you could have—'

His eyes suddenly blazed at me. 'For Christ's sake, stop it!' he cried out. 'Stop it! Do you hear? How do I know they don't arrange for her to come here to Tangier? They may be watching her, trying to follow me. They are there in the background always.' The words tumbled wildly out of his mouth, and then he steadied himself and pushed his hands up over his face and through his hair. 'I have not seen Karen for more than four years.' His voice was gentle, but with a note of bitterness in it. 'And then suddenly we meet . . .' He stared at me. 'Do you think I like to have to turn my back on her?' He shrugged his shoulders angrily. 'I have had too much of this – during the German occupation and after, when the Russians walk in. You don't understand. You were born British. You don't understand what it is to be a middle-European – always to be escaping from something, always to go in fear – the knock on the door, the unopened envelope, the glance of a stranger in the street – to have people checking on you, spying on you, coming between you and your work, never to be trusted or to trust anybody. God! If only I'd been born British.' There were tears of anger and frustration in his eyes and he lay back, exhausted.

'Why did you leave England then?' I asked. 'Why didn't you become naturalised?'

'Naturalised!' He laughed. It wasn't a pleasant sound, for there was a note of hysteria in it. 'How can I become naturalised when they . . .' He closed his mouth abruptly, his eyes suddenly watchful. 'Don't ask me any more questions,' he said. 'You want a doctor for your Mission. All right, you have one. I am here. But don't ask me any questions. I don't want any questions.' His voice shook with the violence of his feeling.

I stood for a moment staring at him. I didn't like it. I knew too little about the man. I'd been prepared for a failure. What else could I expect of a qualified doctor who was willing to come out to North Africa and bury himself in a village in the Atlas? But I hadn't been prepared for this.

'All right,' I said. 'I won't ask any more questions.' And then to ease the tension between us I asked him if he'd like some food.

'No. No, thank you. A little cognac. That's all.'

I got some dry clothes from my suitcase, put them on and went down to the Cypriot café at the corner. When I returned I found he had been sick. His face was ghastly white and he was sweating and shivering. I poured him a little cognac, added some water and handed it to him. His hands were trembling uncontrollably as he took the tumbler from me. 'Shall I get a doctor?' I asked.

He shook his head, quickly and emphatically. 'No. I'll be all right in a minute.' He sipped at the cognac. 'I'm just exhausted physically.'

But it was more than that. It was nervous exhaustion.

'Can I have a cigarette please?'

I gave him one and when I had lit it for him, he drew on it, quickly, eagerly, like a man whose nerves are crying out for a sedative. I stayed with him whilst he smoked. He didn't talk and a heavy silence lay over the room. I watched him covertly, wondering how this odd, excitable man would settle into the quiet, lonely life that I had become accustomed to. It wasn't lonely, of course. There was too much to do, too many demands on one's time and energy. But for a man who wasn't accustomed to it, who wasn't accepting the life voluntarily . . . I had been so engrossed in the idea of getting a doctor out there that I hadn't really given much thought to the fact that he would also be a man, with a personality of his own, a past and all the inevitable human complications and peculiarities. I had thought about it only as it would affect me, not as I and the conditions of life down at Enfida would affect him.

'Have you ever been to Morocco before?' I asked him.

He shook his head. 'No. Never.'

I gave him a little more cognac and then I began to talk about Enfida. I told him how the olives were just being gathered and piled in heaps in the open space outside the auberge and how we would soon be thrashing our own trees to harvest the crop that was part of the tiny income of the Mission. I described the mountain villages to him; how they were flat-roofed, like Tibetan villages, and clung precariously to the sides of great ravines that cut back to the base of the peaks that rose twelve and thirteen thousand feet to form the backbone of the Atlas Mountains. And I tried to give him an idea of what it was like, travelling every day from village to village, sometimes on foot, sometimes by mule, living in the Berber huts and sitting around at night, drinking mint tea and listening to their stories and the gossip of the village.

And then, suddenly, his hand fell limp at the edge of the bed and he was asleep. I got up and took the cigarette from between his fingers and picked up the empty tumbler which lay on his chest. His face had more colour in it now, and it was relaxed. The nerve at the corner of his mouth no longer twitched and his features were smoothed out as though his mind were at rest.

I put his arms inside the bedclothes and then I switched out the light and went out to the café for some food. When I returned he was still lying exactly as I had left him. His mouth was slightly open and he was snoring gently. I went to bed by the moon's light that filtered in through the half-drawn curtains and lay there, wondering about him and about his wife and whether I had bitten off more than I could chew financially, for I would have to get her to join us at the Mission.

In thinking about the Mission, I forgot to some extent the strangeness of his arrival and drifted quietly off to sleep.

I awoke to a tap on the door and a shaft of sunlight cutting across my face. '*Entrez!*' I sat up and rubbed my eyes. It was one of the hotel boys to say that the police and the douane had arrived. 'All right. Show them up.' I got out of bed and slipped my dressing gown on. Kavan was still fast asleep. He didn't seem to have moved all night. He still lay on his back, quite motionless, his mouth slightly open and his breathing regular and easy. I looked at my watch. It was almost ten o'clock. He had had more than a dozen hours' sleep. He should be fit enough now to cope with the immigration formalities.

The door opened and they came in. It was the same sergeant and he had with him one of the Customs officers. I glanced back at the bed, wishing that I'd told them to wait. I'd have to wake him now and he'd be suddenly confronted with them. I hoped he'd be clear in his mind what he was going to tell them. He ought to have mentioned Wade's death to them the night before.

'*Muy buenas*, señor.'

'*Muy buenas*.' I gave the sergeant a chair. The Customs officer sat on the couch. They both stared at Kavan. I felt uneasy and only half awake.

'So, he is still sleeping, eh?' The sergeant clicked his tongue sympathetically. 'I am sorry to disturb him, but it is the formalities, you understand.' He shrugged his shoulders to make it clear that he was not responsible for drawing up the regulations.

'You want me to wake him?'

'*Sí, sí* – if you please. He is all right, eh?'

'Yes, he's all right,' I said. 'He was just exhausted. He had a bad trip.'

The sergeant nodded. 'Of course. And to wreck the ship – terrible. We will be very quick. Then he can sleep again.'

I went over to the bed and shook Kavan gently. His

eyelids flicked back almost immediately. 'What is it?' And then he saw the police and there was instant panic in his eyes. 'What do they want? Why are they here?'

'It's all right,' I said. 'It's about the immigration details. They said they'd come this morning. Remember?'

He nodded, but all the blood seemed to have drained out of his face so that it looked as white as it had done the previous night.

'Señor Wade.' The sergeant had got to his feet.

I started to explain that he wasn't Wade, but Kavan checked me, gripping hold of my arm. I could feel him trembling. His eyes switched from the police sergeant to the door and then back again to the sergeant. 'What do you want?' he asked in fair Spanish and his voice shook slightly and I could feel him trying desperately to get control of himself.

The sergeant was standing at the foot of the bed now. 'You are captain of the boat that is wrecked last night in the Baie des Juifs?'

Kavan hesitated, glancing up at me, and his tongue licked along the sore edges of his lips. 'Yes.' His voice was little more than a whisper. But then he added in a firmer tone, 'Yes, I'm the captain of the boat.'

'What is the name of the boat please?'

'*Gay Juliet.*'

The sergeant had his notebook out now. He was leaning over the end of the bed, his round, rather chubby face with its blue jowls puckered in a frown of concentration as he licked his pencil and wrote down the name of the boat. 'And you are from where?'

'Falmouth.'

'You come direct, señor?'

'Yes.'

'And your name is Señor Roland Wade?'

Again Kavan hesitated and then he nodded. 'Yes.'

'Just a moment,' I said, speaking to him in English. 'This is absurd, you know. You can't go on trying to pretend you're Wade.'

'Why not? Are you going to stop me? Listen.' He grabbed hold of my arm again. 'You want a doctor for your Mission, don't you? It's important to you. It must be or you wouldn't be taking somebody you know nothing about.'

'Yes, it's important to me.'

'Well then, you tell these men the truth and you won't get your doctor. Not me anyway. So you'd better choose. If you want your doctor, don't interfere. If you do, I'll get sent back to England and you'll never see me again.' Though he was blackmailing me, his face had a desperate, pleading look. 'It's only until we get out of Tangier.' He stared up into my face for a moment and then turned back to the sergeant. 'I'm sorry,' he said, reverting to Spanish.

'You sail here alone?' the sergeant asked.

'Yes.'

'There is nobody with you?'

'No.'

He looked up from his notebook then and stared at Kavan. 'Do you know a man called Dr Jan Kavan?'

I heard the slight hissing intake of Kavan's breath and felt the muscles of his hand tense. 'Yes.'

'We were told that he was sailing with you.'

'Who told you?' The sergeant didn't answer, but his small, brown eyes stared at Kavan watchfully. 'No, he didn't sail with me,' Kavan added quickly. 'He – changed his mind.'

I felt sure that slight hesitation must have been as noticeable to the sergeant as it was to me. But all he said was, 'Can you tell me, señor, why he changed his mind?'

'He wouldn't tell me,' Kavan said. 'He came on board the night before I was due to sail. I was leaving with the tide at 4 a.m. and when I woke him, he said he had changed his mind and wanted to be put ashore.'

The sergeant nodded and wrote it all down. 'So you sailed alone, señor?'

Kavan nodded. His eyes were fixed on the sergeant and little beads of sweat had broken out on his forehead.

'That was very dangerous, surely, señor – to sail alone? It is a big ship for one man.'

'I have sailed a great deal – often single-handed.'

The sergeant turned to me 'Twice last night you asked the señor here about another man. You thought there were two of them on the yacht.'

'Yes,' I said. 'That's correct.'

'Who was the second man? Was it Dr Kavan?'

'Yes.'

'Why were you so sure that Dr Kavan was on board the boat?'

'He wrote to me to tell me he was sailing with Mr Wade.'

'I see. Do you know of any reason why he should have changed his mind?'

I shrugged my shoulders. 'No, but there are easier methods of reaching Tangier than by sailing in a yacht.'

'Of course.' He nodded towards the bed. 'Can you confirm the identity of the señor here?'

'No. I had never seen him before last night.'

'*Sí, sí*, it is understood. So you think Dr Kavan changed his mind?'

I glanced down at Kavan. His eyes were watching me, very blue and with the same expression in them that they'd had when he'd implored me not to take him to a hospital. 'Yes,' I said. 'I think he must have changed his mind.'

I felt the grip of Kavan's fingers on my arm relax. '*Bueno!*' The sergeant closed his notebook. 'You have the papers for this boat?' he asked.

Kavan nodded.

'I would like to have the papers. What is the port of registration?'

'Southampton.' Kavan's voice had dropped to a whisper.

'Also we would like to have your passport, señor. And if you have the record of the voyage . . .' He stopped then, for Kavan had suddenly closed his eyes. He leaned over, clutching at me and retching violently. His hand reached out automatically for the pot, gripped it and the retching sound went on and on – dry, rasping and foodless, a horrible sound in the sullen stillness of the room. And then he dropped the pot and keeled over, his body suddenly limp.

I got hold of him and pushed him back into the bed. He was sweating and his face was ashen. I wiped his lips with my handkerchief. His eyes opened and he stared past me at the sergeant. 'I'll bring the papers later,' he whispered, and then he closed his eyes again and seemed to pass into unconciousness.

I glanced at the sergeant. He was shaking his head and making little clicking sounds with his tongue. 'He is bad, very bad. I am sorry, señor.'

'I'll get a doctor,' I said.

'*Sí, sí*. That is what he need – a doctor.' He turned to the Customs officer and they began talking quickly, shrugging their shoulders and gesticulating. Several times they glanced at the man's body lying there on the bed, and their expressions were sympathetic. At length the sergeant turned to me. 'Señor. Do you know if he has his passport?'

'No,' I said. 'I don't know. I think he had some papers with him, but I don't know what they are. If you like I can bring them down to you?'

The sergeant nodded. '*Bueno*. If you will take them to the office of the douane down by the harbour, señor, they will be stamped. There is no necessity for him to come himself. Also, there is this paper to be completed.' He handed me the usual immigration form. 'As soon as he is sufficiently recovered, perhaps you will have him fill it in and bring it with you to the douane.'

'Very well.' As I opened the door for them, I asked the sergeant why the police were interested in Dr Kavan.

'Oh, it is not we who are interested,' he replied. 'It is

the British Consulate. It is they who ask us to watch for him.'

'But why?' I asked. 'Were you going to arrest him or something?'

'No. They just wish us to check his papers and report to them. I will inform them that he did not sail after all. *Muy buenas*, señor.'

'*Muy buenas.*'

I closed the door and turned to Kavan. His eyes were open now and he was listening to the tramp of their feet as they descended the stairs. He was still pale, but his eyes were alert. 'Were you shamming?' I said.

'Ssh!' He gestured for me to be quiet. 'Go to the window and check that both of them leave the hotel.'

I walked to the window and pulled the curtains. A jeep was parked down in the street. As I peered out, the sergeant and the Customs officer came out of the hotel and got into it. There was the sound of a starter and then it drove off, turning down towards the plage. 'They've gone,' I said.

He breathed a sigh of relief and pulled himself up in the bed. 'Now we'll fix Wade's passport. After that everything is straightforward. Will you telephone for a doctor, please?'

He was suddenly calm. He seemed to have no conception of the position he had put me in. I was angry and a little scared. Why couldn't foreigners behave rationally? And now there was the problem of papers, passports, and official documents. I had committed myself without thinking about that. 'You know the British Consulate are making inquiries about you?' I said. And then, when he didn't answer, I asked him why he'd had to pretend to be Wade. 'What have you done that you have to hide your own identity?'

He looked at me then and said quietly, 'I haven't done anything.'

'I don't believe you,' I said sharply. 'When you saw the police, you panicked. You must have done something. If you want my help, you'd better tell me—'

'I have done nothing,' he repeated. 'Absolutely nothing. Please, you must believe me. I have done nothing that you or any other British person can object to. I give you my word.'

'Then why pretend to be Wade?'

He pushed his hands through his hair, which was still dull and sticky with salt water. 'No,' he said. 'Not yet. Maybe when I know you better – when we are out of Tangier.' He lifted his head and stared out of the window. 'I came here to start a new life. I have to sail here because it's the only way I can get out of England. I am a stateless person, you see. And then the owner is lost overboard, the yacht is wrecked and, when I'm brought ashore, I find the police waiting for me there on the beach and asking me if I am Dr Jan Kavan. And then the man Kostos mistakes me for Wade.' He looked up at me quickly. 'What would you do? What would you do if you were in my shoes? It's a gift from the gods. I accept it.' His shoulders sagged and his voice fell away to a whisper: 'And then I find my wife waiting there to greet me also – and she turns away because I have said I am Wade.'

He stared down at his feet, his pale hands gripped

convulsively round his knees. 'Last night – I thought and thought, trying to find a way out. And then, this morning, I wake up and find the police here, and I'm scared. When you're scared, the mind works very fast. I suddenly knew this was the only way out. I must be Wade. I must continue to be Wade until I am safe inside French Morocco. If I admit I am Jan Kavan, then there will be an inquiry into Wade's disappearance and—'

'Why should that worry you?' I demanded. 'You said last night—'

'I told you the truth,' he cut in quickly, and then glanced at me nervously as though trying to discover whether I believed him or not. 'But I can't tell them the truth,' he added. 'Once they know I'm Jan Kavan' – he hesitated – 'they will send me back to England. I know they will. I feel it. And I must get to Morocco. I must get to Morocco.' He looked at me. 'Please. You want a doctor, don't you? You want a doctor for your Mission?'

'Yes, but—'

'Then you must let me enter French Morocco on Wade's passport.'

'But why should they send you back to England? What makes you think—'

'Oh, for God's sake!' he shouted at me. His voice had that upward trend that it had had the night before when he'd been half hysterical with exhaustion. 'Just leave it at that. Leave it at that.'

'All right,' I said, for he was in a desperately nervous state. 'But if you enter Morocco on Wade's passport, your own papers will have no entry stamp. You can't work at the Mission unless your papers are in order.'

'I understand.' He nodded, his forehead wrinkled in thought. 'But that is something we can sort out later. Maybe I lose my papers, maybe I forge the necessary stamp. I don't know. But first I must get to Morocco. That is the important thing. And I can't do that except on Wade's passport.'

'But, good heavens, man!' I said. 'You're not Wade's double, surely. There's the photograph – the description and his signature, too – you'd never get away with it.'

'Nonsense,' he said, his tone suddenly more confident. 'Do you think I learned nothing during the war? I was six years working in the laboratories at Essen and passing information to the British. Besides, don't forget I have been shipwrecked.' He dragged himself to his feet, standing a little unsteadily. And then his voice was suddenly agitated again. 'Where's the oilskin bag? I had a little oilskin bag tied round my neck. I had all the papers in it – everything. Did you see it? It wasn't left on the beach, was it?'

'No, it's here somewhere,' I said. I crossed over to the bed, wishing now that I'd had a look at it last night. 'It's among the bedclothes. I threw it here last night.'

But it wasn't on the bed. It had slipped off on to the couch and was lying under the counterpane. He almost snatched it out of my hand as I held it out to him. 'You'd better have some food,' I suggested.

But he shook his head. 'Not until I've seen a doctor.' He suddenly smiled. It was almost as though the feel of that oilskin bag in his hands had given him back his confidence. 'If he's a good doctor, he'll tell me I'm suffering from lack of food and if the police bother to enquire, they will not be surprised if I recover quickly.'

Curiously, I found myself liking him. Behind the nervous tension and the almost neurotic fear of the authorities was a man of considerable personality, a man of drive and energy. Whatever he had done, whatever he was afraid of, he had guts. 'What are you going to do about the passport?' I asked.

'Oh, that's not too difficult,' he said, shaking the contents of the oilskin bag out on to the bed. 'Wade was about my build and colouring. He even had blue eyes. He was thinner and more wiry, that's all.' He tossed the blue-covered British passport across to me. 'I'll have to fix the photograph, of course.'

The passport was slightly damp, otherwise there was nothing to show that it had come through the surf of Jew's Bay. On the first page there was the man's name – Mr Roland Tregareth Wade – and on the next his description: Profession – Company director; Place of birth and date – St Austell, 10 April 1915; Residence – France; Height – 5 ft 11 ins; Colour of eyes – blue; Colour of hair – black. I turned the page and looked at the photograph. It showed him to be a rather good-looking man with a square forehead and black hair. But the cheeks were a little heavy, the broad, full-lipped mouth rather too easy-going, and there were little pouches under the eyes. It wasn't a dissipated face and it wasn't a dishonest face, but somehow it wasn't quite frank – it was the face of a man about whom one would have reservations.

I looked across at Kavan. 'What about the photograph?' I asked him.

But it didn't seem to worry him. 'They're not to know that the passport was wrapped in oilskin,' he said. 'By the time they get it the pages will be damp and very dirty. The beard helps, too.' He rasped his hand over his chin.

'You seem to have it all worked out,' I said.

He shrugged his shoulders. 'A kindly Providence worked it all out for me.'

'Well, I hope Providence realises its responsibility.' My mind was running over the possible snags, conscious that I was thoroughly implicated in the whole business. I glanced down at the passport again, turning the pages. The visa section showed that Wade had travelled extensively – Germany, Austria, Czechoslovakia, Roumania – most of the satellite countries – and Egypt, as well as Britain and France. He had visas for French Morocco, Algeria and Spanish Morocco, but these were not counter-stamped with dates of entry. The final pages for currency were a mass of entries. I tossed the passport back on to the bed beside him. 'I'll go and get the patrone to ring for a doctor,' I said.

He nodded. He had already picked up the passport and was padding across the room to the wash-basin.

By the time the doctor arrived Kavan was back in bed and the passport, now crumpled and dirty, was drying in the sun by the open window. I checked it through. The ink on Wade's signature on the first page had run badly, so had the figures giving his height which was a good two inches taller than Kavan, and the upper half of the face in the photograph was almost obliterated by a dirty stain. The yacht's certificate of registration had been treated in the same way, and Kavan had completed the form which the police sergeant had left, the signature shaky, but not unlike what could be deciphered of Wade's signature.

The doctor was a young, thoroughly efficient Frenchman. He examined Kavan carefully and, after questioning him about what had happened, wrote a prescription for a tonic and advised a diet of meat broth and steak for the next two or three days. He left with a little bow and a handshake, and I went across to the Cypriot restaurant and got Kavan a tray of food. It was the first hot food he had had for over sixty hours.

The passport was almost dry and I took it, together with the other papers, down to the Customs House. There was no difficulty. The sergeant was there and he only gave a cursory glance at the passport before stamping it. Officially Kavan was now Wade and I walked out into the hot sunshine with a light heart and a feeling of relief. The way was now clear for me to return to Enfida.

It was odd, but I felt no qualms, no sense of apprehension. Just as soon as Kavan was fit to travel, I could shake the dust of Tangier off my feet. That was all I was thinking about as I walked back to the hotel. Wade was dead. An investigation into how it happened would serve no useful purpose. There remained only the yacht. The waves were still pounding heavily at the sands and one of the Customs officers had told me that the wreck was breaking up fast. The Lloyd's representative would have to be contacted about the insurance to avert suspicion. After that, the Wade who had arrived in Tangier could simply disappear.

I imagined Kavan would be sleeping after his food, but instead there was the sound of somebody talking beyond the closed door of my room. I hesitated, and then I heard a voice that I recognised say, 'What you are running is no business of mine. I am interested only in the deeds of Kasbah Foum.' It was Kostos.

Kavan made some reply that was inaudible, and then the Greek's voice cut in: 'You are lying. I know that you visited Marcel Duprez's lawyers in Rouen. I know that—' He stopped abruptly as I pushed open the door.

Kavan was sitting up in the bed, the blankets pulled tightly round his naked body. Kostos was standing by the couch. They were both looking towards the door as I entered. They were quite still like a tableau, and the tension in the room was something that you could feel. 'What are you doing here, Kostos?' I demanded angrily.

'Nothing. Nothing that is to do with you. You keep out of this, Lat'am.' His eyes switched to Kavan. 'Think it over, my friend.' He began buttoning up his raincoat. 'Ali is a fool. I tell him that when I know that in Cairo he arranges for you to act as the contact man. Your reputation is no dam' good. But you double-cross me and you find yourself out on the Marchan with a knife in your back.' He fished in the pocket of his waistcoat and flipped a piece of pasteboard on to the blankets on Kavan's feet. 'Come to my office as soon as you are recovered. An' no more nonsense, you see. This is not Europe. This is North Africa, and all out there' – he waved his hand towards the uncurtained windows – 'it is an Arab world with only a thin layer of white peoples who tread a careful step.' He put his hat on, pulling it down with a quick tug at the brim, and then turned to go.

As he passed me, he paused, tapping the side of his nose. 'Not a sparrow falls. Remember, Lat'am. An' don't do nothing silly, eh?' He pushed past me and went out, slamming the door behind him.

I turned to face Kavan, who was still sitting up in the bed. 'What's all this about?' I demanded. 'What did Kostos want?'

'Some papers – a cargo. How the hell do I know? Kostos is a part of Wade's world.' He shrugged his shoulders. He wasn't scared; not the way he had been when the police had been in the room. But there was a tautness in his voice that showed his uneasiness. 'Wade was a crook,' he added.

'Then why in God's name did you sail with him?'

'I told you before – because I am a Czech and a refugee and it's the only way I can get out of England.'

'But if you knew he was a crook—?'

'I didn't discover that till later.' He lay back and put his hands behind his head. 'He came and saw me in London and it was agreed that I should sail with him to Tangier. I knew nothing about him, except that he wanted—' He stopped there. 'Can I have a cigarette please?'

I handed him the packet and lit one myself. 'Well, when did you discover he was running something?' I asked.

'We ran into a gale off Ushant,' he said. 'We could easily have slipped into the lee of the islands through the Chenal du Four and put into Brest. Instead, he stood out into the Atlantic, beating into the teeth of it to clear the coast of France. He said he wasn't taking any chances. That's how I knew.'

'But what about the Customs when you left Falmouth?'

'We didn't clear Customs. He said there was no need.'

'What was he running?'

He shrugged his shoulders. 'Currency, securities – how do I know? When I asked him, he told me to mind my own damn business. He didn't talk about his own affairs.'

'Did you know Kostos would be waiting for you when you arrived?'

'Of course not.'

'But when he came up to you on the beach – why didn't you tell him you weren't Wade?'

He pushed himself up on to his elbow. 'Because the police are there. Because I have to escape from myself, from all the past. Now leave it at that, will you?' He lay back, breathing heavily. 'I'm sorry, Latham,' he murmured. 'It's just that I'm tired. As soon as we're clear of Tangier—'

'But we're not clear of Tangier yet,' I reminded him. 'What exactly did Kostos say? Had he been here long?'

'No.' He hesitated, looking at me uncertainly out of the corners of his eyes. 'He wanted some documents. He said that I'd been employed by an Arab to get them.

He meant, of course, that Wade had.' He paused and then asked me if I knew anything about an Arab called Ali d'Es-Skhira.

'Yes,' I said. 'He's a nationalist; a fanatic. The French deported him from Morocco after he'd caused serious rioting in Marrakech. He lives in Tangier now. Why?'

'Nothing. It doesn't matter.'

'What happened next?'

'I told Kostos I hadn't been able to get the documents, and he got angry and called me a liar. Then you came in.'

'Did Wade mention these documents to you?'

'I told you, Wade didn't talk about his affairs.'

He was trying to hide something. I could sense it. 'Kostos described them as the deeds of Kasbah Foum.' He stared at me sullenly, not saying anything. I went over and sat on the bed. 'Now look here,' I said. 'You're getting yourself mixed up in something dangerous. I know this town. I've been part of it – that was what turned me into a missionary. Kostos is not a man to play around with. And if you're mixed up with Ali d'Es-Skhira as well . . .'

'But I'm not,' he protested. 'I don't know anything about it.'

'Oh yes, you do. You know all about this place Kasbah Foum. When you regained consciousness in this room last night, one of the first things you asked me—'

'All right. I do know about Kasbah Foum. But it's nothing to do with you, Latham.' He was sitting up again and his voice was angry. We stared at each other for a moment and the atmosphere between us had grown suddenly tense. Then he gradually relaxed. 'I'm sorry,' he murmured. 'Maybe later, when we're out of this place, I'll explain. . . .' He lay back and closed his eyes. There was an obstinate set to his mouth.

I hesitated. Maybe I could shock the truth out of him.

'Tell me one thing,' I said. 'Did you get possession of those deeds after Wade went overboard – or before?'

His eyes flicked open and there was a surprised look on his face. 'You mean—' His mouth stayed open slightly, and then he rolled over in the bed so that he faced me. 'Now listen, Latham. I didn't kill Wade, if that's what you're getting at. It happened just as I told you.'

'It was the deeds I asked about.'

'The deeds?' He stared at me.

'When did you get them out of him?'

'I didn't get them out of him.' His voice was angry. 'How could I? He never had them.'

'How do you know?'

'Oh, for God's sake!' he shouted at me. 'Leave it at that, will you? Wade didn't have them.'

'All right,' I said, getting to my feet. 'But it's a pity you didn't bother to convince Kostos of that.' I stubbed out my cigarette. It was no good worrying about it. The thing to do was to get out of Tangier as quickly as possible. 'How do you feel?' I asked him. 'I see you ate the steak I brought you.'

'Yes.' He smiled and added quickly, 'It was the most wonderful steak I have ever eaten.'

'And you weren't sick?'

'No.'

'How do you feel then?'

'Not too bad. A little tired, and my body's still sore. Otherwise, I'm all right. I think I'll try and get some sleep.'

'Do you think you'll be fit enough to travel tonight? There's a train at nine thirty-five. We could be in Casablanca tomorrow morning in time to catch the day train to Marrakech.'

'Is there a sleeper on the train tonight?'

'Yes. I'll try and book berths.'

There was a knock at the door. It was one of the hotel boys. The patrone had sent him up for Kavan's passport. 'What's he want the passport for?' Kavan asked. I explained that it was the custom in Tangier for the hotelier to hold visitors' passports and he let the boy have it. 'And bring the señor's clothes up, will you?' I told him.

'*Sí, sí*, señor.'

When he had gone, Kavan began rummaging in the oilskin bag and produced a rather battered book that looked something like a ledger. 'Do you think you could dispose of that for me?' He held it out to me.

'What is it?' I asked.

'It's the log of the *Gay Juliet*. I brought it ashore with me as evidence of what happened to Wade. It should be burned now. Do you think you can manage that?'

'Are you sure you want it destroyed?' I asked him. 'I could leave it with a friend of mine – just in case.'

'No. I'm sure your friend is reliable, but—' He

shrugged his shoulders. 'And I daren't take it with me, just in case the douane decide to search me. Burn it, will you?'

'I'll see what I can do,' I said. 'What else did you bring ashore with you?'

'My own papers and visas. There's some money, too.'

'How much?'

He glanced at me quickly. 'Quite a lot.'

I explained to him then that the regulations only permitted him to take so much in cash into French Morocco. I suggested that I bank the excess for transfer to the Banque d'Etat at Marrakech and he agreed. Altogether there was over four hundred pounds, mainly in English notes. 'Is this Wade's or yours?' I asked.

He looked at me hard. 'Does it matter? Wade wasn't the sort to have dependants.'

There was a knock at the door and the boy came in with his clothes and my jacket. I slipped the notes into my hip pocket. The boy paused as he was arranging the clothes on a chair. He was staring at the oilskin bag which Kavan still held in his hands. The dark, Arab eyes met mine and then he turned abruptly and hurried out. 'You said you'd lived in Tangier,' Kavan said as the door closed. 'You know it well?'

'Well enough to want to get out of it,' I answered.

'Can you find Karen for me then?' His voice was suddenly urgent. 'I must get in touch with her before we leave. I must tell her where I'm going. Can you do that for me?'

'I don't know.' Tangier wasn't a big place, not the

European section of it. But there wasn't much time. 'The best chance would be through the immigration authorities.'

'No, no. Don't do that. Not the authorities. But you must know people here – somebody would know about her in a place like this. Please. Find out where she's living and give her the address of the Mission. Tell her to write to me there as soon as she's convinced that she's not being watched. No, not to me. Tell her to write to you. That would be safer. Will you do that?'

'I'll try.' I got my hat. 'Better lock the door behind me,' I said, and left him and went down the stairs and out into the bright sunlight of the streets.

I went first to Cook's in the rue de Statut and was lucky enough to get two wagon-lit berths on the night train. Then I crossed the Zocco Grande to the British bank in the Siaghines where I arranged for Kavan's money to be changed into Moroccan francs and transferred to the Mission's account in Marrakech. It was then past midday and I cut up a side street to a small Italian café, and there I sat over my lunch and read *Gay Juliet*'s log.

Until then I think Wade had appeared to me as an almost mythical character. But he was real enough by the time I had finished his record of that winter voyage out from Falmouth. As a kid I had done a lot of sailing – that was back in the days when my father was alive, before he'd gone bankrupt. I knew enough about the sea to be able to interpret, in terms of physical conditions, such laconic statements as: '*Wind Force 7, gusting 8. Direction S.W. Waves 20 feet, breaking heavily. Lay to under bare sticks, everything battened down. Jan very sick. Pumping every half hour.*' This was off Ushant and continued for fifteen hours. Sometimes he was less factual, more descriptive, as in the entry for November 30: '*Light S.E. breeze off the land. Heavy swell with sea oily and black. Moon just lipping horizon. Ghosting along under Genoa – no sound except the grunt of porpoises. They have been with us all night, their movements visible on account of the phosphorescence, which is unusual at this time of the year. Jan fit now and has the makings of a good seaman. Pray God it doesn't start to blow again. Both of us very tired.*'

The log was something more than a bare record of speed, course and conditions. It was Wade's personal record, entered up daily from the chart table data and going back over several voyages: Cannes to Naples and back – Cannes to Palermo and on to the Piraeus, across to Alexandria and back to Nice by way of Valetta – Nice to Gibraltar. The yachts were all different, so were the crews. Sometimes he sailed single-handed. But always the same flowing, easy handwriting, the same graphic descriptive details running through the Mediterranean voyages and on to the final trip out from England. And then, suddenly, two pages from the last entry, the writing changed, became finer, neater, more exact. '*Dec. 12 –* 0245: *Course 195°. Wind S.S.E. Force 3–4. Speed 5 knots. A terrible thing has happened. Roland lost overboard shortly after I relieved him. Time 0205 approx. Heavy swell running. Threw lifebelt to him and gybed to bring ship round . . .*'

Wade was dead and Kavan was writing up his log.

There was a rather touching finality about that abrupt change in the writing. After all those hundreds of sea miles, logged and recorded between the brown board covers of the book, this bald statement that the sea had claimed him.

Whatever else the man had been, he was a fine yachtsman.

I rifled through the remaining twenty or so pages of the book. They were blank, except for the last two which contained odd jottings, reminders of things he had probably planned on the long night watches. They were under port headings, such as Naples – *see Borgioli – Ring Ercoli – Vomero* 23–245 – *Cheaper to slip here and get topsides blown off and repainted* (*Luigi Cantorelli's yard*) *etc.* I glanced quickly to the last entry and there, sure enough, was the heading *TANGIER* and underneath – *Michel Kostos, 22 rue de la Grande Mosquèe.* Tel. 237846. There were several other names and telephone numbers and then a note – *Try to contact Ed White. Wazerzat* 12 (*Lavin, Roche et Lavin*).

I sat drinking my coffee and wondering about this last entry. Lavin, Roche et Lavin was obviously the name of a French firm and Wazerzat looked like the phonetic spelling of an Arab town – Ouarzazate, for instance.

I closed the book slowly and finished my coffee. Reading that log had brought the man to life in my mind. Reluctantly, I called the patrone and had him take me through into the kitchen, and there I thrust the book down into the red hot coals of the range. I found myself muttering a prayer for him as it burst into flames. The book should have been consigned to the sea.

Coming back into the café, I noticed an Arab sitting in the far corner, by the window. I hadn't seen him come in. I suppose I had been too engrossed in the story of Wade's voyages. There was something familiar about his face. I paid my bill and, as I walked out, our eyes met and I remembered that he had been in the bank when I had arranged for the transfer of Kavan's money. He had quick, intelligent eyes and a hard, aquiline face. His djellaba was of the smooth, grey gaberdine favoured by the richer guides and pimps and he wore brown European shoes.

I turned up into the Arab town, climbing quickly towards the kasbah. I wanted to take a look at Jews' Bay – and I wanted to quash the suspicion that had suddenly crossed my mind.

From the Naam Battery I looked down to the sea and across the width of Jews' Bay. The sea was blue and sparkled in the sunshine. The water of the bay was faintly corrugated and there was a fringe of white where the swell broke on the golden sand. It was a quiet, peaceful scene, utterly at variance with my memories of what it had been like down there less than twenty-four hours ago. There was no sign of the wreck, but a small motor launch was hovering around the spot where the yacht had struck. I turned and walked back to the Place du Tabor, and there was the Arab I had left sitting in the café.

It was just possible, of course, that it was a coincidence. There were always guides hanging around the Place du Tabor. I cut down the rue Raid-Sultan, past the old palace – the Dar el Makhzen – and the treasury and into the labyrinth of alleys that run steeply down to the Zocco Chico. It was cool and quiet, but the roar of the markets drifted up to me on the still air like the murmur of a hive. I reached an intersection where the main alley descended in shallow steps through a tunnel formed by the houses. A narrower passage, leading I knew to a cul-de-sac, ran off at right angles and close by a baby sunning itself in an open doorway. I slipped into the doorway and waited.

Almost immediately I heard the patter of slippers hurrying down to the intersection. It was the same Arab. He hesitated an instant, glancing along the empty passage of the cul-de-sac. Then he dived into the tunnel of the main alley and went flapping down the steps like an ungainly bird.

There was no doubt about it now. I was being followed. The thought that a man like Kostos was now in a position to do this to me made me unreasonably angry. I went on down the alley and came out into the Zocco Chico. The Arab was waiting for me there. His face showed relief as he saw me, and then he looked away. I went straight up to him. 'Who told you to follow me?' I asked him angrily in Spanish. He started to walk away, but I caught hold of him by the arm and swung him round. 'Was it Señor Kostos?' Recognition of the name showed in his eyes. 'All right,' I said. 'We're going back to the Hotel Malabata now.' I let him go and turned up by the Spanish Church, walking fast.

He was close behind me as I entered the hotel. I went straight over to the reception desk where the patrone was sitting and demanded my bill and both our passports.

'You are leaving Tangier, señor?' He was a sallow-faced, oily little man with discoloured teeth and a large, hooked nose. I think he was of mixed Arab-Spanish blood. His eyes stared at me inquisitively over the rim of deep, fleshy pouches. His interest made me suspicious. 'My bill,' I said. 'I'm in a hurry.'

He glanced up at the clock above his head. It was just after three. 'Already you have missed the train, señor. The next one does not depart until twenty-one hundred thirty-five.'

'I'm still in a hurry,' I said.

He shrugged his shoulders and started making out the bill. His eyes kept shifting to my face as he wrote. They were full of curiosity. Through the open doorway I could see the Arab waiting patiently across the street. 'There will be a small addition for the other señor.'

'That's all right.'

He put down his pen. 'He can have your room if he wishes.' He stared at me. 'Or do you both leave Tangier together?'

'Give me the bill,' I said. He met my gaze for an instant and then his eyes dropped shiftily.

I settled the bill and he gave me my passport with the change. 'It is necessary for you to complete this paper, señor. It is for the police.' He was smiling at me craftily as he handed me the printed form which I should have filled in on arrival. He knew that the information I had to give included the address of my destination. When I had completed it, all but this one item, I hesitated. Then

I wrote in the Pension de la Montagne. It was the *pension* from which we had seen the yacht being blown into Jews' Bay. In the old days there had been no telephone there. I handed the form back to him and he glanced at it quickly, almost eagerly. 'I'd like my friend's passport, too,' I said.

But he shook his head. 'I am sorry, señor. He must collect it himself and complete the paper for the police.'

I nodded. 'All right,' I said, and went up to the room. Kavan unlocked the door for me. He had had a wash and was dressed in his underclothes. 'I'm glad you're up,' I said. 'Get dressed quickly. We're leaving at once.'

He reacted instantly to the urgency in my voice. 'Why? What's happened?'

'It's your friend Kostos.' And I explained how I had been followed. 'The man's waiting for us outside now. We've got to lose him before we get on that train. And I don't trust the patrone here either.'

'Did you find Karen? ' he asked.

'No. We can do that later when we've got rid of this Arab. Come on. Hurry.' Thank heavens he looked a lot better.

He didn't argue and when he'd got into his clothes, I sent him down to get his passport while I finished packing my case. 'There's a form to fill in,' I told him as he was going out. 'For destination put the Pension de la Montagne. It's out of town and it'll take them some time to check that we're not there.'

He nodded, stuffing the oilskin bag into his pocket. 'I'll wait for you downstairs.'

When I went down to join him, I heard his voice raised in altercation with the patrone. It was something to do with the passport and they were shouting at each other in French. 'Then why did Monsieur Latham tell me to come down here to get it?' Kavan demanded agitatedly. He caught sight of me then and said, 'This idiot says he gave you my passport.'

The patrone nodded his head emphatically. '*Sí, sí*, señor. Did you not ask for both the passports – yours and that of señor here?'

'Yes,' I said. 'But you refused to give me his. You said he must collect it personally and fill in the form at the same time.'

'No, no. It is true about the paper. But I give you the passport.' He turned to the hotel boy standing by the desk. 'Did I not give the señor both the passports?'

'*Sí, sí, sí*.' The Arab nodded.

It was the same boy who had come up to my room the previous night to collect Kavan's wet clothes. And suddenly I knew why the patrone had wanted these clothes. He had been told to check through the pockets. 'Do you know a Greek called Kostos?' I asked him.

The man's eyes narrowed slightly. He didn't say anything, but I knew I was right. Kostos was at the back of this passport nonsense, too. I sent the Arab boy for a taxi. 'If you haven't produced that passport by the time the taxi arrives,' I told the patrone, 'I'm going straight to the British Consul.'

He shrugged his shoulders, but there was a frightened look in his shifty eyes.

'Now come on,' I said. 'Hand it over.'

But he shook his head obstinately and reiterated his statement that he'd already given it to me.

'All right,' I said. 'We'll see what the Consul and the police think of that story.'

Kavan plucked at my arm. 'It doesn't matter,' he whispered urgently. 'I've still got my own papers.' His face was white and the twitch at the corner of his mouth had started again.

'That's no good,' I said. 'They're not stamped as having entered Tangier. You'd never get across the frontier.'

'But—' His mouth stayed open. He was trembling. I thought he was scared because he was a refugee and in a bureaucratic world; refugees have no existence unless their papers are in order. But it wasn't that. 'I'm not going to the Consulate,' he hissed. 'Whatever happens, I'm not going to the Consulate. We've got to get that passport.'

I glanced at the patrone. His greasy face was sullen and obstinate and frightened. 'It's no good,' I said. 'Kostos must have some kind of hold over him. We're not going to get it.'

'But we must. We must.'

'If you hadn't called yourself Wade and got mixed up with Kostos,' I said angrily, 'this would never have happened.' The taxi arrived then and I turned to the patrone, giving him one more chance to produce it. But he only shrugged his shoulders and called on the saints to witness the truth of what he was saying.

'All right,' I said, and I got Kavan out to the taxi and bundled him in. The Arab moved towards us from the opposite corner of the street. 'Le Consulat Britannique,' I ordered the driver. '*Vite, vite*!'

Kavan caught hold of my arm as the taxi drove off. 'It's no good,' he cried. 'I won't go to the Consulate. I won't go, I tell you.' He was wrought up to a point of hysteria. 'Tell him to stop.' He leaned quickly forward to tap on the glass partition.

But I pulled him back, struggling with him. 'Don't be a fool!' I shouted at him. 'You wanted to call yourself Wade. Well, now you've got to be Wade until we're out of Tangier. And you won't get out till we've recovered that passport.'

'There must be some other way. I could slip across the frontier. . . .' He reached forward to the partition again, but I flung him back into his seat. 'What are you scared of?' I demanded, shaking him. I was suddenly furiously angry, fed up with the whole wretched business. 'Why are you frightened of the Consul? What is it you've done?'

'Nothing. I told you before. I've done nothing. Absolutely nothing.' His voice was trembling. He seemed on the verge of tears he was so wrought up. 'I promise you. Please. Tell the driver to stop.'

'No,' I said, holding him down. 'I've had enough of this.' My voice sounded hard. 'We're going to see the Consul. Either that or you tell me why you're scared to go there. Did you kill Wade?'

'No.' He stared at me, his body shocked rigid. 'It happened just as I said.'

'Then what the devil is it you're scared of? Why did you insist on taking his name? Come on now,' I added, gripping hold of his arm. 'If you want any more help from me, you'd better give me the whole story.'

He stared at me, his white, frightened face outlined against the dark leather of the cab. 'All right,' he whispered, and his body relaxed under my hand as though a weight had been lifted from him. 'All right, I'll tell you.' He leaned back in his seat as though exhausted. 'I have told you I am a scientist.' I nodded. 'Have you lived here so long in North Africa that you don't know what that means?' He leaned quickly forward, his face becoming excited again. 'It means you have something here—' He tapped his forehead. 'And because of that your life is not your own any more. It belongs to the State. I am a Czech. If you take me to the Consulate, then I shall be sent back to England, and sooner or later they will get me. Or else life will become so insupportable . . .'

'Who will get you?' I asked.

'Who? The Communists, of course. The Czech Communists.'

'But for heaven's sake!' I exclaimed. 'You're a refugee. You've been given political asylum. You were perfectly safe in England.'

'Safe?' He laughed. 'You say that because you are English, because you have never been a refugee! Listen. When I fled to England in 1949, everything was all right. But then, after the Fuchs business, there was a new screening and it was discovered I had been a Communist.'

'But if you were a Communist—'

'I was not a Communist,' he declared violently. 'I have never been a Communist – not in the sense of the word as it is used now. But I joined the Party in 1938, after Munich. A great many of us joined then. It seemed our only hope. And afterwards, when the war was over, I forgot all about it. I didn't think it mattered after I had fled from Czechoslovakia. I had left my wife to escape the Communists. I thought that was sufficient.'

'I still don't see what you're frightened of,' I said. 'Are you trying to tell me that our people were going to send you back to Czechoslovakia?'

'No, no, of course not. Oh, God! I knew you wouldn't understand. The British refused to let me leave the country. That's why I had to come with Wade in a boat. It isn't the British I am afraid of. But if I go back there . . . Listen, please. When I ignored the offers from Prague, they began sending me Party literature as though I were a member, they stopped me in the street, phoned me at the office, sent anonymous letters to the authorities denouncing me as a paid Communist agent. They even sent me letters in code from Prague. Finally they began to threaten. They were going to arrest Karen and my father. They would have been sent to the uranium mines or, worse still, into Russia, to Siberia.'

'But your wife's here now,' I said.

'I know, I know. But how do I know she is here of her own free will?' He caught hold of my arm, shaking it excitedly. 'Please, please, try to understand. If I am sent back to England, it will start all over again. I couldn't stand it. No man's nerves could stand it. But here . . . Wade will disappear and there is nothing, absolutely nothing, to connect an obscure doctor at a Mission in the Atlas Mountains with the scientist who is missing in England.' He was sweating and his face was all puckered up with the urgency of what he was trying to convey. 'Please. You must help me. There must be some way out of Tangier. There must be some way.'

The taxi was just turning into the rue d'Angleterre. I could see the arched entrance to the Consulate. 'Maybe there is,' I said and leaned forward and slid back the glass partition. 'Drive down to the Zocco Grande,' I told the driver. I couldn't very well do anything else. Half of his fears were probably imaginary, but they were real enough to him. The taxi turned the corner by the entrance to the Consulate and drove on down the hill, and he was suddenly crying. Tears of relief were welling out of his eyes. 'Thank you,' he breathed. 'Thank you.'

Poor devil! I leaned back in my seat, thinking back over the events of the past twenty-four hours. If I hadn't pulled him out of the sea . . . But I had and now he was my responsibility. Somehow I'd got to get him out of the International Zone and into Morocco. It was a problem – the sort of problem that required inside knowledge of the working of Tangier. There had been a time . . .

I glanced at my watch. It was ten past three. Unless they had altered the flight schedules, we could still be at the airport in time to meet the Paris-Casablanca plane. I hesitated, wondering whether Vareau was still a clerk at the airport. Once, a long time back, I had got a man out that way, and his papers had lacked the necessary entry stamp. It was worth trying. 'We'll get another taxi in the Zocco Grande,' I said, more to myself than to him. 'And we'll have to hurry. We've got to buy you a new suit and be out at the airport before four.'

He gripped my hand. 'I shall never be able to thank you,' he said.

'You haven't thanked me yet for saving your life,' I said harshly. 'Better leave thanksgiving until we're both of us safely out of Tangier.'

CHAPTER THREE

We left Tangier by the rue de Fez, along a dirt-edged road where strings of asses trotted through the dust kicked up by battered French trucks driven fast. Out on the outskirts of the Mountain it was all rickety, new-grown development – an ugly pattern of telegraph poles and tin shacks and brand-new concrete factories. And the old ran side-by-side with the new; the over-burdened asses, the bare-legged, turbaned men driving wooden ploughs through hard, dry ground, and the women, shrouded and veiled so that they looked like perambulating bundles of old clothes.

Beyond the development area, a ridge of grey-brown hills covered with stones and scrub ran out to Cap Spartel and the Atlantic. We passed a gang of convicts picking desultorily at the road and there were herds of black goats and drifts of white that were flocks of the stork-like birds that the French call *pique-boeuf*. It was all just as I remembered it, even to the nervous void in my stomach and Kavan sitting tense and rigid beside me as that other man had done.

It was not quite four when we reached the airport. The field was empty. The Paris flight had not yet landed. I told Kavan to wait in the taxi and slipped over the white-painted fence and round to the back of the airport buildings where the buffet was. I was in luck. Vareau was there. 'Monsieur Latham!' He came waddling over to me, a fat, slightly shabby man with a face like a bloodhound. '*Comment ça va*, eh, eh? You wish me to arrange a seat for you on the plane, yes?'

'Not for me,' I said. 'For a friend.' And I drew him aside and explained the situation to him. But he shook his head. 'You know, *mon ami*, I would do anything to help you. But it is too dangerous. The regulations are most strict now. I must put his name on the Paris list and then what happens when the office in Casablanca see that, eh? *Non, non*, it is impossible.'

'Nonsense,' I said. 'It's not impossible. The Casablanca office wouldn't even notice. And if they did, then you made a mistake, that's all. You've got to help me, Vareau.' There was no other way of getting Kavan out, not with his papers correct. And they had to be correct if he were to work with me at Enfida. I pleaded, threatened, cajoled, and in the end he agreed to do it for twice the sum I originally offered him. Even then he wouldn't have done it but for one thing – for personal reasons the air hostesses were being changed at Tangier. It was this factor that made the thing possible.

We went through the details carefully and then I returned to Kavan. He was sitting exactly as I had left him, his body rigid, his face tense. He looked dazed and desperately tired, oddly unfamiliar in his new suit. 'Is it all right?' he asked urgently as I climbed in beside him. 'Did you fix it?'

'Yes,' I said. 'I fixed it.' But all the same I was wondering whether he could carry it through. His nerves were on edge and beneath the stubble of his beard I saw that the corner of his mouth was twitching.

'What do I have to do?' he asked. 'Tell me what I'm to do.'

I hesitated. I was wondering just how much I needed a doctor, for this business involved me deeper than I cared to go. But it was no good getting cold feet now. The man would just have to pull himself together. 'All right,' I said. 'Now listen. This is the drill. As soon as the Paris plane is sighted, Vareau, the French clerk, will come for you. He'll take you to the lavatory and there you'll shave off that beard, so that your appearance coincides with the photograph on your papers. By the way, I suppose your visa for entry into French Morocco is okay?'

'Yes, yes.' He nodded. 'That was all arranged at the French Consulate in London.'

'And you have a labour permit?'

'Yes.'

'Good. You'll stay in the lavatory until Vareau collects you. By then the passengers who are going through to Casablanca will be congregated in the buffet. You will join them. Have a drink or something to occupy yourself. Talk to nobody. If anybody speaks to you, reply in Czech. Vareau will bring you your ticket and anything else you need to get on to the plane. When the Paris passengers are instructed to return to the plane, you will go with them. There will be a different air hostess and your name will be on the list of passengers travelling direct from Paris to Casablanca. If the air hostess or the immigration official asks you anything, you don't understand – you speak nothing but Czech. Is all that clear?'

He nodded and I had him repeat the instructions word for word.

'When Vareau takes you to the lavatory, he will give you an immigration form to fill in. You will complete it in the lavatory and return it to him when he comes to collect you. Only one question on that form is not straightforward. Against *Where have you come from?* you will put Heathrow, London, via Paris. For destination and purpose of visit you state the exact truth – that you are going to work as a doctor in Morocco and that your address will be the English Mission at Enfida. Any questions about that?'

'No. No, I don't think so.' He was frowning. 'But I don't understand how it helps. The authorities at Casablanca will want to know why my papers are not stamped as having come from Paris. When they find they are not stamped, they will know—'

'There's no difficulty there,' I said, and I pulled out my own passport. 'Look!' I had come out to Morocco by air from England in July 1949, yet the only indication was the entry stamp of the immigration authorities at Casablanca. Though I had stopped off two days in Paris no entry had been made in my passport. 'You see. All you have to say is that you've come from England. You left London by the night flight yesterday. All right?' He nodded uneasily. 'You've nothing to worry about once you're on that plane,' I assured him.

'But you're not coming with me?'

'No. I shall go by train. We'll meet in Casablanca.'

He gripped my arm. 'Come with me on the plane. You could get a ticket here. There's nothing to stop you. Why must you go by train?' He was like a child afraid of being left.

'Because I reserved two berths in the wagon-lit. It would look odd if neither of us turned up.'

He nodded unhappily and stared out across the airfield, his fingers drumming nervously on his knee. 'Isn't there some way we could both go together?'

'No. This is the only way that gets you into Morocco with your papers in order. I should warn you there's a French Civil Control office at Enfida.'

'I don't like it,' he said, shaking his head. 'It's dangerous. And if I'm caught—'

'Oh, for heaven's sake!' I said, and took hold of him and swung him round so that he faced me. 'Now just listen. I'm in this as deep as you are. If you're caught, then I'll be in trouble, too. If you don't like this arrangement, then I'm through with you. Understand?'

'Yes. Yes, of course. I'm sorry.' He half shrugged his shoulders. 'Well, if it's the only way . . .' He nodded slowly. 'Very well. I'll do what you say.'

'Fine. You've nothing to worry about. Just convince yourself that you really have come direct from England.'

'I'll try.' He nodded and then asked me where he should meet me in Casablanca.

'At the railway station,' I said. 'The train for Marrakech leaves at 8.45 a.m. tomorrow.'

'And your train arrives when?'

'At seven twenty.'

'I shall be at the station in time to meet your train then.'

'All right. But if we do happen to miss each other, we'll rendezvous in the foyer of the Hotel Metropole.'

'If I'm not there to meet your train,' he said, 'you'd better look for me in the prison.' He said it unsmilingly.

The taxi driver, who had been standing talking to one of the baggage checkers, called out to us and pointed. The silver glint of wings showed above the hills behind us. I pulled open my case and handed Kavan my shaving things. As we got out of the taxi, Vareau appeared round the corner of the airport building and signalled to us. I gripped Kavan's hand. 'Good luck!' I said. 'You're clear on what you have to do?'

'Quite clear.' He nodded and then said urgently, 'You'll contact Karen, won't you? You'll let her know where I am?'

'I'll get in touch with her somehow,' I assured him.

'Promise you won't leave Tangier without—'

'Of course,' I said. 'Now hurry. Vareau's waiting.'

I watched him climb the fence and disappear round the front of the building with the clerk and then I got back into the taxi and sat there, watching the airfield, whilst the Constellation landed and taxied over. It was about ten minutes before the passengers emerged from the plane and came across the brown, burnt-up grass to the airport building.

I was nervous and the minutes dragged by. Cars came and went and my eyes remained on the corner of the building, my mind trying to visualise the scene inside. It was a modern brick building and on the side facing the airfield was a buffet with tall windows looking out to the runway. The baggage counter was between the buffet and the entrance hall, enclosed by doors. The officials would be fully occupied with the papers and baggage of the passengers stopping at Tangier. Kavan should have finished shaving by now. He should be sitting in the buffet with the rest of the passengers bound for Casablanca. The air hostess had gone into the building with the air crew several minutes ago. Vareau should have added Kavan's name to the list by now. He should have got Kavan's immigration form, too.

I got out of the taxi and began pacing up and down. If I could only have been in the buffet to keep an eye on things, to keep Kavan's mind occupied . . . I was afraid his nervousness would give him away, sitting there alone. I tried not to think what would happen if they started questioning him.

I kept glancing at my watch, but it seemed ages before the hands pointed to four forty-five. The air crew strolled out to the plane, their flat hats and dark blue uniforms looking oddly naval. A mechanic was clambering along one wing. Then he jumped down and the air crew disappeared inside the fuselage. It was ten to five. What were they waiting for? Had something happened? Were they interrogating Kavan now? I went to the rail, craning my head forward to see farther round the corner of the building.

And then the air hostess came out, the board with her list of passengers swinging in her hand. The passengers followed in a long, straggling line. I didn't recognise Kavan at first. He was near the end of the line, walking close to a French family. He looked quite different without his beard. He was walking jerkily, a little nervously, his head thrust forward, his eyes on the ground. Once he half-turned and glanced in my direction. His face looked stronger, more positive without the beard. He had a strong jaw and somehow the sight of him looking like that made me feel it would be all right.

The passengers were bunching up now, queueing at the foot of the steps into the fuselage. Gradually the little crowd thinned. I could see the immigration official. He was talking to the hostess, only half his attention on the passengers. And then he was looking at Kavan and my muscles tensed and my mouth felt dry. The air hostess glanced down at her list and I breathed a sigh of relief. Kavan was climbing the steps. I watched him disappear into the fuselage and then I turned and walked rather shakily back to the taxi.

Five minutes later the plane taxied out to the end of the runway. It stood there for a moment, revving its engines, and then it took off, the undercarriage retracting and the starboard wing dipping as it swung south and disappeared in the direction of Morocco.

I told the driver to take me back to Tangier and I lay back in my seat and closed my eyes. In little more than an hour Kavan would be through the airfield immigration check and on his way into Casablanca in the Air France bus – so long as nothing went wrong. But I couldn't do anything about it now. I would mail Vareau his money from Marrakech and that, I hoped, would be the end of the whole business.

For the first time since I had pulled Kavan out of the sea I felt relaxed. Lying back, watching the dusty road stream by, my mind turned to Enfida. Now at last I was able to think and plan again for the future.

The next thing I knew we were back in Tangier and a horn was blaring at us. We had stopped at some traffic lights and somebody was gesticulating and shouting to me from a car drawn up alongside. It was Kostos, and he leaned across the Arab he had with him and wound down the window. 'Lat'am!' he called across to me. 'I like to talk to you. Tell your driver to stop opposite the British Post Office, eh?'

'And I'd like a word with you,' I shouted at him. The sight of him had suddenly made me angry. If it hadn't been for that nonsense about the passport, I shouldn't have had to run the risk of getting Kavan out of the Zone illegally. He could have travelled with me on the train. I leaned forward and told the driver to stop opposite the BPO. The lights changed and we moved forward. Through the rear window I saw Kostos nose his car in behind us. I sat back again, thinking how dangerous it could be to take another man's name when you knew nothing about him – especially when the destination was Tangier. I was consumed with sudden curiosity to discover what it was all about. What were these documents that Kostos was so anxious to get hold of? And this place Kasbah Foum – it had an oddly sinister sound.

The taxi stopped and I paid the driver off. Kostos and the Arab were waiting for me on the curb. 'Where have you been?' Kostos demanded. 'You don't go to the British Consulate. I check that. An' you don't go to the Pension de la Montagne. I just come from there. Where do you go?'

'That's none of your business,' I said. 'There are one or two questions I want to ask you. First, I want that passport. What have you done with it?'

'The passport?' He smiled at me. 'You heard what Lopez say. He give it to you.' He leaned closer to me, still smiling. 'You tell me where Wade is, Lat'am, an' I make it worth your while, eh?'

'He's left Tangier,' I told him.

'Left the Zone? Oh no.' He shook his head, looking down at the suitcase I was carrying. 'He don't leave the Zone with you – not now. So you better cancel that other berth in the wagon-lit. He don't leave till I get what I want.'

'And that is the deeds of Kasbah Foum?'

He nodded, watching me closely. 'Strictly between you an' me, Lat'am, I trade the papers for his passport. You tell him.'

'And if he hasn't got them?'

'Oh, he has them.'

'How do you know?'

'I know because . . .' He stopped there and took hold

of my arm. 'Come. We cannot talk 'ere. You come to the Café Normandie and have a drink with me, eh?'

'All right,' I said.

He nodded towards the Arab, who was about thirty, tall and well-built, but carrying a little too much flesh under his djellaba. 'This is Si Ali bel-Caid El Hassan d'Es-Skhira.' His use of the man's full title rather than the way he said it conveyed his contempt of everything *indigène*. 'Maybe he persuade you, eh?' He smiled slyly, convinced that only money or power would persuade anybody.

I glanced at his companion with renewed interest. So this was the man who had employed Wade to get the deeds. At the mention of his name he had turned towards me and now that I could see his face I realised that he was Berber, not Arab. His features were long and pale, like a European's, with prominent cheek bones and a high-bridged, aquiline nose. It would have been a fine face but for the cruelty of the mouth and a slight craftiness of the eyes. 'Are you from the Atlas?' I asked him in French.

'From the Anti-Atlas. My father is Caid of Kasbah Foum-Skhira.'

'Poor fellow, he is an exile, you see.' Kostos tightened his grip on my arm with unpleasant familiarity. 'Come, Lat'am. We go where we can talk.' And he led me to one of the pavement tables of the Café Normandie, where he ordered two cognacs and a coffee for Ali, and then sat watching me uncertainly. The Berber stared out across the Place de France, his face impassive, his eyes remote. I was thinking they were typical of the cosmopolitan world of Tangier – the crook lured there by easy money and the Berber nationalist deported from his own country because he had been too actively anti-French. The roar of the traffic lapped round us, mingling with the shrill cries of the Arab news-vendors and the sound of Spanish music from the café radio.

The drinks came and Kostos raised his glass. '*Salud*!' He was looking at me with a sly grin. Then he set his glass down and leaned towards me across the table. 'Lat'am. You do something for me, will you – for the sake of old times. You tell me where Wade is.'

'I don't know,' I replied, amused that it was the exact truth.

'Now don't be silly, please.' The smile had gone from his mouth. The lips were compressed into a hard line. His small, dark eyes had hardened, too. 'I am going to have those papers. He is somewhere here in the Zone. If I do not get them, he never get out. Why do you smile? Do you think I don't tell you the truth? Maybe you think to help him slip across the frontier with some Berber caravan. Well, you try. That's all. You try an' get him out like that. You see' – he jabbed a tobacco-stained forefinger at me – 'it is not only me he have to reckon with. It is Ali, also. The word has gone out to the souks.' He tapped the side of his nose and smiled. 'He don't get out of Tangier till Ali has those papers.'

I was almost tempted to tell him how the man he thought was Wade had got out of the Zone. I would like to have seen his face. But it was too dangerous. Instead, I said, 'He hasn't got the papers you want.'

'Then what is your interest in him?' He said it with

something near to a sneer. 'Now come, Lat'am. Let us not waste time. I know he has the papers.'

'How do you know?' I asked again.

'How? Because he come alone.' He leaned forward across the table. 'Down on the beach las' night you are asking about this man Kavan. Well, Kavan is not on the boat. He do not come. Wade is alone an' he has the papers. He must have.'

'Why? What's Kavan got to do with it?'

He stared at me and then shrugged his shoulders. 'Come, my friend. We are getting nowhere.' His voice hardened. 'We talk business now, eh? 'Ow much you want?'

I suppose I should have told him then and there what Kavan had told me – that Wade never had the papers. I should have tried to convince him. But I couldn't tell him that Wade was dead, lost overboard during the voyage, and I hesitated. The trouble was that I was consumed with curiosity about this place Kasbah Foum. Curiosity is something you suck up out of the atmosphere of Tangier. 'It might help,' I said, 'if I knew something about Kasbah Foum.'

'Ah, I understand. You wish to know what these papers are worth to us, eh?' Kostos chuckled. 'All right, Lat'am. I tell you. To me they are worth nothing. Nothing at all. It is to Ali only that they are important.' He turned to the Berber and spoke quickly in French, explaining what had been said.

Ali nodded. 'Kasbah Foum is part of the land that will come to me when my father, Allah preserve him, is dead,' he said, speaking directly to me. 'It is our own land, you understand, not collective land belonging to the tribe. But when the French come into the south of Morocco, what they call the Pacification' – there was the suggestion of a sneer in the way he said it – 'my father is forced to surrender Kasbah Foum to them. A Capitaine Marcel Duprez demand it of him as a personal gift. Now Duprez is dead and my people need that land because the trees are dying of some pest in the palmerie of Foum-Skhira. The date crop has failed and there is little food. But at Kasbah Foum there is water. New trees could be planted and the land tilled.'

'The place is of no real value,' Kostos cut in quickly.

'*C'est ça.*' Ali nodded. 'It is about a thousand hectares of land, mostly mountain, and there is a kasbah, an old mud fort, at the entrance to a gorge. It is of no value, except to my father's people.'

I looked across at Kostos. I didn't believe him. Why should he trouble himself about this if there was nothing more to it than a matter of planting a few date palms? 'Suppose you tell me the truth,' I said, reverting to English.

'You think we lie to you?' His eyes had narrowed.

I didn't say anything for a moment. I was thinking I ought to convince him I knew nothing about the papers and leave it at that. But I was back in the mood of Tangier and I was thinking of that entry at the end of Wade's log. 'Does the name Ed White mean anything to you?' I asked him.

The Greek's eyes were suddenly hard and angry. 'So you know all about it, eh? You sit there laughing at us—' His hand gripped my arm across the table. 'All right, Lat'am. We talk business now. 'Ow much?'

I pulled my arm away. To gain time I turned to Ali and complimented him on his French. The Berber smiled so that his teeth showed through his rather thick lips. 'I was educated in Paris.' He said it with pride.

'And now you are a nationalist.'

His eyes lit up. 'I have dedicated myself before Allah to the task of driving the French out of my country.' He started on a tirade against the Protecting Power, but Kostos cut him short.

'This doesn't get us nowhere.' He leaned towards me across the table. 'Listen, Lat'am. You an' I, we understand each other, eh? You get Wade to hand over those papers an' there is a hundred thousand francs for you. Understand? A hundred pounds sterling, if you like. That's what I bring you 'ere to tell you.'

'It's no good,' I said. 'He's out of the Zone now.'

'That is a lie. He cannot be out of the Zone.' He finished his drink and nodded to Ali. The two of them got to their feet and Kostos came round to my side of the table, leaning over me, his hand resting on my shoulders. 'Tell him I expect him at my office by midday tomorrow. If he comes before midday, I see you get the money. Okay? And don't get some foolish ideas, Lat'am. He is in a fix, and there is nobody will lift a little finger to help him get out of 'ere – not Arab, Berber or Jew. You tell him that.' He tapped the side of his nose and smiled. It wasn't a friendly smile.

They left then and I watched them drive past. Kostos was staring at me, hard-faced and angry. Then they were gone, swallowed up in the whirl of traffic in the Place de France, and I sat there, smoking a cigarette, whilst dust descended on Tangier and the lights came on in the shops. Finally I picked up my suitcase and went across to the British Post Office and phoned the one man I could trust to do something for me and not talk about it, a retired Indian Civil Servant who had been a friend of my father's. But he was out and his servant didn't expect him back till late. It didn't really matter. I could write to him about Karen Kavan from Enfida.

I went to a French restaurant and had some food and after that I walked down to the station and joined the queue waiting in the booking hall to go through the passport check. I wondered whether Kostos would have somebody follow me on the train and I looked about for the Arab who had kept watch outside the hotel. But I couldn't see him. I wasn't really surprised, for Kostos was essentially a Tangerois.

The minutes ticked slowly by on the station clock and the queue moved forward only a pace at a time. As always, it was a strangely mixed crowd – tourists and Spaniards and native tribesmen all jam-packed together. There were several Americans in gaily-coloured shirts and lumber-jackets – construction men from the big new Moroccan air bases. There were two Jews with grey beards and little black skull caps on their heads. And close beside me was a Berber chieftain with fierce, swarthy features and a black beard. The curved sheath of his knife was beautifully worked in silver.

The queue shuffled forward and one of the Americans said, 'Jesus, these Goddamned Spaniards! The way they behave, you'd think we were on Ellis Island.' He had a hard, braying laugh. Beyond his wide-brimmed hat, I could see the face of one of the passport officials framed in the oval of the hatch. And then a hand plucked at my arm and I turned, startled, thinking it was Kostos or perhaps the police to say that Kavan had been stopped at Casa.

Instead, I found Karen Kavan's grey eyes looking up at me. 'I'm so glad I found you.' Her voice was breathless with relief. 'I was afraid I might miss you in all this crowd, or else that you would have arrived early and be on the train.' She was nervous and her face was as pale and strained as it had been the previous night.

'How did you know where to find me?' I asked.

'I telephoned to your hotel. Then I try Cook's, just in case. I wanted to know—' She stopped there, uncertain how to go on.

'It's all right,' I said. 'I know who he is. And you needn't worry. Your husband left for Casablanca by plane this afternoon.'

'Oh.' She closed her eyes momentarily. 'Oh, thank God. I was so afraid. You see, when I telephoned to the hotel, they said he had gone to the Pension de la Montagne. It's not far from where I work, so I walked there. But no guests had arrived there this afternoon and I was afraid the police . . .' The rush of words stopped abruptly and her eyes stared at me uncertainly. 'Where has he gone please? Last night, you said something about him working for you, but I don't remember – I am too *distrait*.'

I gave her my address and explained that her

husband would be working as a doctor at the Mission. 'You'll always be welcome there,' I added. 'When you're ready to come to him, you've only to write and let me know.'

'Thank you. You're very kind.' She breathed a little sigh. 'I was so afraid I shouldn't find you, that I shouldn't know where he had gone. I felt so alone.'

I glanced quickly at my watch. It was already nine thirty.

'How long have you been in Tangier?' I asked her.

'Just two weeks now. I am working as governess for an American family – Mr and Mrs Schulborg.'

Just two weeks! It was an odd coincidence. 'Straight from Czechoslovakia?'

'No. From the American Zone of Austria.' And then her eyes widened as she understood the drift of my questions. 'Surely Jan doesn't think I am here because they—' She stopped there and then added quickly, 'Please. You must explain to him that I received his message and that is why I am here.' Her voice was desperately urgent. 'His message arrived the 15th November. A week later, on the night of the 23rd, I escape across the border into Upper Austria on skis. That is in the American Zone. It was the Americans who find me this job here in Tangier. Please explain to him.'

'Of course I will,' I said. And then I added, 'You must love your husband very much.'

'Yes. Yes, I do.' The shadow of a smile suddenly touched her lips. 'But I hardly know him any more, you know.'

'Well, that's something that can be altered now. But it was a brave thing to do.'

She shook her head. 'No, not brave. It was dangerous, yes, but . . . You see, I was desperate. They had already arrested Pan Rudolph Kavan – that is his father. Fortunately I am away from Prague, staying with friends. When I returned, I was warned that our house was being watched and that I should be arrested also. That is what made me try to cross the border. I had no alternative. Explain to him, will you, please?'

I nodded. I was thinking of what Jan Kavan had told me in the taxi going up to the British Consulate. So it was all true. 'I'll tell him,' I said. 'Come to Enfida and join him as soon as you can.' And I added, 'You'd better write to me, not to him – just in case.'

She nodded. 'Yes, I will write to you.'

'And your address?'

'The Villa da Vinci on La Montagne.'

'Señor! *Deprisa, deprisa*, señor!' It was the passport officer telling me to hurry. I handed him my passport and went through the barrier to the next hatch where I got the necessary forms. I turned to speak to Karen again. A whistle shrilled. A voice called, '*En voiture*! *En voiture*!' There was the sound of running feet. 'Give Jan my love,' she called to me.

'I will. He will be expecting you. Come when you . . .' A blast of steam cut short my words and I saw the train begin to move. I waved to her and dashed on to the platform and scrambled on board.

My last memory of Tangier was Karen's small, pale face staring after me, her hand fluttering as she waved farewell to the only link she had with her husband. I found my sleeper and slumped into my seat, thinking about how she must feel, having come so far, still to be separated from him by two frontiers.

At El Ksar el Kebir there is a long wait. It's the frontier station between Spanish and French Morocco. I hung about in the cool night air until the frontier police returned my passport and then I went to bed. I was tired and I remember little except the usual vague noises of night travel by train – the rattle of the wheels on the rail points and the sudden, deathly silence of the stations where isolated noises become magnified.

When I woke it was daylight. The country was flat and there were glimpses of the sea through the ragged ribbon of factory buildings that lined the coast. We were approaching Casablanca. The buildings became taller, springing up all round the tracks – white concrete gleaming in the sunshine – and then the train was slowing down and we were running in to the station.

I rubbed the condensation from the window and peered at the people standing on the half-deserted platform, suddenly fearful that Kavan might not be there. But as the train jerked to a halt, I saw him a little farther down, standing alone beside some crates of oranges. He was smoking a cigarette and his face looked hard and set as he scanned the length of the train, watching the doors open and the passengers begin to alight.

He saw me as soon as I got off the train, and he rushed over to me and seized hold of my hand, pumping it up and down.

'You got through the immigration officials all right then?' I said.

'Of course, of course. There was no difficulty at all. They asked me whether I'd come straight from England and I nodded and talked to them in Czech and they stamped my papers and that was that. They're like little lambs.' He grinned and put his hand on my shoulder, patting me as though I were a dog. 'First you save my life. Then you get me out of Tangier. You are a wonderful man! Wonderful!' He was bubbling over with excitement. 'And now, here I am in Morocco. My new country! My new life!' His hand gripped my shoulder. 'I shall always be grateful. Always.'

'Wait till you've walked twenty miles in the mountains,' I said, 'and attended dozens of children half blind with trachoma.'

'You think I can't start my life again? I tell you I can. I'm tough. I have a stake in this country now. I shall learn Arabic and soon I shall be more Moroccan than the Moors.' He laughed and then stopped abruptly and said, 'Did you see Karen?'

'Yes.' And I told him how she had met me at Tangier station. He had me repeat everything she had said, and when I had finished, he stood there with bowed head. 'So my father has been arrested.' He blinked his eyes. 'He is an old man, so maybe they will . . .' But then he gave a little shrug. 'He was a fine man.' He used the past tense. 'He did much good in Prague. I'm sorry.' He straightened up and looked at me. 'Thank God Karen got out in time. I was afraid that perhaps . . . But never mind that now. *Give Jan my love!*' He murmured the words to himself and then gave a little awkward laugh that was so near to a sob. 'And she really said that? You heard her?' And when I nodded, he smiled a little sadly and said, 'You know, it is hard to believe that you have actually heard her voice. You're the first person to give me actual words she has spoken in all these four years. There have been messages, of course – through the underground. But you are telling me her actual words.' He cleared his throat briefly. 'Come on. Let's get some breakfast. Now you are here, I find I'm hungry.'

The difference in the man was extraordinary. He'd waited for my train in an all-night café near the station, but, though he was hollow-eyed, he didn't seem tired. And without the beard he looked somehow younger. But it wasn't just his appearance. His whole attitude to life had changed. His mind looked forward now, not backwards, and he was no longer frightened. It was as though the ordeal of passing through the immigration check at Casablanca had destroyed all the nerves in his system. He had arrived in Morocco. His papers were in order. All the past seemed to have been swept out of his mind, except for one thing.

We had barely settled down to our breakfast in a nearby café when he began talking of Kasbah Foum. 'I must go down there and see the place,' he said, and he pulled a map from his pocket. It was Michelin Map No. 171, covering the area of Marrakech and south to the Sahara. 'I got it last night,' he said. 'But it doesn't mark Kasbah Foum.'

'I think you'd better forget all about Kasbah Foum.'

He reacted at once to the sharpness of my tone.

'Why? Did something happen after I left? Was it Kostos?'

'Yes,' I said. 'I had a meeting with him and Ali d'Es-Skhira.'

'You mean you actually met Ali d'Es-Skhira?' He was suddenly excited. 'What was he like? What happened? What did they say?' I started to tell him, but he interrupted me. 'First, is Caid Hassan of Foum-Skhira still alive?'

It irritated me to have him thinking of nothing but this confounded Wade business. He had come out to be a doctor at Enfida. He should have been thinking about that. 'How the devil do you know the Caid's name? I thought you said Wade didn't talk about his affairs?'

'Wade?' He sounded surprised. 'Oh, I see. No, he didn't talk about his affairs, but . . .' He shrugged his shoulders. 'It doesn't matter.' He hesitated and then, as though he couldn't leave the subject alone, he said, 'Well, is he alive?'

'As far as I know. Why?'

'Nothing, nothing. But go on. Tell me what they said.'

To satisfy him I gave a brief summary of that meeting in the Boulevard Pasteur. When I had finished he said, 'So Kostos thinks I won't be able to get out of the Zone, eh?' He was smiling to himself. And then he looked at me, still smiling, and said, 'What do you think he'll do when he finds I've disappeared?'

'I don't know,' I said shortly. 'Nothing, probably.'

'Yes, he must do something. Ali, anyway. I think they'll go straight to Foum-Skhira.' He nodded his head thoughtfully, peering down at the map. 'Yes, that's what I think they'll do. Look. Here is Foum-Skhira.' He twisted the map round for me to see, pointing to a spot about 150 miles south-west of Marrakech. 'Kasbah Foum will be quite near it, I imagine.'

'Now just listen to me,' I said. pushing the map aside angrily. 'I don't know what Wade told you. Something obviously. But whatever it was that's got you so interested in the place, forget about it. You're not Wade any longer. You're Jan Kavan again. You ceased to have any connection with Wade the moment you stepped on that plane. From what you've told me, you've got quite enough worries without getting involved in another man's affairs.'

'But if Kostos follows me—'

'Why should he? He's not interested in you. He's only interested in Wade. Now just try and understand who you are. You're coming with me to Enfida to act as Mission doctor. That should be enough to occupy your mind. And your wife's going to join you there later. Now just shut up about Kasbah Foum. Okay?'

He nodded slowly. 'Yes, of course. I understand.' He folded the map up, but his eyes kept straying towards it as we ate our food in silence, and when we were on the train and steaming out of Casablanca he opened it up again and sat with it spread out on his knees, staring out of the window at the brown, rolling country where camels and mules, harnessed together, pulled primitive ploughs across the arid landscape.

'It's like the Old Testament come to life,' he said, and

then added, 'And I suppose it gets even more Biblical as you go south towards the desert.'

'You'll find all you want of the Old Testament in the souks of Marrakech,' I told him.

We didn't talk much after that and I drowsed off. When I woke we were running out of the Djebilet hills, down into the flat plain of Marrakech, and there, ahead of us, were the Atlas Mountains. An hour later we were sitting at a table, drinking coffee and looking out at the teeming mass of humanity that packed the Djemaa el Fna. The mountains and the plain had gone. We were swallowed up in the dusty hubbub of the great, red-walled Berber city. We went to the bank and then found a cheap little French hotel in the rue Bab Aguenaou.

In the late afternoon I took Jan to the roof-top of the Café de France. The place was full of tourists, rich people from all over the world who had come to drink mint tea on that roof and watch the sky flare to Technicolor and to look down on the seething acres of tribesmen packed into the great square of the Djemaa el Fna. The tide of humanity ebbed and flowed out of the narrow, covered alleys of the souks and the noise of it came up to us in a steady roar of sound. It was evening now and the flat, white roof tops and the red walls and the graceful tower of the Katoubia were flushed with the pink of the sunset and all the sky was an incredible spectrum of pastel shades. Away to the south the Atlas Mountains glistened like sugar icing, a towering rampart of fairy beauty.

'And that's where we're going?' Jan asked. He was staring towards the mountains.

I nodded.

'It's unbelievable,' he murmured. 'Marcel described all this to me so often. And now I am really here—'

'Marcel?'

He glanced at me quickly. 'A man I met during the war.' He turned back towards the mountains and added, 'It was when I was working with Krupps. I was on secret work and I was getting information out to the British. I used the French forced labour battalions and Marcel was my chief contact. He'd lived out here and he talked of nothing but this country and the people. He was a fine man. He believed in victory always, right from the beginning.' He paused and then added, 'He died of pneumonia in a cellar in Essen. I was sorry when he went.' His tone was sad as though he were speaking of somebody who had died only yesterday. 'And now I am here and it's all just as he described it to me. It doesn't seem possible.' His voice was almost awed. He hunched his shoulders and leaned forward, staring down into the huge square.

I was used to it now, but I could remember how I had felt when I first saw it. There were thousands of people down there; people from all over South Morocco – from the desert and the palmeries and from the most inaccessible villages of the Atlas. They crowded in circles round story-tellers and the snake charmers and the troops of dancers, or wandered hand-in-hand among the booths of doctors and barbers and letter-writers. Among them moved the water-boys, festooned with brass cups, their bells ringing an insistent water-note of sound. It was a shifting pattern of colour that sent up a continuous, inhuman roar. And over all the hubbub of the crowds there rose the ceaseless beat of the tam-tams – rhythmic and urgent; the sound that beats like the pulsing of the blood through the high mountains and along all the valley arteries of the south.

'It's wonderful,' Jan breathed. 'Wonderful. Karen will love it.'

I laughed. 'The glamour of it doesn't last,' I said. 'Not when you discover the poverty and disease and inert stupidity that lies behind it all. This is the thousand and one nights, the city of delight, the sweets of a year's labour in a hard, naked land. And the place is rotten with venereal disease, with tuberculosis, dysentery and conjunctivitis, with every running sore that Job was plagued with.'

'You want I show you souks?' A young Arab boy was standing at our table, his dark eager eyes watching us hopefully. 'You come. Jus' look. No buy. Jus' look.'

I glanced at Jan. 'Would you like to see the markets?'

His eyes went momentarily to the tinted crystal of the mountains and then he nodded and got to his feet. A gleam of triumph showed in the little Arab's eyes as he turned away towards the stairs. 'Do we need him to guide us round?' Jan asked.

'Not necessarily,' I said. 'But these boys are good value. It's getting late, too, and you can easily get lost.' We went down the concrete steps and out into the roar of the Djemaa el Fna, skirting the crowds.

'Philip!'

Jan had stopped, his head turned, staring towards the CTM bus terminal building. 'What is it?' I asked.

'Look!' He pointed. 'Do you see? That man.' His tone was urgent.

I followed the line of his outstretched hand, but all I could see was the shifting pattern of the human tide. 'What man?'

'He's gone now.' He lowered his arm slowly.

'Who was it?' I asked.

He shook his head. 'I don't know. Maybe it was the light. I thought for a moment it was Kostos.'

I laughed. 'Nonsense,' I said. 'Kostos is a Tangerois. There's nothing for him in Marrakech.'

The boy tugged at my sleeve. 'Quick, m'soor. Is late. You come quick.'

'Come on,' I said to Jan. 'It'll be dark soon. If you want to see the souks . . .'

He nodded and we plunged into the maelstrom that swirled around the dark mouth of the covered way that led down into the first of the souks. Here were dates and dried fruit and herbs and spices piled in little pyramids on open counters and Arab merchants squatting behind mountains of nuts in the gloom of their stalls. We went through the meat market and then we were in a long, narrow street thatched with palm fronds. The crowds were moving homewards from the souks now and we were fighting our way through a packed mass of people that flowed steadily towards the Djemaa el Fna. 'What you want, eh?' our guide asked, grinning up at us, eyes sparkling and his teeth showing white against the shadowed darkness of his small face. 'You like Berber silver? I show you bracelets. All good work. Very cheap.'

'You speak Arab, don't you?' Jan said. 'Tell him we just want to have a quick look round.'

'No,' I said. 'You tell him in English. I'm just going to be a tourist for once. Besides it's not many boys of his age speak English.'

'Ess, spik good English.' The boy grinned at us. 'I show you fine silver. Is not dear, m'soor. I fix.'

'We don't want to buy,' I said. 'We just want to look around.'

His mouth puckered sulkily and he shrugged his shoulders. 'Okay. You look. I take you good leather shop. No cheat.' We forged ahead slowly against the mass of people. There were only a few Europeans. Night was closing in and already the lights were on in the bigger shops, the shops that were marble-floored and had their walls covered with Moroccan rugs or finely stamped leather pouffes. 'You like carpet? Real Persian. I fix good price for you.'

'No,' I said. 'Take us to the street of the silversmiths.'

'You want silver, eh? Okay.' His eyes brightened.

The crowds were thinning now. A bicycle flashed past us, its bell ringing furiously as the Berber boy with a woolly cap on his head weaved dexterously in and out amongst the people. We turned into the little street where men sat cross-legged in workshops no bigger than cubby-holes stamping out the intricate designs of the bracelets, pouring the inlay from little iron pots of molten metal. There were still a few plump Arab women there, well dressed in grey or brown gabardine djellabas with silk veils over nose and mouth and naughty little gold-embroidered slippers peeping from beneath their voluminous skirts. Some of them already wore an armload of gold and silver bracelets, but they still stood and stared with longing.

As we left the street of the silversmiths, we met five blind beggars weaving their way home through the crowds, loosely linked like a sightless chain gang. They had the tortured, cadaverous features of the crucified and they were singing tonelessly, bobbing along with their shaven heads drawn back as though they'd all been hanged by ropes battened under the chin. They were led by a man with a wooden bowl who had the pitiless eyes of the professional beggar. His five freaks, strung out behind him, were all of them mutilated by disease besides having the blank, staring eyes of the blind. I stopped to put money in the bowl. As I did so there was a cry of warning, the crowd opened out and a small donkey piled high with Moroccan rugs went trotting past. The crowd closed up and surged forward. I was pushed to the wall and when at last I could make headway, I couldn't see Jan or our guide.

I hurried then, fighting my way through the crush and craning my neck to see ahead. But there wasn't a sign of him. I couldn't see a single European.

I began to get worried. He didn't know the language and I wasn't sure about the boy. It's easy to get lost in the souks. The place is an absolute rabbit warren. I fought my way through the silk market to the point where the souks divided. A narrow alley forked right. It was the street of the shoe makers, a dark tunnel crammed with people. I turned back then. The boy must have led him off into one of the side markets. I cut through a wide souk where silks were displayed in the few shops that weren't already shuttered and came out into the parallel street, where the makers of brass had their stalls. But it was impossible to find anybody in the brush of people going home.

For a while I rushed madly up every side alley, searching for him in the intermittent patches of lighting. But in the end I gave it up and made my way slowly back towards the centre of the city, moving with the steadily-flowing tide of humanity, the murmur of the great square acting as a guide. He couldn't really get lost. He'd only to follow the crowd. It was annoying, that was all.

It was quite dark when I reached the Djemaa el Fna and the booths were lit by the smoking jets of a hundred acetylene flares. The whole place, with its milling thousands of tribesmen and its tented booths, had the appearance of an army encamped for the night. The hotel was opposite the Tazi cinema where harsh Arab music blared at the packed crowd waiting to see an American Western.

As I approached the alleyway leading to the hotel, the little Arab boy who had been our guide came out of it. He stopped at the sight of me and his eyes widened. He looked scared and I caught hold of his arm before he could run away. 'Why didn't you wait for me?' I asked angrily, speaking to him in Arabic.

He stared at me with hurt brown eyes, shocked into immobility by the realisation that I spoke his language.

'*Allah ishet elik*!' I cried, shaking him. 'Speak, boy. Why didn't you wait for me?'

'You no come, m'soor,' he said, sticking obstinately to his English. 'We look all souks, but no see. Is late, very late for souks.' His voice sounded scared and his eyes searched the street as though looking for somebody to help him. 'Is no good staying in souk.' He suddenly jerked away from me, wriggling out of my grasp, and with one frightened look at my face, disappeared into the crowd across the road, a small, scampering figure in a brown djellaba and heel-less slippers.

I went straight up to the room we were sharing and found Jan sitting on the bed staring down at the suitcase full of clothes that he'd bought that afternoon. He looked up quickly at my entrance. 'Oh, here you are. Thank God!' His voice sounded nervous. 'I was getting worried about you. Do you think that boy did it on purpose?'

'How do you mean?' I asked, too surprised at his question to express the annoyance I had felt at finding him back here in the hotel ahead of me when I'd been getting worried and searching all through the souks.

'When we got separated by those beggars, he wouldn't go back for you,' he said. 'He insisted you'd cut down one of the side alleys. We went through it and came out into the brass market. But you weren't there and he got very excited, jabbering away at me in Arab, and led me into a maze of streets so that I didn't know where I was. All I knew was that he was leading me deeper and deeper into the souks.'

'Well, at least he brought you back,' I said, sinking into a chair.

'He certainly didn't. I had to find my own way back.'

I stared at him. 'Do you mean to say the boy just left you?'

'Well, not quite. It was really the other way round. I left him.'

'Where?'

'It was in an alley full of those gold-embroidered slippers. He kept on trying to drag me along the whole length of it. But by then I knew the only sensible thing was to come back to the hotel. I told him that and he tried to convince me the best way back was straight down that alley. I knew it wasn't. That way we should have been going against the crowd and I was certain they were making for the Djemaa el Fna.'

'And the boy left you to make your own way?'

'He came a little way with me. Then he gave it up.'

'But I've just seen him outside the hotel.'

Jan shrugged his shoulders. 'Then he must have followed me, that's all.'

'You're certain he was trying to lead you the wrong way?'

'Yes, I'm pretty certain. I always have a shrewd idea where I am in a strange city.' He hesitated and then said, 'There's another thing, too. The room has been searched whilst we've been out.'

'Oh, for heaven's sake!' I said. I felt tired. 'How do you know?'

'The hasps of my case were undone. I didn't leave

them like that. And when I got here, the Arab porter couldn't find the key. He was gone about five minutes before he produced it.' He was wrought up about it, his nerves on edge.

I pulled myself to my feet and examined my case. As far as I could tell everything was just as I'd left it. 'Let's go down and have some food,' I said.

He stared at me angrily for a moment and then he turned away. 'Perhaps you're right.' But he said it without conviction.

However, he seemed to relax in the warmth of the restaurant, and next day, after a long night's sleep, he was quite a different person. In fact, he was almost exuberant when we were finally seated in the Enfida bus, packed in like sardines amongst a crowd of Berber men returning from a night out in the great city. He talked excitedly, asking questions, and when we drove out past the traceried gateway of the Bab Aguenaou on to the road that runs out into the flat plain, he sat quite still without talking, staring at the mountains. Behind us Marrakech, with its nine kilometres of red mud walls and its flat-roofed houses dotted with storks' nests, lay sprawled out in the clear morning sunlight, a sleepy pattern of red and brown and white.

I didn't talk to him on that two-hour journey out to Enfida.

I thought if I didn't talk, maybe he'd find it easier to adjust himself to his new surroundings. Also, I had my own problems. I hadn't given much thought to the Mission whilst I had been in Tangier. Now I needed to plan. There was the surgery to organise and people I wanted to see – people who had been sick or had suffered some misfortune like Yakoub at the olive factory who had lost his little son. And Jan would have to be introduced to Frehel, the Civil Controller, and to the Caid, and then I'd have to take him on a tour of the villages. I had hardly got all these matters sorted out in my mind before the bus was climbing up out of the plain to the fringe of the foothills and we had come to the first of the olive plantations.

Everything looked very wet. There were pools of water steaming in the sunshine and the roadway itself was creamed with mud. 'There's been a lot of rain up here,' Jan said.

I nodded, remembering the paper I had picked up in José's bar. It seemed ages ago. I wondered whether it could have snowed here.

'Have you had somebody looking after the Mission whilst you've been away?' he asked.

'Yes,' I said. 'Two English people – a painter named George Corrigan and his sister, Julie. I think you'll like them. They run an old single-decker bus which they converted into a caravan. They've been touring Morocco in it.'

'Do they know the south at all?'

'Still thinking about Kasbah Foum?' I said. And then, because my tone had sounded angry, I added, 'If anybody knows it, they will. They've been all over the country. For all I know, George may have done a painting of it. One room of the Mission is stacked with his paintings. There are a lot of kasbahs amongst them.'

We had turned up into Enfida now and a moment later we drew up at the bus stop behind a truck piled high with a load of black olives going down to the press. There was a little crowd standing in the mud waiting for the bus and the rushing sound of the river flooding under the bridge filled the town.

Yakoub, the man who had lost his little son, was standing talking to the driver of the olive truck, his woolly cap and ragged djellaba black and stiff with the rancid oil of the press.

'*Salaam ealykum*!' I called to him, but he didn't answer. And when I went up to him, he seemed ill-at-ease and refused to look me in the face. 'What's the trouble?' I asked him.

He moved his shoulders awkwardly and mumbled something about the wrath of Allah being terrible.

'What is it?' I said. 'What's happened?'

'It is the mountain, sidi,' he murmured. 'It has fallen into the valley. It has fallen upon the Dar el Mish'n.'

'What's he saying?' Jan asked me.

'Something about the Mission.' Yakoub had turned away now. The people by the bus were all standing watching me. 'Come on,' I said. 'We'd better get up there right away.' And we began walking up towards the open space by the Auberge de la Ravine, where the track into the mountains started. There was something about the atmosphere of the place and the way the people stood silently watching us that scared me. The air was heavy with the humid heat of mud steaming in the sunshine and the river roared in a brown flood under the bridge. And in the place of olives outside the auberge, the drivers of the asses and the men who bent over the scales stopped and stared, and when I spoke to them they were silent as though they had been struck dumb. A feeling of disaster hung over the place.

PART TWO

THE MISSION

CHAPTER ONE

We came out above the olive trees on to the hillside and everything looked quiet and peaceful in the midday sun. The mountains were a massive line of white shouldering up into the blue sky and the air was still and calm and crystal-clear. Down below us the river wound through the valley, a turgid, brown flood of water, and the only sound was the persistent braying of a donkey. The slope of the ground ahead screened the Mission, but soon I could see the creamy white of the Corrigans' caravan parked in an olive grove down to the left and then I breasted a rise and all the hillside above the Mission came suddenly into view, and I stopped.

Above the road there was a great, raw gash of newly-exposed rock and rubble. It ran from the very top of the sheer hill-slope, broadening out as it swept down, and disappeared beyond the next rise of the road. I stood there, my chest heaving, my whole body suddenly paralysed at what I saw. It was a landslide, and I was rooted to the spot by fear of what I should find when I topped the final rise.

Jan joined me. He didn't say anything, but just stood there beside me, breathing heavily. There was nothing to be said. I started forward again, slowly now, reluctantly. As we climbed the rise, more and more of the hillside became exposed, showing a broader, more chaotic tumble of heaped-up debris. And then, suddenly, we were over the rise and the full extent of the disaster was revealed. A quarter of a mile ahead of us the road ceased, swept away and overlaid by tons of wet, red earth and rock. The Mission had vanished utterly, blotted out as though it had never been. And where the olive trees had stood and the children's playground and the stables I had built for sick donkeys, there was nothing – nothing but raw, broken earth.

The landslide had swept over it all, obliterating five years' work and all my hopes.

I didn't know what to do. I seemed suddenly without feeling. It just didn't seem real to me. This spot was my home, my whole life. It had been beautiful – a long, whitewashed building looking out across the olive groves to the valley and across to the mountains. It was as much a part of me as my body.

I stared uncomprehendingly at the gang of labourers with their long-handled shovels already at work on the road. They were like pygmies trying to shift a mountain. I felt I must have come to the wrong place, that this couldn't really be Enfida, couldn't be Le Mission Anglais – the Dar el Mish'n.

I followed the great red sweep of the landslide down

the slopes to the valley bottom and understood why the river had seemed so brown. It was pouring in a white cascade over the base of the landslide.

I felt dazed – bewildered by the violence, the utter ruthlessness of it all. If it had left something – a wall, part of a building . . . But there was nothing; not a tree, not a stone, not a single vestige of the place. All my personal things were gone, my books, my notes, my clothes, George's pictures, the medical stores, the van . . . every single thing completely and utterly vanished below that ghastly, piled-up chaos of broken hillside.

Jan touched my arm. 'It's no good looking at it,' he said quietly. 'Better come down to the auberge and have a drink.'

No good looking at it! That was true. 'I never want to see the damned place again,' I said savagely. 'All the time, all that effort! You'd think if God . . .' I stopped myself there and pushed my hand through my hair. Then I turned my back abruptly on the spot that had been my home and walked slowly down with Jan to the inn.

And that was where we met Julie, by the piled-up heaps of olives in the open space by the inn. She came towards us, walking slowly, her black hair hanging limp, her face white and strained. I was too dazed by the disaster of it all to notice then how desperately tired she was. I only knew I was glad she was there.

'You've seen?' she asked as she reached us.

I nodded, afraid to trust myself to speak.

'I was hoping to catch you before you went up there,

to break it to you gently. But you didn't tell me you were coming back today.' Her voice sounded flat and lifeless.

'When did it happen?'

'Two days ago; just after three o'clock in the afternoon.'

'Thank God you weren't in the house,' I said. 'Where were you? Did you see it?'

She nodded, her lip trembling. She was suddenly on the verge of tears. 'I was at the caravan, turning out a drawer. George . . . George was doing a painting of the house. He was sitting at his easel down near the donkey stable. He wanted the house and the hills in shadow behind it. It was to be a surprise for you, Philip. A welcome-home present. And then . . .' She closed her eyes and shook her head, the tears welling slowly, uncontrollably from between her tight-pressed eyelids.

'You mean – George?' I was too horrified to move.

She nodded slowly. 'He was there – just below the house. I saw him.' She opened her eyes, staring at me. 'There was a sort of rumble . . . like thunder. I went to the door. I thought it might be another heavy downpour and I had some washing out. But it was clear and sunny. I heard George shout. He shouted to me and then he began to run and I looked up and saw the whole hillside pouring down. I couldn't run. I just stood there and saw the first wave of rocks pour over the roadway, down to the house and then . . . then George fell and the whole ghastly landslide rolled over him. And then it hit him and . . . and suddenly he wasn't there any more.'

I said something. I don't know what it was, but she was suddenly clinging to me, sobbing hysterically. 'It was horrible. Horrible. And I couldn't do anything.' She was trembling and all I could do was stroke her head the way you do a sick animal.

Gradually she stopped trembling and her grip on my arm relaxed. 'I'm sorry.' Her voice was steadier, more controlled. 'It happened two days ago. I should have got used to it by now.' She straightened up and dried her eyes. 'It was just that there was nobody . . .' She blew her nose hard. 'Ever since it happened I've just felt screwed up tight inside. And then, when I saw you . . .' She shook her head as though trying to shake the picture out of her mind. 'I'm all right now.'

'Where are you staying – at the auberge?' I asked her.

She shook her head. 'No. I'm still living in the caravan. I didn't want to see any strangers. I wanted my own things round me. Oh, Philip – why did it have to be George? Why did he have to choose that afternoon? . . . He'd been painting up in the hills for days.'

I took her arm. She was still trembling. 'I think perhaps some tea would help.'

'Yes, of course.' She nodded, clutching at the suggestion. 'If you come back to the caravan I'll make you some.' As she turned, she came face-to-face with Jan. I don't think she'd noticed him till then. The sight of a stranger seemed to brace her. 'You must be Dr Kavan.' Her voice was steadier as she held out her hand to him. 'I'm sorry. This isn't a very pleasant welcome. . . .' She let her hand drop to her side.

He didn't say anything and she turned quickly and led us down to the caravan.

The bus had been converted into two rooms with a shower bath and kitchenette between. She led us through into the front half, which was bedroom, living-room and studio combined and which merged into the driver's seat. It had been George's room. His things were everywhere, his clothes, his paints, the inevitable stack of canvases. It was impossible not to imagine that he was away painting somewhere in the hills and would return today or tomorrow or the next day.

I sat down, feeling dazed, thinking how senseless it was. There were hundreds of square miles of mountains. Why did it have to be here, in this exact spot? I looked up and stared out through the windscreen. The bus was parked facing towards Enfida. I was looking out on to a pattern of silver grey against the sky with the holes of the olive trees dark streaks in the shade. But the tranquillity of the scene only sharpened the memory of that broken slash of rubble lying over the Mission.

Julie came in then with the tea. 'It's no good brooding over it, Philip,' she said in a small, taut voice. 'We must think of the future, both of us. Think of the new Mission you'll build.'

'The new Mission?' I stared at her. She didn't understand. 'There won't be any new Mission,' I said. 'I've no money to start again.'

'But weren't you insured?' Jan asked.

'Against fire and theft. Not against an Act of God.'

'But your Mission Society?' His voice was suddenly tense. 'Surely they will help—'

'Why should they? I put up most of the capital. The Society isn't really interested in a Mission here.' And then I realised what was worrying him. 'You'll be all right,' I added. 'You're a doctor. They need doctors out here in Morocco.'

He gave a nervous little shrug. 'It's not the same. Here I would have been lost to the world.'

We sat in silence after that, drinking tea, wrapped in our own thoughts. For each of us that landslide meant something different. And for each of us the future was uncertain.

As soon as I finished my tea, I got up and went out into the hard, bright sunshine, walking through the shade of the olives until I came to where they ceased abruptly and there was nothing but great, piled-up heaps of mud and stone. It rose higher than the trees, the surface of it drying and caking in the sunshine.

Insh'Allah! I kicked out viciously at a clod of earth. That's what they'd be saying, here in Enfida and up the valleys at Kef and Tala and all the other mountain villages. Like disease and poverty and the loss of crops through water, it was the will of Allah and you shrugged your shoulders and did nothing about it.

I clenched my fists. Somehow I must fight back; show them that disaster wasn't something to accept, but a thing to struggle against.

But how? How?

I bowed my head then, praying to God for some guidance for the future, for some hope; praying that I'd have the strength to go on, that I wouldn't have to turn my back on it and admit that I'd wasted five years of my life.

But the answer to one's prayers comes from inside,

not from outside, and I was too raw and hurt by the shock of what had happened to feel any revival of spirit.

A hand slipped under my arm and Julie was standing there beside me. She didn't say anything and we stood there, looking at what the giant force of Nature had done to the hillside. Twenty thousand bulldozers couldn't have done it in a year, and yet it had happened in a few moments – in less time than it had taken a man to try and run half the width of it.

The slide stretched like a giant scar from the valley bottom to the very summit of the sheer hillside.

'You mustn't be too bitter about it,' Julie said. She had seen my face, knew what I was thinking.

'I don't know where to begin,' I said.

'Something will turn up.'

I stared at her, seeing her standing there, straight and firm-lipped, remembering what she had lost there under that landslide. I should have been comforting her. 'I'm sorry,' I said.

She smiled and shook her head. 'We'd better go down to the auberge now and see Madame Gast.' Her voice was suddenly practical, though it trembled slightly. 'I expect she'll have rooms for you both.'

The news that I'd returned had spread and the open space outside the auberge was crowded with people. There were women there, as well as men – Arab women, their eyes watching us curiously from the safety of their veils; Berber women in their gaily-coloured cottons. The men, standing in little huddles by the heaped-up piles of black olives, carefully avoided my gaze. They were superstitious – curious but frightened; Allah had struck down the Dar el Mish'n and to talk to the Englishman would be unlucky. Men I had helped, whose sons I had trained as mechanics and joiners in my workshops, averted their gaze, afraid to speak to me, afraid to give me even a word of sympathy. They still believed in the Evil Eye. They wore charms to protect themselves against it – the charm of the Hand of Fatima. 'Damn them all to hell!' I muttered with sudden, pointless anger.

Julie's grip on my arm tightened. 'It's not their fault,' she said.

No, it wasn't their fault. But what was the point of going on? Why bother to struggle against centuries of ignorance?

And then we were in the cold, dark interior of the auberge and Madame Gast was sitting, waiting for us, with her cat. She was a Frenchwoman who had married a German in the Legion. But, sitting there in her ugly, Victorian chair, there was no indication of a colourful background. The girl who had followed the Legion had been obliterated by the widow who for twenty years had run an auberge in Enfida and now she was like a huge-bodied female spider huddled in the centre of her web. She fed on gossip and her little eyes sparkled as she saw us. Both she and her cat were immense and shapeless, like the old carpet slippers she wore. Little grey eyes stared at us curiously out of the big, sagging face.

'I have rooms ready for you, *mes enfants*,' she said. She had known we must come to her.

'I'll leave you now,' Julie said quickly. 'Come and see me in the morning.'

Madame Gast watched her go and then she shouted to the Berber kitchen boy to bring us some wine. The room was big and dreary. Down one side ran the bar and in the corner, where Madame Gast sat, was a big white-tiled Austrian stove. The walls were decorated with discoloured posters of French holiday resorts and there was a rack of faded postcards.

The wine came and we sat and drank it, listened to Madame's account of the disaster. Three farms had been destroyed as well as the Mission and the landslide had dammed up the river and flooded several olive groves. 'And they blame me for the disaster?' I said.

She nodded. '*Oui*, monsieur.'

'What else do they say?' This old woman knew everything that was said in Enfida.

She shrugged her shoulders. 'Does it matter, monsieur?' She hesitated and her eyes softened. 'Tell me, what are you going to do now?'

'What are the people expecting me to do?' I asked her.

'They think you will leave Enfida and go back to your country across the sea. They say that it is the will of Allah.'

'And if I stay?'

She folded her thick, work-stained hands in her lap. 'They do not expect you to stay.' There was silence between us for a moment and then she said, 'Monsieur Frehel telephoned about an hour ago. He would like to see you.'

'What's he want to see me about?' I asked.

She shrugged her shoulders. 'I expect, like everybody else, he is curious to know what you are going to do.'

So they were all waiting for me to admit defeat. Frehel was all right. We got on quite well together. But officially he didn't approve of an English missionary at Enfida. A bitter sense of loneliness had come over me.

I got up then. I felt I couldn't stay in that room any longer. It was so cold and dreary. And I wanted to think. 'I'm going for a walk,' I told Jan.

It was brighter outside. A cool wind blew down off the mountains, but the sun was warm. I walked up through the place of the olives, conscious of the stares and whispers of the crowd. I walked steadily up the road until I came to where the landslide had spilled across it and the gang of workmen were cutting into it with their shovels. I turned off to the right then and began to climb up through the olive groves, climbing towards the top of the slide. Maybe the attitude of the Berbers of the mountain villages would be different. There were too many Arabs in Enfida. Tomorrow I would go up to the villages at the head of the ravine.

It was dusk when I got back to the auberge. The single electric light bulb under its white porcelain shade barely illuminated the big, empty room. A table had been laid for the two of us in a corner. I stopped to warm myself at the stove. The cat was sitting in Madame's chair half-concealing a copy of *La Vigie*. A headline caught my eye: *TANGIER YACHT MYSTERY – What Happened to Second Man? – Police Search for Missing Captain Intensified.*

I pulled the paper out from beneath the recumbent

cat and glanced quickly through the news story. It was date-lined Tangier . . . *and it is now known that there was a second man on board the yacht. His identity is being kept secret, but the police state that the search for M. Roland Wade, captain and owner of the* Gay Juliet, *who disappeared from the Hotel Malabata in Tangier two days ago, has been intensified. They wish to question him about the fate of this second man. Wade stated, when he was rescued from the wreck, that he was the only person on board. It is thought that Wade, who is a short, dark-haired man, may have slipped across the International Frontier at some unguarded point into Spanish or French Morocco. A close watch is being kept on all forms of transport and a description has been . . .* There followed a description of Jan as he was when he had shared my room at the Malabata and a brief account of how the yacht was wrecked in the gale. And then: *Wade was last seen when he left the Hotel Malabata in the company of M. Philip Latham, the Englishman who rescued him from the sea. M. Latham is believed to have returned to French Morocco where he is living. Inquiries are being made by the Moroccan police.*

I sat down in a chair and stared at that last line. So they would be coming here to question me! First the landslide, and now this! I dropped my head into my hands. It was too much. Everything seemed to have gone wrong. And then I was staring at that news story again, suddenly conscious of the significance of that word FATE. *They wish to question him about the fate of this second man.* I wondered how they knew for certain that there had been two men on the boat. But it didn't matter. The point was that they knew. I licked my lips, which had suddenly gone dry. The police had leapt to the same conclusion that I had.

I grabbed the paper again and ran up the stairs. It was inevitable. What else could they think? The man they thought was Wade had disappeared and his companion on the boat had never arrived. On the face of it, it could only add up to murder and now they'd go searching and questioning until they found him. I ran quickly from bedroom to bedroom. But they were all empty. Jan wasn't there. I went back down the stairs and shouted for Madame. The kitchen door opened. 'Dinner is almost ready,' she said.

'Where's Dr Kavan?' I asked her breathlessly.

'He has gone out.'

'Where? Did he say where?' I got a grip on myself and added more calmly, 'When did he leave?'

'About half an hour ago.' She paused and I was conscious of her beady eyes watching me curiously. 'He has gone to see Monsieur Frehel.'

'Frehel?' Had the police traced Jan already? Had they guessed at the truth? Oh God! What a mess! And then I pulled myself together and asked Madame to bring me a *fine à l'eau*. They'd discover that he was the man who'd come ashore from the wreck. I crossed the room and sat down at the table that had been laid for us. They'd think he'd taken Wade's identity for fear of being accused of killing the man. What else could they think? I rubbed my hand across my eyes. Poor devil! And there was his wife, waiting in Tangier. She would be brought into it, too. I tried desperately to think of a way out for him, but it was no good. The only hope was to tell them the truth. It would involve Vareau, but that couldn't be helped. They would have to be told the truth.

Madame brought me my drink and settled herself in her chair, holding the cat in her lap, stroking it gently and watching me with a gossip-greedy look in her small eyes. '*Alors*, monsieur – about this affair in Tangier. I see your name is mentioned in the paper.'

But I was saved her cross-examination by the arrival of a car. It was a Frenchman wanting a room for the night. He was a man of medium height and he wore a grey felt hat and a raincoat over a light suit. I didn't really take much notice of him then. He was one of those men who fit quietly into their surroundings. He might have been a commercial traveller. Madame took him up to show him his room and I sat staring down at the paper, not reading it, just wishing I was done with the whole business.

And then Jan came in. 'I had to go down and see the Civil Controller,' he said.

'What happened?' I asked quickly. 'What did he want? Does he know who you are?'

'Of course. I showed him my papers and we talked—'

'I don't mean that. Does he know you're the man who posed as Wade in Tangier?'

'No. Why should he?' He seemed surprised.

'Why? Because the police . . .' But of course, they

couldn't know all that yet. 'Have you seen this?' I thrust the paper across to him.

He picked it up and I heard the quick intake of his breath, saw the knuckles of his hand whiten as his grip tightened on the pages. He dropped into the chair beside me. 'How do they *know* I was on the boat? They can't know. It was dark when I joined *Gay Juliet* and we sailed in the early hours of the morning, before it was light. I'm certain I wasn't followed.' He didn't say anything more for a moment as he read the whole story through. Then he put the paper down and looked at me. 'This is how it started before,' he said. 'There was a lot of publicity about my being taken off secret work, that was how they knew I was worth bringing back to Czechoslovakia. Once the International Police reveal my name to the newspapers . . .' He gave a little sigh and shrugged his shoulders hopelessly. 'They'll be coming here to question you, I suppose.'

I nodded.

'What are you going to do? Frehel wants to see you in the morning. At ten o'clock. He asked me to let you know.' He stared at me. 'What are you going to tell him?'

'The truth,' I said.

'No. You can't do that. Not yet.' His voice was urgent, his grip on my arm like a vice. 'I need time.'

'Don't be a fool,' I said. 'The truth is your only help.'

'How do you mean?' He had completely failed to understand the implication of the story.

But when he asked me to put my thoughts into words, I couldn't do it. He didn't see it the way I did –

the way the police must see it. Perhaps it was better if he didn't. That way his denial would be more convincing. And then he said something that put the thing out of my mind for the moment. He said, 'Philip. I want you to do something for me. I want you to confirm what I have just told Frehel – what you arranged back there in Tangier. I want you to tell the police when they come that I flew out from England direct to Casablanca.'

'It's no good,' I said. 'They've only to check at Paris or London.'

'I know. But I still want you to do it. All I need is four days. In four days I can get down to Foum-Skhira.'

'Foum-Skhira?' I stared at him.

'I have to see Caid Hassan d'Es-Skhira. It's about Kasbah Foum.'

'What's Kasbah Foum got to do with you?' I demanded. And then I was suddenly angry. All the bitterness of the last few hours was concentrated on this one thing. 'You never intended to work at the Mission, did you?' I accused him. 'It was just an excuse. You used my need of a doctor—' But I stopped there. How could he have known then about Wade and Kasbah Foum? I was tired and my mind was confused.

He leaned forward, his hand on my arm again. 'Please, Philip. Listen. I have a proposition—' He stopped abruptly as footsteps sounded on the stairs behind him.

It was the Frenchman. He stood at the foot of the stairs for an instant, staring at us. Then he went over to the table in the far corner.

Jan picked up the paper again. I saw him glance

several times at the newcomer. Then he leaned towards me. 'We've got to talk this over. There's something I haven't told you.'

But Madame came in then and I motioned him to be silent. She went through into the kitchen and for a while the only sound was the ticking of an alarm clock somewhere behind the bar. The darkness and the dreariness of the room, combined with Jan's tenseness, began to get on my nerves. The room had an unreal quality. It looked like a stage set, with its bar and its white-tiled stove and the faded posters on the flimsy wooden walls.

The soup arrived, and then Madame waddled in, carrying a special bottle of wine carefully in her two fat hands. She took it across to the Frenchman. Monsieur Bilvidic she called him, and her throaty voice smarmed over the hard syllables of his name as she bent obsequiously over his table. Evidently he wasn't just an ordinary traveller. He was someone of importance – an official. His face was pale, almost sallow, and there were little pouches under his eyes, like half spectacles on either side of his thin, sharp nose.

Once our eyes met. It was a quick, appraising glance, and it left me with a faint feeling of hollowness in the pit of my stomach.

Madame had seated herself by the stove again. For a while she concentrated on her food, but once or twice she glanced in my direction. At length she said, 'I was asking you, monsieur, about that affair in Tangier.' And when I didn't say anything, she added, 'You've read the paper, haven't you? What happened to this man after he left the Hotel Malabata with you?'

I glanced quickly across at the Frenchman. But he was concentrating on his food. He might not have heard her question. 'Until I read the paper I hadn't realised the police were looking for Wade,' I told her.

'But what happened to him?'

'That's something I shall have to tell Monsieur Frehel in the morning,' I said. A cold sweat had broken out on my forehead. The man was concentrating too much on his food. He must be listening.

But Madame was persistent. She sat there, feeding the cat pieces of fish in her fingers and asking questions. And because I couldn't just sit there and refuse to say anything, I told her about how I had seen the wreck and brought Wade back to my room at the hotel, all the things, in fact, that the International Police already knew. And whilst I was talking I was conscious of Jan's growing nervousness.

The meal was over at last and I got to my feet, excusing myself by saying I was tired. Jan rose, too, and Madame saw us to the foot of the stairs. '*Dormez bien, mes enfants*.' Her little beady eyes smiled at me maliciously.

We went upstairs to the narrow landing that ran the length of the inn. 'Who was that man?' Jan asked.

'Your guess is as good as mine,' I answered.

'You mean—'

'We'll know in the morning,' I said and pushed open the door of my room.

'Philip. I want to talk to you about Kasbah Foum.'

'Oh, damn Kasbah Foum!' I said. 'I'm tired now.'

And I went into the bedroom and closed the door behind me.

What did he want to keep talking about Kasbah Foum for? Hadn't he got enough problems without trying to involve himself in something that concerned people like Kostos and Ali d'Es-Skhira? I was thinking of the Frenchman back there in the bar, talking to Madame, learning all the gossip of the place.

I sat down on the bed and stared miserably round the room. It was a sordid little box of a place with a big, brass-railed double bed that sagged in the middle and the bare minimum of furniture – a wash-stand, a tin slop pail, a chest of drawers, a wooden chair and a small built-in cupboard. The flaking paint patterned the walls with a stipple of little shadows cast by the naked electric light bulb. I shivered in the cold that struck up from the concrete floor.

I had a quick wash and went to bed. Somewhere out in the darkness a tam-tam throbbed, accompanying the queer, wailing cry of women singing. It went on and on, and then a donkey began to bray, a harsh, sobbing note as though it were slowly being strangled. I heard Bilvidic come to bed and then the auberge settled down to sleep and the only sound was the tam-tam beating out there in the night.

Gradually the moonlight filtered into the room. A little wind had got up and I listened to it moaning round the galvanised iron roof, searching for cracks in the old building.

And then I heard a movement in the passage outside. The catch of the door scraped as the handle was turned and the door opened and Jan's voice whispered, 'Are you asleep, Philip?'

'No,' I said. 'What is it?'

He came in and shut the door gently behind him. 'Mind if I put the light on?' There was a click and I blinked my eyes.

'What's the trouble?' I asked.

'Nothing. I wanted to show you something.' He came and sat on the bed. He was still dressed and he had the raincoat he'd bought in Marrakech wrapped tightly round him. 'I've been thinking,' he said. His manner was quiet as though he'd made up his mind about something.

'Well?'

'I'm leaving for the south tomorrow. I would like you to come with me. No,' he added quickly. 'Don't say anything. Have a look at this first.' He pulled an envelope out of his pocket and handed it to me. 'Please. Examine it.'

It was one of those stiff linen envelopes, but it had been softened and creased with age. It was damp, too, and the remains of the broken seal were indecipherable. Inside was a bulky document to which had been attached a note in French scrawled on a sheet of cheap notepaper that was torn and dirty along the creases where it had been folded. I sat up in bed and twisted round so that the light fell across my shoulder on to the document. It opened out into a stiff sheet of parchment covered with Arab writing. The ink was faded with age, but the words KASBAH FOUM, written in capitals, caught my eye. And then, farther down, I saw the name Marcel

Duprez. The name occurred several times and the document was signed *Caid El Hassan d'Es Skhira*, and some sort of seal had been affixed.

'But this is the document Kostos wanted,' I exclaimed.

'Yes.'

'You crazy fool!' I said, staring up at him. 'Why didn't you let him have it? If you'd given it to him—'

'Kasbah Foum belongs to me.'

But I didn't believe him. How could it belong to him? 'You took those deeds from Wade,' I said. 'Wade was acting for Ali and you took them—'

'No,' he said. 'Wade never had the deeds. He offered me five hundred pounds if I'd give them to him and renounce my claim to the place. But I wouldn't sell. Kasbah Foum is mine.' He said it fiercely, possessively.

I pushed my hand across my eyes. 'I don't understand,' I said. 'How can this place belong to you? You've never been in Morocco before. Land like that isn't bought and sold—'

'Those deeds were given me by Marcel Duprez. He was the man I told you about in Marrakech, the man who died in that cellar in Essen.' He stared at me, frowning angrily. 'You don't believe me, do you? Why do you think Wade agreed to take me on his boat? How do you think we met in the first place? I didn't contact Wade. He contacted me.' He pointed to the note pinned to the document. 'If you still don't believe me, take a look at that note. It was written by Marcel Duprez to the lawyers just before he died.'

I smoothed out the tattered note attached to the

document. It was written in French in a shaky hand and addressed to Lavin, Roche et Lavin, of Rouen:

> *Dear Monsieur Roche,*
>
> *The bearer of this note is Dr Jan Kavan, who is here with me in this abominable town of Essen. In the event of my death, he will come to you after the war. You will give him the document relating to Kasbah Foum in French Morocco. This note you will regard as a codicil to my will. Being unable at this time to write to you direct, I hereby instruct you to ignore any illegality there may be in this method of making my wishes known to you and to carry out these instructions. Dr Kavan knows that Caid Hassan's confirmation of this bequest is necessary to substantiate his claim to the ownership of Kasbah Foum and he holds the necessary letter to Caid Hassan, which he will show to you on request.*

The note was signed *Marcel Duprez* and dated 22 September 1944. So the Marcel Duprez who had fought at Foum-Skhira with the Legion and the man who had died in a cellar at Essen were the same! And Kasbah Foum, subject to Caid's confirmation, belonged to Jan. 'But if you're so interested in the place, why didn't you get your title to it confirmed before?' I asked him.

'That's what I should have done. It's what I promised Marcel. As soon as the Allies arrived in Essen and I was released, I went to Rouen. I saw Monsieur Roche and he gave me the deeds. But—' He shrugged his shoulders awkwardly. 'There was so much to do in Czechoslovakia. I returned to Skoda and there was my research work, and then Karen and I were married. To be the owner of a little patch of desert somewhere in Morocco—' He gave a short laugh. 'It was absurd, you know. Even if there was silver there . . . I had plenty of money and I was happy. I put the deeds away and forgot all about them. Also I forgot about my promise. The Berbers meant nothing to me.' He paused and then added, 'But afterwards, when I was in England, I found those deeds among some papers Karen smuggled out to me. And then it wasn't absurd any more. It was all I owned in the world.'

He was staring at me and his voice trembled slightly with the effort of trying to make me understand. 'When you have no country – nothing . . . to be the owner of a piece of land becomes desperately important. It's a refuge, something to dream about. I remembered my promise then and I wrote to Caid Hassan.'

'And he confirmed your title?'

'No. He didn't reply to my letter. And then, a few months later, just after I'd decided to get out of England and had answered your advertisement – Wade arrived. I knew then that my letter had never reached the Caid, but had been sent on to his son, Ali.'

'Wade told you that?'

'No, no, of course not. But I knew, because of what Marcel had told me. Marcel loved the Berber people. He gave his whole life, and his health, to them.' He shifted his position, leaning towards me. 'Listen, Philip. There's an ancient, ruined city at Kasbah Foum. That was why

Marcel was interested in the place. And it was whilst he was doing excavation work there that he came upon the entrance of some old mine workings. It was blocked and he never had a chance to open it up because, shortly after he discovered it, there was a landslide and it was buried, just as your Mission is buried here. But there is a local legend that silver was once mined at Kasbah Foum. That was what worried him when he was dying.'

'Why should it?' I asked.

'The terms of those deeds are rather peculiar. Whoever inherited from Marcel had to get his title confirmed by the Caid and ownership registered with the Sultan's government. If no new ownership were confirmed, then when Caid Hassan died, Kasbah Foum would belong to his son, Ali. Marcel wanted to prevent that. In his view Ali was a fanatic – not interested in the welfare of his people, only in fighting the French. He was afraid that if Ali discovered the mine and developed it, or sold it, he would use those funds to buy arms. At all costs he wanted to prevent unnecessary bloodshed.'

'And he made you promise to get your title to the place confirmed by the old Caid before he died?'

'Yes.' He stared down at the deeds lying on the blankets in front of him. 'I thought it was just a whim – you know how people build things up in their minds when they're feverish. And back there at Skoda after the war it all seemed so remote and unreal.' He looked up at me suddenly and said, 'But it's real enough now – now that I know Ali is trying to get those deeds. When Wade came to me in England, he said he had seen the lawyers in Rouen and they'd told him a man named White had been making enquiries—' He stopped, his head on one side. 'What was that?' His voice shook a little.

'It's only in the wind,' I said.

But he got up quietly and went to the door and pulled it open. There was nothing there. He stood listening for a moment and then shut it. 'That man,' he said. 'That Frenchman. He's a member of the security police. I know he is.' He started pacing up and down. 'Karen and Kasbah Foum – they're all I've got in the world. And they're both here in North Africa. I've got to stay in North Africa.' He was talking to himself, gesturing urgently. He looked suddenly quite wild with his black hair standing on end.

He swung round abruptly and came back to the bed, leaning down and catching hold of my arm. 'Don't tell them the truth tomorrow. Give me a week. A week is all I need. And you've got to come with me. You know the people. You speak the language. We'll see the old Caid. Maybe there is silver there. If so, you'll get your Mission. I promise you. You'll have all the money you need. It's what Marcel wanted; exactly what he wanted. I was to take what I needed and the rest was to go to the Berber people – hospitals and schools.' He stopped abruptly, staring at me, panting slightly with the effort of his sudden outburst. Then he picked up the deeds and thrust them into their envelope. 'Think it over.' His voice had steadied. 'A few days is all I ask. Afterwards—' He shrugged his shoulders. He stared at me a moment as though trying to will me to agree, and then, when I still didn't say anything, he crossed to the door. 'Good night,' he said and switched out the light.

'Good night.'

The door closed and I was alone again. I lay in the darkness, thinking about it all, trying to make up my mind what to do. But my brain wouldn't concentrate and gradually I fell asleep through sheer exhaustion.

The Berber boy didn't wake me until after nine and when I went into the bar room, Bilvidic was already there, sitting at the same table, writing. He looked up as I entered, murmured '*Bonjour*' and went back to his notes. Jan came in a few minutes later and we breakfasted in silence. Only once did he say anything and then he leaned close to me and whispered, 'What have you decided?'

'I don't know,' I answered. I hadn't decided anything.

At ten minutes to ten Bilvidic put his notebook away and came over to me. 'I believe you have an appointment with Monsieur le Contrôlleur at ten,' he said. 'Since I am also going to see him, perhaps you would care to come in my car.'

I thanked him and got up, conscious of Jan watching me nervously. He went out to his Citroën and as he drove me down through Enfida he talked of nothing more alarming than mountain plants. He was a keen horticulturist.

The administration block of Civil Control was a low, brick building and the offices opened off a single long passage. The Tribunal was sitting that morning and the whole length of the passage was crowded with *indigènes* from the country round. As I walked down to the Controller's office I was conscious of a sudden hush.

The men stopped talking and stared at me curiously. Many of them I knew, but they looked away as I approached.

And then suddenly an old man stood in front of me. It was the *chef de village* from Tala. He touched me and kissed my hand, bowing formally, and then in a clear voice he welcomed me back to Enfida and expressed his deep distress at what had happened. I caught his hand and gripped it, and his old eyes smiled at me behind the glasses. 'We understand each other,' he said quietly. 'You will have help from the villages of the Ravine if you build your house again.'

'There are few, like you, who understand,' I said. And I thanked him and we parted. But somehow the morning had changed completely now. I felt suddenly warm inside and full of vigour.

I was shown into an empty office and though Frehel kept me waiting almost twenty minutes, I didn't mind. I was thinking that if I had the villages of the Ravine with me – the very ravine where the disaster had happened – then it was worth fighting to start again. And then I began thinking about Kasbah Foum. Julie had said something would turn up. Maybe this was it. . . .

The door opened and Frehel came in. He was a tall, rather stooped man with lined, leathery features. He looked more like a professor than an administrator and, as always, his Civil Control uniform looked oddly out of place on his long, loose-jointed figure. He shook my hand and apologised for keeping me waiting. And then he began talking about the disaster and about the Mission. 'A terrible tragedy, Latham.' He shook his head and clicked his tongue. 'Will you tell Mademoiselle Corrigan how sad I am about the death of her brother. Terrible! And he was a fine painter.' And then he wanted to know what my plans were and I began to think that that was the only reason he had asked me to come to his office. 'And this Dr Kavan?' he asked. 'You went to Tangier to meet him, I believe?'

I nodded, conscious that there was suddenly more interest in his voice, a look of curiosity in his eyes. He hesitated, his hands in his pockets, rattling his keys. Then he said, 'I am sorry to trouble you at a time like this, but I have a member of the Sûreté here who has come to ask you some questions. It is about something that happened in Tangier.' He opened the door for me. 'If you will come through to my office—'

Bilvidic was seated beside Frehel's desk, tapping his teeth with a silver pencil. 'Monsieur l'Inspecteur tells me you have already met,' Frehel murmured. Bilvidic got up and brought a chair for me. Frehel seated himself at the desk. He was obviously curious and his eyes glanced quickly at each of us in turn.

Bilvidic turned his chair so that he faced me. 'I think you understand, monsieur, why I am here.'

I nodded.

He produced a pack of American cigarettes and handed them round. 'You were telling Madame last night how you rescued this Monsieur Wade from the wreck and took him back to your hotel.' His manner was friendly, his tone almost conversational. 'Would you kindly repeat the story so that I can check it against my notes. I would like every detail, if you please. You understand, of course, that this man has disappeared completely?'

'I read the newspaper story,' I said.

He nodded. '*Alors*, monsieur.'

So I went through the whole sequence of events from the moment I had sighted the yacht trying to make for the harbour at Tangier. He had his notebook in his hand and a sheaf of typewritten pages, and he constantly referred to these, checking my story with neat little ticks in the margin. He didn't interrupt me until I came to the loss of the passport and the odd behaviour of the patrone at the Hotel Malabata. '*Un moment*, monsieur. The patrone says only that Wade had mislaid his passport.'

'That's not true,' I said, and I explained what had actually happened. I was sweating a little and the palms of my hands were moist. I was reaching the difficult part and I found I still hadn't really made up my mind.

'Can you explain why the patrone should attempt to retain Wade's passport illegally?'

'Yes,' I said, seeing an opportunity to gain time. 'I think he had been bribed by a man called Kostos.'

'Kostos?'

'He's a Greek,' I said. 'He used to be involved in smuggling, but now—'

'Yes, yes. I know about Kostos.' His tone was impatient. 'But what is he to do with Wade?'

'He came to see him at the hotel.'

'Ah, *oui*. I wished to ask you about that. We are curious about this Greek. He left Tangier suddenly two days ago. I think we trace him to Marrakech, but we are not—'

'To Marrakech?' I stared at him. Had Jan been right after all?

'*Oui*, to Marrakech.' Bilvidic nodded. 'We believe he was accompanied by a notorious *agent provocateur*.'

'You mean Ali d'Es-Skhira?'

The name slipped out and he pounced on it. 'How did you know that?'

'Kostos mentioned the name that time he came to see Wade in my room,' I said quickly to cover myself.

'Ah, yes. Will you tell me exactly what Kostos said?'

I gave him the gist of it without mentioning Kasbah Foum. And whilst I was talking, I was thinking that it must be true, the whole incredible story that Jan had told me. Ali d'Es-Skhira would never return to Morocco and risk being arrested by the French unless the matter was urgent. There was no doubt in my mind that the pair of them were headed for Foum-Skhira. It was this that finally decided me.

'And now, monsieur,' Bilvidic said when I had finished, 'let us go back to your departure from the hotel. The patrone has withheld Wade's passport and you have ordered the driver of the taxi to take you to the British Consulate. You were going to make a protest, eh?'

I nodded.

'But you did not go there, monsieur. Why? Where do you go after you leave the hotel?'

'Wade changed his mind,' I said. 'He decided not to

go to the Consulate after all. He asked me to drop him in the Zocco Grande.'

'Why?'

'I don't know.'

'What happened then?'

'Nothing. I was leaving Tangier by the evening train. I never saw him again.'

He glanced down at the typewritten notes. 'This would be about fifteen-thirty hours, eh? And your train did not leave until twenty-one thirty. Would you please tell me what you did during the rest of the day?'

I filled in as best I could. And then, suddenly, he said, 'Why did you book two berths on the wagon-lit?'

In all my concern that he might know about my visit to the airport, I had forgotten all about the problem of explaining that extra berth. I improvised quickly: I had booked the extra sleeper for the man I had gone to Tangier to meet and afterwards I had found a letter waiting for me at the British Post Office saying that he was flying direct to Casa and would I meet him there. I think my hesitation could only have been fractional, for he didn't seem to have noticed it. 'And the man you went to meet was this Dr Kavan?'

I nodded.

'And that is the man who is here now, the man you were dining with at the auberge last night? You met him at Casa?'

'Yes,' I said.

'*Bon.*' He seemed relieved. He looked across at Frehel. 'At least there is no mystery about the disappearance of this Dr Kavan from the boat. The British security officers have made an error. He was never on the boat.' He chuckled, and then checked himself as though remembering he was on official business. 'In fact, there is no mystery at all. There are not two men on the boat, only one. There remains only the disappearance of this man Wade.' He glanced down at his notes, and then went back over my statement of what Kostos had said on the occasion he had come to the hotel. I knew it was all right then. Jan was clear for the moment.

We went over several points and then finally he sat back and lit another cigarette. 'You say you have checked Dr Kavan's papers?' he asked Frehel suddenly.

The Civil Controller nodded.

'And they are in order?'

'*Oui*, Monsieur l'Inspecteur.'

'*Bon*.' He looked across at me. 'What do you know about this doctor, monsieur?'

'Not very much,' I said, keeping a tight hold on my voice. 'He's a Czech refugee.'

'Is that all he has told you about himself?'

I didn't say anything and he shrugged his shoulders as though glad not to have to go further into the matter. '*Alors*, monsieur – the statement . . .'

It was almost midday before the statement was typed. When I had signed it, he drove me back to the auberge himself. '*Au revoir*, monsieur,' he said as I got out. 'I am going back to Casablanca now.' His hard, grey eyes looked at me fixedly. 'There is nothing you wish to alter?'

'No,' I said.

'You realise that it will all be checked?'

I nodded.

'*Bien*, monsieur. We will hope there are no inaccuracies, eh?' He gave me a thin-lipped smile. And then he asked me if I should be leaving Enfida during the next few days.

'I don't know,' I said.

He nodded. 'I quite understand. In view of the catastrophe . . .' He gave a little shrug. 'But if you do leave, monsieur, I should be grateful if you would inform Monsieur Frehel and give him your new address. You understand?'

'Yes,' I said.

He nodded again and turned the Citroën in a tight circle, disappearing in a cloud of dust down the road towards the bridge. I turned and went into the auberge, but Jan wasn't there. I called Madame out of the kitchen and she told me that Julie had arrived shortly after I had left. She and Jan had gone off together.

I went up the mountain road then and cut down to the caravan. They must have been watching the track, for they both came out to meet me. But then Jan stopped and Julie came on alone. She looked very pretty with her black hair hanging down over her orange shirt. She was wearing slacks. She looked slender and graceful and cool. 'Is it all right?' she asked. Her voice sounded nervous and I knew Jan must have explained the situation to her. I didn't say anything and she took my arm. 'I'll get you a drink.' And then she added, 'Don't keep him waiting, Philip. It's important to him.'

'All right,' I said. And I called out to Jan and told him he needn't worry for the moment.

It was extraordinary. The man seemed suddenly to come to life. It was as though I had released a spring inside him. He caught hold of my hand and his grip was so tight it hurt. 'I'll never forget this, Philip. I'll never forget it.' He was like a man reprieved. 'What decided you? All through breakfast this morning . . . I wanted to get a decision out of you, but that man Bilvidic was sitting there. What decided you?'

'Kostos was in Marrakech two days ago,' I said.

'So, I was right. How do you know this?'

'Bilvidic told me. And Ali d'Es-Skhira is with him.'

Sitting in the caravan over a large cognac I told them about the interview. And when I had finished Jan said, 'Well, that settles it. We slip out of Enfida tonight. Julie says if we leave shortly after midnight we'd be across the pass by dawn. By tomorrow night, if we drive hard, we can be at Foum-Skhira.'

'We'll need a car,' I said.

It was Julie who answered. 'We'll take the bus.' She was smiling a little sadly. 'I don't want to stay here – not alone. And there's no hotel south of Ouarzazate; not until you get to Zagora, and you aren't going there.'

I sat and looked at her. I thought I ought to say 'No' – that it was stupid for her to get mixed up in it. But seeing the way she looked – keyed up and excited – I thought maybe it was a good idea. It would take her mind off George's death.

There were a great many things to be done if we were to start that night – stores to get and the bus to be literally dug out. We agreed that Jan and I should feed at the auberge and retire to bed there in the ordinary way. We would slip out of Enfida at night, just in case.

It seemed a long evening, sitting there in that dreary bar room, talking with Madame, watching the Arabs who guarded the olive piles at night drift in and out for coffee. But at last it was ten o'clock and Madame was seeing us to the door to the stairs. '*Dormez bien, mes enfants. Dormez bien.*' Her deep, throaty voice was like a benediction and I heaved a sigh of relief. From the window of my room I saw that a light rain was falling. The night was black and quiet.

Two hours later we slipped out by the terrace and the gate leading on to the road. Julie had the old bus waiting for us just below the road. It was exactly twelve as we drove down the winding road and across the bridge and up through the deserted street of Enfida on the Marrakech road. We left the olive trees behind, and the road and the red earth of the plain stretched ahead of us in the headlights. It was like that for hour after hour, except that the plain gave way to mountain-sides that loomed like dark shadows on either side of us as the road began to climb.

The first grey light of dawn found us grinding up the hairpin bends to the top of the pass. Julie was at the wheel and the bus swayed heavily on the incessant bends, the wheels skidding in the loose slush of melted snow that covered the road. And then at last we were at the top and there were the gaunt pylons of the téléférique marching like Wellsian monsters through the cleft in the mountains. We drew in beside a big stone notice – TIZI N TICHKA, alt. 2.250 m., and below were recorded the Army units who had slaved to build the road through the pass.

We were at the top of the High Atlas. We were astride the shining white barrier of the mountains that hide the strange, desert lands of the south. I had never crossed them, but I knew that beyond lay a different world, a world of kasbahs and dusty palmeries set in a land of black stone hills, rounded with age. And beyond those black hills of the Anti-Atlas was nothing – only the limitless wastes of the Sahara, a sea of sand.

We sat there and stared at the pale dawn sky ahead, conscious of a sense of the unknown, as though we were on a peak looking out across a strange sea. I was conscious, too, of a stillness within myself, and within my two companions. I glanced at Jan. His face was tense, his blue eyes fixed with a sort of desperate eagerness. He stood there upon what was for him the threshold of a Promised Land – the thing he dreamed of for himself and his wife, Karen – his last chance of a refuge from the nightmare in which he had lived.

The sun rose and touched the first of the mountain tops. Without a word Julie started the engine and we began the long run down to Ouarzazate. Nobody spoke. Our eyes were fixed on the sky ahead and the road winding down through the mountains. Somewhere, down there among the black stone hills, was Kasbah Foum.

PART THREE

ZONE OF INSECURITY

CHAPTER ONE

The mountains changed abruptly the moment we were across the divide as though to emphasize that we were entering upon a wild, strange land. Where, on the northern side, there had been scrub and small trees and slopes of snow glimmering white in the dawn, there was nothing now but naked rock. The sky was pale, a duck's egg, pastel blue, and above us to the left rose piled-up cliffs of sandblasted stone that flanked the valley in a long ridge, their battlements picked out in gold as the sun rose in the east.

It was a beautiful, pitiless country.

We stopped for breakfast where the road crossed the first big torrent of melted snow. It was bitterly cold with a chill wind whistling down the valley from the peaks behind us. Yet, by the time the tea was made, the sun had risen above the red rock fortresses of the ridge, the wind had gone, and it was suddenly hot. The abruptness of the change was startling.

It was then that Julie remembered she had some

letters for me. There were two from England – a Bible Society tract and an offer of old clothes from some association I had never heard of. The third was post-marked Tangier and was from Karen Kavan. As we had agreed, she had written to me, not to Jan. It simply announced that her employers were taking a trip south and would be staying at the Hotel Mamounia for Christmas and then going on to Ouarzazate and Tinerhir. She was travelling with them and she gave the telephone numbers of the hotels they were staying at. The number of the *gîte d'étapes* at Ouarzazate was 12. It was the same number that Wade had noted down in the back of his log against the name of Ed White.

I was still thinking about this as I handed Jan the letter. 'It's from your wife,' I said. He scanned it eagerly and then asked the date.

'Today is the twenty-third,' Julie said.

He folded the letter slowly and put it away in his breast pocket, staring out through the side window along the grey ribbon of the road leading south towards Ouarzazate.

'Is she all right?' Julie asked.

'Yes.' He nodded quickly. 'Yes, she's all right. She'll be in Ouarzazate on the twenty-sixth.' There was a sort of wonder in his voice as though he couldn't believe it was true.

'Then you'll see her.'

He looked across at Julie and smiled. 'Yes. Yes, I hope so. It would be wonderful!'

He was thinking of his wife, stopping there at the *gîte d'étapes*. And I was thinking of this man White. If

Wade had planned to phone him there . . . 'You remember you mentioned a man called White,' I said to him. 'When you were telling me about Kasbah Foum.' He nodded. 'Do you know anything about him?'

'No, nothing. Except that he'd tried to contact me through the lawyers.'

'Wade told you that?'

'Yes.'

'You don't know why?'

'No.'

'Weren't you curious about it?'

'Yes. I asked Wade. But he wouldn't tell me. Why do you ask?'

I didn't say anything. I was thinking that perhaps it was White who had started this whole chain of interest in Kasbah Foum. He had been down to the south here. He might even have been to Kasbah Foum. Was that the reason Ali had instructed Wade to purchase the deeds from Jan? 'Was White ever at Kasbah Foum?' I asked.

'I don't know.' He shook his head, staring at me with a puzzled frown.

'Wade told you nothing about him?'

'No, nothing. Only what I've told you.'

I hesitated and then said, 'What about Wade? Had he ever visited Kasbah Foum?'

'No.' He said it slowly and then added, 'But I think he intended to.' He paused for a moment before saying, 'As I told you, Wade was a crook. I have an idea he didn't intend to play straight with Ali.'

'How do you mean?'

'I think, if he had got the deeds, he would have

gone straight to Kasbah Foum. When he discovered I wouldn't sell, he tried to persuade me to go into some sort of partnership with him. He said there was money in it. I think he knew about the possibilities of silver. Right up to the end I think he believed that when we reached Tangier I would agree to his proposition. I didn't discourage him. I wanted that passage out and I didn't trust him. If I had definitely refused . . .' He shrugged his shoulders. 'Anyway, it doesn't matter now.' He glanced at his watch. 'It's time we went on.' He said it almost brusquely, as though he didn't want to think about what had happened on the boat.

The road ran gently down the valley of the Imini and emerged on to an arid, stony plain. The mountains dropped behind until I could see them in the mirror as a long, brown wall topped with snow. I was driving. The others were asleep – Julie in her own compartment at the back of the caravan, Jan sprawled out on the berth behind me. I was alone at the wheel with the road reeling out ahead of me and the blazing sun and the blue sky and the parched earth stretching brown to the horizon – just the two colours, blue and brown, and the grey ribbon of the road. I had an odd sense of space coming down out of the mountains. It was as though I could feel by the lie of the land that the way was open to the south. Ahead were the humped shapes of a range of low, dark hills. Beyond them was the Sahara.

It was strange and a little frightening. This was the most recently conquered part of Morocco. Barely twenty years ago Marshal Lyautey and his troops had still been fighting there. The whole area was run by the military – by Les Officiers des Affaires Indigènes. There were few Europeans and until quite recently it had been known as the Zone of Insecurity.

We passed the turning to the manganese mines of Imini and then we were running through Amerzgane and El Mdint. The white kasbah of Tifoultout stood like a fairy castle on a little rise on the far side of the river and after that the road was straight and tree-lined, ending abruptly in a hill with a fort on it. We were driving into Ouarzazate. The town was largely French, a single street pushed between two small hills. On the right was the Military Post. The road leading up to it was signposted TERRITOIRE. And then I saw a second signpost – GITE D'ETAPES. I turned up a sharp hill, climbing to a long, low building with a tower built like a kasbah.

'Why have you turned up here?' Jan asked, roused from his sleep by the change in the engine note.

'I want to phone Frehel,' I said. 'Also, your friend Ed White stayed here.'

I told him about the telephone number noted down at the back of Wade's log as we went into the hotel. The place was centrally heated and very warm. Beyond the reception desk was a bar and on either side were two big glass cabinets, one displaying Berber jewellery – silver bangles and coin headdresses, blanket pins and long necklaces of intricately-worked silver and beads – the other filled with specimens of minerals found locally. A French officer seated at a table reading a magazine glanced at us idly. Then Madame appeared and I asked her whether she knew a Mr White.

'*Mais oui*, monsieur. An American. He has stayed here several times.'

'On holiday?' I asked.

'*En vacance? Non, non*, monsieur. He is a prospector.'

'A prospector!' Jan's voice was suddenly interested.

'Is this Monsieur's first visit to Ouarzazate?' Madame asked. And when Jan nodded, she said, 'Ah, well then, you must understand that all this country south of here is very rich in minerals. We have many prospectors who stay—'

'Is he staying here now, madame?' Jan asked her.

'Monsieur White? *Non*, monsieur. He has not been here for several weeks now.'

'Do you know where he is?'

'*Un moment*.' She went behind the desk and picked up a notebook, running her finger down the passages. 'Ah, *oui*. He left instructions for us to forward his letters to the office of Monsieur le Capitaine at the Military Post of Foum-Skhira.'

So, Ed White was at Kasbah Foum!

'I suppose he didn't say what he was prospecting for?' Jan asked.

'*Non, non*.' Madame laughed. 'Prospectors do not talk about what they are searching for. But probably it is uranium.' She shrugged her shoulders. 'Always they dream of uranium now.'

'Did a Monsieur Kostos stay here last night or the night before?' I asked her.

'*Non*, monsieur.'

I phoned Frehel then and told him where he could

find us. And whilst I was doing that, Jan wrote a note for his wife. He left it with Madame and we went back to the bus, driving out of Ouarzazate by a road that forded the river not far from the great Kasbah of Taourirt. Everything was very still in the sunlight and as the wheels splashed and bumped over the stones of the river bed, we could see the kasbah reflected in the water. It was a completely walled town, crowding up out of the palmerie in tower after tower, standing out against the blue of the sky like a part of the desert country in which it was built.

And then we were clear of the water and climbing the narrow, ploughed-up surface of the piste, climbing up through a long valley that led into the foothills of the Anti-Atlas. All about us were dark, sombre hills, shadowed by the stones that littered their slopes, closing up behind us and hemming us in so that we could no longer see the clean, white wall of the High Atlas. A little wind rose and drifted dust between the stones. Gaunt skeletons of heath and tamarisk marked out the drainage courses in dusty green.

'Marcel called this country Le Pays Noir,' Jan murmured. 'He said it was geologically much older than the High Atlas and full of undeveloped mineral resources.' He was dreaming of Kasbah Foum again.

All afternoon we struggled through those dark, satanic hills. Dust seeped up through the floorboards in choking clouds from the fine-ground powder of the piste. It got in our clothes and in our nostrils. It powdered our hair grey. Once a jeep passed us, and for an hour after that we caught glimpses of it, a little cloud of dust far ahead. We climbed steadily upwards and then dropped down to a rocky basin in which a lonely kasbah stood subsisting on a few dusty palms and the herds of black goats that roamed the stunted vegetation. After that we climbed again, up a steep escarpment to a lonely watch tower and the pass of Tizi N Tinififft, more than five thousand feet up. Here we were in a land of sudden deep gorges, dark in shadow, that descended in shelves of rock. For an hour we wound round the tops of these gorges until, as the sun set, we came out on to a hill-top, and far below us saw the Draa Valley, a green ribbon of palm trees. And there, on a little hill, was the Military Post of Agdz.

We had a meal then and slept, and at two in the morning we drove through the sleeping Post of Agdz and down the valley of the Draa. The piste was white and ground as fine as talcum powder. It followed the line of the river, winding along the edge of the palmerie, past kasbah after kasbah, and in every open space the kasbah cemeteries showed as patches of desert littered with small, up-ended stones, mute testimony to the countless thousands who had lived and died here over the centuries. We came at length to a fork: a little-used piste turning off to the right and running south over low hills. There was no signpost, but we took it, relying on the map.

Julie was driving again. I could see her face in the light from the dashboard; an intent, serious, competent face. Her black hair was grey with dust, her eyes narrowed as they peered ahead along the beam of the headlights. The stony, desert country ground past us, always the same – an unchanging yellow in the lights, and then suddenly black as it disappeared behind us. Her hands were brown and slender on the dusty ebony of the wheel and every now and then she beat at her knees to restore her circulation. A bitter wind blew in through the chinks in the windscreen, but our feet were warm in the heat of the engine, which came up from the floorboards with a musty smell of dust mixed with engine oil.

Looking at her, I wondered what she'd do now that her brother was dead. She'd have to do something, for I was pretty sure that George would have left her nothing but a few pictures. George hadn't been the saving type. He'd spent money as he made it – always travelling, always painting.

I was remembering how I had first met them. It must be seven years ago now, when I was in Tangier. Their mother had died and left them some money, and they'd come out to Tangier because in Tangier there are no taxes. I had helped them get their money out. That was how I'd met them. Julie had been little more than a schoolgirl then, wide-eyed, excited by everything, deeply concerned at the poverty she saw side-by-side with the rich elegance of the crooks and tax-evaders who occupied the villas on La Montagne. They had stayed for a few months, and then they had gone to Greece and on to Turkey and Syria. Occasionally Julie had sent me a postcard – from Baghdad, Cairo, Haifa, and one, I remember, from Lake Chad after they had done a trip from Algeria right across the Sahara. It wasn't difficult to understand why Julie had stayed with her brother. He had given her all the excitement and colour she had wanted. And it had suited George, for he was interested in nothing but his painting.

She glanced at me suddenly and our eyes met. 'What are you thinking about, Philip?' she asked. 'About what an odd trip this is?'

'No,' I said. 'I was thinking about you.'

'Oh,' Her mouth spread into a smile and the corners of her eyes crinkled with laughter. But she didn't say anything further, just sat there, her gaze on the faint track of the piste.

'I was wondering what you were going to do now,' I said after a while.

She shrugged her shoulders. It was a very Latin shrug. But she didn't answer my question and I was conscious of the stillness between us, It was as though we had suddenly touched each other and then as quickly withdrawn. I felt a softening in the marrow of my bones and I sat back, watching her face, absorbing the straight line of her nose, the smallness of her ears, the way her hair curled at the back of her neck. I'd never thought of her quite like that before. When I had first met her she had seemed very young and then, when they had descended on the Mission three months ago, she had just been George Corrigan's sister. That was all.

And now . . . Now I didn't quite know.

'What's that? Up there.' Jan's voice cut across my thoughts, tense and excited. He was leaning forward over my shoulder and pointing through the windshield. We were climbing now, and far ahead, high up where the dark shadow of a hill cut across the starry velvet of the sky, the yellow pinpoint of a fire showed.

Our radiator was boiling by the time we reached it. It was a petrol fire flickering ghostlike out of a pile of stones beside a battered jeep. Four men were huddled round it. Three of them were town Arabs, but the fourth was a Berber and behind him his two camels stood motionless, hobbled by the foreleg. I signalled Julie to stop and called out to them, enquiring if the piste led to Foum-Skhira.

The Arabs stared at us nervously, whispering together, the whites of their eyes gleaming in the headlights. It was the Berber who answered me. '*Iyyeh, sidi.*' Yes, Foum-Skhira was beyond the mountain. The piste had been washed away by the rains, but it was almost repaired now. The souk at Foum-Skhira had also been washed away. He shook his head gloomily. 'Thanks be to Allah I have left that place.'

The three Arabs had got to their feet. They were moving nervously towards their jeep, which still carried the American Army star. 'I'm going on,' Julie said.

'No, wait . . .' But already her foot was pressed down on the accelerator and as we moved off she said, 'I didn't like the look of them. I'm sure that jeep wasn't their own.'

I had been thinking the same thing, but I didn't say anything and we climbed steadily up the mountainside. Out on the top it was bitterly cold. There was nothing between us and the snow-capped peaks of the Atlas, and the sense of space was immense. We stopped where the road dipped down on the other side. The sky was already paling in the east. We made some tea and watched the sun rise, turning the dark hills first pink, then gold, then a hard, arid brown.

I took over the driving then and we started down the mountain, which was black in shadow and cleft by the start of a deep gorge. Below us lay a brown valley broken by the green of a palmerie, which was shaped like a fist, with the forefinger extended and curving towards the base of the mountain away to our right. From the centre of the fist rose the sun-baked walls of a kasbah. It was Kasbah Foum-Skhira, and close by were the forts of the French Post.

Away to the south the valley opened out, vanishing into the morning haze as though running straight out into the sands of the Sahara: it was like a broad estuary, and on the far side – ten, maybe fifteen miles away – the containing hills were ruler-straight as though cut from the bed of an ancient sea. The sky was palest blue, the earth almost yellow in the clear, dry air. The piste leading to Foum-Skhira was a faint line drawn across the valley floor like the tracing of a Roman road in an aerial photograph.

We swung down in sharp curves until we came to a crumbling cliff and looked down a thousand feet into the black depths of a gorge. The piste seemed to hang on the very edge of the drop and as we rounded the cliff, we came upon a road gang cutting their way through a fall of rock. 'Look!' Jan gripped my arm, pointing down towards the entrance to the gorge. A walled kasbah with four mud towers, two of which had crumbled away, was picked out in the slanting sunlight. And beyond it, on the edge of a stream bed, was a little cluster of tents.

Kasbah Foum! It couldn't be anything else, standing like that in the entrance to the gorge. And those would be Ed White's tents. I glanced at Jan. Though his face looked tired under the dust-white stubble, his blue eyes gleamed with excitement. 'We're almost there,' he breathed.

But it was half an hour before we were driving into Foum-Skhira. The Post consisted of two large forts with a big, open space like a parade ground between them and a single European house. One of the forts was white, with adobe roofs that made it look like a mosque. I learned later that it had been built by the Legion. The other, built by native Goumiers, was of mud with embrasured walls and little square towers like a kasbah. They were both of them empty and as we drove past they had the silent, deserted look of lost cities. A Tricolour fluttered from a white flagstaff outside the European house.

I suggested to Jan that we make contact with the French officer in charge of the Post first. But he said, 'No. Drive straight on to Kasbah Foum. If those were White's tents, I'd like to find out what he's doing before I talk to the French.'

I drove on, past the European house, down towards the palmerie where ruined mud walls marked the site where the souk had been. There were camels hobbled there and mules, and there was a large crowd of people who stood and stared at us, not curiously and not hostilely, but with a strange air of waiting for something. It was the same when we skirted the walls of Ksar Foum-Skhira, the village of the kasbah. The place teemed with people who stood and watched us go by in silence. The women, clustered round the well holes, let go of the ropes so that the long poles for lifting the water stood curved against the sky like the gaffs of dhows. But all the palmerie seemed deserted and the cultivated patches had a neglected look, the little earthen banks to contain the water flattened almost to the ground.

Dust rose in choking clouds through the floorboards as we ran along the edge of the palmerie. Gradually the trees thinned and fell away so that we could see the dried-up stream bed we were following. 'There it is!' Jan cried, leaning forward. 'Right at the entrance to the gorge. And there's the old city and the watch tower just as Marcel described it to me.'

I screwed up my eyes, seeing for the moment only the white glare of the piste and the black bulk of the mountain slope down which we had come. And then I saw it – the little kasbah with its two ruined towers standing out yellow against the black, shadowed immensity of the gorge. I could see the watch tower, too, and all the hill below it was strewn with the debris of an old city. In places the walls still stood, a yard thick and some twelve feet high, and one stone archway remained intact. But all the rest of it had been thrown down as though by some natural upheaval. And yet it was impressive, for this was a land of mud buildings, and I wondered who these people were who had built in stone.

Just short of the kasbah was the huddle of tents we

had looked down on from above. We were very close now. A flash of light momentarily dazzled me. It was a mirror reflecting the sun. A man stood, watching us, a razor in his hand and half of his face white with shaving soap. He wore a singlet and green-khaki trousers tucked into half-length boots.

'He looks American,' Jan said, and then his gaze switched to the mouth of the gorge.

I pulled up outside the tent and we got stiffly down, our clothes white with the coating of dust we'd picked up crossing the valley. My eyes felt gritty and tired. It was hot already and there were flies and the smell of bacon frying.

The man who had been shaving came towards us. He was tall, broad-shouldered, slim-hipped, with a young, rather square face and a crew cut. He was undoubtedly American – his features, his clothes, everything about him. He was wiping the soap from his face as he came.

'Are you Mr White?' Jan asked.

'Yeah.' He waited, watching Jan uncertainly.

'I believe you were recently in touch with a firm of French lawyers in Rouen.'

'That's right. You must be Wade, I guess.' There was interest, but no enthusiasm in his voice.

'Wade was in touch with you then?' Jan's tone had sharpened.

The man frowned. 'You mean you're not Wade?' He sounded puzzled.

'No. I'm not Wade.' Jan said, and then he nodded towards the ruined fort. 'Is that Kasbah Foum?'

'Yeah.'

There was a short, awkward silence. The two of them stared at each other. Jan's gaze shifted to the tented camp and then followed the broad track that ran up into the entrance of the gorge. The track looked as though it had been made by a bull-dozer, for where it passed below the kasbah it had been levelled out by thrusting aside the stones and rubble of the old city.

'Well, what do you want?' White's tone had hardened. He looked very young with his fair, cropped hair and freckled face – very young and very Nordic.

'Would you mind telling me what you're doing up there?'

'What business is it of yours?'

Jan reached into his breast pocket and brought out the crumpled envelope. 'I hold the deeds to this property,' he said.

White stared at him. His mouth had opened in an expression of surprise. But he shut it suddenly and his whole face hardened, so that he looked big and tough and a good deal older. 'Is that so?' He seemed to tower over Jan as he took a pace forward. 'What the hell goes on here? Is everyone screwy? Yesterday it was a Greek telling me the land belonged to him. Now you come here and tell me—'

'Was the Greek's name Kostos?' I asked.

White seemed to notice me for the first time. 'Yeah, that was his name. Kostos.' The name seemed to bring the anger that was in him to a sudden head. He swung round on Jan. 'Now you get the hell out of here. Both of you. D'you hear? I got a concession from the Sultan's

Government. That's good enough for me. If you think you own the land, then you go an' tell them so. Okay?'

'I have the documents here,' Jan said quietly. 'All I want to know is what you're doing up there. You're a prospector, aren't you?'

'Goddammit!' the other exploded. 'I'm not interested in documents. The guy who came yesterday had documents. You go an' sort it out with the authorities.' His voice was excited, nervous. 'Jesus! I got enough trouble, what with the Ay-rabs bellyaching because I use bull-dozers instead of employing them and Captain Legard at thc Post getting scared I'll upset the water. Now you and this Greek telling me I've got no right to operate here.'

'I didn't say that,' Jan put in mildly.

'All right. You didn't say it. But that's the inference, isn't it? Now suppose you get out. I've work to do.'

Jan stood there, uncertain what to do next. The man seemed oddly belligerent. 'Why don't you talk it over,' I suggested to White. 'You haven't looked at the documents yet.'

'I looked at enough documents yesterday.'

'If Kostos showed you any documents they were forgeries,' Jan said. His voice had risen slightly and his shoulders were beginning to move excitedly. 'Kostos is a crook and if you—'

'You're all crooks as far as I'm concerned,' White cut in.

'That's not a very nice thing to say.' It was Julie. The American looked at her, screwing up his eyes against the sun. I don't think he'd noticed her before.

'I'm sorry,' he said. And then he turned to Jan again and added, 'I don't know who you all are, and I don't much care. I'm telling you the same as I told the Greek yesterday – go and sort it out with Caid Hassan and the authorities.'

'If you'd just look at these deeds,' Jan began, but the other cut him short.

'What sort of fool do you take me for?' he cried. 'Do you think I'd start work here, spending my own dough, without finding out who owns the place? It belonged to a man called Duprez. It was given him by the Caid here. And Duprez is dead. I found that out from his lawyers. He's dead and he passed the deeds on to a guy called Kavan. Now, according to the Greek, Kavan's dead, too. Anyway, he never got his title to the property confirmed by the Caid, which he had to—'

'But I am Kavan,' Jan said.

White opened his mouth to say something and then stopped.

'You'd better know our names,' I said. 'This is Dr Jan Kavan, the man to whom Duprez gave the deeds of Kasbah Foum.'

'I don't believe it,' he said. 'Wade wrote me he'd be bringing the deeds out with him. Why should Kavan come here and not Wade? Kavan never took any interest in the place. The lawyers didn't even know where he was. And the Greek said he was dead.'

'Well, he's not dead,' I said a little irritably. 'This is Dr Kavan, and he has the deeds with him. And this is Miss Corrigan.'

He stared at her for a moment and then turned back to me and said, 'And what about you?'

'My name's Philip Latham.'

'I mean, what's your interest in this?'

'I haven't any,' I told him. 'I'm an English missionary out here.'

'A missionary!' He stared at me, open-mouthed.

'There's a most delicious smell of bacon,' Julie said, pointedly sniffing at the air.

He stared at her, still frowning. 'Oh, sure – yeah.' He looked at the three of us uncertainly. He was bewildered and a little uneasy.

'We've been travelling all night,' Julie said.

That was something he could understand. He seemed to relax and a gleam of warmth came into his eyes. 'If you haven't had chow . . .' His friendly nature asserted itself. He turned and shouted, 'Abdul!' And then he laughed awkwardly and said, 'I forgot. I'm cook this morning, I guess.' And he glanced a little angrily round the camp.

'Are you on your own?' I asked. There was accommodation for at least four in the tents.

'Yeah. Yeah, I guess so.'

'Where's the rest of your party?' I was thinking of the Arabs with their jeep parked beside that fire in the mountains.

'Oh – they left this morning. . . .' He stared at us and then added quickly, 'To get stores and things, you know.' He turned back to the mirror. 'I'll just finish shaving: then I'll see about some food.' He gave a little laugh for no apparent reason except that he seemed nervous. There was a streak of blood on his chin where he had cut himself. He slapped irritably at a fly that was trying to settle on it.

'Would you like me to cope with breakfast for you?' Julie asked hesitantly.

He glanced at her and then nodded. 'Sure. Go ahead. There's tinned bacon, biscuits, jam and coffee.' He watched her disappear into the cook tent, glanced quickly at us and then turned back to the mirror again.

'You're mining up here, aren't you?' Jan asked.

'I told you – I've got a concession from the Sheriffian Government.'

'What are you mining?'

'That's my business.'

Jan started to ask another question, but then stopped and stood staring up the newly-made track to the entrance to the gorge. An uneasy silence developed between us. The morning was very still. There wasn't a breath of wind and the air was clear and crisp with that freshness that occurs in desert country before the sun bakes the land to arid heat.

'What about a wash?' I suggested.

Jan looked at me and nodded. 'Yes. A wash would be good.' We got our things and scrambled down the steep bank where a few dwarf palms thrust dusty fronds above the sand. Then we were in the rock bed of the stream and the only vegetation was the feathery sprays of the tamarisk and the needle-pointed tufts of the reeds. A heron rose from the edge of the muddy-flowing stream, its wings beating slowly, cumbersomely. Occasional banks of dark sand were white-crusted and marked by the feet of birds and when I rinsed out my mouth I found the water was slightly salt.

'He was expecting Wade,' Jan said suddenly. And then, after a pause, he added, 'He doesn't believe I'm Kavan.'

'He'll get used to the idea,' I said.

He bent down and washed his face. As he stood up he said, 'I was right, you know.'

'What about?'

'Wade was going into partnership with him.'

'You mean he was double-crossing Ali?'

He nodded.

'You may be right,' I said as I towelled my face. 'The point is, what do we do now?'

'First I'm going up to have a look at the gorge.' He was standing with his towel slung round his neck, staring towards the entrance which was a black canyon of shadow.

'Well, you'd better have breakfast first,' I said.

'Yes, of course.' He nodded, laughing excitedly. Then he turned to me, his expression suddenly serious. 'Philip. You've no idea what this means to me; to be actually here, at Kasbah Foum. It was like a dream come true. Back in England, as things became more difficult, I thought of nothing else. It was my dream – a sort of El Dorado.' He laughed a little self-consciously and, in a more practical tone, added, 'After we've looked at the place, perhaps you'll come with me to see Caid Hassan?'

'Of course,' I said. 'But I think we'd better see this Capitaine Legard first. You don't want to upset the French.'

Julie joined us then. 'Breakfast is ready,' she said. She washed her hands and face and then came and stood beside us. 'It's a queer, wild place.' She said it a little breathlessly, as though she was uneasy about it. 'Why do you think the others left him?'

'How do you mean?' I stared at her and saw that her eyes were troubled. 'They went to get stores. You heard what White—'

But she shook her head. 'I've been inside the big tent. All their things are gone. And there are three empty beds there. You remember those men sitting round that petrol fire on the other side of the mountain?'

'The three Arabs with the jeep?'

'Yes. They came from here. I'm certain of it. That was his jeep. They were frightened. They stole the jeep because they were frightened and wanted to get away.' She stared up at the entrance to the gorge. 'I don't like it, Philip. He's frightened, too. I can feel it. He's trying to hide something, but he's frightened.'

'Who? White? Nonsense,' I said. 'You're imagining things.'

'No.' She shook her head. 'I'm not imagining things. There's a queer atmosphere about the place. And those people down by the souk.' She hesitated and then said, 'A little boy came into the tent while I was cooking. Apparently Abdul used to give him scraps to eat in the mornings. He told me he sleeps up in the ruins of that kasbah. His father keeps his flock of goats there. He daren't bring them down into the palmerie in case they get stolen. Since the souk was destroyed they're very short of food here.'

•

'Why?'

'I don't know.' Her voice trembled slightly. 'There's a feeling of . . .' She didn't seem able to put it into words.

'Oh, come on,' I said. 'You're tired and you need some food.'

She looked up at me uncertainly. Then she smiled and, with a sense of relief, I saw the smile spread from her lips to her eyes. 'I expect you're right. Let's go and have breakfast. Maybe I'll feel differently afterwards.'

We breakfasted under the extended fly-sheet of the larger tent and from where I sat I looked through into the tent, to the three empty camp beds. I, too, began to feel Julie's sense of uneasiness. It wasn't only the fact that the tent looked deserted. It was White himself. He was oddly talkative. And once started, he talked quickly, eagerly, as though he had to go on talking to keep his mind off other things. He talked about himself, about North Africa – about anything that came into his head. He was from the Middle West and he had worked with Atlas Constructors for eighteen months, building the big American bomber base at Sidi Slimane near Fez. 'Hell! That was a tough job. But I needed the dough. That eighteen months made it possible for me to come down here with my own outfit.'

'You'd been prospecting here before, I suppose?' Jan said.

'Prospecting?' White frowned. 'No, I hadn't been prospecting.'

'But you knew the place? You'd been down here—'

'No. I'd never been here before.'

Jan stared at him. 'But how did you know? . . .' He stopped, a puzzled expression on his face.

But White didn't want to talk about Kasbah Foum. He slid quickly away from the subject and began talking about Morocco. He talked about it with an odd disregard for the French as though he had no idea what the country must have been like before they came. And yet he knew more about the history of the Berbers than I did, and when Julie asked him about the old city that lay in ruins on the slopes above us, he talked with authority. 'I'd say it was six or seven hundred years old,' he said. 'Maybe more.' And he went on to describe the ruins in detail, a sudden enthusiasm in his voice as though they touched him personally.

In his view the people who had built it had come in from the desert. 'It's a very complicated history down here in the south. And it isn't helped by the fact that it's been passed on by word of mouth from generation to generation. Some of the officers of the AI have done some good work on reconstructing it, but I guess nobody will ever really know. Basically, it's quite simple though,' he added. 'Nomadic tribes move in from the desert, become date farmers and goatherds in the palmeries, get soft and then themselves fall victim to another wave of tough guys coming in from the desert. It's a cycle that went on repeating itself. But the people who built this city, they were something bigger. As you see, they built in stone.'

He had been staring up at the ruins as he talked, but now I saw his gaze shift to the track running into the gorge. It had become very hot and the whole place seemed to brood in the shimmering light.

'And what about the kasbah?' Julie asked.

'The kasbah? Oh, that's later. Much later. It was the first kasbah built here in the valley. Legard says it was originally called Kasbah Foum-Skhira. Then, when the palmerie developed and they built a bigger kasbah and a new village, they called that Kasbah Foum-Skhira, and the deserted fort here became just Kasbah Foum. To differentiate between the two, I guess.'

Jan leaned forward and touched my arm. He had the deeds of Kasbah Foum in his hands. 'Will you check through this and see if it says how far the property extends?' he asked me.

It took me some time to decipher it, for the ink was very faint in places. As far as I could tell, it took in all the shoulder of the mountains on which the watch tower and the kasbah and the old city stood. It took in both sides of the stream from well below the camp and included the whole of the entrance to the gorge.

'How far back into the gorge does it extend?' Jan asked.

'As far as the first bend.'

He nodded. 'Good!' And then he looked across at White who had been watching us curiously. 'You know Caid Hassan, I suppose?'

'Is that the old Caid at Foum-Skhira?'

'Yes. Have you met him?'

'No.'

'But it is Caid Hassan. I mean, it's the same Caid that ruled here before the war?'

'Oh, sure. Legard says he's been Caid here for more than forty years.'

'That's all right.' Jan folded the deeds up and put them back in their envelope. Then he got to his feet. 'Come on, Philip. Now we'll go and look at the place.'

'Just a moment,' White said.

Jan turned to face him.

'You say you're Kavan?'

'Yes.'

'Did Wade get in touch with you?'

'Yes. But I wouldn't let him have the deeds.'

'I see.' He stared at Jan, frowning again. 'I'm surprised he didn't write me again and let me know.' He said it more to himself than to Jan and then he gave a quick tug to the waistband of his trousers and turned away as though dismissing the whole matter. 'Go on up there if you want to,' he said.

But as we went back up the track, I glanced back and saw him standing by his tent, watching us. His face had a sullen, worried look. Julie had noticed it, too. 'He's like a child with a toy,' she said. And then she added, 'But the odd thing is, he's glad we've come. He doesn't want to be here alone.'

We had a look at the kasbah first. It was built with its back against a section of the old city wall. The sand had drifted in from the desert, piling against the walls, and there were goat droppings everywhere, dried and powdery. There was nothing of interest there. We climbed down to the track and walked up it into the entrance to the gorge. 'Do you know where the mine entrance was?' I asked Jan.

He nodded, his eyes searching the dark cavern of the gorge, comparing it with the mental picture he had been given. We crossed the sharp-cut line between sun and shade, and immediately we were in a damp, chill world of cliffs and tumbled rock. Ahead of us, in a crook of a bend, stood a plantation of fig trees, their stems twisted and gnarled and white like silver. And on a ledge above, a little almond tree clung in a froth of white blossom.

All above us to the right was a great spill of rock. The track had been slashed through the base of it and the debris shovelled into the bed of the stream, damming it up to form a lake. The water was still and reddish in colour. Skirting the base of the slide, we came upon two bull-dozers, white with dust. They looked insignificant in that huge, natural chasm – forlorn pieces of man-made machinery. They had been cutting into the slide to expose the face of a shallow cliff of grey rock, piling the rubble out into the lake so that there was a big artificial platform.

Jan made straight for the cliff face White had been exposing. 'This is the spot,' he said. 'He's almost reached it. Marcel said the mine shaft was at the base of this cliff.' He looked back at the towering cliff that formed the opposite side of the gorge as though to check his bearings. 'Yes.' He nodded to himself. 'Another few days and he would have exposed the entrance.' He stood there, staring at the cliff. 'Marcel should have been here,' he murmured. 'He should have been the person to open it up, not an American. He would have opened it up and used it to help the people here.' His eyes were clouded. In his mind he was back in that cellar in Essen.

'What's this?' Julie asked, holding out a lump of rock to him. I think she wanted to distract him from his thoughts.

He stared down at it. One half of the rock was a strong reddish colour. 'Iron oxide,' he said. 'What you'd probably call red ochre.' He moved back a little way, staring up at the slope of the slide above us. 'It looks as though it's fallen from up there.' He pointed high up the slope to a crumbling cliff from which much of the slide had come. 'I hope there isn't another fall whilst we're—' He stopped, turning to face the entrance to the gorge, his head on one side, listening.

A car was coming up the track from the camp. We couldn't see it because of the slide, but the sound of its engine was thrown back to us by the cliff opposite, beating in upon the stillness of the gorge. It grew rapidly louder. And then a jeep appeared, roaring and bumping round the base of the slide. It stopped beside the second bull-dozer and a European got out. He wore a light grey suit with a brown muffler round his neck and a wide-brimmed town hat.

It was Kostos. His suit was crumpled and dirty, and his narrow, pointed shoes were covered with a white film of dust. He looked uncomfortable and his city clothes seemed out of place against the towering background of the gorge.

'So! It is you, Lat'am, eh?' He glanced at Julie, and then his small, dark eyes fastened on Jan. 'Hah!' He was suddenly smiling. 'For a minute I do not recognise you without your beard.'

'How did you know we were here?' I asked him.

He tapped the side of his nose, smiling. He was so close to me that I could see the skin peeling from his cracked lips and the individual hairs of stiff stubble that darkened his chin. 'Not a sparrow falls, eh? Even 'ere in the desert.'

'Well, what do you want?'

'What do I want? Don't try to be stupid with me, Lat'am. You know what I want.' He moved across to Jan, leaning slightly forward and speaking confidentially as though he might be overhead. 'Come now, my friend. The papers. They are of no use to you. You cannot make claim to this place just because you have Duprez's papers. Duprez is dead and any successor to the ownership of the property must be confirmed by Caid Hassan.'

'I know that,' Jan said.

Kostos chuckled. 'Maybe you know it now. But you do not know it when you take the papers from that poor devil Kavan, eh?'

'What makes you think I took the papers from him?' I think that at that moment Jan was amused that the Greek still took him for Wade.

Kostos looked at him and there was a little gleam of triumph in his eyes. 'You do not kill a man for nothing, my friend.' His tone was gentle, like a kitten's purr.

'Kill a man!' Jan stared at him with shocked surprise. Knowing how it had happened and that it was an accident, the idea that he might be charged with murder was still quite beyond his grasp.

'You don't suggest Kavan *fell* overboard from your boat, do you?'

•

'What do you mean?' Jan's face was suddenly white. 'Who told you anyone fell overboard?'

'So! You do not listen to the radio, eh?'

'No, we haven't got one,' I said. 'But we saw the newspaper report. It was inaccurate.'

Kostos spun round on me. 'You keep out of this, Lat'am. It is nothing to concern you. I make you an offer in Tangier. You remember? That is finish. You lie to me. But now I have a stronger hand, you see, an' I deal direct.' He turned back to Jan. 'This is a new development, my friend. The body of Dr Jan Kavan, Czech refugee scientist, has been washed up on the coast of Portugal. This is what the radio said. It is two nights ago and they give your description – all very accurate, except for the beard which is gone now.' He moved a little closer to Jan. 'The police would be interested to know what motive you had.'

'How do you mean?' Jan's body was rigid, his mouth slightly open.

'If I tell them about the deeds you get from Kavan, then they know it is murder – they know you push him overboard.'

'No.' The denial burst from Jan's mouth. 'I didn't push him. It was an accident. And it wasn't—' He checked himself as though a thought had suddenly occurred to him.

'Now, perhaps you understand, eh?' Kostos was smiling. 'We make a deal. You and I. You give me the papers and I keep silent. Maybe I help you get out of Morocco safe. But if you do not give me the papers, then

I—' He stopped and turned at the sound of footsteps echoing along the cliffs of the gorge.

It was White. He wore an old fleece-lined flying jacket, open at the front to expose the dirty white of his T-shirt. 'What's going on here?' he demanded. And then he recognised Kostos.

'Oh, so you two have got together, have you?'

Kostos smiled and looked across at Jan. 'Yes. That is just about what we do, eh?' He jerked the muffler tighter round his neck. 'I give you to tonight, my friend. I will be 'ere—' he glanced at his heavy gold wrist-watch – 'at five o'clock. If you do not meet me then, ready to come to an agreement, then I will know what to do, eh?' He smiled and nodded and walked back to the jeep. The engine started with a roar that reverberated through the gorge and then he went bumping and slithering over the rocks at the base of the slide and was lost to sight.

'Who was that frightful little man?' Julie asked. 'What did he mean about—'

'I'll tell you later,' I said quickly. I was looking at White, wondering how much he had heard.

He seemed to hesitate a moment. And then he half shrugged his shoulders and turned and walked over to the nearest bull-dozer, his tall, slim-hipped body moving easily, rhythmically as though he belonged in this wild place.

'White!' I called after him. 'Do you know how we contact the Caid?'

But he climbed on to the seat of the bull-dozer without replying, and a moment later the engine started with a shattering roar. The tracks moved and the dull, rock-burnished steel of the blade dropped to the ground, scooped a pile of rock out of the slide and thrust it to the edge of the dumping ground. The gorge echoed to the splash and rumble of a ton of rock spilling down the slope into the water.

I tapped Jan on the shoulder. 'We'd better go down and see Capitaine Legard at the Post. He'll take us to the Caid.' I had to shout to make myself heard above the reverberating roar of the bull-dozer.

He nodded and we went back down the track to the camp. 'Do you think it is true, what Kostos said?' he said.

'He'd hardly have invented it,' I said.

'No, I suppose not.' He looked worried. 'It must be Wade's body that was washed up. But why should they mistake Wade for me?'

'Don't forget they're convinced Wade is alive,' I pointed out. 'And your papers showed that you aren't unalike. The body wouldn't have been in too good shape.' I hesitated and then said, 'Was Wade wearing any of your clothing?'

'I don't know.' He hesitated. 'He could be. You know what it's like in a yacht – oilskins, windbreakers, sweaters, everything gets mixed up. One's too tired . . . Maybe he was wearing something of mine.' He said it slowly, considering the matter, and he walked with quick, nervous strides, his eyes fixed on the ground. 'If it's true what Kostos said,' he murmured half to himself, 'then officially I'm dead.'

'You'll have to explain that it's Wade's body that's

been found in Portugal,' I told him. 'And you'll have to explain how he died.'

'That means publicity.' The words seemed to be jerked out of him. 'There mustn't be any publicity. It was publicity that started it last time. I told you that. I must keep my name out of the papers. At all costs there mustn't be any publicity.'

'That can't be helped.' I said. 'The man's body has been found and his death will have to be explained.'

He didn't seem to hear me. 'If I'm dead,' he murmured to himself, 'then it's Wade who is alive. It's as simple as that.' He said it almost wonderingly. And then he strode on ahead until we came to the camp. He seemed to want to be alone.

And when we drove down the piste towards Foum-Skhira he was strangely silent. It was a queer day now. It seemed to have changed. The strength and clarity had gone out of the sun and the sky was no longer blue, but opaque and hazy. A little wind had sprung up from the mountains and it blew the dust from our wheels out in streamers in front of us. We stopped at the house where the Tricolour flew. There was a sign-board half-hidden by sand. One arrow pointed to the mountains – Agdz, 44kms.; the other south towards the desert – Tombouctou, 50js. . . . Fifty days! A dog raced out to meet us as we stopped. He stood barking at us furiously, a big, rangy animal, oddly reminiscent of the medieval hunting dogs depicted on old tapestries.

'Look!' Julie cried. 'A baby gazelle.' It was in a wire enclosure; a small deer, beautifully marked with long, straight horns.

A Berber servant came to the door of the house and stared at us. I called out to him, asking for Capitaine Legard, and he pointed to the fort, telling us to go to the Bureau.

The sun had disappeared completely now. Yet there was no cloud. It seemed to have been overlaid by an atmospheric miasma. It had become very cold and the wind had risen further, driving little sifting runnels of sand before it. The whole great open space between the two forts seemed to be on the move as the powder-dry top surface of sand drifted along the ground. We were shown into the captain's office by an immensely large, black-bearded orderly wearing a turban and a blue cloak. He was a Tuareg, one of the Blue Men of the desert.

By comparison, Legard seemed small and insignificant. He was short and stocky with sallow, tired features. There was no heating in the stone-floored office and he sat huddled behind the desk in a torn and dusty greatcoat with no insignia of rank on the shoulders. A khaki scarf was muffled round his neck. He glanced at Julie and then pulled himself to his feet, staring at us in silence from behind thick-lensed, horn-rimmed glasses. The glasses caught the light so that it was impossible to see the expression of his eyes. But I felt he resented our intrusion. Moreover, though he might look insignificant, he conveyed a sense of power, as though whatever he wore or however ill he looked, he was conscious of being the ruler in this place.

Faced with the authority of the man, Jan remained silent, leaving me to explain who we were and why we had come to Foum-Skhira. 'We hoped you would be willing to take us to see the Caid Hassan,' I added.

'Caid Hassan is an old man now,' he said. 'Old and sick.' He got Julie a chair and went back to his seat behind the desk. 'Also, you come at a bad time.' He made little explosive noises with his lips and stared at Jan. 'So! You are now the owner of Kasbah Foum, eh?'

'It has to be confirmed by the Caid,' Jan said.

'*C'est ça.*'

He stared at us from the protection of his glasses and the stillness of the room seemed to crowd in on us. His hostility and the chill drabness of the office with its bare, map-lined walls had a depressing effect on me.

'And if the Caid confirms your title, what do you intend to do about this American?' He said 'this American' with undisguised contempt.

'I understand he's been granted a mining concession,' Jan said.

Capitaine Legard grunted. The grunt seemed to express what he thought of people in Rabat who granted mining concessions in his territory. There was silence again, and then he said, 'You have documents to prove your ownership of the property, monsieur?'

Jan produced once more the crumpled envelope and passed it across the desk. Legard pulled out the deeds and examined them. Then he glanced at the covering letter. He read it slowly, carefully. Then he looked up at Jan. 'This letter is from Marcel Duprez?'

'Yes.' Jan cleared his throat. 'Perhaps you knew him, Monsieur le Capitaine?'

'*Non.* But everybody has heard of him. Capitaine

Marcel Duprez was one of the finest officers of les Affaires Indigènes.' There was sudden warmth in his tone. 'Tell me, monsieur, how was it he came to leave you this property? Are you a relative?'

Briefly Jan explained how the war had brought them together and the part Duprez had played in helping him to get information out to the British. And as he talked, I saw Legard's face soften and relax. 'And you were with him when he died?' he asked. And when Jan had described the scene in that cellar in Essen, Legard nodded his head slowly. 'He was a fine man,' he said quietly. 'I am sorry he died like that. He was what the men who sit at desks in Rabat call an officer of the *bled* – of the country. It seems that he was not an executive type but only a leader of the people. He understood the Berbers as few of us will ever understand them. If he had not been half-dead with dysentery and undergoing a cure in France, the Germans would never have captured him.' He shrugged his shoulders and again those little explosive noises blew his lips out. He glanced at his watch and got quickly to his feet. He seemed suddenly alert and full of vigour. '*Alors*. We will go back to the house. We will have a drink and you will perhaps tell me the full story. Then I will phone *mon commandant*. He will be interested. He served with Duprez. He was with him when they took Foum-Skhira. Duprez told you the story of that, eh?'

Jan nodded.

'*Eh bien*.' He took a battered and dusty pill-box officer's hat from a nail on the wall and led us out through the drifting sand to his house. Like all houses in

Morocco, it was built for intense heat. The floors were tiled, the walls cold, white expanses of plaster, their severity relieved by a few hand-woven rugs. There was a gramophone and some books and a small collection of brass sugar hammers, beautifully inlaid with copper and silver. When Julie admired them, he said, 'Ah, yes. Once Foum-Skhira was famous for its silver craftsmen.' He turned to Jan. 'There is an old story that your Kasbah Foum was built on the site of a smelting place – for extracting silver from ore. But—' He shrugged his shoulders. 'Like all these stories, it has come down by word of mouth only. Maybe it is true. Duprez excavated some old fire-places there and now there is this American . . .'

He shrugged his shoulders again and took us through into his study. There was a big desk with a field telephone on it, and the walls were lined with books. Magazines, some of them American, littered the floors. On the mantelpiece were some family photographs framed in silver and above it a delightful oil painting of a Paris boulevard. He saw me looking at it and said, 'That one I picked up in a little gallery I know on the Left Bank. It is by a man called Valere. He is not much known yet. But I think he is good. In the other room I have another by him and also one by Briffe. But this is the one I like best. It is a great pleasure to sit here at my desk and look at Paris, eh? I am a Parisian, you see.' He laughed and then turned to one of the bookshelves. '*Regardez*, monsieur.' He pointed to a beautifully bound collection of volumes, all on art. 'I like to look at the works of the great painters, even if I can never afford to own one. I like pictures.' He turned abruptly away, as though he had revealed too much of himself. '*Alors*, mademoiselle. *Qu'est ce que vous voulez boire*? Vermouth? Cognac? I have a good cognac that I have sent out to me from France.'

'I'd like a cognac then,' Julie said. He pulled up a chair for her and then shouted for his Berber servant, who came and poured paraffin on the pile of wood in the grate so that it went up with a roar as he lit it. Legard poured us our drinks. '*Santé*!'

'*Santé*!'

The fire blazed with heat. The room was suddenly warm and friendly.

'What is the best way for me to contact the Caid?' Jan asked.

'Ah, that is a little difficult, monsieur. I would take you myself, but . . .' He shrugged his shoulders. 'It is as I have said – you come at a bad time. I cannot leave the Post until the food trucks arrive. I have two trucks bringing food here to these people, and they have both broken down.' He made rude, angry noises to himself. 'Our transport is all from the war. It works, but it needs servicing.' He began to cough. 'Like me,' he said as he recovered, and he grinned at us sardonically. 'The trouble is that everything – even the wood for the fire – has to come across the Atlas from Marrakech.'

'Could you provide a guide then?' Jan said. 'I have to see Caid Hassan. It's urgent.'

Legard looked at him, frowning. 'You have waited ten years, monsieur. What is the hurry?' And when Jan didn't answer, he smiled and said, 'Ah, it is the American that is worrying you, eh? Well, he is worrying me, also.' He leaned quickly forward. 'Things were difficult enough here before. The date crop failed. For two years now we have what is called the Marlatt scale pest here in the palmerie. We have sprayed from the air at the time when the insect comes out to moult, but it is no good.' He shrugged his shoulders. 'Then this fool arrives, paying three Arabs incredible wages to run his abominable machines. I asked him to clear the rock by hand with local labour. He refused. He did not seem to understand that the people here needed the money.'

'His Arabs have left him,' Julie said.

'Yes, yes, I know.' He had risen and was pacing up and down excitedly. 'They departed early this morning.' He stopped and stared at us. 'But do you know why? Does the American say why they left?'

'He said they left to get stores,' I told him.

'Pff! You do not send three *indigènes* to get stores when one would do.'

'Maybe they were told to go,' I suggested.

'Who by?'

'Isn't the Caid's son, Ali, here in Foum-Skhira?'

He looked at me hard. 'How did you know that, monsieur?'

I told him then about the visit we had had from Kostos.

'Ah, *oui*. That man Kostos!' He resumed his pacing. '*Merde*!' The word burst out of him with explosive force. 'Everything goes wrong this year.' He swung round on his heels so that he faced me. 'Did you see the souk when you came in and the road up the mountain?

First the dates and then the rain. And now Ali is here.' He started to cough again and winced, pressing his hand against his belly. He leaned on the desk for a moment and then walked slowly round to his chair, his body bent, and slumped into it. '*Eh bien*,' he murmured, 'my relief will arrive soon.'

'You're not well,' Julie said.

He looked across at her and smiled wanly, shrugging his shoulders. 'Every year I go to Vichy to take the cure. I am late this year, that is all.' He shouted for the house-boy who came running with a glass of water, and he drained it at a gulp.

'Is it dysentery?' Julie asked.

He nodded. '*Oui*, mademoiselle. The *amibe*. With us it is an occupational disease. We do not always stay in the Posts. We have to visit all parts of the Territory, and sometimes we must drink bad water. For the *indigènes* it is different. They are immune. But for us . . .' He shrugged his shoulders again.

'About this man Ali,' I said. 'Can't you arrest him? I understood . . .'

'*Oui, oui*, monsieur. I can walk into the kasbah now, this morning and arrest him. But it would disturb the people, and things have been difficult here lately. Maybe when the food trucks arrive . . .'

The field telephone on the desk buzzed. '*Pardon*, monsieur.' Legard lifted the receiver. '*Oui, mon commandant – ici Legard . . . Oui . . . Oui . . . Oui, mon commandant. . . .*' He looked across at us, the instrument still held against his ear, and his eyes fastened on Jan. '*Oui. Exactement . . . Vraiment?*' His tone was one of astonishment. For a moment there was silence whilst he listened to the voice at the other end of the line, and then he said, '*Je le ferai. . . . Non, non, ils sont justement arrivés. . . . Oui, oui, je comprends parfaitement.*' He asked about the food trucks then and after a short conversation on the subject, he nodded. '*Oui, je le ferai . . . Ça va bien. Adieu, mon commandant.*' He put the receiver down slowly on to its rest. Then he stared at the three of us, a little startled, a little angry. 'Your papers, monsieur,' he demanded, looking at Jan and holding out his hand. When they were handed to him, he went through them slowly, glancing up every now and then as though to check that they really did relate to the man sitting opposite him.

'And yours, monsieur,' he asked, addressing me.

He checked my passport and then he looked up at the two of us and said, 'I regret, but I have orders to retain your papers temporarily. You are to remain in this district until you have permission to leave.'

'What exactly is the trouble?' I asked.

'There is no trouble. It is solely a matter of routine.' He pushed back his chair and got to his feet. 'If you require accommodation . . .'

'We sleep in our vehicle,' I said.

'*Bon*. Now, if you will excuse me, I have to leave for Agdz.'

'Don't you want to see my passport?' Julie asked.

'It is not necessary, mademoiselle.'

'But if it is a matter of routine.' She held out her passport.

'I repeat, mademoiselle. It is not necessary.' He

shouted for the house-boy. 'If there is anything you require for your comfort,' he added formally, 'Mohammed will see that you have it.' He indicated the Berber boy and then ordered him to escort us out.

Disconcerted by the abruptness of his change of attitude towards us, we went without another word.

Little runnels of sand had drifted under the front door despite the sacking that had been placed there. And when Mohammed opened it for us, we were met by a cold blast of wind that flung a cloud of stinging sand in our faces. We thrust our way out, too battered by the impact of the storm to think. The door closed behind us and we hesitated, huddling together for protection. The palmerie had disappeared completely. The Foreign Legion fort was no more than a vague blur in the sand-laden atmosphere. The whole surface of the ground seemed to be on the move, rustling past our feet and climbing into the air with a singing sound on each gust, swirling upwards higher than the flagstaff.

We fought our way to the bus, hauled open the door and staggered inside.

'What happened?' Julie asked us as she got her breath back. 'What was that phone call about?'

'I think the police have discovered that Jan didn't come straight out from England,' I said.

But she shook her head. 'No, it wasn't that. Legard is an officer of the AI, not a policeman, and Jan was a friend of Capitaine Duprez. His attitude wouldn't change because he was in trouble with the immigration authorities.'

'No,' I said. 'But it would if his commandant had

thrown doubt on Jan's identity.' I glanced at Jan. He was sitting on the berth, his head in his hands, frowning. 'Well, what do we do now?' I asked him.

He lifted his head and looked at me almost in surprise. 'We find Caid Hassan. That's the first thing. Afterwards . . .' He shrugged his shoulders a little wearily. 'Afterwards, I don't know. But first we'll see the Caid. As soon as the storm is over.'

I glanced at my watch. It was just after twelve. And at five Kostos would be at the camp again.

CHAPTER TWO

Though we had parked in the lee of the Foreign Legion fort, the sand still found its way into the interior of the bus. I would have liked some sleep, but sleep was impossible. We just sat and watched the sand whirl past the windscreen, sifting like water over the long snout of the bonnet. A jeep passed us, battling against the swirling clouds of sand like a little mechanical toy. Legard was at the wheel, muffled in his Spahis cloak. He was driving towards the mountains.

'Why did he have to go to Agdz?' asked Jan. 'He said he couldn't leave the Post until the food trucks arrived.'

'Well, I'm glad I haven't got to drive through this in an open jeep,' Julie said.

'He'll be clear of it in the mountains,' I pointed out.

'Why don't we go to the mountains then?'

I glanced round at her. She had her eyes closed and she looked tired. 'We could go back into the house,' I suggested.

'No, we can't sleep there. Besides, we need some food.'

'All right. I'll drive up to the foot of the mountains then.' I leaned forward and pressed the starter button.

'Why not go to the Kasbah Foum?' Jan suggested.

'If you like.'

It wasn't easy driving. Sand was sifting along the ground so thick that it was difficult to see the piste. It was like driving through a dead world. But at length the palm trees thinned, and as we climbed towards Kasbah Foum, the weight of the sand lessened. Soon we could see the mountains, a vague shadow looming up ahead of us like a heavy cloud formation photographed in sepia. There was the watch tower and the ruined city, and there, straight ahead of us, was the kasbah and the dark gash of the gorge.

In that queer half-light the place looked inhospitable, almost hostile. There was a deadness about it. The tumbled graveyard of the ancient city seemed to be spilling down the hill on to the kasbah. The gorge was a yawning cavity in the mountains, remote and sinister. I glanced at Jan. Those last lines of Browning's came into my mind: *And yet dauntless the slug-horn to my lips I set, and blew. Childe Roland to the Dark Tower came.*

I pulled up close to White's tent and switched off the engine. The camp was deserted, but from the entrance to the gorge came the sound of a bull-dozer working, carried to us faintly on the wind. 'We'll have some food and then you'd better get some sleep,' I told Julie.

As soon as we had finished lunch, Jan left us, walking quickly up the track to the gorge. To Julie and me who watched him go, he looked a small and pathetically lonely figure against the immensity of the mountains. 'What will happen to him?' she asked.

'I don't know,' I said.

Her hand touched my arm. 'How deeply are you involved, Philip?'

'With the police?'

'Yes.'

'Oh, I shouldn't get more than ten years,' I said, trying to make a joke of it. But her eyes looked worried. 'Get some sleep,' I said. 'There's nothing to be done about it now.'

She hesitated, and then she nodded and went through into her compartment of the caravan. I stretched myself out on the berth behind the driving seat and pulled a rug over me. I must have slept, for I woke up with a start to the sound of a car drawing up alongside. It was a jeep and for a moment I thought it was Legard. But then I saw there was a Berber at the wheel, and it was Kostos who climbed out of the passenger seat. He saw me and waved his podgy hand.

'Lat'am. Where is Wade gone to?'

'Wade?' And then I laughed because the name sounded so odd now. I pointed up to the mouth of the gorge and he nodded and climbed back into the jeep which shot off up the track. I glanced at my watch. It was just after five. The wind had died away and all the sky over the palmerie was shot with red and gold and a soft blue violet as the sun sank.

I pulled on my shoes and hurried up the track. The gorge was already beginning to get dark and there was a damp chill about the place. It echoed to the thunder of machines and as I rounded the base of the slide, I saw that both bull-dozers were in operation. White was driving one and Jan the other, as though they had settled their differences and gone into partnership.

The jeep was parked close to the point where the rubble was being tipped into the water. Beside it stood Kostos and the Berber driver. The Berber, in his white djellaba with the hood drawn up over his head, seemed so natural, so much a part of the scene, that he emphasized the incongruity of the European in his crumpled suit and the great, blundering machines. Every time Jan's bull-dozer rumbled past him, Kostos moved forward, shouting and gesticulating in his endeavour to make himself heard above the roar of the diesel engine. As I came up, Jan stopped and switched off his engine. Seeing this, White stopped his engine, too, and in the sudden silence the Greek's voice, raised to a scream to make himself heard, was like the cry of some wild bird.

' . . . do not stop, we will leave at once, do you hear?' Kostos was waving his plump hands and his face was red with the effort of shouting. It was rather comic.

And then I saw that the Berber standing beside him was Ali d'Es-Skhira.

'We would like to talk to you privately,' Kostos said.

'Anything you have to say, you can say to me here,' Jan answered.

Kostos hesitated, glancing quickly round at White and myself. The movements of his head were jerky. 'Well, what have you decided?' His voice sounded small and peevish against the silence of rock and cliff and water.

Jan didn't say anything. He stared down at Kostos from his seat at the bull-dozer, and his gaze shifted to Ali. The only sound was the soft tinkle of water seeping through rock.

'Come on now,' Kostos said. 'You make your mind up, eh?'

'I've made up my mind. The answer is No.'

Ali took Kostos by the arm and they conferred together in a whisper. And all the time Ali was looking at Jan. Finally he spoke to him in French. 'You are not the man I am expecting to meet here.'

'No,' Jan said. 'He's dead.'

Ali nodded his head. His face showed no surprise. 'But you have the deeds of Kasbah Foum?'

'Yes.'

Again Kostos and Ali conferred together. '*C'est ça.*' Ali nodded and folded his hands in the sleeves of his djellaba. 'My friend says that the original offer still stands,' Kostos announced. 'For the papers, five hundred thousand francs.'

There was a silence. Nobody moved, nobody said anything. It was like a tableau. Then Ali turned his head slowly and gazed at the cliff face, now rapidly being cleared of debris. His features were impassive. Only his eyes betrayed his interest. They were dark and brown, but they gleamed in the fading light.

He glanced at Jan, staring at him as though to imprint the shape of his face on his mind. Then he turned without a word and climbed into a jeep. Kostos hesitated, looking from one to the other of us uncertainly. He seemed nervous, almost reluctant to leave. He was a European, and I suddenly got the impression he was uneasy. Then he turned, ducking his head in a quick, awkward movement, and scuttled back to the jeep, his thin-soled shoes making a frail, scraping sound on the rocks. The jeep drove off and we watched it go, not moving or speaking until the sound of it died away and was lost in the stillness.

'He knows now,' Jan said to me.

I nodded. 'Yes.'

'The wind has dropped, hasn't it?' His voice trembled slightly. 'I think we should try and see the Caid right away.'

'We should have gone before,' I said.

He nodded. 'Of course. But it seemed a pity that this bull-dozer should not be operating. And we're so close to the entrance now.' There was warmth and excitement in his voice again. 'White doesn't know the exact location of the entrance. But I do. Marcel gave me bearings. Another two days' work . . .' He stopped there, his excitement damped by my silence. 'What's the matter, Philip? You're worried about Ali. Is that it?'

'Yes,' I said. 'It's a pity we didn't see the Caid this afternoon. So long as Ali thought you were Wade, there was no reason for him to oppose the visit. But now . . . it may be dangerous.'

'I'm sorry.' He climbed down off the bull-dozer. 'I didn't think . . .' His shoulders moved awkwardly and he made a gesture with his hands that embraced the cliff-face, the whole gorge. 'I was too excited.'

•

Ed White came over to us then. 'It looks like you really have got the deeds of Kasbah Foum,' he said.

Jan nodded.

'I see.' He stood staring at us for a moment. 'That makes a difference, doesn't it?' He seemed about to say something further, but instead he turned and walked slowly back across the rubble and climbed up on to the driving seat of his bull-dozer again. The engine started with a roar and the lumbering machine turned back towards the cliff-face.

'Come on,' Jan said, gripping my arm. 'We must see the Caid right away.'

'It'll be night before we get there.'

'I know, I know. But that may help.' He glanced back as a beam of light cut the gloom of the gorge. Ed White had switched on his headlights. 'I was a fool. I forgot all about Kostos coming here at five. Once I got on that bull-dozer . . . It was good to be doing something constructive. I worked with a bull-dozer in Germany for a time – before they discovered I had other uses.' He laughed quickly, nervously. 'We'll go and have some tea with Julie. You English are always less pessimistic after you've had some tea. Then we'll go to Kasbah Foum-Skhira.'

'We'll need a guide,' I said.

He didn't say anything and we walked in silence out of the gorge. The sun had set and a velvet twilight was rapidly descending on the valley. But the palmerie was still visible and I could just make out the brown of the kasbah towers rising above the dusty green of the palms.

•

I wished we had visited the place in daylight. 'If Legard had taken us there it would have been—'

'Well, he didn't,' Jan said sharply.

'No, but—' There was no point in dwelling on it. The palmerie had faded into the dusk already. Everything was very still. It seemed impossible that the pale surface of the land could ever have been whirled up into the air in a cloud of sand; it looked solid and petrified in the half-light. 'What are you going to do about White?' I asked him. 'Don't forget he holds a concession.'

'Oh, we'll probably come to some agreement. I like him. He's easy to get on with. He's a construction engineer and he fits this sort of country. If the Caid confirms my title to the place . . .' He didn't finish. I think that the 'If' was too big.

We walked on in silence and as we neared the camp I saw something move along the darkening bed of the stream. It was a black, compact mass of movement. I strained my eyes and it resolved itself into a herd of goats being driven by a small boy. Jan had seen it, too, and he said, 'Perhaps the boy would guide us to the kasbah?'

'No,' I said. 'A boy's no good. He hasn't the necessary authority. They might not admit us. But if we could get his father . . .' I was thinking that a man who had a herd of goats would almost certainly be conservatively minded and a supporter of the Caid's policy rather than of Ali's fanaticism. I turned off the track and scrambled down the bank. Jan followed us.

The boy had stopped now and was watching us nervously. I called to him in his own language to come and speak with us, but he didn't move. And when we came up to him he stood, regarding us with wide, solemn eyes. He was like a startled animal and at any moment I was afraid he would turn and run. But the goats had stopped and were nibbling at the reed tufts. The boy was watching them all the time and I knew that so long as the goats were there, the boy would remain. They were in his charge and the responsibility was a heavy one, for they represented considerable wealth in this starved, arid land.

I explained to him that I wanted to speak with his father, but he stared at me out of his large, awed eyes and said nothing. I repeated my request slowly and clearly. He looked at the goats as though he were afraid I might spirit them away by magic whilst I held his gaze with my strange talk. Then his eyes came back to me as though fascinated. Probably I was the first European who had ever spoken to him.

In the end I put my hand in my pocket and pulled out two hundred franc notes. I held them out to him. He smiled shyly, eagerly, and shook his head. But his eyes remained on the notes. Again I asked him if he would fetch his father for me.

I knew he understood and I waited. His gaze alternated between my face and the notes in my hand. Then suddenly he leaned forward, swift as a bird, grabbed them from my fingers, and with a little shriek of excitement went scampering away after his goats which had gradually merged into the dusk as they drifted from reed tuft to reed tuft.

We watched him rounding them up with shrill cries

of *Aiya, Aiya*, driving them towards the ruined kasbah. 'Will he bring his father to us?' Jan asked.

'I think so,' I said, and we went on to the caravan.

We had just settled down to tea when the boy's figure went flying past, bare feet scuttering over the sand, scarcely seeming to touch the ground; a small, flickering shadow in the gathering dusk.

I turned the bus then and switched on the sidelights, and soon afterwards the boy appeared with his father. He was an oldish man, tall and slightly stooped, with a long, pale face heavily lined with years of sun and sand. We exchanged greetings and I invited him into the caravan. He sent the boy off and, after slipping his feet out of his sandals, he climbed in and seated himself cross-legged on the berth. From an inner pocket he produced the two hundred franc notes I had given his son and held them out to me. 'My son is not to be paid for bringing his father to you, *sidi*,' he said.

I insisted that he return the money to the boy and then Julie brought the coffee I had asked her to make and we talked. His name was Moha and he was the chief of a small village at this end of the palmerie. He was a man of some substance, with fifty goats and more than a hundred palm trees, and he had a daughter married to the son of the Khailifa, the Sultan's representative at Foum-Skhira. He talked about the failure of the date harvest and how a year ago French experts had examined the trees and then the 'machine like a bird had arrived and covered the date palms with smoke'.

'And didn't it do any good?' I asked.

'*Insh'Allah*!' He shrugged his shoulders and smiled.

But the smile didn't extend to his hard, grey eyes. 'The French officer has told us that it is the only hope for the trees and we believe him because he is wise and like a father to us. But this year I have no dates, *sidi*. No man is sure any more.'

It was the perfect situation for a man like Ali to exploit. I asked him if he knew that the Caid's son had returned to Foum-Skhira. He nodded and I was conscious of a stillness about him, a sudden mental wariness. His eyes were hooded by the pale lids and the curved, predatory beak of his nose made him look like an old hawk.

'Do you know why he has returned?' I asked. But he didn't answer. He had finished his third cup of coffee and, according to Berber etiquette, he would now take his leave. 'You are a friend of Caid Hassan,' I said.

He nodded, gathering his djellaba about him.

'We wish to see him tonight. It is important. Will you take us to him?'

'He is a sick man, *sidi*.'

'I know. But we have to see him. Will you take us?'

'Tomorrow perhaps.'

'No.' I said. 'It must be tonight. At least guide us as far as the kasbah.'

He stared at me, his eyes narrowed slightly. Then he shook his head. 'He is sick,' he repeated.

Jan got up then. 'Ask him,' he said, 'whether he was here when Lieutenant Duprez drank tea with Caid Hassan between the lines.'

The Berber's eyes lit up suddenly as I asked him the question. '*Iyyeh, sidi*. I was there.'

I told him then that Jan had been Duprez's friend, that he had been with him when he died, and he stared at Jan, smiling and bowing as though greeting him for the first time. 'He has a message for Caid Hassan from Capitaine Duprez,' I added. 'It is important.' And then I asked him again if he'd take us to the kasbah.

He got to his feet then. 'Very well.' He nodded. 'I will take you to Caid Hassan.'

I opened the door for him and he stepped out into the night.

Jan followed him. Julie caught hold of my arm. 'Do you have to go with him, Philip?'

'You'll be all right,' I said. 'Ed White will be down from the gorge soon and—'

'It's not that,' she said quickly. She was staring up at me. Then she turned away. 'Well, be careful. This place isn't like the mountain villages round Enfida.' She picked up the coffee things and went through into the kitchenette.

I stepped down to the ground and closed the door. The little lit world of the caravan seemed suddenly small and remote, an oasis of light in the desert of darkness that surrounded it. The sky was clear and the bright starlight showed us the shape of the mountains crouched above the camp. The sound of White's bulldozer came down to us from the gorge. There was no wind, but already the air was cold, with that still, frosted cold of a land where the soil had no humus to absorb and retain the heat of the sun.

We followed the piste down until, looking over my shoulder, the bus was no more than a yellow pinpoint of light in the immense black shadow of the mountains. Then we entered the palmerie and the trees hid even that small indication of human existence. We were alone in a cold, alien world.

It was very dark under the palms and we stumbled along countless small earth banks built to retain the water in the cultivated patches where millet would be grown. But finally we came out on to the bank of a deep irrigation ditch. The path was like a switch-back, but the going was easier. Occasionally a star was reflected below us. It was the only indication that there was water in the ditch. We followed the glimmering white of Moha's djellaba through a world of almost complete blackness. All my eyes consciously saw was the still, fantastic shapes of the palm fronds standing darkly against the stars. My feet seemed to develop a sense and a feel for the ground. They found their way by a sort of instinct that was quite divorced from the control of my brain.

We came to a bridge of palm trunks spanning the ditch and there our guide told us to wait whilst he went into his village. We could hear him beating on the wooden door of his house and there was a dog barking. Then there was silence again. 'I suppose you've got the deeds with you?' Though I kept my voice to a whisper, the sound of it seemed loud.

'Yes,' Jan said. 'And Marcel's letter.'

I didn't say anything. I was thinking that the only documents establishing his claim to Kasbah Foum were on him at this moment. I didn't like it. If the guide sent a runner on ahead of us . . . If Ali knew . . . I felt a shiver run down my spine. It was cold and very quiet standing there on the edge of that ditch in the palmerie. It was like being in a dead world.

A shadow moved in the darkness. It was our guide, the white of his djellaba almost hidden by the blanket he had wrapped round himself. He led us on along the top of the ditch without a word and soon we caught the faint beat of tam-tams far ahead. The sound was a guide to our progress and as we neared Ksar Foum-Skhira the harsh, lilting chant of the singers joined the rhythmic beating of the drums. *Yaiee-ya Yaiee-ya Yaiee Yai-i . . . Yaiee-ya Yaiee-ya Yai-ee Yai-i-ee*. The chant was repeated over and over again with only slight variations. It was insistent like the drumming of the wind or the singing of a sand storm.

We reached a well with its pole uplifted against the stars and then we were on a beaten track with walls on either side. And when we came out into the open again, the noise of the tam-tams and the singing was suddenly very loud. *Aiee-ya Aiee-ya Aiee-yaiee-ya*. We were close under the walls of Ksar Foum Skhira now and there were people about. I breathed a sigh of relief. *Aiee-ya Aiee-ya Aiee-yaiee-ya*.

We crossed an open space and ahead of us, on a slight rise, the darker bulk of the kasbah showed in the darkness. We passed through the arched gateway of an outer wall, crossed an open courtyard of sand and came to the main entrance, barred by a wooden door. Our guide beat upon the wood and the noise seemed very loud, for the kasbah had the stillness of a place that had been deserted for a long time. A kid bleated softly somewhere in the darkness and from near the outer wall came the rude belching of a camel. A light showed through a crack and then the wooden securing bar was lifted and the door was pulled back with a creak of hinges. A swarthy, bearded man, his head swathed in a turban, stared at us suspiciously. He carried a carbide lamp in his hand – an elementary light made of a metal container with a long spout rising from it, at the end of which was a two-inch jet of flame that wavered in the draught.

Our guide explained that we wished to see the Caid. The thick, guttural sounds of the Arab dialect were tossed back and forth between them. 'My companion,' I said, indicating Jan, 'was a friend of Capitaine Duprez. He has a message for Caid Hassan.'

The turbaned porter held the flame high so that he could see us. The light gleamed on his brown, inquisitive eyes. Then he nodded and stood aside for us to enter. The door closed behind us, the wooden securing bar was dropped into place and, with a quick little gesture that was part welcome and part a request to follow him, the keeper of the gate led us into the black cavern of a passageway. From nails on the wall he took two more carbide lights. The place was like an underground tunnel, dank and chill with walls and roof of mud so that it looked as though it had been hewn out of the earth.

We passed a rectangular opening that was a doorway leading to a courtyard. I had a glimpse of stars and the outline of one of the kasbah towers. We turned left here into another passageway. A yellow gleam of light showed at the end of it. It was the entrance to a room and, as we went by, I saw the glow of a brazier and figures huddled round it. The only lights were the carbide flames flickering from their wall hooks. Steps led upwards then – a staircase that followed the square walls of a tower. And suddenly we were out in the open on a roof top. Below us stretched the darkness of the palmerie and away to the right the shadowy bulk of the walled village of Ksar Foum-Skhira, from which gleamed little points of light – the gleam of braziers and flickering flame lights in rooms that had only holes in the walls for windows.

We crossed the roof top and entered the open doorway of another tower. There was a shallow flight of earthen stairs and then we were in a square room with two thick window embrasures, the small, square openings of which were closed by broken wooden shutters. The place was very cold and had a musty smell. It was completely bare. The floor was of hard-packed earth and the walls of dried mud. The ceiling was high, raftered with the soft wood of palm stems. The man who had brought us here lit the two carbide lamps, hung them on hooks provided in the walls and then left us without a word, taking our guide with him.

It was bitterly cold. The temperature was just on freezing and a little wind was driving in through the cracks in the shutters and the carbide flames flickered wildly. 'They'll bring cushions and rugs in a minute,' I said.

Jan nodded, glancing uneasily about him. 'Can I smoke?'

'Yes.'

He brought out a packet of cigarettes and lit one. The only sound was the whistle of the wind in the chinks of the shutter and the singing from the village and the beat of the drums, which was so clear that they might have been in the courtyard below. *Ai-yai-yee Ai-yai-yee Ya-ee Ya-ee Yai-i.*

'There's a fire in Ksar Foum-Skhira,' Jan said.

I went over and peered through one of the broken shutters. In some courtyard of the village flames were flickering in a lurid glow that lit up the corner of a tower and the piled-up walls of some houses. 'They have to have a fire to heat the drums and so stretch the hides to the required pitch,' I said.

The drums were beating faster now. The tempo of the singing increased, became shriller and then stopped abruptly. The drums went on for a few seconds and then ceased on a beat. In the sudden silence we heard the murmur of voices below us in the kasbah and then the scuffle of sandals on the stairs. Men crowded into the room, their arms piled with cushions and silks and hand-woven rugs. A big square of carpet was spread out on the earthen floor, the cushions were arranged round it and draped with rugs and silks. A brazier was brought, a red glow of warmth, and stood in the corner. A copper kettle was set on it. A great silver tray was placed on a low table that was barely six inches from the ground. Coloured glasses were carefully arranged and a silver tea chest and a white cone of sugar were placed beside it.

One of the men who had carried these things up was

Moha and I reminded him that we were relying upon him to guide us back. He nodded and disappeared with the rest of the men. The room was suddenly empty again. We sat down cross-legged on the cushions and waited.

The minutes ticked slowly by. I found myself wishing the singing would start again in the village. Harsh and primitive though it was, at least it was a reminder that there were human beings around. The kasbah seemed quiet as the grave.

But at last there was movement again on the stairs and then an old man entered, walking slowly. He wore a spotlessly white djellaba of soft wool, the hood neatly arranged to frame his features. His beard was white and rather sparse, cut like a goatee, but extending along the line of the jaw almost to the ears. His skin was pale, far paler than mine, and his eyes were a steely blue. He was of pure Berber stock, unmixed with Arab or any of the desert races that so dilute the Berber blood of the south. '*Merhba bikum*!' His gesture of greeting had great dignity. He motioned us to sit and he himself sank on to a cushion, folding up neatly and gracefully despite his age. Summoning one of the two men who had entered with him, he bade him make the tea for his guests, at the same time apologising to us in French for not doing it himself. He then made us a little speech of welcome in a frail voice that only occasionally paused to search for the right word. 'You should have given warning that you were coming to visit me,' he finished reproachfully. 'I would have arranged a *difa* for you.'

'It is very kind of you,' I replied. 'But things are difficult for you now.'

'Yes, I know. But for our friends it is still possible to entertain them as I would wish. It is my people who suffer.' He paused and then said, 'You were with Monsieur le Capitaine this morning?'

I nodded.

'Did he say when the food would arrive for my people?'

I explained about the two trucks that had broken down.

'Yes, yes, I know,' he said. 'But why does he have to go to Agdz? Is he gone to bring the food here?'

I couldn't tell him that Legard had gone to Agdz because of us. 'Yes,' I said, 'he has gone to bring the food trucks.'

'Good. But he must come soon. The people lose so much of their supplies in the disaster of the souk.' He said this to himself rather than to us, nodding his head slightly. His age showed then, for he looked suddenly peevish and irritable.

'They'll be here tomorrow, I expect,' I said.

He shrugged. '*Insh'Allah*!'

'I believe your son is here in Foum-Skhira?' I said.

'My eldest son, you mean? Ali?' He nodded. '*Oui*. There is dancing in his honour in Ksar Foum-Skhira tonight. You know him perhaps?' His eyes had clouded.

'Yes, I met him in Tangier.'

The pale lids closed almost wearily. In those dropped lids I saw suddenly a similarity between the son and his father. He sighed and changed the subject, talking about the rains and how the souk had been destroyed. And then the tea was made and the hot, sweet, mint-smelling glasses were placed in our hands. '*Alors*,' the Caid said, 'you say that you are friends of the Capitaine Duprez.'

I explained that it was Jan who was Duprez's friend and that he had been with him when he died. The old man nodded and motioned the men, standing like shadows in the doorway, to withdraw. Only the man seated behind the silver-laden tea tray remained. He was small-bodied with a cast in one eye, but he had the old man's features and he was called Hassan, so that I presumed he was one of the Caid's sons.

'Now,' the Caid said. 'You have come to talk with me about Kasbah Foum, eh?'

I nodded to Jan to go ahead, and he told him how he had met Duprez, how they had worked together against the Germans in Essen and how Duprez had died there.

The old Caid shook his head and sighed. 'It is a sad end for him,' he said.

'He was serving France,' Jan pointed out.

'*Mais oui*. He always served France. He was a Frenchman. But he should have died here. This was his home and my people were his people also. He was a fine man.' Remembering what Ali had told me, I was surprised at the warmth in the old man's voice.

The man behind the tea table rose and replenished our glasses. 'It is many years ago then that Monsieur le Capitaine died.' There was a hard shrewdness in the old man's eyes as he stared at Jan. 'Why is it only now that you come to tell me how it happened?'

Jan tried to explain why he had not come before,

what his life had been since the war, but it was clear that the Caid didn't really understand. He was not ignorant of the world beyond Foum-Skhira, but to him it was a French world. The complications of other European powers were largely outside his knowledge. 'I think,' he said, 'that you have come because the tall, fair man from America with the big machines is arrived to work at Kasbah Foum.'

'No,' Jan said. 'I came because I had to. I did not know about the American.' He produced the battered envelope and another smaller envelope containing the letter from Duprez. The Caid waved it aside. 'I have been told,' he said, 'that you are not the man to whom Capitaine Duprez handed the papers. It has been suggested that you killed the man to whom he gave them. First, before I see the letter Capitaine Duprez wrote, you must give proof that you are in reality the man who was with my friend when he died.'

'How can I do that?' Jan asked. 'What can I tell you that will prove it to you?'

The old man thought for a moment. 'Tell me exactly how he looked and what he told you of his talks with me.'

For several minutes Jan talked, telling him about Marcel Duprez quoting long speeches that Duprez had made to him, about the Caid, about Foum-Skhira, about the Berbers and the country of the south. Only occasionally the Caid interrupted him to clarify a word or to ask a question. Jan was still talking when there was a disturbance at the foot of the stairs below the room where we were seated. Several men were talking, quickly, angrily, in Berber, and then there was the light patter of sandals on the earthen stairway.

The Caid turned his head towards the entrance, his forehead contracted in a frown.

The footsteps ceased. The figure of a man stood in the doorway. His brown djellaba merged into the black rectangle of the entrance so that he was no more than a vague shape in the darkness. His face was hidden in the hood of his djellaba, but his eyes caught the light of the carbide flames and glinted, as did the curved silver knife at his waist; the eyes and the knife were all that was visible of him. '*Skun ya*? Who is that?' the Caid demanded.

'Ali.' And the man stepped forward into the light, his head and body only slightly bowed in respect for his father.

'Why do you disturb me? Can you not see that I have guests?' The Caid's voice quavered slightly.

'It is because you have guests that I have come,' Ali d'Es-Skhira answered. He had moved to his father's side, towering over the old man who seemed suddenly shrunken and much older.

'Where have you been? What trouble have you been stirring up among the people?' The old man's voice sounded frail and peevish. And when Ali did not answer, he said to him, 'Go. I will talk with you later.'

But Ali did not move. Tangier and his own rebellious nature seemed to have destroyed all the respect and obedience due from a Berber son to his father. He pointed to us and said, 'These men come like thieves in the night, O Sidi, to steal from us the wealth of Kasbah

Foum.' He was still speaking in the Arab dialect and his voice throbbed with violence. 'They are evil men and your people have need of their share of the wealth the foreigner may find in the gorge. Do not be deceived by them. They are thieves.'

'We are not thieves,' I answered him in his own tongue, and his eyes blazed at me in the flickering light as he realised that I had understood.

'You thought that my friend was the man you had employed to purchase the deeds of Kasbah Foum,' I continued, still speaking the Arab dialect. 'But this afternoon, when you came to the gorge, you realised that he was not that man, but the true friend of Capitaine Duprez. That is why you have come here now in haste – because you are afraid that your father will discover the truth and will know that this man is the man Duprez chose to prevent you from using Kasbah Foum for your own selfish purposes and not for the benefit of the people of Foum-Skhira. It is you, Si Ali, who are the liar and the thief.'

He took a step forward, his sudden in-drawn breath sounding loud in the stillness of the room. 'It is the talk of a man who is not sure of himself, *sidi*,' he said to his father and gave a quick laugh.

Caid Hassan's eyes were closed, his body relaxed as though trying to gather energy together inside himself. At length he turned to Jan and opened his eyes. 'You have told me much that has convinced me,' he said, speaking in French again. '*Alors*, monsieur, one final thing. Did my friend tell you how it happened that I gave him Kasbah Foum?'

'*Oui*,' Jan said.

'Then tell me the whole story, and I shall be convinced.'

'You took tea with him in the middle of the battle,' Jan said. 'It was then that you first learned of his interest in Kasbah Foum and the ruined city.' The old man nodded and Jan continued.

It had been in the spring of 1934, at the very end of the pacification. The tribes of the district of Foum-Skhira were particularly warlike. Their resistance under Caid Hassan had been stubborn and the fighting had dragged on. Marcel Duprez, then a lieutenant, was among the French forces. He had been an officer of the AI in Algeria and four years before he had come in alone from the desert to prepare the way for the pacification and persuade the tribes that resistance would be pointless. He knew them all. One afternoon, when both sides had withdrawn after a day of particularly savage fighting, he had calmly walked out into the no man's land between the two forces, accompanied by two Legionnaires. They were unarmed and all they carried was the paraphernalia for making tea.

He had set his brazier down midway between the two forces and, after quietly performing the ceremony of the making of the tea, had called upon Hassan and his chiefs to come and drink it with him. And they had come, knowing the officer and admiring his bravery. And over the tea table he had persuaded the Caid and his chiefs that the French must win in the end and that there was no point in continuing the fight. He had then talked about their history and, in particular, the history of the ruined city. As the sun was setting, terms were agreed, but for the sake of his young warriors' pride Caid Hassan had insisted on continuing the battle for one more day, though it was decided that the fighting should not be pressed by either side. Duprez had then gone back to the Legion's lines and all next day the two forces fired on each other with a great deal of noise, but little loss of life. And in the evening Hassan had come to capitulate.

'You were taken to the tent of the general commanding the Legionnaires,' Jan added. 'But you refused to surrender to him. You said you would only surrender to the officer who had come out and served tea to you. They told you that Marcel Duprez had been wounded in the day's fighting. When you heard this, you insisted on being taken to the hospital tent where he lay, and there, with the general looking on, you surrendered to Lieutenant Duprez.' Jan stopped there and stared at the Caid. 'That is how Marcel told it to me. It was because of his interest in the place and his plans that you gave him Kasbah Foum. Also, he loved your people.'

The Caid glanced up at his son. 'Well, Ali, is that correct?' he asked.

Ail said nothing. His face was impassive, but his eyes glinted angrily in the flickering light.

'Say whether it is correct or not,' the Caid said, and there was an edge to his voice.

'It proves nothing,' Ali answered. 'Legard or the Commandant at Agdz could have told the story to him.'

'And all the other things he has told me?' The Caid stared up at his son and I was conscious again of the tension between them. Then he held out his hand to Jan. 'Give me the letter Capitaine Duprez wrote.'

Jan handed him the letter. Lights were brought and placed at the Caid's feet and, whilst he bent forward to read the letter, our glasses were refilled for the third time. The Caid held the letter in such a way that his son, leaning down over his shoulder, could not read it, and when he had finished it, he folded it up and slipped it inside his djellaba. 'This is not a simple matter,' he said, speaking slowly in French. 'There is an old belief that silver was once mined at Kasbah Foum and that belief has been revived because of this American. I had hoped that it would be Capitaine Duprez who developed that place. He would have used it for the benefit of the people here. He had plans for hospitals and schools. I had hoped that perhaps I was giving him the means to make those plans come to life. But now he is dead and you are here in his place. How do I know I can trust you?'

Jan's eyes were steady as they met the old man's gaze. 'I have come to live here,' he said quietly. 'Morocco is my home now. I have no home anywhere else in the world.' He leaned forward slightly, a note of earnestness in his voice. 'If there is wealth at Kasbah Foum, it shall be developed for the benefit of the people here. That is what I promised Marcel, and I shall keep my promise.'

He had spoken seriously and with force. The old man nodded. But he was still uncertain. 'You are not a Frenchman,' he said. 'And you have only recently arrived in Morocco.' He hesitated and then added,

'What you say may be the truth at this moment. But a man easily changes his mind when his roots are not deep in the soil of his promise.'

'I have come to live here,' Jan repeated. 'Morocco is my country now.'

The Caid glanced up at his son and then stared at Jan. It was as though he were weighing up the two men in his mind. There was a long silence. Finally he said, 'Allah be my guide in this. It shall be as Capitaine Duprez wished it. I will give you—'

'No.' Ali's hand descended on his father's shoulder, gripping hold of it, digging his powerful fingers into the old flesh. 'These men are strangers. They want the silver. Nothing more. They do not love our people.'

'I do not believe it,' the old man said, trying vainly to pluck his son's hand from his shoulder.

'Do this thing,' Ali said, 'and, as Allah is my witness, there will be trouble among the people.'

I stared at the scene with a sense of shock, scarcely able to believe that this was a son speaking to his father. In strict Berber etiquette the man should be as a child in the presence of his father, even to the point of making a request through an intermediary. Yet Ali's manner was openly hostile, even contemptuous. The others in the room had noticed it, too. They were whispering and muttering among themselves whilst the two men – father and son – stared at each other. They were like two adversaries who had battled a long time. Finally the Caid gave a little sigh and his eyes, as they turned away, had the vacancy of the very old; it was as though they looked beyond the flickering walls, back through the dim vistas of the past. Slowly he pulled himself to his feet. Ali made no move to help him. His face was cruel with the look of satisfaction. 'My father is tired,' he said in French. 'I must ask you to leave and permit him to rest.'

We waited for the Caid to speak. He stood there a long time, staring into vacancy. And all he said in the end was, 'Yes, I am tired now. We will talk of this some other day.'

Jan started to say something, but Ali silenced him with a gesture. He took his father's arm and led him out. The Caid did not protest. But he paused in the doorway and looked back. His eyes fastened on Jan. And suddenly they weren't vacant any more. They were intensely alive as though he were examining Jan's features for a sign by which he could come to a decision. '*Barak allaho fik*!' he murmured. 'Allah bless you!' His voice was gentle, like a monk saying a benediction. And then he was gone.

They brought lights and escorted us down the narrow stairs, across the open space of the roof top and into the bowels of the kasbah. A hand gripped my arm in the half dark. 'I don't like it,' Jan whispered. 'Ali is in control here.'

His words echoed my thoughts. We were in the dark tunnel of the entrance passage now. It was intensely cold and I tried to convince myself that that was why I was trembling. We passed the rectangular gap lit by the red glow of the brazier. Figures were huddled around it, as they had been when we arrived. They did not seem to have moved. It was just a brief glimpse and then the carbide flames were flickering on blank walls again, silhouetting the cowled, shadowy figures round us.

With a sense of relief I heard the scrape of the securing bar, the creak of the heavy wooden door. There was a rush of fresh air, a murmur of polite farewells, and then we were out in the cold, bright glitter of the star-studded night.

I turned, surprised that we were, in fact, outside the kasbah. For a moment the carbide flares lit the passageway and the swarthy, aquiline faces of our escorts, framed in the cowls of their djellabas. They were outlined for an instant, motionless like a tableau, and then the door thudded to and we were alone. It was only then, whilst the wooden securing bar was being dropped into place, that I realised we had been shown out without our guide.

Jan had noticed it, too. 'Where's Moha?' he asked. His voice was a hoarse whisper. 'Do you think . . .' He didn't finish the sentence, but I saw his hand reach into his breast pocket to make sure he still had the deeds there. 'Do you remember the way back?' he asked.

'I think I can find it,' I said. We had started to walk across the courtyard. We reached the archway and there ahead of us was the dark, towering shape of Ksar Foum-Skhira. There was no singing now. The village seemed as quiet as the grave. We came to the first of the wells and then we were under the shadow of the walls.

We stopped there as though by mutual consent and stood listening. There was no breath of wind and in the stillness my ears picked up small sounds – the grunt of a camel, the cry of a child; sounds that were innocent and yet, because they were not of our own world, disconcerting. 'Do we have to go back through the palmerie?' Jan said. 'Couldn't we cut across the Post and get on to the piste?'

The thought had been in my own mind, too. We both of us felt the need for open country round us. 'All right,' I said and we turned back, skirting the walls of Ksar Foum-Skhira, moving slowly, feeling our way in the darkness. Once we stumbled into a caravan of hobbled camels who champed and belched in the darkness, shifting their positions with nervous grunts.

We were on the south side of the village now and the going was slow, for we were in an area of intense cultivation and all the ground was criss-crossed with small earthworks about a foot high to retain the water when the irrigation ditches were allowed to flood. The palms thinned out and we were suddenly in soft sand. Here the desert had moved in on the palmerie, killing the trees and half burying them in steep dunes. We were a long time getting through the dunes, but at last we came out on to hard, flat desert and there, straight ahead of us, were the walls of the ruined souk.

After that we had no difficulty in finding the piste. We struck away from it to the right, making straight for Kasbah Foum, taking our bearing from the shape of the mountains hunched against the stars. The going was rough and uneven and we stumbled repeatedly over stones or fought our way through patches of dry, brittle scrub. It seemed a long time before we saw the faint glimmer of light that marked the position of the camp. We made steadily towards it and gradually the light separated into two lights and we could see the shape of the bus and, beyond it, the tents.

We couldn't have been more than two or three hundred yards away, when there was a sudden cry – a yell that rose to a scream; high-pitched, sudden and frightening. It was cut off abruptly. I checked at the sound of it and in the same instant the headlights of the bus were switched on. They cut a great swath through the desert night and figures leapt to view, a huddle of Berber men bending over something on the sand of the piste. They straightened up and stood like frozen figures caught in some fearful act that should have remained cloaked by the night.

The horn began to blare then and they broke and ran. I was running, too, now. I shouted something – something in English. I caught a glimpse of White peering out of his tent. There was a stab of flame and the crack of a gun. Then he started to run. We were all running – running towards a still body that lay in a tight bundle on the piste. By the time I reached it, the man's assailants – three or four of them – had vanished into the darkness that lay outside the beam of the headlights.

The body lying on the piste was alive. I saw that at a glance. The man was breathing heavily, his heaving chest thrusting the air out in great gasping sobs. But there was blood on the sand. 'I didn't hit him,' Ed White panted. 'I fired over their heads to scare them.'

'Of course,' I said and turned the man over.

It was our missing guide – Moha. There was a cut above his right eye that extended across his forehead and into his hair. It looked as though a stone had hit him. But down by his waist his djellaba had been ripped open with a knife and there was more blood. Jan thrust me aside, tearing the djellaba apart to expose the torn flesh of the man's buttocks. He examined the wound quickly and then nodded and said, 'He's all right. Just a flesh wound.' He sat back on his haunches, staring at the inert body. The man was still panting as though he had just flopped down after winning a race. 'Why did they attack him?' he asked, twisting his head round and looking up at me.

'I don't know,' I said. 'We'd better get him up to the camp.'

As we lifted him up, I saw he had something tightly clutched in his right hand. It was a roll of paper. I prised the fingers from their grip on it and then we carried him to the larger of the two tents, where we laid him on one of the camp beds. Julie joined us there, carrying a bowl of water and some bandages. Whilst she set to work to bathe the man's wounds, I took the crumpled paper over to the pressure lamp. It was written in Arabic, the writing thin and shaky, but recognisably the same as the writing on the deeds of Kasbah Foum. It was signed Caid El-Hassan d'Es-Skhira.

I touched Jan on the shoulder as he bent over the knife wound in Moha's body. 'Here's the answer to your question,' I said. 'He was attacked because he was bringing you this.'

'What is it?'

'Confirmation of your title to Kasbah Foum.'

'But I thought the Caid—' He almost snatched the paper from me and stood staring down at the writing.

'Does this mean Kasbah Foum belongs to me?' he asked, and he held the paper out to me so that I could read it.

'Yes,' I said, peering over his shoulder. 'The letter states quite clearly that the Caid agrees to Duprez's choice of a successor to the title and requests the authorities to make the necessary registration. It further states that so long as you live, neither he nor any member of his family shall have any interest in the property.' I hesitated.

'What is it?' he asked quickly.

'He doesn't mention your name anywhere. He simply refers to you as "the bearer of the deeds".'

'Probably he couldn't remember my name.' He was holding the paper tightly in his hand as though afraid it might vanish. 'Does it make any difference, do you think?'

'I don't imagine so. You have the deeds and you have his letter confirming the title. It should be all right.'

He shook his head slowly. 'I don't understand, Philip. I never thought he'd agree to it so quickly. I thought he'd want to talk to Legard and make some enquiries . . . What do you think made him do it in such a hurry?'

The man on the camp bed groaned and moved. I turned and saw that he had recovered consciousness. 'Maybe that's your answer,' I said. 'The old man knows his son only too well.'

There was a movement in the entrance to the tent. It was the goat boy from the old Kasbah, Moha's son. He stood there with wide, shocked eyes, staring at his father. Then he looked at us and there was anger and fear on his small, immature features. It was best that the boy knew the truth of it and I asked his father what happened.

Apparently Moha had received a message from the Caid to attend him in his room. He had found him alone on his couch writing a letter. This he had handed to Moha with instructions that it should be delivered to us with all possible speed. He had left with it at once, but, as he came through the palmerie, he realised that he was being followed. He was past his village then and all he could do was run on in the hope of reaching our camp before his pursuers caught up with him. He had almost made it.

We patched him up as best we could and then drove him down the piste to the nearest point to his village and escorted him to his house. Afterwards we drove back to the camp and had a meal. That night I insisted on Jan moving into Ed White's tent. The American was the only one of us who had a gun. I had Julie lock herself in her own compartment and I was just settling down in the passenger seat where I should be within easy reach of the controls, when the door was flung open. It was Jan. He was half-undressed. 'What is it?' I said, for he was excited about something.

'This.' He threw something into my lap.

It was a small blue book – a British passport. And when I opened it I saw that it was Wade's. 'Where did you get this?' I asked him.

'It was in my suitcase.'

'But—' I stared at it. 'How could it be in your suitcase?'

'I think Kostos must have put it there this morning. You remember there was nobody at the camp that first time he came here. We were up in the gorge.'

'But why should he return it to you like that?'

'I don't know. That's what I wanted to ask you.'

It occurred to me then that Kostos, suspecting Jan of murder, was getting rid of the one piece of evidence that involved him.

I didn't tell Jan this, but long after he'd gone back to the tent I was still thinking about it.

The passenger seat made an uncomfortable bed and I slept little. Nothing happened during the night and when dawn broke and showed me the empty expanse of desert leading down to the palmerie, I transferred myself to the bunk and slept through till almost midday.

By the time I had washed and shaved and had some coffee, Jan and Ed White were coming down out of the gorge for their midday meal. They were talking together and laughing as though they had known each other all their lives. Julie came out of the cook tent and stood beside me, looking up the track, watching them approach. 'I'm glad,' she said. I glanced at her and she added, 'If Ed hadn't been as nice as he is . . . it could have been horrible here if they'd hated each other. They're so completely unalike.'

'I don't know,' I said. 'They have things in common. They're both strangers in a new country. And there's the mine. They're both absorbed in Kasbah Foum.'

'Philip!' Jan's voice reached me on the light breeze. He seemed excited. 'We've found it,' he shouted to me. 'We've found the entrance to the mine. There's just one corner of it exposed now, but by tomorrow we'll have cleared it entirely.'

'Fine,' I said and sat down on the step of the bus and lit a cigarette, looking down across the sand and the dusty green of the palmerie to the Post gleaming white in a sudden shaft of sunlight. I was thinking that Legard would be back and wishing I had Jan's power of concentration, his ability to shut his mind to everything but the immediate problem.

'Jan's right,' Ed said. His eyes, too, were aglint with excitement. 'I guess we'll have the entrance fully exposed by tomorrow. After that, all we've got to do is to clear the rock fall inside the shaft.'

Their enthusiasm should have been infectious. But I felt strangely flat. Whether it was the place or just the fact that I saw the situation too clearly, I don't know, but my gaze kept turning away from the gorge down the piste towards the Post.

It was an odd sort of day, almost English. Julie had laid the table out in the open under the fly of the big tent. The air was cool, despite the periodic bursts of sunshine, and there was a lot of cloud about, especially towards the west, where it was banked up in great cotton-wool piles of cumulus. 'I've been ransacking your stores,' Julie said to Ed. 'I opened up some of your tinned turkey. I hope you don't mind.'

'Why should I?' Ed laughed. 'That's what it's there for – to be eaten. Besides I owe you people a debt of gratitude anyway. If Jan hadn't turned up when he did, it would have been a week or more before I found the entrance.'

Julie was standing over the table. 'You boys are so interested in what you're doing, I'll bet you haven't any idea why I'm serving a turkey dinner.' There was laughter in her eyes.

Jan stared at her with a puzzled frown. It was Ed who suddenly laughed out loud. 'I got it,' he cried. 'I got it.' And he thumped the table with his fist. 'By God, it's Christmas Day.' And he jumped to his feet and dived into his tent, coming out with a bottle of cognac. 'Merry Christmas!' He was laughing as he held the bottle up.

'Do you mean it's the twenty-fifth today?' Jan's voice sounded surprised, as though time had crept up on him unawares.

Julie put her hand on his shoulder. 'And tomorrow will be the twenty-sixth. Your wife will be in Ouarzazate tomorrow. Remember?'

He nodded. 'Tomorrow.' He repeated the word as though it were something unattainable and I saw him glance towards the Post.

Julie turned to Ed. 'Afterwards, I'll drive you down to the Post. There's probably some mail for you.'

'Oh, don't bother.' He turned to Jan. 'We got more important things to talk about.'

'But you must have your mail on Christmas Day,' Julie said. 'There'll probably be some presents—'

Something in the expression on his face stopped her. He was standing with the bottle in his hand looking round at the tent. 'I've been too much of a rolling stone, I guess. And I've no family anyway.' He came over to the table. 'Come on, let's have a drink.' And he began to pour us each a cognac.

We drank a toast and then we started to feed. Every now and then Jan glanced uneasily down the piste towards the palmerie. It was as though he were waiting for something to happen, for tomorrow – the future – to catch up with him.

About halfway through the meal he suddenly stopped eating, his eyes staring down towards Foum-Skhira. I turned in my seat and saw a little puff of sand scurrying along the edge of the palmerie. It was a French truck driving fast along the piste towards us. 'Do you think Legard is back?' he asked me.

The truck drew up by the tent in a cloud of sand. The bearded orderly from the Post was at the wheel. 'Bureau,' he shouted, pointing urgently towards Foum-Skhira.

I got up and went over to him. 'Who wants us to go to the Bureau?' I asked the Berber.

But he insisted on sticking to his limited French. 'Bureau,' he repeated. '*Vite, vite*, monsieur.' It was clear that for official business he regarded French as the only language to talk to Europeans.

I asked him again who wanted us, whether Legard was back, but he remained obstinately silent, merely repeating, 'Bureau, monsieur.'

'*Ça va*,' I said and went back to the others. 'I think we'd better go and see what's happened,' I told Jan.

He nodded and we continued our meal in silence, whilst the orderly sat stolidly waiting for us in his truck. When we had finished I got to my feet. 'I'll drive you down, shall I?' Julie said. Ed sat watching us. His freckled face was puckered in a frown. Jan drew me to one side. 'I'm just going to have a word with Ed,' he said. 'Then I'll join you. We've come to an understanding – a sort of gentleman's agreement. I want him to realise that whatever Legard's instructions about me, he's free to go ahead on his own.' He turned back to the table then, and Julie and I went out to the bus.

As we climbed in, she said, 'I've got something for you, Philip. I wanted to give it to you before the meal, but I couldn't because of Ed.' She went through into her section of the caravan and came out carrying one of George's canvases. She turned it round so that I could see it. It was a painting of the ravine at Enfida, showing the Mission house as a small white building above the green of the olive trees. 'It's just to remind you of us – to hang in your room when you build your new Mission.'

I looked at her, feeling a sudden lump in my throat. I took a step forward and then stopped. 'But you've so few of his paintings. I couldn't possibly—'

'Please. I want you to have it. He would have wanted it, too. I told you, he was doing a painting for you when – when it happened.'

She held the canvas out to me and I took it, still staring at her. Her eyes were wide and close to tears. A pulse beat in her throat. 'I don't know what to say,' I murmured. 'I haven't words to thank you.'

'Just remember where I have asked you to hang it.'

I looked down at the painting, not knowing how to tell her what I felt. And then Jan came in. Julie went past me to the driving seat and started the engine. We drove past the tent where Ed White sat alone and down the piste towards Foum-Skhira, the orderly trailing us in his truck.

The day had clouded over completely now and the wind was getting up so that all the sky beyond the palmerie was brown with sand. It was like it had been the day before. But the wind was from the other direction now and as we ran along the edge of the palmerie, we were sheltered from the drifting sand and all we experienced of the rising wind was the thrashing of the palm fronds as the soft, springy trunks bent under the thrust of it, though away to the left, between us and the mountains, the sand was on the move everywhere. We didn't catch the full force of it again until we drove past the remains of the souk and out into the open space between Ksar Foum-Skhira and the forts. And here, besides the sand, the windscreen became spotted with rain.

There was a Citroën parked outside the Bureau and we drew up beside it. 'That's not Legard's car,' Jan said. 'He had a jeep.'

'Maybe somebody gave him a lift back,' I said. But I noticed as we walked past it that it wasn't an Army car. Under its white coating of dust it was black. I had a sudden sense of being trapped and glanced quickly at Jan. He was frowning and his eyes were looking around him uneasily.

The orderly hurried past us, his cloak flapping in the wind. We followed him into the passageway of the Bureau. He went straight to Legard's office, knocked and went in. I hesitated, trying to catch what was being said, but they spoke softly. And then the orderly emerged again and beckoned to us.

Julie went in first and then Jan. They both stopped and there was a look of shocked surprise on Jan's face. Then I, too, was inside the office and the sense of being trapped was overpowering.

It wasn't Legard sitting at the desk in there. It was Bilvidic.

He rose as he saw Julie. 'Mademoiselle Corrigan?' he asked.

Julie nodded. 'We were expecting to see Capitaine Legard.'

'Ah yes. But he stayed to organise his food trucks. My name is Bilvidic, of the Sûreté in Casablanca.' He paused and regarded Jan, who had turned automatically towards the door as though seeking escape. But the door had closed and, standing against it, was a man who was obviously a policeman in plain clothes. He was tall, thick-set, with sallow features and a flattened nose. Bilvidic motioned Julie to a seat. 'Tell me, Mademoiselle Corrigan, how long have you known this gentleman?' He indicated Jan.

'Not very long,' Julie answered. 'Why?'

'And all the time you have known him as Dr Kavan?'

'Yes.'

'And you agreed to drive him down here to Foum-Skhira?'

'Yes.'

'Why?'

'Miss Corrigan has nothing to do with this business,'

I said quickly. 'If you want to ask questions, please put them to me.'

'Very well, monsieur. Since you wish it.' Bilvidic's grey eyes stared at me frostily over their little pouches. 'Why did you lie to me? Why do you say this man has flown from England? You knew that we would check.'

I looked across at Jan. But he didn't say anything. He was standing with his hands clasped behind his back, his head slightly bowed; quite still like a man considering a problem.

Bilvidic, waiting, produced his pack of American cigarettes and lit himself one. '*Eh bien*,' he said, and sat down on the corner of the desk and inhaled the smoke from his cigarette. 'Since you do not wish to talk, I will tell you what we have been doing. First we check with Paris and London. There is no Dr Kavan leaving London Airport on the night of the eighteenth. There is no Dr Kavan leaving Orly Airport in Paris for Casablanca on the morning of the nineteenth.' He glanced at Jan. 'But you were on that flight from Tangier to Casablanca and you are shown on the list of passengers as having booked through from Paris.' He made little clicking noises with his tongue and his eyes switched to me. 'Why did you do it, Monsieur Latham? It was stupid of you. Now you must come to Casablanca for questioning.' He turned to Jan. '*Alors*, monsieur. Your name is Roland Tregareth Wade, yes? And you are the owner of the yacht that is wrecked near Tangier on the night of the eighteenth.'

I waited for Jan to deny it, but he didn't speak.

'What's the charge?' I asked and my voice sounded nervous for I thought it would be murder.

But Bilvidic said, 'There is no charge. He is being held for questioning. That is all. And we have to be in Casablanca by the morning.'

'By tomorrow morning?' It was over three hundred miles across the mountains. 'It means driving all night. If there's no charge, surely it isn't as urgent—'

'My headquarters insist that we are there by the morning.'

'But why?'

'It is nothing to do with us, monsieur. I do not wish to drive through the night any more than you do. Nor do I enjoy being here in the desert for Christmas Day,' he added sharply. 'It is because of the British authorities. This man' – he nodded towards Jan – 'has been masquerading as Dr Kavan. They insist that the matter of his identity is resolved immediately. If you do not like it, then you have only your government to blame.'

'But I tell you he *is* Dr Kavan.'

'*Non, non.*' He shook his head. 'It is no good, monsieur. Undoubtedly he is Wade.' He tapped a sheaf of notes that lay in front of him on the desk. 'You see, the body of Dr Jan Kavan was washed up on the coast of Portugal near Cape St Vincent four days ago.'

There was a sudden silence in the room. Jan had moved forward slightly as though to ask a question. But now his eyes were fixed on the floor again. I was conscious of the tenseness of his body.

Bilvidic rose and moved behind the desk. 'Tell me,

monsieur, how much did Kavan tell you about himself when he applied for the post of doctor at your Mission?'

'Not very much,' I said. 'Just that he was a qualified doctor and that—'

'He did not tell you he was a famous scientist? Ah, well then, you would not appreciate the interest this matter has aroused. It is in all the British papers. But now that his body has been discovered his disappearance is no longer a mystery.'

'If you're certain the body was from the *Gay Juliet*, then it is Wade's body.' I looked across at Jan. Why the devil didn't he say something? 'What makes them think it's Kavan's?' I asked Bilvidic.

'It is definite, monsieur. We have a full report at headquarters. The state of the body, of course, was not good. But the general description is exact, and he is wearing a windbreaker purchased in Dur-ham, which is where Kavan worked. It even had the name Kavan on it and in the pocket is a watch inscribed in Czech which was given to Kavan by his wife.' He shook his head. 'There is absolutely no doubt, monsieur. But the British insist that we check the identity of your friend here, and also there is the matter of illegal entry into Morocco.'

'Listen, monsieur,' I said. 'I assure you that this man is Kavan. There were two men on the boat – Kavan and Wade. It was Kavan I pulled out of the sea at Jews' Bay.'

He shrugged his shoulders. 'Tell me one thing,' he said. 'Did you ever meet this Dr Kavan – when you engaged him to be your doctor, for instance?'

'No. It was all arranged by letter.'

'Exactly. In fact, you have never seen the real Dr Kavan. You have no idea what he looks like.'

'I assure you—'

But he cut me short, leaning quickly forward. 'Have you had occasion to call on this gentleman's services as a doctor?'

'No, not personally, but when—'

'So you do not know if he is a doctor or not. Have you ever heard him speak Czech?' I looked across at Kavan. 'Well, have you, monsieur? Has he ever spoken one word of Czech since you have known him?'

'It's no use, Philip,' Jan said quietly, speaking in English.

'Oh, don't be a fool. All you've got to do is talk to him in your own language.'

'I know.'

'Don't you realise what this may lead to?'

He didn't answer me, but turned away towards the window and stood there, staring out at the drab expanse of rainswept sand. He seemed suddenly to have withdrawn from the room.

I was angry and a little scared. 'Are you crazy?' And when he still said nothing, I turned back to Bilvidic. 'I give you my word that this man is Kavan,' I told him in French.

He frowned, annoyed at my insistence. 'You admit, monsieur, that he is the man you rescued from the sea at Tangier?'

I nodded.

'And he is also the man who shared your room at the

Hotel Malabata, the man you put on the plane at Tangier Airport?'

'Yes.'

'And yet you still insist that he is Kavan?'

'Yes.'

'Very well.' He shrugged his shoulders. 'Then we will settle it finally.' He nodded to the plain-clothes man standing against the door, and he opened it and disappeared. There was a momentary silence as we waited, and then footsteps sounded on the bare concrete of the passage. There was the man's heavy tread, and also the shorter, lighter tap of a woman's heels.

We were all of us facing the door as it was thrust open and she entered. It was Karen Kavan and she stopped in the doorway, her face frozen with the shock of seeing us there. Her gaze went straight to Jan. But he made no move. He just stood there, looking at her, his face expressionless. She turned to me then. There was a desperate, bewildered look in her eyes – it was as though she was pleading for me to tell her what to do.

And then Bilvidic's voice cut the stillness of the room. 'One question, madame.' He pointed to Jan. 'Is this man your husband?'

I saw her hesitate. I thought she was going to tell him the truth. But then Jan turned away again towards the window and her face froze so that there was no sign of recognition in it. 'No.' She was looking straight at the detective, her face white and strained, just as it had been in the café by the waterfront in Tangier, and she was twisting at the gold band of her wedding ring. Her features might have been chiselled out of stone, they were so controlled.

'Have you ever seen him before?'

'Yes.' Her voice was scarcely above a whisper.

'What is his name, please?'

Again the momentary hesitation. 'So far as I know it is Monsieur Wade.'

'Thank you.' Bilvidic nodded and the plain-clothes man opened the door for her. She paused a moment. Then she went quickly out, and Jan made no move to stop her going. He had turned at the sound of her footsteps, that was all, and he stood there, staring at the open doorway through which she had passed, his face empty of all expression. I couldn't stand it.

'For God's sake!' I cried. 'Tell them who you are. Have them bring your wife back again. Don't you see what you're doing to her?'

I had spoken in English, but he replied in French. 'It is useless.' His voice was harsher now, suddenly determined.

I stared at him. If he had just said one word to her. I turned to Bilvidic. 'Monsieur. I want you to bring the girl back. These two—'

'Philip!' Jan's voice was suddenly angry. 'This is nothing to do with you. Keep out of it. You hear?' He turned to Bilvidic and said in French: 'You say I'm not under arrest?'

'No.'

'I have important work to do here. We're opening up a silver mine. Since I'm not under arrest, is there any reason why I should have to come to Casablanca with you?'

Bilvidic shrugged his shoulders and smiled coldly. 'If you refuse to accompany me voluntarily, then I have orders to arrest you on a charge of entering Maroc under another man's name and with another man's papers.'

'I see.' Jan hesitated and then turned towards the door. 'Very well. The sooner we get started the better,' he said and his voice sounded tense. I listened to his footsteps going slowly down the passage. He didn't pause as he went out to the waiting car.

'Monsieur?' Bilvidic was looking at me. His assistant came in and he ordered him to follow Jan. I glanced at Julie. She was looking pale and a little scared.

'What do you want me to do, Philip?' Her voice trembled slightly. 'There must be something I can do?'

'Do you think you could drive the bus alone as far as Ouarzazate?'

'Of course.'

'Go to the *gîte d'étapes* there and phone the British Consul at Rabat. Tell him the whole thing. Make him understand that this man is Dr Kavan.'

'But how do you know—' She stopped abruptly. But she had said enough. I suddenly realised that she, too, wasn't certain about Jan's identity. 'I'm worried about you,' she said. 'Not him.'

'Just do as I ask.'

She nodded. 'Yes, of course. And then I'll come on to Casa.'

'It's too long a drive.'

'I'll leave the bus at Ouarzazate and come on by CTM.' And then she smiled. 'Don't worry. I'll be there to bail you out.'

Bilvidic must have understood the gist of what we had been saying. 'If you are going to Ouarzazate, mademoiselle,' he said, 'then perhaps you will be so kind as to take Madame Kavan with you. She also has to go to Ouarzazate . . .'

I slipped out of the office and walked down the passage. I had seen Karen standing by the open door of one of the other offices. She heard me coming towards her and turned. Then she went back into the office. When I reached the door she was standing by the window, staring out at the desert. She couldn't see the car from there. She was staring out at nothing, deliberately trying to avoid me. She was quite still and her face was set hard like a mask.

I went over to her. 'Why on earth did you say he was Wade?' I said. 'Can't you see it doesn't matter any more? You're safe. You're both of you safe. There was no point in it.' She stared at me as though I were a stranger to her. 'For goodness' sake tell them the truth. I don't know what Jan's idea is, but it'll only land him in real trouble. Come back now and tell Bilvidic who Jan is.'

But she made no move. 'If that is what he wants, he would have spoken to me.' She said it flatly and without hope.

'He doesn't understand,' I said. 'He doesn't know what he's doing. A body has been found in Portugal and sooner or later the police will—'

'It is my husband's body.' Her voice was toneless as though she was repeating something in her sleep.

'Oh, for God's sake!' I said, and I caught hold of her and turned her towards me. 'Go out to the car and talk to him. Tell Bilvidic the truth.'

She stared up at me, her eyes wide with sudden hostility. I thought for a moment she was going to struggle, but then her body went slack under my hands and her eyes were blank. It was as though she had withdrawn completely inside herself. 'Don't you understand?' I cried, shaking her. 'If you let the police go on thinking he's Wade, he'll face a serious charge. Wade had a motive for killing your husband. For God's sake tell them who he is.'

But she said nothing and her face remained quite blank. I let her go then with a feeling of hopelessness. Years of living in a police state had taught her this one refuge – silence. But surely there was some way I could persuade her. 'You're not in Czechoslovakia now,' I said. 'Please try and understand that I want to help you.'

She remained quite still, her lips tight shut. It was as though I hadn't spoken. She was as obstinately silent as Jan had been earlier. I felt a sense of futility and exasperation. 'Can't you understand how the police—' I stopped there, for footsteps sounded in the passage.

'You are ready, monsieur?' It was Bilvidic. He had paused by the open door, waiting for me. I glanced at Karen. There were tears welling from the corners of her eyes. I was shocked. I'd never seen her cry before. 'Tell him now,' I said.

But she turned her head away. It was a movement of denial, a final refusal. 'Come, monsieur,' Bilvidic said.

I turned then and went to the door. There was nothing more I could do. 'Madame,' Bilvidic said, speaking to Karen. 'I have arranged with Mademoiselle Corrigan for you to travel with her. There is not room for more than four in the Citroën. She will take you to Ouarzazate.'

'Thank you, monsieur.' Her voice was no more than a whisper.

Bilvidic hesitated. Then he touched my arm and led me out to the car. '*La pauvre petite*,' he said and his voice was softened by sudden pity for her. 'She had hoped so much that her husband wasn't dead.'

I didn't say anything. There was no longer any point. The two of them together had effectively convinced Bilvidic. I was glad Karen was going with Julie. It might help, and anyway it meant that she and Jan wouldn't be sitting side-by-side for hours on end in the enclosed space of the car stubbornly refusing to acknowledge each other. When we reached the Citroën Jan was already seated in the back with the second police officer. It was raining and the wind was thrashing through the palmerie. There wasn't a soul in sight. The forts, the souk, the track leading down to Ksar Foum-Skhira – it was all empty and lifeless.

'It is strange weather for this country,' Bilvidic said. 'I have never known such a winter.' He said it for the sake of making conversation. He motioned me into the passenger seat and went round to the other side of the car. He glanced towards the mountains, his eyes shuttered against the rain. Then he shrugged his shoulders and climbed in behind the wheel.

Jan was sitting, staring straight in front of him. He didn't look at me. He didn't seem to be looking at anything. His eyes were quite blank and he seemed to have withdrawn inside himself as his wife had done and again I was conscious of this as something learned in a country that was outside of my experience, in a police state. It was as though the line of mental contact between us had been suddenly cut.

The engine roared and we swung round, slithering on the wet sand, spraying it up behind us. I glanced back and saw Julie and Karen walking out towards the bus. I looked at Jan again. But he hadn't moved. He was staring straight ahead; not at the piste, nor at the mountains – rather at the future that was in his mind. A jagged line of lightning stabbed the darkness of the sky above the gorge and the noise of thunder went rumbling through the hills. Then the rain came down and the mountains were blotted out.

CHAPTER THREE

A **gust** of rain swept over us as we went out past the Foreign Legion fort. It drummed on the bonnet and stabbed into the sand. A grey murk enveloped us. Looking back I saw the old bus turn and begin to lumber along in our wake. The rain came in gusts. Nobody in the car talked. The only sound was the click-click of the windscreen wipers. The wheels spun in a soft patch, flinging sand up in sheets like a brown spray. I wondered how the bus would behave on the sticky surface of the piste. It was a heavy vehicle for a girl to drive and the going would be bad through the mountains unless the rain eased up. 'You should have let me go with Mademoiselle Corrigan,' I told Bilvidic angrily. I was thinking of the section of road overhanging the gorge where the road gang had been working.

He shrugged his shoulders. 'I am sorry. But it is not possible. They will be all right.'

A heavier gust hit the car. The wheels slithered and spun. The rain was turning the powdered sand of the piste to a thick, red paste. The mountains were blotted out entirely. I glanced back. I could see nothing but wet sand and rain through the rear window. The bus, like the mountains, had disappeared from sight and I cursed the Frenchman under my breath. It was no weather in which to make two girls drive a heavy vehicle over mountains on a narrow, treacherous track. Once more I tried to persuade him to let me change places with Karen and keep Julie company in the bus, but he shook his head. '*Non*, monsieur. We must be in Casablanca by this morning.'

'You'll never make it in this weather. You might just as well . . .' The full weight of the storm hit us then and the rest of the sentence was drowned in the roar of the rain. It sheeted down, bouncing on the bonnet, drumming on the roof, cutting visibility to practically nil. The wheels churned in the mud of the piste. The car slithered and swayed. And then the rain slackened again and there were the mountains right ahead of us.

We reached the harder surface at the foot of the mountains and began to climb. Away to the left I saw the watch tower above Kasbah Foum, and the debris of the ruined city gleamed blackly through the rain. Sections of the track were running with water and in places there was a soft surface of mud. The car had front-wheel drive and the engine laboured as the wheels spun in the soft patches. We reached the spot where the road had been repaired and I looked down into the black gulf of the gorge. The whole place seemed to be streaming with water and, on the remote fringe of visibility, I saw the towers of Kasbah Foum looking withdrawn and hostile as they stood guard over the entrance to the gorge.

'If we could have had two more days.' There was a note of bitterness in Jan's voice as he said this and he was leaning forward in his seat, peering down the mist-wrapped length of the gorge.

Then we had turned the corner under the cliff overhang and the gorge was behind us. Far below us down the mountain slope, I glimpsed the bus nosing its way across the flat valley floor. Then it was lost in a curtain of rain. 'They'll never make it,' I said as the Citroën's wheels spun again on a soft patch and Bilvidic fought the wheel to regain control of the car.

'Then they will stop and wait,' he replied impatiently. 'The girl is not a fool. She will not try it if it is not possible.'

But I wasn't sure. Julie knew it was important for her to contact the British Consul. She'd go on as long as she thought there was a chance of getting through. And Karen was with her. Karen would want to go on, too. 'I think we should stop,' I said.

'No.'

'They could go over the edge in these soft patches.'

'Stop worrying, monsieur. They will be all right. They will be going uphill. Downhill, it would be different.'

'You forget that the bus has rear-wheel drive. You can easily skid the back wheels. . . .'

'They will be all right, I tell you,' he repeated angrily. And then he was fighting the wheel again and suddenly the whole road ahead was blotted out by another storm.

•
•

It swept down on us like a cloudburst, drumming on the car, beating at it as though trying to flatten it into the mud of the piste. A little spill of stones slithered in a trickle of water down the bank to our right. It had become very dark and all we could see was the rain and a few yards of mountain stretching ahead of us. The rain was solid like a million steel rods thrust at an angle into the ground. The car juddered, the engine roared. Mud spurted up past my window as the wheels clawed at the surface.

I glanced back. I didn't know what I imagined I would be able to see. I was scared for Julie. I wanted to reassure myself that the bus was all right. But I could see nothing – only the rods of rain gleaming dull like steel against the utter blackness of the storm. I turned and gripped Bilvidic's arm. 'You must wait,' I shouted at him. 'You must wait for them.'

He glanced at me quickly, his eyes sharp and alert, measuring my mood. But he drove on. It was then that I became conscious of Jan's increasing restlessness in the back. He kept twisting round and peering out through the rear window. Once, when I turned round, I met his eyes. 'Do something!' he said. He looked worried. He was thinking of Karen back there with Julie in the bus.

We turned a bend that overlooked the gorge and began to climb a straight stretch of track beside a shallow rock cliff down which rainwater streamed, glistening blackly. 'Do something to stop him, can't you?' he said urgently. We were coming up to the point where the piste hair-pinned round the very head of the gorge. I caught hold of Bilvidic's arm. 'You must stop,' I shouted at him. 'If you don't stop . . .' There was a blinding flash of lightning and the crash of thunder right overhead.

'*Attention*, Georges!' Bilvidic threw my hand off as he called the warning to his assistant. I heard Jan struggling in the back and then I reached for the ignition key. Bilvidic caught hold of my hand. The car swayed wildly. We were coming up to the bend now and as I flung him off and grabbed again for the key, the wheels hit a stone and suddenly the rock wall of the cliff closed in against my window. There was a crash and I was flung forward, striking my head against the windscreen. The car stopped dead. 'Imbecile!' Bilvidic screamed at me. 'Imbecile!'

I struggled back into my seat, momentarily dazed. 'Look what you have done!' Bilvidic's face was white with anger. All the right-hand wing and the front of the bonnet were crumpled.

'If you'd stopped when I asked you—' I said.

He gave an order to his assistant. It wasn't really necessary for he already had Jan pinned down by his arm. The starter whined. But nothing happened. Bilvidic kept his finger on the button. The motor went on and on, but the engine didn't fire. It was completely dead. The rain was torrential, water pouring everywhere, glistening on the rocks, running in little streams. Now that the engine was silent, we could hear it: the hiss of the rain, the drumming of it on the tin body of the car, the little rushing noises of water carrying small stones down the mountain.

And then suddenly all movement ceased inside the

car. The rain had lifted slightly and we could see the bend ahead. A brown flood of water was pouring across it, frothing white as it plunged on down the gorge. All the water from the slopes that formed the very beginning of the gorge was collected in the bottom of the V to form a torrent that was slowly eating into the piste. Already there was a jagged gap and, whilst we sat and watched, it widened as the rocks that formed its foundation were shifted and rolled down into the gorge. There had been a culvert there once, but that was gone, or else the weight of water was too great. And every minute the volume of it and the noise of it seemed to grow.

Jan began struggling again in the back. 'Let me go!' he shouted. 'Philip. We must get back to the bus.'

Bilvidic gave an order to his assistant. One of the rear doors of the car was thrust open and I saw Jan standing there in the rain, staring back down the piste. 'In all the years I have lived in Morocco,' Bilvidic said, 'I have never known a storm like this.' He got out of the car then. He had given up all hope of reaching Casablanca. The piste was hopelessly cut. It would take several days to repair it. I scrambled across the driving seat and got out. 'I think we should get back and stop Mademoiselle Corrigan from coming up,' Bilvidic said.

I nodded. 'Come on!' Jan called to me. He had already started off down the piste. Bilvidic and his assistant were searching in the car for their raincoats. I started to run after Jan, splashing through the water that ran almost ankle-deep down the rutted surface of the track. I was soaked through and steaming by the time I caught up with him. Side by side we went back down the piste, loping down with long strides, our shoes slithering and squelching through the mud and water. Neither of us spoke. We were both intent on getting back down the mountain as fast as possible. The rain died away, but we scarcely noticed it. We were hurrying down through a dead world of mist and streaming rock, and the sound of water was all about us.

The mist gradually lightened and a gleam of warmth softened the blackness of the mountain sides. A wind sprang up, the mist swirled streamers over our heads, and then abruptly it cleared and we were in bright sunshine. All the wet, glistening landscape of rock smiled at us. But above and behind us the sky was black with storm.

And then we saw the bus. It was caught on a bend far below us. The sound of its engine, revving violently, came up to us faintly on the wind, an angry sound like a buzz-saw. But we lost it almost immediately in the roar of a small avalanche of stone on the other side of the gorge.

'The sooner we're out of these mountains the better,' Jan panted.

We had reached the section that had only just been repaired. All along under the cliff face little cascades of rock had built themselves up into small piles and the outer edge of the new-made piste was already sliding away into the gorge. Kasbah Foum was picked out in sunshine as we had first seen it and from far below came the steady, insistent roar of water.

We finally found the bus at the next bend. It had

slewed half across the track, its wheels deep in mud. Karen was kicking rocks under the spinning tyres as Julie revved the engine. The engine died away as they saw us coming down the track towards them. Karen stood quite still, almost breathless, as though she couldn't believe it was true.

Jan had stopped. I glanced back over my shoulder. Bilvidic and his assistant weren't in sight yet. They knew we couldn't escape. 'Listen, Philip.' Jan gripped by arm. 'I'm going back to Kasbah Foum. The whole valley is cut off now. It may be several days . . .' He was staring down towards Karen. 'In two days we might have that shaft opened up.'

'That won't do you much good,' I said. 'Not now.'

'Who knows?' He looked up at me and he was smiling. He seemed suddenly to have found himself. It was as though at this moment, with his wife standing there waiting for him to come to her, anything was possible. 'I'll take Karen with me,' he said. 'At least we'll have a little time together. . . .' He glanced back up the track. The rain was closing in again and visibility was lessening. Then he started down towards the bus. 'Karen!' he called. 'Karen!'

She came running to meet him then. They were both running and he was calling her name and she was answering him, her eyes shining, her face suddenly quite beautiful. They met in the rain and the mud there and he caught her in his arms, hugging her to him.

And then they parted, almost guiltily, as though they hadn't a right to be so happy. They stood there, looking at each other a little shyly, their hands locked, talking quietly.

I turned away, looking down towards Kasbah Foum. I could just see the top of the watch tower. The tumbled rocks of the mountainside would be hard going. Then the rain swept over the tower, blotting it out. 'You two had better get going,' I said. 'It's a goodish way to the camp.'

'Oh, we'll make it before dark,' Jan answered. He said it as though he were going on a picnic, his voice was so full of happiness.

'What do you want me to tell Bilvidic?'

'Tell him Monsieur Wade has gone down to Kasbah Foum.' He laughed, but I knew he meant it. He was looking up at the curtain of rain that was sweeping over us and there was an obstinate set to his mouth. Then he called to Karen who had run back to the bus and was speaking urgently to Julie. Jan ran down to her and took her hand, and together they crossed the Piste and dropped on to the steep slope of the mountainside.

'Don't forget, please,' Karen called back to Julie.

In a moment the two of them had disappeared into the driving mist of rain. 'What happened up there?' Julie called out to me from the cab of the bus. 'Couldn't you get through?'

I climbed in beside her and was in the middle of explaining to her about the crash and the piste being washed away when a voice hailed us out of the rain. It was Bilvidic. He was panting and his thinning hair was plastered down by the rain. 'Where's Wade?' he demanded, his eyes searching the roadway and the limited area of mountainside visible in the downpour. He wrenched open the door of the bus. 'Where is he?' he demanded angrily.

'He's gone to Kasbah Foum,' I told him.

'I don't believe you. Why should he do that? He cannot go down the mountain in this weather. Georges!' His assistant came running and he ordered him to search the vicinity. 'The fool!' he exclaimed angrily. 'He cannot go far in this rain. He cannot sleep on the mountain.' He looked at Julie. 'And where is Madame Kavan? Why is she not with you?'

I started to explain, but Julie stopped me. 'She's not very well,' she told him. 'She's resting.'

'Where?' Bilvidic demanded suspiciously and he began to climb into the bus.

'*Non, non*, monsieur,' she said quickly. 'I cannot allow you to disturb her. She is lying down on my bed in the rear compartment. She is quite exhausted, poor thing.' And then she added, 'It was a great shock to her to discover that that man is not her husband. She had hoped . . . You understand, monsieur?'

Bilvidic nodded, clicking his tongue sympathetically. 'Of course, mademoiselle. I should have realised.' He jumped back on to the piste and began to walk up it, shouting, 'Wade! Wade!'

I turned to Julie then. 'Why did you say that, about Karen?'

'She asked me to. Bilvidic would be suspicious if he knew she'd gone off to Kasbah Foum with a man who is supposed to be a stranger to her.'

'It's madness,' I said.

Julie shrugged her shoulders. 'It was what she wanted, anyway.'

That meant it was what Jan wanted. 'So he's determined to go through with it,' I said and leaned back in the seat, staring at the water streaming down the piste and wondering what would be the end of it all. The storm was passing now and in a moment there was a gleam of sunshine. Bilvidic abandoned the search then. 'He cannot get out of the valley, unless he walks. And if he does that one of the Military Posts will soon be notified.' He stood for a moment staring down towards Kasbah Foum. Then he turned abruptly. 'Now we will go back to the Post. I must phone the Chef de Territoire.'

With him guiding me, I started to back the bus down the hill. There was no room to turn and I had to go on backing until we reached the level sand at the foot of the mountains. And there we bogged down. The piste was a sea of mud, and even the sand beside it was impassable, for it was layered with two inches of glutinous paste that filled the treads of the tyres.

Finally Bilvidic left with his assistant for the Post. It was beginning to get dark and Julie and I watched the two Frenchmen go, sitting in the bus in our stockinged feet, thankful we hadn't got to trudge three miles through that mud.

We spent the night where we were, and in the morning the sun shone out of a clear sky. The air was clean and fresh after the rain. We did the chores and then sat around waiting for the piste to dry, not talking much, just enjoying the sense of being alone. It was the first time Julie and I had been alone together and I think we both felt that these were precious, stolen hours. 'You might have been in Casablanca now,' Julie said once. 'I loathe Casablanca.'

Everybody loathes Casablanca. The thought of the place emphasised the clean beauty of this desert country. The fact that we were cut off here gave it an unreal quality. I glanced at her, seeing the smooth, clear-cut line of her features, the black hair swept back and softly curving to her shoulders. She looked as fresh and sparkling as the day. 'When we've got ourselves out of the mess we're in, I'd like to come down here again and travel through this country.'

She looked at me. 'Like this?' And I knew she meant the two of us and the old bus. She smiled. 'Yes, let's do that.' And she looked away again towards the mountains.

The desert sand dried quickly and by midday we were able to travel on it. As I drove across the open space between the forts, I saw that the French truck was still parked outside the Bureau. Its bonnet was up and both the orderly and Bilvidic's assistant were working on the engine. There was a big crowd gathered by the ruins of the souk. They stared at us in silence as we drove by, a sullen, menacing group. And as we skirted Ksar Foum-Skhira along the edge of the palmerie there seemed a brooding stillness. There was nobody drawing water at the wells and, apart from a few children, nobody moved outside the walls.

'The village looks deserted,' Julie said. 'It's too

quiet.' Her voice sounded taut and strained and I remembered her reaction on our first arrival.

'They're short of food,' I said. 'That's all. As soon as the piste is open again and the food trucks—'

'It isn't that. Something's happened. They wouldn't all be gathered round the souk like that if it hadn't.'

I thought her sudden change of mood was due to the fact that in a few minutes now we should have rejoined Jan and Karen and that the reality of the situation would have closed round us again. 'I'd rather be here than in Casablanca anyway,' I said, trying to make a joke of it.

But all she said was, 'I wish Legard were here.'

The camp looked empty when we reached it. The sides of the tents had been rolled up; clothes and bedding were laid out to air in the sun. The stream was much wider now, a surging flood of rust-red water. As we got down, Karen appeared at the entrance to the cook tent and waved to us. I barely recognised her. She was wearing a pair of Ed White's khaki trousers and a bush shirt several sizes too large for her. She was bare-foot, trousers rolled up almost to her knees and the waist held in by a broad leather belt. 'You look like a castaway,' Julie said.

She laughed. 'I'm cooking. Isn't it wonderful!' She tossed back her hair, her eyes sparkling. I tried to see in her the girl who had sat waiting in José's café in Tangier. But it was impossible. She was somehow different, more alive, almost beautiful. 'Where's your husband?' I asked.

'He is up in the gorge.' The laughter died out of her eyes. 'And please, you must not call him my husband. He has told Ed that his name is Wade. We are sleeping in different tents and we came here together only because we got separated from the rest of you coming down the mountain.' She hesitated. 'I have to be very careful not to give Jan away. I keep my eyes on the ground and never look at him when he is here. It is not easy after so long.'

'Good God!' I said. I was appalled at the self-control required. It shocked me that he'd asked it of her. 'And what about Ed?' I asked. 'Is he convinced?'

'I don't know whether he is convinced or not. He doesn't say much. He thinks only of the work up there in the gorge. I don't think he cares.'

'Jan's being a fool,' I said. 'You know about this body they've found. You realise the risk he's running?'

She nodded. 'Yes. I realise.'

'Have you talked to him about it?'

'Yes, we have talked.'

'And you didn't try to dissuade him?'

'No.' She hesitated, and then said, 'Please. You must try to understand. They think Jan Kavan is dead. It is the answer to everything.' She stared up into my face, her eyes pleading. 'You saved his life. You got him out of Tangier. You must help him now.'

'How?' I asked. 'What does he want me to do?'

From the entrance to the gorge came the muffled thud of an explosion. Karen turned her head sharply, an anxious expression on her face.

'What are they doing?' Julie asked.

'Blasting. He and the American. They have cleared the entrance to the mine and they are blasting to break up the rock falls inside the shaft so that they can clear it away by hand. He warned me what they were doing, but I don't like it. When we came down last night we went too far to the right and had to come down the shoulder of the gorge. All the rock there is crumbling away and the stones kept moving under our feet.'

'Have you been up into the gorge?' I asked her.

'Yes.' She gave a shudder. 'I don't like the place. It is cold and a little frightening. I prefer to cook.' She said it with a little laugh. And then she looked at me, her face serious again. 'That American – why is he so afraid?'

'Afraid of what?' I asked.

'I don't know. But last night, when we got here, he was waiting for us by his tent with a gun in his hand. He was terribly pleased to see us. I think he's frightened to be here by himself.'

'I'm not surprised,' Julie said. 'I would be myself.'

They were both of them looking up towards the gorge. Then Karen began to collect the blankets and fold them. Julie went to help her and I walked up the track into the gorge. Water was pouring in a cascade over the lip of the lake. It was a violent brick red. The whole gorge was full of the sound of water seeping down from above and it was cold and dank despite the noonday heat of the sun. The bull-dozers stood idle. There was no sign of Jan or Ed White. But the rubble had been cleared from the base of the cliff to expose a round opening from which a cloud of rock dust drifted. It was like the entrance to a cave. 'Jan!' I shouted. 'Jan!' There was no answer, but back from the wall of the gorge opposite came the echo – *Jan! Jan!*

I walked towards the entrance to the mine. A little

pile of clothing lay beside a plain deal box which was marked in red – EXPLOSIVES: Danger – Handle with Care. The top of it had been ripped off to expose cartridges of dynamite with slow-match fuses. The dust was thick by the shaft entrance, hanging like an iridescent cloud where the sunlight struck through from above. There was the sound of a stone shifting and Ed White appeared, staggering under the weight of a rock he was carrying. 'Oh, it's you, Latham.' He dropped the rock on to a pile they had made just outside the entrance. 'I thought I heard somebody call.' He glanced up at the cliff top on the far side of the gorge, and then he gave a quick, nervous hitch to his trousers and came over. He was stripped to the waist and the dust had caked on the sweat of his body in a white film. He had his gun fastened to his belt. 'Well, we've made some progress since yesterday. We've cleared the entrance and we're working on the rock falls now. But we need some local labour. Wade thought you might help there. You know the language.'

'He's told you then?' I asked tentatively.

'About his name? Yeah, he told me.'

'It must have come as a bit of a shock to you.'

He looked at me for a moment and then said, 'Between you and me I don't care what he calls himself. All I'm interested in is getting through those falls before my dough runs out. This is a new country and what a man was before he came out here doesn't interest me. All I know is I like the guy and we get on together. Have done from the first. Which was more than I expected from the tone of his letters,' he added. And then he hitched up his belt and turned away towards the entrance to the shaft.

At that moment Jan emerged, blinking in the sunlight. 'Philip!' He came quickly forward. He, too, was stripped to the waist and the dust was white on his thick, hairy body. 'I'm so glad you've come. We need your help.' He stopped and his voice was suddenly nervous. 'Bilvidic isn't down at the camp, is he?'

'No.'

'That's all right.' It was almost a sigh of relief. 'Look! We need men up here. There's tons of rock to be hauled. We need twenty men at least.' The eagerness was back in his voice again. 'I thought if you could go down and have a word with Moha, maybe we could hire men from his village.' He seemed to have no thought in his mind except the opening up of the shaft. 'Come here. I want to show you something.' He switched on the big torch he had slung on his belt and dived back into the shaft.

'What is it?' I asked Ed, for Jan's voice had been excited.

'He's found traces of silver,' he said and he pushed me towards the shaft entrance. 'You go ahead. I'll follow.' I climbed the piled-up debris and ducked into the entrance to the shaft. It was dark inside and the air was thick with dust. The yellow light of Jan's torch flashed ahead. We went in about forty feet and then we were crawling over piles of broken rock. 'You see,' Jan said. 'The roof collapsed. We're having to blast and clear by hand. Now. Look here.' He had stopped and was directing the beam of his torch into a cavity half blocked by the fallen roof. 'We've just cleared this.' He gripped my arm and thrust me forward.

The cavity seemed to be a long, narrow fissure in the rock. I couldn't see it very well. Only a small part of it was so far exposed. But it ran well back, for the beam of the torch failed to reach the end of it. 'What is it?' I asked.

'Part of the mine,' Jan said. 'It's where a seam of ore has been removed.'

'How do you know?'

He shifted the beam of the torch to the sides of the fissures. 'See the marks of their tools. And look at this.' He pulled a piece of crumbled rock from his pocket. 'That's polybasite – a complex ore, but one where the extraction of the silver is a simple, quite primitive process. Probably that's what Marcel found.'

I turned to Ed. 'Do you agree with him?'

'I wouldn't know,' he said. 'But if he says so, then I guess he's right. He's like a walking encyclopaedia. All I know is that this mine must date way back. It wasn't being worked five hundred years ago when the landslide sealed this shaft.' He started to back out again. 'Come on. The sooner we have those natives on the job, the better. I want to get through this fall.'

We scrambled back over the debris and then we were out in the open again, blinking our eyes in the bright sunlight. Once more I saw Ed's gaze go straight to the cliff top on the far side of the gorge. 'Look at him – the bastard!' he cried, and his voice was pitched a shade higher than normal.

'What is it?' I asked, shading my eyes.

'Can't you see him? Look!' He took my arm and pointed. 'I noticed him there for the first time yesterday. He was sitting there all day and again today – just sitting there, watching us.'

I saw him then, a small, turbaned figure, sitting cross-legged and motionless in a natural niche right at the top of the cliff. 'Who is he?' I asked.

'How the hell should I know? They change the guard about midday and a new guy takes over. They never move. They just sit there, watching us.' He turned away to get his clothes. 'It gives me the creeps.'

I looked at Jan. 'Ali?'

'I imagine so.' He hesitated and then drew me aside. 'Did Karen tell you?'

'About the name? Yes, she told me. Look, Jan,' I said. 'This is crazy. You'll never get away with it.'

He gave me a quick, sidelong glance. 'All right, it's crazy,' he said. 'But I don't have to convince anybody. They're convinced already.'

'And what about the British authorities?' I asked.

But he smiled and shook his head. 'Their only worry would be if they discovered I was alive. So long as I'm dead they don't have to try and explain the disappearance of another scientist.' He looked up at me anxiously. 'It's up to you now, Philip.' And then he added with sudden violence, 'Don't you see? This is the perfect solution.'

I shook my head. He seemed utterly blind to the real problem. 'You seem to forget that a body has been washed up.'

'Well, it was an accident, wasn't it?' And then he

added quickly, 'Whether I'm Wade or Kavan, I've still got to explain that.'

'I suppose so,' I said. 'But you've entered Morocco illegally.'

He nodded, but he didn't seem worried about it. 'I think I can make them understand. If Kostos keeps his mouth shut, I know I can. And if we could prove this mine . . .' He glanced towards Ed White who was pulling on his clothes. He was frowning again. 'Did Karen tell you what happened when we arrived at the camp last night? Ed met us with that German Luger of his in his hand. He seemed scared stiff. He was all packed up, too, ready to clear out.'

'Why? Because Ali has men watching him?'

Jan nodded. 'That and something that happened yesterday afternoon. He had a visit from the Caid's younger son – the man who made tea for us when we visited the kasbah that night. He rode out on a white mule to give Ed a message from his father.'

'Well, what was the message?' I asked.

'The man only spoke a few words of French. But he kept pointing to the Post—'

Ed White's shadow fell between us. 'I got the idea anyway,' he said. 'I was to get out, and quick.'

'Why?' I asked.

'How the hell do I know why? Could be that the food trucks haven't arrived and the people are getting sore. Could be that your friend Ali is just trying to scare me. I don't know. But I can tell you this; I was plenty scared last night.' His gaze swung again to the watcher on the cliff. 'Those three Ay-rabs I had working for me were paid good dough. They wouldn't have quit for nothing.' He shook his head angrily, buttoning up his bush shirt. 'I suppose Miss Corrigan is down at the camp now?'

'Yes.'

'At least those two girls ought to go down to the Post. I don't mind staying on here so long as you guys are with me. But they should be down at the Post. They'd be safe there.'

His attitude made me feel uneasy. 'What are you expecting to happen?' I demanded.

He pushed his fingers up through his hair. 'If I knew that, I wouldn't be so Goddamned jittery.'

Jan had scrambled down the rock tip to the water to wash the dust off his body. He was out of sight and for a moment Ed and I were alone. There was something I had to find out and now was the time to do it. If Jan had really convinced Ed, then there was just a chance he could get away with it. I hesitated, wondering how to put it. 'Sooner or later,' I said, 'the police will want a statement from you.'

'From me? What about?'

'About him,' I said, nodding towards Jan.

'Well, they won't get much out of me.' He seemed to consider the matter. 'The only intelligent comment I could make is that he doesn't seem British the way you do. And he talks differently.' He said it slowly, as though it were something that had been on his mind for a long time.

'He's Cornish,' I said, remembering the details of Wade's passport.

'Cornish? Oh, you mean dialect. And then he's knocked around a bit. I guess that would make him different.' He nodded to himself, frowning slightly. And then he shrugged his shoulders. 'Well, Mrs Kavan should know. I feel sorry for that girl. When she came down here she must have been thinking there was a chance that her husband was alive. Instead, it's a stranger, impersonating him. That's not very nice, is it?' He had been staring down at his boots, but now he looked up at me. 'Wasn't Kavan going to act as doctor at your Mission?'

'Yes,' I said.

He nodded, staring at me, and then turned away. 'What I've seen of the people here, they could have used a doctor.' Jan climbed up from the water and he called to him: 'Come on. Let's get some food.'

Jan picked up his clothes and joined us. 'Pity about that shaft,' he said, glancing back over his shoulder. 'Fortunately Ed had that dynamite and he knows how to use it. But even so, it may take several days to break through the falls.'

I knew he was thinking about Bilvidic and I asked him how long he thought he'd be allowed to stay up here. 'I don't know,' he said. 'I hope he'll leave us here until the piste is open. He knows I'm here. That orderly from the Post rode out to the camp on a mule this morning to check that. And he knows I can't get out – not unless I walk, and the Military would soon be informed if I tried to do that.' His eyes lifted to the slope of the mountain above us. It was very steep and about five hundred feet up there was a sudden cliff face, not high, but sheer and crumbling. It shone red in the sunlight. 'I didn't like it when I first saw it,' he muttered. 'But now that we're blasting . . .' He shook his head and turned and started to walk down the track towards the camp.

'It's the Ay-rabs that worry me,' Ed said. 'Legard's away and with the piste cut, God knows when the food trucks will get through. And now there's this discoloration of the water.'

We had reached the entrance of the gorge and in the sunlight the water pouring down the stream-bed was almost the colour of blood against the yellow of the sand. 'How far does the discoloration extend?' I asked.

'Right down into the palmerie,' Jan said over his shoulder. 'There was quite a rush of water coming out of the gorge last night.'

None of us spoke after that and we walked down to the camp in silence. We were thinking about the water and the watcher on the cliff top. For the moment I had forgotten about Jan's personal problems. But it was impossible to forget about them once we had reached the camp, for Karen was there to remind me. She ignored Jan completely. He might not have been there, and not by a single glance, even when Ed's back was turned, did she betray the fact that she was conscious of him. Her self-control was so rigid that I began to understand how it must have been for her in Czechoslovakia.

Lunch was laid out in the open under the fly of the big tent as it had been on Christmas Day. But the atmosphere was very different. There was a sense of strain. As though conscious that she was partly responsible, Karen announced at the end of the meal that she had arranged for Julie to take her down to the Post. 'It will be better if I go.' She said it to Ed, but it was directed at Jan. He stared at her for a moment and then turned abruptly away.

'What about you?' I asked Julie.

'I'll drop Karen and then bring the bus back here.'

'No, don't do that,' I said. 'Stay down at the Post. It'd be safer.'

'My view is we should all go down to the Post,' Ed announced. 'When Legard gets back—'

'No,' Jan said, almost violently. 'I'm damned if I'll leave here now. A day's work might see that shaft opened up. And if it is a workable mine . . .' He hunched his shoulders, staring up towards the gorge. He was thinking that it would give him a stake in the country. That was the thought that was driving him.

'Well, of course, I see your point,' Ed said. 'I'm pretty interested myself to know whether there's still silver to be got out of it. But that isn't the reason I'm here, as you know. The way I see it—'

'Then what is the reason?' Jan demanded.

'Exactly what I told you.' He sounded surprised. 'I never knew there was a chance of finding silver—' He checked himself. He was staring at Jan with a puzzled frown. 'Didn't you bother to read my letters?'

Jan's eyes widened slightly with the shock of realising that he had nearly given himself away. It was Karen who covered up for him. 'But I thought you were a prospector, Ed? When we stopped at Agdz on the way down I heard Capitaine Legard talking about you to Monsieur Bilvidic. He said you had been granted a mining concession.'

'That's right.' Ed was grinning to himself like a boy. 'It seemed the smart thing to say. I didn't want people asking a lot of questions.'

'But if you're not a prospector,' Julie said, 'what are you?'

'An archaeologist.'

'But why ever didn't you tell us?'

He shrugged his shoulders, still grinning. 'Nobody bothered to ask me.' And then he turned to Jan. 'Anyway, you knew. I explained it all in that second letter. Or didn't you get it?'

'But I thought you were a construction engineer,' Karen cut in. 'You were telling me last night—'

'Sure. That's right. I am a construction engineer. But I got a bee in my bonnet about this place Kasbah Foum. Look,' he said, facing the two girls. 'Maybe I'd better explain. Archaeology is a sort of a hobby I picked up in college. Old cities and things; they fascinated me. Well, a friend of my father's was a collector of books and he used to let me browse around in his library when I was a kid. There was an old manuscript there that particularly intrigued me; it was the diary of an Englishman who had turned Muslim and lived in North Africa as an Arab trader in the early fifteen hundreds. It was an incredible story – of wars and love-making and long camel treks through the desert. In it, he described a great stone city built at the entrance to a gorge down here south of the Atlas. He had traded from that city for several years and he knew it well. And this is what interested me. He described a shaft or tunnel running into the cliff face at the entrance to the gorge. There were rooms cut back into the rock from the sides of this tunnel and these had been used partly as the city treasury and partly as an arsenal. He went to Mecca and on to Arabia, and some years later he came back to the same city. It had been sacked and was partly in ruins. And a great landslide had poured down the mountains, completely covering the entrance to the tunnel.' He glanced round at us. 'Well, two years back I got this job at Sidi Slimane air base and I came down here – just out of curiosity. And there were the ruins of the city and there was the slide he'd described.' He had turned his head so that he could see the entrance to the gorge. 'I just had to find out whether that shaft did exist and, if so, what was in it.'

'But it's fascinating,' Julie said. 'You might find all sorts of treasures there.'

'Maybe,' Ed said. 'On the other hand, the people who sacked the city may have looted the treasury. But whatever I find, when it's opened up, I shall be the first man to set foot in there for almost five centuries. That's pretty exciting. At least to me.' He turned and glanced at Jan. 'That's why my angle on this is different from yours. A few days one way or the other won't make any difference to me. But if I open it up and there's trouble – well, I don't want a lot of ignorant natives getting in there and maybe busting up stuff that's priceless. There could be things in there dating back to . . .' He laughed. 'Oh, I don't know – to the first nomadic infiltration from the desert.'

'Not if it were originally the shaft of a silver mine,' Jan said.

'No. That's right, I guess.'

A silence settled on the table. I was thinking how strange it was that these two – the Czech refugee and the American construction engineer – should be working together to open up this shaft for two such different reasons.

Jan suddenly got to his feet. 'You do what you like,' he said to Ed. 'But I'm going straight on clearing the debris out.' He turned to me. 'Will you go down and see Moha about labour for me, Philip?'

'Now wait a minute.' Ed, too, had risen. 'Get this straight, Wade. Our interests don't conflict. But mine come first. Okay?' He was much taller than Jan and he had moved towards him so that he towered over him. 'If I decide that we wait until Legard returns and things have settled down—'

'All right,' Jan said. He was looking up at Ed and then his eyes shifted towards the gorge. 'I understand your point. But suppose we have another rainstorm like we did last night? It could bring the whole mountainside down and cover the entrance again.'

'Yeah. It could.'

'The mine won't run away any more than your antiques will, if they're there. But if the mountain comes down . . .' He stared up at Ed and then said, 'I think we should push straight on with opening up the shaft.'

Ed stood there, considering it. His gaze, too, had shifted to the gorge. In the end he nodded. 'Okay,' he agreed. 'Maybe you're right.'

'I'll go and see Moha,' I said. 'How many men do you want?'

'As many as he can let us have,' Ed answered. 'Twenty at least.'

'And how much are you prepared to pay them?'

'Whatever he asks, within reason. I leave that to you.'

I had Julie drive me down in the bus to the point on the piste nearest the village, and then I entered the palmerie and crossed the irrigation ditch by the bridge of palm logs. Even here the water was strangely red, instead of its normal muddy colour. I knocked at the wooden door of the chief's house and was admitted by one of his sons and taken to an upper room. Moha lay on a bed of cushions and rugs. There was little light in the room and it was very cold. The lines on his face were more deeply etched, the gash on his forehead a brown scab of dried blood. His wound, he said, did not worry him except that he could not sit and if he walked it started to bleed again. He lay there, watching me, and I had the feeling that I wasn't welcome.

Briefly I explained the purpose of my visit. He didn't answer for a moment, but just lay there, staring at me. At length he said, 'The people are angry, *sidi*. They will not come to work for the man of machines who has destroyed the water.' He raised himself up on one elbow. 'My father and his father and his father's father have lived here in this place. In all the time we have been here, the water has never been like it is now. The people are afraid to drink it. They are afraid that their trees will finally be destroyed.'

I tried to explain to him that it was only mineral discoloration, that it would soon pass, but he shook his head and murmured '*Insh' Allah*.' His people might need money, but nothing I could say would make him send them up to work at the mine. I offered them as much as five hundred francs a day – an unheard of figure – but he only shook his head. 'The people are angry. They will not come.'

In the end I left him and walked back to the bus. I didn't tell Julie what he had said. It had scared me badly, for in the south here water was the same as life, and, if they thought the water had been poisoned, anything could happen.

As we drove up to the camp we passed several villagers, sitting on the banks of the stream bed. They stared at us as we went by, their tough, lined faces expressionless, their eyes glinting in the sunlight. 'Where did they come from?' I asked her. 'They weren't there when we drove down.'

'They came out of the palmerie. There are some more over there.' She nodded to the open country between ourselves and the mountains. There were about twenty or thirty there, sitting motionless as stones in the hot sun.

'Which direction did they come from?' I asked.

'I didn't see. They were just suddenly there.'

Karen was alone at the camp when we drew up. 'Where are the others?' I asked her. 'Up at the gorge?'

She nodded and I walked up the track. The sun's light was already slanting and the gorge was black in shadow. I had to go into the shaft to find them. There, in the light of the torches and amongst the debris of the rock fall, I told Ed what Moha had said. 'Until this matter of the water is cleared up,' I said, 'you won't get any of them to come and work for you. I think we should get down to the Post.' And I explained about the group of villagers who were waiting within sight of the camp. 'I don't like it,' I said. 'It may be just curiosity, but I had a feeling they were expecting something.'

We stood there in the torchlit darkness arguing for some time. Jan was angry. Time was running out for him and he desperately wanted to get through that rock fall, to know what was on the other side. But time meant nothing to Ed and he was all for packing up the camp and getting down to the Post. 'If we can't get labour, then we can't and that's that. The only thing for us to do is go down to the Post and wait for Legard to return. He'll have a talk with the Caid and then maybe we'll get somewhere.'

We went out into the daylight and they washed and put on their clothes. Jan was in a sullen mood. When he was dressed, he walked over to the entrance to the shaft and stood there looking at it. I didn't hear what he said, but I guessed he was cursing that fall of rock. Twenty men could probably have cleared it in a couple of days. As it was, he'd have to leave it. He turned suddenly and stared at me. 'If only we could have got down here two or three days earlier.' He said it as though it were my fault that we hadn't.

'Come on,' Ed said. 'There's no good beefing about it.'

'What about the bull-dozers?' I asked him.

'We'll pile all the gear and that box of explosives on them and take them with us. I'm not leaving them to be fooled around with by curious villagers. Come on. Give me a hand and let's get started. It'll be dark before we get down to the Post, anyway.'

We had just started to collect the tools when we heard the sound of footsteps in the entrance to the gorge. We stopped, all three of us, for they were a man's step, but light, as though he had sandals on his feet.

But it wasn't a Berber. It was Kostos. He saw us and jerked himself into a shambling run. His clothes were white with dust and his shoes were cracked and broken, the thin soles breaking away from the uppers. He was shabby and tired and frightened. 'Jeez!' Ed exclaimed. 'He looks like a piece of white trash.'

'Lat'm! Lat'm!' Kostos came to a halt and his eyes watched our faces nervously. 'I must stay 'ere. I must stay with you.' He was out of breath and his eyes seemed to have sunk back into the dark sockets as though he hadn't slept for a long time. He was unshaven and the blue stubble of his chin emphasised the pallor of his face. A drop of sweat ran down the bridge of his sharp nose and hung on the tip.

'What's the trouble?' I said. 'Why do you suddenly prefer our company to Ali's?'

His body shivered. It may have been the coldness of the gorge, for his clothes were all damp with sweat. But he had a scared look. 'Caid Hassan is dead,' he blurted out. 'Ali is in control of Foum-Skhira.'

'Hassan dead!' I exclaimed. 'But we saw him only . . . How did it happen?'

'I don't know. I am not there, you see.' He said it quickly as though it were something carefully rehearsed that he had to be sure of saying. 'I am in the village, in a pigsty of a house. It happens suddenly. That's all I know.'

'When?'

'Last night.'

I glanced at Jan. His face was hard. He was thinking of the old man who had found it necessary to send him the confirmation of his title to this place secretly because he was afraid of his son. He looked as though he could kill Kostos. 'We don't want you here,' he said angrily. 'Why don't you go to the Post if you're scared?'

'Because at the Post are two men from the Sûreté. I don't like to be so close to the Sûreté.' Kostos looked at me almost pleadingly. 'You understand, eh, Lat'am?' And then his tone changed to truculence as he said, 'Well, I am 'ere now. So what you do? It is a public place, this gorge. You cannot throw me out of it.' He looked at Ed and his small, black eyes fastened on the holster at his belt. 'I see you 'ave guns. That is good. You will give me a gun, eh? I am very good shot with a pistol.'

Ed laughed. It was a hard, tense laugh. 'What do you think we are – an arsenal?' He turned and looked at me. 'Is this guy nuts or something?' He was trying to shrug the whole thing off, but the tremor of his voice betrayed him.

Kostos noticed it, too. He crossed over to Ed and caught hold of his arm. 'Please now. You give me a gun. You give me a gun and I stay here and—'

'Are you crazy?' Ed threw his hand off angrily. 'We haven't got any guns. This—' He tapped the Luger at his waist. 'This is the only gun in the place.'

'The only gun!' Kostos stared at him, and then his eyes darted quickly round at Jan and myself. 'But you have women to protect. You must have guns. You couldn't be such fools . . .' His voice died away as he saw from our eyes that it was the truth. 'Oh, *Santo Dios*!' he cried, reverting to Tangier Spanish, and he wiped his brow on a filthy handkerchief, his eyes darting round the sides of the gorge as though looking for a way out.

Jan moved slowly forward then. 'What's happened to make you so scared?'

'Nothing. Nothing.' Kostos backed away from him. 'You keep away from me. You keep away.'

'What about that passport?'

'I never had your passport.'

'Don't lie. Why did you slip it into my suitcase when you came up here that first morning?'

'All right. I tell you. Because I want no part of any killing. The passport is too dangerous.'

'And now you come running up here.' Jan was still walking towards him. 'Let's have the truth now. You're scared of something. You've seen something or done something that has frightened you out of your wits. What is it?' He lunged forward and caught Kostos by the arm. 'Why have you abandoned Ali? What's he done that's frightened you?' His grip tightened on the Greek's arm and he began to twist it back. 'Come on now. Let's have the truth.'

'Look out!' I said. 'He may have a knife.' I had seen the Greek's other hand slide under his jacket.

Jan flung the man away from him and turned angrily back towards us. He pushed his hand up through his hair. 'I can't believe it,' he said. 'The old man dead. He was ill, I know, but . . .' He turned again and stared at Kostos, who was standing there, breathing heavily, his eyes watching us uncertainly. 'He knows something. I'd like to beat the truth out of the swine.'

'I think you'd better go down to the Post,' I said to Kostos.

'No. I am staying here.'

'Then suppose you tell us—'

'Philip!' It was Julie's voice and it rang shrilly through the gorge. 'Philip!' There was a note of panic in it and I started to run, the others close behind me.

Julie stopped as she came round the base of the slide and saw us. Karen was with her and they stood there, panting. 'What is it?' I cried. 'What's happened?'

'I think it's Ali,' she panted. 'There's a whole crowd of them coming up out of the palmerie. Some of them are on mules. They're heading straight for the camp.'

'Julie saw them first,' Karen said. 'I was in the tent. She called to me and then we began to run, up here.'

'Okay,' Ed said. 'Let's go and see what it's all about.'

We didn't have to go far. From the entrance of the gorge we could see them swarming over the camp and round the bus. 'Goddammit!' Ed cried. 'They're looting the place.' He had unbuttoned the holster of his pistol and was pulling it out.

'Better put that away,' I said, 'till we find out what they want.'

'Do you think I'm going to stand by and see my whole outfit vanish under my nose?'

I tightened my grip on his arm. 'How many rounds have you got on you?'

He stared at me. 'Only what's in the magazine,' he said sullenly and began cursing under his breath.

Just twelve rounds and there were a hundred men milling around the camp. 'Then I think you'd better regard that gun as being for purposes of bluff only.'

He nodded sullenly, staring at the scene with hard, angry eyes. A murmur of sound came up from the camp. They were like wasps round a jam pot. They were looting the food and all the time a man on a white mule was shouting at them. It was Ali and he was trying to get them to follow him up towards the gorge. The crowd increased steadily. It was being joined by little groups of men coming in from the desert and up out of the palmerie. A wisp of smoke rose in a blue spiral from the cook tent. It drifted lazily up into the still air and then died away as the tent disintegrated. The other tents were on fire now and then the bus was set alight. We could hear the crackle and the roar of the flames above the steady murmur of the mob.

'The bastards!' Ed cried. 'The bastards!' His eyes glistened with tears of rage and frustration. I kept a tight hold of his arm. The situation was explosive enough.

A hand touched my sleeve. It was Julie. She was staring at the bus which was now well alight and I knew she was thinking of her brother. It was her last link with him, apart from a few paintings scattered up and down the world. 'Why are they doing it?' she whispered. 'Why are they doing it?'

'The Caid is dead,' I said. 'And they think the water is poisoned.' I turned and glanced back at the gorge. The sides were too steep to climb. We should have to retreat back into it until we could climb out. 'Come on,' I said to the others. 'We'd better get started. I don't think they will attack us.'

Jan nodded. 'Yes. We'd better go.' The mob was breaking away from the tents now and starting up towards us, packing close round their leader on his white mule. They weren't shouting. They were, in fact, quite silent, so that we could hear the sound of the flames. Their silence was full of menace. 'Come on,' Jan said, and we went back hurriedly into the gorge.

But when he came to the bull-dozers, Ed stopped. He had his gun out now. 'I'm staying here,' he said. He looked very young and a little frightened. But his tone was obstinate.

'You'll only get hurt,' I said. 'Come on now. There are the girls to think of.'

'Okay,' he said. 'You go back with the girls. But I'm staying here.'

'Don't be a fool,' Jan said.

Ed stared at him sullenly. 'These machines represent all the cash I got in the world. If you think I'm going to run off and let these bastards . . . Latham. Will you stay here with me? I don't speak their language. But if you were here, maybe we could—'

'No,' Julie said. 'Please, Philip. Don't stay.'

But Ed caught hold of my arm. 'You're not afraid to face them, are you? I've got a gun. I can hold them off. If you'll only talk to them, explain to them.'

'All right,' I said, and I turned to Jan and told him to get the girls back up the gorge.

'Do you rate a couple of bull-dozers higher than your own life, or Philip's?' Julie demanded. 'Please, Philip. Let's get out of here.'

'It's all right,' I said. 'You go on. I'll just have a word with Ali and see what I can do. They won't harm us.'

She turned and faced Ed. 'Damn you!' she cried. 'Damn you and your bloody bull-dozers.' She was crying with anger.

'I'm sorry, Miss Corrigan,' Ed said, his voice quiet and restrained. 'I appreciate how you feel. But those bloody bull-dozers cost me eighteen months' work. No man likes to pass up eighteen months of his life without a fight.' He looked at me. 'You do what you think best, Latham.'

'I'll stay, for the moment,' I said, and told Jan to take Karen and Julie back up the gorge. Julie hesitated, her jaw set, though her face was white and frightened. 'Please,' I said. 'I'll be with you in a few minutes.'

I turned to face the mob that was now coming into the gorge round the base of the slide. As I did so, I caught sight of Kostos. He was beside the bull-dozer nearest the mine entrance and he was bending down, stuffing something into the pockets of his jacket. 'Kostos!' I shouted. 'Get back with the others.' And as he didn't move, I shouted, 'What are you doing? Get back with the others.'

He straightened up then and his pale, haggard face was twisted in an evil, frightened grin. He held out his hand so that I could see what he had been picking up. He held a stick of dynamite. 'One gun is not enough,' he said. 'I like to be certain.' And he bit the slow-match of the cartridge off short.

'Kostos!' Ali's voice rang through the gorge. He had halted his white mule just in sight of us, sitting it very still. He was wearing a turban now like his followers and it gave him height, so that he looked a commanding figure with his aquiline face and his blazing eyes. His exile hadn't made him a stranger to the land that had produced him. He belonged, and sitting there, with the sides of the gorge reared up on either side of him, he looked like some virile leader out of the Old Testament. The tribesmen were bunched together behind him. 'So. This is where you are hiding. Come here! At once! You hear me?' He had spoken in French, but Kostos didn't move. And when he saw that the Greek wasn't going to come, he turned and gave an order in Berber to the men who were mounted on mules close behind him. They thumped the flanks of their mounts with their bare heels and came riding forward at a trot, their voluminous clothes billowing out behind them.

I shouted at Kostos to come down and join us, for there was panic in his face. He was city bred with no sense of this country or these people, and I was afraid he'd light the fuse of that stick of dynamite and fling it without thought for the consequences. If he did, the Berbers would attack. There would be no holding them.

But instead, he broke and ran, flinging himself at the steep slopes where the fig trees grew.

'Don't shoot,' I warned Ed. 'For God's sake don't shoot.' He had the gun in his hand and it was aimed at the men who were riding their mules towards us. But he didn't shoot and they swept past us, headed towards Kostos.

The mob was now packed tight in the entrance of the gorge and Ali was coming forward again, his mule stepping daintily on the stones of the track. The men of Foum-Skhira closed up behind him, shoulder to shoulder like a herd of goats. They were mostly young men and they were silent as though awed by the place and by what they were doing. I called on them to halt and began to speak to them in their own tongue, telling them that what they were doing was a wicked thing, that the wrath of Allah would fall upon themselves and their families if they did harm to anyone. I started to explain that there was nothing wrong with the water, telling them that if they wished I would drink it myself. And all the time I didn't dare look round to see how far up the gorge Julie and the others had got, though I was conscious of the movement of rocks and the scrape of feet as Kostos was hounded up the slopes.

Ali's voice suddenly cut across mine. 'Monsieur. These people are angry. They have no food and the water is bad. This place belongs to Foum-Skhira and they believe there is great wealth here that will save them from starvation. Leave this place and you will not be hurt. But if you stay, I cannot be sure what my people will do.'

•

That mention of 'my people' reminded me of the Caid's death and I called out to them again in Berber: 'Men of Foum-Skhira! Two nights ago I saw Caid Hassan. Because of this man' – I pointed to Ali – 'he was not permitted to say what he wished. He had to send a secret messenger. That messenger was set upon by the men of Ali. They tried to kill him. Now Caid Hassan is dead and I must tell you . . .'

'Silence!' Ali screamed at me in French. 'Silence!' And then he was shouting at his followers, screaming at them in a frenzy, inciting them to attack. And they answered him with a low murmur like an animal that is being roused to fury.

'We'd better get out of here,' I cried. But Ed didn't need to be told what that low mob growl meant. 'I guess it's no good,' he said, and his voice was resigned.

And as we backed, so the mob advanced, and the sound that emanated from their throats filled the gorge like the growl of a monster. Then, suddenly, they rushed forward. We turned and ran for it.

The others were already well up the side of the gorge on a shelf of rock that slanted up from the bend. And, as I ran, I glimped Kostos, cut off from the rest of the party by his pursuers and being forced out along the cliff top above the entrance to the mine.

Ed, just ahead of me, turned and looked over his shoulder. And then he stopped. 'It's all right,' he said as I halted beside him. 'They're not following us.' I turned and stared back. The gorge was full of weird howls of triumph and blood lust. But it wasn't directed against us. All their warlike instincts were concentrated on the two bull-dozers. 'Goddam the bastards!' Ed breathed. The men of Foum-Skhira were clustered round the machines like ants. They shouted and yelled and as though by magic the bull-dozers moved. They trundled them down across the tight-packed rocks of the dumping ground and toppled them into the water. There was a splash and then the waters closed over them and the place was suddenly as God had made it again.

And then they moved towards the entrance to the mine shaft. Ali was already there. He had got off his mule and was standing in front of the entrance. My eyes travelled upwards and I saw Kostos balanced precariously on the rocks of the slide almost directly above him. He must have dislodged a stone, for Ali was looking up now. Whether the two men could see each other I don't know. I think it likely, for Kostos wasn't looking at the Berbers creeping over the rocks towards him. He held a stick of dynamite and he was looking down at Ali and the scene below him.

A pinpoint flicker of flame showed for an instant in his hand.

My eyes went involuntarily upwards. Not four hundred feet above, the crumbling cliff, that Jan had pointed out to me, towered above him. The flicker of flame was replaced by a wisp of smoke. I wanted to shout, to tell him not to do it. The men were packed tight below him. It was murder. Stupid, unnecessary, pointless murder. His arm swung back and the wisp of smoke curved through the air. From where we were Kostos was no bigger than a puppet and the wisp of smoke curving downwards into the close-packed mob looked as harmless as a feather floating through the air.

It fell into the centre of the crowd which mushroomed out away from it with an instinctive sense of fear. We could see it sizzling away on the ground now, and I felt a sudden relief. Kostos had left too long a fuse. It would injure nobody. But then Ed gripped my arm. 'The dynamite!' he whispered hoarsely. 'Do you see it? That box.'

It was a small, square patch of yellow close beside the sputtering wisp of smoke. I saw it for a second, and then there was a flash. It was followed instantly by a great, roaring burst of flame. The whole area of beaten rock on which the mob stood seemed lifted skywards. Rocks were flung up and men flattened to the ground. I saw Ali thrown backwards into the mouth of the shaft. And whilst the rocks were still rising in the air, the sound of that explosion hit us and the blast of it rocked us on our feet. It was an ear-shattering, indescribable crash in that confined space. And the noise went on, hammering at the cliff faces, rolling upwards over the mountain slopes, and drumming back at us in a stupendous cacophony of sound, whilst the rocks stopped heaving upwards and began to fall back to the ground.

The sound of the explosion began to diminish as the echoes reverberated back from farther and farther away. And just as a deep, mutilated silence seemed to settle on the gorge, there was a rumble like thunder out of the sky. I looked up. And then Ed's hand clutched my arm and I knew that he'd seen it, too. The sky was blue. There wasn't a cloud to mar the pastel shades of sunset.

But against that blue the cliff face where Kostos stood was slowly, lazily toppling outwards. It was catching the reddening rays of the sun so that the rock glowed. It was like something in Technicolor, remote and rather beautiful.

But the sound was not beautiful. It grew in volume, a great, grumbling, earth-shaking roar. The whole cliff was toppling down, hitting the slopes below and rebounding. It was as slow and inevitable as a waterfall, and the dust rose like spray.

I glanced round me in sudden fear, expecting all the cliffs around us to be toppling. But it was only that one cliff and below it Kostos stood, his body twisted round so that I knew he was looking upwards, seeing the ghastly thing he had let loose, but standing transfixed, knowing it was death that was pouring down upon him in the form of millions of tons of rock and unable to do anything to save himself. And below, by the entrance to the mine, the men of Foum-Skhira lay dazed, barely aware of what was descending on them from above.

All this I saw in a flash and then my gaze returned to the mountainside. The cliff was hidden now by a cloud of dust that shone red in the sunlight, and below it, the great tide rolled like a tidal wave, and as it rolled it seemed to gather the mountainside with it, so that the whole slope on which Kostos stood was thrust over the lip of the cliff, taking him with it, still oddly standing erect staring up at the main body of the landslide.

And in that split second in which my eyes recorded his fall, the whole gorge was suddenly filled by chaos. The sound pounded at the ground under our feet. Pieces of cliff from the farther side were shaken loose. Small avalanches were started. And all the time the noise gathered volume, the dust rose white like steam till it caught fire in the sunlight, and all the mountain poured into the gorge, thundering and crashing and filling it with rock.

Long after the movement had slowed and the weight had gone out of the sound, Ed and I stood there, incapable of action, stunned by the terrible vastness of it. It had a sort of horrible fascination. It took an effort of will-power to make me turn my head and look behind me, up the gorge, to see that the others were safe. Thank God, they were. They were in a little huddle as though clinging to each other, and they were as motionless as we were.

I looked back again at the scene of desolation and felt slightly sick. The dust was settling now and the sunset colours on the mountain top were flaming into vivid beauty. And into the dark cavern of the gorge a stillness was creeping, not a graveyard stillness, but the deep, satisfied stillness of Nature. And then, clear across that stillness, came a cry. It was a high, piercing cry, and I heard the name of Allah. Down by the gorge mouth, clear of the outer spill of the slide, was a little knot of men. They were waving their arms and calling down curses on our heads. One of them, a big, bearded man, was shaking his fist at us and clawing his way towards us across the debris of the slide.

I turned and started up the slope of rock towards the others. 'Come on,' I shouted at Ed. 'Hurry, man. We've got to be out of this gorge by nightfall.'

He caught the urgency of my voice and came

hurrying after me. 'There's only a handful of them left,' he said breathlessly as he caught up with me. 'And anyway it was that damned Greek that caused the explosion. It was nothing to do with us.'

'They don't know that,' I said. 'He was a European. That's all they know. If they catch us in these mountains at dawn . . .' I didn't bother to finish the sentence. I needed my breath, for we were climbing at a desperate rate to join up with the rest of the party.

CHAPTER FOUR

The trek out of that gorge was a nightmare. It wasn't that we were followed. The men who had screamed their need of vengeance at us were fully occupied searching the debris for their dead. But the sun was setting fast and if darkness overtook us before we had climbed out of the gorge, we should be trapped there, and when dawn came we should be hunted down amongst the rocks of the mountainsides and killed.

The ledge up which we were moving gradually narrowed until it finished abruptly at a sheer rock climb of twenty feet or more. It sloped slightly and there were hand- and footholds, but except for Ed we were all wearing shoes, and we had nothing with which to rope ourselves together. Below us was an almost vertical drop of some four hundred feet to the bottom of the gorge. We paused there a moment, looking back. The slide filled the whole mouth of the gorge and water was already building up against this natural dam to form a wider and deeper lake, red like a gaping wound. The flowing robes of Berber men moved ghostlike amongst the debris of the fall, searching for their dead.

There was no going back and we turned to face the cliff of rock that towered above us. 'We'll never get up there,' Karen said.

'Sure you will,' Ed said cheerfully. 'There's nothing to it.' He had her take her shoes off. 'I'll be right behind you,' he said as he started her off. His tough, rubber-soled boots gripped the rock as he climbed, encouraging her all the time, sometimes bracing her foot with his hand. Jan stood with his head back, watching her until she reached the top. 'Come on,' Ed called down to us. 'It'll be dark soon.' He climbed back down the face of the rock and met Julie halfway, helping her up as he'd helped Karen.

The climb wasn't really difficult, but it took time. The sun had already set before we had all gathered at the top. The gorge was cold and dark now, and, above us, the slopes of the mountain seemed to stretch into infinity. We started up, climbing as quickly as we could. But we made slow progress. Karen slipped a great deal in her leather soles and Jan was out of training for this sort of thing. 'Latham!' Ed called back to me. 'I'll go ahead to find the track. It'll be too dark to see soon. I'll call directions down to you. Okay?'

It was the only thing to do. 'Yes, you go ahead,' I told him.

He was fit and seemed to have the feel of the mountains. He climbed fast and in a few minutes he was lost to sight over the brow of a hump. Darkness fell swiftly. It was odd the way it came. Our eyes adjusted themselves to the diminishing light and even when the stars were out I could still see my way ahead. Then I looked down to negotiate a tumbled patch of rock and when I looked up again I could see nothing – only the vague shape of the mountain humped against the studded velvet of the sky.

I shouted and Ed's voice hallooed back to us, very faint and far away. Sound was deceptive, curving round the larger rock buttresses, so that we worked too much to the left and found ourselves up against a cliff. It took us a long time to negotiate it and then, when we could climb again, we found ourselves in an area of massive great rocks as big as houses with deep gashes between that appeared as dangerous as crevasses in a glacier. We called and called, but could hear no response.

I worked away to the right then, calling all the time. But a wind had sprung up from off the top of the mountain and we heard nothing. I kept on working to the right, hoping to get downwind from Ed and hear his calls, but I must have gone too far, for we reached an area where the rocks were piled in absolute confusion. I tried to cross this, still attempting to get down-wind, but it was a very bad patch. Loose rubble slid away from under our feet and even some of the bigger rocks showed a tendency to move. And then, as I was climbing round an extra large piece of rock, my foot braced against it, the thing moved. I shouted a warning to the others and clutched hold of the ground above me. The rock crunched as it moved. I could see it as a vague shape moving gently over on to its side. It hung there a moment and then moved again, dropping away out of my field of vision. We stood there, braced against the slope, listening to the sound of it crashing and banging down the mountain, gathering stones in its path so that there was a rustling, slithering sound of rubble behind it. There was a heavy splash and then silence.

I knew then where I was. I had come much too far and we were right out on the face of the new slide with the broken, crumbling cliff above us. It was already past nine. We had been clambering and stumbling across the face of the mountain for almost three hours. I tried to estimate how far across the face of the slide we had come. 'Do we go forward or back?' I asked Jan, trying to remember which side of that cliff face was the better going.

'If we go forward,' Jan said, 'we'll be on the route Karen and I came down last night. With luck I might be able to find my way back to the piste.'

'And if we go back?'

'I don't know.' His voice sounded nervous. We were both thinking about the chances of getting across the slide without disturbing it and starting the whole new slope on the move.

I asked the two girls which they would prefer to do. They both agreed. 'Let's go on.' And so we inched our way forward across the face of the slide, scarcely daring to breathe, let alone put our weight on to any of the rocks. Stones clattered down, little drifts of scree and dirt were started. Occasionally a larger rock shifted and then went bouncing and thudding down the slope. And each time the sound ended in a splash of water.

It took us nearly two hours to cross the face of that

slide and all the time the retina of my memory carried the picture of how the slide had been after Kostos hurled that stick of dynamite. The picture was appallingly vivid and every time I heard a stone shift or a trickle of rubble start, my heart was in my mouth and the sweat stood cold on my forehead. And each time I cursed myself for having led them too far to the right, for not having realised that we hadn't climbed above this obstruction.

But a little after ten-thirty we came out on to undisturbed mountainside and lay there, panting and exhausted, with a bitter cold wind drying the sweat of physical and nervous exhaustion on our tired bodies.

After that Jan took the lead. We moved very slowly. He was just about all in and so was Karen. She was slipping a lot and she had cut her head open on a rock. Her hand, when I helped her over a bad patch, was sticky with blood.

About an hour later we heard Ed calling from higher up the mountain. The sound of it came to us quite clearly on the wind. But I knew it was a waste of breath to answer him and we climbed doggedly on until we found the piste. I left the others there and trudged on up to the bend where the piste had been repaired. From that point I was able to make contact with Ed. A few minutes later he joined me. 'Where the hell have you been?' he demanded. 'I've been waiting up there for hours, bawling my head off. What happened to you?'

I explained as we went down to join the others. 'Well, thank God you're here now,' he said. 'I'd just about given you up. Once I heard some rocks crashing down . . .' He didn't say anything for a moment, and then he murmured, 'It's a terrible business, that landslide. There must have been thirty or forty of them buried under it. But it wasn't our fault,' he added quickly.

'They're not to know that,' I reminded him.

'No, I guess not.'

When we rejoined the others, we found them discussing whether we should make for the Post or go on up over the pass towards Agdz. It was over forty kilometres to Agdz and the Berber tribesmen from Foum-Skhira could easily overtake us on the piste. At the same time there would probably be a road gang working on the break in the piste higher up the mountainside. There might be transport there. But even so, it was a stiff climb and I wasn't sure we could make it. 'What do you think, Ed?' I asked.

There was a long pause and then he said, 'I didn't tell you this before, but the reason why you lost me was that I had to stop calling down to you. I'd almost reached the piste when I heard mules coming up from the direction of Foum-Skhira. They were Berbers and they passed quite close to me, about ten of them, going up towards the pass and riding hard.'

That decided us. We headed downhill, back towards Foum-Skhira and the Post.

It was then just on midnight. It didn't take us long to reach the foot of the mountain, but from then on the going was heavy in the deep sand of the piste and our progress became slower and slower, our stops more frequent. According to the map it was five kilometres from the foot of the mountains to the Post, but it seemed infinitely farther and it took us nearly three hours. And for the last hour of that journey we could hear the sound of wailing from Foum-Skhira. It was a high-pitched, quavering sound, strangely animal in the darkness of the night, and it grew steadily louder as we approached the Post.

At last the dark shape of the first fort loomed up, the domed roofs curved like some Eastern temple against the stars. We left the piste, making a wide detour round it, so that we approached the Post from the south. We went slowly, not talking, moving cautiously. They might have a lookout posted to watch for us. I didn't think it likely, but it was just possible. A dog barked – a sudden, harsh sound in the stillness. And beyond the sound of the dog was the remote, persistent sound of the women of Foum-Skhira keening for their dead.

I think we were all a little scared. We were bunched close together and I could just see that Ed had his gun in his hand. We were braced mentally against the sudden, blood-curdling yell, the rush of an attack out of the night. It is easy to be frightened at night in a strange country among a strange people. Darkness should be the same everywhere. But it isn't. This was desert country. These were desert people. We could feel the difference in the sand under our feet, see it in the brightness of the stars, the shadowed shape of the bare mountains. The chill of it was in our bones. It was as alien as the moon, as cold and naked. And the agony of that death-wailing froze our blood. The dog barked incessantly.

'Goddammit!' Ed muttered. 'Why can't that bloody dog keep quiet?'

A hand gripped my arm. It was Julie. 'I wish we'd crossed the mountains and made for Agdz,' she whispered.

We were in the open space between the two forts now. The shape of one of the towers was outlined against Orion. 'Where do we go now?' Ed asked. 'The Bureau?'

'That's no good,' I said. 'There won't be anybody there.'

'No, but there's the telephone. We need to get on to the Commandant at Agdz, and quick.'

'Well, we can try,' I said. 'But they probably lock the Bureau at night.'

'What about Bilvidic?' Jan asked. 'He'll be at the house, I imagine.'

We turned the corner of the fort and struck the beaten path that led to the Bureau. The French truck was still parked outside. The door of the Bureau was locked. 'Let's try the sleeping quarters,' Ed said. 'Maybe your friend Bilvidic is there.' The guest rooms were built on to the Bureau in the form of an L. The door was locked and Ed beat on the wooden panels with the butt of his gun. The noise seemed shatteringly loud in the night stillness. The dog's barking became frantic. The sound of the wailing continued unchanged – insistent and agonised. The building outside which we were clustered remained silent as the grave.

'We'd better try the house,' Jan said.

Ed beat once more upon the door, but nobody answered, and we trudged, coldly, wearily, through the sand to the house. The dog barked his fury at us from the wired-in enclosure. Once more Ed shattered the night with the hollow thudding of his gun-butt against wood. A window was thrown open and a voice demanded, '*Qui va là*?' It was Bilvidic. I never thought I should be glad to hear his voice. 'I'll come down immediately,' he said as soon as he discovered who we were.

It was bitterly cold standing there waiting outside that door. The sweat lay against my body like a coating of steel. The dog had stopped barking now and there was utter silence except for the sound of wailing which came to us loud and clear on a chill breath of wind. A light showed between the chinks of the heat-contracted woodwork of the door. The bolts were drawn back and there was Bilvidic. He peered at us in the beam of the torch he carried. 'Come in,' he said. His face was puffed with sleep and his voice sounded irritable.

It was as cold inside as it was out, except that there was no wind. 'You must phone Agdz immediately,' Ed said in his halting French. 'They must send troops. Something terrible has happened.' He glanced quickly round the room. It looked bare and chill in the hard beam of the torch. 'Where's the telephone?'

'The telephone is broken,' Bilvidic said. 'It is cut when the piste is destroyed.'

So that was that. 'We should have gone over the mountains,' Jan said.

'If we'd done that we might all be dead by now,' I answered sharply.

Karen had slumped into an easy-chair. 'It's so cold,' she said. She was shivering and I glanced at Julie. Her face was pale and she looked desperately tired. We were all of us tired.

Bilvidic's assistant joined us then. He was angry at having been got out of bed. 'What's happened?' he demanded. 'Why have you returned here at this time of the—'

But Bilvidic cut him short. 'Georges. Go to the Capitaine's room and bring the cognac and some glasses.' He turned to us. 'First you have something to warm you and we get a fire lit. Afterwards we talk, eh?' He went to a door leading out to the back and shouted, 'Mohammed! Mohammed! *Venez ici. Vite, vite!*' My estimation of him soared then, for he must have been consumed with curiosity and a man is seldom at his best when rudely woken in the small hours.

Mohammed came and was ordered to produce a fire immediately. We moved into Legard's study. Paraffin blazed in the wood-piled grate and Bilvidic handed each of us a quarter tumbler of neat cognac. '*Eh, bien*. Now we will talk. What happened last night at Kasbah Foum? There were rumours that the Caid was dead and that several *indigènes* had lost their lives. What happened, monsieur?' He was looking at me.

I told him the whole thing then, sitting there by the fire, sipping my drink, my body gradually relaxing with the warmth.

When I had finished he sat quite silent for a long time. He was frowning and his fingers were beating a tattoo on the desk where he was seated. At length he said to me, 'Do you know this country? Do you understand the people here?'

'No,' I said. 'This is the first time I have been south of the Atlas.'

He clicked his tongue. 'That is a pity, for I also do not know it. This is a military area and there is seldom any reason for us to come down here.' He scratched his thinning hair. 'It is a pity because it would be helpful if we had some idea what they would do. It is an extraordinary situation, quite extraordinary.' He was using the word in its literal sense. 'First there is the failure of the dates, then the piste is cut so that the food trucks, which are delayed anyway, cannot get through. Then they are frightened by the change in the colour of the water that feeds their palmerie and the wells. Their Caid is dead. And now this. It is too much – too much for any primitive and warlike people.' He looked across at me. 'I agree with you, monsieur. There is likely to be trouble.' He paused and scratched his head again. 'The question is – what do we do? Soon they will know that you are here.'

'If we could get to Agdz,' Ed said.

But Bilvidic shook his head. 'Unfortunately, the only vehicle here has something the matter with it. And you cannot go on foot. It is a long way. Also it is too dangerous.' He pulled a pack of American cigarettes out of the pocket of his jacket which he was wearing over his vest. He made a spill from a strip of paper and lit it from the fire. Then he started pacing up and down, taking quick, nervous puffs at the cigarette.

I leaned back and closed my eyes. The drink and the warmth of the fire were enveloping me with sleep. I seemed to slide away into darkness, engulfed by a beautiful lethargy.

I awoke to the sound of voices raised in argument. I opened my eyes and blinked in the brilliance of the light. It was morning and the room was full of sunshine. Jan lay asleep in the chair opposite me. The grate was piled white with wood ash. A single log was still burning, its flames obliterated by the brightness of the sunshine. 'I have sent a runner to Agdz by mule,' Bilvidic was saying. 'What else can I do?'

'But it'll take him all day to get there,' Ed cried.

'Perhaps.' Bilvidic shrugged his shoulders. 'But there is a chance that he will find transport up there where they are repairing the piste. Also I have told him to get the road gang to try and repair the telephone.'

'Yeah, but that'll take hours. Meantime anything can happen.'

'What's the trouble?'

Ed swung round. 'Take a look out of the window.'

I crossed the room and peered out. The open space between the forts was full of people. They stood or sat in little isolated groups, silently watching the house as though waiting for something to happen. And from the direction of Foum-Skhira came the sound of tam-tams beating. It was a sound without rhythm, an insistent, urgent tattoo like drums beating to quarters. I glanced at my watch. It was just after nine. 'You should have woken me earlier,' I said.

'There was nothing you could do,' Bilvidic declared quietly. 'There is nothing any of us can do now except wait here and hope they do not attack.'

'Attack?' I stared at him, my brain still dulled with sleep. 'Do you mean you think they may attack the Post?'

He nodded his head slowly. 'Yes. I have just had a visit from Hassan – that is the Caid's second son, the man who is now, in fact, the Caid. He came at some risk to himself to warn us that he had not the influence to hold his people back and that we were in imminent danger.'

'They know we're here at the Post then?'

He nodded. 'I cannot understand how they know, but they do.' He swung round at the sound of the front door opening. It was Georges. He carried a rifle slung over his shoulder. 'You found the armoury then?' Bilvidic said.

But Georges shook his head. He had searched the Bureau building, but he had failed to find it. The rifle he had found in the orderly's room, but there had been no ammunition with it. Bilvidic went through into the main room where Julie and Karen were peacefully asleep in easy-chairs with blankets wrapped round them. He pulled open the door leading to the back premises and shouted, 'Mohammed! Mohammed!' But there was no answer. We searched the whole place, but there was no sign of him.

'Looks like he's cleared out while the going was good,' Ed said. 'Isn't there somebody else around here to tell us where they keep their weapons?'

'Only the orderly,' Bilvidic said. 'And that is the man I sent to Agdz.'

'But there is a Military Post,' I said. 'There must be some troops here.'

Bilvidic shook his head. 'Not at the Post. Farther south there is the Camel Patrol. But here Legard has only two orderlies and the other is away.'

'And you didn't ask the man you sent to Agdz where the armoury was?'

'Why should I? I had no reason then to believe that we should be attacked.'

'But we told you there'd be trouble. We told you that a party had been sent out into the mountains—'

'Yes, yes, but that does not mean they will attack a French Post. It is many years now since a Post was attacked.'

'Monsieur. Here. Quick!' It was Georges and his voice was urgent. He was standing by the front door, his head on one side. 'Listen! Do you hear?' He turned the key in the lock and pulled open the door. We heard it then. It was a sound like the sea breaking along the sands, the murmur of many voices and the tramp of many feet. The tattoo of the tam-tams had ceased and in its place was the single, menacing beat of a drum giving the time to an army on the march. And then we saw them, coming up out of the palmerie just to the left of the souk. They were a great mob of people and they flowed over the sand towards the house like a tide. There must have been a thousand or more, including the children running on the outskirts. I felt my heart hammering and my mouth was dry. If they attack in a body . . . I glanced at Julie, still sleeping peacefully in her chair.

'What are we going to do?' It was Jan. He had come through from the study and was standing, looking first at his wife and then through the open door at the advancing mob. 'We must do something.' He rubbed his eyes, half-dazed with sleep, blinking owlishly. 'Shall I wake them?' He was looking at the girls again.

'Let them sleep on,' I said. 'There's no point in their knowing about this till they have to.' I turned to Bilvidic. 'Exactly what arms have we got?' I asked.

He put his hand into his pocket and brought out a French service pistol which he tossed across to me. 'That is Legard's. We have plenty of rounds for that. Also Georges and I have each an automatic with a full magazine and one spare.'

'And I have my Luger,' Ed said.

Four pistols! I stared out of the door at the approaching mob. It wasn't much if they really meant business. 'We ought to move to the fort,' Ed said.

But Bilvidic shook his head. 'It is too big. We could never hold it.'

'But we could hold one of the towers.'

'Yes, but we must be near the telephone. That is essential.'

'The Bureau then,' I suggested.

But again he shook his head. 'They could come at us across the roof from the fort. Here we have an all round field of fire. It is not good, but it is the best we can do. Close the door now, Georges.'

The door slammed to. The key grated in the lock. We could no longer hear the angry sound of the mob. Only the beat of the drum penetrated the room. 'I think,' Bilvidic said to me, 'that you should get all your people upstairs.' He was staring at the advancing mob, searching it with his eyes narrowed over their little pouches. 'I do not think they have a leader. Without a leader they will not attack unless they are given cause. They have only been told that you are here. They do not know. And if they do not see you, then they will begin to doubt and lose their nerve. Get your people upstairs.' His voice was more urgent now. '*Vite*! Hurry! And when you are up there, do not show yourselves at the windows.'

'But that leaves only the two of you down here,' Ed said. 'If they once get inside this place . . .' He hesitated. 'What makes you so sure they won't attack?'

Bilvidic turned and looked at him. 'I know about mobs, monsieur,' he said in a quiet voice. 'In Casablanca I have had to do with many riots. Now hurry, please.'

I knew he was right. It was no time to argue, anyway. I woke Julie and Karen and bundled them up the stairs, explaining the position to them as we went. Jan followed close at my heels and Ed was behind him.

There were Venetian blinds in one of the upper rooms and through the slats we watched the mob slow down and come to a halt in front of the house. Bilvidic was right. It had no leader. It was moved only by the sense of being a mob. Those behind pushed forward and spilled out to the sides, spreading round the house. The people who had been watching and waiting in the space between the forts moved into the herd as though drawn by instinct. The inarticulate murmur of the mass gradually died into silence. It was like a brute beast standing with his head down, wondering whether to charge.

I could pick out individual faces now. They were curiously blank. Many of those in front were young men. They were awed by the stillness of the house, by the Tricolour floating from its flagstaff and by the looming mass of the forts behind, mute evidence of France's mastery of this land. A little knot gathered in the centre and a young man was pushed forward. He was too young to have any hair on his face and he was scared. But he had women behind him who goaded him on and he suddenly clutched the silver hilt of the knife at his waist and ran forward.

But all he did was to peer in at the windows and then he ran back to the crowd, which opened out and sucked him into its bosom. He was shaking his head and then the mob had closed up again and I could no longer see him. But it wasn't a silent crowd now. The people were talking and becoming individuals again in the process. It was no longer a headless, dangerous mass, but a thousand individuals all full of their own opinions. Looking down on it was like looking at some disease through a microscope. It writhed and seethed, splitting up into little eager groups.

The danger, for the moment, was over.

I breathed a sigh of relief, for there were women in the crowd, many of whom would have lost menfolk in the disaster at Kasbah Foum. If this bonfire was to catch fire, it was they who would set the match to it. And the mob was armed. Apart from the knife which every Berber carries at his waist, I counted at least two dozen, perhaps more, with long-barrelled, old-fashioned guns.

'What will they do now?' Julie asked. And it was only then, as I glanced at her and saw her face close to mine, that I realised that I had my arm round her shoulder. 'Nothing,' I said. 'They will talk and talk. And then they will get hungry and go home.'

A buzzer sounded downstairs. It was an odd, mechanical little sound in the stillness that had descended on the house. It stopped and then started again. I heard the scrape of a chair on the tiles and a man's tread as he crossed the main room towards the study. 'By God, it's the telephone,' Ed cried. 'We're through to Agdz.' And he went clattering down the stairs. I shouted at him to stop, but all he said was, 'I want a word with the Commandant myself.'

'Ed! Come back!' I flung myself down the stairs after him.

The stairs descended into a recess between the main room and the study. As I reached the bottom Ed was already in the study. Bilvidic was seated at the desk with the field telephone pulled in front of him and the receiver to his ear, and behind him, framed in the window, was the lined, gaunt face of an old Berber. He was staring into the room and he saw Ed moving towards the desk, his mouth opened slightly to reveal a solitary tooth, like a fang hanging in the muzzle of an old dog; and then the face was gone and I heard Bilvidic saying, '*Oui, oui, tout de suite*.'

'Let me talk to him,' Ed said. I think he thought they'd take more notice of an American.

But Bilvidic waved him away. 'Get back upstairs.'

There was the sudden crack of a gun and a splintering crash. A bullet thudded into the woodwork above my head. Glass from the shattered window-pane rained on to the desk. Bilvidic shouted to us to get down. But Ed was standing dazed in front of the desk with blood welling from a cut on the side of his head and trickling down his face. He turned slowly to the shattered window. A big, wild-eyed man was standing staring at us, the long-barrelled gun with which he had fired the shot still smoking in his hand.

Ed's reaction was instantaneous. His hand grabbed at his Luger. 'Don't fire!' Bilvidic screamed at him. 'For God's sake don't fire!'

For an awful moment there was a stillness in the room. Then Ed lowered the gun. He put his hand up to the side of his head and stared at the blood on his fingers. 'He tried to kill me,' he said in a dazed voice.

I didn't say anything. Bilvidic wiped the sweat from his forehead. 'If you had fired,' he said slowly in a small, quiet voice, 'the lust for blood would have entered into that mob out there. You would have been committing suicide – for yourself and for all of us.' He turned to me. 'You take the gun, monsieur; and get him upstairs out of sight of these people.'

Ed turned to me then and gave a little shaken laugh. 'I'm sorry,' he said. 'I guess I shouldn't have come down.' He glanced towards the window, listening to the roar of the crowd who had become excited at the sound of the shot. Blood dripped from his chin to the floor. Then he turned to Bilvidic who was busy explaining to the man at the other end of the line what had happened. 'Monsieur. You must get them to send troops. That's what I came down to tell you. We need troops here, and we need them quick.'

Bilvidic looked at me and nodded towards the door. 'Get him upstairs,' he said. 'And get one of the ladies to see to that cut.' And then he was back on the telephone. '*Allô. Allô*. Monsieur le Commandant? *Est-ce que vous avez . . .*' Ed stood there listening to Bilvidic's request for a military detachment to be despatched immediately.

'Come on,' I said.

He nodded and moved towards the door, his handkerchief held to the side of his head. 'Well, at least they know what's going on. They'll send troops now.'

I got him back up the stairs and handed him over to Julie. Fortunately it was only a superficial cut from a piece of flying glass and it had missed his eye.

'So they know we're in the house now,' Jan said when I had explained what had happened.

I nodded. 'I'm afraid so.'

He turned on Ed. 'You damned fool!' And then he was looking at Karen. He was scared and angry, for he was standing by the window and the roar of the crowd came up to him.

'It wasn't his fault,' Julie said. 'He did it for the best.' She was bandaging Ed's head with a strip torn from a sheet.

I went over to the window and looked out at the crowd. They were like cattle, bawling and milling around, waiting to stampede. And then suddenly, above the solid, heavy roar came a liquid sound, an ululation made with the tongue like a yodel. It was just a little sound at first, but it swelled rapidly, a female sound that swamped the male.

My blood ran cold, for I knew that sound. I had heard it in the High Atlas. But then it had been a greeting, a ceremonial welcome. Now I was hearing it for the first time as I had been told it was really used: a repetitive sound like the singing of crickets to drive the men to a frenzy of excitement, to goad them into battle.

I went to the window and saw that the women were gathering together, closing up behind the men, their mouths open, their tongues moving; and the shrill, insistent cry gathered greater and greater volume.

I turned then and ran down the stairs.

'Where are you going?' Julie cried out.

I didn't answer her. I think I was too scared of what I knew had to be done to say anything. But she seemed to sense what was in my mind, for she came after me. 'No, Philip. No.' She caught hold of my arm. 'Please.'

Bilvidic met me at the foot of the stairs. His face looked very pale and he had his gun in his hand. 'You can give the American back his gun,' he said.

'You know that sound then?'

'I know what it means – yes. But it is the first time I have heard it.' He smiled a little wryly. 'Get your men down here. The ladies should remain upstairs. We may beat back the first rush. After that . . .' He shrugged his shoulders. Ed came down the stairs then, his face very pale under the blood-stained bandage. Bilvidic made no attempt to blame him for what was going to happen.

I stared out of the window at the gathering men

standing silent, staring at the door. That throbbing, tongued cry of the women seemed to fill the air. 'You understand mobs,' I said, turning to Bilvidic. 'There must be something that would stop them?'

'Yes,' he said, his pale eyes staring into mine. 'If I went out there and faced them and told them why their men had been killed in the gorge – that would stop them.'

'Then why don't you do it?' Julie said quickly, breathlessly.

'Because, mademoiselle, I do not speak Berber, only Arab, and the mass of them would not understand that.' His eyes came back to me and I knew he was thinking that I must speak Berber since I'd been a missionary at Enfida.

'That's what I thought you'd say.' I turned and walked towards the door.

But Julie caught hold of my arm. 'Not alone. Not like that.'

'I must.' I was trembling and my stomach felt cold and empty.

'I won't let you.' She was dragging at my arm.

'Let me go!' I cried.

'I won't.' Her face was white and her dark eyes looked at me with a steady gaze. 'I love you, Philip.'

I stared at her and a sudden glow of warmth filled me. It was as though her declaration had set light to something inside me. I felt suddenly calm and at peace. Gently I released her fingers from my arm. 'You'd better have this,' I said, and handed her Legard's pistol. And then I walked to the door and opened it and went out into the hard sunlight and the noise to face the stare of a thousand hostile, half-animal eyes.

They were bunched out fifty feet back from the house, a compact, solid mass of men that thinned out towards the edges, spreading in a crescent round the house as though formed by instinct into some old order of battle. I was not conscious of their individual faces. They were just a blur in the hot sunlight, a solid mass of flowing robes that ranged from white to brown and matched the arid sand. I was only conscious that they were of this naked land, a living and integral part of it, and that I was an alien.

I tried to marshal my thoughts, but my mind was a blank as I walked out towards them. I couldn't even pray. And they watched me walk out to them like a herd of animals, pressed shoulder to shoulder; and there wasn't a single individual among them – they were a mass and they felt as a mass, not thinking, only feeling. That mass feeling seemed to hang in the air. I sensed it physically, the way you can smell something mad. And behind it all, behind the evil expression of their mass feeling, was that damned female noise, that many-tongued liquid, frenzy-making sound, beating at my brain, thrumming through it until I could feel it against the raw ends of my nerves, stretching them beyond the limits of strain.

And I was afraid; desperately, horribly afraid. My mouth felt dry and there was a weakness in the marrow of my bones. I prayed God to stop me being afraid. But the prayer was not a real prayer and I stopped and looked at the sea of faces, that blur of figures, and I was afraid then that they would know I was afraid.

For a moment I could say nothing. I could think of nothing. I stood there twenty paces from them and stared at them. And they stared back at me, silent and motionless, but strong in the strength of their mass feeling. And behind them was that sound that seemed an expression of the very wildness and primitiveness of the land.

And suddenly it maddened me. I was angry, with myself and with them, and my anger killed my fear. I found my voice then and heard myself shout at them for silence in their own language. I shouted several times for the women to be quiet and gradually the sound lessened and died away. Abruptly the silence was complete, the whole crowd of them so still that I could hear the small sound of the breeze blowing through the dark green sprays of the tamarisks that acted as a windbreak for the house.

I had them then. I could have talked to them. But my eye was caught by an individual face. It was the bearded, wild-eyed face of the man who had fired into the study. He was standing right in front of me and as our eyes met, I was conscious of the hatred and violence that seethed inside him, and it appalled me. He had his gun clutched in his left hand and with his right he pointed a finger at me. He cursed me in the name of Allah. 'You have killed my son and my brother and my brother's son,' he accused me.

'I have not killed anyone,' I said. 'The men who came to Kasbah Foum died because of Ali d'Es-Skhira.'

My voice was steady and it gave me confidence. I began to tell them exactly what had happened there in the gorge. But in spite of myself I found I was speaking to this one man and not to the whole crowd of them, and I saw his face become set and wooden as he made himself deaf to what I was saying.

Slowly he shifted the gun to his right hand and slowly he raised it to his shoulder, moving it slightly so that the long, heavy barrel pointed straight at me. I tried to ignore him. I tried to look at the sea of faces, to talk to them as one composite individual. But my eyes were fascinated by the round hole of that barrel. It didn't waver and it pointed straight into my eyes and I heard my voice falter and slow. His eyes were looking straight at me along the barrel. They glinted with sudden triumph, and in that instant I knew he was going to fire.

I ducked, flinging myself sideways. There was a report and the bullet hit my shoulder, spinning me round. Somehow I kept my feet. Pain shot through my arm and my whole body seemed to grow numb with the shock. I could feel the blood flowing. I could feel, too, the blood lust of that crowd growing.

What came to me then, I don't know. I would like to think that it was courage. But it may only have been the instinct of survival, the knowledge that if I failed to face them now, they would charge and trample me underfoot. I felt suddenly quite cool and a little light-headed, and I was walking towards them.

I walked straight towards the man who had fired at me, never shifting my gaze from his face. His eyes stared back at me for a moment and then I saw guilt and fear in them and he looked down, shuffling his feet and beginning to back away from me. The crowd opened up, so that a narrow gully formed in the mass of it. I walked straight into it. They could have killed me then with their bare hands, but nobody moved, and I felt the power of dominating them, of holding their attention with what I was doing.

The man backed until he could retreat no farther. He was held there by the weight of people behind him. I walked straight up to him and took the gun from him. I didn't say anything to him. I just turned my back and walked out till I was clear of them. The concrete signpost stood at the entrance to the house. I swung the gun by the barrel and brought the breech down across the post, using all the strength of my sound arm, and the stock splintered and broke off. I tossed the useless thing on the sand and walked down the path and in through the open door of the house.

In the sudden shade of the room I could see nothing. I felt my brain reeling. I heard a murmur like surf as the crowd gave voice to its reaction and the door closed, shutting it out. A hand touched mine. I heard a sob. And then my legs gave under me and I passed out.

When I came to I was lying on the couch. There were voices talking. 'But there must be troops down here.' It was Ed speaking. 'How else would you hold the country? If you're properly organised you should be able to have troops at the top of the pass by—'

'I tell you, there are no Goumiers nearer than Boumalne.' Bilvidic's voice sounded cold and angry. 'That is more than a hundred and fifty kilometres away, and they are not motorised.'

'What about the Legion?'

'The Legion is in Indo-China. All our troops are in Indo-China.'

'Oh, to hell with that for a story. You'll see. The Commandant knows there's trouble. He'll have troops here fast enough. It's just a question of whether they get here in time.'

I closed my eyes, wondering what there was about the Americans and the French. They always seemed to get on each other's nerves. I felt a little weak and my left arm was cold. It had been bared by cutting away the sleeve of my jacket and shirt at the shoulder. I moved it gently, flexing my fingers. The muscles seemed all right. I was conscious of somebody close beside me. Fingers gripped hold of the arm and there was a stinging pain in the wound halfway between elbow and shoulder. I cried out, more with surprise than with pain, and Julie's voice, close to my ear, said, 'I'm sorry. I thought you were still unconscious. There's no damage. It's just a flesh wound and I'm swabbing it out with iodine. The bullet nicked your arm.' Her voice was cool and soothing.

'I lost my nerve,' I said.

'Don't be silly.' She gripped the arm as she began to bandage it.

But I was remembering how I had ducked and the man had fired. 'If I'd walked up to him, he'd never have fired. I let him dominate me.' My voice sounded shaky.

The others crowded round me, salving my wounded pride with kind words. 'It requires courage, *mon ami*, to face a mob like that,' Bilvidic said. There was a warmth in his voice that soothed me, but I had a feeling that if he'd been the one who had spoken Berber, he would have outfaced them.

As soon as Julie had finished bandaging my arm, I swung my feet off the couch and sat up. 'What's happening outside?' I asked.

'*C'est ça*,' Bildivic said. 'You have given them something to talk about. For the moment they are no longer a mob.'

I got up and went over to the window. It was true. They were no longer bunched together in a solid mass. They had split up into groups. Some were sitting down well away from the house as though content to be merely spectators. Others were drifting back to Ksar Foum-Skhira. 'It is very hot today.' Bilvidic had come to my side. 'I do not think they will do anything during the heat of the day.' There was a note of reservation in his voice.

'And afterwards?' I asked.

'Afterwards . . .' He spread his hands with a Gallic shrug. 'Afterwards, we shall see.'

'Where's the man who fired at me? Is he still out there?'

There was a momentary hesitation, and then he said, 'He has gone back to the village.'

'Because he was ashamed or afraid, or what?'

It was Jan who answered. 'He couldn't stand their taunts.'

'Their taunts?'

He nodded. 'They jeered at him because you had taken his gun from him.'

'If you hadn't taken his gun away, he would have reloaded it and killed you,' Bilvidic said. 'They laughed at him and threw stones at him because he had been afraid of you.' He turned abruptly away as though he were afraid to talk about the incident. 'I think we should have some food.'

We split into two watches, one half keeping guard, the other half feeding. The time passed slowly. It was a weird business. We dared not go out of the house and, it seemed, the mob dared not attack it. We played through all Legard's records on the gramophone, opening the windows so that the people outside could hear our music and would know that we weren't afraid. By midday the crowd had thinned to no more than a few hundred who sat or lay stretched out quite peacefully on the sand. The rest had gone back to Foum-Skhira. We had lunch and played cards. It was cool in the house, but we could feel the heat outside – the heat and the stillness. 'Why the hell don't they send those troops?' Ed cried, suddenly throwing down his cards. 'This waiting is getting on my nerves.'

Nobody answered him. The waiting was getting on everybody's nerves. 'They must have a garrison at Agdz. Why don't they send them?'

'Oh, shut up,' I said angrily. My arm was stiff and painful. That and the waiting was making me irritable.

A sound drifted through the open windows, the beat of drums coming faintly across the sands to us from Foum-Skhira. The tam-tams had started again. And almost immediately that harsh, wailing chant of the women took up the rhythm. *Ayee-ya-i-ee Ayee-ya-i-ee.* Ed, who had been pacing up and down, stopped to listen. 'Can't you do something? Get on the phone again to Agdz. Tell them to hurry. Tell that darn fool commandant—'

'What is the good?' Bilvidic asked. His voice was calm. 'He knows what the situation is.'

'Jesus!' Ed's fists were clenched with anger. 'Are you going to sit there and do nothing while they whip themselves up into a frenzy again? Will you telephone Agdz or will I?'

Bilvidic shrugged his shoulders. 'Do as you please,' he said. 'But I assure you that everything that can be done—'

'Okay. Then I guess it's up to me.' And Ed turned and stumped off into the study.

Bilvidic looked almost apologetically at the rest of us. 'He is very young,' he murmured. 'It is over forty kilometres from Agdz to this place and the piste is cut up near the pass.'

'They could send planes,' Jan suggested.

Bilvidic turned down the corners of his mouth. 'This territory is controlled by the AI. It is a military responsibility. They will handle it themselves.'

'Well, they'd better hurry,' Jan muttered. He looked across at Karen. Bilvidic was watching him. 'It's a pity you had to bring Madame Kavan into this,' Jan said.

We listened to Ed trying to get through to Agdz. He tried for almost a quarter of an hour. Then he came back into the room. 'The line's out of action again.'

Bilvidic nodded. 'Yes, I know. I tried to telephone them after Latham was wounded. I could not get any reply.'

'Why the hell didn't you tell me?'

'There is no point in telling you,' Bilvidic answered quietly.

Georges called down the stairs then. He was acting as lookout on the roof. 'There are some riders coming in now,' he said.

'Troops?' Jan asked hopefully.

'No. Berbers on mules.'

We went to the windows. They were riding in across the open space between the forts, their robes billowing out behind them. They paused to speak to some of the people squatting on the sand. Then they rode on towards Foum-Skhira. 'I guess those are the guys that passed me up on the mountain road last night,' Ed said.

'It is possible.' Bilvidic was staring through the window towards the palmerie. Then he turned abruptly. 'Georges. Go back to the roof. Watch the palmerie.'

'*Oui, oui. Ça va.*' His assistant hurried back up the stairs.

'Let us continue our game of cards,' Bilvidic said and took up his hand again.

But we couldn't concentrate any more. The drums were beating faster now and the sound, though faint, seemed to throb through the room. It was nearly four. 'I'm going to make some coffee,' Julie said. Her voice sounded small and taut. She and Karen went out together into the kitchen.

We had ceased all pretence at playing. We were just

sitting, listening to the drums. 'It won't be long now,' Jan murmured. He rubbed his hand across his face. 'It's funny,' he said to me, speaking softly. 'For more than five years I have been wishing for Karen to be with me. And now . . .' He half closed his eyes. 'Now I wish she weren't.' He looked across at Bilvidic who had joined Ed at the window. 'I'm sorry for him, too.' The detective came towards us across the room. 'Are you married?' Jan asked him.

Bilvidic nodded. 'Yes, and I have two children also – a boy aged eleven and a girl nine.'

'I'm sorry,' Jan said.

Bilvidic's face softened into a friendly smile. 'It does not matter. It is my work. There is always some danger. The boy – François,' he added, 'is in France now. He has gone to Dijon to stay with his grandmother for the New Year.'

The drums were growing louder and a moment later Georges called down that the mob was coming out of the palmerie. Bilvidic muttered a curse as we went towards the windows. 'It is those men who came in from the mountains. They have whipped up the people into a fury again.' The mob looked different this time as it swept past the ruins of the souk. It was led by a man on mule-back, and it seemed to have more purpose. 'There is going to be trouble this time.' Bilvidic turned to the stairs. 'Georges! Can you see anything moving on the piste from Agdz?'

'No, nothing. *Un moment.* Yes, I think so. Just one man; riding a mule, I think.'

Presumably it was a straggler from the party who

had already arrived. '*Ecoutez*!' Bilvidic said. 'There is to be no shooting. You understand? No shooting. We retreat up the stairs and then up to the roof. Only then do we fight. As long as there is no shooting we have a chance.'

Julie came in with the coffee. She poured us each a cup and took the rest upstairs. We drank it scalding hot, conscious of the growing murmur of the advancing mob. It wasn't such a large mob, but it seemed more compact. It was bunched up behind the man on the mule and there were very few women in it. Knives flashed in the sunshine as they neared the house. Several men carried swords and one a lance. There were guns, too.

There was no hesitation this time. They came straight on towards the house. The leader trotted his mule up to the door and shouted, 'Give us the men who killed Ali. Give us the slayers of the men in the gorge.' He was a tall, bearded man with dark, aquiline features. He was the man who had shaken his fist at us from the entrance to the gorge after the slide.

'Get up the stairs,' Bilvidic said to me. And when I hesitated, he added, 'There is nothing you can do to stop them this time. Get upstairs. Georges and I will hold them. Take everybody up to the roof. Hurry, monsieur. I don't think they will hurt the women.'

The man was looking in at us now. I saw recognition in his eyes and the blaze of a fierce hatred. He shouted something and then his face vanished abruptly. The next instant a lump of concrete was flung with a crash through the window. He was screaming at the crowd and they answered with a deep, baying roar, split by wild cries as they swarmed forward.

'Up the stairs, all of you,' Bilvidic shouted.

We backed away from the room. I motioned Jan and Ed to go on ahead. The two Frenchmen were also backing across the room, their guns in their hands. The tide of the Berber mob rolled against the house, breaking against it, lapping round it. Windows crashed in, the frames splintered under heavy blows. Men climbed through over the sills. The door fell open with a crash. The room was suddenly full of them.

Bilvidic and Georges were in the archway between the main room and the study. The Berbers, finding themselves in unfamiliar surroundings, hesitated – uncertain and suspicious like animals. They stood, silent and baffled, facing the two Frenchmen. Their momentary stillness was full of fear.

Then the study windows were broken in and Bilvidic was forced to move back to the stairs. The tribesmen thrust forward, milling into the alcove between the two rooms. A gun was fired and a bullet slapped the wall above our heads. Bilvidic was backing steadily. It was only a matter of time. I turned, gripping my gun, and ordered everybody up to the roof top. 'Keep down though,' I shouted. 'Keep down below the parapet.'

A ladder led from the top storey on to the flat roof. Julie was waiting for me there and our hands gripped. Karen went up and then Jan and then Ed. We were alone on the landing with the guttural jabber of the Berbers lapping the house. She was looking up at me and my grip on her hand tightened. And then suddenly she was in my arms and our lips touched, a kiss that was without passion, that was a physical expression of what we were suddenly feeling for each other, of the love we had found. Then the door behind us was flung open and crashed to again as Bilvidic and Georges thrust their shoulders against it and turned the key. '*Montez*! *Montez*!' Bilvidic shouted. 'Up on to the roof. Quick!'

I pushed Julie up and followed quickly after her. And as my head emerged into the slanting sunlight, I heard Jan shouting something excitedly. Georges followed me and then Bilvidic. The noise of the mob milling round the house was terrifying. A gun fired and a bullet whined over our heads. I pulled Julie down. Bilvidic and Georges were hauling up the ladder whilst blows rained on the door they had locked against pursuit. It splintered and burst open and at the same moment they dropped the trap-door leading on to the roof.

And then I heard what Jan was shouting. 'Look! Philip. Look!'

I lifted my head above the parapet. A lone horseman was galloping across the open space between the two forts. It was a French officer. He rode bent low over the horse's neck, his round, pale blue hat screening his face, his cloak streaming out behind him. The horse, a big black, was lathered white with sweat and dust.

Julie and I stood up then. It was so magnificent. He was riding straight for the house, urging his horse on as though he intended to ride the mob down.

The roar of voices that circled the house gradually died as the horse, almost foundering, was pulled on to its haunches on the very edge of the thickest of the mob where they milled around the front door. 'Abdul! Hassan!' The rider had singled out two men from the mob and ordered them to take charge and clear the crowd from the doorway. 'You. Mohammed. Drop that gun!'

It was Legard. His body sagged with exhaustion, his eyes blazed with tiredness. His horse could barely stand. Yet he and the horse moved into the mob as though they were reviewing troops on parade. Here and there he singled out a man and gave an order.

In a moment the mob was moving back away from the house. They were going sheepishly, their eyes turned away from the Capitaine. They were no longer a mass. They were just a crowd of rather subdued individuals moving quickly away from the scene, anxious to avoid recognition. They were like children and he scolded them like children. 'Moha! Why are you not looking to your goats? Abdul! You should be teaching the children today. Youssef! Mohammed!'

He picked them out, one by one, riding his horse in amongst them. He seemed to know them all by name and what they should be doing. And at no time was his voice raised in anger. It was only pained.

'Mohammed Ali. You here, too? Why do you make me ride so hard today? Yakoub. I have been to get food for you and now you have brought me back.'

He knew them all and they ducked past him, their heads bowed in respect and contrition. '*Llah ihennik, O Sidi* – Allah keep you in peace, O master.' And they scuttled away across the sands in ones and twos, like whipped dogs with their tails between their legs.

The noise of the mob died into the whisper of individuals and then into silence. Even the voices immediately below us, searching for a way up to the roof top, became subdued and receded into silence. One by one the men who had invaded the house came out, and Legard sat his horse, watching them – and to them he said nothing. They murmured their greetings, grovelling before the sternness of his face, and then they slunk away.

The last to come out was the man who had been their leader. He stood for a moment facing Legard. Neither spoke and the man's head dropped and he ran quickly to his mule and left.

We rigged the ladder then and went down. Legard was standing in the door of the house surveying the wreckage as we came down the stairs. He looked at us in silence. He was drooping with tiredness and I saw that it wasn't only the dust of travel that made his face grey. He looked desperately ill. His eyes glittered as they fastened on us. 'Imbeciles!' he cried, his voice savage with anger. 'You are here two days and you cause trouble.' He began to cough. 'My relief has arrived and now I have to come here and deal with this. All because of you, because you are so stupid that you . . .' His words were lost in a fit of coughing. He staggered forward to the settee and collapsed into it, clutching at his stomach, his eyes half closed. 'See to my horse,' he croaked. 'Somebody see to that poor devil of a horse.' He began to cough again.

Bilvidic sent Georges out to look after the animal. 'What can I do for him?' Julie whispered.

'Get him some water,' I said. I went over to him. 'Monsieur le Capitaine,' I said. 'I'd like to thank you – for us all.'

His eyes stared at me coldly.

'I'd like to thank you, too,' Ed said. 'But why the hell did you have to come alone?' he added. 'What happened to the troops?'

'What troops?' Legard asked harshly.

Ed turned to Bilvidic. 'Didn't the Commandant promise to send troops?'

'Why should he?' Legard pushed himself up on to his elbow. 'What did you want troops for? These men aren't vicious. They're like little children. Anyway, there aren't any troops. We have no troops down here.'

Ed hesitated and then he grinned and shrugged his shoulders. 'Okay. Whatever you say. But thanks all the same.'

Legard didn't say anything, but I saw the severe lines of his mouth relax into the ghost of a smile which spread up into his eyes so that they were slightly crinkled at the corners and he looked younger and less ill. Julie brought him the water and he gulped it down. '*Alors*.' He pushed himself up into a sitting position. 'Now explain to me everything that has happened. I have already sent for Caid Hassan and for the Khailifa. What happened? Monsieur Latham, suppose you tell me.'

'Caid Hassan is dead,' I said.

'Yes, of course. I had forgotten.' He closed his eyes, screwing them up as though they were still half-blinded by sun and sand. 'It is a pity. He was a fine old man.' He pressed his fingers against the balls of his eyes and then got to his feet with an abrupt, determined movement. 'Bilvidic. A word with you, please.' The two Frenchmen went through into the study.

A sudden stillness descended upon the room. It was an uneasy stillness and I glanced across at Jan. He was standing with his back to the fire, his hands behind him, the palms open to the blaze. The muscles of his face were rigid and his head was thrust a little forward. He was frowning and there was a look of concentration on his face as though he were listening to their conversation. But the curtain had been drawn across the study entrance and all we could hear was the drone of their voices. There was a question I wanted to ask him, but I couldn't because Ed was there.

Mohammed came in, his sandals slapping the tiles as he crossed the room. He went into the study and announced that the Khailifa and the old Caid's son had arrived. 'Tell them to wait for me at the Bureau,' Legard said and Mohammed went out again. The stillness of the room became unbearable. Ed walked over to the window and stared out towards the mountains. 'Well, that's that, I guess.' He was speaking to himself.

Jan's head jerked up. 'How do you mean?'

'Well, it's obvious, isn't it? That shaft will never be opened up now.' He was still gazing towards the mountains, seeing in his mind again the landslide thundering into the mouth of the gorge. 'All that work for nothing.'

'You mean you're giving up?' There was a note of surprise in Jan's voice.

Ed turned towards him with a quick, irritable

movement of his body. 'What else can I do? I can't clear that slide away. There's too much of it.'

'We know the position of the shaft. We could tunnel down to it.'

'How? I've no equipment and I'm just about broke.'

'We could use local labour. As for money, there's the insurance on your bull-dozers.'

'They weren't insured. I didn't think there was any reason to insure them.'

He had turned back to the window. Silence descended again on the room. Jan was standing very still. His hands behind his back were clenched now and I saw that his gaze had shifted back to the entrance to the study. And then the curtains were pulled aside and Legard and Bilvidic came out. 'I will arrange for the mules to be ready at nine o'clock,' Legard said. '*Ça va*?'

Bilvidic nodded. Legard picked his blue stiff hat up off the table where he had flung it and slung his cape round his shoulders. As he went towards the door he paused and looked at Jan. 'At least, monsieur, you seem to have succeeded in carrying out Duprez's wishes.' He stared at him for a moment and I realised with a shock that Jan was incapable of meeting the man's gaze. Then Legard twitched his cloak closer round his body and went out. The door banged to behind him.

The sun had set now and night was closing in. The room was growing dark and I could no longer see Jan's face clearly. My shoulder hurt and I was feeling drained of energy, wishing we were away from the place. Bilvidic shouted for Mohammed and ordered him to light the lamps. But even in the soft lamp-glow the room had a cold, alien look. The sense of tension was still there.

And then the telephone buzzer sounded. Bilvidic went through into the study to answer it. He was gone a long while and when he came back he paused in the archway between the two rooms. He was looking at Jan. 'Monsieur Wade. You will please come through into the study. There are some questions I have to ask you. You, too, Latham,' he added, turning to me.

The moment I had been dreading had arrived. I pulled myself to my feet. Jan was already following Bilvidic into the study. Karen was staring after him, her body rigid, her face pale and taut with strain. Her small hands were clenched as though she were trying to will with all the strength of her body that everything would be all right.

I went through into the study, conscious that my footsteps sounded very loud on the bare tiles. Bilvidic was already seated at the desk. '*Asseyez-vous*, monsieur.' He waved me to a chair. 'That telephone call was from Casablanca. I have orders to phone through a preliminary report on this matter to my headquarters tonight.' He pulled out his pack of American cigarettes and lit one. 'Monsieur Wade.' He was looking across at Jan. 'From the time you entered French Morocco until I confronted you with Madame Kavan you had assumed the name and identity of Dr Kavan. Why? Explain please.' He was the policeman again: cold, precise, logical.

I looked at Jan. His hands gripped the arms of his chair and his body was braced. He hesitated momentarily. It seemed an age. Then he shifted his position. 'Because I had to,' he said.

'Why?' Bilvidic's voice was still and hard.

'What else was I to do? Kostos had taken my passport. But I still had Kavan's papers and I had to get to Kasbah Foum.' His voice sounded nervous.

'Why did you not report the loss of your passport to the authorities? The International Police were the proper people to deal with the matter.'

'But that would have taken time. Listen, monsieur.' Jan leaned forward and the nervousness was suddenly gone from his voice. 'I was with Kavan over two weeks in the confined space of a small boat. He told me the whole story – how Duprez had given him the deeds and had made him promise to get his title to Kasbah Foum confirmed before Caid Hassan died. If he didn't, the property, with all its potential wealth, would have passed to Ali. You know the sort of man Ali was. He would have used that wealth against France. He would have purchased arms. Kavan was dead. I accepted his responsibility as though it were my own. It was the least I could do.' He stopped then. He was breathing heavily.

'Nevertheless,' Bilvidic said, 'you should have reported the loss of your passport to the police.'

'Damn it, man. Don't you understand?' Jan's anger was genuine. 'Kostos was waiting for me there on the beach at Tangier. The matter was urgent. Latham understood. That was why he agreed to get me out on Kavan's papers.'

'Very well, monsieur. It is understood. But why do you have to go on calling yourself Kavan?'

'What else could I do? I was here in Morocco on Kavan's papers. Besides, Caid Hassan wouldn't have confirmed the title to anyone but Kavan.'

'Ah. That is the real point, eh?' There was a cold glint in Bilvidic's eyes. 'You had to be Kavan in order to obtain the title to Kasbah Foum.'

'Are you suggesting I arranged for Kostos to steal my passport?' Jan demanded. 'Do you think I enjoyed getting out of Tangier the way I did and coming down here under an assumed name? It was dangerous. But I had to do it.' He got up suddenly and walked over to the desk, leaning on it and staring down at Bilvidic. 'What you're implying is a motive of personal gain. What you should be considering is the alternative. Your troops are all fighting in Indo-China. Caid Hassan is dead, and if Ali were now alive and the owner of Kasbah Foum . . .' He thrust his head forward slightly, staring at Bilvidic. 'Be thankful, monsieur, that it has turned out the way it has. If there is silver there, then it will be developed for the benefit of the people. It was what Kavan wanted. It is what I promised Caid Hassan.'

I glanced at Bilvidic. The whole thing was so logical that I almost believed it myself. The detective was staring at Jan. He didn't say anything and a silence settled on the room. Jan had turned away from the desk. I wondered how long he could stand the silence. There were beads of sweat on his forehead. And then I saw Bilvidic relax in his chair. He drew gently on his cigarette. 'Perhaps you will go and join the others now,' he said to Jan. 'I would like a word with Latham alone.'

Jan hesitated and glanced at me. He looked tired.

Then he turned without a word and went out through the curtains. I moved uneasily in my chair, turning to face Bilvidic. He was watching me, his cigarette held vertical between two fingers and a thumb. 'How is the shoulder?' he asked me. 'Painful?'

'A little,' I said, waiting.

His face softened to a smile and he offered me a cigarette. 'There are one or two questions I would like to ask you. First, who suggested that method of getting him out of the International Zone – you or he?'

'I did.'

He nodded. 'That is what I thought. I have seen your security report. Perhaps you have had previous experience of that method, eh?'

'Perhaps,' I said.

He shrugged his shoulders. 'Well, that is for Tangier to worry about. Now, this matter of Kavan being lost overboard from the yacht. Did our friend tell you how it happened?'

'Yes.'

'In detail?'

'Yes.' I explained when he had told me and he nodded. 'Good. He would have been tired then. Will you repeat it to me in the exact words he used, as far as you can remember them.' I did so and he sat for a long time, tapping his pencil against his teeth. 'Have you sailed yachts at all?' he asked suddenly.

'Yes,' I said. 'Quite a lot when I was a boy.'

'And do you believe this story? Could a man fall overboard like that – or would it be necessary to push him? Remember, the storm was finished.'

'You don't need a storm for a thing like that to happen,' I said. 'It can happen quite easily.' I was determined to convince him on this point. 'The guardrails are often no more than thirty inches high – less than a metre,' I explained. 'Even in a quiet sea a man can go overboard, if he's careless – especially if there isn't much wind and the boat is rolling.' He made no comment and I added quickly, 'In this case, though the storm was over, there was still a big sea running. If you make a quick move out of the cockpit in such conditions and the stern of the boat falls away in a trough . . .' He still said nothing. 'They were both very tired,' I said. 'That was confirmed by the log.'

'Ah. So you have seen the log, eh? Where is it? Has he got it?'

'No.'

'Where is it then?'

I explained how I had burned it and he said, 'Why? Why do you do that?'

'He asked me to.'

'Why?'

I didn't know what to say. For a moment there was a tense silence. And then he gave me the answer himself. 'Was it because he was afraid Kostos might get hold of it?'

'Yes,' I said. 'Yes, I think that was it.'

He leaned slowly forward across the desk. 'Why should that matter, monsieur?'

It was a trap. I realised that too late. There was no earthly reason why Kostos shouldn't have seen the log. If it were Kavan who had gone overboard, then the writing in the log would have remained unaltered. I couldn't think of anything to say. Bilvidic waited a moment and then he got up and crossed the room and pulled back the curtain. 'Wade. A moment please.' Jan's eyes were fixed on my face as he came in, walking jerkily, his hands thrust into his pockets. 'There is something I don't understand,' Bilvidic said. 'Why did you ask Latham to destroy the log?'

Jan's hesitation was only momentary, then he turned slowly to face the detective. 'It was the handwriting, monsieur,' he said in a tone of surprise. 'I could not take Kavan's identity and still carry about with me all those pages of my own handwriting.'

It was so simple, so logical. I felt a sense of relief. Bilvidic wasn't to know that the decision to get out on Kavan's papers had been taken after the log had been destroyed. The detective turned back to the desk. 'Now then,' he said, 'let us get this down in the form of a statement.' He looked across at me. 'I think perhaps, Latham, you would be more comfortable in the other room. Keep warm by the fire.' His expression was almost friendly.

Julie and Karen were standing by the hearth. There was no one else in the room. The lamps and the fire gave a glow of warmth to the bare walls. Karen turned and moved slowly, almost reluctantly to meet me. 'Is it all right?' she asked in a whisper.

'Yes,' I said. 'I think so.'

Her lips trembled slightly and then she turned away her head. I think she was close to tears. Julie's fingers closed on my hand. 'You're cold,' she said. 'Come and get warm.'

Ed came back soon after and we sat and waited in silence. It seemed a long time before Jan came out. He was talking to Bilvidic. 'And you'll make it clear that I had no alternative, won't you?'

'I don't think you need worry,' Bilvidic answered.

'Thanks. And I'm glad you reminded me about the yacht.' He came towards us then, and he was smiling.

'Monsieur White.' Bilvidic's cold, official voice cut across the mood of relief that had filled the room. 'If you will come in here, I would like a short statement.'

Ed went into the study and as the curtains fell to behind him, Jan came towards Karen. 'Well, madame.' For the first time since I had known him I saw him completely relaxed. His blue eyes were twinkling. He looked young, almost a boy again.

'It's all right then?' Karen whispered.

'Yes,' he said. 'Everything is going to be all right now – for always, darling.' Their hands touched and gripped. 'You understand, Karen,' he said. 'We shall have to start courting again. After a decent interval, of course.' And then he turned to me. 'Philip. You will be best man at our wedding, eh?' He was suddenly laughing. 'Tell me. What is the opposite to your saying – It never rains but it pours?' But he didn't wait for an answer. 'Listen. *Gay Juliet* was insured for £15,000. As Wade I collect that money. Isn't that damn funny?' His laugh was a little nervous, as though it were all too good to be true. 'You come and help us open up that shaft, and after that we'll do something about your Mission.'

The door opened behind us and Jan and Karen moved quickly apart. It was Legard. He put his cloak and his hat on the table and came over to the fire. He stood warming himself for a moment and then he turned to Jan. 'I have been talking to Caid Hassan's son,' he said. 'He was present at your meeting with his father.' He paused and then added significantly. 'He speaks French.'

The sudden look of shock on Jan's face showed me that he had understood the implication.

Legard stared at the fire for a long time and then he gave a little shrug. '*Eh bien*,' he said. 'Perhaps, if you stay here long enough, you will cure me of the *amibe*, eh?' He looked at Jan, his tough, leathery face unsmiling – but the corners of his eyes were crinkled up. Then he walked to the door and shouted for Mohammed to bring him some water.